CONVENIENTLY
Yours

The honor of your presence is requested
at not one but *three*
weddings!

Three unusually *convenient* weddings

But wait!
Even the brides and grooms
don't know it, but

CONVENIENTLY
Yours

is about to become **Lovingly Yours**
after the weddings....

Relive the romance...

By Request™

Three complete novels by your favorite authors!

About the Authors

Rita Clay Estrada—As befits the cofounder and first president of Romance Writers of America, Rita is the winner of numerous publishing awards and her deeply emotional romance novels have gained her countless fans around the world. Rita, a former airforce brat, now makes her home in Texas and is the author of well over a score of books.

Bobby Hutchinson—Author of almost twenty romance novels, Bobby's wacky and romantic stories can't hold a candle to her own life. When this former teacher of deaf children and a mother of three fell in love with a father of two, she married him—in sign language! Bobby and her ex-Mountie husband live in British Columbia.

Sally Bradford—This award-winning writing team is made up of Sally Siddon, a former journalist, and Barbara Bradford, a former teacher. Friends as well as partners, Sally and Barbara both live near Washington D.C., with their families.

CONVENIENTLY
Yours

RITA CLAY ESTRADA
BOBBY HUTCHINSON
SALLY BRADFORD

Harlequin Books

TORONTO • NEW YORK • LONDON
AMSTERDAM • PARIS • SYDNEY • HAMBURG
STOCKHOLM • ATHENS • TOKYO • MILAN
MADRID • WARSAW • BUDAPEST • AUCKLAND

HARLEQUIN BOOKS

by Request—Conveniently Yours

Copyright © 1994 by Harlequin Enterprises B.V.

ISBN 0-373-20103-6

The publisher acknowledges the copyright holders
of the individual works as follows:
TO BUY A GROOM
Copyright © 1990 by Rita Clay Estrada
MEETING PLACE
Copyright © 1986 by Bobby Hutchinson
THE ARRANGEMENT
Copyright © 1987 by Sally Siddon & Barbara Bradford

Printed in U.S.A.

CONTENTS

She needs a husband—fast!
He needs a million dollars....
Solution: Marriage!

TO BUY A GROOM

Rita Clay Estrada

For good friends Diane Levitt, Faye Ashley,
Pat Leonard and Mom

1

JOSEPH LOMBARDI hated horses. No, he amended, he hated taking care of horses. He loved horse racing. He was trying to decide which emotion was stronger, when a soft voice interrupted.

"Mr. Lombardi? Mr. Joseph Lombardi?"

"Yes," he answered, annoyed. He continued to examine his prize thoroughbred's hoof.

"I'm Sable LaCroix. I have an appointment with you." Her voice was low and slightly hesitant, but the words were a reminder, just the same. "One of your men said you were out here in the stables."

Joe sighed heavily, dropped Ahab's hoof and patted the horse's neck before turning around. Mrs. LaCroix was another problem in a day filled with them. He'd deliberately avoided the appointment. He didn't have time for wealthy socialites with strange requests for meetings without a stated purpose.

The barn filtered sunlight and shadows, and the woman standing inside the entrance seemed to gather both around her like a silver cloak. She was tall, probably about five foot seven or eight without her heels. Her figure was breathtaking. Full breasts, softly rounded hips and long, slender legs. Beautiful. Very beautiful.

And from what he could see, she was dark-headed—his weakness.

"I remember now, Mrs. LaCroix. My attorney said you're looking for an investment for your dead husband's money. Right?"

He saw her wince at his crass words. "Right."

"And you thought horse racing in Texas was right up your alley, since racetracks and betting will be here in a matter of months."

"Right."

He took off his hat and wiped his face on his sleeve. "Fine. Then do some more talking to my attorney. Mike can handle everything."

She shifted her weight onto one hip; the movement made her legs look longer than ever. "This can't be handled by attorneys. There are some strings attached that *you* have to deal with," she said, her voice melodic, like a gentle waterfall.

Her white suit was crisp and cool. Just looking at her made him feel as if a soft, Southern breeze had touched his skin. A wide-brimmed, black hat shaded her eyes, so he couldn't see their color. His eyes dropped again to her long legs, legs that were designed to be kissed all the way up to . . . Damn! Not liking his reaction to her, Joe made his voice hard. "What strings? And what makes you think I might be interested? I have a lot of work to do. Make it quick."

She hesitated for only a moment. "I need a husband with a good background and a stable career. You need money. I'm willing to offer you a million dollars on the day of the wedding."

Joe stared at her blankly, then shook his head. Obviously the heat was affecting his hearing.

He saw her nod. She must have read his expression. "You heard correctly, Mr. Lombardi." Her voice held a hint of amusement. "I'm asking for your hand in marriage."

That was it. He threw his head back and laughed, slapping the hat against his leg. Her proposal was the stupidest thing he'd ever heard, but at least it was funny.

He became aware that his visitor was patiently waiting for his laughter to stop. Her stance relaxed, a smile played at the corners of her beautiful lips.

His laughter slowly died. He narrowed his eyes. His lips tightened. "Lady, you aren't kidding, are you?"

"No. I'm not kidding."

"Why?"

"I need a husband. You need an investor for the new track you want to build."

Gripping Ahab's lead, he walked the horse out of the barn toward the nearest paddock. It was always best to ignore drunks and crazies, no matter how beautiful they might be. He wasn't sure which category she fitted into and he wasn't about to find out.

Joe opened the paddock gate and led the thoroughbred inside before unsnapping the lead. After a swat on the hindquarter the horse trotted away as Joe exited.

Aware that the beautiful stranger had followed him, Joe turned toward her. Her businesslike demeanor was betrayed by her tight grip on the black-and-white clutch purse, he noted. Did it hold the million she was trying to bribe him with? After hearing her offer, he thought she might be stupid enough to carry it with her.

"I repeat, Mrs. LaCroix. Why?"

"Because I need a respectable husband and the semblance of a family life. You can give me that."

Her claim intrigued him. Silently he led her to his rambling ranch home. He'd listen to her—very politely, just like his daddy had taught him—and then he'd kick her out on her little butt. Her very enticing little butt.

Allowing her to enter the kitchen before him, his eyes lingered on that very appealing part of her anatomy. She turned to face him. "Mr. Lombardi?"

His eyes darted to her face. One brow was raised as if in demand. He might as well get this interview over with. "Who sent you here?"

"Would you believe my husband?"

"No."

"He did. You remember John LaCroix in Vietnam? You two were buddies, trapped in the same section of the jungle. Then after you were wounded, you were roommates in the hospital. He mentioned you often. I've even read the letters you two exchanged for a while, after you both returned home. John said you were the most dependable man he'd ever known—always willing to help."

His eyes widened at the flash of memory. He and John LaCroix had been two disillusioned, eighteen-year-old kids, wondering what had happened to the glory of war and pride in defending one's country. They had been the best of friends, until the normalcy of life returned once more and soothed their nightmares. "You're that LaCroix's wife?"

She nodded. In the sunlight he saw her eyes were brown. Big and round and brown. As soft as a doe's hide.

"For three years," she answered.

"Then what happened?"

"He died."

John was gone. Joe could hardly believe it.

She pulled out a kitchen chair and slid gratefully into it, almost as if she'd been carrying a heavy weight. Lifting the wide-brimmed hat off her head, she tossed it onto the table.

He wanted to moan—both in delight and frustration. Her hair was the exact color of her name—Sable.

"It's funny, isn't it?" she said bitterly. "He lived through everything war could throw at him. Then he died in an airplane crash, trying to make it home in time for our son's first birthday party."

Hands stuffed in his back pockets, Joe stared at her. Somehow none of this seemed real. She was mourning for a lost husband; he was sorry about the boy he had known so long ago. "I'm sorry," he finally said, awkwardly. "I didn't know. He was an all right guy."

Anger flashed in her eyes and her back stiffened. The reaction was short-lived, and she slumped back into her chair. "Yes. But he was more than that. He was a wonderful, compassionate man."

"When did it happen?"

"A little over two years ago."

Memories he thought he'd buried, surfaced, quick and sure, cutting to his heart. So many friends had been lost. And the worst of it was that afterward it was hard to remember what had been real and what had been just a nightmare. He'd forgotten those feelings, but he hadn't forgotten John.

Now John's widow was sitting with him, trying to talk him into taking John's place. It left a bad taste in his mouth. People didn't replace other people.

"So you're looking for a replacement for this wonderful, compassionate man," he jeered, trying to quell his conflicting emotions. "Well, sorry, lady, but I'm not either one of those things. I don't like wives and I'm not partial to kids. Now if you'd given birth to a thoroughbred—"

"I did."

"What?"

"The LaCroix name and wealth are very well-known. They're fourth-generation Louisianans, with enough money to buy the state." She leaned back, closing her eyes for a moment, letting her guard down enough for him to see how tired she was. When she opened her eyes he almost fell into their soft, brown depths. "And I own thoroughbreds, Mr. Lombardi. Three, compliments of my husband's estate."

He leaned against the chair in front of him, baring his teeth as he smiled. "Your in-laws are very generous to want to help John's old buddy by setting him up with their son's widow." He couldn't help the sarcastic tone. This whole conversation was ridiculous, yet here he was, when he had a hundred other things to do!

"No," she said, so quietly he had to strain himself to hear her. "They want my son."

He felt the sadness, the loneliness in her voice, but it was no concern of his. "Why would two old people want a youngster? They certainly couldn't take care of him properly."

"They want him as another LaCroix possession, but they'll only make him weak and worthless. John fought against them, and so will I. They wrapped John in cotton batting until he almost suffocated from their love. I don't want that to happen to my child."

This deserved a drink. He reached into the refrigerator and pulled out a beer, popped the top and guzzled, then wiped his mouth on his sleeve. "What do you want me to do, lady? Fight them off with my bare hands?"

"I want you to be a respectable husband, so my child can have a complete family—a mother and a father. Then the LaCroix can't take me to court and sue for custody of my son."

"You're kidding!"

"Mr. Lombardi," she said slowly, patiently. "My attorney contacted your attorney last week. Didn't he even mention why I wanted to see you?"

"Not a word, lady. Not one damn word." Why hadn't Mike said something? He'd been out at the ranch only yesterday, hemming and hawing about money and how much it was going to take for Joe to get the track and stables ready for the racing season. But he hadn't actually *said* anything—just mentioned in passing to come by the office next time Joe was in town, because he might have a solution....

"You're the solution," Joe muttered, tightening his grip around the beer can until the sound of popping aluminum filled the air. Beer spilled over his hand and dripped to the floor, but he ignored it. He was staring at the woman seated at his table, the woman who looked as if she nibbled on exotic flowers for breakfast.

Sable looked startled. "The solution to your money problems? Yes, I suppose I am. Just as you're the answer to mine. If you want my horses as well, you can have them. I need a husband."

Joe tossed the can into the sink on top of the breakfast dishes, which were on top of the dinner dishes that hadn't been done the night before. The place was a mess. Every square inch of counter was covered with dirty dishes, pots and pans. But the table was clean. He was particular about where he ate his thrown-together meals.

"Look," he began, hoping he sounded reasonable. "I'm sorry you're having problems with your in-laws, but I'm sure if you talk to them, explain to them, they'll see things your way. A child needs his mama. Grandparents aren't always young or energetic enough to raise a little guy. They'd be worn out in a month."

"Wrong. They'll do anything to gain custody. I heard them." She stood, bracing both exquisitely manicured hands on the table and leaned toward him to make her point. "They want him because he's a LaCroix. They won't raise him, just indoctrinate him with cute little phrases like, 'A LaCroix would never work for charity, just donate to it.' Then they'll give him to someone else to raise and bring him downstairs from the nursery to show off to their friends. The same way my husband was raised. He hated it. I hate it, too." She straightened and stared him straight into his baby blues. "I want him because he's *my* son. *My* child. I want to be there when he goes to school, falls down playing ball, swims his first lap across a pool."

She reached for her purse and hat. "But if you don't want to get involved in this, then fine. Not everyone is afraid of money. I'll find someone else to help me."

He watched her walk out of the kitchen and down the hallway toward the front door. That tight butt swayed from side to side.

"Who?" The word was out before he even realized he'd thought it.

She turned, her hand on the doorknob. Her eyes had to be the saddest, brownest eyes he'd ever made the mistake of losing himself in. "I don't know yet, Mr. Lombardi. But I'll find some-one who needs my money as much as I need his help. I guess John was wrong about you."

Then she opened the front door and walked out, closing it quietly behind her.

Joe stood rooted to the foot of the stairs, his eyes still trained on the spot she had occupied. A powerful engine revved in the driveway, then the sound diminished as she drove away.

Had he dreamed her? He wasn't sure. But if he was dreaming, at least he'd fantasized about someone beautiful. She was drop-dead gorgeous. And she was trouble.

Shaking his head at her outrageous request, he walked out to the barn. He had too much work to do and not enough time to get it done.

SABLE PULLED OVER to the side of the dirt road and leaned her head on the steering wheel. She was trembling. *Her plan had failed!* she cried to herself. Taking deep gulps of air, she told herself over and over to calm down.

It had only been a business meeting—one that hadn't turned out as she'd hoped. Joe Lombardi had been as nice as could have been expected under the circumstances. After all, he'd had no prior warning of her offer. Was that an omen? she wondered. Would any man take her seriously?

She leaned her head back and closed her eyes, willing tense muscles to relax before she went any farther. She still had an hour's drive to Hooks Airport, just north of Houston, where she'd take the LaCroix private airplane back to Baton Rouge, Louisiana—in defeat.

It was just as well that Joe Lombardi hadn't accepted her of-fer. His type frightened her. He was one large package of raw, blatant masculinity. Handsome in a craggy, rugged way, he could probably get any woman he wanted. And once he had her, he probably knew exactly what to do with her. Visions of him tangled in soft, percale sheets had Sable's heartbeat quickening.

She opened her eyes and sat up straight. Joseph Lombardi was nothing like John. John had been soft and sweet and tender and understanding. He'd been vulnerable to others' opinions, yet excited about life, not touched by the world-weary attitude many men exhibited.

He had been everything that the man she'd just left wasn't. John could never have been tough. Rough. Raw-edged.

She still missed John's sage advice, his strong, quiet ways. She missed having someone to talk to.

John would never have grabbed a beer and glugged it down from a can.

For a moment she gave in to the tears that pressed on her lids. Two and a half years had only begun to heal her pain over the loss of the man who had been friend and brother and lover to her. Because of him she'd grown up and taken charge. She'd been the strong one; he'd been the wise one.

Again her thoughts returned to Joe. Strange that two such diverse individuals had been friends. War did exceptional things to otherwise ordinary mortals.

Enough of Joe Lombardi! It was time to work on an alternate plan. Somewhere out there was a suitable man who would be willing to marry her for a million dollars. She just had to find him.

Sable ignored the panic that was never far away. She had to find him fast. According to the LaCroix's attorney's secretary, John's parents would file custody papers soon. Over the past two years they had become fed up with Sable's restrictions, allowing Jonathan to visit them for no longer than a day instead of the weeks and months they'd at first requested, then demanded.

The LaCroix didn't know she had overhead them discussing their plans with the family attorney, or that his secretary was also her good friend. She knew she might not win in court. Louisiana still had its share of less than upright citizens in politics. Those who lived by whom, rather than what they knew, could still rule the courts. And her in-laws had influence like that.

No. She couldn't let the suit get to court. There were too many arguments against her case and in favor of the LaCroix.

Marriage, especially to someone living out of state, was her ace in the hole. But having lived a cloistered life since John's death, she knew of no eligible bachelors strong enough not to cave in to her in-laws. If she hadn't been cleaning out John's papers three weeks ago, she wouldn't even have remembered about Joe.

She had another week or so before the LaCroix filed their custody papers. She had to work fast. . . .

"Dammit!" she cried, hitting the steering wheel with her fist. It hurt, overriding the pain deep within her. "Why couldn't you have agreed, Mr. Beer-Drinking Lombardi? Who are you to laugh in my face? If you had agreed, everything would have been so easy. . . ."

Easy? She laughed aloud through her tears. Perhaps it was better this way. Joseph Lombardi was a reminder that she had limited experience with men. She might have been able to housebreak a kitten like John, but never a wildcat like Joe.

JOE HAD WORKED UP a great case of justifiable anger against his friend and attorney by the time Mike arrived.

"Why the hell didn't you just spit it out when you were here two days ago?" Leather-gloved hands on his hips, Joe stood beside Mike's car. "I felt like a damned fool, listening to John's widow explain in simple terms why she wanted to marry me!"

"Now, Joe," Mike began, stepping out of the small, red sportster. "I didn't realize she would follow through this quickly. That's all." He glanced warily at his client. "She's a good-looker, I hear."

Joe glared back. "She's a good-looker with a problem I don't need. What the hell possessed you to even consider such an offer for me? You're my attorney. Why didn't you tell her attorney to go to hell?"

"Because I thought you ought to hear her out. You need money immediately, and the bank's not willing to offer you another loan. Your new barn brought your credit limit to an end. You're overextended, Joe, and we both know it. Even though you have a racetrack license, you don't have the money or the backers to go forward with your own horses. If you had time, it'd be different. But you don't. When the state commission finds that your credit has run out, your license will be yanked. Quick."

Joe rubbed a gloved hand on the back of his neck. It was another hot day. Texas was filled with them. "If we had a few more weeks, I know we'd find some out-of-state backers."

"You'd have all the money you want and more if you took Sable LaCroix up on her offer."

Joe's eyes narrowed. "What do you know about her?"

Mike shrugged. "You knew her husband. That should be worth something."

"I don't know *her*. What do you know?" Joe repeated, his frustration barely held in check.

"That she's telling the truth. The LaCroix family wants its own. They're angry with her for taking their only grandson and moving away from the family home in New Orleans and into a house in Baton Rouge, out of range of their influence. Her husband was an only son who never quite made it out of their sphere. Now they want to raise their grandchild the same way."

Why was he listening to this? Marriage to anyone was out of the question, let alone this marriage to this woman! "And her?"

"Born and gently bred in Mobile, Alabama. She and a baby sister were raised by a widowed aunt, who'd never had children of her own. The aunt died about a year ago. When Sable met John, it was apparently love at first sight. He swept her off her feet. They were married three months after they met, and moved in with his parents. It was John's second marriage. His first wife died."

"I remember," Joe said slowly. Over the years Joe and John hadn't seen each other much, though they had exchanged occasional letters and Christmas cards, but finally even that small connection had faded.

A loud, male voice called his name. He muttered an oath and turned toward the sound. Two of his stallions were getting too close. Some fool had put them in adjoining paddocks.

"Look," Mike said quickly, pushing a file toward him. "Take a look at this and think on it. You don't have to make a decision right away. Just think about it."

Joe's head swiveled quickly. "Are you crazy?"

"No. I'm just trying to find a solution to your problem. I believe this is it."

Loud voices from the paddock area called again. Before Joe realized what was happening, his attorney was in his car, waving as he drove off.

Joe looked at the file in his hand, angry with himself for being unable to take care of two things at one time. "Son of a . . ." he cursed, sticking the folder inside his blue plaid, flannel shirt. He'd go through the papers later. Right now he needed to chew somebody's butt for the trouble in the paddock.

TALIA WATCHED her sister park the rental car along the edge of the airstrip and slip the keys into the glove compartment, then walk toward the plane and its occupants, who were eagerly awaiting news of Mr. Lombardi's decision. She crossed her fingers. Talia prayed Sable's expression didn't reflect what had happened between herself and the man she'd picked to be her husband.

Once Sable appeared in the doorway of the private plane, Talia couldn't keep quiet any longer.

"Well? Did it go okay?" She continued to sit on the plushly carpeted floor, a child's plastic block in her hand. Her fingers clutched it like a talisman.

Little Johnny, his eyes brightening, stood up and ran toward her. "Mommy! Mommy!" he cried as he was swept into Sable's arms. His hug brought tears to her eyes. A lump formed in Talia's throat as she watched. No one, especially someone as sweet and vulnerable as her older sister, should have to fight so hard for what was hers. And Jonathan was hers.

"He said no," Sable announced over the youngster's shoulder. She looked as if she was using every ounce of control to remain calm.

"Damn!"

"Don't swear," Sable admonished, giving her son a kiss on his pudgy cheek. "Hello, dumpling."

"Sorry," Talia mumbled, standing up and sweeping imaginary lint from her jeans. She pushed her hair out of her eyes and glared. "Did he give a reason or just laugh in your face?"

"Both. He doesn't want to be married and he has no use for a child—or my money." Johnny squirmed, and she set him down, so he could run to a toy that had caught his interest.

Toys littered the roomy interior. The LaCroix family plane revealed how prepared her in-laws were to take custody of Johnny. All the boy's needs were kept on board, as they were at the three LaCroix homes.

Automatically Talia began rounding up the toys, preparing for takeoff.

"I'll do that," Sable said, reaching for the rest of the blocks and placing them in the playbox.

"Never mind," Talia told her, grabbing the toys randomly and throwing them into the lidded boxes. "Just tell me what we're going to do next."

"I don't know."

"Did you tell him about me? Did I jinx the deal?" Talia tried not to let her fear show in her voice, but she knew by her sister's expression that she'd failed.

Sable smiled reassuringly. "I didn't even get to you, honey. He cut me off at the pass."

"Well, it's his loss," Talia declared defensively. "How could the man be so stupid? If he was a friend of John's, he had to have *some* intelligence."

"It doesn't matter. It's our loss, too," Sable pointed out softly.

The pilot came on board. "Are we ready, Mrs. LaCroix?"

"Ready." Sable stood and placed her son in the seat next to hers, then strapped both of them in, while Talia did the same across from them.

"We'll be in the air in just a minute. Baton Rouge in an hour and a half, ma'am."

"Thank you," Sable said tiredly, and Talia's heart went out to her. People always assumed Sable was strong, because she shouldered so much responsibility, but Talia knew how hard it was for her. Sometimes Talia felt older than her sister, as if she were nine years the senior.

The pilot disappeared into the cockpit, and she sat back and closed her eyes, listening to Johnny bubble in delight at the pictures of the hard-paged book in Sable's lap.

Thanks to Joe Lombardi's decision, it looked as if the war was over, and they hadn't even fought one battle.

Just then Sable looked over at her. "Don't worry, Spike," she said over the roar of the engines. "The fight isn't over. Not yet."

Talia grinned at her childhood nickname. "You bet." She wondered what she could do to ease the pain she saw in her sister's eyes, but nothing came to mind.

Sable's marriage to an older man had been perfect for her. It had allowed her to grow and learn what her capabilities were. Normally a homebody, Sable had found she was an efficient hostess and party-goer when the need arose. But she was happiest caring for babies and cooking and keeping the neatest house on the block. All the things that Talia hated.

Talia had always gotten whatever she went after. Why couldn't Sable have what she wanted? It didn't seem fair. Suddenly things weren't black and white anymore, but blending shades of gray.

At seventeen she was beginning to realize just how complicated life could be. She hoped it wasn't a permanent affliction. She liked thing simple and straightforward.

JOE RAN THE FIGURES through the calculator again, then compared them to the computer tape printout. They matched. He had hoped they wouldn't.

Mike was right. If he didn't raise half a million dollars within the week, he'd lose the chance of a lifetime. Only three racetracks were to be built in Texas. The other two were corporate enterprises, and his was the only private one. He knew of at least seven other men who could quickly take his place, once the racing commission found out his letter of credit had been withdrawn.

Sable's million dollars was the answer. It dangled in front of him like bait before a hungry bass. He tried to ignore the vision, but the offer was tantalizing.

Ahab, his prized thoroughbred, hadn't won enough races yet to be considered worth a million dollars. Not to a banker, who needed more reassurance than his trainer Totty's word. If Ahab won the next two big ones, however, Joe might be able to claim he was worth that much. But by that time it would be too late....

With Sable LaCroix's million he could *immediately* obtain a letter for another million and open the track on time.

He had no choice—not if he didn't want to lose control of the entire operation by bringing in corporate investors, who would also be major stockholders.

He needed Sable LaCroix's money.

What he didn't need was her problems.

He didn't have a choice.

Before he changed his mind, he reached for the phone and dialed Mike's number.

His words were to the point. "Mike, tell Sable LaCroix the deal is on. I need the money in my account within the week."

"When do you want to get married?"

"How do I know? That's her problem. Tell her to make all the arrangements, and I'll be there." He tapped his pencil against the desk calendar. "One more thing. She has to live here. I expect her to be a wife, not a flittering social butterfly. I also want a prenuptial agreement. When the marriage is over, we each go our separate ways with no financial attachment to the other. Is that clear?"

"Perfectly," Mike said dryly. "Do you want me to draw up the divorce papers while I write out the prenuptial agreement?"

"Why not? I doubt she'll last a year, if that long. This isn't exactly heaven for a female out here. Especially not her kind. The grocery store is over twenty miles away, to say nothing of the nearest boutique."

"I'll call her," Mike promised him. "But I can't guarantee she'll buy all your provisions."

"She will." Joe knew he sounded far more confident than he felt.

It was done. He didn't dare look too closely at why he had agreed to the marriage. Financial need was a good enough excuse for what he was doing. He refused to admit to any other reason.

SABLE HUNG UP the phone and tapped her pencil against the desk calendar. Hope blossomed in her breast. She smiled.

He had agreed!

The prenuptial agreement was fine with her. She had to protect Johnny's future. If Joe hadn't mentioned it, she would have brought it up herself.

With the exception of the million dollars needed to buy the groom, her money would remain hers, and his money would remain his. She had also stipulated separate bedrooms, and her attorney and Mike, Joe's attorney, would draw up a marriage contract. They were to remain together, at Joe's home, for a minimum of five years, with neither having lovers nor affairs, or the agreement would be dissolved. If Joe broke the agreement, Sable's money had to be returned within ninety days. At the end of the contract they could divorce, as Sable believed by then the LaCroix would no longer be interested in gaining custody of her son.

Sable would have no problem keeping to the terms of their deal. She hoped Joe wouldn't, either.

The wedding arrangements were left to her.

She studied the calendar. In one week she would be married and living out of state. The LaCroix family might have influence in Louisiana, but their influence didn't reach as far as Texas. Let them try to prove her an unfit mother, when she was the wife of a man whose name was as well-known in Texas as their son's in Louisiana. She had just bought her guarantee that Johnny was hers.

Talia stuck her head around the door. "Everything okay?"

"Better than okay. How would you like to be a bridesmaid?" Sable saw her little sister's eyes widen. "Who bought it?"

"Joe Lombardi."

If it was possible, Talia's eyes opened even wider. "Really?" she squeaked, bouncing into the room and perching on the side of the desk. "When?"

"Next week."

Talia frowned. "Have you told him about me being part of the package deal?"

"Not yet. I'll tell him when the time is right."

"You don't think I'll jinx the deal, do you?"

Sable's hand covered her sister's. "Not a chance. He's marrying me because he needs the money. I'm marrying him because we need a protector. We both get what we want. It's a simple business deal."

Talia glanced down, then back up at her sister, her brown eyes showing her vulnerability. "Does he know why you won't fight for Johnny in court?"

Leaning back, Sable stared at the hand that lay on top of her sister's. They were still together. "The custody suit you and I went through has nothing to do with him. It's none of his concern."

Talia looked at her—wise beyond her years, Sable reflected. "Regardless of the fact that you were the one our parents fought over?"

"That's not true and you know it. Dad fought for me because I was easier to care for, that's all."

"Honest?"

Sable smiled. It was the truth as she saw it. They had never really discussed it, although both had thought about it plenty. Talia had gone through hell in those days. She still bore the emotional scars inflicted by parents who hadn't been mature enough to behave like adults. But with lots of love Talia had pulled through—no thanks to their parents. Sable would not let Jonathan go through the same pain.

"Honest."

Talia's expression eased. She sat down in the red leather wing chair and leaned forward. "Good. Now, business or not, this is a wedding. What are you going to wear?"

2

SABLE PACED her study for a full hour before she finally found the nerve to dial Joe's number. She found him intimidating and highly frustrating, so she had put off their conversation until there were too many unanswered questions to be ignored. For three days she had not only been planning a wedding, but also a change of residence for herself and two others. And Joe Lombardi had never called her.

She let the phone ring—seven, eight, nine times. She was afraid that if she hung up she'd never have enough nerve to try again. Besides, it was better to try to reach him while she was still angry with the LaCroix's latest move. They had just informed her that they wanted Johnny to remain in Louisiana whenever she used the company plane. They were still ignorant of her wedding plans, and she wanted to keep things that way until the last moment but she still worried that they might suspect.

On the eleventh ring the phone was picked up. "Tejas Stables," Joe barked into the receiver.

If his tone was any indication of his mood, this phone call was going to require all her strength and tact.

"Mr. Lombardi?" she questioned hesitantly, praying it was someone else.

"Yes, what is it?"

This was going to be harder than she thought. "This is Sable LaCroix. I need some questions answered. Are you free for a few minutes?"

"Right now?"

"Yes." Her answer was firm. Her knees were weak.

A heavy sigh filled the wires. "I've got exactly five minutes, honey. Ahab's getting loaded onto a truck, so Totty can drive him to a race in Louisiana. Start asking."

Honey? He had some nerve! Sable wished she had time to count to ten. And who in the world was Totty? Instead she plunged ahead. "Is the entire house furnished?"

Silence.

She tried again. "How many bedrooms are there?"

Silence.

"How many baths?"

A sigh.

Now she was getting somewhere, she just wasn't sure where. "Do you have a washer and dryer?"

A groan, but still no answer.

"How large is the garage? Are there shelves for books? Is there enough storage area or should I rent a space? Is there a dishwasher?"

She stopped for a breath and waited.

Still no answer.

"Mr. Lombardi? Are you there?"

His voice was low, sounding tired. "Honey, I think you should come here and look around. I've lived here over five years, and I never thought of noticing half of what you're asking. It's not important for me to know. But if it is to you, then pick a time when I'm gone all day, and you can answer your questions to your heart's content."

"I don't have time, Mr. Lombardi," she stated firmly. "I'm trying to do most of the plans for the wedding from here, so I won't lose time packing. But I need answers, so I know what to pack and what to discard."

"Just pack a suitcase—one for you, one for the kid—and get your rump to Texas. You can handle the rest from here. Anything that doesn't go in a suitcase, you don't need."

He knew better than to make stupid statements like that, and this man wasn't stupid, so he was having fun by harassing her. It wasn't going to work. She wouldn't be put off.

Ignoring his comments, Sable plunged ahead. "As for the wedding, Mr. Lombardi, it's being held in your living room. I have a right to have my things around me, as much as you have a right to have yours. I'm only trying to work out a compromise in the easiest way possible."

"Then come and look around before moving in. I don't have time to answer questions. I've got a racetrack to build."

Her anger rose in response to his rudeness. "May I remind you that without answers to these questions, I might not marry you," she told him coldly. "Then you wouldn't have the necessary money to complete your pet project."

"Suit yourself, honey. I can always find other backers, but I still have to get the racetrack ready."

She tapped her nails on the edge of the rosewood desk. He was calling her bluff. She didn't know how much truth there was in his last sentence—and didn't have the nerve to find out.

"All right, Mr. Lombardi," she said reluctantly, resigning herself to the inevitable. "I'll be there in two days."

"Fine," he answered. "The front door's always open. Just walk in and make yourself at home."

"Thank you," she said stiffly. "I will."

"Don't I know it," he muttered before hanging up. Sable was left with a dial tone in her ear and a thousand curses in five languages on the tip of her tongue.

She had two days to count to ten—five thousand times. Maybe then, and only then, she could control her temper enough not to lose it within the next three minutes of conversation with Mr. Joe Lombardi!

JOE JUMPED into the truck, gunned the engine and sped out of the yard toward the dirt road leading to the track.

He felt ashamed of the way he'd just acted toward Sable, and shame always made him act overly tough and aggressive.

Couldn't she understand? His prize thoroughbred was on his way to a sweepstakes race. He was in the middle of building a racetrack, with the Texas government breathing down his neck. And she was asking about dishwashers!

She needed to get her priorities straight!

Wasn't he helping her out enough by marrying her? The dirt swirled around the fast-moving truck as his thoughts raced further ahead. He needed money, and she needed a respectable husband.

Well, he could live with that. What he didn't need was a wife, helpmate and leech, who would want his time and whine over his every move. He'd been single too long for that nonsense.

There had always been women when he'd needed them. Today's women only asked for equal treatment and a good time.

He gave them both. Then, with neither guilt nor regret, he moved on to the next one.

But Sable LaCroix wasn't that kind of woman. He doubted if she knew what bra burning was all about. She was a throwback to gentler, Southern ways. And so their conversation had been rougher than normal, because he was trying to make a point. He was his own man, and she wasn't going to change his life-style. Period.

He hoped she'd gotten the message.

TWO DAYS LATER, Sable drove her station wagon over the Montgomery County line in Texas with a smile of satisfaction.

Joe Lombardi had told her to answer her own questions—and she would do just that. Instead of one suitcase, however, she had a matched set of six, a box of toys for Johnny and five cases of books. The moving company would bring the rest.

She turned onto a farm-to-market road, an antiquated Texas term left over from the times when farms surrounded the cities, and counties built just a few good roads for farmers to travel with their produce. This one led to Joe's place.

Sable had a feeling that Joe enjoyed his bachelor freedom too much to give it up lightly. He probably thought threats and rough talk would make clear his intention to be boss in their marriage. He didn't know her very well. In fact he didn't know her at all. Obviously no one had told him that hens usually ruled the roost, and that the rooster was there only on sufferance.

But when it came to her son, Sable was a tigress. She'd do anything to keep Johnny. Anything—including marrying a bully of a man. And if the man didn't like it—tough luck. According to his attorney, he'd already agreed to her terms. Besides, whom was he fooling when he said he could find backers? If that had been the case, he wouldn't have agreed to this marriage in the first place.

After thinking through his threats, Sable had realized that Joe Lombardi had as little choice as she did. And that kept her smiling.

After following a dirt lane about half a mile off the main thoroughfare, she pulled up in front of Joe's house. It was a big, rambling ranch house that looked as if each owner had built an addition to it with no regard for an overall, architectural design. However, despite having wings and windows placed at odd angles, it all came together very well, reminding Sable of an old grande dame who still wore feathers and pearls with her silk dresses and high-buttoned shoes. A unique style, it was unacceptable on anyone else. On this old lady it was perfect.

She pulled up to the porch that ran the length of the front and one side and stepped out. Paint had bubbled and flaked away around the eaves. The porch floor, although sturdy, also needed a new coat of paint.

She opened the screen door to find the front door wide open, as Joe had said it would be. Joe was either trusting or foolhardy to leave his home unlocked this close to a huge metropolis like Houston.

But as she wandered through the rooms, she began to see that the only damage an interloper could do here would be to spray-paint the walls—and considering their condition, that just might be an improvement.

The living-room furniture was in colonial style and at least twenty years old. Sable lifted a couch cushion and wrinkled her nose. Hard-candy wrappers and bottle tops were scattered here and there, along with crumbs of what looked like potato chips. She'd bet the furniture had never been cleaned.

The dining-room set was solid mahogany. This she knew only because she wiped off at least ten years of dust to find the grain and color. The china cabinet held beautiful, floral-patterned dishes and cut crystal water and wineglasses, along with sterling silver serving pieces. Or rather she thought they were silver beneath the tarnish.

All four bedrooms were furnished with plain, sturdy pieces. But nothing matched. The spreads and curtains were in keeping with the furniture—nothing matched there, either.

Mr. Joseph Lombardi was consistent in his taste: he had none.

The kitchen, however, was the masterpiece. Dishes were stacked on one side of the sink, while the other side was clean and clear. The sink itself was filled with pots and pans soaking in sudsy, cold water. She peeked into the dishwasher. It was spotlessly clean and empty. Joe Lombardi obviously didn't use this appliance.

The blue-gray Formica table was spotless, but the floor was a mess. The tile could have been either gray or white, Sable couldn't tell. Now it was a spotted tan with dirty-brown boot marks in strategic places, like the doorway and in front of the refrigerator and sink.

Just off the kitchen she could see a utility room with a washer, dryer and a set-up ironing board piled high with clothing, as well as an upright freezer.

Carefully Sable opened the refrigerator and peeked inside. She found ketchup, mustard, relish, mild and piquant sauces and milk. Two open containers of luncheon meat and cheese completed the food list. The rest of the space on the shelves was filled with at least three twelve-packs of beer.

She wrinkled her nose in distaste. "Mr. Lombardi, you're in for quite a culture shock," she announced, firmly shutting the door.

Sable retraced her steps to the front of the house and descended the steps to unload the car.

Half an hour later as she reached for the last box, she spied dirt swirling on the road to the house. "The cavalry, no doubt," she panted, carefully balancing the box as she headed up the porch steps once more. "And just in the nick of time . . . for one of us."

Before the truck pulled to a halt in the driveway, she managed to open the screen door and make it down the hallway to the bedroom she'd declared her own. All she had to do was inform the master of the house—after she'd moved in.

Wiping suddenly damp hands on the back of her slacks, she walked back and casually leaned against the doorjamb while Joe came toward the house. She tried for a condescending smile. Better to let him know now how it was between them than to find out later she hadn't written the right guidelines.

She felt his gaze dissolve every piece of clothing from her body. His eyes told her he appreciated what, but not necessarily whom he saw.

He was raw virility.

His blue plaid shirt brought out his golden tan and the matching blue of his eyes. His broad chest and muscled arms strained against the fabric.

He was as handsome as sin.

"Hello, *sweetie*. I didn't expect you to be waiting at the door for me," he said as he strode up the steps, only to stop within inches of her. "But these days it's not enough just to be decorative. Next time have an open beer in your hand."

And he was quite obnoxious.

"Look closely, *sweetlings*," she said stiffly. "Because you'll never see me in this domestic-bliss position again, let alone with a beer in my hand."

His brows rose, but a smile still lurked at the corners of his mouth. A very male, very smug smile. "Are we upset about something, darlingkins?"

"Nothing in particular, *honey bun*, except that you choose to live in squalor and I won't."

Now his voice held an edge. "Then clean it, *sweetlings*."

"No way, *darling*. It's not *my* dirt. It's yours."

Joe's chest expanded as he took a deep, exasperated breath. "Dirt is dirt. I don't pander to helpless little females, so if you want a clean home, clean it yourself."

Sable stood even straighter, her eyes blazing. "I am a very good housekeeper. Probably the best you've ever known. But I will *not* clean years of accumulated dirt that I had nothing to do with. Nor will I live in it."

Joe cocked his head. "So what do you plan to do about it, brown eyes?"

She smiled, and for just a fleeting second she saw the fear her reaction gave Joe. "I expect you to have a cleaning crew in here within the next three days to scrub this place from top to bottom. If they don't, then we can call the whole deal off."

He believed she'd do it! "Just like that?"

Sable nodded, her gaze steel-hard. "Just like that."

His eyes narrowed. "And what other conditions do you have up your sleeve?"

"That's it, Mr. Lombardi. I will keep *our* house clean from the wedding on. But I refuse to clean your old mess for you."

A war was raging inside him, she could tell. Sable held her breath. She had no idea if he would remain obstinate, but this first confrontation would tell what kind of man he was. She crossed her fingers behind her back and waited.

"Okay. I agree," he finally muttered. "It isn't fair for you to clean what isn't your dirt. I'll have a crew in here immediately."

She let her breath out slowly and smiled. Joe took a step back, then swung around and went inside the house. But just as she turned to follow, pleased with his answer, he ruined it all.

"But mind you," Joe threw over his shoulder as he walked to the kitchen and opened the refrigerator door. "I expect you to keep this place spotless after that. You're home all day with nothing to do."

"Nothing to do?" she repeated softly. "Nothing to do?" she practically shouted. "I happen to have a son who is in the middle of his messy period. And for the past two years I've been chairman of several charities, to say nothing of my foundation to help the hungry children in America!"

Joe popped the top of his can and took a long, thirsty pull. Wiping his mouth on his shirt sleeve he grinned. "La-di-da, soon-to-be Mrs. Lombardi. Your charities are in Louisiana, not here. My wife will drop those things that have nothing to do with this state."

Her next words dripped poison. "You mean like invest in a beer distributorship? Or find great locations to drop off the weekly barn-mucking offal? Or perhaps I could volunteer at shelters for the battered and neglected wives of racehorse owners."

His face was a thundercloud, his tone a soft warning. "Don't push, Sable. This whole situation is hard enough already."

It was obviously time to try a different tack. "You're right," she said, her eyes demurely downcast. "There's no sense arguing right now. We can work it out later. Together."

His eyes narrowed as he stared at her. She gazed back, her expression bland. *Let him make what he wants of it*, she thought, she wasn't going to queer the deal now. Not when he'd agreed to hire a cleaning crew. Sable had an idea that when it came to women, most of him was bluff and the rest indecision. She'd have plenty of time to test out her theory later.

"By the way," she asked softly. "Do you mind if I take the bedroom across the hall from yours? It's the perfect size, and there's a connecting door to what will be Johnny's room. That way, if he's restless, you won't lose sleep. I can be with him in an instant."

"Be my guest," he replied, though his expression was anything but gracious.

"Thank you." She smiled sweetly.

Joe let out a grunt of exasperation. "What are your plans for moving in?"

"I'm returning home tonight to pack the rest of my things." She gave him a coy glance through her lashes. "You don't mind if I have the moving company bring a few pieces of my furniture, do you? Jonathan needs his own bedroom set, and of course I have my own, too."

"Anything else?" he asked dryly.

She knew her act wasn't fooling him, but she went through with it, anyway. "Oh, there's a few pieces of furniture I'd like to add to yours, if it's all right. I promise it will only enhance the rooms, not crowd them."

"Now listen carefully," he admonished, his face stern. "I don't want my life-style changed. I like my furniture. I like the way it looks. It's neat, and there's no fussy gewgaws around to collect dust or get broken."

"Really? Early bachelor decor appeals to you, does it?"

"Yes." He bit the word out.

"Well, a little more style appeals to me," she told him, barely containing her temper. "And there doesn't appear to be a drop of it in this house."

"Fine. Just keep it confined to your bedroom."

She tilted her chin. "If that's the way you want it."

"I do."

Sable turned on her heel and marched down the hall to "her" bedroom, slamming the door behind her.

Leaning against the cool wood, she breathed deeply, trying to calm her pounding heart. Damn that man! He gave orders like a king! Giving orders as if he owned the place!

He does own the place, her too logical mind answered.

Her temper dissolved. She felt a smile quirk the corners of her mouth. The smile turned into a giggle, which grew into laughter.

JOE STOOD at the kitchen window, taking several deep, cleansing breaths. Blood pounded in his ears, and he wasn't sure if it was due to anger or arousal. Either way his reaction was the same.

Sable had a way of getting under his skin and scrambling his thoughts, until he didn't know what he was saying anymore! Her sparkling, brown eyes, her light, flowery scent twisted his tongue and made him sound like a schoolboy. The sight of her long-limbed body encased in expensive, clinging slacks and a sweater that probably cost as much as his feed bill drove him up the wall.

So here he stood. They'd just had an argument, and she'd had the audacity to walk away from him into "her" room. He wanted her back in the kitchen. *His* kitchen! The whole house was his!

What was the matter with her? Hadn't he just graciously given in and said she didn't have to clean the house? Hadn't he said he'd get a cleaning crew in here, pronto? Was it too much to ask that she keep it clean from then on? Or was she too spoiled to see the leeway he'd willingly given her?

No, that wasn't quite true. He'd been riding her ever since that last phone call, and they both knew it. He had purposely used harsh words and curt actions to keep distance between them. Obviously it wasn't working, or he'd be in better shape than he was right now. The symptoms were more than apparent: he was in his cavemanlike, kiss-her-or-kill-her mode. But he was a civilized man and would wait for the feelings to subside. Confusion always made him feel aggressive.

He admitted, at least to himself, that he didn't know much about the workings of a woman's mind. He'd never had time or inclination to study them. On a one-to-one basis he'd always found they were either nice or they weren't. That was all he needed to know, or so he'd thought until now. Suddenly he wished he understood those small nuances that some men seemed to have a knack of picking up. He was lost.

A sigh left his lips and anger drained with the breath. He wasn't scared of Sable LaCroix. He was scared to death of his reaction to her. And he was even more afraid to let her know. This was a business proposition. She'd made that fact clear from the beginning. The least he could do was to remember that. Then he wouldn't find himself making a pass, only to be turned down and embarrassed.

A sound—faint at first—filtered down the hallway to the kitchen. As it became louder he recognized it. Sable was laughing. Laughing! Behind his closed door and while he was frustrated and in pain, Sable was laughing!

He didn't know how he got to "her" bedroom door, but his hand had turned the knob even before he realized he was there. He pushed against it, and with little resistance it opened.

"Something funny?" Joe's tone was acerbic as he stared into her twinkling, brown eyes.

"Yes," she gurgled, still barely able to keep the laughter under control. "I was laughing at myself. I was so angry at you for acting as if you owned this house. Then I realized that you did. Own it, I mean."

"And that's funny?"

She nodded, her brown hair catching the last rays of the afternoon sun. "Don't you think so?"

His mouth quirked against his wishes. "Yeah," he finally admitted. "I guess so."

Sable giggled again, and the sound sped sensuously down his spine. "I'm surprised that I didn't order you out of your own house," she chortled. "Can you imagine?"

He couldn't hold his smile in check any longer. "And I'd have reminded you whose house it was."

"And left me speechless and totally without dignity!"

He glanced down her enticing figure, then back up to her eyes. She was desirable. And absolutely beautiful. "This is dignity?" he asked, knowing it was either tease her or kiss her.

"This is as good a try at dignity as I'm going to get under the circumstances," she teased back. "At least I'm trying."

Sable took a deep breath to control her laughter. He was sure she didn't realize what she did to him when she placed her slender hand against his chest. "I'm sorry," she said. "It's just so darn funny."

"Sable LaCroix, you're something else." Joe took a step closer to her, leaving barely an inch of space between them. "Something very unusual."

Her smile drifted away as she stared into his eyes. He hoped he wasn't reading her reaction wrong, because he was going to kiss her, no matter what.

"Really?" she asked. Her voice was soft, wispy, and he was drowning in her big, brown eyes.

"Really," he growled, just before covering her lips with his. Her mouth was soft, her breath as warm as a summer day. And he absorbed it until he could feel the freshness of her down to his toes.

His tongue asked for admittance and she acquiesced. She wrapped her arms around his neck as he pulled her closer and deepened the kiss, feeling her body flow against his in molten delight. How had he gone so long without knowing this wonderful feeling? he wondered. Then his mind went blank as pleasure took over.

Somewhere in the distance a car backfired, and with the sound reality returned.

Joe eased away.

Sable was startled to find herself feeling bereft. It was a struggle to open her eyes and stare up at him. She wanted to feel him, not see him.

"Are you all right?" His voice was as rough as coarse sandpaper.

She nodded, then cleared her throat. "I'm fine." What a stupid thing to say! She was not fine! She was fraying at the edges from a kiss that had robbed her of all sense!

"We shouldn't have done that."

She shook her head. "No, you shouldn't. This is a business deal. Nothing more." Her insides still quaked from his touch. *It was just a kiss!* she told herself, still stunned by the strength of her reaction.

"On the other hand," he continued, ignoring her gentle rebuke. "Maybe it's good we got this out of the way now. We would have always wondered what it would be like to kiss. Now we know."

Sable stared blankly at him. "Now we know what?"

His lips turned up in a smile, displaying a deep dimple just below one eye. His finger traced the outline of her lips before he answered, and she found herself pouting in reaction to his touch. "Now we know what it's like to kiss. Our curiosity is abated."

"Right," she murmured, her mind still dazed. "Our curiosity is abated."

"Now we can get on with this business arrangement and not let our, uh, personal observations get in the way."

Sable finally took his point. "Your curiosity is abated. Mine was never piqued."

His husky chuckle filled the air. "You make one hell of a lousy liar, Sable. But if that's what it takes for you to feel better about yourself . . ."

Her backbone stiffened, as if all the vertebrae had suddenly been glued together. "No lies, Mr. Lombardi. Just the plain and simple truth. It never occurred to me to make your kisses a fantasy of mine. Your kiss was nice, but please don't worry about my panting to repeat it. It was just another kiss. That's all."

Joe's smile disappeared and a frown creased his forehead. "Right," he snapped. "Now what are those boxes doing in the corner?"

She followed his gaze. "Those boxes are books and Johnny's toys. Since I had to come here, I brought them to save moving time."

"Do you have your answers now?"

"Yes."

"Good. Don't bother telling me what you found out. I'm not interested. You can go on your way, and I can get back to work before I lose the entire day fooling around."

"If you 'fool around,' as you so aptly put it, then it's not my fault. I got my answers on my own, unpacked on my own, and now I'm leaving. On my own."

"Then we don't have a problem, do we?" he practically shouted.

"No problem at all," she answered in kind.

After a hard, blue-eyed stare, he left her. His steps echoed down the hallway to the front door. The screen squeaked open, then closed with a resounding bang.

Sable held her head in her hands and prayed for control. She had more problems than she could shake a stick at, and all of them had to do with her husband-to-be, Joe Lombardi.

JOE SLID into the front seat and fired up the truck, gunning the engine as soon as it started.

No problem, he'd said. Whom was he kidding? He had more problems than he could cope with! For two cents he'd call the whole thing off. But for a million he'd try to make the best of it. All he had to do was remember that Sable LaCroix was more of a problem than he could handle, and that would remind him to keep his distance.

Somehow the idea of keeping his distance wasn't as reassuring as it should have been.

3

IT TOOK the cleaning crew three days. They cleaned in places Joe didn't even know existed and some he didn't want to know about at all. They even went through his personal closet, then straightened out the linen closet, which had become a catchall over the years for anything made of fabric, including the mending.

He had to admit that Sable was right. The place had only been surface-cleaned in the past, and years of dust and dirt had made their way throughout the house. After the carpeting was steam-cleaned he realized the rug was rust-colored, not brown.

And much as he hated to admit it, Joe liked the "new" look.

What he didn't like was Sable pointing it out to him. Dammit, he'd been too busy earning a living to be a hausfrau, too! Besides, he was only home for morning and evening meals and to sleep. Almost all his free time was spent with the men in the bunkhouse, where they made plans for the next day's work or watched televised sports.

Now his life was changing. Sable was coming to live here, and no matter how hard he tried to pretend that things would remain the same, he knew they would not. Any woman was bound to upset his life. That the woman was Sable . . . he stopped his thoughts whenever they strayed to her.

After duly admiring their work, he paid off the cleaning crew and ushered them out. At last the house was quiet once more. He reached into the fridge for a beer and pulled the tab.

There was no sense in going back out to the track. It was almost quitting time for the men. Besides, he'd run from his thoughts ever since Sable had left. He needed to confront them and get himself back together before she returned at the end of the week.

He was marrying Sable LaCroix on Sunday afternoon.

He plopped onto the couch and stared out the front bay window at the towering pines that shielded his home from the farm road beyond. He lived in a forest that hid his personal paradise, giving him privacy to relax, away from the prying eyes of the civilized world.

He was almost there.

His life-style had reflected his goals: Keep Your Nose to the Grindstone—and look neither left nor right, unless you're changing lanes. He liked his life that way. It had been easier to know he had to plow forward rather than run in circles. Until now.

Ever since he'd left the service and moved to Conroe, where he'd worked on a thoroughbred ranch, he'd been knee-deep in plans and saving every dime he earned for his dream. Knowing he had a knack, an instinct with animals and the races they could win, he'd pursued that dream. He'd vowed he would have his ranch someday, and six years ago his dream had come true. He'd been happy from the moment he'd signed the papers to this place.

In those days he'd even attempted to clean it on a regular basis. Occasionally a female came over and fussed, showing how domesticated and necessary she was to him, but then she'd leave, and Joe would go back to his own ways. That had been before his horses won a few of the more important races and he learned the value of a good reputation to the world of finance. Nothing was more important than his career.

Thanks to Ahab's stud capabilities and the right combination of genes, he now had three blue-ribbon winners. They'd made him a millionaire. His dream had come true.

Having attained one goal, he began looking around for another.

Then last year the state of Texas had decided that horse racing—with betting—was a legitimate business. Everyone and his brother tried out for the licenses. Out of over three hundred entries, his and four others had passed muster. Three other horse breeders and Mike, his attorney, had formed a partnership. Then had begun the long process of completing the necessary paperwork.

The racing commission checked him over each step of the way, cross-examining him in public courts, testing the truth of each of his words by double-checking, and then making him cool his heels before they gave him the next set of red tape to work through. His friends had supplied the commission with glowing recommendations. His luck had held, and the racetrack was to be the only one in the fourteen surrounding counties.

Since the other investors were silent partners, to all intents and purposes this was *his* track, his baby. He had to channel all his efforts and energy into this demanding task, or fail.

Sable's million dollars meant that Joe retained the controlling interest; it would be used as collateral for another two million. He needed the loan desperately. The other investors were tapped out—broke—until they received a return on their investment. Just as broke as he was. Everything he had or ever would have was tied up in this deal. He wanted to own the best track in the state. In the country. Landscaping alone was costing half a million. He was sparing no expense, providing larger-than-theater seats, public and private lounges, and elaborate quarters for both horses and jockeys. Someday he'd have a national race at his track, one equal to the Preakness Stakes or the Kentucky Derby.

And in the midst of all these crises he was getting *married*.

Joe leaned his head back and closed his eyes. Maybe once all this wedding hoopla was over and they settled into some kind of routine, it wouldn't be so bad. After all, she had a child and a house to care for and shower attention on, while he went about, doing his own thing.

The memory of their kiss came back to haunt him. It was unlike all the other kisses he'd ever had, and he resented that. But while resentment built in his mind, his body had a whole different list of possibilities and reacted every time he thought of her. Even now his skin flushed, and he tingled all the way down to his knees. He wished she were here to repeat it . . . just to see if it was as good as his memory kept telling him.

Whom are you kidding, Lombardi? he demanded. *That kiss was as close to fire as you've ever gotten. Only intense fear made you end it. Fear of getting involved with a woman who could take you away from your goal. Repeat it and you might get burned so badly, you'd never recover!*

All his instincts told him to run from Sable as quickly and as far as he could. But he had to ignore those instincts. He had no choice in the matter. Not if he wanted to continue building his dream.

And the racetrack, he kept reminding himself, was what this whole charade was about. The track was his first love and the one that counted. The one he stood to lose, if he didn't continue to concentrate on it.

The thought stiffened his resolve. Right. He had no choice. From now on he'd be nice and kind—and keep his distance from Mrs. Sable LaCroix. That way they'd both be able to stick to their parts of the bargain. Otherwise, he was sure he'd live to regret it.

His fingers tightened on the barely touched beer can. Forcing his eyes open, he banished the image of Sable staring up at him, brown eyes sultry and half-closed. He'd wanted to ravish her there and then. He still did. But he was a grown man. He should be able to handle temptation by now. Especially considering what was at stake.

Sable was just a woman—and he was just a man. Two ordinary people. That was all. Just because they were man and woman didn't mean they had to play Adam and Eve. Hell, he'd seen lots of beautiful women in his time and still hadn't gotten emotionally involved.

He sighed. "Get off your rear, Lombardi," he chided himself. "And finish the paperwork you've been putting off."

He proceeded to do just that.

SABLE STARED around her study. She would miss this small, but comfortable room. It held an antique lady's desk in Queen Anne style, two chairs, a filing cabinet and several small paintings she'd collected over the years. The colors were light: peach and green with sprays of white. It was a restful place, next to Jonathan's room, so she could listen for him in the evening. His room was also done in pastel colors, but its walls were hung with pictures of balloons and teddy bears.

She was excited, but there was also an overriding sorrow. By this time next week she would be Mrs. Joseph Lombardi. The end of one life and the beginning of another.

Married. She vaguely remembered feeling this way when she'd left her aunt's home to marry John. She'd been young and impressionable, scared and unbelievably excited, even though her aunt had at the best of times been what the kids now called a "downer," pouring cold water on everything fun.

Looking back, Sable had often wondered if she'd married John as much to get away from the older woman's influence as because she was in love with him. But she banished those thoughts immediately, because they smacked of treason to John's memory.

The truth was, she had met and fallen in love with him as a teenager of nineteen and married him the day after her twentieth birthday. She had admired him almost as a father figure because he was eleven years older. But over the first two years of their marriage their roles had slowly shifted. She'd become the mother, nurturing him as if she were taking up where his mother had left off. Now she wasn't sure how their marriage would have developed in later years.

When John died, Sable had never dreamed she'd marry again. He'd left her with a child she adored and more than enough money to keep her in style for the rest of her life. Every time she saw her financial statement, her inheritance staggered her. Ironically, it was John's money that had bought her new groom.

She'd thought she'd never have to marry again, because she had her own form of independence. Weren't money and love two of the main reasons most women married? Wasn't financial security the main reason for most second marriages?

Yet here she was, getting married again. Love had nothing to do with it. Money did.

Three years ago she'd been content, caring for her son and sister, and living with the sweetest and gentlest man she'd ever known. John. Now she was contemplating a life where she would be a wife in name only—and she was *paying* the man to agree to it!

The office door opened slightly, interrupting Sable's reverie. Her sister gazed through the widening crack. "Getting prenuptial jitters?" Talia asked.

When Sable chuckled, Talia knew it was okay to enter. She walked in and perched on the arm of the wing chair.

"Hardly," Sable stated dryly. She was unwilling to admit her feelings of confusion to anyone, even to Talia.

Talia studied Sable's expression. "Then why the frown?"

"There's just so much to do and such a short time to sort it all out." Sable tried to contain her sigh. She couldn't admit to jitters, but they'd plagued her ever since she'd overheard John's parents discussing how to obtain custody of Jonathan.

"Anything I can do to help?"

Sable smiled. "Not so far, but I'll keep you in mind for some of the bigger problems."

"Right," Talia drawled, knowing full well her sister wouldn't let her handle anything larger than an occasional frying pan. "Have you told your future husband about me yet?"

Sable shifted in her seat. "Not yet."

Talia stared. "Why not?"

"The subject just hasn't come up yet."

"Liar," her little sister declared. "You're chicken." Then Talia's eyes widened. "Are you afraid he'll say no to the deal if he finds out about me?"

"Not really," Sable hedged. "I just thought it'd be easier to present you as a fait accompli."

"What's that?"

"It means that it's already done."

"*After* the wedding?"

Sable nodded, hoping her sister wouldn't feel too bad about being kept a secret.

"You really think that's wise?"

"There are so many other things to worry about right now. I can't see where telling him later will do any harm."

Talia furrowed her brow as she worried through the information. She was far more clinical than Sable, dissecting and rearranging information like a capable computer, then spitting out the options. "Hmm, might not be a bad idea at that," she mused. "That way he can't renege on the deal."

Sable's breath came out in a relieved whoosh. "That's right."

"Say," Talia began again, still frowning. "You're not thinking of shipping me off to boarding school, are you? It's bad enough that I have to move before my senior year. I want my family with me wherever I am."

Sable relaxed and let herself smile. "No one is putting you anywhere. You'll be with me, just like we always planned," she stated firmly.

Talia relaxed but persisted with her concerns. "It's just that I could understand if you wanted a year or so to get accustomed to this, uh, new arrangement."

"There's nothing to get used to, darling. This is a marriage of convenience. Nothing more." Sable's voice was calm. At least she knew what she was talking about on this subject.

"Okay." Her little sister shrugged, but Sable knew she was relieved. "So what happens next?"

"Next the movers begin packing our belongings tomorrow morning. On Friday we leave for Texas. All of us."

"Have you told your esteemed in-laws yet?"

"Not yet. Not until Friday morning."

Talia grinned. "Don't shoot the in-laws till you see the whites of their eyes."

"Remember the Alamo," Sable retorted, wondering if it was going to be her dying cry.

With Joe Lombardi on her side, could anyone be sure who would win the war?

SUNDAY WAS BEAUTIFUL, perfect for a wedding. The sun was buttery bright, but not too hot, and a light breeze soothed like gentle fingers.

Sable stared at herself in the mirror and wondered why she was so nervous. Looking calm and collected, the woman in the mirror stared back. At least her usual façade was still in place, even though her stomach churned.

Her wedding dress was of pale aqua silk, her hat a gauzy material that matched the dress and shoes. Simplicity and style, perfect for her height and figure.

Sensing the doubts running through Sable's mind, Talia gave her sister a hug. "You're a knockout," she stated with just a touch of envy.

"Thanks." Sable forced a smile. "I needed that."

"I don't know why. You're gorgeous. And the groom is a perfect match. He's so handsome."

Sable faced her sister. "You've seen him?"

"Yes. He's tall, dark and exciting. What he does to a tuxedo could only be described in a romance novel."

Romance novels were Sable's weakness. She read them by the ton and Talia knew it.

"That good, huh?"

"That good. He's dy-na-mite. And just as nervous as you are."

"I'm not—" Sable began, then stopped, unable to deny the emotion that was turning her bones into putty. "Is everyone here?"

"It looks like it. The place is crawling with people."

"Do you recognize anyone?"

"Well, it looks like everyone from the guest list is here, including your attorney and his secretary, along with two women from the foundation office," Talia reported. "The rest are all Joe's friends and business associates. Plus a few characters." Talia chuckled. "There's a bald-headed, bowlegged man who's got the face of Gabby Hayes and the voice of the Strangler. Joe calls him Totty, which should be the name of a chic model—or a Barbie doll's best friend."

Sable nodded, smiling at her sister's astute comment. She hadn't invited anyone other than those Talia had mentioned. "Are the caterers having any more problems? They couldn't decide where to set up the tents earlier."

Talia shook her head. "No. They set up the tents in the front. And the makeshift kitchen is a marvel to behold."

"No one's bothered me for the past hour," Sable said, suddenly worried. "Are you sure everything's okay?"

"Promise." Talia crossed her heart.

A knock on the door stopped Sable from asking more questions.

"Mrs. LaCroix? The minister says it's time." One of the maids hired for the occasion stood just outside the doorway with a warm smile of admiration. "And you do make a beautiful bride."

Sable smiled gratefully. "Thank you. I'll be right there." As the woman backed out, Sable stopped her. "Wait," she said. "Your sister is taking care of Johnny, isn't she?"

The woman nodded. "He's taking his nap right now, but when he wakes, she'll feed and play with him for a while, then bring him down to the reception."

"Tell her thank you again for me, will you?"

"I will," the maid promised. "And don't worry. She's raised three of her own. She knows what to do."

When the door closed, Sable took another deep breath and smiled. "Are you ready, Sis?"

"Ready," Talia answered, brushing the skirt of her pale peach dress. She looked much older than her seventeen years, Sable reflected. But luckily Talia still thought that meeting boys was a game. She hadn't yet reached the stage of regarding them as trophies to be won. Sable hoped things stayed that way for a little while longer. Talia had grown up so fast in so many other ways, it was nice to know that boys weren't part of the picture—yet.

"Let's go!" Sable declared with bravado. All the way down the hall to the living room, she prayed she was doing the right thing. Doubts assailed her from all directions, and they all centered on her husband-to-be.

Her gaze locked with Joe's. He stood by the side of the fireplace, his expression as stern as a schoolteacher's. Then suddenly he winked. With an inward sigh of relief she smiled, calm once more as she placed her hand in his. They turned toward the minister to speak their vows.

ALL OF JOE'S DOUBTS about the marriage hit him with stunning force, when he turned and saw Sable standing in the living room doorway.

She was beautiful. More than beautiful. Every man's dream of a bride. And she was his. Not to touch. Not to share. Just to give her his name. He had even signed a contract to that effect earlier that morning.

How was she going to manage, now that she was out of her own, exclusive element? This was no cosmopolitan city, not even a suburb. It was just a ranch house in a rural area. And she looked as if she couldn't swat a fly, let alone run a household or keep the home fires burning for her tired and overworked man to return to.

The second thought that came to mind astounded him.

She was an orchid. He was just a plain old wildflower. The two didn't go into the same corsage, let alone grow side by side.

This is a business marriage. Remember? he chided himself. But it didn't work. When she walked across the room and gave him her hand, his clasp was as light as a cobweb; he was afraid of hurting her.

Women like her belonged in the big city. Every woman he ever dated had sooner or later tried to get him to move to where the action was, in downtown Houston. Sable wouldn't be any different.

Afterward, others told him the marriage vows were perfect. But he didn't hear a word, didn't see anyone except Sable. He didn't give a damn about anything but getting through the ceremony. He was waiting for the kiss.

Then it was time and he got to do what he wanted. Joe lifted her veil and stared into eyes that were as uncertain as his. As vulnerable as a child's. As sensuous as those of a fully grown woman.

He was trapped. He knew it. And right now he didn't care.

His lips captured and held hers. He'd promised himself that it would be a short kiss, a kiss to seal their bargain. But he betrayed himself.

When his lips touched hers, every muscle in his body tightened to the breaking point. He forgot there was an audience, a minister, as his fingers tightened on her tiny waist. He pulled her closer, fitting her slender frame to his own hard body.

Her resisting hands scorched his chest as she pushed, to no avail. It took several seconds before he realized she was trying to push him away. He raised his head and stared down at her, his breath coming in short puffs.

Her eyes were enormous. "Joe," she whispered. "Everyone's waiting."

Her voice sounded like he felt: high and strung tight. But her words finally penetrated the fog in his brain. With a glance around the room, he pulled away.

Clearing his throat, he turned to the gathering. "Friends, may I introduce my wife, Sable LaCroix Lombardi."

The crowd clapped.

Still holding her hand tightly in his, Joe thanked the minister. Mike was best man and Talia had acted as bridesmaid. Suddenly Joe was glad his buddy was close by. He needed to get away from Sable if he was to think clearly.

Actually he needed a drink.

The guests engulfed them, expressing congratulations and good wishes, laughing, kissing and shaking hands. It was a nice feeling, one made nicer by the fact that those same people were separating him from Sable. Distance was imperative if he was at least to get his body under control. His mind might never be the same.

As his heartbeat evened out and his body relaxed, Joe returned to his senses. The desire to possess his new wife was still at the forefront, but he could handle it. It was just the nature of the situation, he told himself. Any man was allowed to become aroused on his wedding day—even if his wife was a nag. And Sable was not a nag. She was a thoroughbred.

Smiling as he made his way through the crowd of guests, Joe headed for the bar and ordered a beer. Sipping it, he watched the people surrounding his bride. Obviously she was bred to gracious hostessing. Their faces told him she'd charmed them, just as she had charmed him.

Wishing he was in his favorite jeans and shirt, he ran a finger around the collar of his tuxedo shirt. He wished he was in the barn. He'd never felt more like mucking out a stall so much in his life as he did right now.

Propping an elbow against the portable bar, he wrapped his fingers around the cold mug and frowned across the room at his new wife.

Mike came and stood beside him. "Congratulations, Joe. Sable is quite some woman."

"To say nothing of her million," Joe stated dryly, attempting to maintain his role as cynic.

"You mean to tell me you married her only because of her money?" Mike's voice was filled with disbelief.

"Of course," Joe declared evenly. "You ought to know. You arranged this little merger."

Mike grinned. "You might want to believe that tripe, but I know better. You couldn't have been hog-tied into marriage unless you wanted to be hog-tied. And that kiss was hardly platonic. The room temperature went up ten degrees."

Angry with himself for having revealed so much, Joe managed a shrug. "So what? She's a beautiful woman. I'm a normal man. End of story."

"Beginning of romance," Mike murmured, focusing his eyes on the group in the middle of the room.

Joe followed his friend's gaze. His eyes locked with bewitching, brown ones. Sable's expression was enigmatic, but somehow he knew that she was just as scared as he was.

The room full of guests disappeared. Only he and Sable remained. Joe couldn't turn away, couldn't look away. He couldn't do anything except remain caught in her gaze.

You kissed me as if you meant it, her eyes seemed to say.

You're beautiful. It's our wedding day, he answered.

But this is a business deal, not a springtime romance!

Did you like it? he questioned.

Too much.

So did I.

We shouldn't.

Let's pretend that we are really man and wife. Just for today. Let's be as happy for us as our friends are.

And when our friends leave?

The day is over.

And so is the game of Let's Pretend?

Yes.

Her sadness was as palpable as his own. Joe tried to convince himself that her responses were only in his imagination, but when he held out his hand to her in silent invitation, Sable responded by walking to his side and placing her hand in his. Her smile would have melted the hardest of hearts, but it was given to him.

People came up to them, and once more they played host and hostess. This time they stood together, holding hands. Both seemed content with the arrangement.

TALIA STUDIED Joe's young attorney and good friend. She had stood with him in front of the minister, unnoticed, acting as maid of honor to his best man. It didn't matter that he wasn't aware of her. He would be. She'd see to that. After all, she always got what she wanted. And she wanted Mike.

HER HAND firmly encased in Joe's, Sable smiled and chatted with their guests. But her mind was working overtime, replaying the earlier episode between Joe and herself.

When she'd looked up and met his admiring gaze, she'd been relieved. *Am I doing all right?* she had asked him silently.

You're doing fine, his look had answered. *I'm proud of the way you're handling everything.*

Then help me, she had requested. *Make certain that those who will carry details of the wedding back to Jonathan's grandparents in Louisiana will be satisfied with our motives.*

He'd held out his hand—and she'd been both relieved and sad. He was willing to help—but the whole day was a farce. They weren't in love. They weren't looking forward to spending the rest of their lives together. They were acting out parts in a play.

But right now that didn't matter. For the first time since she'd overheard the attorney and her now ex-in-laws discussing Jonathan's custody, the panic had subsided.

Everything was going to be all right. She knew it.

TALIA MADE HER WAY over to Mike, who was watching the guests as if he were conducting the orchestra, rather than being an item on the program.

"Nice crowd. Do you know everyone?" she asked.

Startled out of his reverie, Mike looked down at her. "Talia, isn't it?"

An impish smile played around her mouth. She nodded. "Since I was born."

"Which couldn't have been all that long ago."

His words were meant to emphasize the age difference between them. "Lucky, aren't I?" she queried lightly. "I still have the best years of my life ahead of me."

Again he looked startled. "Right," Mike finally drawled. "I wouldn't want to go through all those years again if I had a choice. It was too riddled with doubts and problems, to say nothing of acne."

Her smile grew broader. So he *was* interested. But her age was a definite drawback. "I agree on the problems and doubts. But I'll learn the answers with time. As for acne, I have no idea. I've never had it."

Mike laughed. "Does your sister know how precocious you are?"

"Alas, yes. She also knows my habit of going after what I want. Hence the nickname Spike, after a pit bulldog we knew."

He clearly understood her message. Mike took a step back. "I hope you're old enough to have learned to pursue only sure things."

"That's right." Her eyes twinkled with delight. "And the older I get, the more discerning I'll become."

He nodded sagely, but his eyes still held that wary look. "That's right."

"However," Talia added and grinned mischievously. "Wisdom doesn't automatically come with age."

"Then I'd ask someone older for advice. Your sister would have sound thoughts on the matter."

"What matter?" she asked innocently.

"Any matter," he snapped, obviously unnerved by what she was intimating, yet not sure if he was reading her correctly.

"Oh." She breathed slowly, then smiled at him again. "Well, it's been nice talking to you, Mike. I know we'll see each other often."

She turned to leave, but his hand lightly captured her arm. "Often?" he repeated.

"Yes. Didn't you know? I'm living here, too."

She was aware of his gaze on her as she walked away. Mike was twenty-eight, young for a man in his position. Her age was the problem. But eleven years weren't an insurmountable problem. Time and persistence would overcome his reservations. Sooner or later Mike would be hers.

ALL THE GUESTS, catering people and maids had left. Jonathan was sleeping, and Talia had gone off to her bedroom. The house seemed curiously empty.

Joe felt as empty as the house. Mike, thinking he already knew, had told Joe about his permanent "houseguest." Sable hadn't said a word—that was what hurt.

He didn't mind Talia living with them. It was the fact that Sable had purposely failed to mention it. He should have been consulted, dammit!

Sable was in the kitchen. It was time for a confrontation.

"Sable?" he called, pushing open the swinging door.

"Don't shout," she said calmly, putting a glass into the now pristine cupboard before turning to face him. "Johnny's asleep."

Her last words stabbed him deeply. He'd been married six hours, and already they sounded like an old, married couple. Her child was now his responsibility, too.

"Why didn't you tell me Talia was part of the package deal?" Instead of anger, he heard the soft query in his own voice.

Her gaze dropped to the floor. "I'm sorry. I should have, but I was afraid you might call off our . . . agreement."

"So I had to find out from Mike that you two are a pair?"

She nodded, her expression so contrite that he couldn't find the fury he had initially felt. "I was going to tell you now, only Mike beat me to it."

He leaned a hip against the wall, reminding himself not to go near her, or he might repeat the wedding kiss. That would never do. "What's the deal?"

"Talia is my sister," she said simply.

"And?"

"I've raised her this far, and I intend to continue to do so. John understood this, so I assumed you would, too."

Joe stood up straight. "First of all," he stated, "don't assume. I'm not John. You married him under different circumstances. I don't give a flying bat's wing what John understood. I'm the partner in this deal, not him. You should have been up-front with me." He ran a hand through his hair, his anger returning, though now it was tempered with caution.

"Look," he began again. "I understand your desire to have your sister with you. I just wanted to be told before the rest of the world knew. If John had been here to tell me about this, I wouldn't be in this situation—you'd still be married to him."

She looked as if he'd struck her, but he couldn't take back his words. They had to establish their relationship, and it had to be done now. "From now on, tell me what's going on before it happens," he told her, then waited in a cold sweat for her answer.

"You're right, of course," she finally agreed. "No one should go into a business deal without knowing all the facts. I'm sorry."

He raised his brows. "Is there anything else you've forgotten to tell me?"

"Such as?"

"Visitors? Other relatives who might want to move in?"

"No. None," she said softly, looking as guilty as a child caught playing hooky.

He wanted to comfort her. He wanted to kiss her. He wanted to bury himself in her and claim her as his own. Instead he nodded perfunctorily. "Good night."

"Good night."

He barely heard her answer; he practically ran down the hall. Closing the door behind him, he plopped onto the bed and cradled his head in his hands.

This was his wedding night. Something he'd always looked forward to. Yet here he was, sitting on his bed alone and wondering what the hell the rest of this marriage was going to bring. He couldn't act like a normal bridegroom and celebrate his own wedding. Instead, he was alone and insanely jealous of a man who, when he was alive, had been his best friend.

It was a hell of a way to spend a wedding night.

SABLE LET OUT HER BREATH in relief. She'd done it. She'd told him about Talia. Well, it had come out. So he'd found out before she could tell him. The result was the same. And though he had blustered, he'd also agreed.

She thought back over the wedding. The few guests she'd invited would go back to Louisiana and let her now ex-in-laws know the details. They'd been impressed with Joe, she could tell. When young Jonathan had come down to the party, Joe had made him laugh by talking nonsense. At that moment she'd known her decision to buy Joe as a bridegroom and a father for her child had been the right one.

She seriously doubted that the LaCroix family would try for custody now. But just in case, her attorney in Louisiana was keeping his ears open, ready to block any efforts they made. Now that she was living in Texas, instead of Louisiana, the LaCroix would have to file their suit here, and their influence didn't reach this far.

Her attorney had also informed her that Texas had a grandparents' law, one which stated that grandparents had the right to see their grandchildren, whether parents approved or not. And most states honored that law. That was all right with her. She had always given John's parents the right to see him, just not the right to raise him.

With a smile and a light heart, Sable flicked off the kitchen light and made her way to her bedroom. After checking on her son, she climbed into bed and sank into the plush pillows.

Remembering this was her wedding night, she had a momentary pang. Strange to be alone at such a time. Then, reminding herself that she'd found an excellent solution to her deepest fears, she smiled again.

Her smile still in place, she picked up one of the newest romances she'd bought and opened it. She settled deeper into the pillows and began to read.

Things couldn't have been better.

4

SUNLIGHT POURED through Sable's bedroom window. Pale peach percale sheets tangled around her legs as she rolled onto her back. With a groan of protest she pulled a pillow over her head to dull the light. But she didn't succeed in suppressing the sounds of Jonathan and Talia's laughter; both were apparently having a whale of a time in a pillow fight.

Children had absolutely no respect for an adult's exhaustion. This was the day after her wedding. One of the most tense days she'd ever lived through. Didn't they realize that? Apparently not, her fuzzy mind answered.

Opening one eye, she glanced at her watch, then bolted straight up in bed. It was after eleven in the morning! Within five minutes she was dressed in slacks and shirt and out of the bedroom, moving toward the sound of the ongoing pillow fight. Surprisingly, she felt terrific.

"Well, good morning, you two." She grinned.

Both were children; there was just a difference in size and sex. Talia's hair was sticking out all over her head, while Jonathan's pajamas, unsnapped at the back waist, drooped over his little bottom.

Jonathan stopped in midjump, his bright eyes wide and round as he tried to judge his mother's mood. Sable's grin grew larger, telling him he wasn't in trouble—this time. He giggled, then stuck his thumb into his mouth.

Talia ran one hand through her hair, attempting to tame her wild curls. "Hi. I thought you were sleeping."

"I was, until I heard the fun you two were having."

Talia glanced guiltily at the little tyke. "Were we loud? Did we wake up Joe, too?"

"I don't know," Sable said slowly, unwilling to admit that she had forgotten about him in her rush to see her family. "I'll go check. Meanwhile, how about you two getting dressed? I'll make breakfast."

"Brunch," Talia called after her.

"Pancakes!" Jonathan shouted.

"Prune juice," Talia substituted, knowing that was his least favorite drink.

Jonathan protested.

Although she halted before Joe's closed door, Sable wasn't brave enough to open it and see if he was still sleeping. She continued into the kitchen, hoping he'd be in there.

She was greeted by a note, in strong, masculine handwriting, propped up on the table. As Sable read, her hand tightened on the paper, practically crushing it.

I leave for the track around seven every morning. I like coffee and toast for breakfast. I'm usually home around noon, except for today. I've got a lunch appointment.

I'll be back around six or six-thirty for a hot meal. I'm a meat and potatoes man and I like to eat early so I can do my paperwork at night. Tonight we'll discuss your budget for the house and the type of meals I want. I let you sleep this morning, but I do expect you to be up when I am.

Sable read it again. Anger seared her body. The man had a way with words. Then she balled the message in her hand and threw it against the wall, watching it land on top of the refrigerator.

"We'll discuss my budget all right, my dear husband. But not on your timetable!" She gritted her teeth as she uttered the words. "And not until you learn some manners—how to request with sugar instead of vinegar, for example!"

The rest of the day was spent organizing rooms and belongings. The movers had brought in everything she needed, but not everything she wanted. Boxes still stacked in the garage had to be emptied.

She made at least four lists of things she needed to find or buy. At three o'clock Sable piled Talia and Johnny into the station wagon and headed toward Huntsville, where she had been assured was a large grocery store.

With a little forethought, she bet she could find enough shopping to keep her busy until way after "six or six thirty." By that time Joe would have returned home to find *her* note propped on the kitchen table beside a foil-wrapped roast beef sandwich, a can of cream of potato soup and a can opener.

He wanted meat and potatoes? He'd get meat and potatoes! At least two weeks' worth!

JOE PACED THE KITCHEN with Sable's note clenched in his fist. The food he'd found beside her message was untouched.

The message was short and to the point.

I've taken Talia and Jonathan grocery shopping in Huntsville. Like a dutiful wife I'll cook your meals, but it must be done with the proper ingredients. There are none in this kitchen.

I can't wait to return so we can have our "discussion."

P.S. Salt and pepper are not the only ingredients with which to cook.

She was angry. It hadn't been hard to find his balled-up note to her on the top of the fridge. It stood out in the spotless kitchen.

All right, so he'd been reprimanded. It wasn't until he'd read his note through her eyes that he realized how abrupt it was. But what did she expect?

The telephone had woken him before dawn with Totty on the other end, telling him that Ahab had won the race. Not realizing the businesslike relationship Joe and Sable had, Totty had assumed Joe could not be disturbed last night—his wedding night.

He'd been in a hurry when he'd written that note.

Besides, he dealt with men all day long, and the best and easiest way with them was to be as direct as possible. That way no one misunderstood. Admittedly he needed a little practice in dealing with women. He could keep up good manners as well as the next man, but this woman was now his wife. Did he have to have good manners forever?

He knew the answer. At least he could try. His foster mother used to say that good manners were the same as courtesy, and courtesy was the same as respect. He certainly respected Sable and the capable way she handled both the toddler and a head-strong, teenage girl. And he'd tell her so as soon as he could.

So why wasn't she home yet? His six-or-six-thirty deadline had passed more than three hours ago. Now he was concerned. He refused to think of the word "scared."

But he couldn't stop picturing the possibilities. Her car could have broken down. She could have had an accident. He didn't know if she carried their phone number with her. Did she even have the address? If something had happened to them, who would know to contact him? All her identification probably still carried the Louisiana address.

Unable to wait any longer, he reached for the kitchen phone to call the police. Just then, car headlights angled down the driveway. Relief flooded through him as he recognized Sable's car.

By the time she entered the house, he had worked himself up again for a major confrontation. The only thing that made him hold his tongue was Johnny was asleep in Sable's arms. Talia was right behind her sister, carrying their purses and a large bag of groceries.

Sable met his gaze. Signaling to him to be quiet, she continued down the hall to the child's room. Joe had no recourse but to follow Talia to the kitchen.

"What happened?" he demanded. "Did the car break down?"

"We got lost," Talia answered, wearily dropping the grocery bag onto the kitchen table. "It seemed like we were wandering around forever."

He'd thought of everything but that. "How long were you lost?" He softened his tone. Talia looked as if she was about to cry. She didn't need to hear his own frustrated anger.

"Since about six. Somehow we got the farm-to-market roads mixed up and we took the wrong one. When we realized it, it was dark and we stopped for directions. Nobody seemed to know exactly where we wanted to go, but they all had ideas."

"The roads aren't hard to follow. You'll get used to them soon."

"It's not Louisiana," Talia told him, sniffing. "We were all tired, and none of these darn roads are marked, except for an occasional sign you have to get out of the car to read, 'cause it's so dark. I never would have gotten lost at home."

Joe had a feeling most of Talia's reaction was due to moving to a new place. And it had put a strain upon everyone, something he'd not considered while worrying about how his life was being changed by the marriage. Three other people had gone through changes, too.

Joe watched Talia, tears of frustration sheening in her eyes as she began to automatically empty the bag of groceries. Overwhelmed by a feeling of protectiveness, he reached out and gave her a sympathetic pat on the back. Her slight shoulders quaked as she accepted his comfort. A moment later she looked up, giving him a brilliant smile that reminded him of her older sister.

"Thanks," she said, rising on tiptoe to place a kiss upon his cheek.

"You're welcome." He felt awkward somehow, not quite sure how to respond. "Are there more groceries in the car?"

"Plenty," she confirmed, putting cans into the cupboard. "I don't understand it. For a woman who only eats fish and chicken, we've got more meat and potatoes than you can shake a stick at."

Joe grinned. Sable might have been angry, but at least she paid attention to his requests. "I'll get them."

After he carried in the last of the bags, Joe felt Sable's presence as surely as if she'd tapped him on the shoulder.

He turned. Her tired eyes were half-closed, her lips slightly parted. Her shoulders drooped with the sheer effort of standing.

"Hi," he said softly. He wanted to hold her. He wanted to give her the comfort of his body as much as he needed the comfort of hers. But he wasn't sure how to go about it.

"Hi," she repeated.

"You okay?"

"We got lost."

Joe nodded. "Talia told me all about it. It was the one thing I didn't think of."

Her glance was rueful. "Frankly, neither did I, but everything looked different as the sun set. Then all those tall pines made the narrow road look even narrower."

"How did you finally manage to get here?"

"I went back to town and retraced my steps, trying not to look at anything but the lefts and rights."

Relieved, Joe let out a pent-up breath. At least they were safe. "I'll get you an up-to-date map of the area. That should help. I'll also make sure you have all the phone numbers you need. You could have called me earlier on the car phone or pager."

She closed her eyes for a moment. "I didn't have any numbers on me, including the house phone. I didn't even have the address. It's in my briefcase. It didn't dawn on me that you had a car phone."

"I figured that," he said gently.

She opened her eyes and stared up at him. "Were you worried? Or were you angry?"

He grinned sheepishly. "Both. But I was worried most."

"I'm sorry. I didn't mean for this to happen."

"It won't again. I should have given you all the information before you needed it." He stood in front of her. "I'll write it all down in the morning and put it into both glove compartments. That way neither you nor Talia will get lost again."

"Thank you," she said, stifling a yawn.

He smiled. "Why don't you go on to bed? Talia and I can put away the rest of the stuff."

"It's already done," Talia announced with a tired grin. She folded the last bag and placed it with the others in the utility room.

"Thanks," Sable said. "I'm on my way."

For a brief moment her eyes locked with Joe's. Both stood completely still.

Then Joe moved to break the spell. "Good night," he said gruffly.

"Good night," Sable answered, turning to go back to her room.

"Oh, and Sable?" Joe called. She glanced over her shoulder at him. "When I said meat, I didn't mean just beef. Chicken and fish are fine, too. Occasionally."

She smiled and his blood warmed, flooding his body with feelings best left alone.

"I'll remember that," she murmured, then disappeared down the hallway and into her room.

Joe whistled softly as he pulled a beer from the fridge. He'd been too crass and too abrupt with Sable. He needed to try a little tenderness, as the old song said. He'd get more from her if he treated her with a little respect.

How much more? the devil in his mind asked. A real marriage? His make-believe wife in his very real bed? He pushed that thought aside. He'd signed the contract for money, and that had been what he got: enough to finish his beloved racetrack.

"Good night," Talia called.

Joe jumped guiltily, as if the thoughts plaguing him were written across his forehead for everyone to see.

"Good night," was the best he could manage. Those other, more provoking thoughts would have to wait. Right now he was starved, and there was no one around to cook for him. He unwrapped the sandwich Sable had fixed for him earlier and took a healthy bite.

Not bad. Not bad at all.

BY THE NEXT MORNING the truce was over.

"I support my family, Sable. Not you. And we'll live within my means." His tone brooked no argument. "It's worked for hundreds of generations, and it's gonna work in this marriage, too."

Sable's back straightened. Her tension was palpable. "Joe," she began, slowly turning to face him. "If I were working at a job in town, would I be allowed to participate in paying the bills? In buying things for the house?"

His look was wary. "Yes, but you're not working—not that way." He held up a hand to forestall her triumph. "And you're married to me. That means that I take care of you."

"No," she declared, equally firm in her beliefs. "It means I'm married to you. No more, no less. I can still spend my money any way I see fit. That was the purpose of our prenuptial agreement—our separate property remains our separate property. You have no right to tell me how to spend my money or when I can spend it."

"This is my house and you're my wife. You will live within my means," Joe maintained. "I pay bills and groceries. The rest you can handle."

"There is no 'rest' after those two things!"

"Exactly."

His look was so smug that Sable could barely control her intense desire to kick him.

"And while we're on the subject of duties, I think we'd better get some things straightened out between us," Joe went on, obviously determined to bull his way through this meeting.

"Such as what?" Now it was her turn to be wary.

"Such as who takes care of your three horses."

She raised her brows. "And who does?"

"You do. My crew has enough to do without adding to their work load. You can groom them and muck out their stalls. After all, you're home all day."

"I hate horses. I kept them only because I thought the fillies might breed a winner. The colt is Jonathan's when he gets older."

"You take care of them, except for the feed and exercise. The men can do that when they're handling the other horses."

"Anything else?" she queried sarcastically.

"That's it." Joe folded his arms over his broad chest and smiled.

She knew he was waiting for fireworks to go off, but she wouldn't give him the satisfaction of seeing her lose her temper.

Instead she smiled sweetly. "Then I have a few dos and don'ts for you. First, you gave me the schedule for meals, so I expect you to abide by it. All meals will be on time, and unless you call and let me know you won't be home, you'll be sitting at the table when I serve them."

Joe frowned, but nodded in agreement.

"Next, let me remind you that this is our home, not the bunkhouse. No more boots on the furniture or sweaty hats on the chairs. That goes for all your employees, too."

"What makes you think we do that?"

"Because no coffee table could be so scuffed, unless a thousand pairs of boots had rested there."

Again he nodded agreement, and the light blush on his cheeks confirmed her assessment of the situation.

"And lastly, no heavy drinking."

Joe opened his mouth to protest, but shut it again. "Fair enough. But I can't and won't control what goes on in the bunkhouse. None of the men are drunks, but they can drink what they want to, when they want to, as long as it's not on the job. I'm their boss, not their father."

"Fair enough," she mimicked.

Joe unfolded his arms and glanced at his watch. "Now that we've gotten that out of the way, I've got to get to work. Is there anything else you need clarified?"

He deserved a slap. He deserved a punch! He was always so cocksure and arrogant!

She clamped her hands on her hips to stop herself turning thoughts into deeds. "And what are my other duties, master?" she inquired in a taunting tone.

"The usual things any normal wife does." He stopped, letting his gaze feed on her mouth. "With the exception of the one thing that seems so repugnant to you, of course," he finally said. "According to our contract, you're not required to be in my bed."

His derisive tone hurt. The fact was that she was beginning to wish she hadn't stipulated that they weren't to sleep together. Her pride had been the main reason. Did she have to pay him to sleep with her, too?

"If I recall, you didn't seem to mind that addendum at the time."

"You were offering me a million dollars, darlin'," he drawled, clearly intent on giving as good as he got. "Was I supposed to disagree with the basic terms?"

"You could have."

This time it was his turn to move away. "It seemed like a good idea back then. It just isn't reality now. It's unnatural for two people, married or not, to live in the same house and not consummate the relationship."

"What's unnatural about it?" Sable found herself asking. "I have my room, you have yours. That way there is no temptation."

Joe shrugged as if dismissing the thought. "Fine. I'm not arguing the point. We both agreed. I'm just saying that it's hard to act as if this is a marriage made in heaven, when it hasn't been *made* at all."

The bluntness of his accusation slapped her in the face. The worst part was that she knew he was right. How could either of them act naturally as a couple, when a major portion of the marriage—the bed—was not being shared?

She didn't have an answer. With determined steps she walked to the door. "You pay the bills and groceries. I cover the rest," she repeated, as if nothing else had been said. "Now I've got laundry to do. Excuse me."

"You're excused," he muttered before she was out the door. "And dammit, you're stubborn, to boot."

SABLE KEPT HERSELF BUSY in the laundry room until she heard Joe's truck driving off. She'd been afraid of what else she might say or do if she remained in the same room with him.

Didn't he know how degrading it was to have to buy oneself a husband? The few men she'd known in Louisiana had run in her in-laws' circle. And they had treated her as if she were not to be touched.

At first she hadn't minded. Her memories of John and the constant attention the baby and Talia had needed made up a full and busy life. Contrary to what society thought of her, she'd always been happiest at home. She loved the quiet atmosphere, the little things that constantly needed to be done for the smooth running of a house. It had been John who insisted she attend public events and join charities. She had continued with those obligations to fill the lonely void John's death had created.

But at night she roamed her house with no one to talk to. Her in-laws were not people she could turn to to assuage her solitude. She had had no one to laugh with, to talk over problems with. She had no man to love.

She wanted to repeat the best moments of her marriage with John—when she'd curled next to him in bed and talked about the things that bothered her, and he'd soothed her with his gentle, caring touch.

She missed that the most.

Joe was another matter entirely. Joe didn't comfort her, he excited her. She wanted to touch him, feel his skin next to hers. She wanted to make love to him. And that was scary. She'd never felt that way before, and she didn't want to now.

With Joe everything was physical. His look, his words, even his voice seemed to touch the very core of her. He made her think of things best left alone.

Alone in bed at night, her imagination ran riot, exploring what she refused to think about during the day. Like the way his hands might feel on her body. Like curling next to him in bed and talking about the day's happenings, while he stroked her back and waist and placed small, butterfly kisses upon her forehead and cheek. Like his possession of her, and her triumph over his carefully controlled emotions....

She'd obviously been reading too many romances.

She took a deep breath and straightened her spine. This wasn't getting her anywhere. With determined movements, she placed the rest of the clothes in the washer and set the dials.

Keep busy. That was the answer.

"Is Joe gone?" Talia asked as she and Jonathan came in from a walk around the property. The boy ran to her, and Sable picked him up, giving him a big hug and a kiss under his chin. He laughed in response, his chubby little hands pushing hard against her.

"Yes," Sable said as she put him down.

"And did you have a good discussion?"

"Yes."

"And who won?" Talia continued as she set the grubby Jonathan on the counter and began taking off his muddy sneakers. It was too late for the kitchen floor, but he could still make a mess of the recently cleaned carpet. "Joe?"

Sable couldn't think of an answer, so she continued to busy herself with the dirty clothes.

"Was it a dead heat?" Talia inquired, not allowing her sister any leeway.

"More or less."

Jonathan squirmed, nearly falling off the counter. Talia caught him, then let him stand in his stocking feet. Immediately he ran off down the hall toward his bedroom.

"I like him."

Sable went on trying to look busy, although for the life of her she didn't know what she was doing. "You'd better. He's probably the only nephew you'll ever have."

"No, I meant I like Joe."

Picking up a particularly dirty shirt, Sable placed it on top of the washer and treated it with a spot cleaner. Anything to stay busy. She was unwilling to look at Talia. "Do you?"

"Yes," Talia stated emphatically. Like all her decisions, she'd stick to it single-mindedly. "He's nice, he's funny and kind."

"You've gotten all that from three days of living in the same house with him?"

"That and more. Did you know that when I was almost on the verge of tears last night, he gave me a hug? Just like Dad—" Talia's voice broke off and she stared out the window.

She turned and faced Sable once more. "Why don't you go for broke, Sable, and make this a real marriage? One you could have kids in and enjoy? It beats all the fencing that's gone on in the past few days."

Sable looked her sister in the eye. There was no use in being subtle when it came to Talia. She refused to allow anyone to hide behind a facade. "It's none of your business, Talia, and there has been no fencing."

Talia eyed her sister. "Then why did I have to take Jonathan out of the house this morning, when he was shaken by you two shouting at each other?"

"He was upset?" Concern laced Sable's words. She'd had no intention of upsetting Jonathan. Nothing was worth that. After all, she ought to know. She'd experienced enough of it in her younger days.

"Yes, and it was your voice that was rising in anger. Not Joe's."

"You're living up to your nickname again, Spike," Sable warned.

"Yes, and the one who calls me that is more stubborn than me," Talia retorted.

"Only because the man's pigheaded." Sable stalked out of the utility room and into the kitchen, pouring herself a glass of water to soothe her dry throat.

"And so are you. But that doesn't mean the marriage couldn't be a real one. Jonathan could have sisters and brothers to enjoy." Talia's voice softened. "Johnny needs a family. Just like we did, Sable. Where would I have been without you?"

"He's got a family. You and me." In spite of Talia's look, Sable continued. "I'd do anything for you two," Sable said, her throat still dry and scratchy. "But I already bought myself a husband, Talia. I'm not about to purchase a baby as well. At that rate I'd be broke in no time. Jonathan will just have to live with being an only child."

"I know it was awful when Mom and Dad went to court over us, but that won't happen again, Sable—thanks to Joe. The LaCroix would have to be insane to file for custody. Don't you think this could work as a real family? For all of us?"

Sable swallowed. How could she explain that she simply couldn't grovel? What scraps of pride Sable had left, she wore like a full-length coat made of her namesake.

"I'll think about it."

Talia began to say something else, but the look on Sable's face stopped her. "I'll check on Jonathan," she said, hastily beating a retreat.

The large, black-and-white clock on the wall said it was only ten-thirty in the morning. Having already gone through two emotional scenes, she wished the day were over.

Her head tilted to one side, she continued to stare at the clock. It was definitely ugly, its black cord hung down the wall like a snake. Even if she had built her own prison, there was nothing in the agreement to say that she couldn't decorate it the way she wanted.

A sad smile crossed her lips. She knew the source of her frustration, but activity was the panacea. Activity was the one thing she could control.

Even before she opened the letter, she knew it contained bad
news. The LaCroix insignia was on the flap of the envelope; it
looked as intimidating as it was formal.

Johnny's grandparents wanted Sable to send the little boy to
live with them, so they could place him in one of the best private preschools in Louisiana, ensuring that he would have the
right friends and connections for his future. It wasn't so much a
request as a demand.

Implied was a threat that if she didn't give up Johnny volun-
tarily, they would find a way to force her. Seething with fury, she
was dialing their number to tell them exactly where they could
put their fancy paper, when the truth dawned on her.

She had bought her security.

The LaCroix could threaten, but they couldn't win—not as
long as she was married.

She would ignore the letter.

It would drive them crazy.

Sable enjoyed turning Joe's house into a home and having no
one underfoot to tell her this was wrong or that would be better.
It was the first time she'd ever had that luxury, and although the
housework was constant, it was also a source of pride—and it
kept her too busy to lure Joe to her bed.

She'd decided not to tell Joe about the letter. She was sure he
wouldn't quite see it in the same light as she did. Jonathan was
her child, and she knew what was best.

Joe seemed as wary of another confrontation as Sable was, so
they stayed out of each other's way as much as possible. That
allowed them to get along fine for the rest of the week and
weekend.

But because he wasn't always around—because she missed
him?—Sable noticed every little thing about him. At meal-

times, when they were forced to be together, she got to watch him up close. There were a thousand little items she hadn't known about the man, but enjoyed learning.

For instance, Sable was amazed by how firmly but gently Joe handled Jonathan. The boy quickly grew to worship his new father figure. He talked constantly as he followed Joe through the house, gardens and barns. And Joe never lost patience with him. In fact, Sable thought he enjoyed his new role.

Joe and Talia teased each other mercilessly. The rapport they had built was obvious to everyone. Talia went around the house singing Joe's praises until Sable had to tell her to stop or go to her room.

She couldn't have bought a better father figure if she'd tried. But husband material . . . Joe was not.

He cussed like a cowboy. He never asked for her opinion. He never held her or whispered sweet nothings in her ear. He didn't seem to be interested in doing anything other than snarling at or ignoring her. He certainly wasn't like any of the heroes she'd read about in her romances—so why did she dream about him?

He scuffed the floor with his boots. His hats were always tossed carelessly onto a chair. He read the paper and invariably dropped it onto the floor. Rather than put his dirty clothes into the hamper in his bathroom, he left them on the floor behind the door, neatly piled, but on the floor nonetheless. And late at night he always raided the freezer for a bowl of ice cream—any flavor except chocolate. Then he'd leave the rinsed bowl in the sink, not the dishwasher.

It was disturbing—to her housekeeping and her psyche. She couldn't make a move without being reminded of Joe.

Every time she saw Joe's arms bared by a short-sleeved shirt, her heartbeat quickened. Images flashed through her mind of those same arms circling her waist, holding her close to his hard body. Even his long-legged stride reminded her of other, more intimate movements. She was beginning to wonder what pristine scruples were keeping her from Joe's bed.

But the bottom line was that she was afraid. No woman wanted to believe the only way a man would be interested in her was because she'd paid him for the services. And paid him dearly. No matter how many times she tried to forget that fact, it was there.

She'd bought a groom. She couldn't quite believe that he was as interested in her as he had been in her money.

She had to keep busy if thoughts of Joe's touch, Joe's kisses were to be overridden enough to allow her to function as a homemaker and mother.

Two kisses do not a fantasy make, she told herself—and knew she lied.

JOE STOOD just inside the huge, barn doors and stared at the house Sable had turned into a home. She had done wonders, moving knickknacks here instead of there, hanging a painting or print on a different wall, and the room's whole complexion had been changed. Even that big, ugly clock in the kitchen had been replaced by a brass-and-white thing that suited the area much better.

As much as he hated to admit it, he was glad she'd taken the house in hand. He liked it.

But swallowing those words wasn't his problem. That would be easy compared to his one, big obstacle.

He wanted her. Day and night he wanted her. But their stupid agreement was in the way.

From their first meeting Joe had been fascinated. Then he'd been stunned. Sable had actually stated she'd had no choice but to marry him! That had hurt his ego. While they were getting to know each other better, he'd honestly believed she was as drawn to him as he was to her. The sparkle in her eyes when she looked at him matched his own.

True, he had needed her money—money he vowed he would pay back to her, if it was the last thing he did. Only the pressure from the bank, his partners and Sable had forced him into this marriage.

That wasn't quite true.

No matter how much he lied to everyone else, he couldn't lie to himself. Part of him, a large part, had wanted this marriage. Otherwise wild horses couldn't have made him walk to the altar.

But that same damn money that was enabling him to finish building his track was also keeping him from his wife's bed. He saw dollar signs in her eyes every time he looked at her. He was sure she didn't think that way, but the fact that he'd been forced into taking the money was like a sore spot on his male pride. Whenever he thought of Sable, he also thought of the money he owed her.

His thoughts shifted to Jonathan and Talia, his ready-made family. Sable had thought she was pulling a fast one when she "forgot" to mention that her little sister was part of the deal. And he had to admit he hadn't been all that thrilled. But what he'd thought would be a hassle had turned out to be a joy. Talia was a bright, witty, older-than-her-age teenager. She didn't mind lending a hand with anything that needed doing, and her quick tongue was fun. And Jonathan . . . well, what could be wrong with an almost-three-year-old boy who had the good taste to idolize him?

The family was his. In such a short time they had learned to love him and he to love them. Now if he could only get Sable to follow their direction . . .

Joe groaned wearily and closed his eyes. All week long he had attended one business meeting after another until late into the night.

His maintenance chief had resigned because of a heart problem, and now he had to find a replacement. Interviews for the executive jobs had been squeezed between staff meetings, but he wasn't satisfied with the applicants. A friend had tipped him off that an out-of-state racetrack's chief wanted to return to Texas. Joe had called him, and the man had agreed to fly out for an interview today. They were to meet at the Houston Intercontinental Airport's private lounge tonight.

It was just one more pressure added to all the others. And all he could think about was a woman whose eyes matched her name. A woman who shared her money with him, but not her bed. He'd rather have had the bed.

There was only one thing to do. He had to forget about the money—until he could pay her back. Instead he would work on their relationship. When he gave her the money, he had to give her a reason to stay.

He had to seduce her. He had to woo her, as if she were a woman he'd just met and was . . . attracted to. He wouldn't allow himself to think of a stronger word. If he was to get any peace during the day and any sleep at night, he had to win her over to his way of thinking. Starting right away.

He could learn how to please her. But first he'd have to know what it was that made her smile, and the only way to do that was to spend time with her. If nature took its course while he was doing that, then all the better.

He found himself smiling. He stretched his arms high above his head in the cool shadows of the breezeway. He had a new challenge. He loved challenges.

SABLE SAT DOWN at the kitchen table and took a deep breath. She'd felt tired all week. Tired of fighting Joe. Tired of fighting with herself.

She'd been a waitress in one of Mobile's better restaurants when she'd met John. He'd sat at her table once, then returned again and again. She'd known he was wealthy. He'd known she wasn't.

After their marriage, a host of servants had taken care of their home. She'd been considered a socialite, but what she'd wanted most was to be a wife and mother, busy with the things wives and mothers did. Not a grand ambition, she'd be the first to admit, but it was hers. And somehow she'd always thought she'd do it for love of her family. Then she had discovered that being John's wife with nothing to do was boring.

Now she was twenty-six years old, and ironically this pretend marriage was the closest she'd ever come to fulfilling her dream.

She heard Joe's heavy-booted tread on the back porch steps, and her heart picked up its beat in anticipation. She remained seated, her ears following the sound of the motions she knew he was making. Then the door opened, he stepped in and smiled.

Her heart beat faster. She smiled back.

"Hi," she said, unable to remove the huskiness from her voice.

"You look bushed." His voice was low, sexy and sweetly concerned. He could read a feed list in that tone and she'd listen to every word.

"I'm a little tired," she admitted, suddenly not feeling quite as weary as she had before.

Joe glanced around at the sparkling counters, the spotless floor, the neat little decorations that made the kitchen glow with a country look. Then his gaze returned to her. "Where's Talia?"

She raised her brows questioningly. "She's reading in her bedroom."

"And Jonathan?"

"Taking a nap. He should be awake in a few minutes."

His smile expressed satisfaction. He pulled out the chair kitty-corner from her and sat down. Taking her hand, he interlaced his sun-darkened fingers with hers, his thumb rubbing sensuously against her palm.

"I have to go to the airport in Houston to interview a man."

"For employment at the track?"

"Yes. We lost our maintenance chief. This guy may take the job."

She nodded, suddenly wary. He usually announced his meetings in a most casual manner. This was anything but casual.

"Come with me."

Her eyes widened. "Now?"

It was his turn to nod.

"Why?"

"Because you've worked so hard since we got married, and I think you could use the break." His grin was endearing. "Besides, it's a long drive and I don't want to go alone. I'd rather have a quiet drink with you while I wait for the guy to arrive." He tightened his grip. "It'll do us both good to get away for a little while."

"But what about the kids?"

"Talia can baby-sit. If an emergency comes up, she only has to phone the bunkhouse and twelve men will come running."

"What about dinner?"

"We'll eat out. It won't hurt the kids to eat sandwiches for dinner this once."

"Give me half an hour."

"Fifteen minutes, or I'll come get you," he teased, his blue eyes crinkling at the corners.

Sable had a feeling that he'd do just that. "Twenty," she bargained.

"You're wasting your fourteen minutes." He stood and pulled her to her feet. Before she could react, he kissed the tip of her nose. "Twenty minutes," he whispered.

She felt buoyant. Her feet were at least six inches off the floor. "Twenty minutes," she promised before darting out the kitchen door and down the hall to her room.

Sable had never dressed so quickly. Knowing Joe was wearing exactly what he had on, she decided on peach-colored pants and a front-button summer sweater with nubby, silk leaves of copper, tan and green spilling over one shoulder. It was dressy, but not too much so. She put on low heels in the same shade of green. With deft fingers she twisted her dark hair and pinned it with a plain, gold barrette atop her head. Instead of her usual stud earrings, she chose gold hoops.

Exactly twenty minutes later she walked down the hall to Talia's room, only to find that Joe had already informed her sister of the impromptu arrangements.

"Have a great time," Talia called as she picked up a still-sleepy Jonathan and watched them climb into the jet-black truck and drive off.

Sable felt almost as if she'd been let out of jail, which wasn't really fair, she had to admit, since she'd chosen to remain at home this past week. She hated to acknowledge it, but she was happy because Joe had asked for . . . wanted . . . her company. It was a heady experience.

"You look wonderful." With a look of endearment, he touched the hand that rested on the seat between them. "Are you still tired?"

"I'm fine," she said with a laugh. "I'm just a little giddy at the thought of eating something I haven't cooked."

"You've been working too hard."

"No harder than you."

"It's different for me. The racetrack is my dream. My baby. Everything I have or ever wanted to have is tied up in it."

"The house and those who live in it make up my dream," she said softly. "Everything that matters to me is there."

"Touché," he murmured before releasing her hand and pulling onto the paved road that led to the interstate.

Sable leaned back and relaxed, watching the scenery pass by in a series of blurred, variegated greens. The ground was lush with last fall's leaves composting in the forest. And the ground gave off the scent of fresh earth and the tang of pine needles.

They passed through Conroe, the self-contained community of the Woodlands, and on down through Spring, another small town. Then they turned toward Houston's huge Intercontinental Airport.

Joe broke the companionable silence. "What are you thinking?"

"Just that I was amazed when I flew into the airport to visit you the first time and saw so many trees. I always thought Houston and the surrounding areas were in the middle of a prairie."

Joe chuckled. "Houston sits just south of the edge of Big Thicket, the largest, densest section of forest in the country. The Comanche Indians, runaway slaves and even a few well-known bandits used to hide there."

"I know," she said dryly. "It extends into Louisiana. I just didn't know it was down here, too."

Joe drove up the spiral ramp and parked in the garage attached to the airline terminal. With tender care he helped her from the car and toward the elevators that carried them to the lobby and the bar.

For the first time since the wedding, Sable felt like part of a married couple. Joe held her arm as he led her into the private, airline club room and toward a small table next to the wall. He ordered their drinks as if they'd been together for years.

Yes, she decided, they looked like an old married couple—until he looked at her.

His gaze was as hot as molten lava, burning her insides with its heat and stirring embers she thought long dead and forgotten. Her face flushed and her skin tingled.

His hand covered hers, cupping her fingers against the coolness of her wineglass. "You're beautiful," he told her softly. "You know that."

She swallowed the dryness that had attacked her throat. "It's nice to hear."

"You're the most beautiful woman I've ever seen."

"Thank you," she murmured, barely managing to speak. Her mouth was still as dry as a desert. Her mind told her she'd heard the words before, but they had never meant much to her. Now she wanted to hear more, craved more from him and yet felt guilty for the craving.

She couldn't stand seeing the desire in his blue eyes anymore and stared down at the glass in her hand—in their hands. His fingers interspersed with hers, made a pattern of light and dark against the gold-filled goblet. She could imagine their limbs entwining in the same golden aura and her heartbeat quickened. She was caught in a spell she couldn't shake.

Before she realized it, she had spoken the words. "You're weaving a spell around me."

The corners of his eyes crinkled. "I wish I could. At least as strong as the one you've woven around me."

Her eyes widened. "Have I?"

He nodded slowly. "Oh, yes. And I love it." His smile was like a breath of sunshine. "But I don't think the workers are too fond of me right now. I go around preoccupied. My mind is on you instead of my work."

She didn't know what to do so she pulled her hand away and entwined all ten fingers in her lap, so she couldn't be tempted to touch him.

"The racetrack will be ready soon." Her voice was unsteady, she knew, she was trying to focus her thoughts on anything but his nearness.

"Soon," he echoed in a husky voice.

"And then you can relax a little."

He nodded. "A little."

Her eyes darted to his, then back down to her glass. When he took his hand from the glass, she saw his fingerprints there. His clasp had made an impression against the chilled glass, just as it had on her entire being.

"Joe!" a man's voice called, and the spell was broken.

After the introductions, Joe began the interview. Sable leaned back and enjoyed the hum of conversation as the two men talked business. It was enlightening to listen to them and learn just a little more about the behind-the-scenes working of a racetrack. She had no idea there was so much to do or that so many people were involved. Joe's racetrack would give jobs to an area that had no industry of its own.

Sipping on her wine, she allowed her eyes to drift about the private bar and waiting room. It was tastefully finished with large, comfortable, padded chairs and small tables. Along the walls were desks, along with several copy machines and even a fax machine or two. Small, stylish telephones dotted the conversation tables. Everything about the room was expensive. Apparently only high-powered businessmen and -women could afford the dues to this private club. Sable was pleased to note that there seemed to be an almost equal number of men and women.

This was all new to her. She had never traveled much, and when she did it was in John's family plane, with no stopovers between their home in Louisiana and their destination.

Joe stood suddenly and shook hands with Mr. Tramore.

When the man held out his hand to Sable, she took it. "It was a pleasure meeting you, Mrs. Lombardi," he said.

"It was nice meeting you, Mr. Tramore," she said, startled by her own name. *Mrs. Lombardi*. It was the first time she'd really thought of herself as Joe's wife. It felt good.

The man tipped back his Western hat with two fingers. "Y'all be careful gettin' home," he growled as nicely as he could.

Sable couldn't hide her grin. Both he and Joe were apparently very similar when it came to women. Both were shy. But Joe hid his shyness by blustering, while this gentleman hid behind his manners.

"What's so funny?" Joe asked with a puzzled look as the man left the room.

"Men in general," she answered, still chuckling.

"And me in particular?" He took her arm and escorted her out of the room and into the large lobby.

When the elevator doors closed behind them and they were alone she whispered her answer. "Yes."

His eyes, focused on her, burned. She felt as if she'd just swallowed a rich, golden brandy. . . .

"Am I that funny?" His lips were mere inches from hers.

She shook her head slightly, moving her lips even closer to his. "No." The word came out as a breath that Joe stole.

"You're playing with me," he muttered. "Beware, Sable. Two can do that." His lips sealed hers, the pressure so slight that she leaned toward him for more. Her head reeled, but with strong hands anchored on her hips, he kept her firmly in place, letting her come no closer than he wanted her.

She wanted more. Ached for more. Craved for more.

Then the elevator doors opened. He pulled away and smiled benignly at the people grouped around the doors, waiting to get on.

As he escorted her off, he raised his voice so that it would carry to the others. "Lady, I'm sure you're every bit worth the two hundred you're asking, but I only have a ten on me."

"Forget it, then," she said just as loudly, walking away from him. "I'll just drive my Cadillac home. Good night, mister."

She felt Joe's hand on her shoulder and she turned to face him. "Don't ever do that to me again." Her voice was sweet and syrupy, but she knew her eyes blazed fire.

His jaw snapped shut. "No, ma'am. Never," he promised. "It was only a little joke."

"I won't be the butt of any man's joke. Not even yours."

"No, ma'am," he repeated as she stood in front of him. "I promise."

"Good. Now can we get something to eat? I'm starved!" She started toward their parked truck.

Joe followed without another word. It wasn't until they were in the cab of the truck that they looked at each other and Joe began to chuckle.

"Why did you go along with me?"

She shrugged, holding back a smile. "It seemed like the thing to do. I wasn't about to let you have the last word."

Then, seeing his expression, Sable couldn't help it. She chimed in. A few seconds later they were both laughing until tears streamed down their cheeks.

"Lady," he said when he caught his breath. "You're full of surprises. I would have thought you'd be at a loss for words. Instead you one-upped me."

"It's only fair," she told him between chuckles.

"Yes, ma'am," he stated emphatically as he started the engine and pulled out of the parking lot. They wound down the circular driveway and headed toward town. "And now I'm warned."

"Exactly. Now are you going to feed me?"

"Next is dinner," he agreed, a gleam of respect in his eyes. He took her hand and raised it to his lips in silent apology.

But the moment his lips touched her hand, all the humor of the moment was gone, replaced by excitement.

Refusing to admit to her desire, Sable snatched back her hand, and sat primly, hands in her lap like a schoolmarm.

"Something wrong?"

"No, nothing."

"Then why the chill?" Joe asked, his voice as smooth as the darkness. "I thought you forgave me."

"I did. I do."

Joe breathed heavily, and the sound hung in the silence between them, creating even more tension.

The restaurant was crowded. People filled the rooms, laughter and conversations spilling around them. Sable felt safe once more. It wasn't Joe she didn't trust. It was herself.

They went into the bar to await their table, and once again Sable realized that she thoroughly enjoyed his company. Joe seemed more relaxed, too. In fact, looking back over their short relationship, she didn't think she'd ever seen him this open and easygoing.

"And then, at the ripe old age of twenty-four, I discovered horses. I read countless books on the subject. I rode more than two hundred horses before I finally chose Aruba."

"Aruba?" Sable frowned. She thought she knew the names of all the horses in the barn, but that one didn't sound familiar.

He nodded. "She was a mare with foal, and I loved her the moment I saw her. Two of my horses are hers, a mare and a stallion. She died last year of an overstressed heart. But she was my beginning."

"Most females are," Sable said dryly, aware that there was a twinkle in her eyes.

Joe chuckled. "They're also usually the end."

"Of a good relationship?"

"Of adolescence. Until a boy meets his first woman, he's just a kid."

Sable blushed, and Joe had the audacity to laugh.

"I'm sorry," he said. "I just can't help it. I enjoy getting a rise out of you."

"You enjoy making me feel . . . inadequate."

"No," he corrected softly. "I enjoy watching you blush." He reached out to touch her hand, but withdrew his own at the last moment. "I'm not the perfect gentleman. Hell, half the time I forget my manners entirely. But that's what comes from being around just men for most of my life. There was no sweet-smelling mama to teach me the finer things in life."

"Everybody has a mother."

He nodded, staring into his drink. "And I'm sure I had one, too. But instead of looking at me and deciding to treasure me for the rest of my life, she dropped me into the nearest trash container in Austin, then went blithely on her way. I was raised in a welfare home most of my life, but they didn't take me because I was sweet, either. Harold and Gladys had five children to raise, and I was a little extra money in their pockets."

This time it was Sable who reached across the table, her slight hand covering his. "I'm sorry."

His gaze held hers. "Don't be. I'm not one to complain much about fate. But maybe if I hadn't been raised that way, I wouldn't be where I am today."

She smiled. "You have a point. But no little boy or girl should be without a mother. Have you ever thought of looking for her?"

"When I was young I thought about it a lot. She would find me and be so sorry. She'd cry and beg my forgiveness. And I was going to be a gentleman and do just that. But as I got older it dawned on me that she was probably a young, scared student who didn't know what to do and panicked. Austin has more students than any other city in Texas. None of them seem to be prepared for life, let alone being on their own. I imagine it was tough over thirty years ago. Especially on a woman."

It hurt to think he had no family, no one who cared. "Do you ever see the people who raised you?"

"No. I was just one in a long line of welfare kids for them, and since my middle name was Trouble, I think they were relieved to see me go."

"How long did you live with them?"

"Until I was sixteen. Then I split. One year later I joined the army and saw the world," he said, his voice suddenly filled with sarcasm.

She closed her eyes, imagining being alone during her growing years and knowing the hardship it would have entailed. The thought brought tears to her eyes. "I'm so sorry. No one deserves such a childhood."

"I didn't tell you to gain your sympathy."

"I know."

Their hands intertwined. Sable blinked rapidly to keep the tears at bay. But she couldn't seem to keep out her compassion. She stared down at their hands, then closed her eyes once more.

Joe leaned forward and kissed each eyelid.

"Thank you." His voice was low.

She opened her eyes and smiled through the tears. "You're welcome," she answered.

IT WAS long past eleven when they reached the turnoff to the house. Conversation had flowed so easily and readily at the restaurant that neither had wanted to call an end to the evening. Sable had had three glasses of wine, and that was nice, too.

"Not too much nor too little."

"Too much nor too little of what?" Joe whispered into her ear. That wasn't hard, since her head rested on his shoulder. He was so comfortable....

"Wine."

He chuckled. "Just right," he observed.

She lifted her head and stared at the firm lips shadowed in the dash lights. "What's just right?"

"You are."

She smiled, burrowing her head back into the solidness of his shoulder. "Mmm."

He pulled the car up to the back door and flipped off the ignition. The silence was as relaxing as the drive had been. His head rested against hers and she moved her cheek back and forth, loving the feel of his stubble-roughened chin. Men and women had so many intriguing differences.

Unwilling to put her feelings into words, Sable lifted her face to his. She followed the thick arch of his brow with a fingernail and marveled at the texture. The pad of her forefinger felt the pulse at his temple, amazing her how alive his skin felt. He was beautiful.

She could sense the leashed strength and, like Pandora with her box, she was tempted by it. To open it up, go wild....

She parted her lips.

Joe groaned, and his lips covered hers in a kiss that sought and seared her very soul. His mouth was hungry, moving over hers as if she were the very substance God had created in order for him to be whole. His every action both terrified and excited her, and she loved it.

His arms enfolded her. Then, turning her body, he pressed her against him. Her breasts were first flattened against the hardness of his chest, then swelled in anticipation of more. The low, purring sound she made in the dark, cozy interior of the cab seemed far away.

She wanted his touch with a craving that drove away all thoughts of possible consequences. She pressed even closer, willing to be absorbed by his heat, his masculinity.

The catch in his breathing echoed around her, adding to her readiness. "I want you." His voice was as soft as a whisper, as rough as pebbles on a streambed. "I want you so badly, I don't think I'd live if you said no."

She took a breath, knowing he was asking for her commitment to their marriage. "I'm not saying no," she admitted. "I want you, too."

His breath sighed from his body. "Then shall we go inside, or would you like to continue this right where we are?"

This was a dream and she wanted it to continue. Just like this. They were alone and no one, nothing could interfere. The truck was like a haven from the house, bunkhouse, horses and the world.

"Here."

He chuckled. "Okay, darling, but we'll have to be pretty agile. Right now I have a steering wheel in my left rib."

She pulled back, her hand stroking his side. "I'm sorry. We'll go inside."

His arms tightened around her, pulling her back to his broad chest. "No. We'll stay right here in our own little world." He had understood her reluctance to leave the confines of the cab.

His hand slipped down and hit a button, allowing the seat to slide back as far as it would go.

She smiled in the dark and moved to the flow of his body, loving the feeling. Her lips caressed his chest, pecking light kisses up to his neck and jawline. "You smell so good," she murmured.

"So do you," he answered, but his voice sounded lighter than hers. His hands moved restlessly from her hips to her breasts, then back down again.

He moved her higher against him and stretched his legs the length of the seat. With a soft moan of contentment he kissed her again. Her weight was fully supported on his body, her arms encircling his neck as she gave him kiss for kiss, touch for touch, soft sound for manly harsh groan.

After undoing the buttons of her blouse, he slipped his hand inside to the soft warmth of her breast, his fingers seeking, then finding, the nipple that awaited his attention.

She pressed her fullness against his palm, loving the texture of the calluses on his hand as he touched her.

With a twist, the front snap of her lace bra was undone, and she was free of the material. Bending his head, his lips teased her nipple into his mouth. It was pure, unadulterated pleasure. It was torture. Even he couldn't stand the torment anymore and enclosed her breast with his tongue.

"You taste so good," he murmured, stealing another kiss from her parted lips. "Like heaven and hell all rolled into one."

"You feel the same way," she whispered, her fingers stroking his jaw and nape. His strength was always a surprise to her. Corded muscles jumped and played with each stroke of his shoulders. "It's wonderful."

"Better. Better than wonderful."

Sable didn't know when he had undone her slacks, but when he touched the juncture of her thighs, her breath caught in her throat at the wonder of it. Every thought fled her mind. Sensation after sensation washed over her, and she felt as if she were going to die. She arched her body, following his directions as he settled her closer to his lap. His touch was magic, his fingers stroking her as if he knew her innermost secrets and desires.

She wanted him so much! Realizing she was unprotected, she mentally flipped through the calendar of the past month. She should be safe right now.

She reached between them to touch him the same way, but Joe stopped her. "Easy, darling," he murmured, his breath warm on her temple. "Soon," he promised. "Soon."

When he finally entered her, it was as if they'd been born to fit that way. He thrust and she clung to his broad shoulders. He was the only thing anchoring her to the earth. Her breathing was short, matching his as they exchanged kisses. Her mind was numb, overwhelmed by a flood of emotions. She'd never felt—never responded—this way before, and his every move sent her closer and closer to the edge. It was frightening. It was wonderful. Ecstasy began immediately, filling her with more love for him than she'd ever thought herself capable of.

She felt him clench his muscles and knew he was feeling the same thrill she was, and her surprised and delighted laughter filled the air.

Joe's arms tightened, then he moved her against him for a final time, and her laughter became a moan of incredulous delight.

6

IT WASN'T until the early morning hours that Sable and Joe, arms entwined, strolled through the back door into the house. The moon lighted their way, smiling benignly, as if giving its blessing.

When they reached Joe's bedroom, he turned her toward him and gently teased her mouth with tiny kisses. This time intimate contact took precedence over passion. His stroking hands spoke volumes, telling her that most of all he loved holding her and didn't want to let her go. He made her feel warm, wanted, cared for.

But still unwilling to admit that her feelings matched his, Sable pulled away, then rested her head on his chest. The deep, steady thud of his heartbeat sounded in her ear as she relaxed against him. Closing her eyes, she pretended the moment would last forever. They were both very still for a long, peaceful time.

When at last she looked up, she touched with exquisite gentleness the few strands of gray at his temple, her fingers caressing his pulse points as her heartbeat matched the rhythm of his.

She was still stunned by her reaction to his touch. It was a shock to realize she had such passion imprisoned inside her. And Joe was the one who'd released it.

She brushed her lips against his, savoring the contact. "Good night," she said softly.

Holding her, he leaned against the doorjamb. "You're not going to spend the rest of the night with me?"

Not trusting her voice, Sable shook her head.

"Why not?"

"Give me time," she finally pleaded, ignoring her own reluctance to leave him. How could she say that she couldn't think clearly around him? She needed to sort through her emotions. Right now she felt both wonderful and frightened. And she wasn't capable of making a decision. Any decision. Besides, it just didn't seem right to let those in her world know what had happened this night. Not yet. She needed time to realize it herself. "This has all happened so quickly."

"It doesn't make sense," he whispered in a deep, growling tone. "We can't just ignore what happened between us." He threaded his fingers through her hair, framing her face with his hands. His blue eyes locked with hers. "And it *did* happen."

She understood, but his presence left her no room to think things through. "Please," she begged, curling her hand on his chest. "Don't rush."

Joe took a step back, and her hand dropped to the space left between them. His eyes narrowed, taking in her pale face. Violet circles rimmed her eyes, visible even in the dim light of dawn. She was exhausted and probably a little confused. And so was he.

"Okay." He sighed. "Just this time."

"Thank you." She kissed the tip of his chin.

"Sleep well."

She smiled. "I'll try."

His kiss on her forehead was slow and sweet, sealing their earlier actions. She pulled away and walked toward her room across the hall.

Joe backed into his own room and softly closed the door.

Undressing in the moonlight, Sable mulled over potential problems they might have created during these past wonderful hours. But her thoughts still couldn't focus on them. Everything was too new and shiny, and her emotions were too jumbled.

She slipped between the cool sheets, believing she would be awake for what remained of the night. Instead her eyes closed almost instantly and she fell into a deep slumber.

JOE TOSSED his pants and shirt into a corner and got into bed. But his eyes refused to close. The bed was too empty, the room too cold. Moonlight was dimming outside his window, but he wasn't ready for the new day.

There was only one solution to all his problems: Sable.

An hour later, the answer was still Sable.

Joe slipped from the bed and reached for his robe. He slung it over his arm, opened the door and listened to make sure the kids were still sleeping. Then he walked across the hall to Sable's room and slowly twisted the knob.

Standing at the foot of the bed, he gazed. She was asleep, curled in a small knot on one side of the bed. Against her back, where Joe should have been, was a pillow. She looked vulnerable, contented and . . . beautiful.

The deep well of tenderness he felt as he stared at her took him by surprise. It was more than lust. It was more than loneliness. Shaking his head, he refused to label it. But it scared the hell out of him.

He couldn't resist. He walked stealthily around the side of the bed and slipped between the sheets. Carefully he moved the pillow from her back and replaced it with his own body. Edging his knee between hers, he rested one arm on the slim curve of her waist. She wriggled closer; the imprint of her body against him was heaven. Sighing contentedly, he closed his eyes. With her body nestled in his arms, he slept at last.

TALIA'S VOICE ripped through Sable's dream.

"Sable, we've overslept!" she cried, opening the bedroom door. "It's after nine, and I'm supposed to be at cheerleader tryouts—"

Sable stirred. It was so very cosy here in her bed. A small, satisfied sound echoed in her throat, and she snuggled closer to the welcome warmth. Perhaps, if she didn't open her eyes, Talia would disappear.

A male chuckle resounded in her ear and sent a shiver down her spine. A soft breath touched her temple. The weight that felt so good on her waist moved. Her body grew rigid. She had to be wrong. She must be wrong. Cautiously she straightened her leg, only to encounter someone else's flesh. Muscled flesh. Talia's giggle told her she was right. Joe was in bed with her.

And apparently as stark naked as she was.

Her first reaction was to flee. Sable rolled away and sat up, clutching the sheet to her bosom like an outraged spinster. Totally ignoring the goggle-eyed teenager, she turned to Joe. "What are you doing here?" she demanded.

Talia giggled again.

Joe grinned. "Sleeping."

"But you're not supposed to be sleeping here!"

"Well, not anymore today," he agreed evenly. "Now I'm going to get up and go to work. We overslept, as Talia so kindly informed us."

She glanced over her shoulder at the teenager. "Talia, leave, please." Then she turned to Joe once more. "I mean you shouldn't be here!"

He raised his brows. "Why not? It is legal, you know. I'm your husband."

"I know! But—" she began.

Sable's gaze darted back to her young sister. Behind her stood Jonathan, his eyes button bright as he looked with undeniable interest from his hero to his mama.

"Mommy like Joe?" the little boy asked.

Sable couldn't answer that question. Not now. "Talia, take Jonathan and leave, please." Her voice shook with anger. At least she told herself it was anger. She wasn't ready to face being found in bed with the man she'd married in name only. And she wasn't ready for the questions she was sure Jonathan would ask. But most of all she wasn't ready for the commitment this action implied.

Talia looked disappointed. She took the youngster by the hand and slowly moved toward the door. Their eyes remained on the couple in bed.

"Now, Talia," Sable urged.

When the door closed behind them, Sable focused all her anger and frustration on the cause of this problem. "What the hell do you think you're doing in my bed?"

"Sleeping," was his prompt reply.

"You were supposed to sleep in your own bed. You agreed," she said, trying to fill her voice with grit.

Head tilted to one side, he stared as though examining her for some rare disease. "I know, but I changed my mind. Is something going on in that tousled head of yours that I don't know about?" he asked quietly.

"Don't try to avoid the issue." Sable bit out each word. "You weren't supposed to come in here, and I want you out. Now."

His eyes narrowed. "You mean I'm good enough to make love to in the cab of a truck, but I'm not good enough to take to bed?" Obviously his patience was ending, too. "What am I? A yard dog with fleas? Good enough to play fetch outside, but not good enough to bring into the house?"

"Of course not!" She took a deep breath to calm the quaking that seemed to permeate her body. "But you promised I'd have time to think this through! Then you climb into my bed and announce to my family that we're sleeping together, without bothering to think how I'd feel about telling them."

"We're married."

"I know." She pulled at the sheet, wrapping it around herself as she stood. She needed to get away. "But this wasn't the way it was supposed to happen. My son shouldn't have to find a man in my bed without my explaining all this to him."

"Why not? We're not strangers."

"Don't start with me, Joe Lombardi!" Sable took another step backward. "You were supposed to stay in your own bed...your own room, until we worked this out. Our contract stipulated that you and I maintain separate bedrooms and all that that entails. I want to keep it that way." She pushed back an errant strand of hair and glared at him. He had no right to look so calm, as if this happened every day.

Apparently oblivious to his own nudity, Joe let the blanket fall away and got up, his tanned form beautifully outlined by the sun from the window. "Correction. You were the one who needed to work things out. I know what I want." His voice was hard, his features carved in granite.

"And just what was it you want, Joe?" she asked sarcastically. "Sex? A little fooling around before you leave for a hard day's work?"

Joe surprised her by nodding his head. "Yes," he answered. "But that's not all. I also want a little stroking. You know, some of the comforting things a *wife* does."

She didn't miss the mingled hurt and sarcasm in his voice. And for just a second she felt she'd let him down. But the feeling led to defensiveness. "You want sex, plain and simple."

"I haven't denied it. But as I said, that's not all I want."

"Get out," Sable ordered, suddenly unable to continue this conversation. If she'd been confused last night, it was nothing compared to now. Her chin tilted upward, warning that she was ready for battle.

"But throw something on first," she said coldly. "Remember there are others in this house."

His face mirrored his frustration as Joe took a threatening step toward her, but he stopped at the end of the bed. "Forget it," he said disgustedly, reaching for his robe. "You have some pretty deep-seated problems, lady. You're right. I shouldn't have come in here and tried to extend our wonderful time in the truck. I thought you were an adult as well as my wife. You're the person I should be thrilled to live with in wedded bliss. As you've just proven, you're not worth the aggravation or the trouble."

Joe opened the door. "Call me when you have your act together. Maybe, if I'm still around, I'll consider an apology."

It was her fault. Their lovemaking had ended in warfare.

One phrase had really hit home. *The person I should be thrilled to live with in wedded bliss!*

Since her marriage she'd thought only of the sacrifices she'd made for her son and sister. She had chosen her way of life, then found a man to help her do exactly what she wanted. But she'd given no thought to Joe's sacrifices, his personal needs, his lifestyle.

For the next five years he'd given up the right to be seen in public with other women.

He couldn't even think of having a relationship with a woman.

Because of this marriage, he'd probably never have children of his own. By the time they got divorced and he found a woman to love, he could conceivably be in his forties and decided the time for fatherhood had passed him by. Then all that joy would never be experienced.

He'd lost his freedom and, in his own home, he'd lost his privacy.

He received a million dollars for giving up those rights! a little voice argued.

They'd both been dumb.

It had been easy to sit in an attorney's office and spout off living conditions. After the wedding they'd learned the difficulty of living up to rules and regulations written in ignorance. And as time went on, the stress of their day-to-day married lives had worsened.

Until last night.

Guilt hit her hard.

And so did memories of last night.

Joe had been so attentive all evening that Sable had let her guard down. By the time he kissed her, she'd been ready to ignore the small voice inside, telling her to slow down.

Now, clutching the sheet still wrapped around her like a Grecian robe, Sable sat on the edge of the bed.

She should have seen where this was leading, instead of just riding the crest of the wave of sensuality. But it had been so new, so incredible. So overwhelming. Joe's touch had lured her into an uncharted land.

It was all her fault. Maybe if she'd treated the whole episode as lightly as he had, no one, including little Johnny, would have thought anything unusual about it. But she'd blown it all out of proportion.

After firmly telling Talia that she would have nothing to do with the man on a physical level, she'd been embarrassed to be found with him in her bed. That knowing look in Talia's eyes had turned her embarrassment into anger and she had exploded at Joe, instead of the real culprit: herself.

JOE CURSED LOUDLY in the shower stall. He'd made a perfectly sane decision to court Sable. He had planned to show her just how gentlemanly he could be. How considerate. In fact, he'd shown her what a jackass he could be.

He wasn't sure what kind of relationship she'd had with John, and wasn't certain he wanted to know. But he had realized that, for a married woman, Sable was very innocent when it came to acknowledging her own sensuality. Yet she had responded with openness and passion he'd never thought he'd find, making their lovemaking all the more incredible. That should have given him a clue as to her confusion, had he thought about it for even a minute.

Instead he'd crawled into her bed. He'd ruined the whole damn thing by forcing her into an open relationship, before she had absorbed all the changes. He'd forced her into displaying their attraction to her family, when she hadn't even admitted it to herself.

He'd rushed her.

He'd fumbled it.

Another muttered curse rang off the tiled shower walls.

But the worst sin, he told himself, was that he didn't know what to do next. He'd lost his temper this morning and said things he didn't mean. But his ego had been pretty bruised. He'd reacted out of instinct, lashing out at her, rather than thinking things through and trying to salvage something from the chaos.

He owed her an apology. But something told him that spitting in his face would give her greater pleasure right now.

Stepping out of the shower, he dried off and stepped into his work clothes.

He had faced the jungles of the Vietcong. He had fought off thugs in a dimly lighted parking lot. He could stare down an irate banker at ten paces. But he was going to run away from one small female who was even more vulnerable than she was feisty.

Replacing the hairbrush on his dresser, he stared at the man in the mirror. "Sounds safe to me." The words echoed defeatedly around the room.

SABLE REHEARSED several apologies but she never had a chance to speak to Joe, because he avoided her. He came in after midnight every night and was gone before seven in the morning.

"I don't see what's so wrong about the situation." Talia's voice startled Sable as she wound the cord on the vacuum cleaner.

"What situation?"

"You know," Talia drawled, dropping into a plush, upholstered chair. "Between you and Joe."

"It's none of your business." Sable couldn't count the times she'd said that in the past week.

"Well, I still don't see anything wrong with it."

"I'll pretend you never said anything, so I won't have to be angry. But one more word of warning, Talia. Please don't bring this issue up again. I just want to forget it."

"Boy!" Talia exclaimed. "You tell me to be strong, make decisions, accept what mistakes you make and go on! Maybe you should follow your own advice."

With as much dignity as she could muster, Sable ignored Talia's last comment and left the room, wishing her thoughts could be left behind as easily.

She decided the kitchen needed a thorough cleaning. Jonathan was napping and the house was quiet. The only way to occupy her mind was to keep busy.

She glanced at the note on the table, then focused on the sink full of dishes. She knew the note—all Joe's notes—by heart. They had been communicating all week by notes left on the kitchen table. She wrote her answers to the messages written in the morning and left them on the table for him to find at night.

She filled the sink with sudsy water and sighed. Maybe washing the dishes by hand would take her mind off Joe. The whole situation would be comical if she didn't feel the way she did about the man.

She loved Joe. She loved him so much, she was afraid of his rejection. So instead of approaching her husband and telling him she cared for him, she avoided him. Just as he avoided her.

Tears filled her eyes, and she tried to blink them away. Every time she remembered the passion they had shared, she wanted more—so much more.

She wanted Joe to feel the same way she did. She wanted him to stride in the door, take her into his arms and kiss her until she swooned. Was that too much to ask? Yes! came the resounding answer.

Despite her efforts to forget it, there was the issue of the money. He wouldn't have had the chance to make love to her if she hadn't bought him. He'd still be free and single and probably making love to some other lucky woman. And Sable would have never known just what she was missing.

She had to do something!

She'd give Joe some time to make the first move, but if, by this time next week, nothing had happened, she would approach Joe, kiss him, then apologize.

Maybe he would take the initiative. She straightened her shoulders. It didn't matter. She'd made the decision. She would hold herself to it.

SEVEN DRAGGING DAYS PASSED, and Joe still made no move in her direction. He continued to stay out of her way.

On the afternoon of her self-imposed deadline she took Jonathan to the barn, and they mucked out the horses' stalls.

By the time they'd finished, she was hot and tired and sweaty. "Okay," she told the horses. "You've been given the equivalent of clean sheets, and I don't have to worry about you for another week." She wiped her hands on her jeans.

Johnny stood in a ray of sunshine, chubby hands wrapped around the handle of the rake as he smiled up at her. Suddenly all was almost right with her world.

"Oh, you think that's funny, do you?" she teased.

Johnny nodded. "Horses don't talk, Mommy."

"Well, some do! They just wait till we're not around, then they tell stories about how funny we humans are."

Johnny shook his head. "No."

The sound of boots hitting concrete caught her attention. Her hand still on the boy's shoulder, Sable turned.

Joe strode toward them. His hair was damp. His shirt clung to broad shoulders, chest and arms. His blue eyes were narrowed, focused on her. She felt like a butterfly caught on a pin.

Joe halted in front of her and stared down.

Her heart beat frantically in her breast. "Hi." Her voice was a whisper.

"Hi, beautiful." Wrapping his arms about her, he pulled her close to the lean hardness of his body. When his head came down and his lips claimed hers, she responded instantly. Heartbeat quickening, she curled her arms around his neck and clung to the strength of him. His mouth, hard, possessive, breathtaking, answered with the same fervor. A soft sound came from somewhere. It didn't register at first that she'd made it.

When the kiss ended, she felt bereft. He placed her head against the solidity of his chest, and his lips grazed her ear. "I'm sorry," he murmured into her hair. "I didn't mean to hurt you."

"I'm sorry, too." Relief flooded her, soothing away her worries. Joe had apologized to her!

"And we have company."

"Here?"

He nodded. But it wasn't until he turned to one side and pulled away that she saw two figures on the threshold. Then Jonathan gave a happy cry, dropped his rake and ran toward them.

Sable and Joe turned to face the visitors together.

Her heart sank.

Jonathan's grandparents stood there, rigid and uncertain, awaiting recognition.

With his arm about her waist, Joe guided Sable toward them. Still dazed, it took her a moment to bid the pair a cool welcome.

How could they face her, when they'd written such an awful letter just weeks ago, demanding she give them Jonathan? How could Joe act so cordially, so hospitably to the people who wanted to tear her family apart? If only she'd told him about the letter. Once more she'd fouled up by not telling him everything.

But Jonathan clearly had no reservations. He was in his grandfather's arms, hugging him as fervently as Sable had hugged Joe.

"We just wanted to see Jonathan," Mrs. LaCroix said with a catch in her throat.

Sable stared at her, their eyes meeting and warring. The older woman looked away first, and Sable realized that she had won. John's parents would never have come here if they hadn't been told they could not win custody of Jonathan.

For a moment Sable felt sorry for the exquisitely dressed older woman. All the money in the world wouldn't bring her son back. It couldn't even buy visitation rights to her grandson.

"We're glad you came," Sable replied. "This is my husband, Joe Lombardi. He and John were friends."

Joe nodded at the woman and held out his hand to John's father.

"Where did you know my son?" the older man questioned.

"Nam. We were foxhole buddies," Joe explained.

Sable slipped her hand through Joe's bent arm. "Come inside. Iced tea should help stave off this August heat."

Jonathan was still in his grandfather's arms when Sable and Joe led the couple into the living room.

Quickly Sable went to the kitchen and made the tea. She added sprigs of fresh mint to the glasses, then placed them on a tray with the sugar. After a moment's hesitation, she decided to leave everything exactly as it was. After all, she lived a simple life now. No silver or crystal.

And Joe was Joe. It didn't really matter whether John's parents liked him or not. They were no longer her in-laws. They were just Jonathan's grandparents.

Taking a deep breath, Sable picked up the tray and walked to the living room.

Joe was sitting cross-legged on the floor. Jonathan, wrapped around his back, giggled as he tickled his stepfather's neck.

The LaCroix looked on.

"He's quite a guy," Joe commented to André LaCroix.

"I agree." The expression on the older man's face reflected his pride. Sable knew that, though there was little resemblance between Jonathan and his father, André saw his son in his grandson.

"Here it is," Sable said, forcing a cheery note into her voice. She placed the tray on the coffee table.

Suddenly thoughtful, she watched everyone. Had she made such a fuss about the big, bad LaCroix that she'd blown the whole situation out of proportion? She didn't think so. Anyone who tried to take away a child from his parent to be raised by hired help was untrustworthy. And that letter *had* been a threat.

"Where's your sister?" Mrs. LaCroix asked. "I thought she lived with you."

"She does," Sable said, choosing her words carefully. "She's finishing her school supply shopping."

"So you're still raising her."

"She's still living with me, yes," Sable amended. Talia had always been too outspoken for the LaCroix to enjoy.

Arms outstretched, Johnny came to Sable. "Drink, please," he said as he climbed into her lap. Proud that he remembered his manners in front of his grandparents, she kissed the tip on his nose and tickled his stomach.

He gave an endearing grin. With a tender smile she allowed him a sip of her tea.

"You look very well," Mrs. LaCroix said softly.

Sable's surprised gaze darted to the older woman. "Thank you. I'm happy."

"I can see that. And so is Jonathan."

Sable nodded. "Jonathan's always happy as long as he has his way," she answered.

"Don't I know it! His father was the same way, always smiling as long as I gave him what he wanted. . . ." Her voice faded; she'd evidently realized she was speaking of Sable's first husband in the presence of the new one. "Oh, I'm sorry!" she exclaimed, holding one hand to her cheek in dismay. "I didn't mean to . . ."

"It's okay." Joe's voice was gentle, but firm. "John was my friend, too. And I want Jonathan to know about his father."

Sable could have kissed Joe when she saw relief in the expressions of her former in-laws. Without Joe to defuse some of the initial awkwardness, this visit would have been disastrous.

The rest of the visit was calm, without the usual tension Sable felt with the LaCroix. In fact, she was surprised to find it a pleasant visit.

They walked the older couple out to the driveway. Mr. LaCroix stood uncertainly at the side of the car. "We only want to see our grandson."

"And you can." Sable knew her smile was forced, but she meant the words. "But I can't allow you to spoil him rotten. Children need strong guidelines and a lot of love."

"May we visit again soon?" the older man asked, his hand outstretched toward Joe.

"Anytime," Joe told him, before Sable could answer.

As they drove away, Joe stood with one arm holding Jonathan, the other around Sable. The older couple waved goodbye and the car disappeared into the distance. Still holding her firmly, Joe turned and directed Sable up the porch steps.

Jonathan ran into the house and off to his room to play.

Sable looked up at Joe, marveling at the strength and gentleness he always displayed. "Thank you," she said softly.

"Nothing to it," he muttered, suddenly embarrassed.

She placed her hand on his arm. "Yes, there was. And I thank you for making it easier."

His eyes narrowed as he looked at her for the first time since the LaCroix had left. "Sable, why did you marry me?"

Her eyes widened. "So I could keep Jonathan. You knew that."

"No," he declared quickly. "I mean the real reason. What was it? Did you like being married? Or did you want your own home, without the bother of battling your way out of theirs?"

Sable wrinkled her brow in puzzlement. "The threat of Jonathan's grandparents fighting for custody *is* the real reason."

"That's an excuse, Sable." His voice hardened. "Those people might think about taking Jonathan, but only if their grandparental rights were threatened. As long as you didn't keep them from seeing their grandson, there wouldn't be a problem."

So that was it. He'd taken them at face value. And she hadn't helped any by not telling him about the letter. "You're wrong," she told him firmly. "I know them. I heard their attorney try to reason with them, but they wanted custody. They were willing to fight for it. In court."

Joe opened his mouth, but she held up her hand to stop him. "And just two short weeks ago they wrote another letter, telling me they wanted to raise my son and send him away to school. Those people mean business when they speak or act, Joe. And I know a challenge when I see one."

Joe shook his head. "Maybe, but I don't think so. I think they just wanted the right to see their grandson, and were afraid you were taking that right away. That's all."

Her hands shook so hard, she placed them on her hips. "You don't know them. You weren't there. I was."

"And you panicked. In your rush to ensure custody of Jonathan, you offered me a million dollars for a marriage you didn't need and obviously don't want." His voice was sad and heavy.

"And you agreed."

"No," he corrected. "I agreed to marry you. I don't believe that they were trying to take away your child."

Frustration filled her. "What do you care? Jonathan's not your responsibility. You never stayed up with him at night, watched him cut his first tooth or cried when he fell and hurt himself. You weren't there. I was."

"And if you had your way, I think you'd like to keep Jonathan away from me, too, Sable. You'd love to have him all to yourself, with no one else to claim his attention. That's not right, for you or for Jonathan." Joe's voice still sounded as tired and defeated as he looked.

He walked inside, then stopped and looked back at her. "Though you didn't have to marry me, you did. Now you'll have to make the best of it. Because this is all we have."

"And you?" she asked, trying to read his expression. "Why did you marry me?"

"One reason was money," he admitted in a tone of finality. He turned and headed toward the back door. "I'll be at the track," he said over his shoulder and left the house.

"Wait!" she called, running after him.

But the truck was pulling away as she ran down the back steps. Fists clenched at her sides, she watched him drive around the house and toward the road. "We're not through yet, Joe Lombardi," she muttered. "Not by a long shot."

SCHOOL BEGAN, and Talia was caught up in the hectic process of making friends and settling into classes. Talia had a talent for fitting in and getting whatever she wanted. She'd already passed the cheerleading tests. Sable had helped her sister develop her self-confidence because she was aware of how sorely she lacked it herself.

Now she even doubted she was capable of gaining Joe's attention by being a wonderful wife and mother. It would be so much easier to just give up. But a small, inner voice told her to believe in herself, and so she continued to try.

These days Sable hardly saw Joe and when she did, he was distant and preoccupied. She knew he was fighting both a deadline and the Texas Racing Commission.

Because gambling was to be legal for the first time since the turn of the century, every detail of policy had to be carefully evaluated. Whatever the board did, they checked with other state commissions first, to see the process before setting up their own. And all of it created more paperwork and headaches for Joe.

Sable prepared gourmet meals, but Joe never came home to eat. Exasperated, she decided at last that she'd go to him.

She dressed with great care and standing before the mirror, decided the effort had been worthwhile. Her long hair swung about her shoulders and her makeup was flawless. Outwardly she appeared cool and assured, but inside she quivered.

Resolutely she marched into the kitchen and placed her husband's hot meal in a plastic container.

At least he'll eat one of my meals, she thought grimly.

Leaving Talia to watch Jonathan and to do her homework, Sable drove toward the racetrack. This would be her first visit to the track and the closer she came, the guiltier she felt. After all, they had been married over a month. She should have shown

more interest in what was her husband's consuming passion—
what kept him away from her.

The road to the stadium was lined with tall pines, and late-
afternoon sunlight sent dappled shadows across the double-lane
road. Entering the grounds, she gasped in surprise when she saw
the huge building.

The structure could have been taken from a 1940s romantic
movie set. A five-story, stucco building, ornately balustraded,
rose through the trees. Walls in a rich cream and carved, dark
wood balconies were interspersed with enormous, floor-to-
ceiling windows, perfect foils for the brown bark and forest-
green background of towering pines.

A row of booths for ticket takers and valet parking atten-
dants flanked broad, semicircular steps leading up to the wide
front entrance.

Sable let the car coast to a slow stop. When she turned off the
ignition, the droning noise of a saw and the intermittent sound
of a hammer echoed hollowly in the distance.

Holding the plastic dish as if it were a talisman, she stepped
outside, then wondered what to do next. Her first impulse was
to get into the car again and drive off. A home-cooked meal
seemed a flimsy excuse to interfere with a project as big as this
one.

Just as she was about to retreat, she heard a shout. "Hey, boss!
You got company!"

Looking up, she saw a workman standing on one of the side
roofs, as if he had all the world under his control. It took her a
moment to realize that the man holding the hammer was her
husband.

She waved weakly.

Joe didn't return her greeting. Instead he turned, walked up
the roof and disappeared over the edge.

Now what should she do? Wait? Disappear? Pretend she
hadn't seen his rebuff? Her heart pounded. She was filled with
indecision. Then she spied him, hammer still in hand, walking
toward her through the enormous lobby. The sound of his heavy
boots rang through the building. When he reached the top of the
shallow steps, he stopped. His plaid shirt was tucked securely
into old, body-hugging jeans, but the day's heat had obviously
forced him to unbutton his shirt. He looked gorgeous.

"Is everything all right?" he called.

Sable nodded, then cleared her throat. "Yes. I just brought you something to eat."

His brows rose. "Come on up."

The command held no note of anger, so she did his bidding.

As she reached his side, she stopped, hands still clutching the dish. "This building is beautiful!" Her awestruck tone added emphasis to her words.

"Yes," he agreed quietly, his dark eyes resting on her face.

Sable raised a hand to her cheek. "Is my makeup smeared?"

His grin was slow and easy. It drew her like a magnet. He took her arm and escorted her through the impressive entrance doors, adjusting his longer step to the cadence of hers. "Your makeup is perfect. Let's go into the office, where I can see what you've brought me."

Just inside the lobby was a bank of elevators. Joe ushered her in and, without taking his eyes from her, pushed the button for the fifth floor. His smile was still turning up the corners of his lips.

Now she became even more nervous. "What's the completion date?"

He shrugged. "If I win, it's a month from tomorrow. If the racing commission wins, it's within two weeks."

"And what are the chances of the commission winning?"

"Fifty-fifty," he muttered, still holding her arm as the elevator doors opened.

They stepped out and he ushered her down an area that apparently would become a large, glassed-in gallery facing the track. She was enthralled with the view.

A wide track encircled an oval of green lawn. Within its boundaries was a beautifully landscaped pond. Swans and ducks glided over mirrorlike water and paraded up and down grassy knolls created especially for them.

"The track is finished!" Sable exclaimed in surprise.

"Yes. So are the barns, quarters and most of the offices. The parking lots and the building itself are all that's left. A personnel company in Conroe is hiring the employees now."

"Oh?" Her eyes darted around the complex, straying here and there even as he led her to another door. "How many do you need?"

"About a thousand."

They entered a large office with the same enchanting view as the gallery beyond.

"A thousand people?" she asked incredulously.

"Yes. One thousand," he repeated gently.

"But what will a thousand people do?"

"Some will be trained to place the bets and calculate payoffs on computers. Others will keep the grounds up, work in the restaurants, the bars, the office or the stable."

He took the plastic-covered dish from her and placed it on the desk. "What's this?"

"Swiss Bliss," she said absently, still staring at him.

How could he be so calm, knowing he had to hire a thousand people in less than a month? Knowing he had to have a payroll for that many people?

"What's Swiss Bliss?"

"It's meat, potatoes, carrots, onions and tomatoes, all baked together with assorted spices," she answered distractedly.

"It looks delicious. Did you bring a fork?" Dipping his finger into the tomato and onion gravy, he tasted it.

"Oh, yes." She reached into her purse and pulled out napkin-wrapped utensils. Her mind whirled. How could she not have known what a huge operation this was to be? "Can you manage that large a payroll?"

He nodded, then took his first mouthful of the meal she'd cooked. "If we don't have any more problems. The first race will help us out there."

Her glance was wary. A thousand-person payroll was a large amount of money. "When is the first race?"

"When we open."

"But you're not sure when you open."

Realizing she wouldn't be happy until all her questions were answered, Joe began explaining. "The first race is one month away. That's why I don't want to open until then. Two nights before the race we'll have the grand opening. A catering firm in Dallas has been handling those arrangements for the past several weeks. If the commission insists, I can open in two weeks, but I want the extra time to train the workers and work the bugs out of the computer equipment."

"Oh." She tried to pretend that it made sense. "But if the first race is a month away, why does the racing commission want you to open earlier?"

"Because, since they're not sure what they're doing, they need the time to teach their men. They want the government men to be established before racing starts."

"What government men?"

Joe sighed, then patiently continued. "Racing committee policies are set by the director of racing. Three men are racing stewards. Two represent the track before the racing commission and one represents the state. Then there are the IRS men who must be available, in case someone wins big. Uncle Sam gets his cut off the top."

"I didn't know," she said, shocked by how little thought she'd given to his work. She'd only been to a racetrack once, during the first year she and John were married. "Will they give you any leeway on the time dispute?"

"If Mike is the crackerjack attorney I think he is, the answer is yes."

"I see."

She watched Joe enjoy his lunch. At least there was something she could do right, even if it was only cooking a meal for her man. *Her man*. What an obsolete expression! And she loved it.

"Delicious," he commented. "And spicy," he added.

"I always make it spicy. It's the best way."

He leaned back in the plush, leather chair. "Only if you don't have an ulcer."

That startled her. "Do you have one?"

He nodded. "Uh-huh."

"Why didn't you tell me?"

"Because you were so busy hating me. I was afraid that if you found out, you might make your meals even spicier," he admitted ruefully.

She shook her head. And she had thought there was one thing she was doing right! "I'll grant you that I'm opinionated on occasion, Joe. But I'm not vindictive."

"I know that now." He scooted his chair back. "Come here," he said, patting his leg.

Sable's heart lightened. For the first time in weeks, Joe was relaxed and happy. She'd missed him.

Sorely tempted to do as he asked, she was nonetheless unwilling to look too eager. "I came here on a mission of mercy. I didn't come for hanky-panky," she lied.

"This will be a mission of mercy," he promised. "Come here. Please."

That did the trick. Cautiously she perched on his lap, her back straight, hands resting stiffly on his shoulders.

"There, that's better," he murmured, laying his head against the softness of her breast. His sigh penetrated her soul. The masculine scent of him rose to her nostrils, and she took a deep breath.

But still wary, Sable held her breath, waiting for his next move. She wanted to run her fingers through his springy, dark hair. His warm breath penetrated her light blouse, touching her skin as surely as if it had been his hand.

"You smell so good." His lips touched the curve of her breast, teasing her nipple.

She swallowed. "So do you."

His light clasp at her waist tightened ever so slightly. "And feel so good," he added.

"So do you."

Finally she gave in. Her fingers lost themselves in the thick texture of his hair. She could feel her body relaxing, responding to his closeness.

Joe breathed deeply, his head settling ever closer to the point of her breast. His arms encircled her and his hands, lightly rubbing her back, followed the slender curve of her spine.

She rested her cheek on his head, trying to clear her thoughts and come up with the apology she had composed earlier. Nothing came to mind.

"Sable."

"Hmm?" Her hands seemed to have a will of their own. They wanted to touch the length, breadth and strength of his shoulders, back and neck. He was strong and he smelled like hot sun and fresh earth. He was intoxicating.

"I want more."

"More what?" Her mind was fogged, slow.

"More from our marriage."

Those words got through. The payroll came unbidden to her mind.

She sat up, pulling away from him. "More money?" she asked, her voice thin. This was what she'd always dreaded. Joe had married her for money, so why wouldn't he ask for more? "Are you asking to commingle our assets?"

She saw Joe stare up at her, his blue eyes suddenly narrowed. "Do you really believe that?"

She shook her head. When she was with him, she couldn't believe that money was all he wanted. Only when she was alone did doubts gnaw away at her. "Well, you told me about the payroll and wanting to wait until just before opening."

"And you thought it was an invitation for you to contribute to the cause."

"I don't know. I'm asking you."

Joe's hands slipped down to her waist and tightened their grip. With one smooth movement he helped her stand, then stood himself. His lips brushed hers, leaving her speechless. Was he angry with her? Or was he telling her that he did want the money?

He turned away and began putting the silverware he'd used into the plastic container.

"Thank you for dinner," he said, placing the plastic lid on top. "It was good. Goodbye."

Before she realized what he was about, he was striding through the door. "Joe!" she cried. "Wait!"

"Can't," he called over his shoulder. "There's work to do. Goodbye."

By the time she forced her legs to move to the door, he was in the elevator.

He was gone. Again.

Suddenly anger filled her. "Okay, Lombardi!" she shouted through the empty building. She didn't care who heard, as long as Joe did. "Run away again! That's all you've been doing since we got married!"

The only answer was the faraway whirr of the elevator as it descended to the ground floor.

As silence fell, she became aware of how ridiculous her accusation had been. If he had wanted more money, he wouldn't have insisted on the prenuptial agreement. Nor did he have to play papa to a three-year-old or an older brother to Talia.

Sable didn't understand why, but Joe brought out all her insecurity, the craziness she'd never known she had—until now. Her feelings seesawed around him. Joe made her happier than she'd been in all her life. He made her feel more alive—and more angry—than she had ever thought possible. And she'd behaved foolishly—throwing insults down the elevator shaft!

Before their marriage, fighting Joe—fair or foul—hadn't been a problem. But since their wedding day he'd run in the opposite direction every time they had exchanged words.

Sable felt a small, sad smile touch the corners of her mouth. Poor Joe! He wasn't the only one running away.

It was time for both of them to face a few homegrown truths....

JOE MARCHED to the back of the building and began climbing the ladder to the first roof.

"Hey, boss! Where's your lovely lady?" one of the crewmen called out.

"She's on her way home. So you can quit ogling and start working again."

He stepped gingerly over the red-tiled roof to check the flashing around the pipes. But his mind was elsewhere. He could still see the wariness in her eyes when she'd asked if he needed more money. More of *her* money! That hurt. What was she thinking of, asking that? Did Sable honestly believe he was after her money?

He had tried so hard to show her how much he cared, but it seemed that everything he did backfired on him. Was asking her to love him, the way a woman loves a man, too much?

What he wanted made him face his feelings for Sable. The plain, stark truth was that he loved her. She couldn't have hurt him this much if he didn't.

He wanted to be her lover.

He craved to be her hero.

He just didn't know how.

The only thing he knew how to be was a lover. He'd had no practice at anything else. Being a lover was easy. You sweet-talked the woman, took her to bed and showed her your emotions in action.

But Sable needed more than that. He just didn't know what. Hell, for fear of making a bad situation worse, he'd even gone out of his way not to argue with her! But instead of being happy about it, it seemed to have made her even angrier.

"There's just no pleasing her," he muttered.

That wasn't true, but he wasn't sure anymore what the truth looked like. He was confused. And the only other person he could blame beside himself was Sable.

He'd stay out of her way until he came up with another plan of action. Sooner or later he *would* win over the fair Sable to his way of thinking. They were going to have a real marriage, and he was going to win her trust. . . .

SABLE PACED THE KITCHEN, waiting for Joe to return home. By nine o'clock, she knew it was going to be another of his "late" nights. Emotionally drained, she sat down at the kitchen table and dropped her head into her hands.

Talia strolled in, placed her manicure set on the table and slouched into a chair across from her sister. "What's the matter?"

"Nothing."

"Sure," Talia drawled, creaming her cuticles.

"Joe didn't come home for dinner," Sable said disconsolately.

"I noticed he wasn't in his usual seat. Maybe he's still pushing for the original date for the track opening."

Sable glanced up. "You know about that?"

"Sure. Don't you?" Talia looked as surprised as Sable felt.

"Yes. But how did you find out?"

"Joe told me."

"When?"

Talia shrugged. "A week or two ago."

Sable's expression told her to continue.

"I couldn't sleep, so I came in here and made some cocoa. Then Joe came in and we talked about the track. He said he was fighting the deadlines and that he thought he could make the racing commission's contract, but it would take hard work."

"I see."

But Sable didn't see. How could he talk to Talia so easily and not speak to her at all? She was his *wife*, for heaven's sake! He should be able to talk to her about everything!

That wasn't true.

To keep him from finding out how vulnerable she was, she had purposely put up barriers he couldn't penetrate. She'd kept things from him, telling herself that he wouldn't understand. But she'd thought he wanted it that way, too. Could she have been wrong? And if so, how many other things was she wrong about? She was afraid to guess.

"Sable?" Talia's voice pierced her thoughts. "Did you and Joe make up today?"

"No," she admitted. "We started out fine, but ended up in a shouting match. Or rather, I yelled. He just walked away, as usual."

"Really? What's he trying to do, steal your act?"

"I don't walk away."

"No? So you've discussed the fact that our father was a drunk? And that's why there's no liquor in the house?"

"That's our business. Our *old* business. No one else needs to know that," Sable declared stiffly.

"I see," Talia mused. "And have you mentioned the LaCroix letter to him?"

"I mentioned it," Sable said, aware that she was hedging.

"And what did he say?"

"Not much," Sable muttered reluctantly.

"Boy! For a man who likes to talk as much as he does, he sure acts strange around you." Talia gave her an innocent look. "I wonder why?"

"I don't know."

"And he talks to Jonathan all the time, too," Talia added, her gaze still glued to her sister.

"I know," Sable said morosely. She didn't need to hear about the difference between Joe's attitude toward her and toward others.

"Yet the one woman he wants to talk about, he doesn't seem to talk to."

Sable stared through narrowed eyes at her sister. "What are you hinting at, Talia?"

The girl quickly began buffing her nails. "Nothing. I just think it's odd. It sounds as if the man has a bad case of love."

Sable bristled. Love? It was ridiculous. She'd had a man in love with her once. She would certainly recognize the signals. What Joe felt for her was more likely. . . lust. Damn!

"You're insane, Talia. That's the teenager in you. You think every problem has to do with love. In the adult world it's very different."

"Can't tell by me," Talia said breezily, holding her hand out for inspection. "I know about money problems and health problems. I know about puppy love and teenage problems. I even see great similarities. But if you say they're not the same, I guess you're right. I'm not all that familiar with adult hang-ups."

Sable's patience came to an end. "Well, the next time you think about love, think twice."

Talia stared at her for a moment, a frown etching her brow. "What would you say if I told you I was in love?"

"I'd say you're too young." Sable stood and smiled down at her younger sister. "And I'd say that, though the symptoms look the same, in your case it has to be puppy love."

"Really? What makes my feelings of love any different than yours?"

"Because I'm older."

Talia grinned. "Then you admit you love Joe."

"I didn't say that." Sable knew she was hedging again.

"Not in so many words. But you *did* admit it. Don't forget, you were only a kid when John swept you off your feet."

"And I was still too young to understand the kind of commitment it took to make a marriage work. I was just lucky that John cared enough to allow me to grow up and make my mistakes."

"So," Talia said thoughtfully. "As an adult, Joe is the only love interest you've ever had."

Sable gave up on her younger sister's logic. "Don't play word games with me, Talia. I'm too tired. In fact I'm going to bed."

"Sleep well." Talia's singsong voice grated on Sable's nerves as she walked down the hall to her room.

Sable realized that she was past being tired. She was punchy with exhaustion. Why else would she want to pull the covers over her head and hide from the world?

Instead she reached for a new romance novel and tried to concentrate on reading. But her heart wasn't in it and she finally gave up. It was another, long half hour before she slept. Every time she closed her eyes, she imagined Joe's head resting against her breasts, his arms around her waist and back. And his dark hair touching her cheek. He'd felt so wonderful....

JOE WALKED in the back door in a mean mood, one he couldn't quite justify.

Talia, eyes bright with interest, was seated at the kitchen table. She watched him walk to the refrigerator and pull out a chilled beer. "And a good evening to you, too," she murmured.

"What are you doing up, squirt?" He drank down the beer and threw the can away.

Talia waved her hands at him. "My nails aren't dry yet."

Joe's gaze darted about the room. "Did Sable go to bed?"

Talia nodded. "She said she was exhausted. Even though she wanted to talk to you, she couldn't keep her eyes open."

"What does she want to talk to me about?" Joe opened the fridge door again, scanned the shelves and took out a plate of fried chicken wrapped in clear plastic.

"I don't know. Something about an apology, but I'm not sure. She wasn't in a good mood."

"She wasn't?"

Talia shook her head.

Joe smiled and put the chicken onto the table. It was nice to know he wasn't the only one who had problems understanding this complicated marriage.

"Any clues?"

"None. Sable was always pretty secretive, even as a teenager. It's her nature." Talia leaned closer and spoke in a low tone. "When she was young, she didn't have anyone to confide in, so she kept it all inside. Not like me. I had her to talk to. She'd solve all my problems and make me feel good about myself into the bargain. Too bad there weren't three of us. Then she could have had a big sister to confide in."

Talia hadn't mentioned their mother. Joe had a feeling that Sable had played that part.

"No friends at all?" he asked, a skeptical look in his eye.

"None," Talia told him him. "Our aunt never approved of anyone Sable brought home. So Sable stopped trying. Personally I think that's why she's so shy. She hides behind a bluff."

Joe took a bite from his chicken drumstick, then put it back onto the plate. His appetite had disappeared. "What made Sable jump to the conclusion that the LaCroix wanted to take Jonathan away from her?"

"The LaCroix family," Talia answered promptly. "To tell the truth, I don't know if they would have or not now. But we wouldn't take that chance. I'd say, judging by their visit, that they've finally seen the error of their ways. It's a good thing, too. We wouldn't want Jonathan to go through what we did."

Joe's gaze pinned Talia to her chair. He saw her squirm uncomfortably. "What do you mean, go through what you did?"

"Don't you know?" Talia was as surprised as Joe seemed to be. "I was just three when our parents divorced, so I only remember the later stages of the mess."

Joe still looked blank.

Her tone was somber as she slowly began the story. "Our parents fought over custody of Sable and me for more than two years. My mother accused my father of bedding every woman in Mobile and the surrounding area at least once, and some twice. My father maintained that my mother had done even worse—everything but sell state secrets."

"They sound like real nice people." Joe's voice was laced with sarcasm.

"They tore each other apart, both in and out of court."

Understanding flooded Joe. "No wonder," he murmured under his breath.

Talia's tone grew bitter. "They didn't care about us. They just wanted to get back at each other. They were willing to say or do anything to mortally wound each other."

Joe stared at the teenage girl. "What happened?"

Talia gazed at her fingers as if she were memorizing the curve of each nail. She glanced up, then back down, her face pale. "Well, the kicker to this whole thing is that two years after my mother won us in the custody suit, she died. And by that time our father had disappeared."

"You mean you never saw him after all the court battles? He never visited you two?" Joe asked, incredulous.

"No. Once the trial was over he disappeared. When the court tracked him down in Atlanta, he didn't want us. He told the judge he didn't know what to do with children he no longer knew, but the court, being just, gave us to him, anyway."

"You weren't raised by him, though, were you?"

"No." Talia shook her head, her eyes still staring down at the table. "After a few disastrous weeks with him and his new wife and son, we were given to his maiden aunt in Mobile. She took us—and a healthy check—once a month."

The breath whooshed from Joe's lungs. "It sounds like a childhood in hell."

For the first time he saw a sheen of tears in Talia's eyes. She shrugged. "It wasn't Aunt Diedra's fault. She just didn't know what to do with two girls. She did the best she could in the best way she knew how. She just didn't know how."

"And your dad?"

Talia closed her eyes, then blinked rapidly. "My father didn't want us to interfere with his new life. He didn't want us to see that his drinking had ruined another family. His second family."

"Do you ever see him?" Joe asked as gently as he could.

"We received a notice that he'd died, just weeks after John did. He was drunk and driving home in a rainstorm. Everything he had was left to his son." Talia glanced up, but she still couldn't look at Joe. And there was a very distinct catch in her voice that she couldn't hide. "It makes sense, I guess. Our half brother was the one who had to live with that pitiful man all those years. Not us. We got Aunt Diedra instead."

"Sounds as though neither was a bargain," Joe observed, realizing now why Sable was so fearful of drink. Talia and Sable had probably seen things he never had, experienced pain he'd never had to live through. For the first time in his life he saw the advantages of being an orphan.

"No wonder you're so grown-up for your age."

A dimple tempered the sadness in Talia's young face. It was then that Joe realized Talia was as good at hiding the truth of her emotions as her older sister.

"Thank you, kind sir, for noticing. Remember that the next time I try for a new curfew."

"If I don't, you'll remind me," he stated dryly, hoping to wring another small smile from her.

He succeeded. "Right on."

Joe stood up, wrapped the remains of the chicken in its plastic shroud and put it back into the refrigerator. "But right now it's time for bed. Curfew or not."

"No school in the morning."

"No, but you still need your beauty sleep," he teasingly reminded her. "Unless you want to look old before your time."

"No, thanks." Talia manufactured a sigh as she gathered up her manicure set. "Someday some man is going to be grateful that I look young and vibrant."

"Anyone I know?" Joe inquired with a grin.

"Yes." She ducked her head and walked under his arm as he reached for the light switch. "But I'm not telling, so don't bother to ask."

"I won't," he whispered as they reached the bedroom wing. "I've got my own troubles."

Joe smiled at the girl. He couldn't help feeling protective toward her. She was the sister he'd never had.

Talia rose swiftly on tiptoe and brushed a quick kiss onto his cheek. Before he could react, she was down the hall, entering her bedroom. "Good night," she called softly. "And thanks for listening."

"Good night. Sleep well," he answered. Her door closed, but Joe remained in the darkened hallway. He stared across the small space that separated his room from Sable's.

So Sable had had every reason to panic at the thought of a custody suit for Jonathan. She was nine years older than Talia and had understood everything that happened. Watching your parents tear each other apart was bad enough, but knowing they didn't want you as much as they professed to had to be a horrible experience.

Now it all made sense. Sable was cool and aloof with everyone—except Jonathan and Talia. With them she was as protective as a lioness sensing danger for her cubs. The only time she'd let her guard down with him had been when the LaCroix came to visit, and he'd screwed that up royally. He'd jumped in and accused her of wanting marriage for some reason other than her son.

He'd been wrong. Dead wrong.

She had never wanted Joe personally. She had wanted exactly what she'd said up front: a marriage to guarantee she'd keep custody of her son. He was the one who had assumed she wanted more.

He'd acted like a stupid fool.

He walked across the hall and slowly turned the knob. Opening the door, he stepped inside.

"Sable?"

There was no answer. Joe walked quietly to the side of her bed and stared down at the slim form nestled there. She was curled on her side, facing the window. The sheet was pushed down to her waist, displaying creamy-vanilla skin and the sensuous fullness of her breasts. His hands itched to touch the slope of waist, hip and legs. Her scent seemed to permeate the room, reminding him of sunshine and flowers and soft, spring breezes. Memories of making love to her brought back his hunger for the sweet taste of nectar on her skin.

His legs went weak at the thought of lying beside her, then taking her into his arms and holding on for dear life as she took him to heaven.

He had to get out of here. Right now. With her image burned on his brain, he walked out and into his own room.

Checking on Sable had been a mistake. His body told him that leaving her had been another. But he'd had no choice. It was either love or conquer. And something also told him that conquering Sable in bed would be no victory. The ultimate test would be to overcome her doubts, so that he could live happily with her. Forever.

PROBLEMS continued unabated at the track. The pump system for the pond broke and had to be replaced. Six of the newly planted trees died within a week. The bar refrigeration system wouldn't cool.

Joe was gone at dawn and came home after midnight. But now it was because he had no choice. Now, when he wanted to be home, he couldn't be. He missed his early morning playtime with Jonathan. He missed Talia's funny bantering.

But most of all he missed Sable.

Sometimes, working at his desk, he was able to totally concentrate on the problems of the racetrack. But Sable always hovered at the edges of his mind. And whenever he did manage to focus his attention on business, Sable invariably appeared with his lunch.

The opening was less than three weeks away, and for the past two days rain had all but stopped the workmen's progress. After a brief glimpse of sun, the sky had clouded up again. As Joe walked the grounds to check on what remained to be done, he was afraid they were in for another unproductive day. He couldn't afford the time.

But if the workmen had to wait for the weather to change, Joe had a desk piled high with paperwork. He walked into his office wet and edgy. A hot casserole dish, sitting in the middle of his desk, told him that Sable had been there. The place setting was perfect. Knife, spoon and napkin were on the right, the fork on the left. Still-warm, crusty bread and a light fruit salad were in two other containers. And today she'd given him a choice. A mug and a glass stood on either side of his plate, along with a thermos of hot coffee and one of iced tea.

Joe found himself grinning. No matter what, Sable would neither buy nor drink beer.

He lifted the heavy plastic lid and sniffed. When the savory aroma of fish stew filled his nostrils, he realized he was hungry.

Sandy, Joe's right-hand man, appeared in the doorway. "Hey, boss . . ." He broke off and stared at the feast. "Wow. The rest of us are eating dried-out fast food, and you're being catered. Now *that's* what being a boss is all about."

"Quit your complaining," Joe said with a chuckle. "My wife cooked this and brought it over."

Sandy's eyes rounded. "Think she might send enough for two?" he asked hopefully.

"Not a chance," Joe told him firmly. "You've got your own wife. Let her do the cooking."

Sandy stretched out in the chair across the desk, taking off his worn baseball cap to wipe his brow. "Never mind. I think I like fast food better than her cooking."

"It can't be that bad," Joe admonished, biting into a crusty piece of bread.

"It isn't. It's just that I'm not into kiddy food. She grills peanut butter sandwiches and makes pancakes in weird animal shapes. And at night she thinks that macaroni and cheese and a salad are a complete meal."

Joe shivered. "That's disgusting."

"Yeah." Sandy looked woeful. "I manage the best I can," he added with a sigh. They both avoided looking at the slight potbelly Sandy was growing.

"Well, you'll have a good meal when we finish this project. On the last day I'm having a barbecue for the crew." Joe's eyes twinkled.

"Really? Wow, that's great!" Sandy exclaimed. "Are we allowed to bring our spouses? You know, so we can kinda brag about the jobs we done?"

Joe hadn't thought about it, but the idea did make sense. After the enormous pressure they'd been under this past month, everyone needed a break. "Why not? We'll invite the families, too." Joe grinned. Sable might enjoy it.

Sandy stood up. "I'll tell the guys. It'll give them something to look forward to."

"Fine." Joe leaned back, pleasantly full. "I'll set it up and let you know the date."

Sandy surveyed Joe's suddenly relaxed attitude. "You know, boss, marriage must agree with you. At least you don't look bone edgy anymore."

"And that's supposed to be due to marriage?" Joe inquired, raising his brows.

Sandy shrugged. "Why not? Nobody can take care of a man like a good woman."

"And what does the woman get?" Joe leaned back. He'd never really discussed marriage with anyone before. Hell, he didn't even know what it took to make a good marriage. Sandy's observations might be helpful.

"Oh, you know women. They like to feel needed," Sandy said as he strolled toward the door. "They also like to have you around some. You'd be a lot better off if you took more time to just sit still for a while."

"I'll do that," Joe said dryly. "Right after we're finished."

"Have you ever heard of delegation? You used that word a lot when we first started. But in the past month it seems you decided to finish this place all by yourself."

"Maybe," Joe hedged. "Maybe not."

"Delegate," Sandy muttered, walking away. "I always liked the sound of that word. It sounds like big business. And success."

Joe got his point. Sandy was right. He'd been running so hard, he wasn't getting as much accomplished as when he'd had weekly staff meetings to distribute the work. Then he'd been able to concentrate on problem areas. Perhaps it was time to go back to the system that worked best.

Something else Sandy had said made a lot of sense. Women like to feel needed. It was worth a try.

He picked up the phone. When Sable answered, he decided to plunge in without giving her time to stall, or worse, hang up on him.

"Sable, can you do me a favor and find a good catering company for a barbecue? We'll need a beer company for at least six kegs. Maybe some wine for the women and soft drinks for the kids."

"When and where? How many people?" Her tone was all business.

"It's for the contracting crew when they finish this project. It will be two weeks from Friday, and there should be . . ." He totaled the number of people on his payroll and tripled it. "Three hundred people. One hundred crewmen, and the rest are wives and children." He took a deep breath.

"You're really asking me to arrange this?" Her voice seemed to dance down his spine. He could get addicted to its lilting tone.

"If you can." He swallowed hard. It wasn't easy to talk to her and not react.

"Of course I can. I'll start the arrangements, then go over them with you."

She sounded so happy. Suddenly he wished he was home with her. He should be grateful for small favors. At least she was talking to him. Maybe he'd call her more often. They seemed to get along much better this way.

"Joe?"

"I'm here." He tried to focus on her words, not the sensuous notes that were turning his body to fire.

"Can you give me more information?"

"I will as soon as I have some," he promised. "By the way, lunch was delicious. Thank you."

"You're welcome," she said softly, then hung up.

For the rest of the problem-filled day Joe Lombardi had a smile on his face.

BY THAT EVENING Sable had figures from two local catering companies, as well as the cost of beer kegs. She had put together several possible menus for the barbecue. She also had a lot of questions.

Excited though she was, disappointment took over when Joe didn't come home for dinner. Again nine o'clock rolled around with no Joe. At midnight she curled up in bed and reached for a romance novel. She tried to pretend everything was okay, but felt so low that she could have easily crawled through the house on her stomach.

For a little while this afternoon Sable had believed the cold war was over. She'd thought that she and Joe might start talking to each other again. Maybe that would help restore their faltering marriage. Then Joe might think about entering her bed once more.

The hero in her book didn't hesitate to talk. He told the heroine everything—especially how much he loved her.

But how many heroes were bought? she wondered. *Stop it!* she told her wayward thoughts. It wasn't fair. She'd asked him to take the money, and now she resented that fact.

It didn't make sense.

As she drifted off to sleep, the hero in her fantasies looked just like Joe.

She woke to hear water splashing against tile. The clock told her it was past five in the morning.

Slipping on her robe, Sable followed the sound across the hall, through Joe's open door and into his wide-open bathroom. Steam fogged the mirrors and hung in the air. The see-through shower curtain was also misted, but she could see Joe's silhouette, his bent head directly under the shower. Water streamed off his broad shoulders and back.

Her pulse beat quickened at the sight. Sable cleared her throat. "Joe? Are you all right?"

His head snapped up. "As right as I'll ever be," he muttered, spewing water from his mouth. "What are you doing up at this hour?"

"I could ask you the same thing."

"I just got home," he said tiredly. "The air conditioning system wouldn't filter properly, and we spent all night working on it."

"You need some sleep!" she exclaimed. Then she realized that he already knew that and blushed at the absurdity of her remark.

"I need to sleep with you. But I guess that isn't possible." He turned the water off. "So I suggest you get your sweet little body out of here, while I grab an hour's shut-eye before my next meeting."

Sable stood quite still. His words had touched her own sleep-fogged emotions, harmonizing with needs she'd pretended didn't exist. As she watched him reach for the navy bath sheet hanging on the rack behind him to dry his hair, her needs burst into flame.

He dried off quickly with precise movements, wrapped the towel snugly around his waist and pulled the curtain aside. "Looking for something?" His tone was dry, even gruff. His eyes scanned her body impersonally.

"A bed partner."

He stared at her a moment, then slowly shook his head. "Oh, no, you don't. The last time you issued that invitation, I got chewed out for being in the wrong place at the wrong time. Never again."

Guilt flooded her, but didn't suppress the desire to be touched. "I'm sorry," she whispered.

"So am I." He eased past her to the counter and brushed his thick, wet hair into order. When it held a semblance of style, he dropped the brush and headed toward the bed. "Good night, Sable. Close the door on your way out."

He set his alarm and put it back onto the nightstand. With a brief tug, the towel dropped to the floor and Joe slipped into bed, his strong, tanned body covered by the sheet.

Sable still didn't move. Even after Joe flipped off the light above his head, she stood there, staring into the darkness, torn between running to Joe and running away.

"Good night, Sable." His voice was firm.

"Good night," she answered.

Then she closed the bedroom door and joined him. Pulling aside the sheet, she slipped into bed, next to him. Suddenly she stopped, at a loss. What came next? She hadn't planned that far ahead. In fact she hadn't planned at all.

She lay stiffly beside him, afraid to move, embarrassed to be there. Why hadn't she thought this through before making a complete fool of herself?

"Are you comfortable?" Joe growled, his voice menacing in the dark.

"Yes," she lied.

"Well, I'm not," he complained.

Turning over, he pulled her into his strong, warm arms. Crooking one leg over her thigh and laying his head next to hers, he sighed and fell instantly into a deep sleep.

Surprisingly, so did Sable.

SABLE BARELY HEARD Joe, leaving with Johnny. She slept until almost noon, awakening only when the sun streaked across Joe's bed. Stretching, she stared at the ceiling. She quivered, remembering Joe holding her tightly against him while he slept.

Happy, she went about her tasks, remembering how bold she'd been.

After school, Sable took Jonathan and Talia into Conroe for some shopping. Talia had been wanting new clothes befitting her senior status. Luckily, the little city just twenty-five miles from Houston had some nice boutiques filled with the usual fad fare for teenagers.

Waiting for Talia to emerge from the dressing room, Sable became aware that time was passing too fast. At this time next year, her sister would be entering college. She had spent so much of her life looking after Talia that she didn't know how she would deal with it.

Talia reappeared, twirling for her little nephew.

"I just realized. You'll be starting college this time next year," Sable said quietly.

"I know." Talia's eyes lighted up with excitement. "I'm aiming for Vassar. But if I can't go there, I'll try Harvard."

A lump grew in Sable's throat. "So far away? I thought we discussed Tulane?" The university was only one state away.

"We did. But that's my third choice, not my first. And with my grades and activities I should be able to qualify for any Ivy League school. I'm already filing my preadmission applications."

"I see," Sable said slowly.

Talia slipped back into the dressing room. Sable's good mood was gone. She was losing a part of her family, and there didn't seem to be a thing she could do to change it.

"Mommy cry?" Jonathan stroked her cheek softly. His big, beautiful eyes were full of sympathy.

Sable picked him up and gave him a squeeze, loving the little-boy scent of him. "No, darling. Mommy's fine."

He rubbed his nose against hers. "Tally crying?"

"No, honey. She's fine, too."

"Good," he said, getting down to explore a shirt rack next to them. As long as everyone he cared for was fine, so was he. Sable wished her feelings were so simple.

On the way home, the subject was brought up again, this time by Talia. "Sable, you know that no matter what college I choose, I'll be living in a dorm, right?"

"Of course. I just didn't realize it would be so far away." She smiled, trying to disguise her sadness.

With Talia gone, Sable's loneliness would be even more pronounced. She didn't have any close friends, and couldn't even talk to her husband. She'd have no one to share her thoughts with.

Talia's hand briefly covered Sable's on the steering wheel. "It's one of the reasons I was so pleased to meet Joe. He's perfect for you. You could be the housewife you always wanted to be, and I wouldn't have to worry about you. You could even have more children, which is exactly what you and Jonathan need. You always said you wanted half a dozen."

"You worry about me?" she asked incredulously, zeroing in on her sister's admission.

"Do you think you're the only one who worries?" Talia asked. "Sometimes you're such a babe in the woods. I worry about people taking advantage of you. Joe wouldn't do that. That's why I like him."

"You don't know Joe," Sable protested, suddenly realizing what Talia had said about children.

"I know him better than you do," Talia declared. "Joe and I have talked lots at night. You two have so much in common."

"Yes." Sable tried to keep her voice from shaking. "We both have a nosy teenager under our roof."

"There you go again!"

"What do you mean?

"Every time I try to tell you something, you bring up my age as a barrier to common sense. It's as if you don't want me to be right!" Talia exclaimed. "Are you so darn afraid of the truth?"

"I'm not afraid of anything." Sable turned the car into the driveway. "And you constantly put your nose in where it doesn't belong. Joe and I will work out our problems because they're our problems, not because you've interfered."

Talia faced forward and crossed her arms over her chest. "Not if you're not forced to, you won't," she muttered. "You've spent a lifetime trying to make peace by keeping quiet or running away. Why change now?"

"I never run away!" Sable answered tersely, wondering where in heaven her little sister could have gotten such ideas. "And there's nothing wrong with trying to keep peace. If I hadn't done it when you were growing up, your home life would have been even worse."

"Right. Our aunt might have had to change her tune on a few things—if she'd been bucked. Instead, we did whatever she wanted, and she never knew how much she hurt both of us. Auntie could quote us to the penny exactly how much we owed her for our room and board and the trouble she went through. And you always agreed—verbally, at least. It was easier to run away than stand up to her and quote the amount of money our father gave her every month to take care of us."

Sable couldn't fight that. It was true. Sometimes she'd wanted to say what she felt, but she'd never found the nerve. "And if anyone runs away in this situation, it's Joe."

"Great. Now we have two people who run away. And you're supposed to make a home together," Talia said, plainly disgusted.

"That's it," she stated, teeth clenched in anger. "You can keep your opinions to yourself from now on. I will handle Joe. I'm his wife."

"Hooray, you noticed," Talia answered sarcastically, just seconds before jumping out of the car and stalking to the back door.

"Talia!"

Sable's call was ignored.

Frustration welled inside her, but there was little she could do at the moment except carry in the shopping bags. Once more Talia's darts had hit home, and once more Sable hadn't been agile enough to dodge them. Her life was topsy-turvy, and Sable didn't seem to have the know-how or experience to straighten it out.

TALIA DIDN'T come out of her room all evening. For that Sable was grateful. She wasn't up to handling a confrontation with a teen whose energy level in sleep was more than Sable's awake.

But late that night as she lay in bed, staring at the dark ceiling, Sable wondered how much of what Talia said was true. Sable had accused Joe of running away, but was she doing the same thing? Was she avoiding issues? Did she fear problems that might end their relationship?

The answer was a resounding yes.

Her biggest stumbling block was that, having paid for a groom, she didn't believe the affection he showed her. Anything he did could be motivated by guilt, after all.

Last night she had secretly hoped that being with Joe, showing that she cared for him, would somehow make their past arguments fade away. It was a stupid wish but it was what she'd dreamed of—an easy solution.

She fell into a troubled sleep. It wasn't until she was securely held in Joe's strong arms, his warm breath caressing her shoulder, that she slept deeply.

When she awakened again, Prince Charming was gone.

JOE CONTINUED to push himself to ensure that the racetrack would run smoothly. His investment was his lifeblood. The track had to pass the racing commission's standards. He was dead on his feet, yet afraid to go home early, for fear Sable would confront him with more problems—problems he couldn't handle. At least at work he knew there was a solution. That wasn't the case at home.

Every time he remembered the morning Sable had slipped into his bed, his body tensed. She was the sweetest, most desirable, most stubborn woman he'd ever met. And he wanted her. Completely.

It was really funny, he thought. Her money had brought them together. But right now it was keeping them apart. He had to open this track on time, so he could pay her back as quickly as possible. That would be one obstacle out of the way. Then he'd only have a million others to deal with.

Then another solution appeared. The wife of one of his workers did housework, he learned, so he hired her to help take some of the cleaning chores off Sable's back. The house, after all, was huge, even though Sable had never complained about being designated housekeeper. In fact she hadn't complained about anything he'd thrown her way—except himself.

On that subject, he remembered, she'd been extremely vocal. Even in front of Talia.

He wished an answer to his dilemma would spring forth, but his mind was a blank. It didn't work the same way a woman's did, he decided. And frustration was the price he was paying for that. But when the track was completed, he would tackle the job of understanding his recalcitrant wife.

In the meantime he'd sneak home just in time to catch a little sleep with her. It was the only thing she seemed to want or allow. And although restraint wasn't the most pleasant feeling in the world, it was better than not having her in his arms at all.

It had taken a while to face the bitter truth about himself. And the revelation hadn't come like a thunderbolt, but more like a light spring rain. He loved Sable. He loved her in all the ways a man could love a woman. He wanted to share his life with her, to have her by his side in times of triumph and trouble.

He wanted Sable to love him as much as he loved her.

"Work on the possible, Lombardi," he muttered. "Don't wish for the impossible."

He remembered that she had seemed thrilled when he gave her the party plans to work on. Maybe if he included her in more of the everyday workings of the ranch, she'd enjoy that, too. The thought brought a smile to his face.

Picking up the phone, he dialed home. When Sable's voice came over the line, his body tensed. She always affected him that way.

"I was wondering if you could do me a favor the next time you're in town," Joe asked.

"Sure. What is it?" She sounded a little breathless. He liked that. "Go by Smitty's and pick up four cases of beer for the bunkhouse. Put it on my tab."

"Four cases of beer?"

"Yes. Because we're so far out of town, I keep beer on hand for the boys. That way they can relax in the evening without leaving the property. I don't have to worry about them going on a toot."

"Isn't four cases a lot? They could get drunk."

"They're big boys," Joe replied, amused. "They can take care of themselves.

When he hung up, he was still smiling.

SABLE STARED out the kitchen window, wondering how many of those beers Joe would drink if he wasn't so tied up with the track. She had to admit that she'd never seen him drunk or disorderly.

Nor had she seen the men in the bunkhouse that way. But that didn't mean they couldn't do it.

She'd go into town for beer in the morning. Meanwhile she'd figure out another way for the boys to be entertained. There had to be something else they could do besides drink beer.

That night she slipped into Joe's bed and read until midnight. When she turned out the light, she fell again into a restless sleep. Only when he climbed in beside her and rested his arm on her waist did she settle down.

As usual, he was gone by the time she awakened. But his scent lingered on the pillow next to hers. She lifted it and buried her face in the soft fabric, wishing for the real thing.

At midafternoon Sable returned from Conroe with the beer Joe had requested. She put the brew into the bunkhouse refrigerator, then hurried back to the house.

A short time later Joe entered the house by the back door and called her name. Sable walked into the kitchen, widening her eyes when she realized she was looking at a little boy in a man's body. "What's going on?"

He grinned, his eyes alight with mischief. "Come on, we're going horseback riding," he said, grabbing her hand and starting to head outside. "The air conditioning system is in and working, and I'm playing hooky."

"Let me get dressed!" she exclaimed, delighted with his happy mood. "But shouldn't you be catching up on your sleep?"

"I need a horseback ride, and no, I don't want to sleep." He stared down at her, his hand still firmly holding hers. "It's the farthest thing from my mind."

The gleam in his eye said he wanted something else entirely. "Let me put on my riding boots," she said.

Lightning swift, she ran to her room and pulled out a pair of Moroccan leather ankle boots. Her movements rivaling the fast forward action of a camera, she changed and ran back out again. Joe was standing in the kitchen, talking to Talia.

He took Sable's hand again and led her out to the barn. His plans had apparently been made before he came into the house, for their horses were saddled and ready to go. Jed held the reins, the smug smile on his face reminding her of the one she'd seen on Talia's.

Giving her a hand up, Joe let his fingers slip down her calf to give her ankle a squeeze. Sable chuckled. It felt so good to do something spontaneously, to have fun for a change.

They began with a canter, Joe leading the way behind the barn and across the field. As they neared a path that ribboned its way through the woods, they trotted. The warm afternoon breeze filtered through Sable's hair and blouse as if proclaiming her freedom.

Her bubbling laughter danced in the air.

Recklessness had never been a part of her makeup, but suddenly she was filled with it. At the end of the trail through the woods, Sable glanced over her shoulder. With a triumphant smile and a light kick to her horse, she urged him into a gallop and sailed past Joe.

His surprise was her advantage. Within a minute or two she was far ahead, aiming for the sloping riverbank. But by the time she pulled the reins to slow down, the gap had closed considerably. Still, when she reached the water's edge and the shelter of a huge willow tree, she waited impatiently for Joe to join her.

A tense excitement stirred the air as he halted his own horse and swung to the ground to stand by her side. In a single swift movement he was lifting her down and into his arms.

His blue eyes no longer danced with mischief. Instead the intensity of his gaze seared her.

"I've finally got you to myself. No prying eyes anywhere in sight. No Johnny, no Talia, no ranch hands."

"No one."

"You're beautiful."

Her fingers traced one dark brow. "If you say so."

There was no doubt as to what he wanted. Every muscle in his body was tense.

Sable reveled in the reckless abandon she saw in his eyes. Taking Joe's face between her hands, she placed her parted lips on his. Her tongue flicked against his moist warmth, and a moan echoed between them like a hollow cry for help.

His arms clasped her waist, pinning her body against his hardness. But it wasn't enough.

He was hungry. He was a starving man.

Strong, impatient hands unzipped her jeans and loosened them enough to cup the ripe softness of her derriere in his palms, cradling her against the jutting hardness of his own need.

Sable stared up at him. His jaw was tight, his breathing shallow.

"Are you going to deny me?" His voice was a mere rasp.

Her hand trailed lightly over his jaw. "No," she whispered. "Denying ourselves would be silly at this point, don't you think?"

Her hands drifted lightly from his shoulders to his chest, and she slowly undid his shirt, exposing the dark hair. Occasionally her hand passed over the curls, watching them spring against her palm.

"Sable," he warned.

Her hand slipped to his zipper. She looked up, her eyes heated with the same fire that inflamed his. "Be patient."

His eyes roamed downward, and her pulse quickened in response. "I don't have any patience left. I need you. Now."

"Not yet." Standing on tiptoe, she pressed soft kisses onto his neck and chest. The fabric shifted off his shoulders and dropped to his wrists. His hands clenched tighter at her waist, pulling her even closer.

Her tongue darted out to flick one small, male nipple. His response was immediate. He took her hand and led her to him, his palm covering hers. Her eyes drooped as she leaned back her head, allowing him full view of her slender throat and the teasing, beginning fullness of her breasts.

"That's it," he muttered. With jerking movements, Joe stripped off his shirt and threw it to the ground beneath the dancing leaves of the trees. In one smooth motion he lowered her to the ground, his body covering hers, crushing her breasts against his chest. It felt so right.

His hands were everywhere, unzipping, unbuttoning, making fabric barriers between them disappear. His mouth pressed teasing kisses against the softness of her skin, until she felt as if her whole body glowed with the intense heat of his touch.

His hands were everywhere. One hand slipped to caress her belly, his fingers teasing, touching, stroking. She drew a ragged breath as anticipation seared through her. When he touched the apex of her thighs, she gasped.

When his mouth captured the peak of one full breast, she felt scalded with pleasure. "Joe, please," she whispered.

He chuckled. "Not yet," he answered, mimicking her. And then he began the most exquisite torture of all.

Sable squirmed with need, and Joe finally appeased her. When he slipped deep inside her, her cry of pleasure echoed through the summer air.

The excitement of having his flesh on hers, in her, his scent surrounding them, drew her quickly to the edge. Joe tried to be gentle. His hands shook as he lifted his torso to kiss her parted lips, the sweet line of a shoulder. But gentleness was not what she needed just then. She wanted his powerful presence to fill her until she couldn't see anything but him.

He understood that and took her to a plane she hadn't known existed. Sable clung to him as they climbed peak after peak, then spiraled back to earth in each other's arms.

His warm breath caressed her ear, his heart still pounded against hers. For a few, very special, moments they had become one perfect being. As the feeling of completeness dwindled away, Sable wanted to reach out and hold it.

But she couldn't.

Flinging his hand against his eyes, Joe rolled onto his back. The fingers of his other hand were wound in her hair, still connecting them. The sun was suddenly cold against her flesh.

Just then, one of the horses neighed to gain their attention, then nudged Joe's booted foot. They both smiled.

"That was quite a ride, lady," he muttered, his voice still a low growl.

Sable relaxed, rubbing her hand against his chest as if to reassure herself that he was still there. "Are you talking to me or the horse?" she teased.

Joe turned to face her, his eyes the darkest, most penetrating blue she'd ever seen. "I'm talking to the horse. There are no words that would begin to explain what you and I just experienced."

"Try," she coaxed.

His gaze seared her with the message that couldn't seem to come forth in words. Finally he sighed and placed a light kiss on her swollen lips. "I can't. I know you need to hear the words, and I want to say what I feel. But I can't."

"Why?"

His finger took the place of his lips as he outlined first her lips, then her chin, watching as his own darker skin touched hers. "Because I'm not sure I have the words." He sighed. "Someday, darling," he promised.

Sable swallowed her disappointment. *She* couldn't find the words to tell him she loved him. So who was she to talk?

Promising herself that soon she'd find the courage to say what was in her heart, she stood up and began to dress.

Joe leaned back and watched every move she made, his naked body gleaming in the dappled sunlight. But the possessive look in his eyes told her what he wanted to know.

It was enough to warm her heart. Someday would be soon.

9

THEIR RIDE back to the house was a slower, sweeter trip, less fraught with tension than when they had ridden out. Occasionally Joe took her hand and squeezed it lightly. Every time he did, happiness filled her, healing the pain of their earlier dissension.

From the moment she first saw him, she'd been drawn to him. And this afternoon, under the graceful willow branches that shielded them from the open, pale blue sky, with a carpet of pine needles for a bed, had been the answer to her prayers. She loved him. Her whole life revolved around him. She wanted it to stay that way. But until he committed himself to her, she'd never be happy.

She cursed the thoughts that had crept in during the dark of night, whispering that her money was the only reason he remained with her. She hated the thoughts that had suggested he was only using her. Their lovemaking was so much more than lust.

Once or twice Joe reined in their horses, then pulled her toward him for a kiss. Fleeting though it was, her heart beat quickly with each one. His touch was gentle, sweet, and he was reluctant to let go. He cared. He had to care or he wouldn't be this charming, this considerate after making love.

It was as if she'd been looking at everything through dark glasses, plodding through life, afraid to look for what might be out there. Then Joe had come along and made her take them off. Now the world was brighter, sweeter, sillier. And for the first time she was in love—as an adult and with an adult. This wasn't hero worship or the search for a father figure.

Everything would be wonderful from now on, she told herself. They could work out whatever little problems came their way. The tension that she'd lived with these past weeks was gone. Making love and being able to smile again made all the difference in the world. Weather forecast, she thought, sunny and mild for the rest of their lives.

Reaching the open area around the house, they sent their horses into a gallop and rode through the wide doorway to the barn together. Laughter filled the air and smiles lighted their eyes.

Totty, the hand in charge of the grounds and barns, stood leaning on a pitchfork, his face a wrinkled road map of frowns. He watched them closely, but not a muscle in his face moved.

Joe swung out of his saddle, then helped Sable dismount, treating her as if she were the most precious thing on earth. He kissed the tip of her nose. Then, pretending to whisper something into her ear, he kissed her there, too. Her cheeks glowed in response as she stood in the protective shelter of his arms.

With his arm firmly around Sable's waist, he turned toward Totty. "What's the matter, Totty? Somebody kill your best friend?"

Totty shot a wad of chaw through the doorway before speaking. "Might well have," he muttered. "Whoever you got to deliver the beer pulled a fast one on you."

Sable felt her smile slip. Not now, she thought. Not now!

"What do you mean?" Joe's arm still circled her waist, but his attention was focused on his oldest hired hand. "It was delivered, wasn't it?" His gaze flashed to Sable, then back to Totty.

"Oh, it was delivered, awright," Totty drawled. "But it ain't beer. It's some kinda soft drink that's supposed to taste like beer."

Joe's arm dropped from Sable's waist, leaving her chilled. "Is that a fact?"

Totty pushed back his battered hat and wiped his forehead with his shirt sleeve. "That's a fact," he confirmed disgustedly.

Why had she been such a fool? Why couldn't Totty have brought this up later—much later?

Unwilling to see the gathering storm in Joe's eyes, Sable grabbed the bridle, walked her horse to his stall and began to unsaddle him.

She'd felt Totty's eyes watching her walk away and realized that he had no idea who had bought the beer. It didn't give her much relief. Soon he'd know. Then she'd have one more man who wondered if there was any substance to the spoiled little socialite.

She couldn't help but hear the conversation between the two men. Her stomach roiled with each word.

"Show me what you're talking about." Joe's voice was empty of the concern and love he'd shown her just moments ago.

"Be glad ta," Totty answered. The sound of their footsteps told her they were leaving the barn and heading toward the bunkhouse—and her purchase of four cases of nonalcoholic beer.

The air whooshed from her lungs. With shaking hands Sable brushed down her horse. She didn't know what to do except to keep busy and hope that Joe wouldn't be too upset with her. Even though she often faced problems head-on, she hated confrontation, so she understood Joe's willingness to avoid an argument.

In her teen years Sable had done quite a bit of that. But when she'd married John and found he did the same thing, she'd been the one to confront trouble and find a solution. She didn't want to be in that spot again. Being a mother to a three-year-old was enough. She shouldn't have to be a mother to a grown man, too.

Besides, with Joe it was different. She was afraid of losing what little they had together if she confronted anything, and at the same time it seemed as if she did things that were intended to annoy him.

As minutes ticked by like hours, Sable felt her hackles rise. So what if she hadn't gotten the beer Joe had expected? People shouldn't be drinking. She had other things to do besides run around the countryside, buying beer for a bunch of men.

Joe's firm, booted tread announced his imminent arrival and she tensed. By the time he appeared at the stall door, she was holding her breath.

"What in the hell made you do such a stupid thing?"

His tone demanded an answer, but at that moment she couldn't think of one. His hard, angry gaze twisted her thoughts into hundreds of small knots that wouldn't unravel enough for her to form a reply.

"No one should promote drinking," she finally answered.

"Just how vindictive can you get?" His words sliced through her like a hot knife. "You take away their beer and give them six different *games* to play with?"

That was unfair! "Vindictive?" She raised her voice defensively. "I wasn't being vindictive. I was *trying* to give the men an alternative to drinking themselves into a stupor!"

"They *don't* drink themselves into a stupor!"

Her hands went to her hips, so she wouldn't be tempted to slap him. "How would you know? You're never with them! You're always worked late."

Eyes blazing with anger, Joe threw down his hat. "You're really something, you know that? You've done everything you could to show me that you hate being here. You hate my lifestyle. You hate me. But I've been too stupid to realize it! I've been hoping that if I was nice and a gentleman, you'd finally see some of my redeeming features, and maybe we could make a go of this farce of a marriage."

He took a step closer. Feeling menaced, Sable backed up.

"But I was dead wrong," he continued. "You'll never change. You'll always be a snob. Women can sit around all day, sipping wine and doing nothing. But a man who's worked all day in the hot sun isn't supposed to enjoy a beer as he sits on the porch at night and watches a ball game. And it's all because you decided to set yourself up as judge and jury for people you don't know and haven't cared to find out about. That's hypocritical, Sable, but I don't know why I expected anything else from you."

Joe bent to pick up his hat; it was all Sable could do not to kick him in the rear.

Anger made her shake with reaction. "That's not true!" she cried. "I've washed and ironed shirts that you could have just as easily sent to a laundry. I've cooked meals you've never eaten, and kept 'your' house as clean and neat as a pin. I've given you everything, including my money, but nothing seems to get through to you. I've got wants and needs and desires, too! But you never noticed that, either. Because you're never home!"

Joe gave her a disgusted look and began to walk out.

But Sable wasn't through with him yet. "Just because I don't earn a salary doesn't mean that I don't work as hard as you and your crew! Twice as hard!" she shouted at his retreating, grass-stained shirt.

Tears filled her eyes. Damn him! Who did he think he was to yell at her like that? Just because she bought a beer substitute instead of the real thing didn't mean that Joe could call her down.

But he hadn't, a little voice said. He'd waited to see the evidence for himself before confronting her—in private.

Oh, shut up, she told her conscience as she stomped out of the stall and headed toward the house. It wasn't worth the effort to fight back. Not when she was wrong....

JOE DIDN'T COME HOME. He left Sable a note, saying he had to go to Austin for a license review, but Sable wasn't sure if that was true.

After a week Joe returned, but seemed to be sleeping at the track. Sable apologized to Totty, who, embarrassed, brushed it off as a lack of knowledge about beer in general. At least he remained her friend, she thought. It was better than Joe's response.

Occasionally in the early evening, when she was cleaning out one of the horses' stalls, Jonathan would run next door and play on the porch with the crewmen, cheering on whatever team they were rooting for. He loved sitting with the men, and she had to admit that they were gentle with him.

But her lonely times taught her three things: she loved Joe with all her heart; Talia and Jonathan missed Joe almost as much as she did; and she wanted to make her marriage work.

When Joe made no effort to contact her, Sable finally remembered the barbecue. She still had the figures and estimates for the party, but he'd never answered her questions. Now was as good a time as any to call and get them. And if she and Joe could carry on a normal conversation for a while, all the better. Somehow she had to give herself a chance to close the gap between them.

But when she called, he wasn't there. Every hour, on the hour, she tried calling his office again. Still no answer.

By the time Talia came home, Sable was pacing the floor. Scraps of paper containing her questions were clenched in her hand.

"Will you watch Jonathan for me?" Sable asked as soon as her sister walked in the door. "I need to go to the site and speak to Joe."

"Sure," Talia replied quickly, fearing Sable would change her mind. "And tell him I said hi and I miss him around here."

"Will do," Sable promised, picking up her purse and practically running for the back door.

The drive to the track was the longest ten minutes Sable could remember. Stepping out of the car, she stared up at the roof, fully expecting to see Joe striding across the tiles.

He wasn't there.

She was amazed at how much had been done since she'd been there last. The open lobby and general seating were finished. Soft mauves and grays and a light peach gave the area a cool, serene appearance. She took the elevator up to Joe's office and was just as pleased with the look of the private club space. Similar-colored tables and chairs were comfortably arranged on every level. Wide four-story-high windows afforded a complete view of the track and gardens.

Her heels no longer echoed on concrete, but glided on pale gray, short-sheared carpet.

She heard Joe's voice as she reached the office door. Sable stopped in her tracks. Her heart pounded heavily in her breast. Her breath caught in her throat.

Then suddenly he was standing before her, a file in his hand. His eyes widened as he saw his wife. "Is something wrong?"

Even though her heart was in her throat, Sable pasted a smile onto her face. "Everything's fine. I just need some information. I thought I'd run over, since you haven't been answering your phone today."

Joe's brows lifted. "I wasn't in."

Sable laughed huskily. "I gathered. But I thought the answering machine would be on."

"It should have been. But my secretary is sick today and I probably forgot to set it."

Turning, Joe walked back to his desk and sat. Sable followed him, leaning against the corner of the desk. His face held no smile for her. There was no warmth, no eagerness to talk.

"What's your question?" he asked in a voice laced with tiredness.

Sable's heart went out to him. His face was drawn, his eyes heavy with lack of sleep. He'd obviously been working too hard. And if the blanket thrown on the long, leather couch was any indication, this really was where he slept.

"You're exhausted."

Joe ran a hand through his disheveled hair. "So what's new?" he muttered, glancing at the myriad stacks of paperwork on his desk. "Just ask me the questions, Sable. I don't need one of our usual discussions. I don't think I could survive it right now."

Sable straightened, mentally withdrawing her emotions. Obviously he didn't want to mend fences or take care of his wife and her petty problems right now. She couldn't stand it. Just the thought of living without Joe made panic well up inside until she was blinded by fear. But that panic also goaded her on.

"I was just wondering what happens next," she told him. "You've been sleeping here, traveling when you want. You haven't even pretended to be the model father our contract stipulated you would be."

She prayed he'd sweep her into his arms and tell her he loved her. But she knew better. His expression told her that much.

"What is you want, Sable?" he asked quietly. "A divorce?"

His question was like an icy slap in the face. She should have expected it, yet she hadn't. Startled, she gazed up at him. He stared back, his expression unreadable. Another stab of pain seared through her.

She swallowed. "Is that what you want?"

"Don't answer a question with a question, especially the same one I asked you," he said softly, a tiny, sad smile edging his lips. "You always were evasive about things that mean a lot to you."

She shook her head. She couldn't find her voice. "I want . . ." she finally managed to stammer, but couldn't complete the sentence. The words she needed just weren't there.

Joe's sigh filled the office, saying more than all the words he could have shouted. "Look, do the barbecue for me and help me get this racetrack opened. After that you can have your divorce. I just need to get this going, so I'll be able to pay back the money you . . . so graciously lent me."

The mention of the money made her flinch. But it wasn't their only problem. She thought of all the things she'd done wrong since they'd married. Guilt weighed heavily upon her, and she had promised herself she would apologize to Joe.

"I'm sorry." Her thoughts had slipped out. "For everything."

He reached out and touched her chin, his thumb outlining the clean, sweet form of it. "So am I, Sable. So am I."

"I'll do your party."

He stood up. "I know."

"And I'll do a good job."

He smiled. "I know."

"And then we'll see."

"Okay."

His hand dropped and a chill brushed her very soul. "Are you coming home tonight?" she asked, stalling for time.

"I don't know yet, Sable. I can't push myself too far. The consequences could make us both sorry."

She nodded. "Okay."

He leaned over as if a strong rope were pulling him. His lips brushed hers. "Thank you."

This time Sable walked out.

Joe watched her go, and his heart felt as if it were being ripped from his chest. He watched as she stood in front of the elevator and waited for its doors to open. By the time she disappeared, the pain was so great that all he could do was walk across the office and slump dejectedly into his desk chair.

She wanted a divorce. The thought echoed in his mind. *She wanted a divorce.* He'd hoped that she would deny it. Instead she'd agreed.

He loved her.

He loved her family.

He needed to feel a part of them. He loved feeling a part of them.

With Sable he felt complete.

How the hell could he tell her he loved her, when the money was between them, forming a wall bigger than the one in China?

Tears filmed his eyes, and he prayed that one of his men wouldn't barge in with some petty demand and find him like this. It would be hard to explain that he wasn't crying, but just feeling sorry for himself.

That inner voice spoke: *You're crying.*

The inner voice was right.

THE BARBECUE was a huge success. Joe made a short speech, thanking all his employees for their devotion to work and their spouses for their patience. The track would open in a week. The office and working crews would begin their training on Monday. Everyone applauded enthusiastically.

Sable's sharp eyes skimmed the tables laden with cooked beef, pork, chicken and sausage. Next to the hot meats were the crisp, cold salads: potato, coleslaw, cold pasta tossed with vegetables, and piles of lettuce, tomatoes and sliced, sweet onions, as well as pickles, olives and relishes.

A five-piece Western band played in the shade of the inner, general gallery. Couples danced, while others stood in groups, talking and watching the children at play.

Joe came up to stand beside Sable and casually draped an arm around her shoulders. She was sure it was simply for effect in front of the workers and their families. But, even though it was a pretense, it felt wonderful.

"Any problems?" Joe asked.

"Not yet," she said cautiously. "The catering firm seems to be doing well."

"So did you. Everything's been arranged perfectly," Joe told her quietly. "Thank you."

"You're welcome."

She didn't discount the amount of work she'd put into this party. And Joe had noticed. That made her feel even better.

A few companionable moments of silence passed before Joe spoke again. "Do you dance?"

Startled, her eyes darted to his. "A little," she admitted. "But I'm not very good.

His smile was beautiful. And heartrendingly sexy. "Don't tell me you never attended dances when you were growing up."

She couldn't stop looking at him. "I never did. I wasn't asked."

"Young boys from Mobile must be stupid," he said, slipping his arm down to clasp her hand.

"Why?"

He led her around the tables to the general gallery. "Because, even if you were only half as beautiful as you are now, they didn't have the nerve to ask. You would probably have danced if you'd been asked."

"How did you know?"

Joe chuckled, a rueful smile etching his mouth. "Because certain boys from Houston weren't too bright at that age, either."

"Neither was I," Sable admitted. "Or I would have asked them. But if you ever quote me to Talia, I'll deny every word."

He stopped in the center of the floor and turned her toward him. "Why?"

"Because she's assertive enough already. I don't think she needs any encouragement."

Joe glanced over her shoulder, then turned her around so she could she what he'd just glimpsed. "I think I agree with you." He laughed. "If I'm not mistaken, she asked Mike to dance. He never volunteers."

Sable saw the uncomfortable expression on the man's face. But she saw something else, too. No matter how much he claimed to prefer sitting on the sidelines, Mike was enchanted by Talia. And Talia glowed with an inner excitement.

Sable frowned, but Joe turned her into his arms, as one slow song blended into another, and she forgot about Talia.

Both his arms rested on her hips, his hands clasped together at the small of her back. She had no choice but to hold on to his broad shoulders. Every time he moved, she felt the tight flex of muscles beneath her palm, and it reminded Sable of other things she shouldn't be remembering at all.

Making love in the cab of a truck. Undressing in the bright, hot, summer sun and feeling the heat flow through every vein in her body, making her one with the earth and with Joe.

Her hands trailed slowly down his shoulders, stopping at the rock-hard muscles of his arms. She wanted to hold him, hug him, lay her head on his chest and tell him that she wanted him back. To hell with the divorce. To hell with everything except the two of them.

"A penny for your thoughts," he said softly.

She opened her eyes and stared up at him. He looked as though his thoughts were as serious as hers. Sable cleared her throat. "They're worth a quarter now. Inflation, you know."

"You can reach in my front pocket and get it."

The thought was enough to make her palms sweat. "I'll trust you," she finally said, her voice barely a husky whisper.

"A shame," he admonished softly. "Cowboys shouldn't be trusted. We act shy, but we know what we want and go after it."

At those encouraging words she screwed up her courage and asked, "And what do *you* want?"

Brilliant blue flashed in his eyes as he focused on her lips. Then, with an almost intimidating slowness, his glance dropped to the low V of her cream silk blouse, tucked snugly into designer jeans. His hands tightened. Then he forcibly relaxed. "No

matter what it is, I don't think there's a fairy godmother with
enough magic dust to give it to me."

Sable prayed he'd catch on soon. She wanted him to drag her
to his office and tell her that he loved her as much as she loved
him. Because of her money she couldn't say those words first.
"If you don't ask, you'll never know."

His eyes narrowed. "If I did ask, I'm not sure I'm ready to hear
the answer."

"Tsk, tsk, tsk," Sable murmured unsteadily. "So fainthearted
for a cowboy who knows what he wants."

Their steps slowed to a stop. Still he continued to stare at her.
"Sable—" Joe began.

"Hey, boss!" Joe's secretary called from the open elevator
doors. "The racing commission is on the phone. They need to
talk to you! Pronto!"

Joe cursed, then reluctantly pulled away. "Hold that thought,"
he said to her, then slipped into the elevator with Judy.

The doors closed and he was gone again.

Sable walked off the dance floor and went outside to check the
tables. Her racing pulse slowly thudded down to a more normal
beat. By the time Joe returned, he'd probably be all business
again. He'd never remember how she'd tried to say everything
but the words that would commit her to him for life. *I love you*
had to be the most powerful aphrodisiac in the world—if those
were the words one wanted to hear.

But if Joe didn't hear them, she'd never know if they could
erase the mistakes of the past and turn their lives toward a rosy
future.

And if he did? He might very well laugh in her face and tell
her, "Tough luck, sweetie. . . ."

She didn't know which thought was more frightening. But she
knew she had to find out.

Tonight, she promised herself. She'd tell him tonight. All he
could do was make her miserable enough to run back to Louisiana like a whipped puppy, with her tail between her legs.

An hour later Joe found her talking to one of the caterers.
Pulling her away, he spoke quickly, but quietly. "I have to be in
a meeting with the racing commission in Austin right away. It
seems that one of the senators who has to sign the licenses has
had a heart attack. We have to work through the final paper-

work without him, or we'll never get it done before opening. Mike's going with me."

"Don't go. Not now," she pleaded.

"I'll be back by the middle of the week." He pulled her into his arms. "So do me a favor, will you? Miss me."

It was an order, not a request. But Sable didn't care. And when his lips claimed hers for a quick, hard kiss, she still didn't mind. Her fingers curled into the fabric of his shirt, unwilling to let him go, unwilling to hold him against his will. His hands tightened at her waist, pulling her into the hardness of his body.

The next moment he was striding toward Mike, who was standing by the gate, Talia at his side. Once Joe reached him, both men kept going.

Neither one looked back.

10

REGRET was a heavy burden. Joe had sounded distracted and businesslike when he called Saturday night to give her his room number at the hotel. And Sable, temporarily open and loving, had closed up like a clam. She told herself he would call again when things eased up. But the days passed and disappointment grew as she waited for a phone call that never came.

WHEN A WOMAN knocked on the door Monday morning and announced that Joe had hired her to houseclean, Sable felt herself turn white. Apparently Joe was already replacing her.

On Tuesday there was still no word from Joe, and Sable was an emotional wreck. When John had died, she'd been devastated. She had clung to Talia and Johnny, not allowing herself to care for anyone else. She'd lost so many people in her life that she wanted to protect herself.

She had also done the same thing with Joe. When he had gotten too close to her, she'd effectively sabotaged their relationship. She'd secretly been afraid of losing him, if she acknowledged her love aloud.

Now that she had an idea of where the problem came from, she was *damned* if she would let it ruin her life. Ignoring their problems was no way to overcome them.

Her resolve once more firmly in place, she picked up the phone and dialed the number Joe had left her.

Joe's voice barked into the phone. "Hello."

"Hi," she answered brightly, her heart thumping so hard, she wondered if the whole world heard it.

"Sable? Is that you?" he asked, the curtness fading from his tone. "Is something wrong?"

"No." She laughed nervously. "I just wondered when you were returning home. I haven't heard from you lately."

"If that's a stab at my communication skills, it'll have to be one more sin to add to the already long list," he stated flatly.

Damn! She hadn't meant to sound churlish. "That wasn't what I meant at all. I was just . . . concerned that everything was going well."

"Everything's going okay, Sable." His voice was softer now, less defensive and more tired. "There's just so many necessary permits—all on different levels of government. And we need them now, even though half the people are out of town. But if everything goes well, we should be home in a day or so. And this Saturday the track can open."

"I'm glad," she said, and meant it. "You've worked so hard to see your dream come true. You deserve it."

He laughed, but it was a brittle sound. "I've worked hard for a lot of things, Sable, but they haven't materialized yet, either."

"How do you know? You aren't home to find out," she told him softly. Her heart did flip-flops as she waited for his answer.

"Oh, I know," he replied, bitterness coloring his voice.

She heard a gruff voice yell his name, and Joe covered up the mouthpiece for a minute. When he returned, he was all business again. "We'll have a long talk when I return, Sable. Goodbye."

Pushing down the receiver button, she held the phone to her breast like a talisman. Nothing had changed—except that now she knew when he was coming home—soon.

LATE IN THE NIGHT, Joe stood naked in the dark room and stared out at downtown Austin. Here he was, in the middle of one of the hottest night spots in Texas, and he couldn't care less. Before Sable came along, he would have been a part of the revelry, whooping it up with the rest of the tourists, instead of sitting in a dark hotel room, mooning over a wife who'd rather be a divorcée.

After the day's meetings, Joe had fallen into bed; weariness had dogged him this entire trip. But sleep hadn't come—it was as elusive as the night shadows beyond his window.

The full moon that hung above the buildings glared down as if it, too, were frustrated by the events of the past and anxious about the present. Joe stared at it and tried to remember how to make a wish. Over his left shoulder? Looking at the moon, or

at a rising star? Since there was no one here to see him, he decided to take a chance.

"Let Sable and me work out our problems."

The words echoed in the quiet room. That really wasn't his
wish. His wish was that she might love him—blindly, unhesi-
tatingly, and with all her heart.

But to say those words aloud would mean that wishes
wouldn't come true. He knew that from experience. As a child
he'd never received anything he asked for. Why should things
change now?

Sable. Her skin was as translucent as the waning moon. Her
hair was the color of a rich, thick, sensuous coat of her namesake. When her eyes flashed, exhibiting her many moods, it was
as though all the colors of the rainbow momentarily appeared
in their depths.

He should have known he was in trouble the day he met her.
In fact he *had* known. He'd just chosen to ignore all the warning
signs.

A loud shout of celebration rang through the night, followed
by a woman's tinkling laughter. The sound reminded him of
home.

Could he have misread her again? Was he wrong to hope that
she wanted to reconcile their differences as much as he did?

He wanted Sable, and suddenly he didn't care who knew it.
He had to let her know how he felt.

She was the most enchanting, infuriating, unusual, wonderful and impetuous woman he'd ever known. Everything was exciting when she was around, yet nothing was more calming than
when she slipped her hand into his. And her smile lighted his
soul.

Determination tightened his muscles. He'd get her, if he had
to hire skywriters to fly over the house morning, noon and night.

Of course, there might be a simpler way. . . .

Joe smiled his first genuine smile of the day. He had a plan that
just might work.

JOE WAS DRESSED AND READY when Mike came by the following
morning to pick him up.

"You look like hell," his friend commented, helping himself
to some of the leftover coffee and cold toast.

Joe watched Mike through heavy-lidded eyes. Now that the sun was up, he was as tired as a bear roused from a long hibernation. "Didn't you get room service for yourself?"

Mike shook his head. "Why should I? You keep ordering food and then don't touch it. Someone should enjoy the fruits of the hotel's labor."

Joe gave his friend a speculative glance. "Speaking of enjoying—what was going on between you and Talia at the barbecue?"

Mike took a long swallow of his coffee. "Nothing, Joe. I swear it. She's just a nice kid who seems to have taken a shine to me." Mike looked flustered as he stared out the window, his coffee now forgotten.

"She's only seventeen," Joe reminded him.

"Don't you think I know that? I've got sisters myself, Joe. I'm just trying not to hurt her feelings. That's all. She's a sweet kid."

Joe sighed, knowing firsthand how tenacious—and how vulnerable—Talia was. She was also the savviest seventeen-year-old he'd ever met. "It's not going to be easy to walk that fine line between friend and romantic idol. It might be better to hurt her now than let her girlish imagination take flight."

Mike turned to pace nervously around the room. "I've tried, but she insists that we can be friends until she'd old enough to change the situation."

Laughing ruefully, Joe stopped Mike by throwing an arm around his shoulders. "Mike, relax," he ordered.

Mike tried to do as he was told. "She's a sharp little girl, Joe."

Joe chuckled. "She takes after her older sister."

"You know, she informed me that her eighteenth birthday was next July, that her favorite flowers were irises and her favorite restaurant was Vargo's on the bayou."

Both men shook their heads. "She spins quite a web, that little spider," Joe commented. "So what are you going to do?"

"I'll send her a bouquet of irises—along with a gift certificate for two for the restaurant—and a letter, telling her to invite the best boy from her school to dine with her."

Joe's brows rose. "Very clever. And very expensive."

Mike pushed up his glasses on his nose. "With the determination this girl shows at this age, she'll be chairman of the board of some major corporation in the near future. It's an investment. I'm hoping she'll hire me for her corporate business."

Joe finally relaxed, doing what he'd told Mike to do earlier. "Good planning," he said, relieved that Mike had the ability to handle a potentially dangerous situation. No wonder Sable had nicknamed her Spike.

Joe grabbed the keys off the top of the TV and headed for the door. "Let's go to that meeting and get this trip out of the way. I need to get home to my wife and sister-in-law."

"Great. Maybe you can keep that junior Mata Hari in line."

"I doubt it, Mike," Joe replied. "But I'll give it a try."

SABLE LOST WEIGHT. "Every other woman would be thrilled to lose weight. But not me. I already have to resemble a scarecrow," she muttered, ignoring the mirror as she stepped from her morning shower and dried one slim leg.

She refused to look into the mirror. Weight loss wasn't her only problem. She knew that a tinge of blue was clearly visible beneath her eyes, showing all and sundry that she hadn't been sleeping well.

What concerned her more was that she was pregnant. This morning, gathering her courage, she'd used one of those early pregnancy kits and confirmed what she'd suspected for the past two weeks.

She was carrying Joe's baby.

She was exhilarated, happy—and frightened, because she had no idea what his reaction would be.

Would he hate her? Would he see her pregnancy as a trap?

After dressing with care and determination, she brushed back her hair into a sleek roll, then studied herself in the mirror. Despite the problems, she wouldn't give this child up for all the world. This would be a baby to love. A brother or sister for Johnny.

Next to having a healthy baby, the only thing she could wish for was Joe's love. But whether Joe was pleased or angry about the baby, she would try her best to be the most wonderful wife in the world. She would be both understanding and supportive. Maybe then his love would follow.

SABLE DROPPED JOHNNY OFF at the nursery school she had enrolled him in so he'd have playmates, then returned to the ranch to wait for Joe. She had just finished seasoning a roast when she heard the car door slam. She tensed in anticipation.

Joe was home. Wiping her suddenly slick palms on her slacks, she pretended to check the oven dials. She told herself it was only natural that she would fear his reaction, both to her declaration of love and to the fact that he was to become a father. Nevertheless, she felt as though lightning sizzled down her spine.

Straightening, she faced the back door. One hand nervously checked to make sure her hair was still sleekly secure in its knot.

But when Joe appeared in the doorway, every word she had rehearsed flew out of her head. He wore a dark blue suit, his tanned skin in stark contrast to the white of his dress shirt. A maroon tie with a blue design dangled from his clenched fist.

"Hi." His voice held the smoothness of velvet and the golden heat of aged bourbon.

"Hi," was all she managed.

"You had the house painted."

"And the porch. It was my treat."

He didn't argue. "The same color."

"I thought you wouldn't notice as quickly."

"I knew I had good taste the first time." His blue eyes stared into hers, searching—for what? she wondered.

"You hired a maid."

He shrugged. "It's only once a week. I thought you could use the help."

She swallowed. "How was your trip?"

"One confrontation after another."

"Was it successful?"

He nodded, his eyes still pinning her down.

"And did you get what you wanted?"

"Almost."

She swallowed again. "What happened?"

He walked toward her, and she suddenly felt cornered, as if she were his prey.

When Joe stood in front of her, his eyes took in her strained expression, the dark circles under her eyes. The anxious biting of her lips.

He narrowed his eyes. "What happened here?"

Sable turned, placing the oven mitt on the counter. "Nothing much."

"Then why do you look as if you haven't slept in weeks?" He took one hand in his and turned it over, palm up. His thumb ran over the light calluses there. "You used to have the softest, most ladylike hands I'd ever seen," he mused.

She snatched her hand away, anger warring with her resolve to be nice. "Now I muck out stalls once a week and do housework for four people," she snapped. "How could you possibly expect soft hands?"

"You work too hard," he said gently. He touched her on the shoulders. Her bones were more prominent than before. "You've lost weight."

"Are you through categorizing my faults yet? Shall I help you?"

His gaze searched her face. She wanted to cry. Tears filmed her eyes, but she stoutly refused to let them fall or allow him to force her to look away. "What are they?" he asked.

She pushed back a loose strand of hair. "I'm rude, aloof, and right now I'm kind of crazy."

"I vote for all of the above."

"How can you not?" she asked crossly. "And I'm sure that if you look hard enough, you'll be able to find something else to complain about."

"There's nothing wrong with you. All I said was you needed more sleep and more help. I didn't know that my observations would open floodgates of bitterness." His voice was soft and teasing.

She stared up at him. He wasn't angry. He was still smiling in that wonderful, indulgent way he had.

Her mood changed abruptly. "I know. I'm not sure I always understand me, either."

"Right," he drawled. Then he pulled a fat, white envelope out of his coat pocket. "I need to discuss something with you right now."

"Yes." Sable took his hand and pulled him into the living room. "I need to talk to you, too. And I should go first." Sable sat down beside him on the couch, one leg curled under her as she leaned toward him.

For the first time since he'd walked in the door, Joe looked wary. "Let me begin—"

"No, I need to apologize, and that has to be done first."

Joe looked shocked. "For what?"

Sable looked down, still holding Joe's hand. His strong, tanned fingers were twined seductively around hers.

Then she gazed back into his eyes. "I married you for all the wrong reasons. I panicked."

His finger traced her cheek. "I know."

It was a sad statement, one filled with enough regret for both of them, and her heart sank.

"I'm sorry. Something happened to Talia and me when we were kids, and I allowed it to color my thinking."

"Talia told me about the custody battle, Sable. It had to be horrible for you both."

"You know all about it?" she asked in surprise.

He nodded. "It explained a lot, but it left my ego in shreds."

"Why?"

He shrugged, suddenly looking like a little boy embarrassed to be caught stealing penny candy. "I hoped you had more than one reason to marry me. That maybe you married me because you were attracted to me."

She tilted her head and stared at him, a question in her eyes and on her lips. "Did you like that idea?"

His grip tightened. "Yes."

"Yes, what?" she prodded, wanting, needing him to say he wanted her. Needed her. Loved her. She held her breath.

Joe sighed. "Yes, I liked the idea. I liked it more than I can tell you."

She was disappointed, but continued to press. "Why?"

"Before I get into that, I want you to have this," he said, holding out the fat envelope.

Sable stared at him, then at the envelope. With shaky fingers she accepted it, then carefully lifted the flap. She pulled out the sheaf of papers and cautiously unfolded them. Her eyes widened. Sable glanced at Joe, then back down at the papers again. "These are Ahab's papers."

Joe nodded.

"They're made out to me."

He nodded again.

"I don't understand."

"Ahab will be worth a million dollars by the time his prize monies and stud fees are calculated over his lifetime. I'm paying you back for your investment in the track."

"But I didn't invest. I gave you the money in exchange for a marriage certificate."

"And I'm giving you back the money." His voice was patient. "This way we're even. The debt is paid."

"And the marriage?"

His smile disappeared. "Is still a marriage. And if you're willing to try again, I think we might be able to make it work, Sable. I just don't want the money to be an obstacle to working out our problems."

"I didn't think it was."

He smiled sadly. "Don't lie, honey. We both know it was. It was the wall between us. Now it's down, and we can concentrate on ourselves."

"You love that horse."

"And I still do. Just because he's yours doesn't mean I won't see him or watch him race. But you'll receive whatever money he makes." A hint of a smile crinkled his eyes, bringing out the tiny dimple on his cheek, Sable noticed. "As well as his feed and vet bills."

She loved his easy teasing. Her hand cradled his jaw. "And now what happens, Joe?" she questioned softly.

Her husband looked away. "This is your apology, remember? I'll tell you what I have to say after you finish."

"I want to hear it now."

"You insisted on going first."

Sable laughed. He'd given away far more than he thought. "Okay." She took both his hands in hers. "I'm sorry about the beer episode. It wasn't fair of me to judge the men. I had nothing to go on but a built-in prejudice against beer."

"I accept your apology on their behalf."

"And I'm sorry about shouting at you the morning, the time—"

"—the morning I climbed into your bed and Talia found us?" he finished dryly.

Sable nodded. "I wasn't able to cope with the changes, so I took it out on you."

"I should have seen that. But I wanted you so much, I didn't stop to think," he told her, his voice filled with regret. "If I hadn't pushed so hard, we might still be sharing our nights."

She looked back up at him. "I love you."

The silence hung between them, as tense as a bowstring. His grip tightened, painfully so.

Then he dropped her hands and reached for her shoulders. "Say it again," he demanded.

Sable swallowed the lump in her throat. "I love you." Then she remembered their child and her resolve returned. Despite her failings, she took care of those she loved. The children were hers. It would be up to Joe to decide whether he wanted to be a part of their lives, as well.

She tilted her chin defiantly. "I love you!" she declared for the third time, her voice stronger now.

"Since when? Since you kicked me out of your bed? Since you screamed at me in my office? Since you snubbed me in my own home? When?"

"Since all of that," she said quietly. "I wasn't supposed to love you. I didn't want to. But I do."

His triumphant laughter shook the rafters. "I knew it! I knew you had to care for me, or you wouldn't have made love with me."

"Well, you don't have to be so vocal about it," Sable told him, pulling away. "It isn't nice to crow."

He leaned forward and kissed her. It was meant to be an old-fashioned buss, but turned into a wonderful, heartwarming, soul-talking kiss.

His mouth never leaving hers, he wrapped his arms around her waist and pulled her into his lap. She clung to him, her fingers losing themselves in his dark hair. His tongue found its way in and captured hers. Somewhere deep inside, Sable realized she was with Joe in their home, but as long as she was in his arms, she knew she was in heaven.

He held her so close, she thought she'd never lose the imprint of his body. But she didn't want it any other way. Joe was gruff, sometimes rough, sometimes tender—and she loved him in every way possible.

Joe rested his lips on her forehead, his warm breath soothing her brow. "We need to cancel that damn contract and write up a new one. You keep your money, I keep mine. Everything else belongs to us. No five-year plans. No other rules. We'll make them up as we go along."

Sable pulled away and stared up at him. Now it was her turn to demand. "Say it."

His eyes burned into hers, but she ignored their message. "Say it!"

His throat constricted, so that his words came out in a whisper. "I love you."

"Again," she demanded softly, finally allowing herself to dream.

His hands circled her face. The last hesitation faded from his eyes. "I love you. Completely. Forever. I love you, Sable La-Croix Lombardi."

She grinned. "It's about time you earned your silver tongue, you devil."

He clasped her close to him again. "You're my world, Sable." His voice teased her hair. "That scares the hell out of me."

"Me, too," she admitted.

"You're staying with me."

"Yes." She bestowed a butterfly kiss upon his white-shirt-covered chest.

"Joe?"

"Mmm?" he asked, his lips touching her hair as his hand stroked her back.

She couldn't resist the age-old question. "When did you know that you loved me?"

His answer came immediately. "When you stood in the doorway of my barn and proposed to me."

She lifted her head and stared at him. "But that was the first day we met!"

Laughter rumbled in his chest. "I know."

"When did you decide it was love?"

"When I heard you shouting at me as I went down in the racetrack elevator. You yelled something about me running away. It dawned on me then that I never did that, unless I was afraid of the love being offered. Of a happy ever after."

She stroked his cheek. "You didn't want to believe?"

His hand covered hers, and he brought her palm to his lips. "On the contrary. I've been searching for love all my life, but when I met you, I was afraid to believe in it, for fear you'd never return my love."

"Believe," she whispered, teasing his lips with hers. "Believe, my darling."

He sighed. "All the way home I was afraid you wouldn't be here."

"Where would I be?"

"I was afraid you'd leave me. I didn't want to know that. I wanted to pretend you were here, even if you weren't."

His words wrapped themselves around her heart and squeezed. She'd read all the signals wrong. They both bore childhood scars. "Oh, darling," she murmured. And then she remembered her secret. At least she knew now that Joe would be happy about the baby. No man could need so much love and not be happy.

The drone of a plane caught Joe's attention, and he pulled her up with him as they went to the front door and down the steps to the yard.

"Look," he said, pointing upward. "This was supposed to be my surprise. I thought if I let the world know how much I loved you, there was a chance you might take pity on me and love me back."

Sable stared at the plane above, which was skywriting *I Love You, Sable* in big script letters.

She had her storybook romance. She'd found her hero. Sometimes real life did resemble romantic fiction. Sometimes real life was even better than the love stories.

She hugged Joe, laughing in delight. "I don't believe it! Joe Lombardi is a romantic!" She stared at him, then again at the words in the pale blue sky. She wanted to cry as much as she was laughing. It touched her so deeply to think that this man cared enough to announce it to the world, or at least to the world of Conroe, Texas. And that this same man had such a hard time forming the words!

"You have a vivid imagination, husband mine," she whispered into his ear as she gave him one more hug. The plane had gone, and the writing began drifting away on the breeze, but the man who'd made it possible was still here with her.

"Then let's play another game of Let's Pretend, darling," Joe said, a wicked gleam in his eye. "We'll start all over again. Just

as if this were the first time we met. But this time we'll do all the
right things." He kissed the shell of her ear. "Make a fresh start."

"A fresh start," she repeated, loving the sound of the words.
She grinned. It was going to be hard to explain a fresh start when
there was a month-old life curled beneath her heart. "Joe? I have
something to tell you, darling."

"No, it's my turn," he told her. "I've asked Jonathan's grandparents to baby-sit, so we can have a honeymoon."

Her mind went blank. "The LaCroix?"

He nodded. "I knew we needed time alone together, without
any distractions, so I asked them if they wanted to take care of
Jonathan and Talia while we're away. They said yes—with a few
conditions."

"What conditions?" Sable asked warily.

He gave her a hug. "Don't worry. They're coming here to stay
for a week. But they're also bringing a maid and a cook."

"Of course!" she chortled. "What else would they do?"

"Well, they did want to bring a handyman and a nanny as
well, but I talked them out of that."

"How?"

"I told them they would have to buy a recreational vehicle for
the two women to stay in, and that if they also brought a nanny,
they might miss the real experience of learning to know Jonathan."

"What about the handyman?"

"I told them we had twelve handymen in the bunkhouse, who
also double as baby-sitters in emergencies." He looked very satisfied with himself.

"And when is this trip to take place? Where are we going?"

"We're having a honeymoon in Ixtapa, Mexico. A friend of
mine has a very secluded villa there." He frowned. "But we can't
go for another week. I can't get away until the track opens."

"Is it far from the ocean?" she asked, thinking of a bikini that
wouldn't quite fit by that time.

"Yes. About two hundred miles as the crow flies."

She dropped a kiss onto his bottom lip. "Never mind. What
your lady needs is you. Alone."

Joe slipped one hand under her knees, the other around her
back, and lifted her into his arms. "Let me explain what your

man needs, lady. He's into anatomy these days, and he'd like to do a little studying."

Joe strode through the front door and down the hall toward his bedroom. Sable wrapped her arms around his neck and let him have his way.

"I thought we were pretending that we're meeting for the first time?" she asked, dropping kisses onto his neck and chest. "That would make this our first date, yet you're heading for the bedroom. What kind of a woman do you think I am?"

"You're my woman," he declared. His voice was low and filled with need. "It's my game, and I'm setting the rules. I'm pretending this is a one-night stand. Forever."

"Okay, big fella," she murmured against the curve of his neck. "But I expect to get my money's worth."

His chuckle echoed through the hall. "Honey, you don't know it, but that's exactly what I had in mind."

She laughed, a husky sound that was almost a purr. "That's forever," she confirmed.

"Right," he answered, finally allowing her feet to touch the ground. His hands went straight to her blouse buttons. With intense dedication, he applied himself to the task of undressing her.

"And when I'm finished with that, I'll begin lessons in teaching you how to drink beer. You have to sip it, smell the bouquet, test the temperature of it on your tongue. It's an art."

"Kiss me, you nut."

"With pleasure, my love. With pleasure." And then words became deeds.

There was suddenly plenty of time to tell him all the things she wanted to share.

After all, they had the rest of their lives....

11

JOE PLACED a soft kiss on the nape of Sable's neck. They stood in a darkened corner of the far, second-story balcony, seeking a temporary retreat from the revelers. A twenty-four-piece orchestra took up one section of the grassy knoll by the pond. Fireworks painted the night sky with glorious streaks of color. Tuxedoed waiters wound through the crowd with silver trays filled with glasses of the finest champagne.

Racing at the Bluebonnet Racetrack would begin tomorrow.

"Talia was certainly excited tonight," Joe commented, his warm breath brushing her cheek. He stood behind her, allowing her to rest against him.

Sable chuckled. "I'm not sure if it was because she received a letter from Vassar, or because she's celebrating here with Mike."

"Mike will be very gentlemanly with her. You aren't worried, are you?"

"No. She's much too young for anything permanent. Especially now, with college waiting in the wings." Sable just hoped Mike could hold up under Talia's assault.

"Happy?" he murmured. His hands clasped her waist to pull her closer to the leanness of his body. She rested her head on his shoulder and stared into the softness of the dark.

"More than I can say."

"Ready for a week at that villa?"

"As long as you're there."

His lips touched her temple. "As soon as the balloons are released, we'll leave," he promised.

The balloons had been Sable's idea. Tucked inside five hundred of them were free passes to the upper gallery to watch the opening day's races.

Sable had a balloon tied to her wrist. She turned in his arms, facing him. "You have to pop your balloon first," she said.

"I thought it was a souvenir."

"No," she corrected softly. "This is a very special balloon. It will reveal your future."

Joe smiled indulgently, popped the balloon and caught the folded piece of white paper that fell from it. Still smiling, he unfolded the paper and tilted it toward the light.

Your wife will bear a child, to be born in the spring. You will live happily ever after.

His blue eyes delved into hers. "Is this a joke?"

She shook her head. Was he thrilled at the thought of becoming a father? Or did he feel cheated because they wouldn't have time alone before they began their own family?

"Are you sure?"

She nodded.

His smile lighted up the darkness that surrounded them. His laugh was deep and honest and full of the wonders of life. His arms encircled her, pulling her close to his warmth. "A child. Our child."

Her heart sang. "Our child," she confirmed.

Joe leaned back and stared into her upturned face. "Are you happy?"

"Yes," she said simply. "It's what I've always wanted."

He kissed the tip of her nose, his hands so light on her waist that she could hardly feel them. "Then we'll have a dozen."

"How about a compromise?"

"Six, then," he amended, pulling her toward him once more. "With Talia and Jonathan that will make eight. A nice round number."

"And we'll live happily ever after?" she teased.

His smile was replaced by an expression of sincerity. "Honey, I pray so. We're damn well going to try."

"We'll make it work," she promised. "We have luck on our side."

"Really?"

She nodded sagely. "After all, luck brought me to you when I was buying a groom. It certainly wouldn't dare desert me now, when I found a husband."

Joe chuckled. Now that the debt was paid, the money seemed such a small matter. And yet that money had given them the one thing they had wanted—each other.

A loud cheer roared around them. Six nets, filled with balloons, had just opened; the bright lights of the track allowed the spectators to watch their multicolored ascent.

Joe and Sable stood quietly on the second-floor balcony. His hand slid across the slick fabric of her full-length sheath and covered her still flat stomach.

Sable leaned back, her heart filled with contentment. For the rest of her life she would remember this moment and the feeling of completeness that encompassed it. His touch was so gentle, so sweet against her flesh. She wanted more.

"I won't break, you know," she told him. "I didn't break last night. Or the night before."

"And you won't break tonight, either," Joe promised. "But just in case, perhaps we'd better grab the limo now and head for home. I'll need to take my time making love to you. I certainly can't rush with you in such a delicate condition."

"You're absolutely right," she said, taking his hand in hers. "Let's go."

"In a hurry?" he inquired with a chuckle.

"Yes," she declared firmly, tossing the words over her shoulder. "To live life. With you."

"Forever," he muttered, swinging her around to fill the curve of his arms as he kissed her once more.

The spotlights caught them, the balloons framed them. But Joe didn't care.

Finally he was somebody's hero.

And he'd spend the rest of his life proving it.

She needs a husband with an American passport.
He needs a mother for his rebellious child....
Solution: Marriage!

MEETING PLACE

Bobby Hutchinson

CHAPTER ONE

"I DON'T CARE if she's a dead ringer for Miss Europe. I'm still not getting railroaded into this preposterous scheme you two have cooked up for me."

Still, Alexander Caine couldn't resist looking at the tiny snapshot he held so gingerly between his fingers. He stared curiously at the face of the girl-woman. No, he corrected himself, twenty-nine is definitely a woman. And it was this woman his father and Uncle Barney wanted him to marry. The woman they'd badgered him about for weeks. The picture showed only her face, a serious face. Her gaze was forthright and faintly imploring, or was that only his guilty imagination? Her cheekbones were slavic, wide and high, and the forehead was broad beneath the crown of dark, luxuriously thick braids.

An attractive face, not pretty but arresting. Her coloring surprised Alex. Instead of the blond Prussian coloring he would have expected with such deep blue eyes, her hair seemed almost black in the photo, her skin tawny and clear.

"She doesn't look like Aunt Sophia at all," he commented absently, studying the slightly exotic tilt to the eyes, the full, clearly defined lips. There was a tiny round mole beside her mouth.

Barney shook his head, and a fond expression crossed his face.

"No, she doesn't take after my Sophia. She's more like old Anna, Sophia's mother."

Alex heaved a sigh of frustration, giving the photo one more cursory glance. So this was the notorious Yolanda Belankova, the woman he was being pressured to marry.

No beauty, he concluded again. Features too strong. Exotic looking, maybe. Unusual eyes. Wide set, thick lashed. Questioning. Accusing? *Forget it, Yolanda. My armor's too rusty for rescuing damsels these days.*

Across the desk, Robert and Barney Caine watched Alex intently, their narrowed glances speculative and cautious. The brothers were slouched in comfortable leather chairs in Alex's inner office, and in the corridors beyond the closed door the everyday business of the Parliament Buildings continued, muted and ordinary despite the grandeur of the setting.

The resemblance between the three men was subtle, transcending the generation between the two older men and the younger. All three shared a certain cragginess of facial lines, a sense imprinted physically of a civilized veneer thinly disguising an almost primitive urge to inflict their will on the world. They had tall, muscular frames more suited to rough woolen shirts and jeans than the carefully tailored expensive suits all three wore. And there was a similarity in the set of jaw, the stubborn expressions on all three faces evinced by a slight tightening of muscles, a flaring of handsome nostrils that hinted these were powerful men who were used to having their own way, one way or the other. By force, if necessary.

"There has to be another solution," Alex stated flatly, tossing the photo down amongst the clutter on his wide oak desk. It landed among reports stamped Ministry of International Trade and Investment, reports Alex should be studying right this minute, instead of having this recurring, insane conversation. Which one of these two had dreamed up the damned scheme in the first place? Not that it mattered once they'd made up their minds.

"You have to think of an alternative, because I'm absolutely not marrying some woman I've never met just to get her out from behind the iron curtain. I'm thirty-nine years old, damn it. I got over wanting to be James Bond years ago." If only Barney and Robert had, Alex reflected.

Alex deliberately folded his arms across his chest in defiance, straining the back shoulder seams of his tweed jacket. "There has to be another way," he growled again stubbornly.

"Well, I'm telling you there isn't." Uncle Barney's voice was booming and aggressive. A narrowing of his nephew's green eyes made him clear his throat and consciously modulate his tone before he went on.

"We've battled, fair means and foul, for five years now. You know that, Alex." Barney Caine lifted his massive shoulders in a gesture of frustration and defeat and scowled at his nephew. "We've tried bribery, we've applied repeatedly for visitor's permits, and we've even looked into smuggling her across the border. That's so bloody dangerous it has to be a last resort. Which we're gonna have to start planning by the look of things, if you won't listen to reason." This time he met Alex's quelling glare with a narrow-eyed stubbornness, refusing to be silenced.

"Look, this kid started out way behind. When she was twelve, her father was shot over that Dubček thing, so her background leaves her under suspicion to start with, and now she's in the soup over some stupid interview. Lost her job, demoted to sewing dresses in a factory, for God's sake. It's driving Sophie nuts." A look of concern and tenderness crossed the big man's face at the mention of his wife's name.

"Sophie's not sleeping at night, worrying about this girl. Yolanda's her only niece. The kid has no other relatives except old Anna, her grandma. Her mother died soon after Josef was shot. Sophie tried to get old Anna out years ago when it was easier, but she wouldn't come." Barney shrugged, his massive hands held out, palms up.

"So fair enough, home's home. But Yolanda, well, the way I see it, she never had a choice. She's Sophie's only brother's kid, and if she'd married like most of them do over there, if she weren't so hardheaded and outspoken, it wouldn't be as dangerous. But in a place like Czechoslovakia, she's heading straight for a lot of harassment, possibly even a prison term. Fast."

His gaze swung out the window to the hazy gray rain of a Victoria winter. The street outside the Parliament Buildings bustled with gaily colored umbrellas, rain-coated people hurrying about their Monday morning business, the reassuring everyday normal patterns of life in a free country.

"I saw a group of women prisoners the last time I was over. Two years ago, when the company had that foul-up at the pulp and paper plant outside of Prague." His soft dark eyes caught Alex's clear green gaze, and his gruff voice was flat and hard, remembering. "It was early in the morning, wintertime. There were maybe twenty prisoners, with one woman guard. She was dressed in a warm coat. Their clothing was shabby, warm enough, I guess. They all looked old, sixty, seventy. They were carrying picks, and they started to break up the pile of rubble on a side street. One of them caught my eye . . . maybe she was younger than the rest—I don't know. She'd been pretty once, you could tell. Anyhow, she glanced up, and her eyes were empty. Nobody home. Her body was there, but whoever she'd once been was long gone.'' His face twisted, and he slammed a fist down on the hard oak desk. "Damn it, Alex, what a miserable waste. Those women should have been like my Sophie, plump and busy, cooking, smiling. Loving some old coot like me. Anything but what they were doing. I asked one of the Czech engineers later what the hell they might have done to be imprisoned, and you know what he said?'' Barney's voice had grown progressively louder again, and he sat on the edge of his chair, hands clenched into futile fists, punctuating his words with impotent downward thrusts.

"He said they'd probably been critical of the system. They'd probably had the audacity to tell their kids that life hadn't always been that way, that they remembered a better time, before the Russians took over. And for that, they were doing a life sentence?'' His booming voice filled the quiet room, and his fist crashed down on the desk, sending papers drifting to the gray carpet. Then he sank back in his chair, breathing heavily. The lines in his face drooped, and Alex studied him, a frown beetling his heavy dark brows. Uncle Barney looked older than his sixty-four years.

"Uncle Barney, calm down. You'll have a heart attack, carrying on this way.''

But Barney ignored the words, instead locking Alex's concerned gaze with his own zealous glare.

"You know I worked over there for four years, off and on, Alex, when the industry made the deal with the Russians to send our engineers over to start the pulp project and teach them to operate it. Sophie was an interpreter, like Yolanda. You remember me telling you how I met her, how scared she was to even be friendly. And that was years ago, before things got really bad. Before Dubček.'' He shook his head, and his thick fine white hair slowly settled back into its customary haphazard order.

"Czechoslovakia is a beautiful country, physically. Politically, I'm not exaggerating the way it is. I feel damned lucky to have met Sophie there, and even luckier to have gotten her out. Even then, marriage to a Westerner was the only sure way. I loved Sophie, so that part was easy." Barney took a huge gulp of his coffee, and his hand trembled slightly when he put the cup down.

"Damn it, Alex, I understand how Sophia feels about Yolanda. Hell, you're my only nephew. What if the situation was reversed, and you were the one trapped in the Eastern bloc, the one I might never see again? Don't you think I'd move heaven and earth to get you over here, give you a chance for a decent life? Just the way Sophie wants to do for Yolanda?"

Barney was capable of dramatics if the occasion called for it. Alex had watched him orchestrate scenes worthy of Academy Awards when an important business issue was at stake.

But somehow Alex doubted this impassioned speech was one of his uncle's calculated performances. The man was sincere. This was hard for him, this favor he was asking. Barney Caine was usually on the giving end of favors, Alex mused uncomfortably.

So was Aunt Sophia. Alex visualized her mischievous smile, the caring warmth she seemed to radiate. More times than he could count or even remember, all during the difficult teenage years when these two well-meaning but rough men roared and ordered and disciplined the motherless Alex in their blundering, loving fashion, Sophie had quietly managed to make him feel she loved him, cared what happened to him, really listened to him.

Barney and Sophia had been there in the past whenever he needed them.

All during the awful year after Dixie's death, they'd insisted he and Tracey join them for dinner twice every week, in spite of the fact that Sophia worked and maintained a busy social schedule.

They'd invited his difficult daughter along on holidays, giving Alex precious time to himself. They'd even had Tracey to stay with them last summer, when Dixie's mother was ill and couldn't care for the girl, and his job had necessitated a trip to Norway. Tracey loved them both, and now she often stayed at their apartment when she was home from school, and Alex had to go away on business. Although lately he was uncomfortably aware that Tracey was neither an easy, nor a pleasant, guest.

No doubt, he owed his aunt and uncle more than he could easily repay, he realized with growing discomfort. Sophia had taken the place of the mother he didn't remember, adding a much needed balance to the "tough love" his father and Barney had employed in raising him. If she seemed as much at a loss in dealing with Tracey as he himself was, it certainly wasn't Sophia's fault.

He shifted restlessly in his seat, and reached to pour more coffee into the thick brown mugs, then added a stiff shot of brandy to each from the bottle of Courvoisier half buried on the desk top.

"Wouldn't it look suspicious, me racing over there and marrying her?" he queried abruptly. "I've never met the damned woman," he added, his stomach sinking when he caught the sudden flash of hope on Barney's face, and the glance he shot at Robert. Both older men were giving him that "atta boy" approving look they'd perfected years ago.

"What could they do about it, son?" Robert Caine spoke for the first time, his quietly reasonable voice a counterpoint to Barney's bluster.

"The girl isn't in prison, at least not yet. Your position with the government here lends you a great deal of credibility and respect, and our company's plant outside of Prague does need attention, so there's a valid reason for the trip. You're single, and your papers are all in order."

Alex felt a wrenching dismay in his gut. Not only was he single, he was absolutely determined to remain single. One marriage, for better or worse, was enough. He wasn't good at marriage.

Barney was saying eagerly, "They'll run us through the usual amount of red tape, but I can't see them being able to block us. Robert and I'll take care of all that. All you have to do is fly over, marry her and bring her home on a visitor's visa. We've checked with immigration, and they have a special policy for immigrants from Communist countries. They bend the rules a little. Once she's here, we'll get her permit extended until she receives landed immigrant status. That'll take about six or eight months. As your wife, they can't stop her from leaving Czechoslovakia, either.''

Robert held up a hand, anticipating the query his son was about to make. ''I know, you're wondering how long you'd have to stay married to her. For sure until she gets her landed immigrant status; then there'd be a discreet annulment as soon as possible—marriage not consummated and all that.'' He cleared his throat, a bit embarrassed. ''Maybe a year, probably less.'' He met his son's gaze squarely. ''There's nobody here you're serious about, is there, son? Nobody going to be heartbroken about a marriage like this? No breach of promise suits?''

It was the one sure way Alex could have ducked out of this whole thing honorably. The foxy old devils. Although they never openly discussed it, Robert knew Alex avoided serious entanglements, just as Robert himself did.

Annoyance mixed with humor quirked the younger man's mouth into an ironic half grin. They both knew he dated Carrie Russell from time to time. They probably guessed he'd spent the odd night at her luxury town house.

But they probably also knew that the ambitious journalist was more of a friend than a serious love interest. Carrie was a career woman, through and through, and the possibility of Alex's marrying her never arose. Which was why he went on taking her out.

''No, Dad. I wouldn't be facing a breach of promise suit.''

The only promise he'd break was the one to himself, the one about living the remainder of his life alone.

In his deepest soul, Alex was still married to Dixie, despite the fact that she'd been dead four years this July. How could he explain that the bottom line in the string of objections he had to this preposterous scheme was really that one plain fact? The illogical but very real feeling that he couldn't marry because he was still married.

He carried the emotional impact of that first, long marriage buried deep in his soul. He remembered Dixie vividly, despite the fact that his wife was dead, had been dead for long enough that everyone but him had begun to forget.

Even their daughter. Even Tracey was slowly forgetting. She never mentioned her mother to Alex. It was probably healthy, this ability in the young to leave the baggage of the past behind. He couldn't seem to do it.

And that was the very reason he couldn't do this, either. He drew in a deep breath, preparing to refuse one more time, definitely and finally this time. *Spare me from aging warriors on a search-and-rescue mission,* he thought. *Especially tough and wily specimens like these two.*

But when he glanced up, he saw clearly that the two men he loved most in all the world were actually growing old. Their eyes had deep wrinkles at the corners, their hands, though still strong, were veined and stained with brown marks of age. And on each lined face was the single-minded conviction that they weren't too old yet, by God. Maybe they might still right one more injustice, rescue one more fair damsel from distress.

Two aging knights with a reluctant apprentice. How long or how short a time before men grew old and ineffectual? A line from Dylan Thomas sprang into his mind. "Do not go gentle into that dark night...Rage, rage against the dying of the light."

These frustrating, infuriating, beloved men were raging.

Alex slumped in defeat, squeezing his eyes shut in horror at what he heard himself saying.

"Okay, damn it. I'll do it. I'll do it. I'll marry her. Make the arrangements."

CHAPTER TWO

"Tu přítomní, Alexander Thomas Caine, *chcete si vzit dobrovolne la*—"

"Do you, Alexander Thomas Caine, take this woman," the nervous voice of the male interpreter echoed the fibrous Slovak in accented English, "to be—"

Repeating the words twice seemed to make this farcical marriage doubly binding, Alex thought ironically. The town hall in the tiny village of Votice, fifty kilometers south of Prague, was crammed to the rafters, and the person conducting the ceremony—Yolanda had assured him the man was a Communist official in good standing with the Party—had now fixed Alex with a piercing gaze, waiting for his response.

"I do," Alex said hastily, and the interpreter faithfully reproduced, in Slovak, his exact tone.

Alex gazed beyond the imposing official to the tapestry that adorned the wall. It was maroon velvet, trimmed in gold tassels, a colorful country scene of trees and brook and bridge. Two golden candelabra stood on the floor, and although it was still afternoon, the candles were lit. Ten candles in all, he counted, adding their golden glow to the afternoon sunshine filtering through the high window.

Yolanda was now making her response, her pleasantly husky voice faltering only a little. "I do," she said in English, and Alex glanced at her. Surely this was as difficult for her as it was for him, this charade of a wedding to a person she'd just met and spoken with perhaps half a dozen times in the past week. She seemed remarkably composed.

SHE'D BEEN THERE to meet him at the airport in Prague. He'd submitted to the passport checks, the rigid currency exchange—so many koruna for each day the visitor remained in the country—then verification and another passport check, luggage retrieval and the thorough inspection of his bags by still another official.

His first impression was of a politically oriented, rigidly controlled country in which one should obey the rules to the letter.

"Papers, please."

The lavish numbers of dark blue uniformed policemen, carrying guns and accompanied by dogs, as well as the imposing presence of numerous army personnel reinforced the impression in Alex's mind. This was a regime that took itself very seriously, indeed, and all of Sophie and Barney's descriptions paled before the harsh and sobering reality of the actual experience.

"Papers, please."

After what seemed hours, he was finally approved, passport stamped, nodded to, papers stamped, peered at and dismissed. Grasping his single large leather suitcase, he strode across the building, wondering irritably where he could rent a car.

She came from behind him, laying a hesitant hand on his arm for just an instant before shyly withdrawing it.

"Alex Caine?" She was taller than he'd imagined, perhaps five eight, and generally bigger than her picture had indicated. Not fat, exactly, but plump and tall.

She wore a scrupulously pressed and outdated two-piece blue suit with a paler blue blouse underneath, revealing luxuriously voluptuous contours beneath the outfit's prim facade. For all her weight, she was well proportioned.

"Excuse me, you are Alex Caine? I am Yolanda. Welcome to Prague."

He noticed both her voice and her eyes. The voice was faintly husky, with a slight break now and then, giving it an enchanting cadence. She called him "A-lexx."

Her eyes, thickly lashed with curling, dusky lashes, were the most amazing shade of sapphire, and seemed somehow translucent. She had absolutely beautiful eyes, and the realization confounded him. He hadn't expected to find her beautiful. He stared at her for long seconds before he said, "Yes, of course, how do you do, Yolanda?"

He extended a hand, grasped her strong fingers in his own, smiled at her, and she was able, with a great deal of effort, finally, to return the smile.

She was intimidated by Alex. Tall, handsome, foreign; he seemed so suave and sophisticated in this echoing place that he might have come from another planet. The pictures Aunt Sophie had sent had done nothing to prepare her for him. He'd looked simply agreeably attractive in them. Nothing had hinted at his size or the force of the animal magnetism he seemed to exude. Broad-shouldered, powerful-looking, he took her hand, and she wondered despairingly why she couldn't have met this man under different circumstances, had a chance to know him in a situation other than this awkward charade.

How ironic, to be so instantly attracted to him. And how dangerous.

THE OFFICIAL, to Alex's surprise, was adding a stern admonition to the legal proceedings of the wedding. The old bird was waxing poetic.

"Your pathways in life have intersected, and of your own free will. You are now man and wife. You must love each other and work hard at making a good life together." He fixed Alex with his gray-blue stare, and Alex held the gaze evenly until the man's eyes dropped. He indicated with a brusque wave that they should sign the register on the small table behind him.

Then, to Alex's relief, the mood altered. A bottle of red wine was produced, and glasses were filled for the official, Yolanda and Alex. There were toasts, and a young woman recited a poem that sounded highly romantic.

Alex's eyes met the clear, translucent blue of Yolanda's, and she swallowed hard at the despair she read there. He hated this performance. Well, so did she. Clearly he wanted to be anywhere but here.

It showed plainly in the tight hard set of his mouth, the slight tick beside his left eye, and irrationally, she felt hurt.

There was still the reception to get through, prepared by *babička* and the village women, sure to last most of the night. Yolanda tried to give Alex a reassuring smile, but her lips felt stiff and dry, and a peculiar sad ache began somewhere in her chest. This was her wedding day.

THE RECEPTION HAD BEEN GOING ON for what seemed forever to Alex.

He and Yolanda had been swept from the town hall by the noisy, laughing crowd, escorted down the narrow street in the first blush of summer evening to this reception hall. The crowd had marched them inside, singing merrily, *"The people from the wedding are coming; the bridal group is coming."* Yolanda, her arm through his, had translated breathlessly.

Then, when all were inside, there had been an odd little ceremony with salt and bread. Alex and Yolanda had placed token bits in each other's mouths, and Yolanda then had taken the plate holding the offerings and smashed it at their feet. Alex was given a broom, and he'd swept up the broken glass to the sound of cheering and laughter.

"It is a symbol," Yolanda explained, "of how two married people, they support one another." She didn't meet his gaze as she said the words.

Next he had to swoop Yolanda into his arms and carry her to the gaily decorated banquet tables set all around the periphery of the room.

He saw the trapped reluctance in her face, and in an effort to console her, he caught her eye and winked. There was simply no way to get through this easily. Alex looped an arm under her knees, careful to encompass the heavy satin of her gown, and swept her into his arms.

She was warm and fragrant and trembling, and not as heavy as he'd feared. She put an arm shyly around his neck, and he saw the long lashes shielding her eyes from his glance.

He felt a stab of remorse for her, for this elaborate and special ceremony that should be a romantic rhapsody and wasn't. He gave her a small reassuring hug before setting her down.

Then, there was the feast. Thin ham rolled around cheese, beef broth with homemade noodles, schnitzel with potato salad. And in front of every single guest, a large bottle of vodka and one of mineral water.

Alex welcomed the vodka and its inevitable blessed blunting of his senses drawing him onward through this dantesque inferno of noise and heat and strangeness.

When the food was done, the lights in the hall dimmed, and dozens of candles were lit. Music began—a four-piece band; guitar, accordion, violin and piano.

"We must dance, in the center," Yolanda explained, "the dance of the bridegroom. Then, the women will pay to dance with you, the men with me."

"Pay?"

"Yes, they will give the money to the master of ceremonies, Rudi, over there. It is the custom," she added anxiously, and he nodded reluctantly.

Well, he would quietly make an anonymous donation to the town tomorrow to make up for what had to be hurtful generosity. These people didn't have much, and yet they were going to pay to dance with him? A sense of despair had been growing stronger in Alex with each passing moment. Memories of another wedding, years before, kept surfacing inside him, and with them, a steadily increasing sense of urgency that this be over, soon.

Yolanda Belankova—Mrs. Alexander Caine, Yolanda Caine, she corrected herself silently, covertly watched the tall stranger she'd married. Despite wide shoulders and a deep chest, his large body was svelte and slim in the elegant dark suit, his ash-brown wavy hair expertly cut to complement the rather craggy face with its slightly crooked nose and square, strong chin. Clean-shaven and tanned, his was a foreign face, guarded and expert at hiding true emotions. Almost a frightening face, with the green eyes cold and unresponsive, the strangely sensual mouth set in polite and disdainful grimace.

No wonder he stood out, with such a remote expression as that amidst the broad, open countenances of her countrymen, the farmers from this village who'd watched her grow up, and her more recent close friends from Prague. They too knew the secrets of subterfuge, perhaps even better than he, but somehow he made them look clumsy.

Alex raised an eyebrow at her questioningly. He thought of her, living with him, in Canada.

Home. It was sane and quiet and predictable. The way he'd been, one short week ago. What in blue hell was a respectable politician from Victoria doing at a wedding—his own wedding—in a village hall in Votice? Barney and Robert Caine would pay for putting him through this, Alex resolved, gritting his teeth, smiling as a bridesmaid, an extremely large and toothy blonde named Ludmilla, claimed him for what had to be her fifth dance.

Across the room, Yolanda studied him as she'd done all day, covertly, trying to discover the reason for the conflicting and disturbing emotions he stirred within her.

Was it something about the way he moved, she wondered, the smooth, gliding motions, precise and understated, yet giving an impression of leashed strength?

Now he bowed and smiled politely, his face a mask above Ludmilla's blond braids. He'd smiled in that same strained way, his eyes a flat and frigid green, when the official had married them this afternoon.

He'd slipped the plain gold band on her third finger as if he were performing a duty. She had no ring for him, believing the marriage too much of a falsehood to emphasize the deceit further.

He's doing his duty, what more do you ask of him? she demanded silently. *This marriage is a farce, whether or not* babička *believes it.*

One of the matrons nearby, Jenda Jaraskova, neighbor and longtime friend of *babička*'s, chose that moment to joke loudly, "He's a handsome one, Yolanda's foreigner. I shouldn't mind taking her place tonight in the feather bed, with one who looks like him. Think he'd notice the difference?" she inquired archly of the appreciative cluster of women busying themselves for the second banquet, which would take place at eleven.

Although Alex was too far away to hear the women's ribaldry, it was still fortunate he understood almost nothing that was said.

Yolanda's nerves tensed, and the blood rushed to her face as she imagined his reaction to such remarks and the many others to come during the late dinner, when everyone would be relaxed and loose-tongued from vodka and dancing.

Yolanda fervently hoped that no one would attempt translation for him. Alex Caine provoked enough reactions in her without the added humiliation of sexual innuendo.

The truth was that Yolanda felt bone tired and more than a little disoriented and unsettled ever since the dance she'd shared with Alex.

If only this celebration hadn't been necessary. Their wedding was, after all, only a formality. The feelings he stirred in her must be suppressed for he must never know what ridiculous fantasies she'd entertained in his arms.

She brushed absently at the filmy ivory veil floating around her shoulders, Grandma's wedding veil, ancient handmade gossamer lace. Her dress was a rich silvery satin that Yolanda had painstakingly cut and fitted and shaped into her wedding gown.

She slid a hand over the fabric's richness, loving the slippery weight of the expensive material, the feel of it against her skin. She had spent nearly all her meager savings on this gown, this celebration, this . . . counterfeit union. If only her wedding was the triumphant happy occasion it pretended to be, instead of a mockery. If only she were marrying the way she'd dreamed of when she was still a romantic young girl, marrying a handsome man who loved her. Someone familiar, whom she understood. A man who would be her friend.

She straightened her shoulders in a typically determined gesture. Romance was an indulgence few could afford. At twenty-nine, she wasn't a girl any longer, she reminded herself stoutly, and nowadays, nightmares were far more common than dreams. Nightmares of soldiers and guns and prison. She forced the specters of her sleep away, but her eyes automatically scanned the crowd and found the deceptively innocent face of the woman who pretended to be her friend. Katya Krajinkova undoubtedly was making mental notes this very minute, to report as soon as possible to the authorities everything that was said, done, eaten, insinuated here tonight.

An old anger surfaced, and rebellion tightened her lips. Let them suspect. They could prove nothing, for all their snooping. Sophie and Barney had been scrupulously thorough in their groundwork for this marriage of convenience, just as Yolanda herself had been.

But Katya's presence forcibly reminded Yolanda of the true purpose of the seemingly joyful festivity.

This wedding was as it had to be—a means to an end, a route to the freedom she'd almost given up hoping for, a way out of the country she hated and adored. Czechoslovakia. Her prison, her joy, her despair.

She raised her chin stubbornly, defiantly, her confused emotions focused on her new husband.

Smile, she entreated him silently. *Really smile at me, with warmth in those gold-flecked green eyes instead of ice!*

Her eyes seemed to gravitate to him, picking him instantly out of the crowd. The eerie awareness he created inside her drew her eyes toward him. Again, the illogical hurt. Obviously the awareness was totally one-sided.

He was bowing politely to Ludmilla, and Yolanda's pulse leaped, alive with excitement she couldn't explain or control, for now he was approaching, moving in that graceful fluid fashion toward her.

"I understand we're supposed to sit down, Yolanda. Come."

Rudi must have prepared him. It was time for another ceremony.

Alex and Yolanda sat side by side, arms entwined, holding glasses of wine. The strong young men of the village grasped the wooden chairs they sat on and raised them high over everyone's head.

"For luck and happiness," Yolanda whispered in explanation.

There was nowhere to look except into Alex's eyes. He met her glance for half a second, then hastily sipped from the stemmed glass she held. She did the same, and the glasses were tossed to the floor, the bridal couple lowered unsteadily by the singing crowd.

With a quick impatient gesture, Alex loosened the burgundy silk necktie threatening to choke off what little air there was in this press of sweating bodies. He lost count of the number of tiny glasses of fiery vodka he assured himself he was obliged to swallow, the number of indecipherable toasts he saluted with the endless glasses of the excellent local wine, unaware that at some point he had stopped pretending and actually started to relax.

The noisy raucous merriment spilled out the open doors, over the humble cottages of the village, or *vesnice* as it was known

here. The sound tumbled over the fields of newly planted potatoes and turnips and cabbage, losing velocity as it rose
through the clear night air, disappearing entirely long before it
reached the heights of the mountains that ringed the village, or
the countries that ringed the landlocked borders of this nation
of Czechoslovakia, this beleaguered tiny area long known as the
geographical heart of all Europe.

Even the stars were gone when the hall finally emptied. Gray
tendrils of dawn stroked the inky eastern sky, and the clear
heady air struck Alex like a hammer, intensifying the effect of
the potent alcohol, underlining the exhaustion he felt. He
forced his aching shoulders back, forced himself to walk
straight and tall down the earthen path. The dark blue Skoda
he'd rented was parked where he'd left it that morning outside
Yolanda's grandmother's cottage and acted as a beacon in the
semidarkness.

He'd suggested driving back to Prague right after the celebration, and now he could only be fuzzily grateful that Anna
Belankova had quietly but firmly insisted they stay there with
her in her cottage for the night.

Alex, touched by the old woman's obvious devotion to Yolanda, had reluctantly agreed to the plan. What did it matter
where he spent one more night in this godforsaken country?
Tomorrow he would leave Prague for four days of business
meetings, touring the pulp and paper plants set up by the
Canadian Trade Commission, and then he would return to
Prague, collect Yolanda, then head for home.

Once in Canada, Yolanda would be Barney and Sophie's responsibility, Alex told himself. That's all this heightened
awareness of her probably amounted to, just an overdone sense
of responsibility. He had to deliver her safely to Barney, and
then he would be free to more or less forget about her.

Tonight, this moment, it was increasingly difficult to think
that far ahead, anyhow. He longed only for a bed somewhere—anywhere—and sleep, for whatever remained of the
night. His wedding night, the second wedding night of his life.

He'd fought the memories all day. After all, there was no
comparison between that long-ago day and this, no similarities except in the solemnity of the two ceremonies. But by some
quirk of irony, the differences made him remember far more

poignantly than likenesses would have. Every difference brought painful memories of that other time.

Yolanda was the antithesis of his first wife. Dixie had been slender as a reed that day, laughing and flirting coyly with him, always touching him, holding his hand, stroking his arm, those seventeen years before. He was twenty-two, and Dixie was eighteen. A girl.

This somber woman had probably never flirted in her life. He cast a quick glance sideways at her. Certainly she didn't make any effort to touch him. She walked beside him, keeping distance between them, and he glanced at her now and then, at the lush ripeness of her. She moved a bit ahead on the narrow path, and Alex watched the unstudied grace of her movements, the proud tilt of her head. The traditional white satin she wore emphasized her breasts, her ample hips. She was...he searched for a word, forcing his muzzy brain to cooperate. She was...erotic. She had flawless skin, golden skin that had tanned a glowing copper shade in the early June sun. And those oval jewellike eyes, with their exotic tilt! The luxurious coils of thick soft dark hair—Dixie's hair had been a pixie cap of red gold curls, her eyes dark brown.

Dixie had been all that was delicate, almost childlike, ultra-feminine, coquettish.

No, this sturdy creature striding along at his side was no Dixie, he reminded himself bitterly.

But he'd married Dixie believing he loved her. And even with that depth of emotion as a firm beginning, his marriage had somehow gone awry.

Yolanda? Yolanda, he reminded himself, was strictly duty. Family duty. He'd do well to remember that. The vodka was to blame for that embarrassing response in his body when they'd danced; the liquor created the ache deep in his groin.

By the time he'd reached Anna Belankova's cottage, the iron discipline he exerted over his limbs in order to make them obey was fast disappearing, and the quantities of vodka and wine he'd consumed had torn down the barriers he usually used to block the loneliness in his soul.

He'd had too much to drink. He was a hairsbreadth away from maudlin. Cautiously he climbed the steep narrow staircase to the bedroom the old woman had shown him to earlier that afternoon.

He closed the bedroom door behind him, sighing with relief to find himself alone at last. He located the light's string after a bumbling search, and the single bulb swinging on the cord harshly lit the tiny area under the eaves, making him dizzy with its swaying.

There was cold water and a fresh cotton towel on a small washstand in a corner. He drank deeply from a glass, then tipped the yellow china pitcher over the basin. He doused his hot face, fastidiously washed away the sweat from his body and smacked his head on the ceiling when he stood upright.

Rubbing the spot, he cursed under his breath and wondered where the hell to dump the water from the basin. He finally found the bucket tucked discreetly under the washstand and cautiously poured out the soapy water.

At the foot of the stairs, Yolanda heard the bang as he knocked his head. She winced for him, and then the bedsprings creaked, the sliver of light under the door at the top of the steps went out. Taking a deep, weary breath, she tried once again, the Slovak words tumbling one on top of the other.

"But *babička*, you know this is not a real marriage, you know the reasons for..." Yolanda's whispering almost hurt her throat with its intensity, but Anna Belankova was adamant. Her leathery skin was like a roadmap, creased and lined and proudly advertising her seventy-nine difficult years of life. Yolanda didn't recognize the stubborn set of the older woman's chin or the narrowing of the faded blue eyes with their slight tilt as a mirror image of the determined expression her own features wore.

The words spurted from Anna's lips. "A marriage is a marriage. You were knotted in the sight of God. It's only right you join your husband on your wedding eve."

"Grandma, he's not really my husband. He married me only because of Aunt Sophie...please try and understand—"

The stubborn expression in the old eyes changed to one of cunning.

"What's to understand? You married him, with witnesses, but words are not enough. A marriage must be consummated, my darling, or it is no marriage. This union more than usual.

What are words, with no physical joining? Pshaw!" The work-worn hands spread, the shoulders lifted and dropped in a graphic gesture. "The marriage can be annulled—he feels no responsibility for you. After all, he has done his duty by simply coming here. But lovemaking, ahhh." She nodded wisely, a reminiscent smile making the thin old lips softer, younger.

"The flesh forms a stronger bond than even the words of God or man. Go to him, Yolanda—I order you."

Yolanda's arms were folded across her breasts, partly to ward off the chill air of near-dawn in the unheated kitchen, partly to help buttress herself against Anna's inflexible will. There was no reasoning with Anna when she made up her mind like this. Patiently Yolanda tried, anyway.

"There isn't any love, *babička*. He married me only because his uncle asked him to, because of Aunt Sophia. To...to get me out. You know that. It would be obscene to...I would feel humiliated if..."

"Enough." The fierce outrage, the fiery anger in Anna's face silenced Yolanda. The old woman had raised her, and that expression, coupled with the single word, had always stilled Yolanda's outbursts of rebellion.

"Marriage is not only love and happiness, the way you young fools think. Marriage is much greater. It isn't meant to be happy at first: you struggle together, you fight the world to make a life, and you grow to really know each other, then you fall in love afterward."

"Is that another one of your Gypsy sayings, Anna Belankova?" Yolanda teased tiredly, gently, hoping to deflect Anna's purpose.

"So what if it is? Do as I tell you, Landa. Please, for your old grandma. I will die soon, and I want to know you are safe and happy before I go."

Her voice quavered slightly, and the suddenly weakened mouth and chin trembled. The drama, the tragic passion in the lined face delighted Yolanda. *Babička* should have been a dramatic actress. *Babička* was a dramatic actress, she decided. A tiny smile tilted her full lips.

"Try to wait until you harvest all those potatoes we planted— it would be a shame for them to go to waste."

"What have I done, to raise such a bonehead, such an un-grateful child," Anna moaned, but there was a flicker of amusement now in the shrewd old gaze, although not the slightest weakening of intent. "I will stand here all night if I must, an old woman deprived of her rightful rest, to make sure you do as I ask, Yolanda Belan—Yolanda Caine." The unfa-miliar name came with difficulty, but Anna emphasized it, her gaze boring into the young flushed face inches above her own. "Go to your husband, as a proper wife should. Go," she whis-pered. An almost frantic note came into the old woman's tone. "Sometimes even in our own homes, the state has eyes and ears. This is your chance, my darling. Please, for me, make certain it succeeds." All trace of acting was gone now. Anna was pleading, and with an angry, defeated flick of her satin skirt and an irritated exclamation, Yolanda started up the steps. After all, where else *was* there to spend the night? The man was asleep, unlikely to awaken. Her very bones ached with weari-ness, and the chairs in the kitchen were meant for sitting up-right. There were only two tiny bedrooms, the one on the right, the room Yolanda had occupied since she came, orphaned and bereft, to live with her grandmother sixteen years before. Where Alex now slept. The other was Anna's. There really wasn't anywhere else to go, with Anna guarding the kitchen like a bulldog.

He would be sound asleep, anyway, she repeated to reassure herself as she halted near the top of the steps. Her heart pounded with nervousness, and she silently turned the knob and slipped through the bedroom door.

Sure enough, deep, even breathing filled the little bedroom. It was dark; the heavy curtains at the window blocked what little dawn light there might be. Yolanda knew every inch of the cottage, and she crept silently over to the wooden hook on the wall where she knew Anna had hung a freshly laundered nightdress, an embroidered white gown of bleached soft linen. She was more aware each second of the mounded form of Alex on the bed, the alien male odors of leather and some sort of citrus after shave, overlaid with a totally undefinable scent she'd noted when he danced with her earlier, the intimate body scent of a clean, perspiring man.

With shaking hands she stripped off her gown. Alex cleared his throat, heaved half over. Yolanda froze, then raced to hang the satin gown on its hanger on the peg and to tug off her long taffeta slip and sturdy white bra. She yanked the voluminous folds of the nightgown over her dark head, fighting a wild panic when a small button caught in the strands of her loosened hair and her body was half exposed in only white panties for agonizing seconds.

But the man on the bed still slept, his breathing the deep, even sighs of exhaustion. After a moment's hesitation Yolanda slipped the panties down and off.

Planning every slightest move before she made it, she poured icy water, drop by nervous drop, into the china basin. Using a cloth to wash away the light traces of lipstick and powder she'd worn, she then laved her underarms and breasts, her stomach and legs, as best she could beneath the folds of the sweet-smelling gown, still redolent of the sachet of herbs and flowers *babička* used in her closets and drawers. With every movement, she listened to the sounds of the man on the bed for signs of wakefulness, but there were none. Silently, stealthily, trying not to disturb the goosedown quilt or touch her sleeping husband in any way, she crawled into her marriage bed.

Her feet were freezing, and every nerve in her body felt as if it were vibrating. In contrast, the body inches from her own was sending out soothing waves of warmth, like the stove downstairs when Yolanda stoked it with coal on winter morning weekends.

Slowly, inch by inch and limb by limb, that comforting warmth and her weariness took over, and she relaxed, still not moving, but gradually slipping uncontrollably into the deep sleep her tired body craved.

HIS DREAM WAS SENSUAL, permeated by a lingering old-fashioned odor of mingling flowers and spice, an elusive, compelling scent that intrigued and excited him unbearably, reminding him of simpler times and forgotten, innocent passions.

Perhaps the softness surrounding him and the evocative summer smell convinced him that he was carefree again, a man with his life still before him, strong and proud of this primeval pulsing urgency in his loins. There was a woman in his fantasy. She wasn't Dixie.

This woman's full breast was lush and comforting in his palm, her nipple responding instantly to his touch, erect and echoing his own fullness. He exulted in his strength and her response, his hardness and her supple yielding, the potency of their desire. He was both intrigued and driven to madness by the softly modest coverings his beloved dream companion wore.

He knew her to be a creature of his subconscious imaginings, soft and all-encompassing, sweet smelling, and best of all, his own companion. His need was almost pain now, and he craved the sweet release he knew he'd find if only he could penetrate these folds of cloth. His tumescence slid unerringly up a newly naked satiny thigh. There was some reason that he should awake, and he fought it with considerable will, desperately denying any return to consciousness. Then, the battle lost, he penetrated the hot soft flesh at last.

She pulsed and burned and drew him irresistibly. She held him tight, luring him into a spiraling ecstasy so intense that he convulsed immediately and moaned. With his final uncontrollable surge of release, he flew upwards from the red and heated wetness of somnolent delight into the grayed and stark images of reality.

The groan he'd emitted from ecstasy swiftly became a choked exclamation of concern as he disentangled himself from Yolanda. The dawn light was enough to reveal her, hazy with sleep and confusion, blinking up at him, and it took only seconds for the full impact of what he'd done to penetrate the numbed, delicious lassitude of sexual tranquility still shivering through his long form.

His curse was graphic, and Yolanda hadn't ever heard that particular expression in English. He rolled off and away from her, burying a fist viciously into the soft enveloping feather tick that covered them both.

"Why didn't you stop me?" he ground out, and she felt her body contract with humiliation at the unleashed fury of his tone. She swallowed hard, and then prayed he hadn't heard the clumsy gulping sound she'd made.

"You ... you are my husband," she whispered, so softly he barely could make out the accented words for the huskiness of her tone. "I was asleep."

She could see him in the gray light, his wavy hair disheveled, the rough bristles of his morning beard apparent on his cheeks and chin. Her face and neck still tingled from the evidence of that beard where his head had rested in the crook of her shoulder short moments before, his breathing stertorous and uneven and sweet in her nostrils. Her heart hammered so loud she imagined she could feel the bed shaking from it.

She'd been drugged with sleep. He was already moving languorously against her body before she started to wake, and the delicious feelings he generated seemed to be a continuation of her dream.

One of his large hands was cupping her breast, circling lazily, gently, making her nipple curl and bud in response, sending sleepy spirals of delightful sensation through her.

She came fully awake then, immobile with shock, and almost immediately felt him enter her, a slow certain entry that took advantage of the unconscious way her tired limbs had sprawled in sleep.

Her body reacted with all the suppressed response he'd generated in her from the moment they'd met. She welcomed him, moist and convulsive.

Her action had been instinctive and totally natural, and her face burned now at the recollection.

Without hesitation, she'd made it easier for him, despite the involuntary tensing of her inexperienced flesh. It had been so many years since ... But before she could join him, he'd stiffened and moaned against her, before she could adjust and respond to the exquisite sense of fullness and heat sending delicious undulations through her thighs and belly.

That quickly, it was done, and she was truly the wife of Alexander Thomas Caine. His seed trickled in a warm stream down her thigh. Trembling uncontrollably, she listened to the low, steady stream of cursing from the man beside her. He rubbed an agitated hand through his hair, and his amber-flecked guilty eyes collided with her quietly furious stare.

"I am twenty-nine years—I am no child," she stated, her voice as steady as she could make it. She desperately hoped he hadn't been able to sense her inexperience. Surely Western women were more sophisticated in these matters.

"If you find me so, so, disagreeable . . ." What did he expect of her now? Her stomach twisted with uncertainty and hurt, but she proudly refused to look away from him. He met her gaze with his own burning green glare in charged silence, his broad chest with the mat of curly hair exposed above the puffy eiderdown. His arms were strongly muscled under the tanned skin, and his hands were large and veined, clenched into fists. Yolanda's own hands were callused, her nails short and stained from planting.

Self-consciously, she kept them under the covers and averted her gaze. The awakening memory of his hand so sweetly on her breast was vibrant and painfully intense.

"Disagreeable? Hell, no. Just the opposite," he burst out, miserable, angry with himself, not able to distance himself yet from that moment of utter bliss he'd known in her arms. He reached out a hand, absently tucked a long strand of silky fine hair back from her cheek, and she wanted to turn her face into his palm, sniff at the skin smell of him.

"I'm furious with myself. I had no intention, I . . . What are you doing sleeping here, anyway? I was . . . I never thought for one minute you'd actually crawl in beside me. Hell, Yolanda, surely you know enough about men—" He stopped abruptly. What was he doing, blaming her? The responsibility was his.

"Sorry, it sure as blazes isn't your fault," he growled shortly. "I apologize."

Her face was burning, and she could only hope that her tanned skin would hide her embarrassment. With all the dignity she could summon, she said, "There are only two beds in the cottage. Grandmother—she's old fashioned—she insists we're married, and I was tired."

How to explain Anna's insistence, her devious reasoning? Translating from Slovak to English in her head was hard enough without the convolutions of Anna's reasoning. Yolanda gave up with a discouraged sigh.

Alex sank slowly back down on the pillows. He felt as though he was sinking deeper and still deeper into this bizarre plot his father and Barney had engineered, and far from simply being a crucial but uninvolved bit player, he had, by his actions of the past half hour, suddenly entangled his life with that of the woman at his side. He didn't want to be involved with her, at least not more than he'd planned. He didn't want to feel this tenderness for her, this insane urge to take her in his arms and replay what had happened in sleep. She was so lovely....

Enough. But against his will, he remembered the delight of his dream, and he shuddered.

How could he have guessed his body would betray him?

CHAPTER THREE

YOLANDA LAY IMMOBILE, waiting for Alex to make the next move. Getting out of bed, sharing the intimate morning rituals of washing and dressing in front of him seemed unthinkable.

How ridiculous, she chided herself, to feel shy with him. Especially now.

The first tentative cheeping came from birds outside, picked up rapidly by others until the chorus was constant. Gradually, too, more light filtered gently through the blue curtains. It was a fine morning. *Babička* would be awake soon.

"What time does everyone get up?" His voice was neutral, devoid of the intensity of the past half hour. He'd bent his arms at the elbow, folding them under his head, staring up at the ceiling. If she turned her own head the slightest bit, her forehead would touch his underarm. She could see his armpit with its curling nest of light hair and the light blue tracing of veins under the skin. His leg, rough with hair, brushed against her ankle.

"Anna is usually up at dawn. If I'm home and it's cold, I always light the stove for her." She drew her legs carefully away from him. "Before, as a translator, I had more days off. Now, as a seamstress, only Sunday," she said matter-of-factly.

"Why didn't you apply for work as a translator somewhere else when they fired you?" he queried. "With your training, it seems a waste to be stuck in a factory, sewing."

She gave her head a single decisive shake. Her blue eyes had grown dark, and her lips pressed firmly together. "If I try to change jobs, my work permit will be revoked, or I will be sent miles away to some remote place. I'm a dissident, you see."

"But your language skills, don't you speak—what, four or five languages fluently?" Alex remembered one of Barney's sales pitches about Yolanda. "Czech, Slovak, German, Russian, French, English," he recalled, slightly awed again by her linguistic abilities. He'd barely mastered French in university.

"Yes, I speak them, some more than others, but of course the work permit determines what job one does." *And how well you obey their rules,* she added silently. She was much better at languages than rules.

"I'm thankful, at least, still I am in Prague. I might have been assigned anywhere. The factory is close enough; I can come home."

He didn't understand her acquiescence at all. He propped himself up on one elbow, studying her curiously. "What did you do, exactly, to lose your job?" Barney had said something about a journalist, an article in the French newsmagazine.

"There was a group of French tourists. One man kept on talking about how fortunate Czech women were, free to have careers, all of us working. Liberated, he kept saying. I was, I think the word is, indiscreet. I was critical of our so-called freedom, saying that what most women have are two full-time jobs, that even though a woman is pregnant and sick, she must still be at work at 6:00 a.m., put in eight hours, go home and cook and clean." The vehemence in Yolanda's voice surprised him. She caught his expression, and her voice trailed off. "I didn't know he was a journalist, you understand."

Alex frowned and lay back on the pillows. Harsh punishment for what sounded insignificant. But her words reminded him of a new subject he'd have to broach.

The silence hummed awkwardly. Her stomach rumbled, and her hands flew down to try and quiet it. Beside her, he moved restlessly.

"Yolanda?"

"Yes, what?"

"I don't suppose, ah, you're using, er, birth control?"

She started to answer and had to clear her throat before speaking.

"No. It has not been necessary for me. There have been no men." The words were so simple, spoken with dignity, revealing more of her than he'd expected to learn. She was touchingly naive in her blunt honesty.

"Well. I wanted to tell you that it's, well, that it's highly unlikely there'll be any problem." After two desperate years of
trying with Dixie, they had adopted Tracey. Unlikely, indeed,
that one dreamy encounter would produce what prayers and
youth and love had been unable to create, although it had never
been proven that the fault was his alone.

"I believe the—the timing is not—" She groped for the
proper expression, desperately translating in her head. "The
cycle, it is not appropriate," she finally managed. "So there is
not needs for concern."

He did his best not to smile at her mangled syntax, and a
frown creased her smooth forehead. This conversation was infinitely worse than any awkwardness involved in getting up with
Alex watching.

She slid out of bed, tugging the high-necked gown down
around her ankles, scooping up her underwear. Her everyday
clothing was in the armoire in the corner, and she hurriedly
grabbed the first thing her hand landed on, a printed polyester
dress with buttons down the front. Her hair floating like a
shawl down her back, she literally tore out of the room, bang-
ing the door behind her. Drawing a deep, quivering breath of
chill air into her lungs, Yolanda escaped down the stairs.

When Alex entered the kitchen half an hour later, she had
already lit the huge blue-and-white tiled stove that dominated
the small room, and its crackling and sparking was sending out
welcome rays of warmth.

Her face was glowing from a recent scrubbing, devoid of any
makeup, but wholesomely fresh and cheerful. Her purple-and-
pink printed dress was buttoned sedately to her neck. The
shining black hair lay coiled on her neck in a bun, and she wore
the incongruous combination he'd seen often in this country—nylon anklets, which Western women wore with slacks,
combined with sensible medium-heeled black pumps. An expanse of bare unshaven leg stretched between the skirt hem and
the nylon sock top. The most disturbing discovery, for Alex,
was that the leg was also curvaceously long and well shaped.

"Coffee?" she inquired, deftly moving a speckled enamel
coffeepot to one side on the stove top. With a miniature shovel
she stoked the fire with chunky lumps of brown coal, then replaced the lid before any smoke could escape into the low-

ceilinged room. Her movements were swift and economical, born of long habit and familiarity.

She poured a mug for him. "Cream, sugar?"

"Black." Even bending to tie his shoes upstairs had been a rash act, swelling his skull to bursting with reminders of excess. "You wouldn't have a couple of aspirins?" he inquired sheepishly, and she flashed him an understanding, almost teasing glance before producing two white tablets and a tall glass of water, which he downed with a sigh of gratitude.

He sat down at the wooden table and watched her prepare a small tray with coffee and a generous slice of fruit-filled bun. *"Kolatchi,"* she identified it. "For *babička.* She won't admit it, but she loves having coffee and *kolatchi* in bed, if ever I can beat her to the kitchen. I will be only a moment." She climbed up the stairs, and Alex heard Yolanda's cheerful greeting and Anna's chiding tones before the door shut.

It would be hard for Yolanda...leaving Votice, leaving Anna, Alex mused. He hadn't considered her feelings much before. Now, watching this little ritual, he remembered the radiant warmth, the generosity and family feeling the villagers had generated at the wedding celebration. Uneasily Alex thought of his own casual family in Victoria. They undoubtedly cared about one another, but the demands of modern living left little time for family socializing. Yolanda would miss all this closeness.

Well, it was a vastly different culture, and she would have to learn to adapt. Still, he felt a tender sympathy stir within him; then he reminded himself sternly that it was her choice to come to Canada.

Yolanda was back quickly, and without asking, set about boiling him eggs, setting out peach preserves, toasted chunks of golden-crusted peasant bread and cherry-filled *kolatchi* atop a snowy linen cloth she spread over the table. She was careful never to meet his eyes, however, and he watched her preparations in silence, thankfully sipping the potent coffee and feeling his head gradually clear.

The kitchen had scrubbed wooden floors, scattered with brightly colored braided rag rugs. The stove Yolanda worked at was ornate, one large flat oval set atop a second, with a row of shiny pots hung above it, an attached reservoir to heat wa-

ter and several roomy baking ovens. Everything gleamed with
cleanliness, but not one modern appliance was in evidence—no
toaster, mixer, electric oven or microwave. He might have
journeyed into a peasant kitchen in a past century.

The walls of the house were at least three feet thick, and
morning sunshine filtered through the several small blue-
curtained windows. Hand-carved brown wooden plates, var-
nished and intricately inlaid with detail were hung on the
whitewashed walls, and near the table were several stern-
looking yellowed photographs in wooden frames. A gray furry
cat purred and wound sinuously around Yolanda's ankles as she
worked, and she spoke to it absently in Slovak.

At last everything was ready. Pouring coffee for herself, and
refilling his, Yolanda sat across from him, aware that he was
inspecting the pictures.

"My father, Josef Belan."

She indicated an imposing young giant in a smart military
uniform, with a swooping handlebar moustache and the burning eyes of a zealot, staring fiercely into the camera's lens.

"He was a handsome man," Alex commented.

Yolanda stared up at the photo, her full lips pressed into a
tight line. "He was a fool," she stated flatly, contemptuously.
"He was a supporter of Alexander Dubček, and because he
never learned to compromise, he died in a silly, useless up-
rising when I was twelve. Within a year my mother caught in-
fluenza and she also died. Of course you know the story of
Dubček and our liberation?" The sarcasm underlining the
word was unmistakable.

Alex remembered well, but he wanted her to go on talking to
him in this unself-conscious way. Her voice was passionate,
with that beguiling break coming unexpectedly every now and
then. The kitchen was a comforting place to be. The aspirin had
dulled his headache; the coffee was strong.

"Tell me, anyway," he demanded, watching curiously as she
neatly arranged her breakfast before her, adding cream to her
cup, breaking the toast into tidy chunks, deftly cutting the top
off an egg.

"Alexander Dubček was elected first secretary by the
Czechoslovak Communist Party in January, 1968," she recited like a good student. "He tried to combine Communist

ideology with democratic rights. For eight months, there was an open window to the West." Yolanda kept her recital dispassionate, concentrating on her food and trying to avoid eye contact with the man whose knees grazed her own disconcertingly beneath the small table.

"Then, in August, Russian tanks rolled into Prague." Her eyes flew to her father's photograph, remembering the last time she'd seen him, her mother weeping hysterically, the quiet determination he'd radiated that fateful morning, and again she felt the anger inside her that always flared when she remembered him. His had been such a pathetic, useless sacrifice.

Hadn't he considered his family, his gentle wife, his daughter? Why hadn't he put them first? Weren't they important to him; wasn't she, Yolanda, important to him? She subdued the old pain, controlling her voice.

"My father was there—he'd gone to school with Dubček. Regrettably he died in the liberation, but Dubček lived. We, the people of Czechoslovakia, benefited. We were set free by the Russian army. Fortunate, yes?"

The slight catch in her voice, the irony of her tone, were all that stamped the words with bitterness and changed their surface meaning. "It was too bad my father chose to die in such a misguided manner, because as his daughter, I am suspect, and will always be under this regime."

He glanced keenly at her, and then busied himself with his breakfast.

She made her features impassive, as she'd learned to do over the years, had to learn in order to survive. Inside, emotions boiled and surged, frustration and anger churning through her. With the kaleidoscope of bitterness a new flicker of hope stirred, as well. Perhaps she could learn to forget. In the new country, perhaps she could stop remembering.

This morning was different, she reminded herself. The past was the same, and its effect on her. The cottage, the village, her homeland, Czechoslovakia, were just the way they'd always been. Her eyes ventured past the curtains at the window, seeing the small carefully tilled field where she and Anna had planted potatoes and turnips.

The difference this morning was that before it was time to harvest, she would be gone. She would be in Canada. For so long, she hadn't dared even to dream, despite the determination and confidence of her Aunt Sophia. It was ironic that now, with the dream becoming reality, she was a hundred, no a thousand times more frightened than ever before. She was afraid of going to Canada with this disturbing man.

What did she really know about his country, or him? All of Aunt Sophie's attempts to describe Alex had fallen far short of reality. Yolanda could only suspect her information about Canada would be just as inadequate. What kind of country could produce a man like Alex?

Yet some things between men and women were universal. Her gaze lifted shyly to him, busy with his egg and toast. Her mind vividly replayed the moment when she'd awakened to find him loving her, and a hot awareness curled through her body.

Those long-fingered hands, occupied now with deftly knocking the end from his egg, had touched her, stroked her expertly, tenderly. She studied his heavy eyebrows, the way they tufted up at the ends, the definite bump where his nose had been broken, the way his mouth and eyes had tiny wrinkles at the corners. Worry? Humor?

He glanced up and caught her staring and quickly lowered one eyelid at her in a teasing wink, so her embarrassment became a smile.

Babička had been right after all; there was now a tenuous bond between them. He no longer seemed as remote and unknowable to Yolanda. He'd pressed himself into her urgently, wetly, needing her terribly. They had shared intimacy, and with that sharing barriers had crumbled. It was possible this morning to ask questions about his country, his life, his job, which she had been much too shy to ask yesterday. Hesitantly she began to question him.

"Please, I know you're a politician; could you explain for me your system of government?" she asked tentatively. And, for the next hour, the night's intimacies, the awkwardness of their situation, even the tiny kitchen was forgotten as two minds and cultures exchanged ideas. She forgot her shyness, intrigued and stimulated by his concise and seemingly open responses to her ten million questions, each couched in careful textbook English, answered in his deep-timbred Canadian accent.

Several times his laugh rang out full and pleasantly masculine when some remark she had made amused him, and she found herself waiting for those responses, intrigued by the warmth that kindled in his amber-flecked eyes.

She already knew much about his life, thanks to Aunt Sophie. She wondered if he realized that fact, if he would be angry to learn that Sophie gossiped fondly about him in her letters.

Regardless, it was enthralling to have him tell her himself, give life to the sterile truths she knew about him.

"My grandfather was a lumberjack," he explained at one point. "Grandpa had dreams of his own timber company, and he started small, but he succeeded. He named the firm Western Forest Industries, and by the time Barney and Dad were adults, the whole thing had become big business. Timber is one of B.C.'s major resources, along with mining and fishing. Like everything else, you don't just go out and cut trees anymore and sell them. It's much more complicated than that."

Yolanda sat, her chin cupped in her palms, nodding when a response was required. She noticed the timbre of his voice, the way a slight frown came and went between his heavy eyebrows.

"Barney became involved first with international sales, and that led to setting up pulp and paper plants in other countries. Dad still manages the company from offices in Vancouver and Victoria, but the whole operation has become pretty sophisticated." His gaze turned to the window, but Yolanda could see he was looking inward.

"And you, Alex? What is your profession?" Aunt Sophia had said only that he worked for the provincial government in British Columbia.

His name came easily to her lips this morning, and he responded with a half grin, again enjoying the way she'd posed her question.

"I was sent to university to study forestry and ended up with a degree in trade and commerce instead, and an avid interest in politics. I'm an international lumber buyer by profession, appointed by the deputy minister of International Trade and Investment in B.C., as an advisor to the department. Although my title is assistant deputy minister, I'm not an elected representative. It's an appointed position."

She knew about such positions and the underhanded benefits they provided. A wave of disappointment overwhelmed her. She had so wanted him to be that rarest of specimens, an honorable man. But she should have known that politics and the resultant payoffs were universal. West and East were similar that way, obviously. Bile rose in her throat, and her next words were harsher than she'd meant them to sound.

"Such a position must greatly benefit your family business." The sarcasm was obvious, and to her amazement, he threw back his head and laughed heartily.

"You sound exactly like one of our backbench politicians who regularly accuse the entire cabinet of pork-barreling." Her totally confused expression also amused him, and he explained, "Pork-barreling is using a position to further one's own interests. It's a shoddy practice, not unheard of in Western politics, but fatal to the politician caught red-handed. Because of my family's business, I'm extremely careful never to breach confidentiality or release privileged information. You see, Yolanda," he said, suddenly earnest, "it's not as if I campaigned for office—I simply had expertise in an area helpful to our present government. Curtis Blackstone, the man I work for, is an elected member. He knew of my interest in both timber and trade and asked me to work with him as an assistant deputy minister during his term in office. I'm not an elected politician. In fact, I'm not at all sure I'd want to be. I'm sort of a...well, a hired hand, you might say."

Anna joined them just then, and Alex rose politely to greet her. Anna Belankova's smug delight in the spectacle of Yolanda sitting at ease, talking comfortably with Alex, shone in her faded blue eyes and it was obvious in the grin she shot her granddaughter. "I told you sharing a bed was a good beginning," her triumphant expression seemed to say. A fiery blush burned its way up Yolanda's neck and suffused her face, and she scowled horribly at the smug old woman.

Now it was Alex whose face registered confusion. He knew there was an undercurrent between the women, but the silent communication baffled him.

THEIR DRIVE BACK TO PRAGUE later that morning was more relaxed than Yolanda had anticipated. She'd dreaded spending this time alone with him in the car for fifty kilometers after the tense silence and painful politeness of yesterday's trip, but the lengthy discussion over breakfast had already made it possible to talk to him. He, too, was more at ease, driving with a one-handed ease that both frightened and thrilled Yolanda.

He wore brown cord pants and an open-necked short-sleeved shirt the color of fresh cream. In the strong sunlight she could detect an underlay of silver in his ash-brown hair, but instead of aging him, it simply made the strong planes of his face seem even younger. He was thirty-nine, Sophie had said. She wondered how and when he'd broken his nose, and then swiftly turned her head to the window when he glanced her way.

"The countryside here is magnificent," he commented. "It changes so quickly from flat cultivated fields to these wooded areas. What kind of trees are those? I recognize maple, oak and fir, but what's that?" He pointed at a copse.

She said, "Acacia, and some basswood."

Hilly fields of rich loamy soil, newly planted, were punctuated by wooded glens resplendent with every shade of new spring green. They drove through a tiny hamlet, passing faded red-tiled roofs and crumbling plaster houses. Each yard had a vegetable garden and a stand of poppies, not, as she explained to Alex, for decoration, but to supply the poppy seeds that were ground and used for filling in cakes and buns. The hamlet looked as it must have looked for centuries, and this morning, she saw through his eyes.

Once again in the countryside, Alex said, "It's not unlike British Columbia. We have higher mountains but the same sort of rugged terrain as this. But of course we also have the ocean."

He pulled out to pass a wide wooden cart pulled by two gray horses, and Yolanda shut her eyes. But they were safely past, and he went on talking as though he'd hardly noticed the near-accident, a trace of nostalgia in his voice.

"My family home, Rockwoods, is situated on a grassy knoll overlooking the ocean, outside the city of Victoria. It's quite isolated, with trees sheltering it on three sides and a view of the water on the fourth."

"You . . . you live there, in this house?"

Yolanda was sure that Sophia had told her he lived in an apartment in the city, a short distance from Sophia and Barney. But perhaps she'd gotten it wrong. Aunt Sophia was, unfortunately, inclined to be vague.

"I lived there with my wife and daughter, but after my wife's death, the house has been empty. It's more convenient for me to live in the city," he explained stiffly, and she felt reproved for asking.

He kept his eyes on the road and added, "You knew I was married—" the next word stuck in his throat, and he cleared it before he went on "—before? And that I have a fifteen-year-old daughter, Tracey?"

Yolanda nodded and said softly, "Yes, Aunt Sophia has told me these things."

Alex seemed to need to tell her himself. He continued talking as if she hadn't spoken.

"Dixie and I were married for thirteen years. She died four years ago of an illness nobody suspected she had. She was thirty-one."

He'd stopped believing that he should have known or could have done something to save her. The doctors had emphasized that it was nothing anyone could have prevented or even diagnosed, and finally, he'd accepted their conclusions. Four years had accomplished that, at least.

"We adopted Tracey as a newborn baby. She knows she was adopted, but it's never bothered her. She's not at home much. Her school is in Vancouver, and she often stays there with her maternal grandparents."

What could he say about his difficult daughter? That she'd been suspended from the strict Catholic boarding school last winter for smoking marijuana, and he'd had to practically beg them to take her back? That she'd run away three times? That she made him feel helpless and hopeless and useless as a father? That he was terrified she was heading for a life of ruin, and that he didn't know how to prevent it?

His knuckles were white on the wheel, and he consciously relaxed them as an oxcart plodded over the next hill. He rapidly steered a course around it without diminishing speed, missing Yolanda's wide-eyed gulp and clenched hands at the maneuver.

"Tracey's at camp just now, but you'll probably meet her before the summer's over."

He felt an uncomfortable sense of relief, knowing Tracey was at camp for six weeks.

His attention was on the highway, and again she watched his rugged profile unobserved. He had sideburns trimmed low around well-shaped ears, and the line of his strong jaw was angular and clearly drawn.

"Where will I . . . where can I live in Canada? I mean, where will it be convenient? Of course, later, I will find an apartment if that is possible, but at first . . ." Where she'd live was a problem she'd worried about for weeks.

Alex had discussed that issue thoroughly with Barney. It had been a loud and lengthy discussion, and in the end, Alex had bowed to logic with little grace or hospitality. It had begun to seem as if one concession—agreeing reluctantly to marry Yolanda—had simply led to more and more disruption in his well-ordered existence.

"You'll stay with Barney and Sophia, and then at my apartment. It's better if there's no suspicion about our marriage being anything but legitimate."

Yolanda noticed the sudden aloofness in his tone, and embarrassment twisted her stomach into a fist.

He'd fought the arrangement tooth and nail, but Barney had insisted that until her waiting period for citizenship was over, the facade was necessary.

"We'll help you find a place of your own, of course, as soon as possible." *The very instant it's possible,* he revised mentally, feeling angry with himself all over again, remembering the previous night. Should he reassure her on that score? He needed reassurance himself. What would happen with the two of them living in close proximity at the apartment?

Confusion made him frown. Damn it, what unholy demon had made him act so stupidly? If only they could both forget it had ever happened.

He glanced over at her. She was quietly watching the countryside slip past, the strong lines of her face almost somber. Her profile was arresting, clearly drawn and powerful. Beautiful? Not quite, but definitely attractive, and again he felt the captivating sensuous aura she exuded, and he frowned and looked again at the road.

She really wasn't what he'd expected, not at all. She had an impressive mind, quick and incisive, and she was amusing. She'd never make a fashion model with those clothes, and yet she had an offbeat beauty. Her eyes made him feel as if he could peer into her soul.

They were entering Prague. The afternoon streets were again all but empty of cars, a fact that had astonished Alex when he'd arrived. No rush-hour traffic here. People simply had no money for cars, Yolanda had explained matter-of-factly.

This part of the city, one of Europe's oldest and most historical, looked as though it was slowly slipping into a gray decay. Piles of rubble littered the pavement.

Newer construction seemed invariably to be cement block, utilitarian but absolutely devoid of aesthetic appeal. Even now, in the first June glory of a European summer, the only color discernable in the streets they drove through were the red flowers planted around the prominent and numerous sculptures of the hammer and sickle, with their two doves and inscription.

"What does it say?" Alex asked curiously.

"Thank you for forty years of freedom," Yolanda translated in a flat and uninflected tone. Alex snorted inelegantly, and she shot him a startled look, then she, too, dared to smile at the irony.

An ominous and heavy atmosphere of life reduced to the most functional denominator—work for all, luxury for none—pervaded the somber city, and yet he knew Yolanda had friends here, had made a life for herself and didn't see the bleakness the way he did. He was, after all, comparing this country to his homeland. She had no comparison.

At her instruction, he stopped the car in front of her apartment in an older, despairingly down-at-the-heels area, where grayness lay like a leaden skin over the littered streets and the crumbling stone. He was now pressed for time—he had appointments Barney had deemed urgent with the Canadian engineers employed by his family's company. Yet strangely, he was reluctant to drop Yolanda there and disappear, even for the three days before their flight to Canada.

As a precaution he'd given her the plane ticket, duplicates of the documents in triplicate translated by Berlitz identifying him by birth, marriage, job, age, character, income. There were copies of everything he'd had to submit to the police: the wedding license, the documents identifying her as Mrs. Alexander Caine—her life, her hope, her future, all contained in a large brown manila envelope.

"No need to come in with me," she insisted. He'd seen her apartment the day she brought him there after meeting him at the airport. It was cramped—an eight by ten foot galley kitchen with a tiny fridge and gas stove, a modest living room, and the smallest bathroom he'd ever been in. The miniscule sink was perched over the equally tiny tub. The plumbing was rusted tin.

The amazing thing was the hominess she'd somehow created: the cheap, colorful pictures carefully tacked to the walls, the green plants, many in bloom, flourishing everywhere, the gaily embroidered pillows and bright curtains over windows hiding a dismal view of a children's muddy playground.

"Please," she'd said to him, "be at home."

And the strangest thing had happened. He'd relaxed. She had the ability to put people totally at ease.

But now he wanted to be on his way, wanted time away from her to think over the events of the past day and night.

At the last moment, as she slid out of the car, he took a thick roll of dollars from his eelskin wallet and pressed them into her hand. When she shook her head in proud dismay, trying to hand them back, he insisted, "Use this money to buy something for Anna, at the Tuzex store you pointed out to me."

She'd shown him the government-operated wonderland of a store where, with this magical Western currency, one could purchase vouchers that would buy almost any necessity or luxury.

"What sort of things?" he'd asked curiously, and she'd shrugged.

"Almost anything, a hot-water tank, soup, soap, a summer cottage," she'd elaborated. "It's an effort on the part of the government to attract valuable foreign dollars into the country."

She'd shrugged again with fatalistic acceptance and added, "Of course, the ordinary citizen never has dollars and never goes there."

He firmly opened her clenched fingers and closed them again over the money insistently. "Buy Anna something from both of us, please," he pleaded. It was the "both of us" that surprised her into keeping the roll of bills. *Both of us* sounded so... married.

Then he hurriedly shook her hand. She had strong, slender hands, he noticed. He climbed into the Skoda, impatiently forcing it into life. "Goodbye," he called, and she stepped back as the car began to move.

"Good luck," he said quietly, watching her tall, sturdy figure grow smaller in the rearview mirror, alone on a side street in the afternoon sunshine.

He wished fervently that the Skoda had a radio, for he needed something to distract him from the confusion of his thoughts.

Yolanda. He didn't want this depth of compassion for her, this awareness of her as a woman.

He braked to let a chain of hand-holding kindergarten children cross the street. All of them were in uniform, red sweaters and blue pants, with serious little faces, and he pictured Tracey as she had been at that age. He fervently wished she still was a sunny child in kindergarten. It was infinitely preferable to the intractable, sullen girl she had become.

"Thank you for our freedom."

Another inscription flashed boldly past on yet another monument, and Alex found himself also wondering again how being introduced to real freedom in the days and weeks ahead would affect the woman he'd married yesterday.

Would Yolanda feel just as alien in Canada as he felt here?

TWO DAYS LATER, Yolanda lined up at midmorning to catch the bus for Votice, attracting curious stares from the few old people and children also waiting to board, partly because of the heavy box she carried but mostly because it was a workday and it was unusual for a young woman to be away from her place of employment. The prickling uneasiness, the nameless anxiety of going against the system, of doing something to draw attention to herself made her sit uncomfortably tense, staring out the window. She avoided meeting anyone's eyes. The bus left the city behind.

In Votice, Yolanda climbed carefully down the high step of the bus, balancing her box. Her arms ached by the time she reached the lane to the cottage, but her heart leaped with the joy of coming home. Today was the last time she would walk up the lane this way, but she wouldn't think of that.

Anna was on her knees in the garden, weeding the rows of budding cabbages.

"*Babička*," Yolanda called impulsively from far up the lane. Anna raised her head, and she wiped her hands on the grubby apron covering her skirt. Stiffly, she slowly got to her feet, still rubbing her hands up and down to cleanse them, then waved eagerly to Yolanda and hurried to meet her, her stride vigorous and forceful.

Anna's face was tanned almost mahogany, making the blueness of her eyes, the faded echo of Yolanda's sapphire, youthful and vivid amidst the wrinkles.

Yolanda set the box down in the grass and wrapped her arms tightly around Anna, smelling the musty, sun-scented hair, the slight odor of mothballs and strong soap that always clung to the old woman.

"So, you've come, have you? I thought you'd come today. And what do you have there?" Anna asked briskly, leading the way to the open door of the cottage, shooing away the gray cat weaving itself around her ankles. "About time, too. I was beginning to believe you'd grown so fond of that new husband that you'd forgotten your old grandmother. What is that there in the box, Landa? So it's tomorrow you go, child. Is your clothing all washed? Did you do as I told you and pack your winter underwear? Sophia has told me this Canada is wet and cold. You know how you take a chill, Landa."

She busied herself at the stove, adding meager bits of coal to boil the water for tea and stirring the thick soup she'd started that morning—Yolanda's favorite. She kept her back carefully turned to Yolanda despite the smoke screen of words and tugged a corner of her apron up, surreptitiously wiping her eyes now and again.

Birds trilled outside the open door, and a dog barked somewhere nearby. The kettle bubbled on the stove. Yolanda looked at the peaceful room with eyes that devoured each item she'd always taken for granted, desperately memorizing color, scent, shape, like someone about to be blinded. Why had she never really seen that delicate embroidery *babička* had done on the throw? It must have been years that it had covered the back of the sofa, yet it seemed she saw it for the first time.

"Tomorrow we leave on the plane in the early morning, Grandma. The arrangements are complete. I phoned to Aunt Sophia as she directed. She sent you her dearest love."

"And your husband? Did you also speak with him?"

"Yes, he phoned last night. He will pick me up in the morning to go to the airport." She lifted the box from the floor to a small table.

"He gave me money for the Tuzex store and told me to buy this for you, *babička*."

Proudly Yolanda removed the tiny television and set it up on a small table, grateful that the cottage had been wired for electricity. Even so, she was relieved she'd bought the long extension cord—there was only one plug here.

Anna eyed the set greedily, her tears forgotten for the time being.

"Jenda Durchnakova's daughter has one just like this, so small. I watched it all one evening. Surely, Landa, this man of yours has more money than sense, sending you to buy a television for me," she scolded, but her attention was caught immediately when the set flickered into life showing a group of Russian folk singers. With a pang Yolanda realized what they were singing.

"Co to za veselie?" the song asked. "What kind of gaiety is this?" It was one of the songs that had been sung at her wedding reception, and the words had struck her then as ridiculously inappropriate and ironic. Here they were ludicrous, with the time of parting hanging like a storm cloud over the cottage.

Nevertheless, Anna sat still, totally entranced, for fifteen minutes.

"Well," she said with a sigh when the music ended, "I can't wait to see Jenda Durchnakova's face when she finds out I have one of these." The smug delight in her voice told Yolanda how perfect the gift had been, and she felt a rush of warmth for Alex's kindness.

Anna set out large dishes of soup, a loaf of heavy bread, pastries and a cucumber salad with vinegar and sour cream.

"Babička?"

Anna was spooning up the savory broth, dunking a thick slice of bread to soften it, but still didn't meet Yolanda's eyes directly.

"Afterward, after I am settled with a job in Canada, if I send for you, please, will you come?" Yolanda had hardly touched the food, and now the words tumbled out between them, voicing the request she'd never dared to make during the long time since Sophia's visit, the beginning of the campaign to get Yolanda out.

"You know that older people can leave freely—there are no restrictions like the young encounter," Yolanda added.

Anna sighed dramatically. "Why do young people make things so hard for themselves? New countries are for the young, Landa. What would I do there? I don't even speak the language. Here I have my pension, my home, my cat, my garden." She nodded her head at the television. "Now, even that." She paused to chew, drink steaming tea. "I am Slovak, Landa. No matter what they do to my country, I am Slovak, with, of course, a touch of Gypsy. This is my home, and I will stay here till I die. It's easier that way when one is old."

"But it would be so simple for you to leave. I will send the tickets...I could get us an apartment?" Yolanda heard the note of frantic pleading in her voice and was helpless to contain it.

Anna shook her head slowly. "Landa, no. You know I grew up not far from here, in the high Tatra mountains. Your grandfather, Karel Belan, came there one summer to work at the haying. My father saw he was a strong young man—our family was only five girls—and Karel looked at me more than the others . . . a marriage was arranged." The blue eyes softened with recollection, and Yolanda felt a poignant tenderness for the older woman. The story was a familiar one, related often, yet always fascinating for Yolanda. It was her history, the way she'd come to be.

"My marriage was not unlike yours, dearest. Arranged, but Karel and I learned to be happy together. We had Sophia, then no more babies came for so long. Ten years, before I was pregnant again with your father, my Josef. His birth was hard, and after him I couldn't have more babies. It was a sadness for Karel. He wanted many sons." Her gaze strayed to the portrait of her son on the wall. "How they quarreled, those two. One a farmer, one a dreamer, father and only son. After their arguments Karel would rage at me, say it was my fault, my wild Gypsy blood that made Josef so." Mischief lifted her mouth into a secret grin. "Always, though, he would make up later. He liked me as I was, Gypsy blood and all, your grandfather."

Yolanda sat still, listening intently, knowing Anna was imprinting these verbal memories as a heritage for Yolanda to carry with her to the new land.

"I was always glad Karel died before his son, before the Dubček thing. He couldn't have stood losing his only son, you know. Men are not as strong as women when it comes to such matters, Landa." Anna reached to refill her mug with tea, absently nibbling a pastry oozing apricot jam. "Karel died when your father was still at the university. He wanted his son and daughter to have a better life than him, to have education. Sophia, she had this gift of languages, and she was an easy child. But your father, was he a bonehead!" Anna clicked her tongue, her head tipped to the side. "It was always politics, politics, and he and his father would argue. Poor Josef. And Karel, too. They never understood each other. Now Sophia, she was lucky, always a gentle, happy girl, easygoing. Funny, she was like my own mother, ladylike always. Perhaps a bit scatterbrained. But you, Landa, oi yoi yoi." Blue eyes met blue, and both mouths quirked ruefully.

"Yes, you are like me, I'm afraid. A little wild, a little crazy. Never able to swallow your words." Anna paused, then caught up the thread of her story again.

"Your Aunt Sophia, sweet as she was, still was too fussy when it came to marriage. Truly, I believed she would never marry—she already was in her thirties. Then, after all, she did so well, when those Canadians came. Although she never had children, I was always sorry for that. You know, when she left, she, too, asked me to go with her to Canada, but in those days we believed it would get better here. And afterward when you came to me after your mother died, taking you out would have been hard." Anna shrugged. "Well, it is all for the best. 'The worse, the better.'"

She quoted the widespread slogan automatically, and Yolanda felt the helpless rage she always experienced when she heard it. "The worse, the better," indeed! To her, the words were a confession of helplessness and utter impotence instead of the brave stubborn maxim they purported to be.

"Landa, I want to live the remainder of my days here, be buried close to my Karel and my son, here in my homeland. Not in some strange country far away, with customs I don't even know. The only traveling I will do is maybe back to the valley where I grew up, before I die. Up in the Tatras, where the snow covers the tops of the mountains all year. Then again, maybe not . . . I don't know. I'm getting to be an old woman, you know."

"Yes, *babička*, I know, but only because you tell me often enough." Yolanda smiled, but the usual bantering was hollow today.

They cleared away the food and washed the dishes with hot water from the reservoir on the stove. Each familiar routine became achingly special for Yolanda. Would she ever stoke this fire again, sweep this floor, gaze out this deep-set window at the tiny *vesnice*?

When the afternoon began slipping into evening, Yolanda and Anna sang together the wild Gypsy melodies and the lilting folk songs Anna had taught her. The hours marched so swiftly. Far too soon, they walked up the lane to the wooden bench where the last bus stopped for the trip back to the city. If only the bus would be late, as usual. There must be a million things they'd forgotten to discuss . . .

The bus came wheezing up almost immediately, and Anna's roughened hand trembled suddenly on Yolanda's. She groped in the pocket of her skirt, drew out a small paper-wrapped box tied with string and tucked it into Yolanda's purse. "It's your father's wedding ring; your mother left it for me to give to you." Her tearful voice strengthened suddenly, and her words had a desperate intensity. "Give it to the one you love, and always remember, my darling," she implored, reaching up to cup her granddaughter's face between her rough palms, "Remember always you are not just Slovak or Canadian. You are also one-quarter Gypsy, and for the Gypsy, all the world is home." Her steely control broke then, and her face dissolved into a crumpled mask of tears.

"Go safely, my Landa. Be happy—don't concern yourself over me. I am still a young, strong woman." Anna pulled herself determinedly away from Yolanda's fierce embrace, stepped back and motioned toward the bus where the patient driver waited. "Go, go," she ordered crossly, sniffing back her tears. "I want to show the neighbors the television."

Blindly Yolanda boarded the bus, paid her fare and stumbled into a seat with all her parcels. It became imperative that she watch Anna as the vehicle pulled away. She staggered to her feet, sobbing openly, lurched into the aisle and bent over an irritable middle-aged man reading a paper to watch helplessly through the dusty window as Anna's lonely waving figure, swathed in dark clothing, grew smaller and smaller in the growing dusk.

Then the bus careened around a corner, and Anna and the village were gone. Yolanda collapsed into her seat, and the tears ran unhampered down her face. Despite what Grandma said, this was her home, this place she was leaving. Unbidden, the words of the Czechoslovak national anthem came into her mind.

"Kde domov můj?"

"Where is my home?"

Yolanda understood for the first time why the land of her birth had the only anthem beginning with a question.

CHAPTER FOUR

"THE LARGE WHITE BOATS down there are provincial ferries," Alex explained, raising his voice to be heard over the steady thrumming of the floatplane's motor. The last portion of their interminable journey was in a much smaller craft than the gigantic Lufthansa aircraft that had carried them to Canada, Yolanda thought nervously. She was heartily sick of airplanes, whatever their size.

"The ferries are essential to Vancouver Island, bringing supplies and people back and forth every hour, every day."

What would it be like, living on an island? Yolanda wondered. Alex flashed her a smile before he turned his attention back to the window, the same smile she'd watched for in vain during the long first hours they'd traveled together. It tilted the rather narrow lips up in a crooked line and reached his green eyes, making the amber flecks seem to dance. He was pleased to be nearing his home, she thought.

They were winging their way across the strip of water separating the mainland of British Columbia from its provincial island capital, and Yolanda hesitantly gazed down at the many rugged small islands scattered through the straits, patches of green and violet in the expanse of gray-blue ocean below. She longed for this journey to end, and at the same time, she dreaded it.

The past two days had been an exhausting, stomach-wrenching series of echoing airports, muffled announcements Yolanda couldn't understand, a barrage of hedonistic meals and drinks and solicitous, efficient attention. Who, in her homeland, could ever imagine such opulence, such sophistication? They traveled first-class, and Yolanda watched and listened as Alex competently managed every detail of their journey and sidestepped all her efforts to recapture the warmth they'd seemed to share the day after the wedding. Somewhere during the days he'd spent on business away from her, he'd become an aloof, unapproachable stranger.

Certainly, he was a gentleman, making certain she was warm enough, wasn't hungry or thirsty and that she had stacks of magazines to read. He made sure she understood the route they would follow on the seemingly endless flights, and what landmarks to watch for when the plane landed first in Frankfurt, then briefly in Calgary and finally in Vancouver.

Yet his was a cold, impersonal kind of consideration, and she watched hungrily at first for the smile she remembered from their earlier time together, needing the reassurance of its warmth, wondering anxiously what she could have done to anger him.

Those first hours, he'd never smiled, never even met her eyes. He'd been silent, his lips pressed together grimly, and he'd avoided looking directly at her. He'd pulled sharply away if he happened to touch her, even during the endless night hours on the flight when they rested tensely side by side, neither of them sleeping.

Yolanda resented this reticence in him, this holding back of himself, the cool polite attention offered as if she were a casual stranger he was accompanying. There was none of the closeness they'd shared driving back to Prague that morning. What could be wrong? she wondered. How had she offended him? The unreal hours passed, and Yolanda struggled to maintain her fragile equilibrium.

The fact was that Alex was exerting a steely control over himself. He'd surreptitiously watched her ingenuous response to the comforts every other seasoned traveler took for granted, and how the predictable airline food delighted her as well as the small, unremarkable services that pleased and surprised her.

He was alarmingly conscious of her beside him. Without having to look, he knew exactly how her deep-set eyes widened at takeoff, how the long dark lashes shadowed the high cheekbones and the full pink lips parted slightly in unconscious awe at the strangeness of flying.

She stirred some deep chord in him, and he felt confused. Vulnerable. Damn it all, he had never wanted to feel vulnerable about a woman again, he reminded himself, and ended up feeling angry.

Alex struggled with his emotions, and the tension his body generated filled the small space between him and Yolanda.

Their exit from Prague had filled her with stark, vivid terror. Even now, countless hours and thousands of miles later, Yolanda felt a renewal of the fear she'd experienced as they'd lined up for official inspection of their documents.

She began to shake uncontrollably as the line shortened, and by the time they were ushered into a tiny private office, she was near panic. Her inbred fear of any sort of uniformed official became impossible to control, even though Alex had explained that every one of her papers was in meticulous order.

He'd walked slightly behind her, his flight bag casually over one shoulder, his briefcase firmly gripped in one hand.

Why couldn't he just touch her this once, take her hand in his free one, she thought wildly, heart beating at triple time as she looked at the grim-faced uniformed official who had the power to block her exit even now, at this last second.

Alex seemed to exude an invisible aura of wealth and authority and calm, while she could hardly walk for the trembling in her legs.

What she couldn't know was how careful he was not to reveal his own nervousness as the series of officials suspiciously examined her papers. He had faith in Barney, and Barney had masterminded these details, these pink forms in triplicate, these signed authorizations, this all-important green passport for Yolanda. But the sense of isolation from the outside world that Czechoslovakia inspired in him made him anxious.

Who knew what could go wrong?

Alex felt dampness grow and spread in his armpits beneath the soft blue cotton shirt, and then a wild surge of relief coursed through him as he watched the papers slowly receive officially stamped approval.

Everything was fine. He drew in a huge, relaxing breath. They were free to board their flight.

With every step she expected them to be called back. Finally she whispered to Alex, "That's all? We are free to go?" Her voice as well as her hands were now shaking as if she had palsy.

Alex gave her a cool glance. "Of course," he said casually. "I told you there'd be no problem."

Her feet carried her along while she absorbed his words. He was acting as if she was on a holiday trip, and he was the cultural guide appointed to accompany her.

Somehow, in a blur of conflicting emotion she didn't care to remember, she boarded the plane to freedom.

But the farther she came west, the more she was aware that she was entering unknown territory. The responsibility for adapting was hers alone, and she'd never been more frightened or felt more insecure.

Frankfurt was busy confusion. An indefinable lighthearted aura pervaded even the airport. Soon they were back on the plane for the longest leg of the journey.

Half a globe and endless hours later, they landed in Calgary.

"You must deplane," the friendly stewardess announced, "and wait in the area provided for international passengers, as you will be clearing customs in Vancouver."

The area was clean, new-smelling, sterile and cold. Outside the windows there were no trees. Everything was flat and arid, and beyond the airport runways rows of identical houses lined up like soldiers on parade with nothing to alleviate the tedium of the horizon. Disappointment surged inside Yolanda, and her spirits sank as she walked slowly from window to window. The day was overcast and dull.

"What do you think of Canada?" Alex queried impersonally.

"There is not much here, is there?" she finally said weakly.

Everything, even the rest room Alex directed her to was different, totally alien, neatly confirming her feeling that she was absolutely stupid and gauche.

How could he, this foreigner, understand that she mourned the loss of her green homeland, of all that was dear and familiar, even as she welcomed the opportunity to escape?

How could he know that she hadn't been able to find the ridiculous button hidden on the floor in the bathroom, the button that flushed the toilet, and she'd been forced to ask a motherly woman with blue hair, who'd then acted as if Yolanda were mentally deficient, taking her by the hand with awful, stupid patience and making her push the button several times?

This indignity, plus Alex's coldness suddenly became too much to bear. She longed desperately for a warm glance, a friendly touch, a word to indicate he knew how she felt, some sign to show her he sympathized. It became more and more important to her with every step she took into this strange country that he accord her some human recognition, a response beyond the duty he performed.

Shaken, she returned to the waiting room and quietly sat down in a chair beside him. He was engrossed in a newspaper.

Her nerves, her confidence in herself, were shattered. She started to weep noisily, floods of burning tears pouring down her cheeks in a torrent she couldn't control, and she was much too miserable to even notice the electrifying effect it had on her companion.

"What the hell? Yolanda, what's wrong? What's happened?"

Feminine tears had always terrified Alex. There had been times in the distant past when he'd suspected Dixie had used them to her advantage, but his reaction never varied. Women crying made him feel responsible, ineffectual. This torrent of tears coming as it did from Yolanda, a woman whom he saw as being incredibly strong and stalwart, reduced him to a state approaching panic.

"Don't cry, Yolanda, for God's sake, don't cry."

The trace of impatience in his tone masked his alarm. She heard it, misunderstood and sobbed harder. Then she got up, stumbled, hardly caring if she fell, knowing only that the tears were uncontrollable, and she must get away from him.

What am I going to do with her? Alex wondered frantically. He took her arm and guided her back to a seat. People were looking sympathetically toward them, and Alex scowled viciously at a heavy man a few feet away who insisted on staring. The man flushed and looked away.

Alex groped in his jacket for tissues, clumsily mopped her satiny tanned skin free of tears, aware of its texture against the roughened tips of his fingers, its poreless natural beauty. He held her chin with two fingers, tipping her face up to his rough ministrations.

"Can you tell me what's wrong?"

Her eyes were brimming, seeming to swallow her other features with their mute expression of primitive hurt. A desperate appeal for human comfort, for tenderness, signaled nakedly in their depths.

He met that gaze with his own, and he couldn't stand it.

"Landa, honey, please don't cry like that." With a deep groan, Alex gathered her close against his chest, the way he'd held his tiny daughter years ago when she hurt herself, when she still turned instinctively to him for comfort.

Yolanda collapsed in an orgy of weeping then, at the endearment, the affectionate shortened version of her name that *babička* had always used, and at the senseless desire to have him go on holding her forever.

He rocked her back and forth, ignoring the onlookers, mumbling meaningless phrases and holding her tightly against him, and he remembered clearly the other time he'd held her, in the dreamy gray dawn in that village far away. The memory stirred feelings that were anything but fatherly, and Yolanda felt him shudder before he drew abruptly away from her.

But this time, the quizzical smile he gave her was warm, driving out some of the cold loneliness in her heart.

"Stay right here, and I'll bring you coffee. And don't cry anymore; I'm flat out of tissues."

The command was gentle, and she sniffed and nodded. She'd stay anywhere, if only he went on talking to her in that gruff, caring way.

A final bumbling swipe at her face with a sodden Kleenex, and he'd hurried off, his tall form disappearing in the wasteland of plastic and chrome and disembodied announcements.

What if he never returned? New panic threatened to overwhelm her for an instant.

But already Yolanda knew that Alex kept the promises he made, and in a few minutes she saw him slowly coming toward her, balancing plastic cups in his large hand, with pastries in the other. After that, Yolanda's desperation had eased.

Now, as this final segment of the journey drew to a close, the plane made a swooping circle above the crowded inner harbor of Victoria, bumped hard, then glided to a smooth, watery landing. Alex half turned to her.

"Welcome home, Landa," he said in the sudden quiet as the motor died. "I see the family is all on the wharf, waiting to greet you."

As she clambered, awkward and suddenly bashful, onto the floating walkway, Yolanda found herself enveloped in the arms of a joyously weeping Sophia, whose gauzy peach dress and firmly plump body sent wafts of lavender up Yolanda's nostrils. Next, she was nearly smothered by the rib-cracking bear hugs of an exuberantly triumphant Barney and hugged by a quietly elated Robert. Both men smelled of fresh sea air, pipe tobacco and spicy after-shave, and both had suspiciously wet cheeks against her own. *They cared,* she thought dazedly. Openly, they were showing her they cared. How big these men were, how reassuring, how welcoming.

"Hi, darlin', glad you got here safely," said Uncle Barney.

"Hello, Yolanda, great to meet you, welcome to Canada," said Robert, Alex's father, so much like Alex, so handsome...

"Darling, I'm delighted you're here at last. How was the...Barney, where are the flowers? Where did I...Alex, dear, over there, I laid them on the bench. I got so excited when I saw the plane. Oh, Alex, thank you for bringing her. My dearest Yolanda, I can hardly believe you've come. I couldn't sleep last night...I was so...oh, dear, do let's go home, Barney. The poor child's probably..."

Everyone seemed to be talking at once, asking and answering questions, the older men avidly pumping Alex for every official detail, Sophia's gentle voice twittering, filling the pauses in conversation as she patted her eyes with a tiny lace-trimmed handkerchief and slid one braceleted arm around her niece.

Somehow, the delicate bouquet of baby's breath and miniature pink and golden roses was retrieved and presented to Yolanda, who buried her nose in it and fought back tears of her own. The cornflowers and daisies had been blooming at *babička*'s cottage too, only three days ago.

With a sense of unreality Yolanda raised her head and slowly looked around, allowing the sights and sounds and smells of this new country to penetrate her senses. Her first blurred impression had been of color, of carefully groomed lushness, and next, the smell of sea air.

The protected harbor was in the heart of the city, full of brightly colored yachts and bobbing float planes. Sidewalks were dotted with ornate lamp standards. From the lamps hung chained baskets of variegated flowers spilling lavishly out of pristine white pots. There was color everywhere.

Was it a holiday? Everything looked so festive. Everywhere she looked, there were people, carefree, chattering, arm in arm. The couples strolling by looked relaxed, happy, beautifully and expensively dressed. Young people in casual blue jeans and T-shirts lounged on a nearby lawn. In the near distance rose a towering ancient gray castle with turrets and graceful lines, and many windows twinkling in the warm afternoon sunshine.

"Our Provincial Parliament Buildings," Sophia explained proudly.

Overhead, sea gulls swooped and cried, their raucous voices joining the swelling chorus of traffic noise, voices, music, and the gentle undertone of the waves slapping against the cement abutments.

"The car's parked over this way, come, dearest Landa," her aunt beckoned.

Yolanda walked with Sophie as if in a dream. The entire city had a gay, holiday feeling, a character so lighthearted that she could hardly begin to absorb its significance.

Happy. This place seemed happy. Could a city exude an emotion?

Yolanda slowed, stopped and turned in a full circle, her hands clasping the flowers Sophia had given her, and Alex, glancing at her from where he stood flanked by his father and uncle, noted the bedazzled look in her wide blue eyes.

He, too, reexamined the lighthearted landscape he'd always taken for granted. Remembering Prague, he knew exactly why Yolanda looked bewildered, and he wanted to reach out to her, touch her arm and whisper, "I understand."

But he couldn't. His rescue mission was over, and it was time to let the others assume responsibility for her. So why didn't he feel more relieved?

The group loaded into a silver-gray car, with Barney at the wheel, Alex beside him, and Yolanda nestled protectively in the back between Robert and Sophia.

Barney pulled the car into traffic with the flourish of a man who loves good machinery, and Alex quietly asked his uncle, "Have you heard how Tracey's doing at camp?"

Barney glanced sympathetically at his nephew and sighed.

"She's not at camp, Alex. She's back at the apartment, waiting for us. She didn't want to come along, and I thought it was better not to make a scene."

Alex cursed softly. "What the hell happened? I paid a King's ransom to send her to that place. What'd she do this time?"

Barney deftly maneuvered the big car through afternoon traffic, and under the excited mixture of Sophie's Slovak and English, he explained, "We got a call from the police. Seems Tracey and another girl took off in the dead of night from that camp, and the cops picked them up trying to hitch a ride into Vancouver. I went down and got her, phoned the camp counselor and straightened it all out." He glanced over at his nephew. "Don't be too tough on her, Alex. She's just a kid. There's no real harm done."

Alex shuddered. Thank God there was no real harm. Fifteen, female, hitchhiking at night. His daughter. Dixie's daughter. Where had they gone wrong? And what was he going to do with her for the next three weeks? He had to attend that conference in London, which meant leaving here no later than Tuesday. He glanced down at the date on the gold watch on his wrist. Three days from now. He'd figured that at least the problem of what to do with Tracey's summer was taken care of. Camp Kelsey had assured him that the "young ladies" they accepted had a wonderful time for two full months. His head ached, and he rubbed a weary hand across the back of his neck.

Yolanda noticed the gesture as she allowed Sophia's voice to wash over her, childishly grateful for her aunt's soft small hand firmly clasping her own, and for Robert's protective arm extended like a benediction across the seat behind her. Somehow these two instinctively guessed how much she needed their physical assurance, and both gave it freely. Perversely, it was Alex's arm Yolanda longed to have resting behind her. What new phase would their strange relationship enter now?

They pulled into the underground parking area of a modern hotel apartment, and within minutes Yolanda found herself whisked to the twenty-fourth floor, down a silent corridor, and into Barney and Sophie's home, the first Western home she'd ever seen.

Its opulence intimidated her. Everything looked new, and luxuriously appointed. She sat gingerly on the patterned brown velvet sofa, nervous about even walking on the thick ginger pile of the rug that stretched throughout the entire area. One entire window wall afforded a magnificent view of the ocean, with a balcony where glass topped tables and brightly flowered lawn chairs shared space with tubs of scarlet geraniums.

Yolanda glanced toward the hallway where the bedrooms must be, and her eyes met the frankly hostile glare of a gray-eyed girl, hovering in the doorway. Before Yolanda could do more than smile hesitantly at the slender blue-jeaned figure whose long braid of auburn hair hung over one shoulder, Alex entered and distracted the girl.

"Tracey, come here," he ordered sternly, motioning her fully into the sun-drenched room. Tracey squared her shoulders resentfully, and her heavily lipsticked mouth pulled into a petulant pout as she slowly came to stand before her father. He slid his hands to his hips, pushing back his sports jacket in a vaguely belligerent fashion, narrowing his eyes. The girl crossed her arms over her chest protectively.

"Tracey, I'd like you to meet Yolanda. As I explained before I left, Yolanda is, um—" he hesitated, clearing his throat "—Yolanda and I are married," he concluded.

"Yolanda, this is my daughter, Tracey." He made the introduction without taking his eyes from the girl, an unspoken warning evident in his expression.

Yolanda stood up uncertainly, smiling and extending her hand. Tracey ignored her.

"You told me it wasn't for real, Daddy. So she's not my stepmother, is she?" The young voice was husky and belligerent, with nasty inflections on key words.

Alex moved a threatening half step toward her, but the girl stood her ground, her chin jutted out stubbornly.

"Tracey." Her father's voice was low and steely. "You're already in a good deal of trouble, young lady. I'd suggest you remember your manners before I forget mine. We're going to have a talk about this camp business right after dinner. Now, I expect you to be polite."

He held her eyes with his furious gaze, and after a second of consideration, Tracey relented.

"Sorry," she mumbled. "How'd ya do." The words were aimed generally in Yolanda's direction. The narrow shoulders sagged.

"I am happy to meet you, Tracey," Yolanda lied, eyeing the girl warily. She was profoundly shocked at Tracey's rudeness. She'd never met any young person the least bit like Tracey. She'd expected a shy child, hovering uncertainly on the brink of adulthood, as Yolanda herself had been at fifteen—polite, serious, keeping her true feelings secret. This girl was of another species entirely. This one was *trâpeni*—big trouble.

"Come now, Tracey, help your old auntie with the food," Sophie said gently, and the tension was dissipated when she took Tracey's hand and led her off to the kitchen. But Yolanda saw the resentful glare the young girl shot at her as she passed, and she felt the palpable hostility surround her like glacial air. She shuddered.

Alex had turned his back to the room, staring out the window, his shoulders slumped.

"C'mon, Alex, sit down here and have a beer," Barney invited, sidling into the room with a tray full of bottles and mugs. Robert followed and brought Yolanda a tall cool glass with a slice of lime in its lip. Sitting down beside her, he gave her a warm smile and a pat on her arm.

"You're probably exhausted, my dear. You're going to need a couple of weeks just to get used to being here. Don't worry if everything seems strange at first," he remarked quietly to her. "Try to relax. We want you to feel at home, look around, take the time to get to know us all." He sipped his beer, and Yolanda smiled at him.

"I am very grateful to you. There is no way for me to thank you for what you have done." Yolanda fervently wished the words didn't sound so stilted and formal, because every syllable came from her heart.

Warmth began to replace the strangeness of everything when he gave her a mischievous grin and a half bow, and said, "Believe me, it was our pleasure. Old men like Barney and me don't get the chance to rescue beautiful young damsels often." She flushed, pleased at the courtly compliment.

Barney, talking quietly with Alex, overheard the comment and warned Yolanda loudly, "Honey, you watch that old silver-tongued devil beside you. He's always been a rogue with the ladies."

The good-natured, affectionate joshing that followed was fascinating to Yolanda. Even though whole phrases escaped her at times—her command of formal English might be excellent, but she was fast realizing there were many idiomatic words and phrases she missed—there was no mistaking the warmth between these giants. Barney, Robert, Alex: these men seemed larger than life, with hearts to match.

Before his death, her father had been away a great deal, although she could vividly recall the excitement that had flooded over her whenever he'd come home unexpectedly. She had still believed, then, that she and her quiet, gentle mother were foremost in his life. How stupid she'd been!

After her parents died and she had gone to live with *babička*, the household was feminine. She knew only the farming men of Votice until she went off to university. She'd never known men such as these, men who seemed to fill a room with their presence, men who laughed with great good humor, who teased each other, whose kindness glowed from mischievous eyes.

No wonder Alex had that air of power and authority, possessed as he was of such a big-boned muscular frame, such a strong, handsome face. He'd inherited his green eyes from Robert, she noticed.

However, there was an intensity, an undercurrent of sadness in Alex that was missing in the older men, and each time his daughter sullenly passed the trays of delicious hors d'ouevres Sophie had prepared, Yolanda noticed that he watched Tracey, his brows knitted into an unconscious frown.

He didn't smile as easily as either Barney or Robert. Barney was vocal, big and blustering, balding on top, with dark, twinkling eyes that nearly disappeared in a network of wrinkles when he laughed, which was often. Robert was quieter, more distinguished, his mane of silver hair becomingly long on his neck and above his ears.

Sophie buzzed in and out of the room, unable to contain her delight at Yolanda's presence.

"Alex, somebody wants you on the phone," she announced now. "Take it in the study. Tracey, go hang up the kitchen extension."

Delicious smells had been emanating from the kitchen, which she wouldn't allow Yolanda to enter, and Sophie stood in the doorway, her face flushed rosy pink, a frilly organdy apron over her dress.

Her aunt was lovely, Yolanda decided. It had been four years since Sophie's last trip to Czechoslovakia, yet she seemed to have aged hardly at all. Petite, with hair like dandelion fluff, she had blue eyes that were several shades lighter than Yolanda's, and her skin was delicate, her dainty hands well tended.

Now, she gestured to her niece, and ordered the men around like a diminutive general. "Yolanda, darling, there's just time to freshen up before we eat, if you want. Barney, come and carve this roast. And Robert, would you see to the wine? Tracey, show Yolanda where the guest bedroom is. I had Alex put her suitcase in there."

Tracey, her back stiff and shoulders swinging defiantly, led the way down a long central hallway to a lilac bedroom with a deeper lilac rug, a tilting white-framed mirror, puffy lace-edged duvet and matching frilly pillow covers. Yolanda's eyes roved over the room, astonished at such lushness, such decadent comfort. Her gaze fell on her own reflection in the mirror. Her blue suit was creased and she looked rumpled. There was a small stain on the white blouse. Her hair was beginning to escape from its chignon. The shoes that she'd thought smart in Prague looked chunky and clumsy here.

She looked foreign, as if she didn't belong in such a luxurious setting. Obviously Tracey agreed. The girl stood behind her, and Yolanda read the contemptuous expression in Tracey's hard gray gaze.

Sauntering over to a closet, Tracey threw open the folding wooden doors with rather more force than was necessary.

"You can hang your clothes in here, I moved all mine out. It doesn't look as if you've got many, anyhow," she spat out venomously. Her eyes were hard as gray agates, holding Yolanda's stunned gaze without flinching. "You managed to trick my father into marrying you—you might as well have my bedroom, as well."

CHAPTER FIVE

YOLANDA STARED SPEECHLESSLY at the angry girl for several moments, and the harsh words echoed between them. Yolanda felt astonished, hurt and defensive at the unprovoked attack. Most of all, she was uncertain how to respond to this kitten with fangs.

"This, this is your room?" Yolanda asked as she crossed the room to Tracey's side, and impulsively put a hand on the girl's shoulder.

"Please, Tracey, I have no wish to take your bedroom. I will tell Sophia—"

Tracey jerked away, crossed her arms over her thin chest and turned her back. Yolanda recognized the action; Alex had done exactly the same thing in the living room, not an hour ago.

Watching the girl, Yolanda was at a loss. Was this brat of a Western teenager as tough as she seemed, or was her behavior simply the cocky bravado of a lonely child? Yolanda studied the tense back, the narrow, childish hips in the tight jeans. The last thing she wanted was to cause a rift between Alex and his daughter, she thought wearily.

"Tracey," Yolanda started hesitantly, "what you said about the marriage of your father and me."

"I," Tracey corrected condescendingly. "Your English isn't very good, is it?"

Yolanda subdued her irritation. "The marriage of your father and I. There was no trick, as you call it. It was a kind gesture on your father's part, and you must know, as he told you, it was a formality only." A wrenching knot of sadness twisted her insides at the admission. Relentlessly she made herself continue.

"As you said, I am not really your stepmother. Your father, your uncles, they are such kind men; they have made it possible for me to come here to your so beautiful country. And dear Aunt Sophia. But it would be..." Yolanda paused, lost for words for a second, intimidated by the girl's stance. Was Tracey even listening? After taking a deep breath, she began once more, the difficult words tumbling over themselves this time in an effort to make her listener understand.

"There is no reason for you to like me, of course. I think it's a big mistake for me to take this room which is yours, most...unfair." Yolanda's tired brain groped for the proper words. "Just as it would be a big mistake for you to think I want to divide your father from you. I did not come here to make trouble for anyone. You understand, Tracey?"

The stiffness of the girl's shoulders held for another long moment, and dejectedly Yolanda decided she had failed. But then Tracey turned. The serious gray eyes met Yolanda's blue ones with less hostility.

"What should I call you, then? I can't go around saying Mrs. Caine—that was my mother. And I can't say 'hey, you,' can I?" The resentment was still plain, but there was less anger now. The question was guarded, testing.

"If you are Tracey, then I am just Yolanda, of course." Yolanda knelt and flipped open the top of her suitcase. "In here, somewhere, I have small gift for you if you will accept...." She finally unearthed a box, carefully wrapped in tissue paper, and held it out to Tracey with a smile and inner misgivings. It seemed like blatant bribery, yet she didn't know what else to do.

Would the girl like it? Would she even accept it? The gift suddenly seemed pathetically insignificant when viewed beside the opulence of this apartment.

Tracey hesitated only a moment before stiffly accepting the box and unwrapping it with her narrow hands. The girls nails were bitten almost to the quick.

The wrapping fell away. Inside was a blouse, fine white cotton, covered with delicate hand-stitched embroidery. The garment was an ornate peasant style, with red, blue, yellow and green intricate patterns worked round the neck, and red trim on the three-quarter sleeves.

Tracey was still child enough to be delighted with a gift. She drew the garment out, and at last her mouth curved into a spontaneous, sweet smile. "Hey, it's sort of funky. Peasant is in right now, too."

Yolanda drew a relieved breath and smiled back, explaining, "*Babička*, my grandmother, she made this for you. The pattern of the design is supposed to bring the wearer good luck—it is Gypsy custom."

"Gypsies? Is your grandma a Gypsy?" Tracey's tone was eager now, curious. "Aunt Sophia never told me that."

"Not full Gypsy, you understand. Only half. It was *babička*'s mother who had full Gypsy blood. So *babička* has half, Sophia—what? One-quarter, and me, only one-eighth, isn't that correct?"

Yolanda's voice was even, but she felt close to tears. It hurt unbearably to speak of Anna and to fully realize how far away she was. "As long as you wear this blouse, no harm can come to you, Tracey."

She made an attempt at lightheartedness, and Tracey held the colorful cotton up against herself, preening in the mirror.

"I better put it on, then," the girl said with a drawn-out sigh. "Because my dad is going to kill me for sure, right after dinner." Now Tracey's voice quavered alarmingly.

Yolanda translated silently, and frowned in confusion.

"This is a joke, yes?"

"Uh-uh." Tracey shook her head and slid cross-legged onto the rug, one hand fondling the blouse. "Daddy's raving mad at me because I ran away from that stupid damn camp, and I just know he's probably gonna make me go back." Her clear voice took on a note of desperation. "I'll run away again, first chance I get. I hate it there. They give you makeup lessons, and play stupid games, and show movies everybody saw ages ago, and call one another silly nicknames. I absolutely hate it. I'll . . . I'll kill myself if I have to go back."

She sounded as if she was on the verge of tears. Yolanda abandoned the suitcase. Her clothing could wait. She sat down on a chair, facing Tracey.

"Your father is very understanding," she fibbed hesitantly. Alex lacked a bit in that area, if she was to be truthful. "If you explain how you feel about this camp, then I am certain—"

Tracey shook her head from side to side, making her braid swing. Her chin quivered. "He won't listen," she stated with weary conviction. "I've tried to talk to him before. It's just hopeless."

These sudden confidences were just as hard to handle as Tracey's earlier animosity so Yolanda felt a great surge of relief when Sophia appeared in the doorway, scolding them because dinner was ready and Yolanda wasn't.

Tracey whispered urgently to Yolanda, "Don't say anything about the bedroom; it's fine with me, honest. I'm in the one just down the hall, anyhow. Actually, I like it better. It's no big deal."

From the bathroom Yolanda heard Tracey a moment later saying cheerfully, "Look, Auntie. Your mother made it. The pattern's a gypsy design. Yolanda brought it for me. Neat, eh? How come you never told me about your mother being part Gypsy?"

As she stripped off the tired blue suit and used a terry face-cloth thick and soft as sponge cake to quickly wash, Yolanda marveled at Tracey's mercurial changes in mood. Sunny, stormy, sunny again.

She shook her head at the mirror reflection of her tired face: lavender smudges inked under the glassy blue eyes, clear skin looking sallow under its tan. Such a face would never do for a celebration. Ruthlessly she doused with cold water and rubbed with the terry towel until she'd created a hint of color in her cheeks. The desire for sleep was overwhelming her. If only she could stay awake during dinner.

It was hard, but she kept her smile intact and her eyes wide open during the next several hours, only to find that when at last she lay between the silky, scented sheets in the fairy-tale bedroom, aching with fatigue, she was, ironically, unable to sleep.

Beneath her chaste white cotton nightgown, her skin had trapped the fragrance of the exotic bath oils and powders her thoughtful aunt had given her for the long, blissful soak in the strange blue tub. She smelled like the delicate lily of the valley plant that grew wild on the banks of the stream running through Votice, and the gown still echoed the fresh air and sunshine of her home, half a world away.

But this was Victoria. Canada. North America. A new and different world, with only fragrance to echo the old.

The cool night air blew the window drapes in and out in a peaceful rhythm, and Yolanda's brain replayed the events of the evening, snippets of information about this family she'd joined. Some things still puzzled her.

For instance, it had gradually become obvious that the family's gathering together for dinner was not a frequent event. "We have to do this oftener. It's a damn shame when people get too busy to spend time together," Barney had declared. "Is it that way in Czechoslovakia, Yolanda?" he'd asked, and she'd found herself trying to explain the long hours of work contrasted with the joy people took in being together whenever they could.

"Grandma and I had no real family in Votice, but the neighbors always included us." How could it be otherwise? she wondered. Didn't people here get together to enjoy the simple pleasures of conversation, a glass of wine at the end of the day?

Pleasure welled up in her when Alex described the wedding celebration people had given them. "They were so welcoming, so full of emotion." His deep voice was pleasingly resonant, and Yolanda, seated across from him, was electrically aware of his every nuance of expression, every glance he sent her way. His hair looked tousled, for it had been finger-combed absently until it had tumbled forward in an unruly wave on his forehead. The chandelier overhead caught the planes of his face, shadowing the rough contours and emphasizing the crooked nose, the strong, square chin. He lifted an eyebrow in silent query when he caught her intense stare, and she quickly looked away.

Conversation turned to the trip Alex would make the following week, and a sense of depression overwhelmed Yolanda as she realized he would be gone for several weeks.

She really must fight her attraction for him, she decided, reject the feelings he aroused in her. It was undoubtedly only the result of having traveled together, of relying on him for everything during the past days. Then a shiver swept over her, and she remembered the wedding night, the weight of his body on her, the burning delight of having him inside her. Her face flamed. Her thoughts had wandered far from the conversation around her.

"We must visit the Parliament Buildings, the Provincial Museum, have tea at the Empress, and of course, drive out and see Butchart Gardens...." Yolanda became conscious of her surroundings with an uneasy start. Sophie was cataloging alarmingly busy plans for Yolanda's first weeks in Victoria.

"Dear Aunt Sophia, this is not necessary." The last thing Yolanda wanted to do for the next few days was to become a tourist, hurrying here and there.

But Sophie was making still more detailed plans. "First, we'll go sight-seeing, and then maybe we'll take a trip over to Vancouver."

Yolanda felt her spirits sink with the idea of such a busy itinerary. She desperately needed a quiet time, a period in which she could begin to adjust slowly, and at her own pace, to her new country. Sophie's plans sounded as if she was about to be captured by a whirlwind.

It was Tracey who rescued Yolanda. Alex had been alternately watching the expressions flit across Yolanda's arresting features and puzzling over his daughter's suspiciously quiet, impeccably correct behavior.

Now, carefully pouring hot coffee to accompany the rich chocolate torte Sophia was serving, Tracey inquired ingenuously, "That's going to take all summer, and I thought you only got two weeks off, Aunt Sophia." Her eyes were wide and innocent. "Meals on Wheels depend on you, don't they?"

Sophie's brow puckered slightly, and she cast a worried frown at Tracey, and made a motion to be quiet with her hand.

"I told them I needed more time off—I'm certain it will be fine. But one of the other drivers has to go into the hospital for tests, and they're short. Of all times! But they're trying." She'd told Yolanda enthusiastically about her volunteer work, driving all over the city to take hot meals to old people who were unable to care properly for themselves. It was evident Sophie adored her job, and Yolanda felt appalled that her aunt would consider neglecting it simply to entertain her. Barney had also wistfully mentioned a trip through the Rockies, jokingly asking if Sophie could fit him into her busy schedule. Yolanda shuddered at the idea of being a burden to her aunt.

In her entire life, she'd never had more than a week of idleness. She wanted to learn to make her own way in Canada as soon as possible, just as she'd always done. "Please, I am grateful for your plans, but it is not necessary...."

Halfway through her stammered objection and Sophie's adamant rebuttal, Tracey suggested smoothly, "This whole thing is crazy. Auntie, you're busy, and so is everybody else except me. I have all summer off and not one thing to do." She carefully avoided Alex's sharp glance. "Why couldn't I show Yolanda around? I know all the places she'd like to see, and I've got nothing to do on my holidays."

Alex's face was unreadable as he studied her thoughtfully.

Tracey's voice grew cajoling when he didn't immediately object. "We could stay at Rockwoods, Daddy. Yolanda would love it there." She drew in a quick breath, and her words tumbled out. "You'll just adore it, Yolanda, there's a beach and everything. We could ride bikes, and I could show you around Victoria on the bus. We could sort of keep each other company."

Although very well aware that the plot was cleverly presented to benefit Tracey herself, this alternative was vastly better than the prospect of being a burden, regardless how welcome or beloved, to Sophie. Yolanda nodded eagerly at Tracey, and then shot a glance at Alex. Ultimately, it would be his decision.

"Before you run ripshod over Yolanda with this scheme, Tracey, remember that you and I still have the matter of camp to discuss." Alex's tone was quiet but implacable. Tracey opened her mouth to argue, then shut it again.

Everyone covertly watched the interplay between Alex and his daughter and tried to fill the nervous silence that fell when the two disappeared into Barney's study directly after dessert. When they emerged three-quarters of a long hour later, Tracey flew across the room and grabbed Yolanda's hand with impulsive glee.

"Daddy says we can stay at Rockwoods if you don't mind chaperoning me. Yolanda, please say you will?" she gasped breathlessly.

Yolanda of course agreed.

Lying in bed later, however, she wasn't at all confident about her ability to be a chaperone for Tracey. The idea frankly frightened her.

As if she were focusing her mind on a mantra, Yolanda concentrated instead on a mental picture of Alex as she willed her body to relax. He'd taken her hand in his tonight as he left to go to his apartment, his strong, long fingers encompassing her own momentarily with firm, friendly pressure, sending messages through her nerve endings that she was sure were unintentional.

His eyes had flicked over her features in that odd way he had of looking at her, as if each feature deserved concentrated scrutiny. He'd centered finally on her lips, and she had the strangest feeling he might have kissed her if the others hadn't been there.

"I'll come by late tomorrow morning," he'd promised. "We'll see about getting you and Tracey settled." He'd given his daughter a light kiss on her forehead, and left. Tracey had remained with Barney and Sophia, and Alex hadn't seemed to even consider that his daughter should be with him.

He and Tracey were like strangers, groping for common ground.

What a strange land, where families don't gather regularly together, thought Yolanda, marveling that Sophia, although she'd grown up and been a part of that other life in Votice, was now totally Canadian in thought and manner. Even though she'd been even older than Yolanda when she'd come here as a bride. She'd adapted to the West totally.

Yolanda, too, was here as a bride. But the difference was that Barney loved Sophia. Did a man's love make it easier to adapt?

She fought a sudden overwhelming feeling of desolation until exhaustion overcame her, and she slept.

THE NEXT MORNING, Alex turned the key in the lock and pushed the heavy cedar door at Rockwoods inward. It creaked, just as it always had, and opened into the wide front hallway. A delicate table stood under a gilt-edged mirror, and an antique coat stand stood huffily at attention to the right of the door.

How long was it since he'd last been here? That one long weekend last fall, at Tracey's insistence. He'd been too busy to come at Christmas. The business trip to Japan had interfered with the holiday, and she'd sullenly stayed with Dixie's parents in Vancouver.

He knew he'd been avoiding Rockwoods the past four years, despite Tracey's love for the place. The smell of an unused house washed over Alex; clean, cold, faintly musty and redolent of memories of the past. Rockwoods. Dixie. She'd chosen that mirror and hung that pastel watercolor over there.

Her girlish presence was so real to him here, where they'd spent most of their marriage. He stared blindly at the three curving stairs leading up into the living room, his arm stretched across the opening, unthinkingly blocking the doorway.

"Daddy?" Tracey's impatient voice came from behind him, where she and Yolanda stood in the morning sunshine, waiting for him to move.

Yolanda wasn't watching Alex. She was staring out over the grounds, the immaculately groomed wide lawns with their careful flower beds stretching in an undulating green carpet to meet the thick woodlot that isolated Rockwoods estate from the road. *So much grass, over an acre. Where were the vegetable gardens?* She turned in a slow circle. Perhaps behind the house? But the house seemed to perch almost on the edge of a short steep embankment, and beyond the sandy beach at the bottom stretched the ocean.

The woods, thick and dappled with every shade of emerald, curved to either side, forming a pocket for the house and lawns. Outbuildings larger than most of the cottages in Votice were gathered in neat groupings a discreet distance away. She couldn't see another house anywhere, and the treed lane effectively blocked out traffic noise. Yolanda pursed her lips and expelled her breath in awe at such opulence.

"Daddy, move, please. This bag's getting heavy." Tracey juggled the oversize sport bag she carried, and Alex quickly led the way into the high-ceilinged entrance hall. Mouse-brown carpeting cushioned their footsteps, and sand-colored walls stretched up to a vaulted ceiling. The stairs led gracefully up to a large L-shaped room, whose interior wall was dominated by an immense fireplace with a raised stone hearth.

Light spilled through the window wall facing the ocean, muted by beige draperies. Yolanda drew them aside and caught her breath, overwhelmed by the panoramic view. Perched near the edge of a low cliff, the house seemed to float above miles of sparkling water, and the wall of glass acted as a frame for the seascape outside, water and sky, boats and faraway islands. The curtain fell back over the window, and the glory was gone.

Tracey, impervious to the view, rubbed her bare arms.

"Brrr. It's chilly, Daddy. I'm going back outside, down to the beach. Why don't we have a fire in here? It smells damp." She skipped across the carpet, and a moment later the door slammed behind her.

Alex moved to the fireplace. "She's right; it is cold in here. Agnes comes in once a month when the place is empty, to air it and dust. I phoned her this morning, and starting Monday, she'll come every day. Agnes Witherspoon. Tracey knows her; she's been our housekeeper here for years."

Alex spoke as if his attention was elsewhere, and Yolanda paused in her scrutiny of the room to eye him curiously.

Why would he think two able-bodied women like her and Tracey needed a housekeeper? she wondered. Perhaps he didn't quite trust her with his daughter or his house? A sense of hurt came over her, but then she reminded herself stoutly that Alex could hardly know if she were reliable or not. He'd met—and married—her in the space of several weeks.

Still. She felt she knew Alex, a strange sense of familiarity, as if she'd somehow always known him. How could that be?

She watched him kneel before the natural stone fireplace, crumple paper, add kindling. He wore casual gray cords with a navy cotton pullover, running shoes with sport socks, and the long line of his back tapered gracefully into a narrow waist as he crouched on one knee, his trousers pulled tight on his long thighs and trim buttocks. His hair curled down his neck, and the muscles bulged across his shoulders. He was—she searched for a satisfactory description, and several graphic, earthy phrases in her native tongue ran through her mind.

Strange. She'd never really understood their meaning before meeting Alex.

A wave of pure sensuality tingled like moths' wings in her stomach, and a glowing surge of desire warmed her. They were alone. If only this marriage was more than just paper. She'd move behind him, stroke her hand down his hair and into the neck of his shirt where the smooth brown skin felt warm and smelled like pinecones.

Nervous tingles made goose bumps rise on her arms, and she reproached herself for being fanciful. Legal or not, there was no real marriage between them, and she must remember that. Homesickness was undoubtedly playing tricks with her emotions.

She forced her attention to a row of photographs precisely arranged on top of the rough cedar mantel, and like a physical blow to the pit of her stomach, she recognized framed snapshots of Alex and his dead wife. His first, his real wife. Dixie Caine. Yolanda's eyes were riveted to the face of the woman Alex had loved. She was tiny, pixielike, beguiling, childlike. She had a delicate figure and wide, innocent eyes. Alex's arm was around her...Alex's head close to hers...Alex was holding her hand.

Yolanda's throat constricted, and she gulped involuntarily. It was stupid, she chided herself, to let the photos affect her. This had been their home together, after all.

Alex held a match to the carefully stacked wood and absently watched as it flared and caught fire. He fed more chips into the blaze, his mind far away, but strangely, it wasn't Dixie's memory that haunted him at the moment. It was last night's phone call from Carrie Russell.

He'd closed the door to Barney's study the previous evening and picked up the receiver.

"Welcome home, Alex. I thought I'd be the first to congratulate you on your wedding." The silky voice was open, friendly, sincere, and Alex felt himself tense. The red-haired reporter was at her most dangerous when she appeared the most ingenuous. It was a trait that had often amused him when he read her interviews with fellow politicians, because he understood exactly how the unfortunate subject had been lured into making the controversial comments that had been quoted. Carrie made verbal indiscretion absurdly simple. Her flamboyant looks, her hearty good nature, charmed then captivated her victims.

Invariably, the subjects of her interviews grew relaxed and expansive, lulled by her easygoing questions, her quick wit, until suddenly they found themselves discussing some issue they had no intention of even mentioning.

Like the matter of his marriage to Yolanda. There was no point speculating how Carrie had found out about it this quickly. The question was, what would she do with the information?

He shuddered at what she could say in her column, considering the press's interest in the Eastern bloc countries, Alex's position with the government, the family's interests in Czechoslovakia.

And Carrie's personal interest in Alex? He grimaced. The redhead had never made a secret of her attraction to him, despite the casual nature of their relationship.

"Hello, Carrie." He'd carefully avoided saying more than that, and after a second she'd laughed softly.

"Just 'hello, Carrie'? You're a cautious man, Alex Caine. You sure don't sound like an ebullient bridegroom on his honeymoon. Haven't you got a few romantic remarks I could quote to my faithful readers? It's not every day one of our most eligible political figures secretly marries 'Anna Karenina' and spirits her home to Canada."

He'd managed to chuckle. "That lurid imagination of yours is working overtime."

"I must admit I'd imagined an entirely different lurid scenario for you and I. It would have been nice of you to warn me, Alex." As if she'd pressed a button, the hint of wistfulness in her tone disappeared, and her voice became businesslike.

"Just so I get the facts straight, can you tell me your wife's name, where you met, and how long you were engaged? Either this was a whirlwind romance, my boy, or you kept it pretty quiet."

The steely undertone was almost indiscernible, but Alex caught it.

"I seem to remember having a drink with you not six weeks ago, and nary a word was said about an upcoming wedding."

Alex cursed silently. Aloud, he tried for casual ease. "These things happen pretty fast sometimes. I'm sure one romance is much the same as the next. Hardly material for a political column, I'd think."

"Then you'd think wrong, my friend. My faithful readers will be fascinated to hear all about West marries East, especially when it involves an assistant deputy minister. But I wouldn't want to get the details wrong, so...?'' The satin voice muffled a threat.

He tersely gave Yolanda's name, and the bare facts that he knew Carrie could dig up, anyway. But he knew better than to hope she'd let the matter go at that. He shook his head in frustration. The last thing an assistant deputy minister wanted or needed was undue interest in his private affairs. Would this marriage bring exactly that, thanks to Carrie?

The fire was crackling and the chill in the room began to disappear. He got up, dusted off his knees and realized Yolanda had been quietly watching him, and he'd been ignoring her. He rubbed a hand across the back of his neck and met her intense blue stare.

The exotically high Slavic cheekbones, the tiny mole beside her generously curved lips registered sensually in a subliminal part of him, and his gaze roved unconsciously over the lush fullness of her breasts then went back up to the wide, honest eyes.

"You are troubled, Alex? If you worry about Tracey, I promise you I will take the best of care with her." Her husky voice was pleasingly soft and earnest, and Alex smiled warmly at her. The complications in his life weren't limited to his marriage, after all.

"I haven't the slightest doubt you will. What concerns me more is what kind of merry chase my daughter might lead you. She's not the easiest child in the world, and I'm afraid that for the past few years..." He paused.

"I think maybe Tracey and I will be friends," Yolanda stated with a reassuring confidence she was far from feeling.

"I hope so," he said fervently. The house was suddenly warmer, his spirits inexplicably lighter, and the quizzical grin she gave him sparked an answering smile. He reached impulsively for her hand and grasped it firmly, liking the feel of her palm against his own.

"C'mon, I'll give you a guided tour of Rockwoods."

Her heart was beating furiously, as if the strong hand capturing hers carried an electrical current straight to her heart. He seemed unaware of her reaction, tugging her along in a playful manner she'd not yet seen in him.

"This place is a mutation, new improvements grafted on to the best of the old. Dad and Barney grew up here. My mother died when I was a baby, and Dad and I and Barney lived here together. Now, we all seem too busy to live outside the city." He gestured to a portrait over the mantel. The old photo was sepia-toned, ornately framed, a posed study of a broad-shouldered, roughly handsome man who looked uncomfortable in his tight white collar and vested suit.

Vividly, uncomfortably, Alex remembered losing his temper with Dixie the day she'd taken the picture down. He'd retrieved it immediately from the attic and rehung it where it belonged. She'd wept prettily, but for once he hadn't given in.

"That's Grandpa Caine, the lumberjack," he said hastily, fighting the flashes of haunting memories with words. "He had foresight, old Gramps. Instead of just drinking and gambling like most lumberjacks are likely to do when they make money, he bought land. Huge tracts of forest nobody wanted. By the time Dad and Barney were young men, lumber had become one of B.C.'s major resources, and because of Gramps's investments, the Caine family was well on the way to being financially solid."

Rich, Yolanda translated. This family was undoubtedly rich.

Without giving her time to absorb details, Alex whisked her through a dining room with a highly polished table, spindly chairs, gleaming silver precisely arranged on a sideboard.

All the furniture was elaborate and looked new, unused. The curious thing was that the delicate French provincial lines seemed unsuited to the ruggedness of open beams and wood, brick fireplaces and window walls. Only the heavy-framed old picture suited the architecture.

Like the living room, where every piece of frail furniture, every tiny satin pillow, every expensive figurine was precisely arranged, the dining room and small study were meticulously ordered. The rooms looked as if no one dared live in them. Here, too, formal frilled draperies covered the windows. It was all Yolanda could do not to draw them rudely aside and let nature in.

He drew her finally into a modern kitchen painted pale green, with a flowered cloth in a deeper shade of green covering a cozy table set in front of another wide window covered in frills. A back door, also with a half window, gave access to a path that curved down to the beach.

Yolanda suddenly felt more relaxed. A kitchen was a kitchen, although it was doubtful that anyone had ever whipped up a messy batch of anything here. She turned to the window and pulled back the curtains, rearranging the hooks so the window was clear.

"Does every room look out over the ocean?" she asked. The view intrigued her. She'd never lived beside a large body of water before.

"The house was designed around the view, by a practical architect Gramps hired." Alex's eyes twinkled mischievously. "Wait'll you see the bedrooms. The guy was definitely ahead of his time, and I've always figured Gramps must have had a wide streak of hedonism under his red long johns to agree to the design. C'mon."

He recaptured his hold on her hand, and he whisked her rapidly along until she tugged him to an abrupt stop.

"What is this hedonism under long johns?" Yolanda's brow furrowed in charming confusion, and Alex had to laugh at the question even as he noted the length of the naturally thick dark eyelashes shading her eyes.

"Long johns. Men's winter underwear." He laughed again, shared laughter as she nodded in understanding. "Hedonism isn't as easily defined. It's the belief that pleasure is the most important thing in life. Enjoying life's comforts to the fullest." He decided to tease her a bit.

"I suspect you'd call it decadence, Yolanda."

"Like Aunt Sophia's bathroom?" she immediately retorted.

He shrugged, puzzled. He'd never really noticed Sophia's bathroom, when it came right down to it.

"She has perfumed soaps and lotions and powders. I think this hedonism is not such a bad thing," she declared decisively, and Alex loved her smug tone of voice and made a mental note to pay more attention the next time he visited the facilities in his uncle's apartment.

They climbed the wide curving staircase to the second floor, and Alex pondered, not for the first time, what there was about Yolanda that created this tangible rapport between them—and also created the unsettling current of acute sensual hunger her presence stirred in him.

Ever since the night of their wedding, Alex persistently thought about the compelling way her most intimate curves had cradled him, the softness and heat of her luxuriant breasts cupped in his hands, the elusive, wildflower scent of her body. He wasn't proud of his actions that night, but neither could he forget the ecstasy he'd found in her arms.

She paused at the round porthole window set in the landing. "Alex, look there, so many birds. Are they sea gulls?" His body brushed against hers as he peered out, and desire stirred.

"Yes, sea gulls. They nest on the cliffs."

Despite the sense of ease he enjoyed in her company, this other, spontaneous response didn't exactly promote relaxation. Even holding her hand stirred emotions he wasn't ready to examine. He released her fingers abruptly and moved ahead to throw open the first door leading off the hallway, turning so he could see her face.

"This room is yours, if you want it," Alex told her. "That door leads to a bathroom, shared by Tracey. Her room is next door."

He watched Yolanda, and her unaffected pleasure delighted him. How stimulating to introduce her to Canada. Seeing Rockwoods through her unsophisticated eyes was a new experience, one that he savored. Dixie had never really liked it here.

He found himself suddenly envying Tracey, wishing he could be the one to show Yolanda around Victoria.

"Ahhh." Her breath escaped in an unconscious sigh, and she hesitantly stepped through the door and into liquid sunlight.

The room was golden, its warm honey-colored rug stretching to meet walls of buttercup yellow. A pale lemon ceiling took on the texture of variegated silk where the reflection of sun on water flowed through the by now familiar window wall, rippling, re-forming, like an ever-changing kaleidoscope. She'd never been in a room that felt this . . . giddy . . . before.

One interior wall supported a tumbled stone fireplace, and louvered doors led to wide closets along another. A long low window seat cushioned in soft, worn amber corduroy lounged invitingly below the expanse of glass. Here, nothing looked new or stiff. There were no swathing draperies choking off the view.

The room had obviously escaped the fussy decoration lavished on the downstairs.

"We never used this bedroom."

"We." Alex and Dixie and Tracey. Yolanda's delight in the beautiful room faded a trifle. Everywhere at Rockwoods, it seemed, the ghost of the lovely Dixie lingered.

"Your room is also on this level?" she blurted, and then cursed herself for asking the gauche question.

Alex shook his head. "Upstairs," he said gruffly, pointing to where a narrower set of spiral stairs curved upward. "It used to be an attic. Now it's the master bedroom," he added, not offering to show her, and effectively breaking the delicate thread that had woven a knot between them.

"Hey, where are you guys? I'm hungry—can we have the picnic Auntie Sophia sent along?" The cheerful tones changed dramatically as Tracey came charging up the steps and into the yellow room.

"Oh, here you are. What are you doing up here, anyway?" Her gray eyes flickered suspiciously from her father to Yolanda, instinctively sensing an intimacy in both the setting and the charged atmosphere of the room. Her face stiffened, tightening into hard lines.

It wasn't hard for Yolanda to identify the feminine jealousy Tracey was feeling, but the animosity she radiated was chilling.

"I think the basket of food is still in the car," Yolanda improvised. "I'll get it." It was a relief to escape, to leave Tracey alone with her father.

Lunch was uncomfortable for Yolanda. Tracey jealously excluded her from the conversation, drawing Alex into reminiscences Yolanda couldn't share. The ham sandwiches and fruit salad lodged in Yolanda's throat. She could understand Tracey's insecurity, but that didn't help the feeling of isolation such intimacies produced, or make it easier to field the triumphantly venomous looks the girl shot at her when her father wasn't looking.

Alex, annoyingly oblivious to his daughter's ploys, answered all her questions absently. His thoughts were far away—lost in memories of the wife he'd lost? Yolanda wondered. His distractedness only made Tracey doubly determined to attract his attention.

"I think I will take a walk along the beach," Yolanda announced as soon as the plates and glasses were loaded in the dishwasher. Tracey had condescendingly instructed Yolanda in the process.

"You mean you've never used a dishwasher before?" she'd asked. "Man, I can't believe it. That's straight out of the dark ages. You can't put that in; it's too big. You really don't know, do you?"

Yolanda longed to get away, to escape the hard-eyed glances Tracey shot at her and the thinly veiled sarcasm. Had the friendliness of the night before been only an act, a show of good behavior calculated to get the girl out of going back to the camp she hated? What was it going to be like, Yolanda wondered apprehensively, to spend the next weeks being responsible for so devious a girl? Yolanda's knowledge of teenagers was sketchy at best.

"We have to drive back in about an hour," Alex announced unexpectedly, finally emerging from his reverie. "There's a meeting this afternoon I have to attend."

Tracey's face immediately lost its expression of sly triumph at Yolanda's retreat, and her attention was fully on her father.

"But I thought we'd stay here all day," she wailed. "How come we have to start back so soon?"

"I told you, I have to go to a meeting. It's a briefing on the trip next week, and I can't miss it." Tracey's whining tone annoyed Alex, and his answer was curt.

"Then I'm coming to the apartment with you, Daddy. I don't want to stay at Uncle Barney's." The look she shot Yolanda silently added, *"with her."* "You and I could go to a movie later, okay?"

"That's not possible, honey. I won't be home till late."

"I'm not a baby, Daddy. I can stay home alone."

"I said no, Tracey. I'm too busy, and I want you at Barney and Sophia's until Sunday. Then I'll drive you and Yolanda out here."

Tracey was standing near the sink, slouching against the counter. She straightened suddenly, her face crumpling.

"Go to your stupid meeting, then," she shouted. "See if I care. You never want me around, anyhow." Tears shone in her eyes, but she turned them to anger, grabbing the first thing her hand touched on the drainboard, a heavy glass bowl Yolanda had put the fruit in.

Before Alex or Yolanda could move, Tracey flung the bowl as hard as she could against the opposite wall. It shattered, and glass shards flew across the room. Alex and Yolanda instinctively put their hands up to shield their faces against the splinters.

Tracey raced to the back door, wrenched it open and slammed it behind her with a crash that shook the house.

For an instant Yolanda and Alex stared dumbfounded at the glass, then at each other. Alex was the first to move. He cursed, and strode out after Tracey, rage evident in his face and his rigidly held shoulders, his balled fists.

The door slammed behind him, and Yolanda let out the breath she'd been holding in a long sigh. Then she found a broom and carefully cleaned up the glass. She smiled wryly as she imagined what *babička* would say and do with one like Tracey. The smile faded rapidly.

What was she going to do with Tracey? She was responsible for her, beginning Monday.

CHAPTER SIX

ALEX LEFT, RELUCTANTLY bidding goodbye to Tracey and Yolanda at Rockwoods. After the drama of that first visit to the estate, Tracey had been morose, sullen and withdrawn.

Barney, Robert, and Sophie were anxious and hesitant with her, as if they didn't know how to deal with her moody silences, her bursts of tears and dramatic exits to her bedroom. Yolanda watched the teenager manipulate her older relatives with ease, watched them pamper and coax her to no avail.

Her moodiness lasted until she and Yolanda were alone at Rockwoods on Sunday evening, and everyone had gone.

Then, like a chameleon, she'd dramatically switched to sunny good behavior. Yolanda eyed her warily, wondering when the other Tracey would again emerge.

"I've told her in no uncertain terms," Alex had related privately to Yolanda, "that she either behaves herself, or she goes back to the camp. At the first sign of trouble with her, I want you to phone either Dad or Barney. If they aren't available for any reason, call this number. It's my hotel in London."

So far, Tracey was fine. The housekeeper whom Alex had promised, Agnes Witherspoon, arrived at nine Monday morning, and it was she who set Yolanda's teeth on edge, not Tracey.

"You Alex's new missus?"

Tracey was still asleep, and Yolanda had been enjoying a quiet cup of coffee at the kitchen table when Agnes let herself in the back door. Tall, with a round face, small eyes and yellow skin, Agnes wore her sparse gray hair drawn into a nubbin on the top of her head. She pulled her wool sweater closer around her concave chest and advanced on Yolanda.

Uncertain as to how one treated a housekeeper, Yolanda stood up and smiled hesitantly. Agnes's beady eyes insolently assessed Yolanda's face and figure.

"Humph. You sure ain't nothin' like Mrs. Dixie, I'll say that. She was the sweetest little thing, bless her heart."

After several more syrupy testimonies to the marvels of Mrs. Dixie, Agnes set to work, and soon the entire house, which Yolanda had thought scrupulously clean to start with, was subjected to latherings of bleach, lemon oil and detergent, interspersed with aggrieved comments from Agnes.

"That girl had better get up. Never seen such laziness."

"That tray don't go there, missis. We keep it up here."

"Miss Tracey, you didn't scrub out the bath the way you're supposed to—what would your mother say?"

Yolanda, and Tracey, too, finally escaped outside.

"Miserable old thing," Tracey commented petulantly. "She's always hated me, even when Mum was here. She was always sickly sweet with her, though."

Although Yolanda suspected that Tracey exaggerated the number of people whom she insisted "hated" her, their mutual dislike of Agnes spun a momentary bond between them.

Tracey soon wheeled two bikes from the garage and suggested they go for a ride. Yolanda enthusiastically agreed. Back in Votice, her battered bike had been the major form of transportation, and she missed cycling.

"This one belonged to my mum," Tracey announced, mounting the yellow cycle. "But I don't think she ever rode it. I used to wish she'd come riding with me. It's great to ride bikes with somebody, don't you think?"

Tracey's references to her mother interested Yolanda. It was perfectly natural for Tracey to want to talk about Dixie but Yolanda suspected that the girl had learned not to mention her mother often to Alex.

"Don't you think this is great, Yolanda?" Tracey persisted.

Yolanda gave her a wide smile.

"This is good idea, yes," she commented gratefully, preparing to climb on the shiny green bike.

"A good idea. You have to use 'a.' Are you really riding in that dress?" Tracey's tone was a blend of astonishment and disbelief. Yolanda looked down at herself, puzzled.

"Of course, yes," she confirmed. Her pink nylon dress had buttons down the front and a flared skirt. She could ride in it easily.

Tracey's strong features screwed into a grimace.

"Don't you have any jeans? Like, nobody rides a bike in a dress."

It was gradually becoming apparent to Yolanda that what women wore here in Victoria was vastly different from clothing styles back home. Yesterday, Tracey had staunchly vetoed the short nylon anklets Yolanda was accustomed to wearing with dresses.

"That's gross," she'd groaned, and then succinctly interpreted gross, using as a further example Yolanda's unshaven legs, then offering dainty pink razors she'd unearthed from a bathroom drawer to remedy the situation.

Yolanda accepted the criticism gratefully. After all, how was she to discern "gross" from "not gross" unless someone told her, she'd assured Tracey.

Evidently a dress on a bike was also gross. Yolanda shrugged and, taking care to avoid Agnes, quickly changed into her only pair of slacks—navy polyester.

Tracey looked her over and reluctantly nodded.

"I guess that'll have to do. But I'm gonna tell Auntie Sophie we need to take you shopping," she muttered, mounting her bike. With Yolanda close behind, they pedaled down the winding drive.

It was overhung with blossoms from ivory-pink Japanese plum trees, and the surrounding woods were redolent of moss and wetness, with salt-scented ocean and burgeoning growth. Rockwoods smelled of summer, and a sudden bird song sent an unbearable ache zigzagging through Yolanda's heart.

Just so were the birds singing in Votice right now. *Babička* would be weeding her garden. Sometimes homesickness clutched at her chest and made it hard to breathe.

The lane snaked through dense woods before it deposited them on Beach Drive, which wound its way along the shoreline and into Victoria.

Yolanda let her mind wander as she followed Tracey's erratic fast-slow-fast pattern.

The past days had given little time for thinking, as Sophie and Barney and Robert showered her with attention and kindness, guiding her around their city, pointing out attractions and landmarks until her mind felt stuffed to overflowing with details, and with beauty. Victoria and the island it was on made Yolanda feel she was in a fairyland at first, a frothy confection of beauty and charm where everything was pleasant and prosperous.

Then Yolanda began to look beneath the surface, beginning to sense the deeper, more profound differences between this culture and that of her homeland, and she saw that not everything was perfect. There was poverty here, and other social ills. For some reason, such inequities made her more comfortable with Canada.

She was eager to learn, to adapt. Most important, she was striving to understand Alex, to know what influences had shaped and molded him. He was seldom out of her thoughts. In fact, thoughts of him pervaded her days and haunted her confusing dreams. As she looked and listened and analyzed, Yolanda compared everything with Czechoslovakia. The Pacific Ocean here, the mighty Vltava River there. More cars here, more bikes there. Here, not as many birds. She especially missed the cuckoos, and the small villages full of kitchen gardens, each cottage with its few chickens or geese.

Those gardens. She steered around a corner, momentarily losing sight of Tracey. "People here must eat grass; they have no gardens," she'd commented to Barney, and he'd laughed uproariously. Wealth probably made the difference, she concluded, pedaling hard.

She was beginning to sweat. Tracey was setting a furiously fast pace, and Yolanda's hair tumbled loose as she recklessly let the bike run free down a hill, her heart-stopping descent uncontrolled and thrillingly dangerous, and she pulled up sharply at the bottom. Tracey was wildly exuberant.

"Way to go. Let's ride into the city, and have lunch at McDonald's. You'll love it, Yolanda."

That meant Tracey would love it.

"Is it expensive, this place?"

Tracey giggled at the question. Yolanda's extreme caution with money both puzzled and amused her.

"It's fast food. Fast food is never very expensive, silly. Besides, we've got the money Dad left. He never asks me for any back when he goes away like this," she said complacently.

Alex had left enough cash to keep four Czech families for a month, Yolanda estimated. It was a shocking excess, she thought.

"How can I know how much it will be if I don't ask?"

In the next hours, Tracey guided her through a more practical introduction to Victoria than Yolanda had yet had. Among other things, she learned where one could get the biggest doughnuts in town, which rock star was appearing in person, and what theaters would let underage teens in to see adult-rated movies. It was an education that left Yolanda's head reeling and convinced her more than ever that Tracey was in serious need of supervision.

The girl had become giddy, chatting boastfully about her independence. In the process, Yolanda accidentally learned several things that horrified her about the exclusive boarding school Tracey attended in Vancouver. Smoking, sneaking out, meeting boys. Surely fifteen was too young for such things even in Canada?

"Why not attend school here in Victoria?" Yolanda asked. They were having hamburgers, fries and Cokes—Tracey had ordered for both of them—and Yolanda decided that this "fast food" was delicious. She dunked her french fries in ketchup the way Tracey instructed and savored the taste of some kind of sauce on the hamburger.

"Nobody has time to have me around much. Aunt Sophia works and plays bridge a lot, Grampa and Uncle Barney go to their office most days. Besides, they're all old. Dad's just never home. There's nobody around, so it's easier if I board."

She looked pensive, and she said defensively, "My dad has a real important job, you know. He has to travel lots."

"I'm sure he would prefer to spend more time with you if he could manage it," Yolanda said.

Tracey shrugged but focused her eyes on the Styrofoam holder the food had come in.

"Nana and Papa Mitchell, my mother's parents, live over in Vancouver, so I see them a lot."

Yolanda sensed that caution was in order. Tracey was flip-pant, as if none of this mattered, but she wasn't wolfing down her lunch as she had been only a moment before. One forefin-ger went unconsciously to her mouth, and she bit the short nail viciously, tearing it off.

Yolanda said casually, "My *babička*, my father's mother, raised me. My father and mother died when I was twelve."

Tracey's eyes widened. "Hey, that's how old I was when..." She stopped.

Yolanda seized on common ground. "Sometimes it was very difficult, because to me my *babička* seemed—" Yolanda searched for the word "—old-mannered."

Tracey's gray gaze was intent on Yolanda's face.

"Old-fashioned," she corrected. "Boy, you got that right. Nana and Papa are nice to me, but man, it drives me nuts. They give all my friends the third degree, and they don't approve of jeans or makeup, and they talk about what a saint my mother was all the time." Realizing what she'd blurted out, Tracey looked appalled, and her words rushed out in a torrent.

"Like, Mother really was something; I know they're right about that. She never got into trouble, or made anybody mad, or anything. She was tiny and pretty and really smart. There's still some of the same teachers at school—it's the same school she went to. They tell me all the time how nice she acted. But I don't figure they know I was adopted. Like, it's not the same if you're adopted, you're not like your mother then, see?"

The wistful plea in the young voice unexpectedly wrung Yo-landa's heart, and she had a flash of inspiration. "*Babička* al-ways wanted me to act just like my Aunt Sophia," she confided. Tracey's eyes once again flew to Yolanda's face.

"Yes, the same Aunt Sophia you know." Yolanda nodded. "When I was a girl, all I heard in the village school was how brilliant Aunt Sophia had been, how polite, how clean, how quiet."

She had Tracey's undivided attention, and Yolanda nodded again, making her eyes wide.

"Truly. The whole time I was growing, *babička* told me also, at least twice a day, how well-behaved Sophia had been, how hard she worked, how good-tempered she was compared to me."

She pressed a hand dramatically to her forehead. "I used to run from the house, way into the fields, and I would stand there and shout, 'Aunt Sophia, I hate you, I hate you, do you hear? I hate you, perfect Sophia.'" Tracey's mouth hung open with amazement. Yolanda took another big bite of her food and chewed thoughtfully. "Afterward I felt better. And Sophia, way over here, never heard me once. Fortunately, neither did *babička*." Yolanda winked at Tracey.

Over the clutter of disposable containers, mischievous blue eyes met uncertain gray ones, and Tracey let out a tiny squeak of a giggle. In another moment, both were laughing, and by the time they left, Yolanda felt the most tenuous of bonds beginning to form between herself and the fifteen-year-old girl, a bond as fragile as a spider's web on a summer morning and just as easily broken.

"Can we go now to the museum?"

Sophia had insisted that Yolanda visit the Provincial Museum near the Parliament Buildings.

"I wish I had time to take you, because, more than anything," Sophia had assured her, "it will give you a feeling for this beautiful province." It had a massive totem pole outside, and beautiful glass, timber and gray granite architecture.

Tracey gave the mandatory groan, but she led the way.

Yolanda stepped through the museum's doors, and stood enthralled.

A larger than life dugout canoe—carved of cedar and peopled with naked Haida Indians hunting a whale—was screened behind a realistic waterfall. It was so lifelike, the expressions on the fierce handsome faces so evocative that she shivered with the message it conveyed of another time, of people adapted to their environment.

She followed Tracey up an escalator, gaped at a wooly mammoth and told Tracey that she felt she could actually smell the ocean from a lifelike beach where sea lions cavorted.

"You can," Tracey said smugly. "This place uses smells and sounds to make you think you're really there."

On the next level they entered a turn of the century British Columbia town. There was a train station, and the old steam train could be heard approaching just down the tracks. On each side of the boardwalk, shops offered glimpses through windows and half-open Dutch doors, and an eerie feeling came over Yolanda. Tracey was right. The sounds and odors made her feel she was actually in the old town.

"Neat, eh, Landa?" Tracey asked, obviously enjoying her role of tour guide. She moved impatiently to the next half-open door, and the scene caught at Yolanda's heart and brought tears stinging her eyes.

It was only a kitchen, an old-fashioned kitchen, like the one in *babička*'s cottage in Votice. A wood-burning cook stove had a tea kettle steaming on its surface. A soiled bib hung carelessly from a high chair, and a wooden table held pie pastry half rolled out. A hand pump stood beside a sink, and above it, red gingham curtains blew gently in and out at the open window. Just outside, a dog barked, horses' hooves clattered up the lane, voices called cheery greetings. The smell of cinnamon pervaded the room.

Warmth, love, family—the room embodied the spirit of home.

Instantly, Yolanda was back in Votice. In another moment, *babička* would walk in and make the tea. Yolanda stepped forward, drawn irresistibly, but the half door banged against her thighs, and Tracey tugged impatiently at her arm. "C'mon, let's go. Hey, are you crying?" She gazed at Yolanda in alarm. "It's only a kitchen, for gosh sakes."

Only a kitchen. Yolanda allowed herself to be drawn away, but before she left the museum, she slipped down once more to stand in the kitchen doorway. This room was important to her. It spoke to her soul, to her loneliness, to her sense of displacement. Somehow, it drew Votice and Victoria together in her heart.

Outside again, Tracey led the way to a shopping mall.

"What're stores like where you come from?" Tracey asked as she efficiently locked their bikes in the rack provided for bikers.

Yolanda was staring with awe at the racks of seedlings and plants casually laid out on the pavement.

"Nothing is displayed like this," she said, and when they entered the wide doors she felt dumbfounded at the magnificent array of goods, the shoppers with their carts, the abundance everyone around her seemed to accept unquestioningly.

She struggled to draw a picture of the stores in Prague for Tracey as they wandered along the aisles.

"The grocery stores. *Potravini*, we call them. Small, neat. Rows of preserves in glass jars. Pickles, sauerkraut, peas, beets. Coffee, rice, sugar, flour."

Yolanda gazed around, and in her arose a sudden awareness that the life she'd known and lived till now was over. She'd been transplanted, like a young tree, and she was suffering root shock. The soil was alien, but she must adapt.

They were passing a display of fruit, and to Yolanda's horror, Tracey calmly reached out and ate a green grape, then two purple ones. Next, she picked up a mushroom, casually wiped it off, and ate that, as well.

Reacting instinctively, Yolanda landed a sharp slap on the girl's fingers as she reached for more.

"What'ya think you're doing? I'm only having a grape, for god's sake."

The camaraderie of the day disappeared as they glared at each other.

"You are stealing," Yolanda hissed, looking around and praying no one had seen. "This is a very bad thing, and your father made me responsible. What would we say to the owner if he saw you doing such a thing?" Yolanda was scandalized.

"Calm down, nobody cares about it. What's a few grapes, anyway? The girls from my school do it all the time. It's called grazing."

"Grazing? Like cows, eating grass?"

Tracey nodded.

"This is not your grass to graze upon. You are forbidden to do this thing anymore, do you understand, Tracey? There are some rules that are universal, and stealing is the same everywhere."

Tracey mumbled sullenly for the time it took to leave the store, but Yolanda was relieved to see that there was a certain amount of embarrassment evident on the girl's face as she unlocked her bike with sharp, angry movements.

"You can go ahead and tell my father; I don't care," she spat out at Yolanda.

"Why should I do that? This thing is between you and me, a private matter," Yolanda said reasonably, struggling with her own lock. "And now it's over," she added. "Tracey, this lock. Show me, please, how it works."

There was a pause, and Yolanda held her breath. Would the girl simply ride away without her? Yolanda waited, and waited.

Nimble fingers with torn, chewed nails took the chain from Yolanda's fingers.

"It's a combination, see, 41-6-18." The lock sprung open, and Tracey handed it casually to Yolanda. She climbed on her bike and balanced for an instant.

"Everybody else always tells my father on me," she said, and then she was pedaling furiously across the parking lot.

"Hurry up," she hollered back to Yolanda. "Aunt Sophia will be home by now, and I'll bet she'll make us some sandwiches when we stop by. I'm starving."

The rest of the afternoon passed pleasantly, and Agnes Witherspoon was gone by the time they stowed the bikes wearily in the shed at quarter to six that evening. Sophie had taken Tracey's complaints that Yolanda had no "decent" clothing in which to ride bikes seriously, insisting they go shopping that very afternoon.

Ignoring Yolanda's panicked objections, the other two had marched her to a store near Sophie's apartment.

Now, the pants she'd worn were in a bag, and she had on a pair of new-smelling, stiff-feeling blue jeans and a fluffy pink T-shirt. She wore deeper pink canvas runners on her feet. She felt weak thinking how much they had cost her—she'd adamantly refused Sophie's offers to pay, and scrupulously avoided using any of Alex's money, either.

Yolanda's small hoarded savings had disappeared like smoke with the purchases, but a purely feminine delight bubbled inside her as she caught a glimpse of herself in the hallway mirror at Rockwoods. She looked almost . . . Western.

It had been a shock, though, to see herself in the triple mirrors at that store. For the first time she'd impersonally evaluated the undeniably plump figure in the mirror, the snug fit of the jeans over her ample hips and backside.

Subconsciously, she'd been comparing herself all day to the women she saw on the streets; casually dressed, incredibly thin, sophisticated women, looking so elegantly beautiful.

She studied her hips and rounded stomach as objectively as she could, and then pulled on the T-shirt thoughtfully.

Well, it covered that roll of fat at her waist, at least. The shell-pink color suited her well enough. But there was all this spare flesh. Sticking her head out of the dressing room, she impulsively called Sophie and Tracey inside and candidly pulled the shirt up, exposing her midriff.

"Here," she pointed, frowning at her waist, "and here," she said, indicating her hips, "and here." They giggled as she cupped her behind. "There is too much of me in these places," she announced. Sophie, tactfully loving, started to object, but Tracey had no such delicacy.

"You need to lose a few pounds, fer sure," she declared candidly, giving Yolanda's figure an assessing once-over. "You don't actually look bad in those jeans, and your boobs are great, but ten or fifteen pounds less would make a difference, all right."

"I joined a diet group, years ago," Sophie announced unexpectedly. "I know I kept all the booklets. It was a good, sensible diet, too. I'll find them when we go home."

She had, and for the rest of the afternoon, they'd mapped out a sensible diet for Yolanda.

"If you're going to seriously diet, we have to find that scale," Tracey fretted that evening. They'd looked in the bathroom on the main floor, and now in their own.

"I know, I'll bet it's in Dad's bathroom." Tracey leaped up the stairs.

"C'mon, Yolanda, have you been up here yet?"

Her heart began to beat a fast tattoo. It was probably unforgivable of her to enter Alex's private rooms without his express invitation. But her curiosity, and the relentless desire burning within her to know all there was to know about him, overwhelmed Yolanda. She slowly climbed the curving iron staircase.

The spacious area had been reclaimed from a high attic, and open beams gave the sensation of airiness, with the inevitable breathtaking vista out of one block of triangular window, which was curtainless.

Deep, rich navy blue carpet stretched from wall to wall, and the furniture was solidly masculine. A terry robe lay tossed carelessly across the deep blue spread. Did it still hold the body scent of Alex?

"Isn't it neat up here? Like a tree house," Tracey chattered, disappearing into the adjoining bathroom on her search for the scale.

"Dad changed the furniture here two summers ago."

So he hadn't slept in this bed with Dixie. But beside the bed, on a table, a studio portrait of her smiled toward the empty pillows. Yolanda swallowed hard. A hopeless, nameless yearning came over her, and a sense of dread. Alex went to sleep each night with that picture next to his bed, with Dixie's memory alive in his heart.

"Come in here, Yolanda. I found the scale."

Tracey was pulling it from a cupboard under the wide sink in the huge bathroom. What drew Yolanda's eyes was the array of crystal bottles, elegant boxes of powder, vials of exotic perfume, eerily aligned on the dressing table. Downstairs, too, she'd found evidence of Dixie's silent presence, but nowhere else had it affected her as deeply as here, in Alex's private bathroom.

He bathed and shaved and dressed with this constant, mute reminder of Dixie all around him. Perspiration broke out on Yolanda's brow, and a sickness rose in her stomach. What a fool she was, to half dream that there might be a future for her and Alex. How could there be, when Alex was irrevocably wedded to the past?

They were hardly downstairs again before the phone rang. Tracey answered, and Yolanda heard her sing exuberantly, "Hi, daddy. You sound awfully far away."

Several minutes passed, with giggles and rapid comments from Tracey. Then Tracey called, "Yolanda, Daddy wants to speak to you."

With her pulse beating heavy and slow, and her hands trembling, Yolanda hesitantly took the phone.

"Yes, hello?" The simple words stuck in her throat. All she could think of was the photo beside the bed upstairs, the endless reminders of Dixie all around her at Rockwoods, and the transient nature of her own relationship with the man on the other end of the line.

"Yolanda, hello." Alex sounded weary across the humming wires, and his voice held a vulnerable note she'd never noticed before. Against her will, she anxiously wondered if he was eating properly, if he was getting sick.

In London it was early morning, hardly dawn. Alex hadn't slept well and finally left the rumpled bedroom and the twisted sheets for the adjoining living area. He had to be at meetings, difficult meetings, all day long, and he felt tired before they even started. Jet lag had caught up with a vengeance, and his body ached. He slumped on the ridiculously hard chair beside the phone.

Outside, a gray drizzle pattered on the hotel's dusty window, and Alex knew a moment's longing for the scene he could see in his mind's eye of Rockwoods, of late evening over the ocean and flags of pink and violet cloud spreading across the gentle silver sky.

Tracey's prattling tale of bike riding and shopping brought a smile to his lips, and a sense of relief from the anxiety he felt about leaving her for Yolanda to cope with. It was obvious that Tracey, at least, was happy and content for once. What about Yolanda?

Her rich, gentle tones with their charming accent made him suddenly close his eyes, creating a vivid picture of her standing with the phone pressed to her ear, her head with its crown of dusky hair tilted quizzically to one side, the way she held herself when she was listening intently or was puzzled about something. When had he noticed that?

"Is, ahm, everything is fine, I take it? Tracey sounds great. Do you need anything? Has Dad been over yet?"

The contained, husky tones of her voice gave the requisite answers, and when he caught himself asking about the weather, he realized it wasn't her answers he wanted. It was the soothing, lilting sound of her voice. For the first time since he'd arrived, he felt unreasonably happy.

What the hell kind of nonsense was this, anyway? Confused, slightly disgruntled, he ended the call abruptly.

"I'll be in touch in a day or so. Goodbye for now."

"Alex?" The accented word came hesitantly over the miles.

"Yes, I'm still here. What is it?"

"Could Tracey and I perhaps have a garden, do you think?" The breathless query came in a rush, and for a second he couldn't make sense of it. A garden? He squinted at the picture on the wall, his eyebrows meeting in puzzlement. The photo was called "The Hunt." He studied the details absently.

"If you want one, of course you can. I told you to make Rockwoods your home, to feel free to do whatever you want. Get Ian Cameron to help you dig it. He's the old gardener who does the lawns—Tracey knows him."

"Ian Cameron? Thank you, Alex. Thank you very much. I'm happy you don't mind if we do this thing. Goodbye."

She was gone abruptly. Alex hung up and decided to go down and see if breakfast was a possibility this early. He needed to shake off the tension that had inexplicably built up during his talk with Yolanda. For a fleeting moment he frowned over the turn the conversation had taken.

A garden seemed a strange thing for a woman to want. It was a new one on him, he mused. It was probably a small flower garden she wanted, an area to grow roses or daffodils or some such thing. She was—he searched for the proper words—an earthy woman, Yolanda.

Well, Ian would manage it. He'd forgotten to warn Yolanda that Ian Cameron didn't exactly see eye-to-eye with Agnes Witherspoon, though. He headed for the bathroom, and the three weeks of his stay hung like an albatross around his neck. For the first time in four years, he wanted to be at home. And he didn't particularly want to examine why.

He suddenly found himself desperately trying to remember what kind of flowers Dixie had liked best. Violets, that was it. He was sure it was violets.

Yolanda undoubtedly preferred sunflowers, but when he found a shop selling bath supplies, he bought gardenia for her. In everything.

"YOLANDA, SHOULD WE PUT the tomato plants here or over there?"

The morning was hot, and Tracey's nose was as red as the tomatoes they planned to grow. She wore an old pair of cut-offs, and her knees were black from kneeling in the earth. Her torn nails were now dirt-encrusted, and a smudge made her look as if she had a black eye. She crouched in the rich loam they'd sweated to prepare for the seedlings they'd bought that morning, and her eyes sparkled with excitement.

Yolanda was just as sweaty, dirty, and excited as Tracey.

"Ian Cameron, didn't you say they needed plenty of sun?" she called out to the gnarled little man raking the soil at the far end of the garden.

"Aye, they like the sun, those." The man's thick Scots brogue was almost another language to Yolanda. She deciphered it, and nodded.

Yolanda studied the garden plot, a trace of unease undermining her pleasure at the destruction of such a large part of Rockwood's front lawn. With a machine called a Rototiller, Ian had efficiently carved the "waste" of front lawn into rather more of a garden than Yolanda had envisioned, putting an extraordinary amount of enthusiasm into the task.

"If it's a wee bit more than ye wanted, plant potatoes in what's over," he'd shouted at her, turning over more and still more lawn.

"Agnes was some mad when she saw our garden," Tracey commented apprehensively. "She said she's phoning Grandpa on us this morning."

Yolanda shrugged with a lot more nonchalance than she felt.

"I asked your father, and he gave permission. Agnes is perhaps just in a bad temper today."

That was putting it mildly. The woman had seemed on the verge of apoplexy when she arrived an hour before and saw what had been the lawn. None of them had dared venture into the house for anything since her outraged retreat. This was silly, Yolanda finally decided. They could all use a drink of water, and she'd love a cup of coffee.

"I'll bring a tray out," she promised the other two bravely.

"A Coke for me, please," Tracey requested. "If the dragon doesn't eat you," she added softly, and Yolanda couldn't bring herself to reprimand the girl. Agnes *was* a dragon.

The kitchen was empty when Yolanda ventured in the back door, and she reached for the coffeepot she'd left half filled at breakfast. It was empty, scoured out, and it had been doggedly replaced on the shelf.

Annoyed at Agnes's fanaticism, Yolanda impatiently re-filled the pot and set it to perk just as she heard Agnes approaching.

"I just finished those floors," Agnes immediately barked, "and now look at the dirt you tracked in. I must say, you sure ain't like Mrs. Dixie, always so fresh and clean she was. Dainty," she huffed, glancing pointedly at Yolanda's less than dainty shorts and sweaty cotton shirt.

"I just cleaned out that coffeepot, too," she grumbled. Agnes shot a sly look at Yolanda. "Mr. Robert is coming by to look at the yard. Don't know what that old fool Ian thinks he's doing out there, but I'll bet he's gonna lose his job, the way he ought to have years since. Rude, he is, and dirty. I've been here lots longer than him, that's a fact, and I'll be here after he's gone. Mrs. Dixie hired me, and I'll be here after the likes of him."

And you as well, the statement implied.

"Ian Cameron is following my directions," Yolanda stated coolly.

"Humph. Mrs. Dixie sure never went around giving directions like that. She wouldn't have dreamed of doing such things on her own."

Yolanda felt a surge of fury, and she levelled a cool stare at Agnes.

"But I am not Mrs. Dixie, am I, Agnes Witherspoon? Mrs. Dixie is dead, and I am Yolanda," she said deliberately and turned to pour the bubbling coffee into the cups. Then she added slowly and succinctly, "This garden, it is mine. I want to hear no more of it, do you understand?" Her hands trembled.

"Well, I never," Agnes choked as Yolanda balanced the tray on one hip and propped open the door. "Don't you take that tone with me, you, you, furriner. Don't even talk the Queen's English, you don't. I don't have to work here, you know. There's plenty asking all the time for good housekeepers."

"Then you should leave." The words were out before Yolanda fully considered their implications.

Shocked, icy silence followed her exit.

Robert Caine arrived after lunch. He pulled his battered truck into Rockwoods' graciously winding driveway with a flourish, braking to a stop close to where Yolanda and Tracey were finishing a row of tiny lettuce plants.

For several long moments he simply sat, and Yolanda could see his snowy hair but not the expression on his face. Would he be angry? All of a sudden she had misgivings. Time seemed to stretch like elastic until Tracey got to her feet.

"Hi, Grandpa," she hollered exuberantly. "Come and see what we've done. We're gonna grow enough stuff here for everybody."

Robert got out slowly, and Yolanda and Tracey walked to meet him. He studied them, their sunburned faces, soil-stained knees and hands. His gaze lingered on Tracey's happy, dirty face, and then his features broke into a wide grin.

His green eyes alight, he declared, "Well, this is one hell of a good idea. Hell of an idea. Used to have to cut that lawn when I was a boy, and I always detested it. Never thought of turning it into a garden, though." The gnawing anxiety Yolanda had tried to subdue all morning disappeared like smoke, and Robert draped one arm around her shoulder, one around Tracey's, oblivious to the danger of dirt on his sport jacket.

Yolanda happened to glance toward the house in time to see a curtain in the upstairs hall fall back into place. Agnes had been watching.

The next morning, the time came and passed when the housekeeper usually appeared. Yolanda and Tracey waited nervously. At midmorning the phone rang, and Sophia's worried tones announced that Agnes had given her "a piece of her mind," and resigned. Sophia tactfully avoided exactly what the "piece" had consisted of.

Yolanda frantically rejected the suggestion of a replacement. "Surely we can take care of ourselves. It will be good training for Tracey, and I will feel better with some work to do."

At last Sophia reluctantly agreed, adding that she and Barney would drop by that afternoon.

Tracey had been eavesdropping shamelessly.

"The dragon's gone, hurray, hurray—" she shouted.

She was a bit less exuberant when Yolanda laid out a strict routine for keeping the house tidy, allotting chores to each of them and suggesting they share the cooking.

"I can't cook," Tracey said, as if that ended that.

"You will learn easily. I will teach you," Yolanda promised.

Within a week Rockwoods had relaxed into comfortable hominess. Best of all, the plants in the garden took hold and began to grow, casting a pale sprinkling of emerald over the rich umber soil, just as they would have done in Votice.

During the next two weeks, Rockwoods was slowly transformed even more.

Cycling beside Tracey down a willow-lined country lane one morning, miles from Rockwoods, Yolanda saw a nanny goat with a broken tether around its neck, trotting jauntily toward them down the middle of the road.

She retrieved the broken leather strap and patted the little animal, scratching its head and chattering to it in Slovak. It was a sweet little doe, and badly in need of milking, Yolanda pointed out to Tracey.

They spent an hour locating the owner, and finally knocked on the door of a dilapidated house trailer set in the middle of a field. A laconic young woman with a baby on her hip and a toddler clinging to her jeans looked out at them, and at the goat.

"Oh," she said disinterestedly, "You found Cinnamon." Then she simply stood there. The little goat butted its head against Tracey's legs, and the woman sighed and said, "I guess I better tie her up again." She set the baby on the floor where it immediately began to howl.

"Show us where you want her, and we'll tie her for you," Yolanda suggested, smiling at the diapered toddler who had his thumb in his mouth.

"She needs milking. I will do it for you if you want."

"I never use the milk, anyway. This trailer's sold, and I'm going to Vancouver to live with my folks," the woman explained listlessly. "But there's that goat and the geese down by the shed." She shrugged. "I'm leaving tomorrow. I guess I can't just leave them here...."

"They'll starve." The horror in Tracey's voice echoed Yolanda's own reaction to the callous suggestion. They exchanged telling glances, and a small amount of money changed hands.

Now Rockwoods had a resident goat named Cinnamon, and two geese Tracey named One and Two.

The tempo of daily life speeded up. The goat needed milking, and it was unthinkable to let the milk spoil. Yolanda made cottage cheese and yogurt, teaching Tracey how to, using well-remembered methods *babička* had taught her. They fed the excess milk to the geese. One and Two were invaluable as scavengers in the garden, eating the bugs and weeds, not touching the thriving plants.

Ian Cameron seemed gleeful at the changes in Rockwoods, and he stopped by daily. He turned an empty toolshed into a pen for the geese, and fenced off half the huge cement garage as a home for Cinnamon.

Yolanda had anxious moments when she also wondered what Alex's reaction would be to all this. But, she reminded herself stoutly, he'd told her repeatedly to do what she wanted at Rockwoods.

And no one could mistake the changes in Tracey. Gone were the sulks, the whining, the sad face. The girl was tanned, lithe and healthy-looking, and if she still complained now and then, the complaints were centered around vacuuming or dusting instead of life in general.

"I can't wait to show Daddy what a good cook I'm getting to be," she repeated over and over. She was learning, as fast as Yolanda could teach her, all the old recipes Yolanda kept stored in her head from her own tutelage under *babička*, and many new efforts they tried together from cookbooks.

"Mother hated cooking," Tracey commented once.

It was Ian who brought the chickens one afternoon. He had one clucking hen under each arm as he ambled down the drive. He never did say where he acquired them.

"There's a fine market hereabout for eggs, and these two are Rhode Island Reds," he declared. "I thought Tracey could earn a wee bit of pocket money," he said innocently when Yolanda made halfhearted objections to these new additions. But chickens meant fresh eggs, and Yolanda soon relented. Tracey was thrilled.

"They'll be good company for One and Two," she assured Yolanda.

The chickens joined the geese and the goat.

Yolanda made manure tea for the garden. Tracey applauded each egg as if she'd laid it herself, and she grew adept at milking Cinnamon.

"Doesn't it smell wonderful?" Tracey sniffed the earthy odors tempered by fresh sea air. Yolanda nodded. It was like home, to listen to the medley of chickens clucking, geese honking, goat bleating.

And, best of all, Alex would return in two more days.

CHAPTER SEVEN

"YES, HELLO?"

The phone had rung just as Yolanda stepped into the house. She'd gone for a walk after dinner, wandering along the windswept shore below the house. Tracey had taken her bike and ridden over to Ian's to borrow a book he'd promised her, a story written by a woman veterinarian. Tracey had confided she wanted to be a vet, adding in typical Tracey fashion that her father probably wouldn't let her. Remembering the remark, Yolanda smiled and shook her head as she picked up the phone.

"Is this Mrs. Caine? Hello, my name is Carrie Russell. I'm an old friend of Alex's, and I just wanted to welcome you to Canada. Yes, I know Alex is out of town just now, that's why I thought it would be nice to introduce myself. It must be a bit difficult, getting used to a new country and not having Alex around to introduce you to anyone."

Yolanda felt both bewildered by the rapid flow of words and intensely curious about this woman with the silky voice who was Alex's old friend. Accustomed as she was to *babička*'s friends and neighbors popping in and out, Rockwoods often seemed isolated and lonely.

Besides, Yolanda told herself she needed to make other contacts. She must soon think about a job, an apartment, a life on her own. The idea made a hard knot of apprehension twist her insides. She must keep reminding herself that she was only a temporary resident here at Rockwoods. And in Alex's life.

Disquieting thoughts flitted through her mind as she listened to Carrie's voice rush on, hardly waiting for Yolanda's answers.

"I understand you're from Czechoslovakia? I'd love to meet you. Perhaps we could have coffee together? Would you like to come into the city, or should I come out there? Oh, yes, of course I know where Rockwoods is. Tomorrow at, say, ten? Great. Fine. I'm looking forward to it. Bye now."

Yolanda slowly hung up the phone. Meeting Carrie Russell was one more way of knowing Alex. Her feminine curiosity had been stirred, and maybe another emotion as well, one she didn't want to examine. What sort of "good friends" were they? Something seemed to stick in Yolanda's throat, and she swallowed hard. Maybe she didn't want to meet this woman, after all. Well, it was too late now. Her practical nature asserted itself. What would she serve for coffee?

Briskly she set to work sifting flour, beating eggs. She would make *babička*'s special coffee cake, and sweet bread with raisins. There were the tender stalks of pale green rhubarb Ian had brought that morning. She'd stew them. There was freshly curded cottage cheese from Cinnamon's milk, and she could make a custard with all those eggs.

It was soothing to mix, beat, and measure in the ancient rituals taught her by Anna, taught Anna by her mother, rituals handed down to daughters like a precious legacy over the centuries from women ingenious at using whatever was at hand to create food for their families and friends. Would she ever have her own small daughter to teach, as *babička* had taught her, as she was teaching Tracey?

Yolanda's floury hands paused over the mixing bowl. During the past few years, her immediate future had been too uncertain to allow the luxury of dreams. Getting through each day had taken all her energy, and the nights had been haunted by fearful images and nightmares.

Thoughtfully she kneaded the sweet dough, rolling it backward and forward between her strong hands on the smooth surface. There hadn't been time to think much about love, or husbands, or children.

Her hands stilled. She wanted children. Small, roughneck boys and girls, chasing chickens and trying to ride the goat. The hard lump in her throat nearly choked her this time, and she had to fight back tears. With something like anguish, she leaned over the counter and closed her eyes, facing fully the truth she'd managed to avoid till now.

She wanted love, the love a man and a woman shared. And not just any man. Alex. From the moment she'd first met him, her subconscious had recognized the truth. She'd known it on the day of their wedding. She loved him, and she longed for his love in return. She wanted to have his children—if she were to have any children at all. Already she was nearly thirty. Time was speeding her past the most fruitful years. Babies would have to come soon, or not at all.

Then, there was Tracey. She wanted to watch Tracey's growth into womanhood.

Ironically, she'd fallen hopelessly in love with her husband, and, she reminded herself harshly, her husband wasn't really her husband. He still belonged to the memory of his first wife.

The back door slammed, and Tracey's cheery voice rang out.

"Hi, Landa. I'm home." The girl bounced over to the table. She'd ridden into Victoria and had her hair cut the day before, and the result had brought Slovak exclamations of horror from Yolanda.

"They have sculpted you," she gasped.

"Scalped," Tracey blithely corrected. "I told them to; it's the style. It's hot."

Hot or not, Yolanda had to get used to the change every time she looked at Tracey. She couldn't imagine what Alex would say, but after all, as Tracey insisted, it was her hair. Actually, she looked like a beguiling nymph, Yolanda decided fondly.

"What're you making?" Tracey asked.

Yolanda managed a wide smile and injected a light tone into her voice.

"Wash your hands, and come here, beside me. I will teach you to make bread, just the way *babička* taught me."

Everything was ready long before Carrie arrived the next morning.

Yolanda dressed nervously, ignoring Tracey's suggestion that she wear her jeans. She slid on the gray skirt she'd chosen to wear. It slid off her waist, and barely held over her hips.

"Tracey," she called in amazement. "Come look at this."

The girl ambled in from her room. Together they viewed Yolanda's reflection in the wall mirror, and Tracey held her thumb up in her familiar salute. "*Awwright!* That diet really worked. But you sure can't wear that skirt. It's hot out. Haven't you got a summer dress?"

Yolanda, at Tracey's urging, took the panty hose and slip off and settled on a green-flowered cotton with a belt she could cinch in, a simple shirtwaist she'd made herself the summer before.

"Our feet are almost the same size," Tracey noted. "I've got some sandals I never wear; they'll be better than those clumpy shoes of yours." She brought them, and Yolanda buckled them on. A glance in the mirror confirmed that the strappy leather sandals suited the casual dress.

Staring at herself, Yolanda saw a stranger with a familiar face. She didn't quite look like the thin, elegant women she'd admired on the streets of Victoria. Her wide, high cheekbones were more pronounced since she'd dieted, and her blue eyes looked larger. There was a quality in her face that would always mark her as foreign, a look that Grandma had labeled "Gypsy wild."

She didn't look Canadian, whatever that was. But neither did she look entirely Czechoslovakian any more. Would she ever be entirely one thing or the other? She shrugged and went to make the coffee.

"YOU SPEAK ENGLISH very well, Mrs. Caine."

"Alex's daughter, Tracey, she is helping me with idiom, thank you, Carrie Russell. Please, call me Yolanda."

Yolanda felt more than a little intimidated by Carrie Russell. A flaming redhead, Carrie's hair was as flamboyant as the woman herself. Shorter than Yolanda, she was reed-slim, and she moved as if an electric current coursed through her. Her movements were quick and almost awkward, punctuated by dramatic motions of her narrow hands, which boasted a flashing ring on nearly every finger. She had intelligent dark brown eyes. Her straight hair was expertly cut, with a fringe that played up her milky skin and the faint dusting of freckles across the diminutive nose.

Carrie picked up one of the framed photos of Alex and Dixie from the mantelpiece, but to Yolanda's relief, she didn't comment. Instead, she stared at it for a moment with the snappy eyes that seemed to miss nothing, and then put it firmly back in place.

She wore tailored gray slacks and a wisp of a silk blouse in a burgundy rose shade that should have been absolutely wrong with her hair, but instead was exactly right, making Yolanda conscious of her own homemade dress and bare legs.

As if by magic, within ten minutes Carrie's pleasing soft voice and stream of artless conversation had set Yolanda at ease.

Tracey had appeared, said a brief hello in response to Carrie's easy greeting, and then excused herself to feed the animals.

"I had no idea Alex was into farming," Carrie remarked, surprise and amusement in her voice. "That's some garden out there."

"It's not really farming," Yolanda tried to explain. "We have the garden, the chickens and geese. And the goat."

"A goat?" Carrie's voice held a strangled note of disbelief.

"Of course, yes," Yolanda replied. "Cinnamon supplies us with milk, and cottage cheese, and that helps feed the chickens, and the geese keep the garden free of bugs and weeds. And later, we will have roast goose."

Carrie blinked, and nodded weakly.

"I guess there aren't any bylaws out here to worry about," she murmured. For the first time, she seemed to run out of friendly patter, so Yolanda suggested they have their coffee.

The table was set under the window in the kitchen, bathed in morning sunshine and laid with a bright yellow cloth. There was thinly sliced and buttered sweet bread, coffee cake oozing melted sugar and plums, a clear glass dish with darkly pink stewed rhubarb waiting to be topped with the soft curds of freshly made cottage cheese sweetened with honey.

"My God, it's a feast," Carrie breathed, slipping into the chair Yolanda indicated. "And it's all homemade. Fantastic. How'd you know I skipped breakfast this morning?"

She attacked the food with the same energy she applied to everything else, and Yolanda nibbled. If Carrie was an indication of how thin Alex liked women, it was probably a lost cause to even try to diet, she mourned silently. She poured more coffee, urging her guest to try another piece of cake.

They talked easily and superficially at first, about clothing styles in East and West, of Yolanda's pleasure in cooking.

Carrie admitted she could barely manage to open packaged bread, never mind bake it.

Then Carrie casually asked, "What work did you do before you came here?"

"I worked in a factory, as seamstress," Yolanda replied simply, deciding not to reveal the problems that led to that particular job. "Days off, I worked with *bab*—with my grandmother. She had a small plot of land. We grew vegetables—smaller than this garden, however."

Carrie laughed. "Alex's garden looks as if he's going to give up politics and start truck farming," she joked.

Yolanda protested earnestly, "Oh, no, I think not. But it helps with expenses, growing enough food for a family."

Carrie shot her a curious glance, one thin eyebrow tilting assessingly above her chocolate eyes.

"I wouldn't have guessed that finances were a problem for the Caines?"

"Every family should be self-sufficient in the matter of food," Yolanda insisted stubbornly. "Here, I have seen people on the television, standing in line for groceries. Yet everywhere are unused acres of land which could be cultivated, like here. It is big mistake to waste in this manner; it surprises me."

Carrie listened. Then she asked casually, "What other things have you seen here that surprise you?"

Yolanda looked sharply at the other woman, and a warning bell sounded.

She said simply, "Why do you ask this?"

The redhead looked away, and a faint stain rose in her cheeks.

Then she said reluctantly, "I have to admit, Yolanda, that I did have an ulterior motive in wanting to meet you. You see, I write a column in one of Vancouver's two daily papers, a column read by a great many women who are always curious about other women, what their lives are like. I wondered if you'd mind my quoting some of your impressions of Canada, of Victoria, just the ordinary things we've talked about here today?"

The woman's admission made Yolanda's stomach clench painfully. It was because of indiscriminate remarks made to a journalist that she'd lost her interpreter's job in Prague. Why hadn't she thought of asking what Carrie's job was?

She'd begun to enjoy their conversation, and she felt acute disappointment at the other woman's disclosure, and a sense of betrayal.

Meeting Carrie's eyes with a forthright look, she said deliberately, "I think you have misled me, Carrie Russell. I welcomed you here as friend of my husband, not as a journalist."

Carrie had the grace to blush deeply, but she held Yolanda's gaze steadily this time.

"And that's exactly what I am, a friend of Alex's. I'd like to be a friend of yours, as well. But you must understand what writers are like. We have to use everything available for inspiration."

She lifted her cup and sipped at the coffee. "Alex, whether he likes it or not, is a public figure. Publicity and politics go hand in hand; he has to accept that. Better that publicity comes from a friend who knows the situation than from a news-hungry stranger. Don't you agree?"

With each passing moment, Yolanda felt more and more that she'd been duped into the meeting, and worse still, that she wasn't at all sure how to handle it. The last thing she wanted or needed was attention paid to her marriage, to the circumstances under which she'd become Mrs. Caine.

"I don't believe Alex's and my private life would be of interest for your readers," she said evenly.

"On the contrary, anything about the colorful Caine family is always interesting. Especially such an exotic marriage as yours. You wouldn't care to tell me how you met ... any romantic details of your wedding?" Carrie hadn't gotten her column by being reticent.

"I would not, no," Yolanda stated firmly. She got up. Her body felt stiff.

"I think perhaps we have talked enough," she said with all the dignity she could muster. "You should speak to Alex about this. He will be home tomorrow afternoon."

Carrie rose unhurriedly and thanked Yolanda for the refreshments as if nothing untoward had happened at all. In a few moments Yolanda heard Carrie roar off down the lane in her sporty red car.

Yolanda drew a deep breath. She tried to shake off the ominous feeling that she'd made a bad mistake in talking to Carrie Russell at all, yet when she reviewed their conversation word by word, she couldn't for the life of her recall anything that would cause trouble for Alex. She cleared away the dishes, put on a pair of shorts and headed for the garden.

The tiny lettuce leaves already needed thinning, and as always, the hot sun and the feel of the earth between her fingers calmed and comforted her.

Tracey pedaled up the lane in another hour and skipped over to Yolanda. "That lady left, huh?" she inquired cynically. "Bet she just wanted to see who got to marry my dad." Tracey snorted rudely. "Broads like her don't fool me any. They just pretend to like me because they think that will make Daddy like them. Boy, I'm glad I never got one like her for a stepmother."

Anxious that Yolanda not misunderstand, Tracey added hastily, "Some of the girls at school have stepparents, and they hardly ever get along with them like you and I do, Landa. But you're not really my stepmother, so that's probably why," she finished guilelessly, racing off to check on Cinnamon. The little goat was showing an amazing ability to chew through any tether and escape, sometimes onto the low roof of one of the outbuildings.

Yolanda stared after Tracey's retreating back. It was pretty certain that Carrie's visit was exactly what the girl said ... a desire to see who had married Alex. Yolanda felt her forehead crease into a frown. Just exactly how many "broads" had pretended to like Tracey, anyway?

ALEX ARRIVED AT THE AIRPORT late the following afternoon, feeling a deep sense of relief at coming home. Even first-class accommodation didn't really allow ample room for his long legs, and this flight had seemed endless.

Robert met him at the airport outside of Victoria.

"I'm sick to death of hotels, of restaurant food," Alex commented as they collected the last of the luggage and loaded it into the back of Robert's battered blue half-ton truck.

He'd resisted the impulse to phone Yolanda each day. There really was no logical reason for him to call apart from the crazy pleasure he felt at hearing her husky voice saying his name.

"Want me to take you straight out to Rockwoods?" his father inquired.

Alex shook his head and reflected that he'd heard men went slightly berserk at forty. Well, he was thirty-nine. There seemed no other logical explanation for the way he was feeling lately, this burning need to get home to Rockwoods. To see her.

"I have to check in at the apartment first, Dad," Alex heard himself saying. For some reason he couldn't explain, he wanted to arrive at Rockwoods alone. He felt strange about seeing Yolanda again, as if in some ridiculous fashion she would know about his persistent presence in his dreams over the past weeks. Erotic dreams, at that.

Robert seemed a bit preoccupied. He slid behind the wheel and then said emphatically, "That Yolanda's a fine woman, son. Salt of the earth. Hell, Tracey isn't the same kid she was when you left—you'll see."

For God's sake, could even Robert pick up his thoughts about Yolanda? Alex slammed the truck door and fussed with the seat belt.

"I'm glad to hear that, because I was ready to strangle Tracey the day I left. Anything's got to be an improvement."

"She's a different girl. I have to admit I was dubious about all the changes at first, but now..."

"I see you're still driving this old wreck, Dad," Alex interrupted, deliberately avoiding the path Robert's conversation seemed to be taking. He didn't feel ready for a lengthy discussion about Tracey, which would lead naturally to Yolanda. He didn't want to talk about her with his father. His thoughts and feelings were far too confused for that.

"What're you doing, keeping the Rolls as an ornament?"

Robert's white Silver Shadow had become a family joke. It sat, gleaming and exquisite, under cover in the garage of Robert's apartment. No occasion ever seemed suitably momentous to drive the magnificent vehicle. Consequently, Robert went everywhere in this battered Chevy truck.

The older Caine chuckled good-naturedly as the faithful motor roared into life. "Reason I like this old truck, son, is that it matches me. Getting old, but still plenty of mileage left in both of us. The Rolls is too much like some women, elegant as hell to look at, but not much use when the going gets tough."

Alex gave his father a wary glance. What had prompted that analogy? Could it be Yolanda again?

"Well, this one's upholstery leaves a bit to be desired, but I guess you're right," Alex agreed lightly.

They were companionably quiet for several miles.

"You know Agnes Witherspoon resigned?" Robert said next.

Alex nodded. "Barney phoned. Did Sophie manage to find somebody?" Privately Alex thought Agnes was no great loss. Dixie had hired her, and he'd never gotten around to firing the woman. Dixie had insisted on having everything hospital-clean and in order at all times. It was one of the things she'd been unreasonable about, in Alex's opinion, and one of the few things they openly disagreed upon.

"Yolanda insisted that she and Tracey could take care of the house themselves, and damned if it isn't a pleasure to be able to spill a few ashes around when I visit, without that martinet of an Agnes glaring at me. Never liked that woman."

Alex slouched comfortably, letting his father's words flow over and around him, not paying too much attention to the details.

It was good to be home. He couldn't remember when he'd so appreciated the lush fields, the grazing animals on the small farms bordering the highway, the distant view of mountains. He couldn't remember, either, when he'd last been so eager to get to Rockwoods.

Robert dropped him at the apartment, refusing Alex's half-hearted invitation for a drink. Within half an hour, Alex was showered and changed, and ten minutes after that, he'd hurried down to the parking garage and into his cherished silver Porsche.

Humming along with the car radio, he drove swiftly along Beach Drive. Sunglasses shaded his eyes, and anticipation made the miles seem longer than he remembered, despite the vista of sparkling ocean.

He approached Seaview Road, and finally the weathered wooden sign, 45 Rockwoods, which signaled the tree-shaded winding lane. Exuberantly, Alex made the turn, screeching the tires and peeling his glasses off, wanting to relish his first glimpse of house and gracious lawn and far-flung ocean without distortion.

The sun was in his eyes as the car burst from the foliage, and all he could distinguish at first were the shining wide windows of the house. Then, the light shifted; the scene unfolded.

"Son of a—" Alex slammed on the brakes without thinking, and the car jolted to a jerky halt halfway down the drive. Momentarily he wondered if he might have mistaken his own address and turned into the wrong driveway.

The car idled, and he automatically turned off the ignition, wrapping both hands around the wheel, leaning forward in the seat and gaping at the scene before him.

Fully half an acre of raw, plowed earth gaped like an open wound on his right, where a carpet of green had spread until it met the wall of encircling forest. Alex blinked, shut his eyes, looked again.

To his left, a goat—a goat?—was tied by a length of rope to the apple tree, busily munching grass in an ever widening circle. Removed from the house, but plainly visible from where he sat, a shed encircled by chicken wire held—two chickens? As his eyes returned in dumb amazement to the garden, he spotted geese happily pecking between planted hillocks.

Chickens. Geese. A goat. *Rockwoods?*

Before he could even begin to absorb it all, Tracey was flying like an ungainly colt up the driveway, all long, slender arms and legs.

"Daddy," she was shouting like a banshee. "Daddy, you're home, you're home." When she reached the car, she stopped all of a sudden, becoming bashful as he opened the door and climbed out.

"Hi, Daddy. Welcome back," she said demurely.

When had she last raced to meet him this way? Not for years, not since she was a plump little thing in a lacy dress. What had happened to...

Alex could only stare at her just as he'd stared at Rockwoods a few seconds earlier. Tracey, too, had undergone a metamorphosis. She was taller. The stooped shoulders were held straight, and what had been long, auburn hair was cut in... Alex swallowed hard. Did they still call that a brush cut?

The sullen expression he'd come to expect was replaced by a wide, crooked grin.

"So what d'ya think, Dad?"

This gamin of a girl radiated tanned good health and high spirits. For the first time he could see the embryonic woman in her waiting to break free, and he had to swallow again, this time because of an awkward lump in his throat.

He reached out and gathered his daughter into a bear hug, then tousled what was left of her hair.

"I used to call you pumpkin, but I better switch to onion now," he managed to say, rubbing a hand over the bristle on her head.

"Oh, gross," she wailed, but her arms were like clamps around his middle, and he realized she'd been tensely waiting for his reaction. "Wait'll you see everything Yolanda and I did while you were gone," she enthused, grabbing his hand and tugging him along the drive.

"You mean there's more?" he muttered, taking another incredulous look to the right and left.

"Where is Yolanda, anyway?" A peculiar tightness accompanied the words, a tension of anticipation.

"She went to gather seaweed for the garden. It's good fertilizer, you know, Daddy. I'll go get her." Tracey dashed away.

Yolanda had just clambered up the beach path, dragging a load of seaweed in a canvas sling, when she had spotted Alex's car pulling into the driveway. Her hair was blown by the wind, and her hands were stained from the green weed. He mustn't see her like this, Yolanda thought, panic-stricken. She ran pell-mell for the house, ducking in the back door.

In a frenzy, she washed her hands at the kitchen sink, smoothed her hair, patted her cheeks with cold water, muttering under her breath like one demented. Her face burned as if she had a fever. She hurried to the front door, jerking it open, and there on the other side was—Alex.

Alex. The nervousness stilled, and her whole being became quiet. She heard her own voice saying something, but the silent words inside drowned out the spoken words, and she was uncertain what she actually said.

I love this man. I am in love with you, Alex. Can you see?

She drank in the sight of him, from the tumbled ash-brown hair with its underlay of silver, the endearingly crooked nose, to the way his thick eyebrows lifted as if he were asking her something.

She'd forgotten he was this tall, this broad. Her head came just past his chin. Her eyes were on a level with his mouth.

Those narrow, hard, sensual lips. She stared at them, unable to look away. A slow, unbearable tension began to grow between them.

Alex had turned for another disbelieving glimpse of what had once been the lawns just as the door was flung open. Turning quickly to Yolanda, he started to say hello, but the word died before he could get it out.

The woman in the doorway was, technically, the same woman he'd married five weeks ago. Yet, like everything else at Rockwoods, this was a vastly different Yolanda than he'd remembered.

"Hello, Alex," she greeted him with a tentative smile. "Welcome home."

The same luminous tilted eyes, startlingly blue, thickly curtained with gold-tipped lashes. Full, slightly parted lips in a face somehow made starkly dramatic, cheekbones carving it into sculptured lines. Mole by the mouth. Curving, slender neck below a cleanly drawn jawline. Husky, accented voice. Golden copper skin. Tendrils of silky dark hair escaping from a thick club of heavy braid hanging over one shoulder—these were more or less the same.

"Hello, Yolanda."

What was it that had changed, then? She was thinner, that was it. High, rounded breasts were outlined under the thin cotton of a white T-shirt, tapering into a narrow waist and delicately flaring hips encased in snug blue jeans. Strength and delicacy melded into total femininity, enhanced by the trace of shyness that brought color creeping up her neck and into her cheeks.

She was less than she had been, yet so much more.

Her eyes seemed to center on his lips like an invitation. His reaction was automatic. He took a half step forward and put his arm around her. When she tipped her head back to give him a startled look, he kissed her, his mouth drawn irresistibly to taste the full, provocative lips, and he knew what it was he'd been hungry for these past weeks.

She was staring up at him when his arms came around her, and his face blurred. Just before she felt his kiss, she touched his face hesitantly. His hands slid around her, spanning her waist and pulling her fiercely tight against him, and she shuddered.

His smell was familiar; a clean, sweet essence of Alex. She remembered the sensation of slightly abrasive male skin against the softness of her cheek.

He nibbled gently for an instant, and Yolanda felt surging excitement and eagerness spring to life within her, trapping her breath in her lungs. She wanted him to kiss her properly. If he released her now, she couldn't bear it.

His lips hovered over hers for less than a heartbeat, and then he claimed her.

His mouth moved on hers, thirsty, exploring, talented and hungry, and a wild elation sprang to life within her. Instinctively her lips opened for him, and his tongue's hard tip memorized their shape, tracing the bow, the full lower lip.

His tongue slipped inside. Her body tingled as small shocks of pleasure touched hidden places within, teasing, hinting of more and yet more. His arms tightened around her, and hers around him.

He made a sound deep in his throat, of wonder and aching need, and her lower body instinctively undulated against the heat of his hardness.

His hand rose, captured the single long braid and tipped her head back so his mouth could explore the long, curving line of her neck, his tongue echoing the pulse that thundered at its base, hot and wet against her skin.

She wanted an unnameable more. With a rushing, pulsing heat in her loins and up into every pore of her body, she wanted his loving. The small sound welling up in her throat was an invitation, a provocative question, totally female and wanting and wordless.

He was the one to remember time and place, to tighten his embrace like a promise and then release her in a tortured effort at control.

He took her chin between his thumb and finger, gazing down at her.

"Yolanda? Landa, is it really you?"

The rough tenderness in his voice was amazement, question, hunger.

Her voice was drowned by delight. All she could do was nod. Whatever he wanted of her, she would give. She loved him.

He looked into her eyes, and a frown came and went on his forehead.

He felt again as if he were gazing down into her soul. Never before had he met a woman this open, a woman so devoid of subterfuge. She could be hurt so easily. She seemed to have no defenses. It threw all the responsibility on him, and he fought the feelings she roused in him, resenting both her and himself. He wanted to throw her down, here in the hall, and make love to every inch of her. He also wanted to turn away, get in his car and leave before he hurt her.

He groaned, drew her roughly against him once more to cradle her in his arms, and they stood silently, trying to recover from what had happened between them, both weak, breathless, throbbingly alive.

"Yolanda? Yolanda, where are you?" The voice was Tracey's. The kitchen door slammed, and there was the sound of hurrying feet pounding across the tile.

They sprang apart, like guilty children caught in mischief. Yolanda tried to steady her breathing, erratic and rough.

"I'm here, Tracey," she finally managed to say, and Alex turned and climbed the entrance stairs to meet his daughter as she burst into the living room, and to protectively shield Yolanda for a moment behind him.

"Where were you? I looked all over," she said accusingly, her gray eyes flitting from one to the other suspiciously. But the desire to show off for her father overcame her momentary doubts.

"C'mon, Dad. I want you to meet Cinnamon, and One and Two, and the chickens. And wait till I show you our garden."

His head turned, and he looked at Yolanda questioningly.

"Go with her, and I'll make dinner. Go."

She was still shaky, and she needed solitude for a time. She'd known the word *desire* in five languages, but obviously she'd never suspected its meaning till now.

It was a power to be reckoned with.

Today, for the first time, she also knew that Alex felt something for her. Was it love? Or was it only the natural need of a man for a woman, the same need with which he'd held her on their wedding night? Would he allow his need to overcome him again? She didn't know.

Her natural practicality refused to agonize over it. He'd held her and passionately kissed her. It was enough. It was a beginning.

But it wasn't at all simple. If her relationship with Alex should ever become intimate, what of Tracey? They couldn't always leap apart the way they just had, hiding perfectly normal emotions from the girl.

Yolanda had come to know Tracey in the past weeks, and she was deeply concerned about her. Somehow, in the midst of all the moneyed luxury surrounding the Caine family, the child had gotten lost. Perhaps when her mother had died, perhaps even earlier. When it had happened didn't matter.

What did matter was that the happiness on Tracey's face remain there, grow stronger and more certain. The girl would never feel an outsider again, Yolanda decided firmly. Not if it could be prevented.

Her hands busied themselves with spreading a freshly ironed cloth, putting out the pretty willow-patterned china, fresh yeast buns, the trays of simple vegetables and fruit she'd disciplined herself to eat, and had even grown to like. There was the fragrant fresh cheese from Cinnamon's milk and the hearty stew she'd made earlier. Preparing food was the same everywhere, and the task always brought her peace. She smiled a little sadly.

How often *babička*'s hands had followed these same patterns, serving food.

And the patterns of the heart. Were they universal, as well? Would she ever find the happiness *babička* had known with her Karel?

There had been only one man in Anna Belankova's long life.

"For some women, that's how it is," Anna had once declared.

That's how it was and would be for Yolanda Caine.

CHAPTER EIGHT

"WHAT'S GOING TO BECOME of the animals when you go back to Vancouver to school, Tracey? You know there's no one here at Rockwoods most of the time, and there's only five weeks of school vacation left."

Alex had avoided the subject until dinner was over, but it had nagged at him as he listened to his daughter chatter excitedly. Yolanda had been quiet during the meal, meeting Alex's eyes squarely, but allowing Tracey to do the talking. The girl's gaze flew to Yolanda now.

"There's a high school near here, one I could ride to on my bike."

Her voice quavered. "Yolanda said to talk to you about it."

Unreasonable resentment stirred in Alex. "Your mother wanted you to graduate from Duncan House," he stated firmly, adding cream to the coffee Yolanda poured for him. She stood poised with the coffeepot still in her hand, her eyes going from Alex to Tracey and back again.

"My mother is dead," Tracey said slowly and distinctly. "Even if she weren't, I'd want to go to school here. I hate Duncan House, Daddy." Tracey's fists were balled into tight knots, one on each side of her plate. Yolanda could see how agitated she was becoming, and she moved to put a calming hand on Tracey's shoulder.

Alex shot Yolanda a glance. He angrily suspected she was aligning herself with Tracey and that she had unwittingly brought this scene about with her garden and animals and God knew what else. "You're going back to Vancouver, back to school at Duncan House, and that's that," he ordered, feeling like a tyrant as soon as he'd said it, baffled anew at his inability to deal with Tracey.

He dealt with politicians, foreign diplomats, touchy international traders, and yet he couldn't carry on a reasonable conversation for longer than five minutes with this child.

The rest of the scene was predictable. She'd throw something, scream and cry, run out... He tensed expectantly.

Tracey's lips trembled, and there were tears in her eyes, but Yolanda's quiet voice intervened.

"Ian wanted you to ride over this evening, Tracey. His grandson is coming to stay for the summer, remember? Why don't you go now, and I'll clean the dishes this time?"

Jerkily, without another word, Tracey got up, not looking at her father, and walked stiffly out. She banged the door, but not as badly as she might have.

Alex expelled his pent-up breath in a slow, tired sigh. Now he'd have to try and explain to Yolanda why it was wrong to encourage Tracey's rebellious attitudes about school. Damn it all, this being the father of a teenaged girl was beyond him.

Two minutes, pregnant with silence, had gone by before the door exploded open, and with eyes round and horrified, Tracey hollered, "Cinnamon got loose, and she's on top of your car, Daddy."

Galvanized into action, Yolanda and Alex flew out the door.

Sure enough, the saucy goat was planted firmly on top of Alex's sporty silver car, her chewed roap dangling from her neck, her sharp hooves making dents in the gleaming paint. She bleated at them, prancing a little, creating new scratches with every movement.

Alex cursed in a steady stream, reached up and lifted the animal down, setting her none too gently on the ground and shoving the tattered rope into Tracey's hands.

He studied the damage. The hood would need extensive bodywork and the whole car would require a new paint job. He used a basic Anglo-Saxon expletive.

"Lock this animal up before I wring her bloody neck," he gritted.

Tracey gave him a wounded, outraged glare before she led Cinnamon away, and Alex rounded on Yolanda.

"Alex, I'm sorry. She chews through her rope, the rascal..." Yolanda began, but nothing would calm him, for the goat had simply provided the vehicle for the maelstrom of conflicting emotions that had warred in him since his arrival.

They erupted now in a burst of illogical fury, fueled by the confusion of his emotions toward her, the intense sexual response and consequent frustration she stirred in him, as well as the recent scene with his daughter.

He jammed his hands deep into his pockets and stepped closer to Yolanda, disturbingly close. He was formidable, with his green eyes cold and narrowed, his voice snarling at her.

"What the hell did you think you were doing, digging up half the estate, filling it with all these damn geese and chickens, and that infernal bloody goat?"

Her answer was deceptively quiet, and she stood proudly, her newly slender body held straight and tall. She would not allow him to intimidate her.

Even in his anger he was disturbingly aware of every tantalizing curve.

"I was doing what you said I should do, Alex. You said I should treat Rockwoods as my home. At first it seemed to me some fancy hotel, not a home at all. I asked you about the garden; you told me to go ahead. I should have discussed the animals first with you, but Tracey loved them, and I was caring for Tracey."

She was quiet, reasonable and right. It infuriated him.

He abandoned that attack for another.

"You had no business encouraging Tracey in this ridiculous idea she has about changing schools. You don't understand the first damn thing about the problems I've had with her."

He knew it was grossly unfair and that his troubles with Tracey certainly weren't Yolanda's fault. He felt ashamed as soon as he'd spoken.

"Perhaps not. But the past is over, and what I understand now is that Tracey feels unhappy and lonely in this school. She has told me things about it which concern me, Alex."

"What things?" He'd been about to apologize, but now he felt on the defensive again. How had Yolanda won his daughter's trust in such a short time, while he was unable to communicate with her?

"The details are a confidence between her and me. But I assure you, this place you are sending her is not good for Tracey." Unconsciously she folded her arms across her chest.

Alex glared at her, but she refused to flinch.

"Are you telling me," he said, his voice low now and silkily lethal, "that in three short weeks you think you know more about what's good for my daughter than I do?"

Yolanda felt that if she released her arms from their grip on each other, she'd fall in a heap on the ground. What was she doing, defying him this way? But Tracey couldn't talk to him and make him understand. Robert, Barney, Sophia—they were older, involved in their own busy lives. Who did that leave to fight for the girl? Someone had to make him understand. She stood her ground.

"Yes," she said bravely. "I do believe that, Alex."

Even when he was furious, he stirred her. His hair was rumpled, the green eyes had darkened to a stormy shade, and the fists in his pockets pulled the casual cords tight across lean hips. The memory of his kisses made her catch her breath.

But this was war, not love. She tilted her chin even higher.

Utter astonishment paralleled his outrage at her words. In the course of his whole married life, he couldn't remember one single confrontation during which Dixie had stood with her arms crossed and outright defied him like this.

Sometimes Dixie had cried, making him feel like a heel. Then there were pouts and long silences to get through uncomfortably. He thrust that memory aside. At other times, she'd wheedled charmingly, and if the issue weren't too important, he gave her what she wanted. But this? Yolanda's blue eyes were icy. She was taking him on, toe to toe, her chin tilted defiantly.

Grudging respect for her stirred in him, but he was at a loss as to how to deal with her.

He resorted to tactics that were effective in the legislature debates when a member was being attacked.

"Exactly what do you mean, Yolanda? Explain yourself."

(Does the honorable member have facts to back up his imaginings?)

She looked around, aware of the incongruity of standing in the middle of the yard and quarreling, while birds twittered and

a soft evening breeze rustled the arbutus trees. Besides, Tracey
might come back and hear them out here.

"Perhaps we should go in the house to discuss this further?" she suggested coolly, proud that she was able to keep her
voice from quavering.

A delaying measure. Aha, she was wily. Fine.

He nodded curtly, stalking off ahead of her, holding the door
politely for her to slip past, his face hard and impassive, his
body rigid.

He was doing his best to ignore the powerful images of
holding her here in his arms, the way she'd felt and smelled and
tasted. Against his will, his nostrils drew in the faint flowery
fragrance she exuded as she hurried up the steps into the living
room. His eyes were on her provocative behind as she gracefully climbed the stairs.

Yolanda felt that if she didn't sit down soon her trembling
legs would give way. By doing this, she was destroying every
chance there might have been for joy with him. What was it in
her that made her unable to curb her tongue and ensure her own
survival?

She sat on a hard-backed chair. He took a similar chair a few
yards away. They faced each other warily. How could she say
what she had to, without making him hate and resent her?

"When I was a child, I attended the village school in Votice,
and I was happy there. But as I grew beyond it," she began
slowly, "I had to board in Prague to go to school, live in a
dormitory with other girls. It was not a good experience for me.
I was a private child, needing to be alone a lot. Groups of young
people are the same everywhere, I think. Either you join them,
or you become the enemy. Tracey knows this."

She gazed out over the calming vista of water and clouds and
distant islands beyond the window, her blue eyes stormy with
memories.

"I was fortunate. I had *babička* to return to every weekend,
to help me set a course for myself. To give me courage not to
join the crowd when I didn't want to. Tracey doesn't have
babička, Alex." She met his eyes squarely, deliberately aiming
for the heart, feeling desolate as she did it.

"She doesn't even have you at home every weekend. You
aren't there for her when she needs you."

He shot to his feet and color rose in his lean cheeks. His jaw
was set so the strong bones showed through the skin.

"Her grandparents dote on her, and she stays with them
whenever she chooses," he said hotly. "Sophia and Barney
keep a room for her."

Her words were stirring a dreadful guilt inside him, a guilt
he'd known was buried, but one he hadn't had the courage to
drag out and examine. It hurt to do so now.

"Sophia, Barney, her grandparents—they all love her, undoubtedly, but they aren't giving her what she needs: guidance, firm discipline." Yolanda was relentless. "Only you can
give her that. When you were a boy, Alex, who was there to talk
with you? I remember you said you grew up here at Rockwoods, with Barney and your father. You must remember how
secure that made you feel, those strong, wise men to rely on.
Tracey needs you, just as you did them."

He stalked to the window, his back to her. Pride made him
hide the effect of her words, the awful realization she was
forcing him into.

Of course he remembered. There had always been his father, his uncle Barney. And Rockwoods. The school he'd attended was in Victoria, and he'd come home, here, every night.
His eyes swept around the familiar room.

In those days there'd been the mounted head of a moose
above the mantel . . . right there, and a huge old rocking chair,
his grandfather's, had sat here. Dixie had had the place re-
done, with flower prints and drapes to cover the windows, and
this light, spindly furniture. All the old pieces were up in the
attic.

He'd accepted the changes, but secretly he'd liked the old
place the way it had been, masculine-looking, relaxed.

Home. With Robert and Barney always there to listen. Blast
this woman. What right had she to dredge up all his misgivings this way?

"Tracey is a girl. She needs to learn things I can't teach her."
It was a line of last defense, and he recognized that.

"She needs you. She needs more than occasional visits with
you. Tracey needs a full-time father." Yolanda was implacable, but it was costing her dearly to see the anguish she stirred

in him. She despised hurting him, ached to rush over and cradle him in her arms, yet she felt angry, too, for Tracey's sake.

When he turned toward her, his tone and his eyes were icy and remote, and he'd erected a wall between them. "You've made your point. Now, if you don't mind, I prefer not to discuss the matter any further."

He strode from the room, and she felt as if she'd been physically beaten. Every muscle hurt from the tension between them. What had she accomplished, except to make him furious with her? Tears burned behind her eyes, but she refused to let them fall. In this instance, tears solved absolutely nothing.

Instead she went briskly to the kitchen and washed and polished, cursing pithy, satisfying Slovak curses as she scrubbed things she normally never noticed. When everything was gleaming so that even Agnes Witherspoon would have approved, she escaped to the beach and walked miles along the rocky shore until it was so dark that she had to feel her way back up the path.

She could hear Alex and Tracey talking in the library, and she crept like a burglar up the steps to her room.

A nightmare she'd had in Czechoslovakia came back that night, a dreadful, formless terror of running for her life, with dogs and men with guns behind her. There was no one to help, no one to care if she escaped or died, and that knowledge was infinitely worse than the danger.

When finally she woke, she lay trembling, ice-cold and afraid to move in the silent darkness. The faint sound of the ocean, the conscious knowledge that she was safe at Rockwoods were of no comfort, because she was still alone. It seemed hours before she slept again.

Still tired when she entered the kitchen the next morning, she was surprised and wary to find Alex already there and the coffee already made. He poured a steaming mugful for her as if he'd been waiting. Her heart pounded at the sight of him, and her throat felt dry.

He wore jeans, and his long, narrow feet were bare. He had the feet of an aristocrat, she thought, glancing at them. His denim shirt was carelessly open, revealing the mat of light brown curls across his chest.

Was he still angry? His green eyes had lost their icy edge, but she couldn't be certain.

"Good morning," he greeted her, pleasantly enough, and his eyes swept over her deep blue flared cotton skirt and faded T-shirt, both Tracey's comfortable hand-me-downs. The girl had delved out an armload of clothing from her immense closets and insisted Yolanda wear whatever she liked.

His eyes took in the early morning freshness of Yolanda, her face shining from a recent scrubbing, her hair braided neatly into a single plait and hanging casually down her back. He studied her closely. He still wasn't used to this slender, graceful creature being the Yolanda whom he'd married.

This bloody-minded, black-determined, stubborn, slender creature, he corrected himself, remembering the quarrel the evening before, the restless night he'd just spent. There was no doubt Yolanda had won the first battle.

His conscience was alive and well, unfortunately. "This matter of Tracey's schooling."

Yolanda tightened her grip on the cup she held, and tension made her knuckles whiten.

"I've thought it over, and last night I had a long talk with Tracey." He was still amazed that the hour he'd spent with his daughter had actually resulted in a productive conversation, accompanied by no tears, no door slamming.

"I think you're right," he said briskly. "She'd be better off over here in a public school. It poses certain problems, however." He was finding it damned hard to admit he was wrong. It wasn't something he'd had to do often, at least in recent years. His lips twisted in ironic amusement. Good for your pompous soul, Caine, he chided himself.

The next part was harder still, because he was aware he wanted her to agree for reasons that had nothing to do with Tracey whatsoever.

"I have to travel a fair amount, as you know. Tracey can't stay here alone, either now or after school begins." Unconsciously he rubbed a hand over his beard-rough chin. He hadn't shaved yet that morning, and Yolanda heard the faint rasping sound. A shiver coursed through her. She'd like to rub her cheek against his, feel that roughness on her skin. Prickles ran up and down her arms and legs.

"I know we'd talked about your getting an apartment soon. Instead, would you consider staying on here at Rockwoods? You'd be perfectly free to take a job in the city, if that's what you wanted. I'll find a cleaning service so you aren't saddled with all the household chores." He did his best to inject a light tone into his words. "I'm not sure I can find one who does chickens and goats, but I'll certainly give it a try."

It was ironic that when Barney and Robert had suggested that she should live with him for a period of time, he'd raged. Now he waited for her to answer with his gut tied in knots. He wanted her here, close to him, of her own free will, more than he'd wanted anything for a long time.

He deliberately avoided putting a time limit on her stay, and he watched her expression closely for a reaction to his words.

There could be no sidestepping with Yolanda.

"Is this what you want, Alex, or only for Tracey?" She held herself absolutely still, steeling herself for his response. It would tell her a great deal she had to know before she could give him an answer.

He let his breath out in a slow sigh. She didn't make anything easy.

"It's what I want. I thought of you while I was away, and I'd like us to spend some time together, get to know each other." He met her eyes squarely, and his voice was slightly harsher when he added, "We'll go slow, Landa. More than that, I can't say."

He was honest. It was all she asked, and more. Her smile flashed and was reflected in her eyes, making him catch his breath.

"Yes," she said matter-of-factly, "I'll stay here with you gladly."

His grin was boyish, lightening the traces of fatigue that lingered on the lines of his face, and a bolt of pure happiness shot through her as she realized how tensely he'd been waiting for her answer. It had been important to him, then, having her agree. *Wonderful*.

"What would you like for breakfast?" she asked, and the hominess of the question pleased her, just as it pleased her intensely to be here with him, in the intimacy of early morning, making his meal.

"Surprise me," he suggested, wishing he had the freedom to swoop her into his arms, carry her up to his bedroom under the eaves, strip her with excruciating slowness and enjoy the breakfast his body insisted it wanted. If Tracey weren't upstairs sleeping, he would have.

How would she taste? How would those lovely breasts feel, cupped in his hands? Like the first time he'd loved her back in Votice? The next time would be slow, he vowed. The next time he'd make damn certain it was good for her; he'd control himself instead of acting like some randy teenager. He'd make her want him, again and again....

With amazement he realized that this was the first time since Dixie's death that he'd acutely desired one particular woman, wanting not a carefully orchestrated physical release with a temporary partner, but true spontaneous lovemaking, the kind where there was a morning like this after a night before, spent eating breakfast, sharing mundane small talk, going back to a rumpled bed... He drew himself up short.

Was he ready to risk loving again? His eyes settled on a photo in the glass cabinet in the corner. Dixie smiled out at him, and not for the first time since her death, he felt uneasy with her memory.

Yolanda hummed under her breath, breaking eggs into a heavy black skillet, slicing fresh bread for toast. With her back to him, she was unaware of his intense scrutiny. His eyes moved from flesh and blood to the photograph.

He'd been a faithful husband to Dixie. He'd liked having a dainty, pretty wife, a purpose to his life beyond his work. She'd stayed at home, sometimes taking courses in china painting or some other womanly thing that interested her. Often, she traveled with him. When she didn't, she'd always been waiting for him, it seemed. Had he disappointed her as often as he thought?

There'd been rough patches in their marriage, particularly before they adopted Tracey. That had been one of the few times she'd really fought with him, too.

Alex hadn't wanted to adopt a child. At times the responsibility for Dixie's happiness and well-being weighed heavily on him, and he was secretly relieved no babies came. But Dixie was adamant about parenthood, and eventually he'd given in, and then fallen in love with the engaging bundle of energy and charm that Tracey had been as a child.

But somehow it had gone bad. Marriage was something he'd done once, and hadn't planned on doing again. His reasons for that decision were hazy. It was an emotional response more than an intellectual one.

Now he was married again—more or less accidentally, to Yolanda—and it was causing him a great deal of confusion, this marriage of convenience. What was he going to do about it?

Yolanda turned and caught the pensive look on his face, not entirely certain of the reason for it, but instinctively aware that it concerned her, and aware, too, that it wasn't something he'd talk about with her. So she used an immediate diversionary tactic.

She set a plate loaded with toast and eggs and small sausages on the placemat in front of him. Her lovely apricot skin was flushed with the heat from the stove.

"Eat," she suggested. "You look hungry."

Her earthy solution lightened his mood, and in another moment they were laughing together as she related one of Ian's dour witticisms.

That light conversation and laughter marked the pattern for the day, and Alex relaxed and enjoyed himself. When the morning's misgivings appeared like shadows in his thoughts, he dismissed them determinedly. He'd think his way through them another time.

Bashfully he gave Yolanda the huge bag of bath salts, oils, powders and soaps he'd brought her, and her delighted reaction made him ridiculously happy.

"Hedonism," she instantly declared. "Now I need only the long johns."

"Winter's coming; that can be arranged," he quipped, and the smile on her lips and in her eyes was radiant.

Robert arrived in the early afternoon, wearing comfortable old jeans and a tattered sweater. Everyone was outside when he drove up. Alex had just completed another guided tour, and he'd been forced by Tracey to comment on and admire every single plant in the monstrous garden.

"What's planted here?" he had just demanded obligingly for what seemed the billionth time, gesturing to a large area where

numerous green shoots were appearing, looking for all th
world exactly like all the other green shoots he'd gazed at fo
the past hour.

"Cabbages. Red and green both. Daddy, can't you tell?"

Several times he'd caught Yolanda's knowingly amused eye
on him, and he'd widened his own at her in mock horror a
Tracey blithely moved inch by painful inch along the garden
rows.

He admired the cabbages, endlessly grateful for his father'
arrival and grateful, too, that Yolanda had made Robert fee
comfortable enough to wear clothing Alex remembered from
years before. Besides, Alex had wanted a cold beer for the pas
forty minutes. Tracey greeted her grandfather warmly, and then
announced, "Grampa, look what Cinnamon did to Dad's ca
yesterday." She obviously wanted a second opinion on the
gravity of Cinnamon's crime.

Yolanda sneaked an anxious glance at Alex. She realized tha
she didn't know him well enough to predict his reactions to such
matters.

Robert took one look at the damage and burst into laughter
His hearty chuckles were contagious, and in another second
Alex found himself laughing, too, somewhat sheepishly.

"This'll teach you to get a sensible vehicle, like my old truck
there, son. Farmers don't drive fancy cars."

The day turned into one of those unplanned, wonderfully
easygoing times. Tracey and Yolanda bullied the men into
helping with the dinner, and then they ate casually on the cement patio outside the kitchen, as the sounds of birds and sea
gulls' cries punctuated their lazy, idle conversation.

Traitorously Alex recalled that Robert had never relaxed this
way during his visits here when Dixie had been alive. Dinners
here then had tended to be rare and formal. Entertaining made
Dixie nervous, and eventually they'd done most of their socializing in Victoria's more sophisticated restaurants.

He dismissed the memory and suggested a walk on the beach
to watch the sunset just beginning over the western ocean.

ALEX HAD TO GO TO HIS OFFICE the next day. For the first time
in years, he would rather have stayed at home, but despite that,

he felt great. He'd whistled to himself during the drive in, and the morning was splendidly sunny.

"Good morning, Ruth," he greeted cheerfully, wondering again if Ruth Prentiss had any life outside these walls. She was always here, no matter how early he arrived, and she was usually still at work when he left, prim, proper, correct. He relied on her to keep things running.

He breezed into his pleasant office, went to the window and looked down on the early morning traffic on Government Street. It was good to be back.

He heard Ruth come in behind him.

"Have you seen the morning paper?"

When he shook his head, she laid the paper and a cup of coffee on his desk and went out. He'd missed having breakfast with Yolanda this morning, as he'd left just as she was coming downstairs. The truth was that he'd lingered until he'd heard her, wanting to have her smile good-morning to him.

He cradled the mug, glancing idly at the morning section.

The paper was folded open to Carrie's column "The Way It Is."

Alex shook his head and smiled fondly. What ingenious mayhem was Carrie's typewriter causing today? He started to read.

If you spend any time around the politicians these days, you're bound to hear about recession and inflation. Everything old is new again, you say? Well, there's a bill before the house advocating a substantial raise in our elected members' salaries. What else is new? Their income just won't match their expenditures, they complain, a problem with which many of us ordinary mortals are all too familiar. However, one of our politicians has a solution that doesn't involve hikes in pay—just good-old fashioned honest labor.

Alex had a nasty premonition. His grip tightened on the paper, and his gaze flew, skimming the remainder of the article, reading it again in disbelief and with a growing sense of outrage.

During a recent visit to Rockwoods, the lovely Caine estate built by the lumber baron Thomas Caine back in 1901, this reporter was astounded to discover that the elegant grounds had been converted to what must be the largest garden plot in Victoria. The spacious double garages have been converted to pens for goats, chickens and geese. Yolanda Caine, newly acquired wife of Assistant Deputy Minister Alex Caine, volunteered the information that these changes are helping the family make ends meet in the face of the economy's belt-tightening. Mrs. Caine believes that if other estates were converted similarly to small farms, Canadian food banks would be out of business.

Well, elected representatives? Man your spades. "The Way It Is," the taxpayers are doing all the digging. With a little help from the Caines.

In stunned disbelief, Alex finished, and just as he read the last word, his phone began to ring ominously.

"Alex, welcome back." It was the bluff, hearty voice of Curtis Blackstone. He asked about the trip and its business results, and then he added innocently, "Say, could you use a load of manure on that farm of yours? I hear the Opposition has a great supply."

It was the opening sally in a barrage of similar comments and queries. Alex's friends thought it hilarious. His adversaries considered the article ammunition. Some of the members regarded it as little short of treason. By four in the afternoon, Alex decided that if one more person whistled "Old MacDonald Had a Farm" one more time, he was going to drive that person's teeth straight down his throat and enjoy watching the blood sully the hallowed marble floors of parliament.

To top it all, he'd forgotten till now that he had to take the goat-damaged car to the garage and try and explain why the roof was covered with hoof prints.

EVERY MORNING YOLANDA read the paper front to back. It was a window on her new world, a way to gauge the thinking of Canadians, a way to discover the character of the people. But this morning, Anna's letter had taken precedence over the news.

Yolanda sat hunched over the thin air-mail sheets with their colorful Czech stamps, reading *babička*'s letter over and over, trying to hear the voice of the old woman in them. Why couldn't Anna write the way she talked, instead of these stilted, formal words that didn't even sound like her?

Tracey's voice interrupted her reverie, sounding shrill and outraged.

"Landa, you absolutely won't believe this. Remember I told you that broad was nothing but a snoop?" She handed Yolanda the paper.

Yolanda scanned Carrie's column quickly, and then reread it slowly, digesting every twisted inference, her hands trembling with outrage. She felt betrayed, patronized. She felt terrified and helplessly angry.

She felt exactly the way she'd felt in Prague on the day when she'd lost her interpreter's job because of the article in the French journal. A thought so dreadful that it made her gasp leaped into her head.

Alex. This was terrible. Would Alex lose his position in the government because of her? It became more probable the longer she considered it. Remorse and anguish swept through her like a windstorm. Carrie's column would hurt him, humiliate him. He would despise her for being so stupid, and she deserved his contempt.

Tracey, involved in her plans for the day, had already dismissed the whole thing. "Ian invited me over to help him and Victor make a new pen for the pigs today; that new sow is coming tomorrow."

"Victor?" Yolanda felt as if her voice was coming from a great distance away.

"Victor, Ian's grandson, Victor. Jeez, Landa, I've told you his name a dozen times already. Victor Martinos. His Dad's Italian. Anyway, as soon as I finish with the animals, I'm gone ... if that's okay with you. See you at suppertime."

With a blithe wave, she left.

Like an automaton, Yolanda went about her daily chores. Her imagination fueled her apprehension.

Unbelievable as it was, this time she had even more to lose than the last time she'd been careless with her tongue. After he read this today in the paper, Alex would probably send her away. Who would want her around, making such stupid comments? She debated packing her things and leaving immediately, not going through the pain and humiliation of a scene with him, but she couldn't run away. She'd have to face him. And then there was Tracey. She wanted to explain what had happened to Tracey.

Oh, the thing got worse the more she thought about it.

She couldn't eat. Her stomach cramped and ached with tension. Trying to maintain fragile control, she showered and dressed carefully as the time approached when Alex would arrive. But it was another full hour and a half before she heard his car in the driveway.

Then the door slammed, and she heard him enter the house. She began to shake. It wasn't his anger she feared. He had every right to be angry. It was the loss of the tenuous bond she'd sensed growing between them. That, and her own pain and shame at having hurt him after everything he'd done to help her.

"Yolanda?" His deep voice seemed to echo through the house, full of portent. Slowly she walked to meet him, feeling as if she were dying a little inside with every step.

CHAPTER NINE

"YOLANDA?" Alex's tone was openly impatient.

He stood in the entrance hall, his tan jacket slung over a shoulder, his tie loose, the buttons at his shirt neck undone. He looked hot, rumpled, casually urbane. He scowled up at her.

"Why didn't you tell me you talked to Carrie Russell?" He strode up the entrance stairwell, taking the steps two at a time, and moved past her into the living room. He tossed his suit coat carelessly on a chair as he passed, shrugging his shoulders as if to ease the tension from them.

She wet her lips and straightened her shoulders.

"Alex," she began. He was standing with his back to her, staring out over the sunlit ocean, his hands casually propped on his hips.

She had trouble getting her breath, and her voice was thin and unnaturally high. She wrapped her arms around her waist.

"Nothing I can say will correct this…" she said, choking the words out. "But I want you to know I apologize. I will leave tonight. I feel terrible to have caused you this trouble, this disgrace, after everything you've done for me."

Feeling utterly miserable, she couldn't seem to stop talking once she'd begun, and she heard herself babbling. "It was ignorance, of course, I am unbelievably stupid. It was a big mistake to talk with this Carrie Russell, but she said she was your friend. I did not at first know she was a reporter," she continued painfully, barely able now to keep the tears at bay, balling her hands into fists.

He'd turned toward her, but she couldn't see his face or his expression. The late afternoon sun filtered through the window behind him, silhouetting him against the brilliant light.

She stood frozen in place, waiting. Why, oh why didn't he say something, rage at her, accuse her? The tension in the room

became unbearable, and she whirled around and half ran
heading for the staircase to her room.

But as she passed Alex, he reached out and grabbed her arm
turning her toward him and anchoring her with his hand on he
other shoulder.

"Hold it," he commanded. "Slow down, and let's go ove
this again."

His hands were firm, his grip far too strong to struggl
against. She looked up at him, and all the anguish she felt wa
reflected in her tear-flooded eyes. She drew in a half sob, an
blurted, "I cannot. I cannot talk about it anymore. I feel to
ashamed, to have said such things. But you must understand
that wasn't really what I did say. I did say these things, but no
in this way, you understand. Please, Alex let me go," sh
begged, on the verge of tears.

Alex was shocked to realize how upset she really was. He'
felt out of sorts, annoyed with both the good-natured joshing
and the more pointed remarks he'd had to endure all day. Cer
tainly, he was irritated by Carrie's damned column, but i
wasn't the end of the world.

He looked at her drawn face, recognized the panic in he
voice. Her body was trembling. Lord, did she think he was go
ing to beat her? Alex reacted instinctively, drawing Yoland
into his embrace, enfolding her tightly in his arms.

"Calm down, now," he soothed. He forgot his own cha
grin, forgot the barbs of the day as he pressed her dark, silk
head to his chest, stroking the fat knot of hair pinned at he
nape.

"Your job, Alex. Will you lose your job because of me?"
Even her voice was trembling. She forced herself to ask th
question, her body a knot of tension as she waited for his an
swer.

"Lose my job?" His tone was incredulous. "Of course
won't lose my job. Just because of a..."

Suddenly he remembered. She'd told him so matter-of-factl
on that morning in Votice, about the journalist, the repri
mands, the loss of her job as interpreter. Perhaps because o
that remarkable restraint of hers, her matter-of-fact accep
tance of absolute censorship and the harsh penalties impose

in her native country for breaking any rules, he'd never given a single thought to how she'd feel today.

His lack of consideration appalled him. Instead of being so damned caught up in the loss of a little dignity, why hadn't he guessed what a calamity Carrie's words would appear to Yolanda?

With a smothered oath for his insular pride, he drew them both over to the sofa, gathering her onto his lap in a crumpled heap of gauzy rose cotton dress and long tanned limbs.

"Now, what's all this about leaving? I'd never blame you for the press and what they consider news. Anyway, that article is only a minor annoyance. It's Carrie's rather perverted version of humor, that's all. People here don't lose jobs that easily."

Convulsively her arms locked tightly around his chest and back, and she burrowed into him. Expecting the worst, preparing herself for his wrath all day, and now being in his arms instead strained her emotions past their limit. Giving up the struggle for control with a smothered whimper deep in her throat, she began to cry, wetting the front of his shirt with hot, copious tears.

He patted her, murmuring comforting phrases, while he thought about the complex woman he held.

The contrast between the defiant, outspoken Yolanda challenging him over Tracey's schooling, and this huddled, soft ball of misery on his lap forced him to examine her vulnerability.

She fought fearlessly for those she loved, and over the past days he'd understood that she'd come to love Tracey. In her convictions as to what was best for the girl, Yolanda was maddeningly confident and infuriatingly secure.

Yet curiously in other ways she was painfully insecure. There had been the tearful scene in the airport at Calgary. She'd had every reason to be terrified during that exit from Czechoslovakia, yet she'd been calm. And then she'd fallen apart because she'd felt that he was indifferent to her, unaware of her feelings, unwilling to talk. "You won't even touch my hand," she'd accused tearfully.

Even now, it wasn't herself she was concerned about, the remote chance this article might raise questions about her application for Canadian citizenship. Instead, it was him, his job, his reaction to her error, his censure of her that had triggered her collapse of serenity.

Her presence made further analysis impossible. He found he was enjoying having her on his knee, with her arms around him. Her newly slender hips were tantalizingly curved and firm. She felt both fragile and strong to the touch.

"Hold still." Following an impulse he didn't even try to curb, he moved one hand up and carefully removed the pins holding her hair in a pristine knot. It cascaded like dusky smoke over his forearm, and he lowered his head to bury his face in its fragrant softness. Flowers. She always smelled of flowers.

Desire didn't come slowly. It surged through him, instantly tightening his body into a hard, aching urgency, and he had to grit his teeth at the sweet agony even her slight movements caused him.

She tilted her wet face questioningly up at him, and of course there was no hiding his pulsing need for her. He groaned and claimed her lips, still tangy with tears, delicately circling them with the tip of his tongue, then drinking deeply.

Alex wanted her. She felt the pounding of his heart against her cheek, the throbbing message of his arousal beneath her hip, and her love for him ignited an answering fire in her body. She let her head fall to his shoulder, and his lips and teeth nipped up and down her throat, sending tiny jolts into her abdomen. Then, with a ferocity he'd controlled until now, he kissed her lips again, ravaging them with his own, silently illustrating with his tongue exactly what he wanted to do to her body.

He was breathing heavily and his uninhibited movements drove her mad with longing. Every part of her seemed to slowly fill with need.

He kissed her, moving his lips down her throat, sliding his hands up and down her body, finding the swelling tautness of her nipples and knowing exactly how to fondle their hard tips so that she uttered a small cry of ecstasy. There could be no question of denying Alex; the thought never crossed her mind.

Small, eager whimpers came from her throat as he touched her, his hand stroking her leg, impatiently pushing aside the folds of her dress, finding her bare inner thigh and slowly, painfully slowly, touching that part of her needing his clever touch so desperately, rubbing gently and persuasively through the flimsy panties she wore, then slipping underneath, alternating rhythms, bringing a panting exclamation from her swollen lips.

"Please, yes, like so, like so. . ."

She writhed, and his own desire surged with her movements. His mouth suckled her nipple, relaying the pattern of her response down to his fingers, back to his lips. He controlled his own craving for release.

"Landa, lovely Landa."

His voice was rough, thick with desire for her, and he wasn't quite sure what he wanted her to answer, only that he needed contact on every level possible with the women he held. Her reply was immediate. "Yes, Alex. Please," she whispered. "You must teach me, tell me what I should do—I know little about this."

Her beautiful simplicity thrilled him. She was completely innocent of the small, coquettish games other women had played when he first made love to them. She demanded nothing more than what he was so eager to give, asked for nothing beyond the moment, no promises about tomorrow, no assurances.

"Where's Tracey?" he asked cautiously.

She had to draw air into her lungs with a shuddering gasp, forcibly pull herself back from the realms of sensation he was creating.

"Ian has invited her to dinner, and later, a movie."

He nodded and lifted her easily from his lap. The flimsy sofa tilted as he moved them to the thickly carpeted floor. The sight of her passion-clouded, starry gaze, her distended nipples poking through the flimsy cloth, her disheveled dress, tumbled high around her thighs, enflamed him.

"Let's get this off you."

He grasped the hem of the garment, clumsily catching handfuls of it as he drew it up over her hips and breasts, freeing her long hair with one hand as he finally pulled the dress off and tossed it aside. His heart thundered as he devoured the sight of her.

She wore a simple white cotton bra, brief flowered panties.

"You're so beautiful," he breathed, and for that moment, she believed him. She felt beautiful with his hands on her, his touch warm and sensitive, fiendishly adept at finding places that made her gasp.

She watched him, drugged with delight. A wave of his hair hung forward nearly into his eyes, and his face was flushed, the amber-flecked eyes half shut.

Reaching up, she shyly slipped his tie over his head, unbuttoned the silky shirt so she could place her palms on his chest and gauge the hammering of his heart against the way her own hot blood pounded in her veins.

He tantalized her, running his tongue from the thundering pulse point in her throat down to her engorged breasts, then stripping the bra away and cupping the fullness in his hands, flicking the hardened tips with his thumbnails and soothing them immediately with his mouth.

"Landa, I ache to make love each time I'm near you," he muttered, sliding a hand down over her satin skin, exploring the downy nest of soft dark curls hidden just under her panties.

He could hardly control his own rush of elation at her indrawn breath, her rhythmic, uncontrollable responses to his sure touch.

He wanted to give her pleasure. The memory of their wedding night haunted him, as well as the burden of his own selfishness. More than anything, he wanted to bring her fulfillment, wanted to watch her writhe, hear her moan as a result of his caresses. She was so moist, so hot beneath his fingers, velvety, liquid, urgent.

He was close to demanding fulfillment himself, dangerously so. There was a primeval sensuality in her that stirred him, excited him as no other woman ever had. He felt tender and passionate and ravenously curious about her.

The pulsing agony of longing grew in her until nothing existed except Alex, his smell and taste and touch pulling her into an upward spiral she couldn't control, didn't want to control. She wanted it never to end, she wanted to rush him to its end.

She cried out, teetering on the brink of release yet holding back, fearful of being so helplessly outside of herself.

"Easy, I'm here, holding you. Now, Landa. Let it happen now." His whisper was both a command and an entreaty.

The release that he controlled intensified, crested and exploded within her. Her arms clasped him convulsively, and his choked whispers were echoed by her low song of wild fulfillment.

After an endless pause, the involuntary writhing ceased, and she collapsed, drowned with satiation, lassitude, peaceful happiness and wonder.

She opened her eyes when he stood up, watching him strip off his clothing with heedless efficiency, his tall form graceful and muscularly firm, swollen with the virile need she'd stirred in him. And then his weight was on her, delightfully heavy.

Her trembling thighs parted to him, and with a single thrust he entered her, pausing to allow her time to adjust, to become familiar with their joining flesh.

His teeth were clenched with the effort of withholding his instinctive drive for fulfillment, and the face above her own took on a savage urgency as he adjusted his motions to the hesitant response he felt her inner muscles giving him, the quivering beginnings of her renewed desire.

He went slowly. She wound her body around his, her arms tight around his neck, her legs entwining him like silken vines, and she marveled at the quickening inside her.

He encouraged her, whispering all the things he wanted to do, watching her face intently to time the moment of her release to coincide with the bursting explosion he suddenly could restrain no longer. He shut his eyes, shuddering with pleasure. The cry that he uttered was guttural and ancient, the sound of a man claiming his mate, and when his cry subsided, hers began.

Afterward, they clung together in sated peace, content at first to hold and be held, gloriously naked and wrapped in each other's arms as twilight fell.

"Alex?" Her voice was warm, thick and sleepy. He held her head pillowed on his chest, one hand in her hair, the other flat on her abdomen, feeling the rich pulsing diminish slowly under the satin skin. Her body held a fascination for him, slender but voluptuous, quivering at his touch.

"Alex," she repeated calmly. "I am in love with you."

The words, the way she said them, demanded nothing of him. Her confession was a random, comfortable truth she felt like telling him in this intimacy of afterlove.

He moved his hand away from her stomach as if he'd been burned. His body tensed, and he had to consciously control his voice. He felt deeply, inexplicably disturbed.

"That's flattering coming from such a beautiful woman, but you don't really know me well enough to love me, Yolanda."

He sounded as if he were reprimanding her, damn it. He didn't want to sound like that. But he didn't want the added responsibility of her love. He had to say something more, to try to make her understand.

"I know it's ridiculous, but I'm still not over the death of my wife. Can you understand that, Landa?" He couldn't see the picture of him and Dixie from where he lay, but suddenly he was aware of it, up there on the mantel.

She sat up and looked down at him, allowing her hand now to stroke back the hair on his forehead, linger on the planes of his cheek. She was aware her words had upset him. How stupid of her, to blurt it out that way, spoiling this miracle between them. But a tiny part of her was hurt and angry and betrayed.

"You're right, of course. It's much too soon to know you." Her fingers strayed into the curls on his broad chest, and she made her voice teasingly light, deliberately ignoring the other half of what he'd said.

"I think you're an excellent teacher, Alex Caine."

He brought her face down to his and kissed her gratefully. The awkward moment was gone. She buried the hurt of his rejection, telling herself it was her own fault she was in pain for once again saying too much.

"We need to have supper," she said practically. "Are you hungry?"

"Starved," he confessed, getting to his feet and pulling her up easily. "But you're not cooking tonight, Landa." He picked her rose dress up from the floor and held it up. The cotton gauze was hopelessly creased.

"I've pretty well wrecked this one. Go put on another dress, and I'll take you out to dinner."

She scooped up her underthings and hurried naked to her yellow bedroom to shower. She heard Alex go to his suite under the eaves. She visualized him looking at the picture beside his bed, the collection of powders and creams in his bathroom, the silent but ominous reminders everywhere in this house of the woman who had been Dixie, and she slammed her fist down on the soft eiderdown of her bed. How could anyone compete with a ghost?

After washing, she dried and dressed in a flowered cotton wrap skirt patterned with huge cabbage roses—one of Tracey's offerings again—and the pink T-shirt she'd bought.

She brushed her tangled hair and decided to leave it loose, tied with a scarf at the nape of her neck.

Alex had said Yolanda didn't really know him. Certainly, she hadn't known Dixie. How could she? It would help to find out what kind of life Alex had lived with the first Mrs. Caine. Yolanda suspected it would reveal a great deal about Alex.

Perhaps she should just openly ask Alex about his former wife, and see what he said.

A small, wry grin twisted her lips as she slowly went downstairs. No doubt about it, she had never really learned to keep her mouth shut.

"Is there anywhere you'd especially like to go to eat?" Alex's eyes admired the wholesome beauty she projected.

"I like McDonald's," she said, loving the way he looked at her.

"I think I'd better decide," he remarked dryly, and he caught her long, thick mane in one fist, drew her near, then planted a playful kiss on her lips.

The restaurant he chose for them was called Chez Armand. It was on Yates Street, in the heart of what Alex called the Old Town. The lighting was dim, and a piano played softly in the background. The menu was written in both French and English.

"Monsieur, madame? Bonsoir."

The maitre d' was suave, a tiny bit haughty, tall and dramatically handsome in his well-tailored suit, with eyes as smooth and softly dark as sable. He had shiny black curly hair, and his body looked as if he worked at keeping it fit.

Quite naturally, Yolanda stated her preference in excellent French. The language unleashed a torrent of words from the man. Smiling at her delightedly, he volunteered the information that he had recently arrived from Quebec with his sister, bought the restaurant and renovated it, and that he loved Victoria but that hearing French spoken so fluently made him feel homesick.

Yolanda smiled back, then complimented him on the decor. He told her of the difficulties he'd had with painters, and inquired about her charming accent. She explained she had recently moved to Victoria and she also was homesick at times, just like him. "Ahh," he purred. "I knew we had a great deal in common."

Alex waited impatiently through all of this, understanding a word here and there, noting irritably the way the man's eyes lingered on Yolanda's long, flowing hair, the way her startling blue gaze responded to the waiter's rapid discourse.

"I am Armand, Armand Mollins," he finally volunteered. He bowed slightly over the hand Yolanda offered, and Alex's smile was only slightly strained as he, too, was belatedly included in the conversation.

But the food was wonderful, delicately prepared and attractively arranged, although, Alex pondered, one would think Armand had more to do than flash that engaging grin at Yolanda all evening.

"My wife would like another cup of coffee."

Yolanda couldn't believe she'd heard Alex correctly. *My wife*. She stared over at him, but he and Armand were silently exchanging an eloquent, masculine look. Armand poured her coffee with a flourish, gave Alex a mischievous, purely Gallic shrug, a wry smile, and left them alone at last.

Alex waited with ill-concealed impatience until her coffee cup was empty.

"Let's get out of here," he half growled, and Yolanda walked to the entrance and waited as he paid the cashier.

"Perhaps you would enjoy meeting my sister, Dominique," Armand suggested. Armand's musical French words came from behind her, and when she turned to him, he handed her a small yellow business card.

"She has this tiny boutique, Foofera, very chic, close to the waterfront. I think you and she would like each other...if ever you are in the vicinity."

He bade her and Alex, who appeared at her elbow just then, an effusive good-night in accented English.

Alex nodded coolly and took Yolanda's hand firmly in his. He seemed thoughtfully quiet as he helped her into the car. He pulled out of the parking lot, turning into the street before he spoke abruptly.

"Shall we drive, or would you rather go to a club for a drink? There are things we need to discuss."

"No club, thank you. Already I feel the wine."

He drove to an area just across the Inner Harbour from the Parliament Buildings, and Yolanda made a small murmur of appreciation for the place he'd chosen. The car engine stopped, and the open windows caught the intermittent salty breeze from the water, carrying the sound of waves lapping on the pleasure craft moored in the inlet. The summer night was balmy, and the sky above the buildings was a deep, almost navy blue with stars scattered across it.

"This is one of my favorite views," Alex confided, and Yolanda nodded in agreement.

The scene was spectacular. The entire facade of the domed buildings gleamed in the night, illuminated by bulbs whose combined golden wattage etched every ornate architectural line in glowing, incandescent light. Windows, doors, spires, cornices were silhouetted both on the central structure as well as the east and west wings.

"I want to talk about our future, Yolanda." His voice was solemn, and her heart seemed to slam against her ribs.

"You are planning a future for us, Alex?" The words were difficult, her voice hardly audible.

"You know everything changed between us tonight, Landa." He turned his body urgently toward her, his arm stretching along the back of the seat, his face shadowed in the reflected light from the water so she couldn't read his eyes or expression.

"It was good, making love to you." He thought about that, and quickly rephrased it. "More than just good, at least for me." He seemed to be waiting and she was grateful for the darkness that hid her hot blush.

"For me also," she whispered.

"Yolanda, we have to make some decisions here. We have to decide whether we want an actual marriage or not. Tonight, well, our lovemaking was certainly unplanned. But from here on, it can't be. I don't intend to go on like this." He sounded almost angry. "It's not as if we're involved in some casual affair. It's the damnedest thing, being already married to you, yet feeling guilty about making love, thinking afterward that I've taken advantage of you, violated the original agreement."

He leaned toward her, and his intensity was obvious.

"You don't feel that, do you, Landa? That I'm taking advantage of you? Believe me, that isn't what I intended." He sounded anxious, and she shook her head vehemently in denial. He was vulnerable, this strong, reliable man. It touched her, and made her tease him gently.

"Perhaps you feel I've taken advantage of you?" she queried softly. "I, too, am a responsible adult, Alex." She turned the tables on him neatly, and after a moment he even laughed a little. Then he was serious again, and his voice became low and passionate, sending shivers through her.

"All the same, I suspect I'm more experienced at seduction than you. The truth is I want you, Landa. I want you in my bed. I realized tonight that subconsciously, ever since that first time in Votice, I've intended to have you again, to feel you move like that under me, the way you were tonight. The softness, the way your eyes get wild ... God, I can't seem to get enough of you. Right here, this minute, I'd like to—" He stopped abruptly, and she had the feeling he'd surprised even himself.

Mischievously she pretended to loosen her T-shirt, striving to add a martyred note to her voice, twisting around and looking at the other cars parked nearby, and at the blue-and-white police cruiser slowly driving past.

"If you really must, then I suppose right here is fine, Alex. If you don't mind these other people watching, and the policeman in that car allows it—"

His grin flashed, and he said slowly, "I should call your bluff, crazy Gypsy." He put a restraining hand on hers and linked their fingers.

"But on second thought, I'll take a rain check."

The tension was gone. "Rain check?" She was puzzled.

"A promise for later," he explained huskily, and she shivered at the velvet depth of his voice.

"Besides driving me mad, you're good with Tracey. You understand her better than I do." The admission hurt. He let her hand go, rubbing his distractedly through his already tousled hair.

"I'm making a hell of a botch of this. What do you think, Landa? Should we give this marriage a try? I'm not much better at being a husband than I am at being a father, but I'll do my best."

The admission puzzled her. There was something in his voice; reluctance, bitterness, perhaps? He was a proud man, and it was obviously hard on him to admit his problems with Tracey. But why did he feel he was not a good husband?

Just a few hours ago he'd insisted she didn't know him well enough to love him. She sensed he wanted no more protestations of love from her. Certainly, he was making none. He wouldn't want prying questions, either.

She was acutely aware of what he wasn't saying, of all the romantic promises he wasn't making. He'd married her out of familial duty to Sophie and Barney. Was he going to continue the relationship because of Tracey? She couldn't agree to that, however much she loved him.

As if he'd read her mind, he said next, "I'm not suggesting we stay married for Tracey's sake, if that's what you're thinking. That would never work."

She was sorely tempted to ask, "Then why, Alex? You don't say you love me, only that you want me in your bed. A marriage is full of many things besides lying together in bed."

But for once, she managed to hold her tongue. She wanted what he was offering, wanted this chance to be his wife in every way he would allow.

"Don't turn down half a loaf when you're starving, waiting for a whole." That had been one of *babička*'s folk sayings, and Yolanda was starving.

She snatched the half loaf.

"Yes, please, I want to try this," she said.

He sucked in a deep breath and slowly let it out again. For a brief moment he experienced jubilation at her calm, husky acceptance of his proposal. He'd needed her acceptance, he realized, however reluctant a part of him had been to commit himself to another, real marriage. It was done now.

After all, he reasoned, there was no other way. If he wanted her this ferociously—and he did—then he had to offer her the security of a future. His own ambivalence about being married again would surely fade as time passed. Anyway, he didn't really understand why he felt as he did.

Then she was in his arms. As long as he held her, there was no need for thought. Her breasts seemed to swell, her arms entwined around his neck. Gypsy. The name suited her. She'd cast a spell on him, and he wanted it to last forever.

"About this rain check." Her whisper tickled his ear. "Perhaps you should drive us home, Alex, so we can get this rain check settled?"

CHAPTER TEN

THEY WERE TURNING INTO Rockwoods' driveway when Yolanda noticed the light from the upper hallway shining out of a small window. For one last moment she let herself believe that it was possible to go with Alex to his bedroom and explore the sensuality they craved, then sleep all night in his arms. Then she faced reality. Legally married or not, there was Tracey to consider.

Softly, dejectedly, she told Alex her decision.

"Until we talk with her and explain this change in our marriage, Alex, I think we must go on as we have been. Another rain check, yes?"

Her voice sounded as disappointed and wistful as Alex felt at this new development. All the way home, he'd been lasciviously plotting the rest of the night in his head.

He'd conveniently forgotten he had a teenage child, because he felt like a virile teenager himself just now. He'd driven fast, expertly maneuvering around curves and up hills, with one arm holding Yolanda tight to his side, stroking her hair and her neck as the miles few by. He'd felt like letting loose with a rebel yell out the open window of the car, just from sheer exuberance. He hadn't felt this way since he was sixteen, full of the joy of a speeding car and the feel of a beautiful girl nestled into his shoulder.

His disappointment was keen, but he had to agree with the sense of Yolanda's suggestion. As he parked the car in the quiet yard, apprehension rose in him as he remembered in a rush all the jealous scenes Tracey had concocted at various times in the past, and the careful assurances he'd given her about this not being a real marriage.

Hell. Now that he thought about it, being both Tracey's father and Yolanda's lover was going to require diplomacy he wasn't sure he possessed.

He kissed her, and the kiss was full and deep and hungry; then she went to her yellow room reluctantly.

Alex spent the remainder of the night figuring out the best way to break the news to his daughter, and feeling grumpily deprived. His brain knew all the reasons for circumspection, but his body insisted that if he was going to have a wife, damn it, he wanted her beside him. Now.

He rose early and out of sorts, pulling on a pair of old jeans and quietly descending to the kitchen in his stocking feet to make some coffee.

He sat sipping the hot brew, running his fingers through his hair and frowning as he rehearsed the best way to explain himself to his daughter.

"Tracey, Yolanda and I have decided to sleep in the same room from now on." Nope, that wouldn't do. Too simplistic. Just how much did a fifteen-year-old girl understand about the physical side of adult love? he wondered. Damned little, he decided, absently watching the ocean turn from formless gray to gray-green, and then become molten as the sun appeared.

"Tracey, Yolanda and I are going to live together as man and wife." Was that better? Would she question him about what being man and wife implied? Surely not. He put too much cream into his cup and had to dump it down the sink. He could hear those stupid geese honking in the shed.

Tracey's school was for females, and it was run by nuns. He was pretty certain they taught basic concepts of sexuality, but the actualities of it all—no, she was an innocent child.

What had he known at sixteen? He grimaced. He'd forgotten some of what he thought he knew then, and it was a good thing. But there was no comparison between a girl and a boy, of course.

He rose and paced back and forth, sloshing coffee on the tiled floor, soaking it up with his stockinged foot.

Tracey had never asked him about sex. Hazily he remembered her asking Dixie where babies came from once. Dixie had become prettily flustered, and she'd bought a dainty little book with pictures that weren't exactly misleading, but definitely weren't graphic. If he remembered correctly, the book had turned the whole process into the development of a flower or something.

She'd undoubtedly progressed beyond the flower stage. But how far? Exactly what sort of things would she want to know about him and Yolanda? She wasn't the type of kid to just accept something without asking a million pointed questions. Damn it, why weren't there courses for things like this? He could hear footsteps coming down the stairs. Maybe Yolanda could help him figure this out. His mood lightened at the thought before he realized there were two sets of feet.

"Morning, Daddy."

"Good morning, Alex."

The two females were dressed similarly in cutoffs and T-shirts, their faces clean-scrubbed and glowing. Alex sent one quick, covetous glance at the curvaceous length of Yolanda's legs.

"Morning. What're you two doing up so early?"

"This is the day we clean Cinnamon's pen," Tracey informed him. She popped bread into the toaster with studied casualness, and he shot her a look. Something was coming; he was sure of it.

"You can help us if you like, Dad." There was a pregnant silence. Then, with her back turned to him, she blurted out, "Yolanda says you guys are going to start having a real marriage, Daddy. She explained it all, like about adults needing companionship, and a physical relationship, and you two wanting to be honest with me. I was a little freaked at first, but I see your point. I'm not exactly a child, you know. I know you need somebody your own age to be with. I can relate to that." Still without turning, she added, "Besides, Yolanda understands about my—my...mother. About her still being my mother, even though..." Her voice faltered, and she cleared her throat. "Landa says she and I'll be friends, and naturally, I'm not jealous of my own father. So, no problem," she concluded, smearing toast with half an inch of peanut butter and adding honey. "Everything's cool." She didn't sound as certain as the words indicated, but her response amazed Alex with its brave attempt at reasonable maturity.

Yolanda watched Alex clench his coffee cup with both hands, until she marveled that it didn't shatter. Then his gaze swung from his daughter, now rooting in the fridge for milk, over to Yolanda, and he slowly raised one thumb in Tracey's currently favorite "all right" signal. His approval made her feel warm and delightfully happy, but she also felt slightly uneasy at how relieved he seemed to be. Should she have insisted he talk to the girl himself?

The opportunity had come up spontaneously, with Tracey's appearance in her bedroom earlier, and some instinct had suggested the issue was better handled woman to woman.

Perhaps she'd been right. Her face flamed at the memory of the forthright questions Tracey had asked. Youngsters were sophisticated. It was better, maybe, that Alex wasn't present.

"I guess you and my father want to sleep together, eh?" the girl had demanded sarcastically. "I guess he's forgotten all about my mother by this time, anyway." It had taken a great deal of honesty to help her understand, and Yolanda felt Tracey still had a great deal of thinking to do before she'd feel easy about it.

But the tender, warm look Alex telegraphed across the table made joy bubble inside Yolanda, and her deepening flush now had nothing to do with Tracey.

"Can I go over to the Camerons' later? Vic and I are going riding. Ian's neighbor has horses he's gonna loan us." Tracey obviously felt they'd exhausted the subject of fathers and daughters and stepmothers.

"Who's Vic?" Alex asked.

"Oh, Dad, I told you. Victor is Mr. Cameron's grandson, Victor Martinos. He's staying here for the summer, maybe longer. He might even be going to the same school as me. He's older, though. His mum and dad are divorced."

Fatherly caution made him demand, "How old is this Vic?"

"Sixteen. Mr. Cameron's going to show us how to saddle the horses and everything. I can go, can't I?" she demanded anxiously.

"I'd like to meet Vic sometime soon, but yes, you can go," Alex answered.

"Perhaps we could plan a picnic on the beach, and you could ask Vic and his grandfather," Yolanda suggested.

"Oh, super," Tracey enthused, all signs of the earlier strain disappearing. "Can we do it next weekend, Dad? We can have a bonfire and a corn roast—okay, Dad?"

Alex would have agreed to much more than just a picnic right then.

"That's fine with me," he said. "Now, are you two ladies going to teach me how to clean out a goat pen?"

He was, in short order, extremely sorry he'd asked.

From that moment on, the long hot weekend slid by, the hours like beads on an abacus used to measure contentment. The garden burgeoned, the animals flourished, and the people smiled a lot at each other.

There were a few awkward moments when Yolanda moved her things into Alex's room. She noticed immediately that he'd removed the picture of Dixie that had been beside his bed. But in the bathroom the perfumes and powders still rested in neat rows. Yolanda found a box and packed every last one neatly, then carried it into the basement. Upstairs again, she arranged the things Alex had brought her from England on the wide countertop.

Alex didn't seem to even notice the change.

Plans for the picnic accelerated. Yolanda and Tracey had expanded the guest list to include Robert, Sophia, and Barney.

"Who else, Alex? Are there friends from work you'd care to ask?"

He shook his head. During the past years he hadn't encouraged friendships. Being a widower was awkward. There was Curtis, but a family picnic was the last place a roué like Curtis would choose to be. Besides, Alex didn't want Curtis lavishing his charm on Yolanda.

"There's my secretary, Ruth. But she'd never come to a picnic."

"Why not?"

He shrugged. He couldn't imagine Ruth outside of the office. He told Yolanda that, and she gave him a scathing look.

"You are being a chauvinist, Alex. I'll phone and invite her myself," she insisted. She did, and Alex was astonished when Ruth promptly accepted.

During the week Alex worked, but the entire parliamentary process slowed down in the summer, and the buildings were all but deserted. His workload was light, and he found himself hurrying home in the early afternoon, eager to change into shorts, drink a beer, even to weed the garden.

Most of all, he looked forward to just being with Yolanda.

"Will you tell me, please, why..." she would begin, and he'd find himself having to view a perfectly ordinary situation from a point of view he'd never considered. They talked incessantly. They discussed newspaper articles, political dogma, hairstyles, the weather. They argued frenziedly, and to his amused chagrin, Alex found himself winning only part of the time.

On Wednesday night she insisted on teaching him and Tracey the finer points of making cottage cheese.

"But I don't even like cottage cheese," he objected.

"You must learn to like it, of course," Yolanda stated firmly. "Otherwise what will we do with all this milk?"

Alex very nearly suggested getting rid of the goat. He still had visions of the damned animal's hoofmarks on the roof of his car. Instead he ladled warm curds into cheesecloth and tried not to gag at the smell. He wondered if there were three people who laughed as much.

Until bedtime came, she was a friend. Until they climbed the stairs to his room, and then the true magic between him and Yolanda began.

There he discovered the other Yolanda, the woman he'd labeled "Gypsy." She was amazingly sensual, naturally so, despite her inexperience. He would love her to exhaustion, leaving both of them boneless and sated. And then she would wriggle against him with mock innocence and the satin of her skin, the wildflower scent of her body mixed with the musk of their love, would ignite him, and desire raged until once again he felt her sheathing him, felt the dainty rippling of her innermost pleasure beginning. It drove him to white-hot frenzy and to depths of release and delight he'd never before experienced.

Once in a while he caught himself comparing the tempestuous abandon of their lovemaking with the quiet occasional sex he'd had with Dixie.

When that happened, he felt angry with himself, disloyal. Dixie had never actually refused him, but he'd sensed quite early in their marriage that she didn't share his deeply passionate nature. Oh, she'd always been welcoming and warm. He'd loved her, and because of that, he'd been faithful to her, even though at times he'd been sorely tempted.

He'd grown more and more aware of subtle signals other women gave him during those years, messages that hinted they would be happy to take on the burden of his virility.

He'd turned to sports, soccer, handball, jogging—exhausting physical ways to control an appetite Dixie didn't share.

It was the opposite with Yolanda. He was intrigued with the contrast between her composed, cheerful daytime self and the moaning wanton she became when they made love. Intrigued, and disturbed. She was like a drug to which he was becoming more and more seriously addicted.

There had been women after Dixie's death, far too many of them. He'd needed to purge a lingering insecurity in himself, a deep-seated fear that Dixie's lukewarm responses had been his fault, as a result of his clumsiness or lack of technique.... He'd been lavishly reassured on that point, at least. Repeatedly. And each of his willing partners had been a delight. But none of them had affected him like Yolanda.

His desire for her increased as each day passed. He thought of her at work, reliving details of the previous night. The need to be with her would become so compelling he'd miss portions of conversations, and Ruth had taken to repeating most things several times as well as staring at him strangely at odd moments. Once, she slipped her half-moon glasses farther down her nose and asked loudly, "Are you sure your hearing isn't deteriorating, Alex?"

She was so typically earnest about it that he'd wickedly held a hand behind his ear and bellowed, "Eh? What's that, woman?"

Ruth had snorted, then marched out of the office.

He would leave early in the afternoon, race his sporty car over the hills and along the winding shore road to Rockwoods like a boy let out of school.

That hot week in August, Rockwoods was sunshine, cheerful voices and the smell of bread baking.

There were only two discordant notes to Yolanda's happiness.

Since their lovemaking that first night, Alex had meticulously taken care of protective measures.

"It's unlikely you'd conceive, but I'd rather not take any chances," he'd explained, his voice suddenly harsh as he added, "I'm not much good at being a father. Even though I'm almost certain it wouldn't happen, I'd rather not ever try it again."

The dim light in the bedroom hid the pain Yolanda's face reflected at his words. With Dixie, he had loved enough to adopt a child. With Yolanda, he was unwilling to accept even the remote possibility of having one.

Did he realize that he was making the decision for her, as well as for himself? She struggled with her emotions, and finally her practicality won. She must welcome what he could give and never demand more. After all, she'd known all along there was a vast chasm between the passion Alex felt for her, and the love he'd had for Dixie.

With morning, she'd put such matters determinedly to the back of her mind. She had more of Alex than she'd dared ever dream of having. She'd make it enough.

The other incident was less important, perhaps, but it hurt all the same.

From the first, she'd felt the house was stiff and unwelcoming with its careful groupings of delicate furniture and the precise arrangements of figurines and china. One evening she impulsively suggested, "Let's move that couch over to here, and fill the vases with wildflowers and sweet peas instead of those plastic roses, and take down all the curtains."

She was already planning further changes when she realized Alex wasn't answering. He was standing stiffly, his face half turned away. She caught a glimpse of his expression, and her heart plummeted.

Unthinkingly, she'd made a dreadful mistake. He looked decidedly unhappy, ill at ease, and his gaze went slowly from one area of the room to another, as if he were seeing more than what was there.

His amber-flecked eyes were apologetic and sad. "Let's just leave the room as it is for now, Landa."

Dixie's ghost had won again.

Yolanda did her best to hide her dismay, throwing herself into preparations for the picnic on Friday. But she fretted over the scene, nervously wondering if she would blunder socially, as she'd managed to do privately with Alex.

It was only a party, she reminded herself sternly on Friday afternoon, the same sort of happy get-together that the villagers planned in Votice after the annual day of mushroom picking. The guests here were mostly family. Still, her palms felt clammy. She couldn't stop imagining she might make a fool of herself somehow. Ruth Prentiss had sounded frighteningly sophisticated when Yolanda had impulsively phoned and invited her.

Promptly on time, with Victor, his tall grandson, beside him, Ian Cameron was first to arrive, wrestling his old Jeep down the driveway.

Tracey quite suddenly became as shy as Yolanda felt, and she scampered into the house, mumbling about putting Coke in the fridge.

"C'mon, Gypsy. This was all your idea, remember?" Alex squeezed Yolanda's hand reassuringly, and his teasing made her smile. All at once, everything was all right again.

Robert arrived, bumping up in his blue truck, giving Yolanda a warm hug and a fond kiss even before he greeted his son.

"That's a hell of a garden you're growing, Alex," he commented, giving in to the urge to tease his son again about the newspaper column he'd found so hilariously funny. "Have you had the minister of Food and Agriculture over here to see it? Seems to me this could go a long way toward solving world famine. Can you drag yourself away from farming in a couple of weeks to come fishing with Barney and me, or will we have to take the goat along?"

"Lay off, Dad," Alex warned. He jerked a thumb at Ian, who did his best to look innocent. "This is the old reprobate who's responsible for that damned garden, and for the chickens, as well. I couldn't even guess what he used for fertilizer, but I've never had to eat so many fresh vegetables in my life."

Or endure as many bad jokes. But he could see the humor in the whole thing now, because the garden had gotten totally out of control, lavishly presenting new tomatoes, zucchini, onions and peas at a rate even Yolanda had trouble dealing with.

Barney and Sophia drove in just then, and right behind them, a bright red motorcycle roared up. Alex's mouth actually dropped open when Ruth Prentiss, smartly dressed in a gray cotton jumpsuit, casually dismounted and removed a shiny red helmet.

From that unlikely moment on, the picnic acquired a personality all its own.

"Ms Prentiss, can we have a look at your bike?" Victor, with a no longer shy Tracey in tow, was eyeing Ruth's machine with religious fervor. "How many cc's? What's the gvw?"

In another few minutes Ruth was demonstrating the gears and braking system and showing them how to start and stop in the driveway. Robert, beer in hand, wandered over to watch, and soon even he was taking short trips up the driveway with a gleeful grin on his face.

Barney asked Yolanda for a tour of the garden and an introduction to the animals, and of course Cinnamon neatly escaped the moment her pen was opened. Ian gave chase, swearing colorfully at the capering goat as it eluded him, and everyone laughed, making outlandish suggestions. Alex brought Sophia a glass of white wine and sank down beside her in a lawn chair, taking a deep swig of his second beer. This was easily the most unusual gathering he'd ever hosted, all right. He was beginning to resign himself to the fact that whatever Yolanda involved him in always ended up just a little out of control.

Sophia prattled on for several minutes and then abruptly said, "Alex, I know men never notice these things, but Yolanda needs a new wardrobe. I tried to buy her several things one day when we were shopping, but she's very proud and independent. She absolutely refused. She insisted on buying herself that very outfit she's wearing. And Tracey told me that when Yolanda lost so much weight and nothing fit her, Tracey gave her some things of hers." Sophia frowned. "I know she didn't have much money of her own. If there's some way we could—" Her voice trailed off uncertainly.

Alex's eyes immediately found Yolanda, slender and girlish looking in her jeans and pink T-shirt, and he suddenly remembered how often she'd worn that exact outfit over the past week.

He cursed himself silently for being a heedless fool and felt ashamed of his insensitivity. Why hadn't he noticed how few clothes she had? Probably because she looked delectable to him in anything she wore. Probably because all he thought of lately was getting whatever she wore off her as quickly as possible.

"I'm glad you mentioned it, Sophia," he said evenly, sipping his beer and watching Yolanda, who was laughing now at something Barney was saying. "Don't concern yourself any longer. I'll take care of it." He was furious with himself for not being more observant, but he also felt irritated with Yolanda. He'd made very sure she always had money, but he'd never dream of asking her what she did with it. Why hadn't she been using it for necessities like clothing?

"I didn't think I'd ever have to encourage a woman to buy clothes," he joked weakly. "Dixie filled so many closets with things she never wore that I could hardly find room for my suits."

Sophia put a gentle beringed hand on his arm, and her voice had a serious note despite its bantering tone.

"You mustn't make the mistake of thinking that just because we're female, we women are at all alike, dear, or the slightest bit predictable. For instance, I noticed the expression on your face when Ruth Prentiss arrived on that motorbike. She surprised you, didn't she?"

Horrified would be a better word, he thought, nodding wryly at his aunt. "I just hope Tracey doesn't get any ideas in her head about learning to ride one," he commented.

Sophia gave him a penetrating look and said spiritedly, "I hope she does. Then she could teach me how, as well."

Alex was greatly relieved to have Barney arrive at that moment and demand a refill for his empty glass of Scotch. There had been an undercurrent to his aunt's words that Alex found vaguely disquieting.

"ALEX, IT WAS a very big success, this picnic of ours, wasn't it?"

It was late, almost morning. They were alone in his room under the eaves, wrapped together in a relaxed lover's knot of entwined arms and legs.

"Yeah, it was. It turned out to be the longest picnic I've ever been at," he teased. "For a while there, I thought they were going to stay all night. And I wanted to be here instead, doing this with you."

He stroked a finger down the line of her back, marveling again at how completely she gave herself to him, innocently and honestly taking the physical satisfaction he delighted in bringing her. He'd controlled himself, using his expertise, holding back his own ecstasy just to watch her desire grow, the delight blossom in her exotic eyes, and burst, as it had moments before, scant seconds before his own.

"Alex? I like your Ruth Prentiss. She has invited me for lunch one day next week. And you know, I think your father liked her also." The smug pleasure in her voice amused him, and he laughed.

"Matchmaker. That woman on the motorcycle tonight sure as hell wasn't 'my' Ruth Prentiss. The Ruth Prentiss I know wears dark suits and intimidates strong men on the phone, and yet I could swear she was flirting with Dad. A motorcycle, for God's sake. Now I suppose Tracey's going to want one."

"If she does, is it so terrible, Alex?" The gentle tones reminded him of the conversation with Sophia, and he frowned as Yolanda went on, "Victor wants a motorcycle, of that I'm certain. I heard him telling his grandfather."

The mention of Vic made Alex suddenly uneasy. Meeting the kid had been a shock. Victor was taller, more muscular, more—everything—than Alex had expected. He looked like a man, an extremely handsome man, at that. He probably already shaved. And Tracey was with him practically every day. He remembered, uneasily, his recent memories of sixteen-year-old males.

He drew his arm from under Yolanda's head and rearranged the tumbled pillows restlessly.

"I don't think it's good for him and Tracey to see so much of each other," he blurted, folding his arms under his head and frowning up at the ceiling.

"They are friends, Alex. Ian has also become Tracey's friend. It's hard for you to accept, but Tracey is growing up. I believe she needs this contact with other people."

As she spoke, Yolanda realized vaguely that she, too, needed contact with other people. She'd been living a rather insular existence. It was time to venture beyond Rockwoods, make new friends beyond the family.

"Maybe you should have a talk with Tracey about Vic. Explain things to her," Alex suggested vaguely.

On the edge of sleep, Yolanda felt a tiny pang of apprehension. Alex was placing the responsibility for Tracey's sex education squarely on her.

It was confusing. Alex chatted easily with his daughter about everyday matters. He teased her and listened to her. But they spoke only about superficial things. When a serious issue arose, an emotional problem, Yolanda found she, instead of Alex, ended up talking to Tracey.

The issue was forgotten as Alex drew the blanket over them, snuggled her into his arms and yawned sleepily.

"Night, beautiful Gypsy. We have to get up and go shopping tomorrow, so go to sleep now."

"Shopping for what, Alex?"

But he pretended to snore rudely, and soon they both slept.

"DON'T MEN IN CZECHOSLOVAKIA buy clothes for their wives?"

Yolanda stood in the expensive boutique, her chin thrust out belligerently, arms folded across her chest. Alex was a bare few feet away, as furiously angry as she'd ever seen him, looking totally out of place and ridiculously masculine in this unlikely setting.

Why hadn't he told her his intentions before they left the house, she thought, so they could have had this quarrel there instead of in this carpeted, perfumed, frightening salon, while the sleek salesperson in her black suit and pearls avidly listened as she pretended politely to arrange a display of lingerie?

"Of course." She shot daggers at him through slitted eyes. "Of course they do. But I am not those women, and I don't want you buying me clothing." It was impossible to explain why, because even she didn't fully understand. It had to do with independence and freedom.

From the first, she'd worried about being a financial burden to him. It mattered not at all that he was obviously wealthy, and ridiculously generous. From the day she'd moved into Rockwoods, she'd kept careful account of all the money he'd given her. He refused to even glance at the neat figures, laughing and teasing her for her thrifty ways.

What mattered desperately was that she maintain at all costs that elusive freedom she'd come here to find. In order to do that, she had to feel she was paying her own way.

So far, she had. By taking over Tracey's care for the summer, she'd spared Alex both worry and expense. The garden and the animals . . . well, they'd served other purposes besides economics. But what Alex was insisting on now seriously threatened her independence.

He was glaring at her ferociously. Alex Caine was not an easy man to fight with, but she'd had training. She'd learned plenty from *babička*. She squared her shoulders.

Alex scowled. The woman was driving him insane. He felt like a perfect fool, but this time, he refused to let her win. He narrowed his eyes, and revealed his strategy.

"Yolanda, you are my wife. Correct?"

She nodded unwillingly. It wasn't a fair question. He knew as well as she did the status of their peculiar marriage. "That is correct, yes."

"As my wife, you'll be meeting people I know . . . going out to lunch with Ruth. There are social occasions we'll have to attend." He was getting better as he went along, improvising. He'd make a politician yet, by God.

She listened, expressionless.

"Yolanda, as my wife, you have a certain responsibility to dress well. People will notice what you wear. Your appearance will reflect back on me."

Her deep-set eyes with their long lashes looked a little uncertain now. Good. He was getting somewhere.

"It's important that we maintain a certain standard." If Barney or his father ever heard that pompous statement, they'd choke to death laughing. But Yolanda was nodding slowly. He was winning. Elation swept over him—too soon, however. He should have guessed it wouldn't be quite so easy.

"I understand, Alex. I agree. You must not be made ashamed of me." It touched him strangely that she would even think he'd be ashamed of such beauty. But he hid his reaction, because he needed to win.

"Whatever you spend today is a loan, which I will repay."

He swore in frustration, and the saleslady who'd been listening raised her plucked brows and sniffed. He would do her serious injury if she didn't move the hell away and stop eavesdropping. He gave her one patently furious look, and she finally scuttled off.

"There's no need..." he snapped, but Yolanda's certain tone cut him off.

"Not for you, Alex. But for me, there is need, yes." There was almost panic in her voice, and he was lying in his teeth when he said testily, "Okay, okay, so we'll consider it a loan."

After that, bags and boxes accumulated swiftly. The older clerk whom he'd insulted, huffily refused to wait on them, which was great, because they were helped by a cheery young salesgirl who had an artist's eye for what best suited Yolanda. She carried armloads of whispery finery into the dressing room, and Alex, seated on a ridiculously spindly chair, considered gravely, then nodded or shook his head as Yolanda shyly appeared in one outfit after the other. He was surprised and touched by her absolute trust in his judgment—not once did she protest or argue about his decision. In Alex's experience, that, too, was a first.

She was dazed by the array. She searched furtively for price tags, but there weren't any visible, and when she asked, she got a wink in response.

"The way you look in these, Mrs. Caine, they're a bargain at twice the price." Alex had given the staff strict instructions.

On each giddy trip out of the cubicle, Yolanda repeated, "Alex, this is enough—surely I don't need so many...?"

He nodded at the clerk. The simple scarlet silk dress with the outrageously exaggerated shoulders was added to the pile on the counter.

"I can only handle one shot at this shopping thing, Yolanda," he warned gruffly. "Once a year it is, so go try on those slacks and the jacket, and stop bitching."

His crooked grin took the sting out of his words, because she wasn't complaining, really. She was starting to actually enjoy the experience. What sane woman could resist trying on these soft rainbow-colored silks, the glovelike leather strappy shoes to match, the jewel-toned blouses and sweaters and skirts?

But how much would it all cost?

She shuddered and slid into butter-soft vivid blue suede pants, a wildly patterned crepe shirt, a matching suede jacket with wide lapels and dramatic blousing narrowing in at her slender hipline.

Alex's nod was emphatic.

A deceptively simple emerald green jersey dress that skimmed her body provocatively was modeled next. It was slit high on her thigh, but the neckline was demure, dipped just enough to hold a necklace in the hollow of her throat. The sleeves were full at the top, narrowing into tiny buttoned cuffs. Yolanda's eyes sparkled when she buckled the ridiculously high-heeled sandals the sales girl proffered to complement the dress.

This time Alex's eyes held banked fires when he nodded his approval.

Finally they were done. Yolanda wearily tugged on the serviceable blue skirt and plain blouse she'd worn into the salon, unconsciously comparing their quality with the clothing she'd just tried on. The new garments would undoubtedly cost a fortune. Her fingers trembled, and she shook her head at such extravagance. Well, she would have to find a way to pay him back.

Alex hastily scribbled an astronomical amount on a check, and the clerk hid it away in the cash register's drawer.

When Yolanda emerged, he casually accepted a handwritten bill for a ridiculously lower figure from the bemused clerk. Yolanda held out a hand, and he gave it to her reluctantly.

She was almost afraid to look, but when she did, it wasn't as bad as she'd expected. She sighed deeply, and the impressive stack of boxes and bags and padded hangers with garment bags took several trips to carry to the car.

Fifteen minutes later Alex made two approaches before he found the courage to enter a women's lingerie shop while Yolanda was in the supermarket buying groceries, and he came out with still another embossed bag, with cold sweat on his forehead and shaking hands.

He'd come close to running out of the store. He'd been the only male in the place. And those confusing stacks—bikinis, hipsters, full cut, French cut—he slumped deep into the leather seat of the car and closed his eyes. He'd give anything for a drink, or several drinks.

But any strain he'd felt was worth it to see Yolanda in those clothes, watch her eyes glow. And her body. He swallowed hard, remembering how she'd looked as she anxiously turned before the mirror, clad in soft, floating things, her slender, voluptuous form graceful and seductively curved beneath the clothing.

Sexual urgency flared so powerfully he clenched his teeth.

Savagely he reminded himself that she was his and that they were going home. Tracey was in Vancouver for the weekend, on a reluctant but long overdue visit with her grandparents.

"You are my wife," he'd reminded Yolanda earlier, although the words had made his gut clench in protest.

Why couldn't he allow himself the emotional luxury of loving her? He was obsessed by their lovemaking, and he enjoyed being with her more all the time. Yet whenever he projected the relationship over a span of years, thought of himself as a permanently married man again, a cold dread crept over him.

He'd admitted long before that he hadn't been able to make Dixie happy during the long years of their marriage. Those painful memories were still strong; the impotent sensations of failing someone he loved, of feeling responsible for her happiness and guilty for being unable to provide her with what she needed.

He grimaced and his hands curled around the steering wheel until the knuckles were white.

He wanted Yolanda, but he'd rather not be married to her. He'd rather not be married to anyone. Ever.

"You are, though, Caine," he muttered bitterly. "You sure as hell are. You're about as married as any man can get."

CHAPTER ELEVEN

THE FOLLOWING TUESDAY Ruth phoned Yolanda and confirmed the tentative luncheon she'd suggested at the picnic.

"Is there anywhere special you'd like to go? I usually just bring a brown bag, so I'm not too familiar with restaurants," Ruth explained.

"I know only two, and one is McDonald's. The other was called Chez Armand, and I liked them both."

"I think we'll choose Chez Armand," Ruth said dryly.

Yolanda was excited the next morning, and also a little nervous.

"Come, please, and help me decide what is best to wear to a luncheon," Yolanda asked Tracey as soon as Alex had driven away.

Tracey had seen and approved of Yolanda's new wardrobe as soon as she'd returned from her Vancouver visit. Everything, that is, but the contents of the bag Alex had abruptly produced at bedtime that evening.

"This is for me, Gypsy," he'd warned aggressively. "Before you blow a fuse and get all independent and huffy on me, you get to wear it, but just remember I bought it for myself."

Mystified, she'd emptied the bag's contents on the dark blue bedspread, and then stood, spellbound, afraid to touch the magical wisps of satin and lace lest they disappear.

There were silk bikini panties, so scant she blushed to imagine how little they'd cover. Each dainty pair had a matching bra, gossamer sheer. The sets were ivory, burgundy, palest powder blue and warm peach. What puzzled Yolanda when she dared examine them closely was that the sizes were exactly right.

"But Alex, how did you guess the size?" Alex was watching her intently, his green eyes narrowed as he waited for her response. Fleetingly she thought he seemed almost nervous, but that was so unlike him she'd dismissed it.

"It wasn't a guess. I wrote down the numbers on one of your sets this morning."

The mental picture of him, laboriously copying the confusing numbers from her underwear, made her give a wicked little giggle. By then she was examining the rest of the lingerie, holding them up, pressing her face into their fragile softness. There were three lavishly lace-trimmed one-piece garments called "teddies," in palest apricot, pristine white and wicked black. They were all more lace than fabric.

Lastly, there were four tissue-wrapped diaphanous thigh-length silk nightshirts, indigo blue, dusky rose, peach and pale vanilla.

"I, um, I like the nightgowns you wear. These were the closest they had." He really did sound uncertain this time. Yolanda looked at him closely. His expression was unreadable, but a tiny nerve ticked beside his eye. It slowly dawned on her that he was actually afraid she wouldn't like what he'd chosen.

Instead of saying anything, she did something she'd never dreamed she'd be wanton enough to do. She stood slowly, and with his narrowed eyes tracing her every movement, she gracefully removed every stitch of her clothing. Deliberately then, one by one, smiling provocatively as she did so, she tried on every single garment he'd bought her, slipping them on and off with loving care, her nakedness even more apparent when covered by the garments. She turned her body this way and that, growing more heated with every movement because of his heavy-lidded gaze.

"You see, Alex? They are a perfect fit."

He didn't move. He stood with one leg propped on a chair, his buttocks resting against the low oak dresser across the room from the bed. But she was all too aware of her effect on him, of the heated flush rising in his cheeks, the increased tempo of his breathing.

He let her finish, let her draw last of all, the rich blue silk nightshirt over her nudity, her tumbled dark hair falling loose down her back in disarray. The lamplight behind her outlined her body, her proudly peaked breasts, nipples hardened in awareness, the inward curve of her waist, the womanly flaring of her hips and the long, beautifully shaped legs below the hem.

"You like these, Alex? You will allow me to wear them for you?"

In two strides, he was holding her against him, making her feel his hardness.

"Witch," he breathed. "Teasing witch. Feel what you've done."

She put her fingers gently on his lips before he could kiss her, holding him away so she could tell him with words what she guessed he needed to hear. "Alex," she said softly, "never have I had things so beautiful as these. I know they are your gift for me. I love them, Alex, and I don't know how to thank you."

He'd shuddered, drawing a long, shaky breath before he'd claimed her lips in a burning kiss and tumbled them both back onto the bed. "I can think of several ways, Gypsy," he'd murmured. "Now pay attention while I show you."

The images of that night were strong in Yolanda's mind as she and Tracey climbed the winding stairs to the bedroom she shared with Alex.

"Tell me why you thought I would not like your gifts," she'd asked him hesitantly that night, lying clasped in his arms so tight she could feel his every heartbeat. He'd sighed, a long, shuddering sigh, but he hadn't answered, and she'd been more and more aware that though he clung to her physically, he still kept her at arm's length emotionally.

The morning's brightness poured in through the triangular windows as they entered Alex's bedroom—her bedroom, too, now, she reminded herself stoutly. Why did she always feel so—temporary—here, in Alex's private space?

"Yolanda, do you like being married?"

Her reverie was interrupted by Tracey, and Yolanda recognized immediately the carefree tone the girl used. It usually accompanied questions or comments that were anything but casual.

Tracey had plopped herself down on the neatly made bed, her gray eyes wide and innocent, emphasized by the street-urchin hair.

"I like so much being married to your father, yes, Tracey." Yolanda moved to straighten the books on the long bookshelf, waiting for the rest of the girl's questions. Something warned her this wasn't going to be easy.

"Lots of the girls at school said they weren't ever going to get married, just have affairs and stuff like that."

Yolanda kept her voice neutral.

"How about you, what do you think about it?"

Tracey's shrug was nonchalant.

"Things are different than they were in the olden days, when you were my age. Women are free to have affairs if they decide to." She rubbed her palms back and forth across the furry spread, her head down, and there was only a slight catch in her voice when she added, "That's probably what I'll do, I guess." This time a nervous gulp accompanied her words. "Most of the girls at school that I hung around with had already slept with guys. They didn't think it was any big deal." Her next comment was hurried. "None of those guys were half as neat as Vic is, either."

The smile that had threatened at the term "olden days" faded quickly, but Yolanda went on methodically removing books and replacing them in almost the same order. Her hands were steady, but her thoughts were in turmoil.

Alex, what do I say to her? What do I tell your daughter?

"Do you want to..." She hastily borrowed Tracey's own phrase. "Are you thinking of having this, this—affair—with Victor Martinos?"

Tracey kept her head bent low, so only the auburn sheen of her spiky hair was visible. Her voice was forlorn.

"I do...don't know, for sure. I mean, sometimes I think so, but it...it's kinda scary, you know?"

Yolanda nodded, giving up on the books and sinking down on the bed herself, imitating Tracey's cross-legged pose. She made a quick decision, and she could only hope it was the right thing to do for Tracey. The girl was mature enough to understand, Yolanda was sure of that.

"I do know. This is not a new thing, Tracey, whatever or not you believe. It is a decision all women come to in their lives. I was several years older than you when I myself decided to have an 'affair.'" Yolanda shook her head ruefully. "I don't know for you, but for me, I assure you it was a big mistake."

Tracey's head snapped up, her startled gaze fully on Yolanda.

"You had sex . . . you slept with . . . how old were you?"

"I was seventeen, but this is not just a matter of age, Tracey. For women, it might sometimes be right at fifteen." Privately Yolanda doubted her own words, but she felt she was walking on eggshells. "Or, I suspect, it could be wrong at twenty-one."

Tracey's voice was querulous. "I don't see what makes the difference."

"It has to do with how you feel, not how many years you have lived." Yolanda was finding this discussion harder and harder as she went along. "With me, I was curious, impatient, eager for what I felt was adulthood. I wanted to know. It had little to do with the man, and everything to do with myself and my impatient nature." She added slowly, "I think for lovemaking to be good, or right, it has to have everything to do with the other person."

"You mean you have to love him?" Tracey sounded skeptical. "All this junk about love. How does anybody ever know if they're in love or not?"

"If you have no doubts, and what you're doing feels not only right, but inevitable, and you care more about the other person than about yourself, then I would say that is love."

Sweat was beginning to trickle under Yolanda's arms. This conversation was the worst yet, harder even than the morning she'd explained to Tracey about her and Alex sharing this room.

"Is that how you feel about my father? Are you in love with him?"

Yolanda felt her tension ease. This, at least, was easier, and she could smile confidently. "Yes," she said positively. "I do love your father, Tracey."

"Why didn't you . . . what happened to that other guy?"

It took Yolanda a moment to catch on.

"Who . . . oh, Antonin." She was silent a moment, remembering. "He went to the army, and I went on to school. He was glad to leave, I think, and I was glad to see him go. We had become a burden to each other. It happens like that if it's not right, and instead of being friends, you finish never wanting to see each other again." A new thought struck her, and she said awkwardly, "Tracey, this school you went to, they taught you about the body?"

"You mean like ovaries and stuff? Yeah, we had life class, it taught us about venereal disease and—and birth control."

Should she take this any further? Yolanda studied the flushed young face now turning to stare out the window. It was unfair to stop halfway.

"Tracey, if you decide to have this affair, do you have a medical person for birth control?"

The girl shook her head. "Only old Doctor Hanes, and I'd die before I'd go to him. He knew my mother and everything. There's a clinic downtown, but it's kind of scary to go alone." Obviously, Tracey had given the matter a great deal of consideration already.

"Think it over, and if you want, we will go together."

Suddenly the impact of what she was doing fell heavily on Yolanda.

"Perhaps you should talk with your father about this?"

Absolute, unmitigated horror registered on the girl's features.

"I can't, oh, Landa, don't make me, don't tell him. He'd never understand. He'd...you're not going to...he thinks I'm still a baby."

Her distress was so acute that Yolanda put an arm around her and soothed, "No, no, you and I are friends and this is a confidence. Only he is your father, and—"

"I can't talk to him about stuff like this."

Yolanda felt torn between her loyalty to Tracey and her responsibility to Alex. Reluctantly, knowing Tracey would never confide in her again if she violated her trust, Yolanda promised.

Then, enough was enough. Bounding from the bed, Yolanda threw open the closet door. "Now, please, important decisions. What do I wear for this luncheon? I now have so many choices, I don't know where to begin."

"YOU LOOK ABSOLUTELY ELEGANT," Ruth said when she greeted her an hour later, and together they walked the short distance to the little restaurant.

Armand Mollins was again very much in evidence, and he welcomed Yolanda like a compatriot, embarrassing her a little as he rattled on in French, interspersing it with English to explain to Ruth that Madame Caine and he were old acquaintances. He escorted them to a choice table by a window.

Ruth waited until Armand was gone, then raised a well-groomed eyebrow at Yolanda before demanding, "Where did you learn to speak such excellent French? And how did you meet that charming man?" An impish look came over her usually stern features. "I do hope Alex is suitably jealous."

For the next half hour Yolanda found herself volunteering a capsule account of her background, with the exclusion of any details about her marriage, and then she concluded, "So, then I married and came to Canada. Enough about me. Ruth Prentiss, it's your turn for biography now."

Ruth looked distinctly different today than she had at the picnic. She wore a no-nonsense brown striped shirtdress, and her soft brown hair was drawn tightly back in a bun instead of becomingly loose the way it had been the other evening. But her regular features and large brown eyes were quietly attractive, and she nodded agreeably at Yolanda's suggestion.

"Fair enough. My life story is singularly dull, however, compared to yours, Yolanda. I was born and raised here in Victoria. I attended school and business college here as well." She sipped her wine from the long-stemmed glass, staring down at her ringless fingers.

"I didn't marry. I'm forty-seven years old, and I've always lived at home. When my father died seven years ago, my mother became bedridden. I cared for her until she died last October." She sipped her wine again, grimaced at Yolanda and said, "There, see? Just as I said, dull, dull, dull." There was a sadness in the lines of her face as she set down her glass, and the two were quiet while Armand served them small pannikins of golden quiche.

"You've left the interesting parts out," Yolanda accused. "How did you come to buy that machine that Tracey talks of constantly?"

Ruth looked a tiny bit sheepish, and a lovely soft pink shaded her cheeks.

"I woke up one morning feeling that my life had gone by, and I'd never really done anything exciting. I saw an ad in the morning paper for a course in motorcycle training, and I registered." Something came and went in her eyes. "I passed the course, marched out and bought the bike. It's become a passion, I'm afraid."

She raised her wineglass rebelliously. "Here's to passion," she toasted throatily, and they both laughed.

Yolanda drank the toast, enjoying the cheery atmosphere and quiet sense of relaxation in the restaurant. At the other tables were well-dressed groups, eating and talking and laughing together. Yolanda found herself wondering idly who the other women in the restaurant were and what they did to allow them time to idle away the afternoon so pleasantly.

Like a dream that suddenly takes on the aspects of a nightmare, she abruptly saw herself in this setting. She looked like a Canadian here, laughing, talking, drinking wine. She wore expensive, smart clothing. She had time to sit and wile away an afternoon. She had money in her purse, thanks to Alex. Was this why she'd left her homeland, to lead this type of life? Where had her sense of purpose gone? Ruth had a career; she'd earned everything she had.

And herself? She'd become decadent, lavish, useless, her Czechoslovak roots accused, and in the space of a heartbeat, her stomach clenched in the by now familiar agony of homesickness. She would never belong in this country, never feel at peace with her past and her present lives. Fighting nausea, she stared at Ruth. Ruth belonged. She was born here.

Would Yolanda ever belong anywhere again? Slowly she fought the sickness. Slowly she became aware once more of what Ruth was saying about her motorcycle.

"I've met new people because of riding it, and I must admit they're people I'd never have spoken to before. It's made changes in my life," she said thoughtfully. "Good changes, but difficult for me. Half of me keeps wanting to stay in the same old groove, while the other half is out there making things happen." She shrugged. "Sometimes I think that's what life means us to do, change every so often. Look at the changes you've gone through, Yolanda." She flashed a warm smile. "It helps to know other women go through the same sort of thing."

It was eerie, almost as if Ruth were somehow aware of how Yolanda had been feeling for the past few moments and was reassuring her. Their situations, their ages, their backgrounds were vastly different, but underneath, the emotions were probably identical.

Was there a universal pattern among women, a set of experiences besides the usual one of childbirth, which formed a bond despite nationality or culture? Ruth must have been reaching the same conclusion as Yolanda, because she lifted her wineglass again.

"To us," she said. "To women everywhere."

The luncheon was a great success. The tentative warmth the two women sensed between them at the picnic had blossomed today into friendship. They talked and laughed and enjoyed themselves immensely.

"Ruth," Yolanda said hesitantly when the other woman reluctantly rose to leave, "do you mind telling Alex I will meet him at his office later and ride home with him? I think I will stay in town for a few hours."

She would do some exploring. Seeing Armand again had reminded her that she'd never visited his sister's boutique as she'd promised. She'd go there right after her next stop. She pulled out an address she'd scribbled from the phone directory just before she left Rockwoods, the result of the disquieting conversation with Tracey.

Tracey's questions that morning had reminded her uncomfortably that she had allowed Alex to take all the birth control precautions, and that it was unfair of her not to share the responsibility.

She was nervous as she entered the modern building with the Planned Parenthood sign on its window, but forty minutes later, she felt reassured and comforted as she left the clinic. Doctor Mary Carlisle had been caring and easy to talk with, as well as thorough. She'd examined Yolanda and ordered tests done at the downstairs lab, but it was closed when Yolanda tried the door. A sign announced Back in Fifteen.

Should she wait? After fifteen minutes, and with no sign of the returning technician, Yolanda decided to come back another day. After all, the tests were routine, and Dr. Carlisle had given her detailed instructions on a product to use until she could begin birth control pills. And there was another, much more appealing visit she wanted to make this afternoon.

She visited the neighboring pharmacy, purchased exactly what the doctor had recommended, tucked the package into her purse and fished out the cheery yellow Foofera card. She asked the friendly clerk for directions, and the man pointed out the proper bus stop, just down the street.

As Armand had indicated, the address was on the waterfront, in an old part of Victoria where brick warehouses had been converted to trendy shops. Foofera was halfway down a block, its bold yellow sign highly visible among the more subdued stores surrounding it. Yolanda hesitated before going in, admiring the clever and eye-catchingly simple window display.

When she opened the door, she was aware of several customers waiting patiently for service at an oak desk that served as a counter. Classical music was playing softly, but the most prevalent sound was that of a small baby crying frantically. The wriggling blanket-wrapped bundle was clamped incongruously in the left arm of a reed-slender, dark-haired woman with a harried expression, obviously the owner.

"I know, *madame*, I promised the hem would be done. But my assistant, who does these things, is ill, and I myself, well..." she brandished the screaming baby helplessly. "As you can see, right now it is impossible. The baby is hungry, and there is nothing for it, I must feed her."

With that, she sat down in a backless rocking chair, calmly undid her stylish purple smock top and began to nurse. The baby made frantic snorting noises and choked several times, waving tiny flower fists in the air as if she were drowning before she finally calmed. The nursing mother, looking like a high-fashion model posing for a motherhood ad, caught Yolanda's amazed stare and gave a typically Gallic shrug, rolling her eyes dramatically.

She rocked gently, stroking her snuffling baby's cheek with one long, well-manicured finger, an expression of resigned acceptance on her face. Yolanda wanted to giggle; it was all so outrageous.

This woman was undoubtedly Armand's sister, for his classically handsome features were more marked on her face in a way that might have been unfortunate but instead was arrestingly attractive. Her black hair was curly, cut boyishly short to accentuate a well-shaped head.

"Excuse me, Mme. Dominique..." Impulsively, Yolanda introduced herself, using rapid French for privacy and quickly explaining that she'd met Armand and come at his suggestion. Hesitantly she asked if she could help in any way.

"I can't feed the baby, but I do know how to sew," she added. Dominique unleashed a torrent of dramatic, grateful French. An angry wail followed from the baby, who'd lost her place while her mother gestured expressively.

Forty minutes later the baby was tucked back in a wicker bassinet, sprawled sound asleep on her full stomach, contentedly giving an occasional wet burp, and Yolanda had the store under control.

Ten minutes after that, Yolanda dazedly accepted Dominique's offer of a temporary job at Foofera.

Yolanda stroked a finger over baby Lili's downy cheek, made arrangements for hours and wages and hurried to catch the bus to the Parliament Buildings and Alex.

Yolanda felt dazed and frightened and exuberant, all at once. She had a job, her first real job in Canada. And she'd found it all on her own.

Alex wasn't as excited as Yolanda when she burst into his office at five forty-five, breathless from hurrying and flushed with her news. In fact, he was surprised at how negative her announcement made him feel.

"Is this job really what you want?"

She stood just inside the office door, her high-heeled sandals planted apart, the dark, shining head with its smooth coronet tilted to the side, considering his question. Her white slacks discreetly outlined the narrow waist, the gently swelling hips, the intriguing curve of her pelvis.

"For always, no. I should like a job where I could use my training in languages. But for one month, Alex, yes, I will love this job."

He rose from behind his desk and strode over to hold her in his arms for a moment and gave her a quick kiss. He did his best to hide his reaction, reminding himself that in the beginning of their marriage the plan had been for her to find a job as quickly as she could, so that she would become independent and self-sufficient.

It was a shock to find that now he didn't want that at all. He wanted her at Rockwoods, ready to give him all of her attention. He wanted her all to himself, and the discovery made him uncomfortable. What kind of a caveman instinct was that for a modern guy to have?

"Tell me more about this Dominique and the madhouse she operates," he said lightly, grabbing his suit jacket and hooking it on a finger. He led her out of the building with his palm resting on the small of her back.

She did, her husky voice full of animation, her blue eyes deepening as she described her unorthodox employer. Involved in her story, she was unaware of the male heads that discreetly turned to follow her progress down the wide marble stairs, the carpeted hallways. Alex noticed, however, and slid a proprietory arm around her waist. They were in the car when he pulled a gold-engraved invitation from the pocket of his shirt and handed it to her.

"We're invited to the fall garden party at Government House," he explained. "Next Sunday."

She read the ornate printing and demanded, wide-eyed, "This is a big deal, Alex?" She drew the words out dramatically.

He laughed, recognizing one of Tracey's expressions. Several ornate teenisms had creeped into Yolanda's vocabulary, amusing him.

"Yup, you could certainly say that. Everybody gets shaved and showered and suited to stand around making polite noises with a glass of sherry in hand, and it can be boring as hell." She turned toward him, and he saw her eyebrows lift quizzically.

"You would rather not go, Alex?"

"I haven't gone for the past several years."

Yolanda translated that statement to mean "since Dixie's death." She waited for him to continue. He wheeled the silver Porsche out of the parking lot, his arm across the back of the seat as he watched the rear window.

"Everybody watches to see who's there and who isn't. It's a big social event. It's colorful and traditional." The little car darted through the afternoon traffic like a ballet dancer, and he savored the low, powerful thrum of the motor.

"I only wish they served beer instead of sherry," he said plaintively, and Yolanda laughed. Her hand rested lightly on his thigh, and she studied him as he drove, thinking how good he looked. He'd tossed his sport jacket over the seat, and his shirt was rolled up on his forearms. His hair was carelessly rumpled over his forehead. The silver in the brown was increasing.

As the years passed, she mused, Alex would undoubtedly develop a silvery white mane, like his father had, and his leonine handsomeness would only increase, as had Robert's.

What would it be like, growing old with Alex? More to the point, did he plan on spending the years ahead with her? His projections for them were invariably short-term plans, never even extending a few months ahead, let alone years.

They were now free of the city, and his mouth twisted into a smile as he whipped the car around the curves and up the hills, driving expertly, but far too fast. He had a streak of recklessness that showed in his driving.

It also showed in his lovemaking. A tiny secret smile tilted Yolanda's lips. Alex made love to her with an intensity almost shocking, a passionate power that left her senses imprinted with his touch. Looking at him like this was enough to remind her of the previous night and make her anticipate the one to come. He was a mysterious combination of wild and gentle lover.

Then, as they turned into Rockwoods, she thought of the visit to the doctor, the package in her purse. A vivid image of Dominique's baby came into her mind's eye, and she dismissed it.

Tracey came to meet them, trailing a leash with Cinnamon bounding on its end. The goat now acted like a faithful dog.

Yolanda immediately told the girl about her lunch, and about her job. Tracey gave her an impulsive hug and the inevitable thumbs-up approval. "A boutique, eh? That's first class, Landa. Bet you'll get ten percent off whatever you buy, too."

Affection welled in Yolanda for this daughter of Alex's. Suddenly she felt sad. She had Tracey to mother, and that was a good thing. But there would be no babies for her and Alex.

IT RAINED THE REST OF THE WEEK. Sunday, however, dawned
with only a light gray cloud cover, and by the time Yolanda and
Alex arrived at the garden party, the sun was making teasing
appearances in an almost clear August sky.

Government House was located on a slight hill just outside
central Victoria, and as Alex parked and gallantly helped her
out of the car, Yolanda had an overwhelming urge to head off
down the hill at a run, away from the discreetly merry sounds
coming from the acres of lawn surrounding the imposing stone
mansion, the official residence of British Columbia's lieutenant governor.

What was a country girl from Votice doing in a place like
this?

CHAPTER TWELVE

"EXPLAIN TO ME AGAIN, please, who this lieutenant governor is that I will meet, Alex?" She stopped walking and put a hand on his arm. Anything that delayed the ordeal ahead suddenly appealed to Yolanda.

"Alex? This lieutenant governor?"

He was thinking how beautiful she looked, and how he wished they'd stayed home. He didn't want to share Yolanda today. He studied her legs and answered absently, "He's the queen's representative. Canada is a member of the British Commonwealth, and we have a governor-general in the nation's capital, Ottawa, and a lieutenant governor in each of the ten provinces. The appointed official is actually a figurehead, giving token royal assent to any legislation passed in his area of responsibility."

"Have you met him before?" Yolanda was beginning to panic at what she considered her social debut among Alex's colleagues.

"Yes, several times. He's a rather stern man. I haven't met his wife. Come on, Gypsy. Let's get this over with."

Gazing at the splendor that was Government House, Yolanda wondered why she was here. Verdant lawns stretched for what seemed miles, separated by a wide semicircular driveway. Rock gardens planted with dramatic and delicate flowers bordered the lawns. Small white tables and chairs were arranged in tasteful groupings, but Yolanda could see at a glance that the crowd was much too large to allow many of the guests to be seated.

"Alex, this was a big mistake," she protested, but he drew her forward. Women dressed in every shade of the rainbow mixed with men in business suits, guards in dress uniform, RCMP officers resplendent in their scarlet tunics, diplomats in

the formal array of their respective countries. It was a visual
feast, a panoply of color and character. It was an "event."

For Yolanda, standing frozen on the periphery, hesitating
with her arm tucked into Alex's elbow, the scene was knee-
shaking, dry-mouth terrifying.

"Alex, do I look correct?" With trembling hands, she
smoothed the shimmery cinnamon-rust silk dress. Twisting
around, with Alex's amused eyes watching, she tried to casually check the sheerness of her hose for runs.

"You're lovely, relax," he whispered in her ear.

Actually, she had to admit she felt attractive today.

Yolanda said a grateful, silent thank-you to Ruth, who'd
helped her choose this dress for the occasion.

The dress was cut in a chemise-style, with the currently
fashionable emphasis on bodice and shoulders. Its dramatic
color wasn't one Yolanda would have chosen, but Ruth had
insisted, and she'd been right. When Yolanda had slipped it on,
the warm cinnamon-gold with undertones of fire played up her
exotically tanned skin tones, showed off her raven hair, contrasted with the clear blue of her eyes, trapping shadows and
mysteries in their depths so they seemed to shimmer.

The dress was deceptively simple and wickedly sexy. It
slipped and slid over her body, enticing and revealing.

"Ruth, you are certain so much of my leg should show?"

One side had a slit that opened as she moved, revealing a
shocking amount of slender thigh.

Ruth snorted. "Fashion is knowing how much and where to
uncover. Believe me, those legs should be uncovered, but discreetly. Now you see them, now you don't. Perfect."

Yolanda gave up and took her word for it.

Too much leg or not, there was no more chance for hesitation. Alex drew her smoothly along the plush red carpet laid on
the lawns. It led to the receiving line where a majestic old man
in tails stood beside a tiny, bejeweled woman, greeting each
guest with a word and a handshake.

"This is my wife, Yolanda Caine. Yolanda, I'd like you to
meet—"

The words were repeated again and again, and half her mind
listened and registered names. The other half was mesmerized
by Alex's deep voice announcing her to the world as his part-

ner. Smiling, nodding, listening, she accepted a cup of tea and nibbled at a tiny rolled sandwich.

Alex introduced clergymen, RCMP officers, judges and members of the legislative assembly with whom he worked. And their wives. Yolanda moved from one group to another, one hand captured in his, her teacup balanced carefully in the other.

She lifted an eyebrow at Alex when he accepted a tiny glass of sherry from a uniformed waiter, and he gave her a comically pained look just as a male voice demanded, "Where have you been hiding this lovely creature, Alex?"

The speaker was a handsome, heavyset man in a navy suit, part of a small group of people standing somewhat apart from the crowd.

"Yolanda, this is Curtis Blackstone. Curtis is Minister of International Trade and Investment. We work together. Curtis, my wife."

Yolanda smiled politely, held out her hand, and found that Curtis was loath to relinquish it.

"I work, Mrs. Caine—may I call you Yolanda?—but I'm afraid Alex, here, simply circles the globe and calls it 'labor.' Where in the world did he find you?"

Yolanda told him, and the dancing brown eyes studied her astutely, feature by feature. "So you're new to Canada. Well, if ever you're lonely while Alex is away, you will let me know, won't you? I'd be most happy to fill in for him, and I'm sure Alex wouldn't mind, would you, old sport?"

"Yes, I would mind. Sorry, Curtis, she's off limits." Alex's straightforward answer amused Curtis immensely, but Yolanda was shocked. She thought the words had a deadly serious undertone, and she glanced at Alex in surprise. He was smiling easily, but there was a hardness in his eyes as he watched the other man's reaction.

Curtis simply threw back his large head and laughed heartily. "A pity you saw her first and married her, my friend. I assure you I'd have given you a run for your money."

Was there a trace of seriousness in the banter, or did these men always talk this way to each other? Yolanda didn't know and there wasn't time to dwell on the question, because Curtis drew them forward to introduce a thin man, impeccably dressed in black suit and white shirt, with a plump little woman beside him.

"This is Sergio Markoff, and his wife, Vasha, from the Russian consulate. I've wanted to get you two together, Alex, because Sergio is here with a group studying reforestation, and with your background in the lumber industry..."

Sergio and Alex were soon deep in discussion. Yolanda had stiffened at the mention of the Russian consulate. Before coming to Canada, she would have reacted to meeting high-ranking Russian officials with frozen, horrified silence, followed swiftly by flight. But these people seemed so ordinary. Surely the shy, nervous little woman beside her could hardly be considered a threat of any sort. She seemed ill at ease, and Yolanda searched her brain frantically for a topic of conversation.

Chitchat eluded her. Vasha stood silently smiling, and Yolanda stood silently smiling back as the minutes lengthened.

"You must excuse Vasha, Madame Caine," Sergio apologized with a little bow, interrupting his conversation with Alex. "She is learning English, but it's slow, and she is shy about her mistakes. Our home was in a rural area, and these gatherings are a little hard for her, you understand?"

How well Yolanda understood! Under her brave facade, she felt the same as Vasha, a stranger in a foreign land.

When the men again were engrossed in a discussion about salmon fishing, Yolanda quietly addressed Vasha in what she feared was Russian grown rusty from disuse.

The effect was electrifying. Vasha's eyes filled with tears, and she grasped Yolanda's hand in both of her own. A torrent of Russian words poured from her, explaining her difficulties with the English language, the aching loneliness she felt for her homeland.

"The children, they make it easier for me; they help with my English," she confided. "You have children, Mrs. Caine?"

"A stepdaughter," Yolanda explained. "She, too, corrects my pronunciation all the time."

"Mine are the same—" Vasha laughed "—even though they were born at home, they speak much better than I."

Born at home.

Home was unquestionably Russia for Vasha, as Czechoslovakia was for Yolanda. Would it always be so?

Sergio overheard them, and he broke off his conversation excitedly again to ask Yolanda where and how she knew his language, and an animated conversation followed between Sergio and the two women.

Several other people joined the group.

A smartly uniformed military band began to play, and under the cover of the music, Curtis said quietly into Yolanda's ear, "Beautiful, and talented, as well. Alex is indeed a lucky man, my dear." Yolanda flushed with pleasure at his compliment.

When the music ended, conversation became more lively. More and more people gravitated curiously toward them, drawn by the frequent sound of laughter and the fact that many knew Curtis and Alex.

Yolanda translated quite naturally for Vasha, and soon found people asking both her and Vasha their impressions of Canada, the things about the country they found most interesting, the social difficulties for newcomers to a strange land.

Yolanda didn't notice Carrie Russell's unobtrusive arrival, or her keen attention at what was being said, for Yolanda had gradually relaxed. She was glowing with the effect of stimulating conversation, laughing readily at anecdotes Vasha and Sergio told of natural, but funny linguistic mistakes and social faux pas they'd made when they first arrived.

They prompted Yolanda to relate some of her own experiences, and she did so humorously, including the tale of the goat and the garden.

With a teasing glance at Alex, she told of Cinnamon's dance on the roof of Alex's beloved sportscar, and that story especially delighted Curtis Blackstone, who seemed to be hovering near Yolanda's elbow.

Warmth emanated from those around her. Sergio and Vasha obviously regarded her as a valuable friend, and Vasha was blossoming shyly now that she understood everything that was being said.

Alex was involved for long minutes by an excruciatingly boring judge who wanted to discuss free trade, and when he finally escaped and glanced around for Yolanda, it was surprising how the group surrounding her had grown. His face grew somber and then wary as he caught sight of Carrie.

"What difference do you notice between women here and women in your native countries? Do you see injustices here that didn't exist back in your country?" The speaker's bleating tones were strong enough to drown out the more general conversation.

"Surely our social programs aren't half as efficient as those in the Eastern bloc," the petulant questioner continued.

Alex knew this unfortunate woman. She was the head of a local women's group and was noted for her radical and partisan views on whatever cause was current. She'd buttonholed Alex several times at social gatherings, and the last time it had happened, he'd deliberately insulted her. After that he'd tried his best to avoid her.

Alex resisted the impulse to hurry protectively to Yolanda's side. Such a move would be too obvious. Glancing at Carrie, who was taking notes, Alex cursed under his breath.

The obnoxious woman persisted. "Now, Mrs. Caine, not long ago I read in the newspaper what you had to say about food banks. Your husband is in government. Does he share your concerns about such matters?"

Alex tensed. Curtis had a wary look on his face, but there was little he could do. The woman was cleverly baiting Yolanda.

Hesitating momentarily, Yolanda finally shrugged and said casually, "Alex believes the necessity for such things is a big mistake. In such a prosperous country, there should be no need for social programs."

He had said something to that effect, in an argument once with Yolanda. He just hadn't meant it to be quoted publicly. Disgruntled, Alex caught Carrie's eye and read the impish, eyebrow-tilted expression there.

Yolanda went on, responding to the other query as well.

"Instead of differences, I see much that is alike between women in Czechoslovakia and women here. Women all want the same things, I think. Home, family, career, and balance between all." The group had grown silent while she spoke, and charmingly she made an effort to lighten the serious tone the conversation had taken. "And, of course, a goat that doesn't climb on cars." The laughter neatly deflected any more serious conversation.

Before Alex had a chance to move, Carrie was beside him.

"Your wife's not quite the little seamstress I was led to believe she was, Alex. More of a philosopher, wouldn't you say? How many other languages is she fluent in besides Russian?"

"English, French, German, Slovak and Czech," he confirmed coolly.

"But not proficient in political double-talk?"

He shot Carrie a really filthy look and stalked off to collect Yolanda.

Yolanda was still smiling when the flashbulb went off, and she turned in surprise to find a young man holding a camera just to her left. Alex suddenly materialized, almost shouldering Curtis out of the way.

"We're going home, Landa."

ROCKWOODS SEEMED DESERTED when they drove in. The geese and chickens were safely penned, and Cinnamon was firmly tethered to a tree trunk at the far back of the property. The unsettled weather had surrendered to sunshine, and birds trilled happily in the silence when the car engine died.

Inside the house, Alex took the stairs to the second story two at a time. He was restless, and he wanted to get out of this bloody monkey suit. He'd already yanked his tie loose and undone his vest.

He felt generally uneasy with the way the affair today had gone, and he'd bet Carrie would make something of Yolanda's innocent comments in tomorrow's column.

Damn it, what was there about Yolanda that attracted attention and that managed to embroil both of them in publicity?

His mouth twisted with the ironic admission that today, at least people would have had to be blind or dead not to notice her combination of sultry, exotic beauty and unusual linguistic ability. Curtis certainly had noticed, far too much for Alex's peace of mind.

Beauty and brains. Yolanda was undeniably intelligent, just as Carrie had said. She simply had an uncanny knack of saying the wrong thing at exactly the right time.

He was passing Tracey's door. She was home, he knew, because rock music from her stereo was blasting loud enough to shake the foundations. He slowed, about to knock and tell her to turn it down when a pause came between tapes, and in the silence he heard the murmur of voices. One sentence sounded clearly, and Alex stood frozen in place.

"Please, Trace. I've told you I love you. You want it, too, I can tell," an agonized young male begged, then added petulantly, "Everybody else does it."

"Victor, I told you, I—"

Without a thought for the wisdom of his actions, Alex burst into Tracey's bedroom.

Tracey was sprawled across her bed, her clothing in disarray. Vic lay facedown beside her, one hand fondling her breast. He'd obviously been kissing her. Both of them were flushed, and their breathing was heavy.

Blood rose in Alex until he could feel his pulse thundering with rage. He'd smashed the door open with such force that it had banged into the wall.

Trembling, his fists balled, he advanced on the now-terrified Vic, who'd leaped up and was taking refuge behind the bed, his hands nervously tucking in his loosened shirt, checking the zipper on his pants.

That particular action brought Alex dangerously near to hitting the boy, smashing his fist into that too handsome nose.

He restrained himself—just—and bellowed, "Out, get out of here. And don't come back."

Vic, obviously terrified, still made an effort to explain.

"Look, Mr. Caine, it's not what—"

"Shut up." Alex was beyond reason. He made a threatening move, and the boy headed for the door and pounded down the stairs.

Tracey had leaped from the bed and was straightening her own clothes. Her face was scarlet, and a mixture of humiliation and rage showed in her trembling lips and sparking gray eyes.

"What the hell is going on in here, young lady?"

Alex's voice held all the impotent rage and fear and disbelief of a parent learning that his innocent child is not so innocent, and no longer a child.

"Daddy, you have no right..." Her voice was quavering. She cleared her throat and bravely met Alex's gaze with a defiant glare.

"There wasn't anything. I mean, we weren't doing any thing."

Fleetingly Alex realized he was handling this situation badly But he couldn't seem to make himself stop.

"Not doing anything? From what I saw," he barked at her "you would have been in another few minutes. Why, you're a baby—you don't even know what the hell you're doing. That bastard of a boy... I've got a good mind to go over to Cameron's and—"

"Daddy, you wouldn't." Absolute horror was on Tracey's face and in her voice. "This is between Vic and me. It's no anybody else's business." Her chin shot up, betrayed by a quiver. "And I'm not a baby, either. I have the right to make my own decisions."

Alex snorted. "You happen to be fifteen years old. That's far too young—"

"It is not." Tracey's fragile control was starting to crack, and her voice had a hysterical edge.

"Fifteen isn't too young, even Yolanda says it isn't."

Alex felt himself grow still inside. Carefully he moved toward his daughter and caught her shoulders in his hands.

"What do you mean, Yolanda says it isn't? What's Yolanda got to do with this?"

Tracey stared back at him, her features rebellious. "Yolanda and I are friends; she talks to me. I'm not stupid, Daddy She said if I needed, needed birth control or—"

"Birth control?" Alex felt dazed. "Birth control?"

Tracey lowered her eyes. "She offered to come with me. But I decided, well, I thought it over, and I decided not to, not to have an affair. And right when you came in, I was going to tell Vic, but then you burst in here like a maniac, and now..." Tears began to roll down her cheeks, and her voice was going up and up, out of control. "I'll probably never even see Vic again after this. Daddy, how could you? Weren't you young once; don't you remember?"

She was shrieking at him now, but her words were barely registering. What was reverberating in Alex's brain was the knowledge that Yolanda had betrayed his trust, had... She'd poisoned the mind of his daughter.

"We'll talk about this later, Tracey," he said abstractedly and turned to the open door. Yolanda stood just outside it. She'd obviously heard most of what had been said.

"Alex, please," she began to say quietly as he came into the hallway, and she reached out to place a restraining hand on his sleeve. "This is not what you think."

Roughly he pulled his arm away. He fixed her with a cold, narrow-eyed look, the kind of look he'd give an obnoxious stranger, and he went up the stairs to their room.

Yolanda stared after him, her stomach churning with apprehension. She must go and talk with him, try to explain Tracey's words. She glanced into the girl's room, and her heart melted with pity for the huddled ball of sobbing misery on the bed.

"Tracey, darling, don't cry so."

Yolanda, forgetful of the elegant dress, hurried over to the bed and took the weeping girl in her arms.

Upstairs, Alex wrenched his suit off, tossing it on the bed. A button flew off his shirt, and he cursed foully and tore the garment off over his head, flinging it on the bed, as well. Every moment he expected Yolanda to come through the door, willed her to come so the outrage building inside him would have a focus. He drew on jeans and a faded T-shirt. He was bent over, tying his runners when she came softly through the bedroom door and closed it after her.

He looked up, and she shivered as a tidal wave of apprehension swept over her. His eyes were icy, remote and hard.

"I understand you've offered to supply my daughter with birth control." His voice was edged with steel. "And that you fully condone a fifteen-year-old having an active sex life."

She walked shakily into the room, trying not to let him see that his anger was frightening her.

"I discussed these matters with Tracey, yes, Alex, but not in the way you think." She made an enormous effort to keep her voice steady.

"The way I think? What way is there to think? Did you or did you not tell Tracey that girls of her age have sex?" He got to his feet, taking several steps toward her.

She stood her ground, but the effort made her tremble. Why wouldn't he listen to what had actually happened?

"Alex, Tracey is not the child you imagine her to be. She is a young woman, and I said she must make her own decisions. I told her only what I believed to be true."

He knew he was being unreasonable, knew hazily that his anger wasn't really directed at Yolanda, or maybe even at Tracey, for that matter. But a demon possessed him, a deep confusion that made him lash out viciously.

"You're not her mother, Yolanda. You have no right to act like her mother. Dixie would never have allowed this to happen."

The words were evenly spaced, lethally cruel. Her face, already pale and drawn under the healthy tan, seemed to whiten even more. She flinched, as if his words were a physical blow, and she wrapped her arms around her breasts as if to shield her heart. But she met his gaze evenly.

"No, I am not Tracey's mother. Just as I am not your wife, not in your heart, am I, Alex? I saw your displeasure today. I say and do the wrong thing—I am not perfect as your Dixie was." The hidden frustration and hurt and anger she felt boiled to the surface. "You want me here as a convenience, isn't that so? To fill the awkward spaces between you and your daughter, to satisfy the needs of your body. But your love belongs to that—" She gestured illogically to the place on the nightstand where Dixie's picture had been and where Yolanda still imagined it to be.

"You belong to that dead woman, just as everything in this house does." She was trembling visibly, and she had to finish before she began to cry. Finish, and leave. He took a half step to close the distance between them, and she held her hand up to him, warning him away. If he touched her, she would never be able to say what was in her heart, and it had to be said.

"You use me as a shield between you and your daughter, and you use Dixie as a shield between you and me. You told me once I didn't know you well enough to love you. Now, I do know you, and I see how little understanding there is in your heart for Tracey, or for me. I wonder, Alex. Were you sensitive to this Dixie you love so faithfully, or does it only seem so because she is dead?"

Her voice broke, and she turned and fled. He heard her running down the stairs, heard the door slam, and he didn't move.

He couldn't. Her words had hammered at him, each truth a separate blow. He didn't need to have her say the final words. He knew what they'd be. Now that she knew him, she no longer loved him. He swallowed again and again, as if he were choking on words that should have been spoken long ago.

Yolanda charged down the beach path, vaguely aware of the incongruity of her dress and high-heeled shoes, but too miserable to care. The heels of the dainty shoes sank deeply into the sand with every step, and when she came to the area where the picnic had been held, she sank down on the log where she'd sat beside Ruth and Sophia.

Loneliness and a dreadful anguish grew in her with excruciating pain. Homesickness—longing for *babička*, the feeling of alienation she experienced so often in this country where she didn't belong—mixed with the things she'd refused to accept in her marriage, and which, today, she'd been forced to face. She didn't belong in her marriage, either. She clasped her body with her arms, rocking back and forth in agony.

Time passed. She gradually became aware of the sound of gulls, wheeling and crying over the ocean, and the stillness heralding evening's approach. Despite the sunshine, she felt chilled. The devastating pain had eased, but what she had to do filled her with another type of pain, a more lasting kind but just as agonizing.

She had to leave. Rockwoods, Tracey, the animals; the thought of leaving them tore her apart. It would be every bit as painful as leaving Votice had been. And Alex? The thought of leaving Alex made her feel as if she were dying. But if she stayed, now that the truth was acknowledged between them, she would die a different way, more gradually, without pride or self-respect, and still without his love.

Better to go now. Her lips twisted in a sad mockery of a smile. She'd heard *babička* lecture a neighbor woman once, saying sternly, "Be careful of pride. Pride is cold comfort in bed."

Yolanda suspected the months ahead would be cold indeed, and devoid of comfort.

CHAPTER THIRTEEN

ALEX WAS GONE when she finally struggled back up the path to the house that evening. His sports car was missing from the garage.

"Grampa phoned about the fishing trip they're taking, and Dad's gone over there. He said he'd be home late," Tracey mumbled, offering Yolanda some soup and a grilled-cheese sandwich, but avoiding her eyes.

"I caused trouble for you, Landa. I didn't mean to... I'm sorry," she finally blurted out. "I made you promise not to tell Dad, and then I did myself." Tears trickled in a woebegone path down her cheeks.

"Oh, Tracey." Yolanda drew the girl into her arms, feeling helpless. How would she explain the confusions adults made for themselves, when she didn't fully understand them, either?

Yolanda drew a deep breath. Tracey deserved an explanation.

"What we have here is one of these 'breakdowns in communication' you and I read about in those women's magazines, Tracey."

The weak attempt at lightness fell flat.

"We were both wrong in not involving your father in such important affairs in your life. He loves you so much, that's why he grows angry when he finds you are growing up. It's up to you to help him. From now on, you must go to him, confide in him," Yolanda persisted.

How to broach the other matter, the collapse of their marriage, such as it was? Sighing, Yolanda said heavily, "The problems between your father and me are most certainly not your fault. It would be ridiculous to think so. He and I—that is an entirely separate matter, private between us."

She bent her head over the sandwich that she couldn't eat, steeling herself against the pain of what she had to tell the girl.

"Darling Tracey, forgive me, but I have decided to live alone for a time."

Her announcement brought hysterical tears from Tracey, and it took all evening and as much common sense as Yolanda possessed to convince the girl that Yolanda wasn't disappearing from her life just because she would live elsewhere.

Then there was the problem of the animals to solve, as well, with Tracey going back to school. Thankfully, a telephone call to Ian Cameron provided the solution. He would "board" Cinnamon and the geese and hens, as long as Tracey came over daily to help with their care.

Yolanda couldn't help but be proud of the responsible way Tracey was behaving. But the girl was badly shaken, all the same, by Yolanda's leaving.

"Please, can I come and stay with you sometimes, Landa? Maybe when the men go fishing?"

Yolanda promised, her heart twisting with pain for the child-woman who felt she was losing still another person in her life. She slumped into a kitchen chair when Tracey finally went up to bed, feeling drained and exhausted.

When Alex's car purred into the driveway an hour later, a cold numbness settled over her. She must end whatever was left between them, and quickly.

When she heard his footsteps approaching, a hollow sickness filled her. His first words made her feel immeasurably worse.

"Yolanda, I'm sorry," Alex said contritely the moment he came in the door. He looped his jacket over the chair back and came over to where she sat in the dimly lit kitchen. She wanted to scream with frustration.

"There's a lot about this business you don't understand," he began, but it was too late. Whatever he said, she reminded herself, nothing had changed between this afternoon and now. The very fact that she sat in the kitchen, avoiding the areas where Dixie's order was evident, was enough to remind her of the silent but very real ghost whose presence lingered here in this house and in Alex's heart.

Fear mushroomed within her as he approached, along with a desperate need to keep him at arm's length. She could only do what she had to if he didn't touch her, if she didn't acknowledge the sadness and appeal in those green eyes.

"I have decided to move, Alex, as soon as possible," she blurted out. "My decision is final, so please, don't make it harder for me."

"Yolanda, we have to talk. There's so much I need to explain to you."

Not for months had she used the mask she'd worn so often in Czechoslovakia, the impenetrable mask of cold silence and indifference she'd used so effectively. She used it now, unaware that it brought painful remembrances to him of another wife, of problems always left unresolved, of guilt he never quite forgot. His anxious concern faded into a cold mask of anger.

He'd put a hand on her arm, and she snatched it from his grasp.

Her face was pale when she looked him squarely in the eye, but her huge eyes were devoid of expression.

"Can you tell me you love me, that you trust me to help raise your daughter? Can you promise the memory of your first wife is only a memory, that she will no longer be there between us? I see you cannot. So I have absolutely nothing more to say to you, except that what has happened between us has been a big mistake."

Her hard, indifferent tone stopped him cold. She got up, fighting the urge to look at him, and with all the dignity she could muster, she marched out and up the stairs, locking the door to the yellow room before the torrent of weeping began.

The following morning she packed her suitcase, stubbornly taking only the clothing she'd brought and the things Tracey had given her. She left the luxurious wardrobe he'd bought her hanging in his bedroom closet. It was simply another part of the fantasy she'd been living, and she had to leave it behind with the rest of the dreams.

In a side pocket of her suitcase she found the small box containing her father's wedding ring, which *babička* had given her when she left. She stared down at the golden band and viciously shoved it back in its hiding place.

Her father's loyalty had been to a dead dream. Alex's loyalty was to his dead wife. There was an ironic similarity to both of Yolanda's losses.

There was a final tussle with Alex, this time over where she would stay.

"I will find a furnished room," she insisted, and was unprepared for the vehemence of his response.

"You will use my apartment in Victoria, Yolanda." The words were a command. "It's empty, and I assure you I'll never bother you in any way, if that's what's worrying you."

Stubbornly she started to argue, but his next words came out harsh and full of pain, and she had to give in to him. "Please, Yolanda, do this one last thing for the sake of what we've had between us. I can't stand the thought of you living in some dingy room, and anyway, you still don't have your citizenship. It's safer this way. And there's room in the apartment for Tracey to come and stay now and then. She's already told me she's staying with you when we go on that damned fishing trip Barney's so set on."

Reluctantly she agreed, and he drove her into the city, to the imposing apartment complex near the park. He unloaded her few belongings: the suitcases and a box of fresh vegetables Tracey had insisted on picking for her that morning. It was that produce that nearly destroyed the rigid and fragile control she imposed on herself while Alex was there. She remembered so vividly how much hilarity the garden had brought them.

He gave her the keys and a list of things about the apartment services.

"You will let me know if there's anything you need?"

His faded jeans were snug on his narrow hips, and his cotton shirt was slightly rumpled. He had dark circles under his eyes, and his jaw tensed and released in grim testimony to the stress he felt.

Alex, my husband, my lover. I need you, I need you, only you.

But the time was gone to confess her love. She ran to the wide window to watch Alex drive away, feeling as if her heart went down the street along with him.

After she'd been in the roomy penthouse suite an hour, she realized that living there would be as bad as staying at Rockwoods, if she wanted to escape reminders of Alex.

There was more evidence of him here than had been at Rockwoods: books he obviously read, pencil sketches of forest scenes, a scale model of a sports car. Most of all, however, was the sense of quiet masculine opulence the apartment exuded, the leather sofa, the huge oak desk in the corner, the butcher block table and sturdy modern chairs in the space-age kitchen. If Rockwoods was Dixie, every corner of this apartment was Alex.

She put her belongings into the bedroom farthest from the one she knew to be his, vowing to find a place of her own, regardless of what Alex had asked. But for the time being she was simply too tired to do anything.

The apartment was well stocked with tinned and frozen foods, and Alex had insisted on having even more delivered that afternoon. It was evening before Yolanda forced herself to go for a walk, and bought a paper to take back with her to the lonely apartment.

She opened it and gasped. There, in the middle section, her own face looked out at her, smiling, animated, happy. She stared down at herself, unable to believe she'd looked that way just yesterday. How could a life change so quickly? Underneath, Carrie's column, "The Way It Is," was subtitled "Light a Tiny Candle."

Assistant deputy ministers don't often comment publicly on our government's social programs or their effectiveness—or lack thereof. So it was enlightening to have Yolanda, beautiful Czechoslovak wife of Alex Caine, state publicly that her husband abhors the need for such programs, believing they should be unnecessary in a well-run country. Could one of government's own sons be lighting a tiny candle in support of what many of us have long believed? Yolanda Caine, pictured above, also commented on the universality of women's aspirations everywhere. She—

Yolanda crumpled the paper, her hands trembling uncontrollably.

The column would be an embarrassment to Alex, the final straw in their relationship. She walked to the window to stare down at the pinpoints of light starting to illuminate the city, and she wished passionately, fervently, hopelessly, that she'd never left Czechoslovakia. She wanted to go home.

Instead she dragged herself out of bed the next morning and went to work.

Foofera was incredibly busy during these first weeks of September, and for that Yolanda was grateful. The demands of each moment mercifully delayed the inevitable hours when she was alone at night.

DAYS, THEN WEEKS, passed in a gray fog of wretchedness. Usually impervious to illness, Yolanda now felt sick much of the time, and she had trouble sleeping.

The only time the shop was quiet was first thing in the morning. Yolanda was grateful for this short respite from customers.

This morning she'd been racked by such acute nausea and weakness that she'd been tempted to stay in bed.

She felt even worse by the time she arrived at the store. Lili was dangling casually from her mother's arm, and milk from her most recent feeding bubbled from her tiny mouth. Dominique plunked the baby into Yolanda's arms and motioned to a chair.

"Sit now, and tell me what makes you look like this. Holding a baby makes one feel better, whatever is wrong, no?"

It was true. The fragrant, squirming bundle was wonderful to cuddle, easing the aching nausea in Yolanda's stomach.

"For the past days I have watched you, the tear-swollen eyes in the morning, the pretense that all is well. Now you look terrible enough to finally tell me what has happened to make you this way. Talk."

Yolanda hesitated, not knowing where to begin. Dominique began for her.

"You moved suddenly into the city, and that handsome husband of yours no longer calls you at the store. You are separated, no?"

"Yes."

"But you love your Alex?"

"Yes."

"He knows that you are pregnant?"

If Yolanda hadn't been sitting down, she would have dropped Lili. She stared into Dominique's sympathetic eyes as if hypnotized.

Dominique gestured at Lili. "I remember those first months well; that certain look one has, the yellow cast to the skin, the sickness." She frowned at Yolanda. "Even the tears. Of course, I might be altogether wrong. But it is possible?"

Yolanda numbly counted weeks in her head. Seven had passed since her period. It was definitely possible.

Suddenly she remembered the doctor's examination, the probing questions she'd asked. And Yolanda had ignored the follow-up appointment two weeks ago. What was the sense, she'd reasoned listlessly, of bothering with birth control now? She hadn't bothered even phoning to cancel.

She stood like an automaton, placed Lili gently in her mother's arms and reached for the phone to call the clinic.

"Let it be so," she whispered feverishly as she found the number and dialed. She couldn't have Alex's love. By some miracle, could she have his baby? "Please, God, let it be so."

And it was. Yolanda was able to get another appointment almost right away.

"I suspected pregnancy in its earliest stages when I examined you, Mrs. Caine," the doctor said as Yolanda waited breathlessly in her office. "The lab tried to contact you for samples, but there was some difficulty in reaching you."

"I have moved. This is my new number." Reciting the digits, Yolanda felt light-headed, as if her voice were coming from a great distance. Alex's child. She would have Alex's child.

"I'd like you to start a course of vitamins," Dr. Carlisle said slowly, studying Yolanda's pallor, the look of fatigue in her eyes.

"You're a very healthy woman, and twenty-nine these days is quite normal for a first pregnancy." She looked up at Yolanda again. "Are you suffering some particular form of stress, my dear? Working too hard, perhaps? You're a bit thin, al-

though your blood count is fine. If it's your job, I would rec-
ommend—"

"No, no. I will be fine now. This baby, this pregnancy... it
makes me happy. I assure you, I will take good care from now
on."

The doctor smiled and pushed her large glasses farther up
onto her nose.

"And your husband? You did come to the clinic in the first
place for birth control. Will he be as pleased as you are?"

The words hung in the small room. The doctor somehow
knew.

"I am no longer living with my husband."

"You will tell him, though, won't you?"

Yolanda hesitated. Then she shook her head. "He will eventually know, of course. But for now, no. I think not."

Dr. Carlisle didn't comment until Yolanda was leaving. Then
she said, "You've chosen a difficult route, my dear. You know,
a great many men have negative feelings about becoming parents. In my experience, those men are often outstanding when
they actually become fathers."

Yolanda said quietly, "My husband already has a daughter
from a previous marriage. He's made it very plain that he wants
no more children." Then she thought to ask, "When do you
think my baby will come?"

"May, early May. Let's see, about the tenth, I should think."

May. The gardens would be sprouting green shoots in Votice, the meadows would be sprinkled with poppy shoots and the
first blue cornflowers.

The cuckoos would be nesting in the trees by *babička*'s cottage.

A baby, in May. Alex's baby.

"Thank you, Doctor Mary Carlisle. I thank you more than
I can say."

WHEN THE PHONE RANG THAT EVENING, Yolanda snatched it
up, certain that it was Dominique. She ached to tell someone
about the baby, and there was no one else she could safely tell.

She had no idea what Alex had told the family about her
moving out of Rockwoods; Barney and Robert and Sophia had
each come to the apartment the first week she'd moved in, si-

lently closing ranks and making certain that she was well cared for and that she had everything their money could provide. And their love. She had no doubts about their love for her.

They'd never asked her to explain her sudden decision, and she hadn't felt strong enough emotionally to offer one without an accompanying storm of tears. She cried so much these days it was a wonder she didn't dehydrate, and they'd looked at her swollen eyes and never probed. She loved them dearly for it.

"Yes, hello?" she said breathlessly, and the silken smooth voice on the other end announced, "This is Carrie Russell, Yolanda. I'm sure you must feel like hanging up on me. Please don't, at least until you hear what I have to propose. I've had a hell of a time tracking you down. Your stepdaughter finally gave me the number, but she practically made me sign in blood for it. She's very protective of your privacy."

Almost an hour later, Yolanda slowly put the receiver back in the cradle and rubbed her ear. It felt as if it were swollen, the same way her mind felt with the idea Carrie had outlined.

Briefly, the columnist had suggested a series of articles—interviews, actually—in which Yolanda would expand on the comment she'd made at the garden party about all women wanting the same things from life.

"I've never had such response to a column as I had to that one," Carrie had explained. "Women have been phoning and writing and even dropping by the news office. It seems you struck a common chord by underlining the sameness of women the world over. The public want to know more about you, about the background you came from, more about Czechoslovakia that isn't simply political. Women want to know what kind of lives their Eastern cousins have, what type of jobs they do, what kind of day care and wages they get."

She paused and with some embarrassment added, "This is ironic for me, Yolanda, because the first column I did about you was definitely mischievous." There was a long pause. "I had, oh, fantasies at one stage about a future with Alex." She gave a self-deprecatory laugh. "I had no basis for hope, except, of course, my rather lurid imagination. So it comforted me to present you as a sort of gauche immigrant. Then, the other day when I realized you were an accomplished interpreter with the charisma to attract crowds, I have to confess I was jealous. Until my good sense took over. Now I'm afraid I'm in the awkward position of hoping you'll accept my apologies and agree to work with me. I've already been approached by several women's organizations, church groups and others, begging to have you come and lecture. They'll pay, and I've got a go-ahead from my editor to offer you a hefty amount for the columns." She named a salary that seemed outrageous to Yolanda.

"What do you say, will you do it?" There was an anxious note in Carrie's voice.

Yolanda was curled into a ball on the leather sofa by then, the receiver propped between her chin and ear. She hugged her legs and shut her eyes tightly. It was all too much to comprehend, too much in one short day. There were many things to consider, now that there was the tiny life growing inside her.

"Please, Carrie Russell, I would like to think this over. I will call you with my decision tomorrow."

Reluctantly Carrie had agreed.

In the end, it didn't take long at all to decide to accept. The job offered a fair chunk of money, which would become important with the baby coming. More than that, the experience offered a chance for Yolanda to test her wings in her new country, learn about the ordinary people who lived here, begin to carve out a career for herself, a life for her and the baby.

The baby. Yolanda sang the words over and over, glorying in the sound. She forced herself not to guess what Alex's reaction might be to the news. She intended to tell him, but she wanted to choose the proper time.

She got up stiffly from the sofa and went to the kitchen to plug in the kettle for tea.

What issues would Alex raise, and how would he react? She put a handful of loose tea leaves in the stoneware pot and leaned against the stove waiting for the water to boil.

First he would be angry. She smiled fondly, remembering Alex's anger. He was a passionate man, with strong emotions, and they had often clashed. The smile faded as she realized that this time the anger would be deeper, colder. He would feel betrayed by her, just as he had felt in the fiasco over Tracey. He'd made his feelings plain many times on the subject of children.

He'd blame her, even though her pregnancy hadn't been planned. He would feel trapped by a situation he'd never wanted.

At the very least, Alex would insist on paying support. He was impossibly stubborn when it came to financial matters. Two delivery men had arrived halfway through her first week in the apartment, leaving several huge boxes. Inside was the entire wardrobe he'd picked out for her. A note was pinned on top.

"Keep these, or so help me, I'll feed them all to Cinnamon."

Instead of smiling, the scribbled note had made her burst into a storm of tears, with the reminder of the small, homey details of Rockwoods. She'd hung all the garments in the roomy closet, poignantly remembering expressions on Alex's face the day he'd helped her choose them, the laughter they'd shared at some of the more bizarre designs, the shy way he'd presented her with the bag of lingerie, wanting her to accept, afraid she wouldn't like her choices.

He'd wanted to give to her, wanted to buy her these clothes. From working in the boutique, she knew that they'd cost far more money than he'd revealed. She'd never paid him for the clothes, either.

In a sudden burst of understanding, she realized that he'd never intended her to pay. He had been so magnificently generous with his wealth. How was it that he gave money so freely and yet hoarded his love? She wanted to give him love in untold measure, yet she felt uneasy with material support. And she instinctively knew that Alex was unable to unlock the Pandora's box in which he kept his emotions, giving money in their stead.

Stubbornly Yolanda determined to earn her own money and support their child herself. If he couldn't give love, she didn't want money. She would take the job.

Carrie had assured her that the newspaper articles would be given final approval only by Yolanda, and if she objected to anything, it would be cut. An ironic smile tilted Yolanda's lips. So much trouble in her life had been caused by the press; it would be satisfying to use the medium for her own interests for once.

She drank her steaming tea, nibbled a digestive biscuit, then went to bed in the king-size bed in Alex's bedroom. For the first time since she'd left Rockwoods, she slept deeply all night.

She called in the morning to accept the job.

"Fantastic, fabulous," Carrie enthused when she heard Yolanda's decision. "How about having lunch together Saturday, ironing out details?"

"Sorry, no," Yolanda refused firmly. Tracey was coming to stay while Alex went fishing. Having time with Tracey took precedence over anything else, even this job. The girl had become her younger sister, her daughter, her friend.

Carrie made an appointment for the following week and rang off.

Yolanda replaced the receiver slowly, and her hands cupped her abdomen. It felt exactly the same as it always had, but she knew that the mystery and magic of life was going on in there at a rapid pace, and a feeling of serenity replaced the deep anxiety that had gnawed at her for weeks.

The anguish of leaving Alex was unabated, but having his child within her somehow eased that pain.

Another of *babička*'s truisms came to mind.

"One door never closes but another opens."

Strange how the same phrases that drove her crazy in Czechoslovakia came back now in Canada to bring her comfort.

ALEX DREADED THIS fishing trip. He'd tried to back out at the last minute, feeling that his utter dejection would throw a pall over the outing, but Barney and Robert ignored his excuses and insisted. As usual with these two, the trip began at the incredible hour of 3:00 a.m.

"No use wasting good daylight," Robert had commented like an echo of bygone years, and with the oft repeated remark, a peculiar sense of déjà vu overcame Alex.

How many times had he sat between his father and Barney in a truck like this one, leaving home hours before dawn, sharing a thermos of tepid coffee between them, just to arrive at the same stretch of deserted river shortly after daybreak?

They'd started taking him along when he was about four, he guessed. He remembered the excitement of those childhood days, so intense he couldn't sleep all the night before they were to leave.

He hadn't slept much the night before this trip, either, but excitement wasn't the reason. He hadn't slept well since the day Yolanda left. It had taken fifteen minutes alone at Rockwoods to begin missing her with a vengeance, and the days since then had been the most hollow of his entire life. Yet something kept him from going to her, making the promises he knew to be necessary. Why? he wondered miserably.

He tore his thoughts away from that painful subject, concentrating on his memories of those other fishing trips.

The trips had been yearly events up until his marriage. Then, he'd felt it wasn't right to leave Dixie alone on a weekend, and he'd reluctantly stayed behind.

Barney and Robert kept up the tradition, though, and they'd never stopped asking him to come along. And he'd never stopped wanting to go with them, until this trip. This was the last thing he wanted to do right now.

The trouble was that he didn't know just what it was he did want. He'd made a damned mess of everything, and he felt about as bad as he'd ever felt.

Tracey treated him with cold reserve, fastidiously cooking meals and keeping things in order with an efficiency that amazed him, for it seemed only yesterday he'd had to tell her to wash and brush her hair. The changes in his daughter's habits had to be Yolanda's doing.

On the other hand, she refused to talk with him about anything but the most superficial topics. She chatted politely about her new school when he asked, or about the need for milk or bread. But when he'd awkwardly tried to broach the subject of Vic, she'd quickly left the room. Alex knew she and Vic saw each other at school and also at Ian's, where Tracey daily cared for her animals.

"I don't care to discuss Vic, Dad," she would say with dignity. And if there was a way to make any woman talk when she'd decided not to, he sure as hell had never learned it.

Neither could he talk to Tracey about Yolanda. The aching, twisting loss inside him, the countless times he reached for her warmth in his sleep, the silence of Rockwoods since she'd left, unnerved him. He blocked her out of his thoughts as much as he could, and the empty ache inside him grew remorselessly, day by day.

"That's the turnoff dead ahead." Barney's deep voice interrupted his thoughts, and he saw the faint path leading off the gravel road that would take them to the campsite.

The clearing was a natural semicircle of flat land, ringed by an evergreen forest of Douglas fir, cedar and hemlock. The variegated greens were already interspersed with fiery sprinklings of autumn-painted maple. The campsite fronted the edge of the wide, shallow Cowichan river.

A few hundred yards upstream, a gravel bar formed a natural pool where the steelhead gathered. Today, the sunlight filtered sleepily down through the trees, falling like dust into the campsite. Jays, sparrows and robins called back and forth, and the smell of the fresh-turned mossy earth blended with the particular odor of the oiled-canvas tent as the sun's warmth released the tent's winter mustiness. The ever-present roar of the river muted the other woodland sounds, making them a counterpoint to the restful melody.

Maybe this was what he'd needed after all, Alex thought. Maybe the peace of this well-remembered place and the easy camaraderie with the two men he loved would help him hold at bay the images that haunted him.

"Get the rods, lad," Barney ordered when the camp was set up.

Lad.

Alex's heart constricted. Thirty-nine years old, and to them he would always be "lad."

Robert wandered down to the gravel bar, and Barney found his own favorite spot. As the sun lazily rose to its zenith and started to dip downward, Alex worked his way along the uneven riverbank, sending his line out and drawing it in the way they'd taught him long ago, until slowly the compulsive rhythm began to bring him a sort of numbed peace.

"Still using that Mitchell spinning reel, I see," Alex commented when he found himself casting near Barney. It was a reel popular thirty years before, an antique like the ancient canvas tent Alex had just set up.

"I think they might have improved those, Barney," he ribbed his uncle gently.

Barney had on the filthy old green cap he always wore for fishing, and under it his dark eyes crinkled with amusement as he expertly sent the lure and line soaring upstream.

"They may look a little different, but the basic pattern's the same," he said mildly. "New equipment isn't necessarily better. It's just newer."

Alex shook his head at this bit of folk wisdom, and then suffered the arch looks his uncle shot him as Barney hooked, fought and landed a magnificent steelhead. They fished side by side in silence after that, working their way aimlessly down the curved path of the river.

They'd rounded a bend when Alex spotted the deer. Half-hidden by a protected gravel cutbank and by their own natural camouflage, two white-tailed Island deer were drinking, spraddling their legs in an ungainly way among the river rocks, dipping and bending in a delicate ballet.

The men stood silently watching until the graceful pair, hardly larger than good-sized dogs, turned and scrambled daintily up the bank and disappeared into the forest.

Deer. It was deer such as these that had launched Alex's sex education. He'd been about five. He remembered Robert holding branches aside for him on that hike through the woods. His father's back had been reassuringly broad, and Alex remembered wondering if he'd ever grow that tall and strong. They'd reached a high knoll, and eaten the lunch from Robert's pack.

Alex begged to use the binoculars, and Robert carefully suspended them around his neck. Looking down into the valley, Alex could see little at first, until his father patiently showed him how to adjust the focus.

Then, the green world below sprang alive, branches and even far-off rocks showing texture. He panned clumsily back and forth, enthralled by the magic of bringing far-off things close. Accidentally, he saw the deer.

They were playing, he thought, two of them in a sun-dappled glade too far away to even see without the binoculars.

"Deer, Daddy. Two deer, I can see them." Excitement was making his hands shake. Robert was stretched out in the warmth with his eyes closed, and he gave a grunt of interest.

Alex sat immobile, the glasses propped on his knees as he strained to see every detail of marking and color.

They were bumping each other; the male with the horns was trying to jump on the female. The glasses picked up the male's swollen penis, and Alex stared unbelievingly. Then, as he watched, the male suddenly mounted the female, and the act of procreation began, seeming so close and urgent that Alex still remembered the shock and the rush of heat he experienced, the way he dropped the glasses to his chest in confusion. The raw energy, the driving thrusts, the way the female stood wide-legged, head down—he'd thought the male was killing her at first.

"What is it, lad? What'd you see?" His father sat up, curious.

Robert took the glasses and seconds later lowered them slowly, meeting Alex's flushed stare with a level easiness.

"It's okay, son. That's absolutely natural."

He gulped, and it took minutes before he mustered the courage to ask, "But what are they doing, Dad?"

Naturally, and with words easily understood, Robert had explained the process to Alex, and finished it by neatly linking it to human reproduction.

Alex remembered the ensuing scene vividly, and his mouth creased with wry amusement. His poor father must have been heartily sick of the whole subject by the time his son's curiosity was finally satisfied.

One of the trickier points, he remembered now, had been to try to relate the number of babies produced by this fascinating process to the number of times the act was performed, and the astonishing information that humans did something similar.

"Is it called rutting, too?" he'd queried, plaguing Robert with questions about mothers and fathers and numbers of times and how it felt and why anybody wanted to do it in the first place.

He could still see Robert now, sighing, rubbing the back of his neck and tipping his face wearily up to the sky as the conversation went on and on. He'd answered every single question, though, as honestly, and openly as he could. Alex remembered that clearly.

It hit Alex like a hammer blow, the sudden connection between the conversations he'd had with his father, and the ones he hadn't had with Tracey. It would have been easy for Robert to ignore the subject that day, but he hadn't. He'd struggled through.

Alex was the one who'd ignored any openings Tracey had presented. He remembered that damned coy book Dixie had bought for their daughter. Why hadn't she told the girl about love herself? The sunshine dappled and danced in the water, nearly blinding him, and his hands stopped their automatic reeling.

Like a hammer blow to his gut, he realized fully for the first time what he'd done all along. He'd fobbed off the difficult task of parenting first on Dixie, then on the boarding school and relatives, finally on Yolanda. What had happened with Tracey that Sunday afternoon was unfortunate, a direct result of his detached attitude as a parent. He'd refused to recognize his daughter was growing up, perhaps because he'd delegated most of her care in recent years to others.

He swallowed, and a lump stuck in his throat as he remembered that final conversation with Yolanda. Full realization came as he stood in the sunlight, watching his line float randomly down the current.

He'd avoided his responsibility, and then blamed Yolanda for taking it on. How could he have done such a thing? He'd always prided himself on being a fair man. The things he'd said to her burned in his head now like fire, repeating over and over like a tape he couldn't shut off.

Alex reeled in his line. He felt suddenly sick.

"I think I'll head back to camp," he said weakly, and Barney gave him a peculiar stare as he walked off, his shoulders bowed with the ordeal of looking clearly at himself. He didn't much like what he saw.

The rest of the day played itself out on two levels for Alex. He joked with his companions, the automatic responses echoing other times like this. He laughed, and he must have sounded fine, because the other two men didn't seem to notice anything unusual.

The long day slipped placidly into evening as the sun made a spectacular splash of color over the western mountains. The turmoil inside Alex grew until he wondered how he would contain it. In his mind's eye, he watched scenes of his relationships, first with Dixie, then Tracey, and most painful of all, with Yolanda, like an actor watching himself on screen.

The tape went on and on, until he couldn't be sure that what he said aloud had no connection to his inner agony, and so he stopped talking.

He sat stupidly beside the dying fire, not drinking the steaming enamel cup of coffee Robert poured him. When the time finally arrived, he crawled into the tent, found his sleeping bag and pretended to sleep until Robert and Barney snored an arm's length away from him.

Crawling outside again, he realized he was trembling. He crouched to replenish the fire and sat with his back against a tree trunk. He still didn't understand all of it, but one fact hammered at him relentlessly. He had fallen in love with Yolanda, somewhere between Votice and here. That love had lain hidden inside him, locked behind barriers he'd erected.

Today, it had demanded recognition, even after he'd done his level best to destroy it.

He laid another log on the embers, watching as the flames glowed and licked at the branches. A loon laughed across the murmuring river, and the fire crackled as pitch dripped into the blaze.

He clenched his jaw muscles against the waves of pain washing over him. The hours of the endless night were marked only by the number of logs he placed carefully on the fire, and the number of times he recognized the agony of loss when he thought of Yolanda.

CHAPTER FOURTEEN

THE BIRDS HAD STARTED their morning chorus, and the dark eastern sky was beginning to streak with sunrise colors. Alex rose, stiff and drained from his nightlong reverie and emptied the dregs of the blackened coffeepot, then walked down to the river for water to make a fresh pot.

"Morning, lad. You're up pretty early, aren't you?" Barney's voice was deep and somehow comforting in the stillness of the early dawn.

Alex tried to keep emotion from his voice, but it was there, anyway.

"I couldn't sleep, so I figured I'd keep the fire going."

Barney didn't comment, instead tipping a generous amount of coffee grounds directly into the cold river water in the pot and setting it on the iron grill to perk. The look he leveled on Alex was intent.

"You remember Mary Ellen Moore?"

The question seemed senseless. Alex stared blankly at his uncle, and then he did remember, vaguely. Mary Ellen Moore had been the first girl he'd been interested in, back when he was . . . how old?

Fourteen. The experience had scared him nearly to death.

Barney adjusted the pot on the coals, and shook his head, remembering.

"I recall asking you if you were real fond of that Mary Ellen, and you finally getting around to telling me you were, but you felt real mixed-up about it all. That you wanted to be with her when you were with your friends, and when you with her, you'd rather be with them." He chuckled, pouring two fresh cups of the biliously strong brew, blowing on his own to cool it. When he looked up again, his gaze was piercing.

"Confused. Doesn't seem to me you've changed all that much over the years, lad. Seems to me you still aren't too certain what you want."

Alex met his uncle's eyes squarely.

"You're talking about Yolanda?"

The query was unnecessary, but he made it, anyway. It gave him time to steel himself for his uncle's reply.

"Yup. Your dad and I feel mighty responsible for what's happened between you and her."

Alex was silent. He'd never talked with either Barney or Robert about Yolanda, and he didn't know how much they'd guessed. Probably everything, he concluded. They were anything but slow.

"It was plain as day you two had fallen for each other, and we were happy for you, Alex. No need to tell you she's one in a million, that girl. And I guess we felt pretty sharp, arranging it all, seeing the difference she made in Tracey, and in you." He sipped his coffee thoughtfully.

"Now Yolanda's moved out of Rockwoods, Tracey looks like a thundercloud each time I see her, and you can't sleep. To say nothing about how skinny Yolanda's getting. Seems to us you're not happy, any of you."

"The whole damned mess is my fault, Barney."

There was a peculiar comfort in admitting it.

Barney drew a fat cigar from his checkered flannel shirt and made a business of lighting it. He glanced at Alex sharply.

"Might help to talk about it, lad. As I said, Robert and I sure as hell aren't blameless in this, either." He carefully avoided looking at Alex, tapping the glowing ash from the cigar into the fire.

"To be honest, we had high hopes all along that you and her would, eh, well, that you'd hit if off. Guess we're turning into meddling fools in our old age." His expression was grave as he studied his nephew. "This whole thing is because of your first marriage, isn't it, Alex?"

The question caught Alex off guard, and he sipped his coffee, stalling for time. In some confused fashion, Barney was right. His ambivalence toward marriage was rooted in his relationship with Dixie. But exactly how or why, Alex wasn't certain.

"No marriage is perfect, son—don't get me wrong. God knows your aunt Sophia can drive me nuts at times with her entertaining and her going places. I'd like to stay home more, but in a marriage, you compromise."

His cigar was slowly burning away, and he tapped the ash off absently, his expression introspective.

"I loved Dixie. We were married a long time," Alex stated defensively. Every time he tried to examine why he felt as he did, that single point seemed to be both the beginning and the end.

"'Course you did, no question of that. Seems to me, though, you struck a bad bargain in that first marriage of yours. No disrespect for the dead, but Dixie was as much to blame for the way things were as you were." He nodded to himself, not noticing the frozen look on Alex's face.

"See," Barney went on, gesturing with the cigar, "you never let her grow up, Alex. Never made her grow up," he corrected. "She was what, eighteen when you got married? And you were twenty-two. I remember thinking it was awful damn young for the pair of you. Then I watched you get older than you should have, fast, while she stayed the same. Flirty, pouty, dissatisfied. Fussy for the wrong reasons. Worst of all, I watched you turning your guts inside out to make her happy."

Barney shook his head sadly. "That's where you were wrong. Can't ever make somebody else happy, lad. They've got to do it themselves. Mind you, you can give them a shove now and then, like I did with Sophia. Like you ought to have done with your Dixie."

Barney paused for a moment to sip his coffee. "Don't know if you remember, but when Sophia first came here from Czechoslovakia, she wouldn't budge out of the house. Scared to talk to anybody. Wouldn't go anywhere without me." He chuckled and gave Alex a resigned look.

"Doesn't sound much like our gadabout Sophia, does it? Anyhow, I made her try. Made her start shopping, go to night school, learn to drive."

A peculiar look of pride came into Barney's eyes. "Now, I've created a monster. The woman's never home." His gaze centered again on his nephew. "But she's happy, and so am I. We're friends, adult friends, as well as being man and wife. We don't expect the other person to do everything for us, be everything to us."

He squinted earnestly at Alex. "I liked Dixie; don't get me wrong. But I love Yolanda. And I'm afraid you've got some cockeyed notion that one marriage might be like the other, that the whole responsibility for whether the thing works or not is on your shoulders. Yolanda's no child, lad. She's a woman, and all that that implies." He shrugged and lifted an eyebrow. "Even when it's great with a woman, it's not easy. It's just worth it." He grinned wickedly. "Know something? I bet women feel the exact same way about us."

"Barney, you ought to get a soapbox instead of a stump. I've been lying there with the sounds of your voice going on and on for well over an hour, and damned if you two haven't drunk all the coffee, too."

Robert joined them, and his teasing words were a cover for the anxious look he shot his son. Alex looked haggard. But inside, he felt relieved, for the puzzle pieces were painfully coming together. Barney had solved part of it for him. He had to figure out the rest himself.

Alex found the old iron skillet, and the eggs and bacon. "Guess you two are just going to sit around and give orders and watch me cook, so I might as well get it over with."

He had a lot of thinking to do, a lot of painful memories to review, revise and discard. He tilted his head back, squinting up at the autumn sky. It was lighter now, and the grayness and moisture in the air might mean rain. The fish would be biting.

There was no better place than a riverbank for thinking. He was sure Barney and his father knew that quite well.

"HI, DADDY. COME ON UP." Tracey's voice sounded cheery on the intercom. He'd buzzed from the lobby, catching sight of his unshaven face in the oval mirror by the elevators. The drawn lines around mouth and eyes were accentuated by the stubble, and his hair looked as if he hadn't combed it all weekend.

He probably hadn't. He badly needed a shower, fresh clothes, a shave, but he didn't give a tinker's damn how awful he looked.

He wanted to see Yolanda. He needed to see her, talk to her, with a hungry, desperate yearning born of the emotional battle he'd waged with himself and won in the past two days, and the clarity that had resulted from it.

It had become irrationally imperative for him to tell her that he loved her. After that was done, he could take the time necessary for the rest of the explanation he owed her. The elevator sighed to a stop, and he strode down the familiar carpeted corridor with a feeling of expectancy rising in his chest. Somehow, he'd manage a few minutes alone with his wife. Somehow, he'd begin to repair the damage he'd done to their marriage.

Tracey opened the door, drawing him inside.

Too late, Alex realized Yolanda had company. He tried to turn and leave, but Tracey was already pulling him into the room.

"Alex, hello."

In that first second—as always when she saw him—she was aware of no one else. Her heart gave its customary lurch, and she took in the bloodshot eyes, the look of exhaustion. What had happened to make him look this way? He was staring at the others in the room, so she couldn't read his eyes.

Awkwardly she bridged the silence.

"Alex, you've heard me talk about Dominique, and you remember her brother, Armand, from the restaurant?"

Armand, suave and impeccable in his casual slacks and wine-colored sweater, rose from his seat beside Yolanda and extended his hand, appearing to Alex like a host comfortably welcoming a visitor. An open bottle of white wine stood on the low glass-topped table. Its label was French, and beside it was a bouquet of violets.

There was only the slightest hesitation in Alex's response, but Yolanda noticed. The room was fraught with tension, even though he made a joking apology for the way he looked, and several comments on the fishing trip. He studiously avoided even looking in Yolanda's direction.

"Come into the bedroom and peek at the baby, Daddy. Her name's Lili, and I got to hold her until she fell asleep. She's so cute."

His tone was curt. "I'm not much with babies. Another time, Tracey."

"Dominique is going to get me to baby-sit. She says I have a way with Lili."

"Get your bag, please." The words came out gruffer than he'd intended, and Tracey shrugged and obeyed, rolling her eyes heavenward in exasperation.

Within minutes, Tracey had given Yolanda a ferocious hug, and Alex had coldly thanked her for having Tracey for the weekend.

Yolanda found herself standing alone in the entrance hall, staring at the door Alex had just firmly closed behind him and his daughter.

Her hands were trembling, and she felt dizzy from fighting the anguish that seeing Alex had caused. He'd been so remote, so cold to her, never meeting her eyes after that first split second. And he'd looked almost ill.

There was absolutely nothing she could do for him, she reminded herself. Alex had made it plain there was no real place for her in his life. What she had to do now was concentrate on the baby they'd started together.

"I'm not much with babies," Alex had said, and she'd felt pain knife through her heart.

She returned to the living room, grateful that Dominique and Armand had come by this afternoon so unexpectedly. The apartment would be unbearable with Tracey gone. The weekend had been marvelous, and the bond between her and Alex's daughter seemed stronger than ever. If only it might have been so with Alex.

"Armand has offered to give us dinner at Chez Armand, despite Lili's tendency to scream the place down and scare the patrons. I suggest we accept before he comes to his senses," Dominique said lightly.

"I accept," Yolanda agreed, bending forward to hide the sudden tears in her eyes, sniffing the violets Dominique had brought. She had made good friends here. It was silly and childish to long for her grandmother when she was a grown woman expecting a child of her own. Tonight she'd finish the determinedly cheerful letter she'd started, and mail it off on the way to work tomorrow.

She'd told *babička* about the baby. She just hadn't told her about leaving Alex.

TRACEY WAS QUIET all the way back to Rockwoods. Alex alternated between desperately wishing that she'd say something to indicate the nature of Yolanda's relationship with Armand Mollins, and desperately hoping she wouldn't.

It had never crossed his mind that Yolanda would begin seeing other men. He understood logically how ridiculous that assumption was—she was a beautiful young woman, and she was no longer living with him. He'd watched her charm Curtis Blackstone and every man in the near vicinity at the garden party. Of course, other men would flock to be with her.

Like Armand, for instance. Alex's hands tightened around the steering wheel until his knuckles were white, and he had to consciously keep his foot from tromping on the accelerator.

Logic had little to do with the blazing jealousy he'd felt when that Frenchman had stood to shake his hand. Alex had had all he could do to stop himself from driving his fist into the unsuspecting man's handsome nose. Wine, flowers. He'd had to get out fast. An icy chill made him shiver with suppressed emotion.

"Warm enough?" he asked Tracey.

She gave him a puzzled stare.

"It's real warm out, Daddy. Maybe you're catching a cold. You're sure acting funny, and you drove right past our turn-off."

They finally reached Rockwoods, and everything was icy and empty.

The house had the musty closed-in smell of disuse. How could it get that way in just a couple of days?

Alex had forgotten to buy bread and milk. He lit the wood in the fireplace in a futile attempt at hominess. "I'll help get dinner as soon as I shower and shave."

Tracey nodded glumly, throwing herself down on the dainty sofa and driving it back several inches along the carpet. One of the ornate feet broke off, and the whole thing tipped drunkenly to one side.

Tracey got up and scurried to recover the broken leg. She shot him an anxious, guilty look, obviously expecting a reprimand, but Alex just shook his head. He was irritated, not with Tracey but with the ridiculous fragility of such furniture.

He wearily climbed the stairs and impulsively headed straight for the bedroom phone. Yolanda wasn't home.

Out of desperation, that evening he came to a turning point in his relationship with Tracey. When he came downstairs again, she was still sitting despondently on the tilted sofa. She didn't say anything or even glance up when he passed her.

He went straight to the kitchen, reached for his best bottle of Scotch, poured himself a hefty drink and added ice. On an impulse, he filled an identical glass with Coke, added ice, and carried both glasses into the living room.

"Care for a drink with your old man?" he asked Tracey.

Things had been much more formal in the past weeks, and she looked surprised. She straightened and swallowed.

"Sure."

He settled into one of the few comfortable chairs in the room and took a hearty swig from his glass.

"You know, Trace," he began thoughtfully, "getting older doesn't necessarily mean getting smarter. I've been pretty dumb about being a father, and I need to talk it over with you and see if you've got any suggestions."

The silence was long, and he wondered if he'd made another bad move.

"What do you mean?" she finally asked cautiously, and he relaxed a bit. Maybe he was on the right track, after all. At least she wasn't saying she didn't want to talk about it, or walking out on him.

"I think it started when your mother was alive," he continued. "I'd grown up an only child, with Grandpa and Barney raising me. Ours was a masculine household. So when you came along, I didn't know how to treat you, and it was easy to rely on your mother. If she said this or that was right for you, I figured she knew."

He glanced over at her. He had her attention, all right. She was sitting absolutely still, and her eyes were riveted on him. The cola glass was clenched between her hands.

"When your mum died, I was completely lost, Trace. I loved her very much." More than he'd known then, perhaps, now that he was beginning to understand a lot of things. "I was also scared, because now there was just you and me, and Lord, what

I didn't know about raising a girl would have filled a whole library."

"Girls aren't that different from boys, Daddy." Her voice was low and defensive.

"I know that now, kid. But I'm one hell of a slow learner."

"You never talk about my mum with me. I used to wish you would." Her wistful tone tore at his heart, and his voice was ragged when he answered.

"I didn't know what to say to you, and I figured I'd just upset you all over again."

"It's there inside all the time, anyway. Talking about it helps." She remembered her Coke and took a quick gulp. The she said tentatively, "Do you still love my mum, Daddy?"

He met her eyes squarely. "Yes, Trace, I do. But I'm still alive, and she's gone." It was a bald statement of fact, and he wondered what her reaction would be. It wasn't at all what he expected.

"You love Yolanda, too, don't you?"

Something in his chest constricted. He drank the rest of his Scotch without a pause. "Yeah, I do."

Her voice was accusatory. "Well, she's your wife now, and I think you should tell her and get her to come back and live with us. I really miss her, Dad. Yolanda's my best friend."

He drew in a deep, shaky breath.

"I think she's mine, too, and I intend to do exactly that, Trace. But first, I think you and I ought to make some changes around here."

He explained what he had in mind, and she agreed enthusiastically.

Getting to know his daughter wasn't the easiest thing Alex had ever attempted, and they had a few difficult silences that first week. But it was hard to stay quiet for long when the evenings were spent carting the old heavy furniture, which Alex remembered from his own youth, down from the attic and into the living room. Alex phoned a charity and offered them the entire contents of the living and dining rooms, including draperies, on the condition they'd come and take everything away.

"You can keep whatever you want, Trace," he offered, wondering if some things might remind her of Dixie.

"That little dancing horse and the photographs are all I want. You ever try dusting all this junk, Dad?"

The "junk" was packed into a box and sent with the furniture. Then the two of them started moving the heavy old pieces out of the attic.

Halfway down the stairs with an armchair that might have been overstuffed with lead, Alex pantingly suggested that Tracey give Victor a call and ask him over to help them before Alex ended up crippled for life.

Victor appeared twenty minutes later, and both the work and the conversation became easier after the first awkward few sentences.

They got through most of the moving that evening. Alex ordered in a pizza, and he was pleased to find that Vic knew a great deal about sports cars. Before the evening ended, Alex knew a great deal about Vic. The boy wasn't that bad at all.

Yolanda's final week of work at Foofera went quickly. When Friday afternoon arrived, Dominique gave her a check with a generous bonus added.

"Most boutiques do not require one to change and cuddle babies in between serving customers," she said firmly. Then she wrapped her long thin arms around Yolanda in a ferocious hug.

"We are friends, yes? And I want to watch this—" she patted Yolanda's tummy gently "—grow to immense proportions, on someone besides me this time." She pulled away and looked earnestly at Yolanda. "Raising a child alone is not ideal, believe me, my dear friend. You know, of course, that Armand is half in love with you. He is a good man, and he knows about babies, not entirely by choice," she added with a grin.

Yolanda could only shake her head. She sensed that Armand wanted more than just friendship, and she liked him immensely. He was amusing and gentle, suave and urbane. She'd also watched him clumsily caring for Lili, swearing softly in French under his breath, a concentrated frown on his handsome face as he struggled to put a miniscule kicking foot into a tiny bootie. He was a warm, caring, uncomplicated man, and she liked him. But there was room for only one love in her heart, and Alex was the one.

Sophia phoned.

"The men all have to attend a board of director's meeting in Vancouver Saturday, so I thought we could have an early dinner, just us women. I've invited Ruth, and I asked Tracey, but she's going with Alex to visit her grandparents."

"Thank you, Sophia. I'd love to come."

The Saturday luncheon meeting with Carrie went much smoother than Yolanda had expected. Carrie was friendly and professional, and after the first few minutes, Yolanda relaxed.

"I've already booked you for two short talks in Vancouver next week, one for a church group, the other for a Voice of Women organization."

Yolanda shivered nervously at the idea of talking to groups. "I will do my best, although that may not be so good," she said candidly.

"From what I've seen, you'll be a smash hit," Carrie lavishly reassured her. "Because the newspaper's based in Vancouver, I figured that's where we'd start." Carrie efficiently planned the trip, and they spent the remainder of their time discussing the subjects Yolanda would talk about.

"I prefer to avoid political matters completely," Yolanda decided positively, and Carrie nodded thoughtfully.

"I agree, but is that because of Alex? He doesn't have any objections to this, does he?" she inquired in her forthright way. Yolanda met the redhead's eyes squarely.

"Alex and I no longer are living with each other." If she were going to work this closely with Carrie, the facts had to be revealed.

Carrie's eyes narrowed, and she held the eye contact for a long moment. Then she put a long, slender hand on Yolanda's shoulder and squeezed comfortingly.

"I'm sorry about that, Yolanda. Doubly sorry if it has anything to do with those columns I wrote."

"Nothing at all," Yolanda managed to say firmly. "It is a personal matter between Alex and me."

Carrie nodded, and when Yolanda didn't elaborate, the matter was dropped. By the time Yolanda rose to go to Sophia's, Carrie and she were well on their way to friendship.

The day was chilly, and rain was falling in a steady drizzle by the time Yolanda reached Sophia's. The apartment looked warm and welcoming, and there was a fire crackling cheerfully in the wide rock fireplace. Sophia greeted her with a hug and reached up to plant a warm kiss on her cool cheek.

"You're getting far too thin, child," she remonstrated. "Promise me, no more of this dieting. Heavens, if only that diet had worked as well for me." She tilted her head and gave Yolanda another long look.

"You've changed, Landa. You hardly look like the same person you were when you arrived in June. You were pretty then, but now—you're absolutely lovely, dear, although your eyes are sad." She hesitated, then blurted out, "I know this is prying, but I had such hopes for you and Alex. Why, last summer it seemed as if at Rockwoods you were both . . . oh, I don't know!" Not knowing what to say, Yolanda followed her aunt into the comfortable living room and took the easy chair she indicated in front of the fire. She would have to tell Sophia about the baby, and soon.

"Sit there—I'll get some tea. Ruth will be along, but first I wanted you to read Mother's last letter. Have you heard from her recently, Yolanda?"

"Two weeks ago, but she didn't have much to say." *Babička* wasn't getting any better at letter writing. The last one had been only a few hastily scribbled lines, mostly about the harvest.

Sophia looked worried, and Yolanda suddenly felt anxious. "She's not ill, is she?"

Sophia frowned, and then shook her head no. "I don't think so. She mentions the flu, a cold, but nothing serious. I suppose I got used to getting long letters from you, with the occasional note from her, and now it seems strange to receive only the notes." She shrugged and took the letter with its colorful stamps out of a drawer in the desk.

"However, that's one reason I wanted to see you today, Landa. Barney is taking me to Czechoslovakia before Christmas. I want to go and see for myself that she's all right." She poured strong tea in a fragile cup and added milk for Yolanda. "I would so love to have you with us, darling. I asked Barney, but he says it would be dangerous to go before your papers are finalized."

Yolanda half listened as her aunt prattled on, reading the letter carefully. *Babička* wrote only of the vegetables she'd harvested, and the fact that summer was nearly over. Then, near the end of the letter, she abruptly added, "Soon, now, I am going to visit in the Tatras. Before winter comes again. Autumn was always beautiful up there."

"Did she say anything about this trip to you, Yolanda?" Sophia was asking.

"Nothing. She used to tell me she'd go someday, but she must have decided quickly, because she says nothing in my letter." Yolanda stared into the fire thoughtfully. "It's strange for her to decide to go now. She hates traveling, and winter's coming." Yolanda reread the message, a puzzled frown creasing her brow. "I think I will write a letter to Jenda, the neighbor across the road, and ask her about *babička*."

"Better tell her not to let mother know we're checking up on her. She'll give us both the sharp side of her tongue if she finds out."

They smiled together, knowing the feisty old woman. The intercom buzzed, announcing Ruth's arrival, and Yolanda laid the letter on the small side table, glancing at it now and then during the evening, wondering. The train journey to the Tatras would be long and complicated. It was out of character for her grandmother, this impulsive decision.

Yolanda greeted Ruth and was amazed at the changes in her. The rather prim hairdo was gone, replaced by a short, fluffy layered cut. She wore subtle makeup and a soft, very feminine pink dress.

She flushed prettily when both women complimented her, and shyly announced that Robert was taking her to dinner the following evening. Yolanda remembered the night Alex had called her a matchmaker and wished she could share this pleasant news with him. There were so many things about their relationship she missed, so many things they used to talk about. And so many things they never talked about, she realized sadly.

The afternoon and evening passed pleasantly until Yolanda's morning sickness capriciously decided to become evening sickness. She fought off the queasiness as long as she could, but the dreadful nausea increased until it overwhelmed her, and she dashed for the bathroom, heaving.

"You have the flu," Sophia said worriedly when she returned, pale and trembling. "I'll get you some tablets that might help."

Yolanda waved her back into her chair and made her decision. They would know soon, anyway.

"I'm pregnant. I am going to have Alex's baby," she stated calmly. "Alex doesn't yet know about it. He made it very plain, you see, that he never wanted a child. And we are now separated, as well." She drew a long, shaky breath. "It's very difficult, because you see, I want this child very badly, and I plan to tell him, but..." Yolanda felt the easy tears begin. "This pregnancy, it makes me weep all the time," she added petulantly.

Stupefied silence greeted her announcement, and then both women began to talk at once. A few moments after that, all three were crying, the older two with their arms around Yolanda. They were wonderful, warm and loving and supportive. They didn't pry or judge or lecture. They made her weak, sweet tea and fed her soda crackers and fussed like two hens with one chick between them.

Once, Sophia shook her head and said, "All those years, Dixie blamed Alex because she didn't have children. I always wondered if perhaps she..."

The comment lodged in Yolanda's mind. How ironic that when he'd wanted children with the woman he loved, he couldn't have them. And yet now...

Ruth drove her home. When they reached Yolanda's street, Ruth pulled her compact car to the curb and turned the key off.

"I won't come up," Ruth said. "I think you need a hot tub and a good long rest." She paused reflectively, then went on, "I knew Alex's first wife, too, and I much prefer his second. Secretary's catch a firsthand glimpse of their boss's lives, and from what I gathered, Dixie was not an easy person, for all her charming ways, and many times—well, who knows. She was childish, and I suspect Alex was too patient." She grasped Yolanda's hand in her own and held it. "He's worth fighting for, my dear, even if he's acting like a blockhead at the moment. Now, one more thing. I wasn't fortunate enough to marry and have children of my own, and I've ended up with considerably more money than I'll ever need. I'd consider it a great favor if you'd allow me to be a surrogate grandmother to your baby, and open an account to help you through the next months."

Yolanda thought of that conversation as she bathed that night, luxuriating in the hot water. Dominique, Armand, Ruth, Sophia, Tracey, Robert, Barney—she had so many friends who made it obvious they cared about her.

And Alex. Would the time come when they, too, could be friends, when the tension between them would ease, when her heart wouldn't pound out of control just at the sight of him?

A spasm of pain replaced the smile. She had to tell him, and soon—before someone else did accidentally. The very next time she had an opportunity to talk with him alone, she would simply say it, just the way she'd told Sophia and Ruth.

"Alex," she rehearsed, "I am going to have your baby."

And what would he say?

Goose bumps rose on her arms despite the heated water surrounding her.

He would never admit it, but he'd secretly feel she tricked him. He would feel he'd somehow betrayed the memory of Dixie, and Yolanda would spend the rest of her life living in the shadow of a ghost woman, just as she'd spent the past few months.

She couldn't bear that. She couldn't stand having his compassion, being his moral obligation. She'd already done that, helplessly standing beside him in that hall in Votice, knowing he was marrying her because of family pressure, and she'd sworn never to be in that situation again in her life. She'd be his lover, his friend, his companion—but never again his duty. Never again.

The only thing left to do was to convince Alex she wanted their marriage ended, before he ever found out about the baby. That way, there could be no question about her intentions.

Grief, and a terrible longing for what might have been—what should have been for this child she carried, and for her marriage—made her press her hands to her face in anguish.

Sunday morning came. Yolanda had slept deeply, exhausted and emotionally drained. She got up carefully, anticipating the usual morning nausea, but she felt fine. She padded over to the bedroom drapes and tugged them wide to see the day, grimacing at the gray, misty fog outside the window.

She wrapped herself in Alex's old blue robe and went to the kitchen to make tea. Coffee seemed oily and thick now, and she could no longer tolerate even the smell.

The intercom's buzzing made her jump. She pressed the button.

"Yes, who is it, please?"

"Alex. May I come up?"

Panic seized her. She wasn't prepared for an encounter now; she was still groggy and half asleep, and she wasn't even dressed. How ridiculous to worry about how she looked. This man had seen her, kissed her, held her against his naked body, morning after morning.

Wordlessly, she released the door for him, and then he was standing in the entrance hall. She looked up at his beloved face. Perhaps the baby would be a boy and look like him.

"I didn't get you up, I hope." He was dressed in a business suit, and he'd loosened his tie as usual and undone the shirt's top button. Tiny droplets of moisture clung to his hair, and his cheeks were ruddy from the cool air. His wonderfully rugged face with the square, strong chin and crooked nose was so familiar to her, and the green eyes seemed less guarded this morning.

"Good morning, Alex, I was already awake. Would you like coffee, or maybe breakfast?"

Without a word, he leaned forward and kissed her, a gentle kiss, the kind he used to give her after lovemaking. His lips brushed across hers, lingered at the corner of her mouth before she pulled away. He smelled of fresh air and the outdoors. He smelled of Alex, and his kiss unnerved her.

"I have to talk with you," he said huskily, holding her startled gaze. "I've just come from the ferry. I dropped Tracey and her friend at McDonald's for breakfast. She'll walk over here afterward."

His eyes devoured the way she looked, that special, dishevelled morning look, with her dusky hair wild and loose on her shoulders, her blue eyes wide and alluring, her lips softly, naturally pink. She was pale this morning. He wanted to tumble her back into the warm bed, strip off whatever she was wearing. It was, in fact, a voluminous old blue robe of his. A thrill of pleasure coursed through him, a feeling of pure male possessiveness that she should wrap herself in something of his.

"Coffee?" she asked again, confused by his kiss, wary of his warm eyes stroking over her. She turned jerkily into the kitchen, filled the automatic percolator and found the filters. The kettle was boiling. She put a tea bag in the pot and filled it with water. What now? He was lounging in the doorway, watching her so intently it unnerved her.

"Tracey is well?" she asked awkwardly.

"She's great," he answered, moving to sit at the butcher-block table. "That's partly what I wanted to say to you. You were right, about my needing to learn to talk with her, get to know her better. You were right about so many things. I'm sorry I lashed out at you, Landa. The change in Tracey this summer is entirely due to you, and I'm more grateful than I can say. Forgive me for being an ass?"

"There is nothing to forgive," she lied briskly, turning away and finding him a mug, trying not to gag at the strong smell of coffee in the room. She must not be ill; she must fight it. She swallowed hard two or three times and poured her own tea.

She sounded remote, far-away, and Alex frowned. He wanted things open between them, and he wanted to tell her the things he'd rehearsed all week as he'd struggled with that bloody furniture, struggled with the new knowledge of himself he'd gained during the past eternity of days without her. He'd waited until he could be sure of the words he'd use and the best way to explain that what had happened between them was his fault, but more important, that he understood why it was his fault.

She sat with her eyes down, staring into her teacup. Why didn't she look at him, receptive and eager, the way she always had before?

"Yolanda." His voice was harsher than he'd intended. She poured him a mugful of coffee, found cream and sugar and a spoon. "Will you stop bouncing around and listen to what I've got to say?"

She sank back into the chair, meeting his eyes unwillingly, folding her hands over her rebelliously churning stomach. If she didn't look at the coffee perhaps she might feel better. The odor filtered through the room.

"I've done a lot of thinking about us. Things were so good there for a while, and I know now what happened to change them. I made a bad mistake, letting you believe that my first marriage was perfect." It was hard to say these things, more difficult than he'd expected. He cleared his throat, took a gulp of hot coffee. "The truth is, I knew there was lots wrong between Dixie and me, but I resented her for it and blamed myself. I never really treated Dixie as an equal, you see, as a mature woman. Then after she died, I felt guilty about the whole mess, felt it was mostly my fault, that I was a failure as a husband, and also as a father, the way Tracey was turning out. So getting back into another marriage wasn't what I wanted or planned."

Yolanda sat still, listening, fighting the nausea, wondering what he was leading up to.

"Then you came along and forced me to examine what I expected of a wife, what a husband and father should be. And Barney said some things that made me see myself clearly. It wasn't easy or pleasant." He rubbed an anxious hand over his tousled head. He wasn't getting any better at this as he went along, and she was making it hard, damn it all.

Well, Caine, what did you expect? That she'd welcome you back with open arms? She's not the unsophisticated woman you married, not any more. A dreadful premonition built inside him.

"What I thought was," he finally blurted, "maybe we could give this another try, this marriage of ours?"

Her face had that total lack of expression again, and he floundered. He wanted to stand up, pull her into his arms with savage force, make love to her on the floor if he had to, force her to let him have another chance.

But this had to be a free choice for her. Up till now, it had been his choices they'd lived by. This time, it had to be hers, or it wouldn't work. He'd never given Dixie enough choices, and he couldn't make that same mistake twice.

To Yolanda, he sounded uncertain. She suspected he was doing just what she'd feared, feeling obligated to make the best of things. She'd been surprised to hear his comments about his marriage, touched by the vulnerability in his face as he spoke. She longed to throw herself into his arms and agree to try again.

Two weeks ago, she would undoubtedly have done exactly that. Now, because of the baby, there was no way she could. If he had once said he loved her, taken her in his arms, told her he couldn't live without her; then, she could have told him about the baby. As it was, it sounded to her as if all he was proposing was another trial, another attempt. Nothing definite. No forevers. And the coffee was making her sicker every moment.

The telephone rang. Alex watched her pick it up, heard her say hello, listened abstractedly as she spoke.

"That was Carrie Russell," she explained when she hung up. "Tomorrow I go with her to Vancouver to begin my new job." She outlined briefly what she would be doing, never quite meeting his eyes as she spoke. She had to conquer her reactions to him, force herself to do what must be done.

"It will be exciting, this new job, and a challenge for me," she said as convincingly as she could. "I am beginning a new life. Therefore, I believe—" she tried and failed to draw a deep breath into her lungs "—I think it would a big mistake to go on with," her voice broke, and she disguised it with a tiny cough, "on with this marriage."

She crossed her arms tighter on her midriff and looked pointedly away from him. "I think we should have, should get, divorced now, as was planned in the beginning."

The pain in her chest and the sickness in her stomach were one. Her glance slid unseeingly across his features, not registering the disbelief and then the pain there, before he masked all feeling.

Through the cold agony her words caused him, Alex knew what must be done. He had to let her go. He'd held Dixie back from independence, until it was too late for both of them. If he loved Yolanda, he had to set her free.

It was too late, he'd waited too long, and he'd lost her.

"If that's what you want, then I'll begin proceedings." The words were toneless, spoken from the well of anguish rising in his chest. "The divorce may have to be postponed until after your citizenship is final, but I can have a legal separation drawn up, if you prefer."

"I think that would be for the best." To her dismay her voice quavered, and she stood up hastily. "I have to, excuse me, I—" She raced to the bathroom, barely able to close and lock the door, turn on the muffling fan, before the wretched vomiting began. It went on and on, leaving her shaking and weak and strangely removed from what had just occurred.

When she rinsed her mouth and reluctantly ventured out, a note sat propped against the sugar bowl on the table.

"Decided to pick Tracey up at the restaurant. Best of luck with your new life. Love, Alex."

She took the note back to bed with her and held it against her cheek until she fell into a deep sleep. When she woke, Sunday was nearly gone, and it was still raining. She bathed and dressed, forced herself to have milk and toast, and then walked as quickly as she could to the Provincial Museum.

The stooped-shouldered guard in the blue uniform nodded and smiled at her. She knew most of the guards by now; she'd come here so often in the past weeks. She rode the escalator up, and soon she stood before the Dutch half door leading to the kitchen.

It was always the same. The smell of cinnamon rose from the pie pastry on the oilcloth-covered table. The pump stood over the primitive sink. The old iron range had a bucket of coal beside it, and a child's doll hung by the arm from a small rocking chair. The kitchen curtain blew in and out with a gentle breeze, and somewhere just outside the sound of horses' hoofs sounded, a dog barked excitedly, a man's voice called.

She closed her eyes, and finally was able to let the pain of the morning grow and grow, until it enveloped her, consumed her. When she could stand no more, she brought the room into focus, concentrating on the comfort it provided.

She'd thought at first the fascination here was the similarity of this room to the kitchen in Votice. Yolanda had always imagined Anna outside, chatting with the neighbor whose dog was barking. Soon, any minute, she'd come back in and put coal on the fire, ladle out the soup for supper.

Now, she saw it as Rockwoods. She'd stepped outside to meet Alex. The room symbolized children, laughter, love, all the things she longed to have with him.

The things she would never have with him. She gripped the wooden barrier, forced her fantasy back again to Votice, and *babička*. Home?

The breeze blew the curtain in and peacefully out again. It was the cottage.

It was Rockwoods.

It was neither. Was there no meeting place for the fragmented pieces of her heart, no tranquil, happy spot, filled with simplicity and contentment?

In Czechoslovakia, she hadn't really belonged.

In Canada, she didn't belong, either.

"Kde domov můj," the anthem asked. "Where is my home?"

The answer wasn't here. She turned and walked quickly away.

DURING THE TWO WEEKS THAT FOLLOWED, Yolanda became something of a minor celebrity in Vancouver as she tried to illustrate the universality of women. Her daily interviews appeared as she continued her simple, straightforward talks, and ever increasing numbers of people came to hear her. She avoided religion and politics and dogma. Instead, she spoke of the lives of ordinary women in Czechoslovakia, their dreams for their children, the traditions handed down from mother to daughter through recipes, and folklore, the methods of housekeeping and cooking one generation taught another, the simple kitchen gardens they planted and tended. She underlined the common bond of female experience, and in doing so she won the hearts of her audience and her readers.

"You're a natural, kid. I knew you would be," Carrie gloated.

Yolanda was quietly pleased, warmed and humbled by the affectionate response she generated, yet in her innermost soul, she was lonelier than she'd thought a human could ever be.

The only thing that gave her joy and comfort was the tiny life quietly growing within her, but even that was mixed with a deep sadness because she couldn't share its magic with the man she loved.

ROBERT'S PHONE CALL CAME EARLY in the morning, before Yolanda was properly awake.

"Yolanda, dear, it's Robert Caine. I'm sorry to wake you up like this, but Sophia had an accident; she's fallen and broken

ter hip. Now, don't get panicked . . . she's going to be fine. It
happened yesterday afternoon. She was working, taking a dinner to an old man in an apartment with rickety stairs, and—
well, the thing is, she wants to see you. Do you think you could
come this morning? I'll arrange a flight for you.''

Barely two hours later, Yolanda sat beside Sophia's high
hospital bed, holding her aunt's hand tightly in her own. Robert had insisted that Barney go with him for lunch to leave the
two women alone.

Sophia looked tiny and softly fragile. Her eyes and her fierce
grip on Yolanda's hand signaled her mental distress, despite the
blurring effect of the drugs she'd been given to ease her pain.
She spoke in Slovak.

"Darling, I'm so glad you've come. There's nothing either
of us can do, but I wanted to tell you myself. I phoned to Jenda
yesterday morning, in Votice, because I was worried about
Mother. I just had a bad feeling, and, oh, Landa, she's sick—
she's very sick. Jenda said—'' A sob choked Sophia's voice,
and she raised a hand like a child to rub the tears away. Yolanda found a tissue, and with her own fingers trembling, tenderly stroked it down her aunt's finely wrinkled cheek.

"She's dying, Landa. She refused to go to hospital; she's so
stubborn. The neighbors are doing what they can, but she has
pneumonia. I arranged for Jenda to get her a nurse, but now I
can't go to her. I want you to phone, make sure she has whatever she needs, anything at all, please, darling. Barney will see
to it, but he doesn't speak the language, and it's so complicated arranging it from here.''

Yolanda somehow found the right words to soothe and reassure her aunt. When Sophie's eyes began to close for longer
and longer periods, Yolanda slipped away. After the initial
shock, she felt calm inside, resolved about what she must now
do.

Babička was dying. She was the last, the only link between
this new world and the old. She was all Yolanda knew of home.

Yolanda must go to her.

It was that simple.

But how to make the arrangements? She couldn't ask Barney or Robert for help. They would forbid her to even con-

sider such a trip. She was still, technically, a citizen of Czechoslovakia, without landed immigrant status in Canada.

That made going home dangerous, but it gave her the right to return if she desired. Carrie had handed her a sizeable check when she left Vancouver, and gave her a hug.

"If I can help in any way, let me know. And come back soon. The job is waiting whenever you're free." Carrie had become a good friend.

The check, plus what Yolanda had saved from her job at the boutique, would mean she had enough money to execute her decision.

Next, Yolanda considered contacting Sergio Markoff, the Russian diplomat she remembered from the garden party. His wife, Vasha, had come to the boutique several times afterward, and Yolanda had enjoyed a casual lunch with her one day. Not allowing herself time to be shy about asking a favor, Yolanda phoned, and within an hour Sergio had made the arrangements, pulling who knew what strings to get her a flight out of Vancouver the following day, with connections in Frankfurt to Prague.

"You have given this careful thought, Yolanda Caine?" Sergio asked her worriedly. "You realize, getting into your country is not a problem. But leaving again? I can be of help only one way, and I am concerned for you. You have discussed this carefully with your husband?"

"I am no longer married, so the decision is mine alone to make," Yolanda said evenly. "And I understand, yes. I am grateful, Sergio. Thank you."

She packed the same suitcase she'd brought with her, the old, battered leather case that had belonged to her father. Tucked into the zippered compartment, she found the ring once more, her father's wedding ring. It might as well go back to Votice with her. Like the wedding ring she still wore, it symbolized only broken dreams.

She tucked it back into the suitcase.

CHAPTER FIFTEEN

RUTH PUT THE CALL through from the Russian Consulate.

Alex, tired and preoccupied, tried to inject a note of heartiness into his voice as he picked up the receiver.

"Hello, Sergio...not at all...of course I remember." He nodded and observed the appropriate social amenities and then abruptly he leaped to his feet, gripping the receiver with enough force to crush it, with the same force that seemed to be crushing his heart.

"When did she leave?" He listened, feeling the blood drain out of his face, feeling stark and vivid fear snake through him.

"Sergio, my friend, thank you for telling me. No, believe me, it's not meddling. Yes, I know, I know it's dangerous. Thank you again—I'll be in touch."

Ruth came running at his mad bellow, and her face, too, grew pale when he told her the news.

"Yolanda flew to Prague four days ago. Barney's at the hospital with Sophia; I'm going there now. Get Dad to meet us, and tell him to hurry."

Ruth hesitated, wondering if she should breach Yolanda's trust and tell him about his baby, wondering if he knew. But by the time she decided Alex was slamming the door of the office behind him.

Barney was in Sophia's room, tenderly and clumsily brushing the tangles from his drowsy wife's tousled hair. He looked up and grinned when Alex entered.

"Well, lad, we didn't expect you this early today. Good to see you."

He doesn't know, Alex realized as he walked over and kissed Sophia, giving her what he hoped was a smile.

"She's just had a shot, so she's kind of groggy," Barney warned softly, but Sophia took Alex's hand and clasped it in her own. Her eyelids were heavy, threatening to close, but she smiled fondly up at him.

"It's nice, having my family here," she murmured fuzzily. "You brought Tracey last night, too," she rambled on. "She's turned into a fine young woman, Alex. She's going to be so thrilled about the baby." Her eyes filled with tears. "I only wish mother could have—" Sophia's eyes slowly opened, and she put a hand over her mouth. "Oh, oh, I wasn't supposed to say, was I? But Alex, you really should forget your differences. Landa loves you so, and now your baby is coming, but mother is... Yolanda said she would take care of every..." Sophia drifted off, her hand relaxing its grip on Alex's nerveless fingers.

For the first time in his life, Alex seriously wondered if he would faint.

"Steady, lad." Barney's arm gripped his shoulder.

Robert strode in just then, holding Ruth's hand in his own. His concerned green gaze immediately singled out his son, and slowly Alex felt strength and purpose replace the nauseous faintness.

Two aging knights and one apprentice. It was enough. It had to be.

"Old Anna's dying, and Yolanda's flown to Prague. Her papers expired a month ago. We have some planning to do, because I'm going after her," he hurriedly explained to the older Caines. "Come into another room, so we don't disturb Sophie."

"Well, guess we'll tag along this time," Barney said easily. "Now, here's what we're going to have to do—" The door swung shut, and Ruth settled down beside Sophia's bed. The Parliament Buildings could run themselves for a while.

THE AFTERNOON OF Anna Belankova's funeral was unseasonably warm for a day in mid-November in Votice. There was a cool breeze, but the sun shone over the autumn landscape, and the air was pleasant.

There was no real reason to feel this icy cold, Yolanda thought, shivering uncontrollably as she began the walk to *babička*'s cottage.

"Get in, Landa, we'll drive you," Jenda had insisted, but Yolanda needed to walk. It was only a mile or so, retracing the path down the twisting, rutted road leading to this cemetery where Grandmother had requested she be buried beside her Karel.

Not far from the raw, new grave with the heap of funeral wreaths was Josef's grave. Yolanda stared at it through tear-swollen eyes, and the old resentment toward her father surfaced.

If he'd made different choices, better decisions, if he'd lived, her life would now be different.

She stood for a moment, thinking she had never, not even in Victoria, felt so alone, and turned away.

Even her passing had been the way Anna Belankova, iron-willed and determined to the end, had wished it. She'd refused to be moved out of her tiny bedroom in the cottage. She'd welcomed death like a friend for whom she'd been waiting calmly and peacefully.

Walking slowly between the fir trees bordering the pathway, Yolanda was aware of the wind, sighing through the empty branches, reminding her of *babička*'s voice.

"I was going to the Tatras," she'd whispered petulantly to Yolanda, her voice whistling through the growing thickness in her chest. "To see my home again. Then it came to me; it wasn't the Tatras I wanted. It was Karel, my Karel." She had had to rest a moment, and then she had gone on, "You have your husband now, your home, so you understand, Landa, how I miss my Karel."

That final night, Yolanda had sent the fussy, annoyingly talkative nurse away, insisting that she could care for *babička* herself until morning, and in the deepest part of the night, just before dawn, she had realized that the old woman's last rattling breath hadn't been followed by another, and the gnarled hand she had held in her own had relaxed it's feeble grip. Yolanda had held her own breath, second after second, waiting, hoping—but finally, she had to draw a gasping lungful of air. *Babička* was gone.

"Alex!" Yolanda had cried out then. "Alex," she'd moaned, over and over in long, hopeless, lonely anguish. The plea had echoed through the cottage, the bedroom where she'd lain in his arms that first night, down the stairwell, out into the blackness of the predawn *vesnice*, losing velocity as it had risen through the cold night air. Votice was ten thousand miles from Alex. Yolanda was ten thousand miles from home.

Dully Yolanda noticed the bareness of the land, the stripped and naked look the fields had after harvest. It was the way she felt inside; it was appropriate.

To the west, the village huddled, naked without its blanket of softening snow. It would come soon, the snow. She would have to make warm maternity clothing for the coming winter. She would have to get a work permit, find a job. For the first time since she'd boarded the plane in Vancouver, Yolanda faced the probability that she would never be allowed to board the flight back. She would try tomorrow, but in her heart she knew the attempt would be useless.

Entering Czechoslovakia had been deceptively simple. The guards had examined her documents closely, and she'd watched them scrutinize her and make endless notations on their endless forms.

"Is your husband traveling with you?" The question had seemed so innocent.

"I am alone. My grandmother is ill—"

"Will Mr. Caine be joining you here soon?"

"I am alone."

They knew. No one, no one, came back before citizenship in a new country was assured. Even her marriage was no protection now. The separation papers must be through by now. Alex was free of her. He'd given her freedom once. His responsibility for her was over.

She couldn't stand to think of the others; Tracey, Barney, Sophia, Robert...Dominique, Armand, Carrie...her friends, her family. Would they understand why she had to return? Did she herself understand the force that had drawn her back?

She shook her head. It was *babička*, of course, she'd had to see *babička* this one last time. But was that all?

She stopped under a tree whose naked branches sighed in the wind. She wrapped her arms around herself, around the small, hard mound that pushed out against the front of her black jersey dress, and she recognized what she had done by returning.

She had jeopardized her unborn child. If, as she suspected, her departure tomorrow was blocked by the officials, her child

would be born here, a native of Czechoslovakia, with all the
problems that entailed. A great shuddering sigh escaped her.

Coming back had been more than a need to see her grandmother. It had been an odyssey, a journey in search of herself.

Home. Curtains blowing in the breeze, the smell of cinnamon. Home wasn't the cottage or Rockwoods. It wasn't
Votice or Victoria or Czechoslovakia or Canada. Home was a
place in the heart, and she'd learned this truth too late.

Coming here was something she had to do, but it could also
be the greatest mistake she'd ever made. How could an action
be wrong and yet right at the same time?

It came to her then, and the admission made her tremble.

She and her father, Josef, had made identical choices, doing
what each of them knew to be dangerous. Josef had died for his
choice.

She'd gone through her life resenting the course Josef had
chosen, because it had drastically affected the pattern of her
life. Yet by choosing to return here, she had made a similar
choice for her unborn child.

She stood, cradling her stomach, staring unseeingly out over
the desolate landscape, the clarity of her new understanding
stark and terrible, until the healing tears, the gentle tears of
forgiveness began to fall at last. Josef had only done what he'd
had to do, just as she had.

"I'm sorry, I'm so sorry," she murmured wearily to her father, her child, herself, and Alex. Then, there was nothing left
to do but walk back to the empty cottage.

Her head down, exhausted beyond thought, she was nearly
in the lane before she saw the blue Skoda parked by the door,
and her heart gave a tremendous lurch.

"It might be anyone—it could be anyone," she cautioned
herself aloud, afraid to hope. Still, she started to run, and the
cottage door flew open.

"Alex, Alex!" she cried unbelievingly, and he caught her, his
arms clamping her so solidly against his body she knew he'd
never let her go again. He swept her up in his arms and carried
her inside, kicking the door shut behind them.

"God, Landa, I'm so glad to find you. You're freezing!
Here—" He sank down with her on the old settee, loosened her
coat, rubbed clumsily at the tears still wet on her cheeks, and

then he became very still, holding her tightly. She could feel his huge body trembling.

"Don't ever leave me again," he whispered roughly, passionately. "I won't ever let you leave me again. You can have a dozen careers, run for prime minister if that's what you want, but with me beside you. I love you, Gypsy. Do you hear me? I love you. I need you as my partner, as my wife."

He cupped her cheeks with his hands, forcing her to look into his intense amber-flecked eyes, and he repeated relentlessly, "Do you understand? I love you, and you must promise me, Landa, you'll stay my wife. Tell me you will, tell me you love me." She drank in the craggy lines of his face, the hard shape of his mouth, the slightly crooked nose, and then she closed her eyes tightly.

"It's not so simple anymore," she choked out. "You see, I am having a baby, Alex. Our baby, and you said you don't want babies."

She gasped as his mouth clamped down over her own in a wild and scalding kiss that choked off the rest of her words. He drew away, and she stared up at him, bewildered by the fierce intensity on his face.

"I know about the baby, but that's not why I'm here. I'm here because of you, Yolanda. We have to settle this matter of our marriage before we get into anything else. I can't even discuss babies until I know you love me, that you want to stay married to me."

He kissed her again, more gently this time, and his voice was harsh and raw when he said, "All this is my fault, for ever letting you leave me in the first place, for not telling you how deeply I love you. Damn my stupidity."

His tone became determined. "Now, either you love me or you don't. If you don't, I'll simply spend the rest of the night showing you why you should. If you do, then for God's sake, say it. I've chased you half around the world to hear you say it, Landa."

Through the almost unbearable relief and joy his words created, she whispered tremulously, "Alex, of course I love you. I told you once, but you didn't want to hear. From the first, I have loved you, and will love you forever." The quiet, growing certitude in her husky voice satisfied him, and his lips once again came gently down on hers, lingered, then lifted. He looked at her carefully, noticed the drawn, pale exhaustion stamped on her clear features and the slight trembling in her body.

"Stay here," he commanded. "I'll stoke the fire and get you hot tea and some food." He slid his hand tentatively, shyly, to her rounded abdomen. "There's plenty of time to talk about this child of ours." His hand stroked upward making her shudder with pleasure as he cupped her breast, traced her shoulder and neck, then each smooth cheek with lingering tenderness. "I've got one hell of a lot to learn, and not just about babies." A roguish gleam came and went in his eyes. "I suspect you'll force me into it, one way or another, won't you?"

Yolanda's eyes brimmed with tears. "This pregnancy, it makes me cry all the time," she sighed in resignation.

"It's okay, I brought some Kleenex with me," he teased, but his heart was at peace, his voice full of compassion and love and understanding of all she'd been through. He sought for words to comfort her, to ease the loss of her grandmother, but nothing he could think of sounded right. At last he simply said, "If our baby's a girl we'll name her Anna."

DARKNESS DROPPED LIKE A BLANKET over Votice. In the tiny bedroom where they'd lain together on their wedding night, Yolanda lay in the arms of her husband. This time, their passion was a white-hot flame that seared and melded and healed with its intensity, binding them together, husband and wife, forever.

She fumbled in her suitcase, found Josef's ring and slid it on Alex's finger.

"This belonged to my father, and *babička* said to give it to the one I love."

They talked then, each baring their soul to the other, revealing fears and hurts and doubts. Alex spoke freely of his marriage to Dixie, and the complicated maze of emotions he'd worked his way through so painfully the past few months.

"It was hard to admit we'd both been wrong. I'd spent so long telling myself the problems were all mine, yet secretly blaming her for not acting like an adult, even when I didn't treat her like one. We weren't partners, Landa, and that's what marriage must be, a partnership you commit yourself to every day of your life." He cuddled closer in the darkness, "As Barney says, 'It takes work.' Sometimes it's easy, and sometimes it tears your guts out, but because you love each other, you do it."

He related anecdotes from his weeks alone with Tracey, funny and poignant blunders he'd made, unconsciously illustrating the new relationship he shared with his daughter. What kind of father would he be to this new baby? He relentlessy subdued his uncertainty. He'd do his best, but would that be good enough?

Slowly, exquisitely slowly, he explored all the changes in her beloved familiar body, made newly foreign by pregnancy. He caressed the full breasts with their swollen, tender nipples, skimmed the warm curve of her rounded belly with his palms, awed by the hard, determined bulge his child made beneath the satin skin. "When will she be born?" he asked, pressing moist kisses across her stomach, making her breath come fast and labored.

"May," she answered.

Suddenly he tore his hand away from the silken curls his fingers were exploring. "Maybe I shouldn't—"

But she laughed softly, found his hand and replaced it. "When the time comes, then I will tell you. But now, this is necessary. The doctor would agree, Alex; this is necessary for my health."

Neither of them spoke again, losing themselves in the sensuous, throbbing delight their love demanded. But after Yolanda had fallen into deep healing slumber in his arms, Alex lay awake.

The ominous and dangerous specter of the Prague airport with the guards and officials and documents, and the scene to be played out the following day on that stage, kept him from sleeping. The arm that locked Yolanda's relaxed form tightly against his body went numb finally, but still he didn't move. He tucked the goose-down comforter more securely around her shoulder and waited grimly for the dawn.

THE UNIFORMED OFFICIAL with the cold, shuttered eyes slapped the green passport down on the desk and shook his head.

"Outdated," he pronounced once again in his heavy accent. "It has not the proper stamp. I am sorry, Mr. Caine. We require the proper authorization."

"But she's my wife, and I'm a Canadian citizen," Alex grated out, and the man looked bored and shook his head again.

"This is not Canada, and Yolanda Belankova Caine is not a citizen of your country, unfortunately," he replied in a brisk tone. "She must have the proper forms and the proper stamp. I am sorry, Mr. Caine."

Where were Barney and Robert? Alex could feel his blood beginning to boil with rage and frustration and anxiety.

This same scene had been repeated three times, up through varying ranks of officials. And three times, the result had been the same.

The flight to Frankfurt was only twenty minutes away. Alex glanced at the clock high on the gray wall, and he squeezed Yolanda's hand reassuringly in his, praying fervently that help was on the way.

Yolanda felt the tension building in Alex, sensed his muscles flexing at the mask of official indifference confronting them, and she laid a cautionary hand on his arm, keeping her own protective mask firmly in place.

Her panic and terror, her despair, were increasing by the instant. Her worst fears, her every nightmare, seemed to be incarnate at this moment, in this place, and she knew with a sick and final certainty that her situation was hopeless. Barney and Robert hadn't managed to work a miracle this time.

She would have to stay behind.

These petty officials weren't being malicious, she thought tiredly. They were simply doing a job, obeying orders by rote, rejecting reason and compassion and humanity because that was what they'd been ordered to do.

She turned to tell Alex so, when there was a commotion behind her, the sound of loud voices, laughter, and Barney and Robert were suddenly on either side of her, and behind them, dozens of men. Official tags proclaimed them to be engineers from the Caines' pulp and paper plant, and as they crowded around, their Canadian accents echoed cheerfully.

The official behind the desk now looked rattled. From the corner of her eye, Yolanda caught a glimpse of two military policemen watching suspiciously, moving slowly toward her.

Barney shoved a folder full of what looked to be important documents across the desk, but the official was shaking his head, refusing to even look at them.

"There are irregularities," he insisted stubbornly. Robert stepped forward.

"This is my son and my daughter-in-law," he said pleasantly. "The gentlemen with us are our engineers from the pulp and paper plant in Ružomberok—I'm sure you've heard of it? It would be unfortunate if we should have to recall these men because of some misunderstanding, shut down the business, lay off the workers. Especially..." He slipped a thick envelope from his jacket pocket and slid it discreetly across the desk. "Especially when all these papers prove that Mrs. Yolanda Caine is not only part of our family, but also has official status as a Canadian landed immigrant. Right here, see?" He waved a form from the stack inside the folder, and the official suspiciously glanced at it. He inched the envelope toward himself and peered inside.

Yolanda could hear the military policemen ordering a path through the press of bodies surrounding them, and she felt herself growing dizzy. The clock on the wall showed fifteen minutes until flight time...*fourteen*...

The envelope of money disappeared.

"What is the problem here?" The words were sharp, staccato.

Yolanda's throat convulsed, and she could smell garlic on the policeman's breath; he was so near.

"No problem, simply documents to be affirmed."

A barrage of stamps banged down like gunshots. Impassively, the official handed her papers with the requisite stamp boldly visible across them.

Thirteen minutes, twelve— She could see the leashed dogs straining at their collars beside the policemen—Alex was half carrying her, with his arm around her, hurrying, but her legs wouldn't work properly. Out the door, deep breaths of cold air, across the endless tarmac, up the ramp. Black spots danced in front of her eyes, and in a red haze, she imagined the guns, the dogs, the cries of the guards. Alex's arm encircled her, and then she was slumped in a seat, the world was whirling, and the floor vibrated beneath her feet.

"Bring my wife some water. Hurry! She's feeling faint."

A rushing tunnel of blurred images passed outside the window, and a sense of weightlessness engulfed her. She sipped at the water Alex was holding to her lips, and the world tilted, straightened. Slowly, as if awakening from a dream, she looked beyond the circle of his protective arms.

The plane was airborne.

Alex's face hovered over her, tense and strained, but a kind of glorious rapture burned in his green eyes.

"That's my girl, that's my Gypsy, better now?" he crooned in her ear. "We're safe, my love, my Landa. We're free; we're going home."

Across the aisle, Barney and Robert frowned worriedly at her until she smiled their way. Then exuberant grins replaced the concerned expressions, and they each held up a thumb to her in Tracey's triumphant salute.

Yolanda turned to the window. The plane was circling high over Prague, and she watched the city below grow steadily smaller, until at last she saw only an innocent patchwork of green and gray and brown.

The sun pouring through the tiny windows made her eyes water. Alex was cradling her against his shoulder. She rested there, and when she looked outside again, the tragic and beautiful land of her birth had disappeared beneath the clouds. All she could see was blue sky and golden light, and the silver wing of the plane.

The strangest sensation made its way lazily through her stomach, a wavering flutter like a tiny sea creature stretching, rippling, inside her. She held her breath, and it happened again.

"Alex," she breathed in awe. "Alex, our baby is moving, here, feel."

She pressed his large warm hand to her abdomen. The ring she'd placed on his finger dug in a bit, and the flutter came once more, stronger this time.

He felt it, and the lingering uncertainties that had plagued him in the night slowly faded, replaced by an incredible joy and a sense of wonder. He'd been given a second chance at loving, and at parenting. This tiny, living being beneath his palm was a symbol of their union, a living part of each of them.

"I hope she looks just like her mother," he said, and reverently he bent and kissed his wife.

EPILOGUE

ONE WINDY AFTERNOON in early May, the skies over Victoria slowly cleared, and cornflower blue replaced the wet gray rain clouds that had hovered for days over the island city, disguising the fact that spring had settled in unremarked, hidden by umbrellas and dampness.

Curtis Blackstone, hurrying out of the Parliament Buildings that afternoon to keep an afternoon tryst with a lady he was courting, noticed the rows of Japanese cherry trees, hung with pearly pink blossoms glistening in the warm sunlight.

Robert Caine removed the cover from his pristine white Rolls-Royce, and drove Ruth Prentiss to Beacon Hill Park just to see the carpet of golden daffodils, rolling nearly down to the sea.

Barney stopped at a market on the corner and bought a purple hyacinth to celebrate Sophia's graduation from daily therapy.

Sergio Markoff noticed that the arbutus trees in his garden had finished shedding their bark, and now the trunks looked warm, amber-shaded, naked.

Newborn. He paused to touch one before he opened the door of his house. Vasha came bustling down the hall to meet him.

"Look, Sergio, what comes today." She spoke to him in English now. The children insisted on it.

"Came," he corrected automatically, giving her a noisy kiss and examining the hand-printed message.

> Rockwoods, 45 Sea View Road, May fourth
> Tracey Caine announces the arrival of her brother
> Karel Alexander Josef Caine
> nine pounds, fourteen ounces.
> Mother excellent, father recuperating, baby noisy.

Across the bottom in phonetic Russian, Yolanda had scrawled "Rosjhani doma." Vasha traced the words with a fingertip, translating slowly into English.

> *"Born at home."*

She needs a man to father her baby—
with no entanglements.
He needs a temporary wife....
Solution: Marriage!

THE ARRANGEMENT

Sally Bradford

To Pell Palace,
where it all began

CHAPTER ONE

BRADY TALCOTT DROPPED the folded magazine on the bar. "Problem solved," he announced, clapping his friend on the back. "I'll be married within a month."

"Married?" Phil Gentry put down his martini and swiveled his bar stool around until he was face to face with Brady. "Exactly who are you going to marry?"

Brady's face broke into a rakish grin. "I haven't met her yet."

"My God! I thought for a minute, there, you were serious." Phil slid down off the bar stool and picked up his glass.

"I *am* serious, dead serious."

"Yeah, and I'm Superman. Come on, let's find a table. What you need is a good stiff drink, and then we've got some business to discuss."

Brady followed Phil toward an out-of-the-way table near the window that gave them a panoramic view of San Francisco, furnished by the late-afternoon sun. "That sounds like my lawyer talking," Brady quipped.

"Your lawyer and your friend," Phil corrected him. "You've got one hell of a problem, buddy, and it's time we quit making jokes about it."

"This isn't a joke," Brady protested, settling himself in a thickly padded captain's chair. He unbuttoned his suit coat and loosened his tie. "I'm trying to tell you, I'm on to something. I really am going to get married. I've finally figured out how to get around my father and his damn trust agreement."

"Your father has been dead for almost two years," Phil observed unnecessarily. He took another sip of his martini, pondering Brady's present state of mind across the rim of his glass. The noise level in the club bar had risen to a low din, about right to give them enough privacy for a serious discussion that was long overdue.

For months Phil had been warning Brady that his time was running out. In another year, Talcott Enterprises was going to be tied up in litigation if Brady didn't meet the terms of his father's trust agreement. Phil could see it coming, and he was powerless to stop it. The hell of it was he couldn't come up with any answers either. Between them they were going to have to figure something out.

"Not only is your father dead," Phil continued, "the terms of that trust agreement of his are coming down to the wire. You can fight it in court—and you'll probably win—but there may not be enough left of the company by that time to make any difference."

"The hell I'll go to court." Brady opened the magazine he'd carried over from the bar and held it near the yellow glow from the hurricane lamp in the center of the table. "If you won't read this yourself, then I'll read it to you. I'm telling you, it's our solution—and don't interrupt till I'm finished."

Brady cleared his throat. He didn't really need the words in front of him. He'd gone over the ad so many times that he'd memorized them. Squinting in the dim light, he read slowly in a carefully controlled monotone:

SINGLE FEMALE LAWYER, age thirty, in search of professional male, age thirty to forty. Must be good looking, intelligent, open-minded. Object: paternity.

"Paternity! Hot damn, Brady—"

"Quiet! I'm not finished," Brady interrupted. "Where was I?

Object: paternity. Current references, résumé with photo, and medical history mandatory. Reply to Box 9046, *Bay City Magazine*.

Phil downed the second half of his martini in one gulp. "You are joking," he said tentatively, almost certain but not quite. He'd known Brady for thirty years, since before he could really remember. The thing that bothered him was that this was the kind of damn fool stunt Brady might try because the man was cornered.

Before Brady could answer, the waiter appeared, his footsteps soundless in the carpeted room, his manner one of deference as he waited for a break in the conversation. Brady ordered Cutty Sark for himself and another vodka martini for Phil before he turned his attention back to their conversation. His whole demeanor changed. "I already told you this wasn't a joke." His jaw was set, his eyes hard. "I'm down to the wire. You know it, and I know it. This is a way out, and I am going to take it."

As Brady's voice rose, Phil looked around warily. So far, no one seemed to be paying any attention to them. As even-tempered as Brady normally was, when he got that look on his face it was an unmistakable signal. Anxious to prevent a public explosion, Phil summoned all his restraint. He could see they were going to have to discuss this idea as though it were a reasonable option.

"Let's back up for just a minute." Phil's voice was noncombative. "Try to look at this logically. The ad says paternity. That's not your problem." Brady's face was impassive, and so Phil continued. "What the trust says is that you have to be married before you're thirty-five," he explained patiently. "It says absolutely nothing about fathering a child."

"Hell, I know all that. We've been over it often enough." Brady picked up the jigger the waiter had set in front of him and poured the scotch into a glass of ice. "I'm three steps ahead of you. It's actually pretty basic when you think about it. Some broad placed this ad because she wants a baby. Right?" Phil nodded silently, and Brady took a sip of his drink. "Now, I come along needing a short-term wife, somebody to marry me for a few months. Are you with me so far?" Phil opened his mouth to answer, but Brady raised a hand to silence him. "So what we do is make a trade."

Phil shook his head. "That is a lousy idea if I ever heard one." He looked hard at Brady. There was no sign of humor on his friend's face. Brady really *wasn't* joking. "Look," he tried again, "your father wrote the trust that way because he believed in it. He wanted you to have a wife and kids and all those things he thought really mattered." Phil leaned over toward

Brady. "You know that marriage clause probably won't hold up in court. Your father probably knew it, too, but he figured it might shove you in the right direction." With a disgusted look at the magazine, Phil took another drink of his martini. "You'd be better off to go to court than to make a stupid move like this."

"And lose months or maybe years just when the company is on a roll?" Brady shot back. "Talcott Enterprises was on the rocks when my father died. In two years—just two years—I've turned the business around." His eyes flashed with determination. "I've got a good thing going with the new toy line, and I'm not going to put that on hold while I fight a court case."

"Come on, Brady, you're about to make a stupid move because you're mad as hell at your father. You realize, he wasn't such a bad guy—he was just trying to do what he thought was right," Phil observed.

"I know that," Brady grudgingly agreed. And damn! He had to admit he did miss him. There were times he still picked up the office phone to buzz his father when unexpected problems arose. And when he went home to his mother's, especially on holidays, the chair at the head of the table seemed empty, no matter who sat in it. But the terms of the trust were something else. "My father has no right to meddle in my private life— dead or alive." Brady spit out the words.

"True," Phil acknowledged. "But that doesn't change the fact that he's doing it."

"Dammit, that also doesn't change the fact that I'll get married—for real—when I'm good and ready and not by some artificial cutoff date." Anger flashed in Brady's eyes. "I'm not going to have some woman I love always wonder if I married her just because of the trust. You know how I feel about marriage."

"Yes, I do know how you feel about marriage. And I also know the trust agreement is part of the reason you've pulled back whenever you started to get serious with a woman."

Brady looked past Phil toward the window where the setting sun had bathed the nearby buildings in gold and had cast deep purple shadows on their neighbors. He and Phil had known each other so long that Phil saw straight through him. Right now Phil was shifting back and forth between the roles of friend and lawyer, and in both capacities he was trying to protect him. Brady wasn't sure he wanted to be protected, not this time. Besides, there wasn't any harm in investigating the idea. If this woman seemed reasonable, he'd be up front with her and tell her about the trust agreement. If she was willing to go along with him they'd both come out ahead. She'd have her baby and he'd have his company, free and clear.

Encouraged by Brady's thoughtful expression, Phil worked on an appeal to his common sense. "I agree you're running out of time, and we're going to have to make some moves. But you're not quite at the desperation stage yet." Phil leaned forward, building his case. "We've talked before about arranging some sort of a friendly buy out, and Talcott Enterprises looks good right now. If we could time it just right, we could probably make some sort of deal so your future is safe—"

"Dammit, Phil, no." Brady slammed his fist on the table. "You know that won't work. I'm not going to give up." His voice dropped lower, the words edged with emotion. "It's not like we sold shoes or paper towels or sheet metal. When you make things for kids—furniture and toys—it gets to be part of you. It's the rest of my life, Phil; it's everything I've worked for. I won't give my company up."

Brady sank back in his chair, withdrawing into a heavy silence, idly swirling the amber liquid in his glass. He knew the ad was a long shot, but it was the best option so far. He'd also known Phil wasn't going to like the idea, but so far his friend hadn't found any fatal flaw in his plan. That was one of the reasons for running it past him. He was going to have to be in on things later anyway. Looking up at Phil, Brady saw the grimace of resignation cross his face.

"All right," Phil sighed. "You've obviously thought this over. Run it by me again."

Brady grinned. He'd figured his friend would eventually come around, at least enough to listen. "It's basically very simple, and the beauty of it is that everybody wins," Brady explained. "I answer the ad. I agree to father the child if she'll agree to a short-term marriage. It's the only way I'd do it anyway—I can't produce a bastard."

Phil shrugged. "I wouldn't think so, but it's often done that way these days."

"Not by me," Brady scowled. "Anyway, we set a cutoff date to end the marriage and then we go our separate ways. Nobody gets hurt. She gets her baby; I get Talcott Enterprises."

"All neat and tidy."

"Right." Brady looked at him smugly and signaled the waiter to bring another round.

Phil picked up the magazine Brady had dropped back on the table and read the ad again, shaking his head. "Come on, buddy. What kind of a broad would run a classified like this? For all you know, she may be playing a nasty practical joke."

"Maybe..." Brady hated to admit he hadn't thought of that. "But I'm banking on the fact that she's a quiet little thing, can't quite make it with men, wants a baby because she's lonely. She'll probably make a hell of a good mother."

"So what if she comes back later and sues you for support? You can't sign away that responsibility, you know."

"I never intended to." Brady's deep-set eyes darkened and his voice took on a hard edge. "I'd already planned to set up a trust fund for the baby. I may be an opportunist, but I'm not a heel."

"I know you're not. As your lawyer I'm trying to keep you out of a mess." He looked directly at Brady. "And as your friend I'm telling you this is a half-assed idea. You're talking about a baby you'll never see."

Brady took a deep breath. "I know that. I can handle it."

Phil's gaze wandered to the window where a panorama of lights punctured the gathering darkness. "That's what Eileen said when she walked out. She said she didn't give a damn whether she ever saw the boys or me again."

His hollow voice silenced Brady. Brady knew how Phil felt about his two boys, and how badly his wife had hurt him. He also knew their situation didn't apply to him. He tried again. "Eileen had problems, or she never would have left. We've been over and over that. What I'm talking about is something entirely different. I've given it a lot of thought—"

"Eileen told me over a year ago that she'd given it a lot of thought, too," Phil interrupted. "She didn't want anything to do with me or the boys ever again. Presto!" Phil snapped his fingers. "Instant release from motherhood. Except it didn't work. You know how often she's tried to see Michael and Timmy."

"I also know what kind of shape she's in," Brady added. "I don't have her problems, and I'm not going to deal with that kind of attachment. I'll never see this baby."

Phil shook his head. "All right, let's go at this from another angle. You think it's going to be so damn easy to end this marriage—"

"It's not a marriage," Brady cut in. "It's an arrangement."

With a sigh, Phil picked up his glass and finished his martini. "You're really hung up on doing this, aren't you?"

Brady shrugged. "Not if you can give me an alternative."

"No alternative—but I'll keep thinking about it." Phil signaled for the check. "Maybe we'll just hope she's already found someone else. Or, maybe..." Phil looked at the ad again. "Maybe you won't meet her criteria. Open-minded, yes. But intelligent and good-looking..."

"Cut it out," Brady chuckled. He picked up the magazine and stood up, while Phil signed the check. "And, by the way," Brady added, "thanks for the drinks."

On the way out of the club, Brady stopped by the front desk to pick up an envelope. Hurriedly he addressed it to the post office box cited in the magazine ad. He pulled a business card from his wallet and dropped it in the envelope. Then he stopped. The ad called for a résumé. If he didn't send one, it might kill his chances. He drummed his fingers on the polished wood counter. He'd never had a résumé, and he wasn't about to write one now.

He deliberated for a few moments before he smiled and sealed the envelope. Sending only a business card could have just the opposite effect. If the lady lawyer had any imagination, she'd be intrigued and follow up the card. The whole damned thing was a gamble anyway. He dropped the envelope in a mailbox on the way to his car.

WHEN THE HASTILY addressed envelope, containing nothing but a business card, arrived in Juliet Cavanaugh's office, she almost tossed it into the wastebasket. Her ad had specified a résumé, and this applicant was the only one who hadn't complied.

She slipped the card under the edge of a brass paperweight on her desk and in the crush of work forgot about it. A week passed before she noticed the card again, and this time her curiosity got the best of her. What kind of man would have the audacity to send nothing but a business card? It might be interesting to interview him and find out, she decided.

When she saw the name J. Brady Talcott on her list of appointments several days later she questioned whether she should have arranged the interview. But that was before Brady arrived.

From the first moment she saw him, Juliet knew she'd made the right decision. Being careful not to reveal her interest, Juliet stood up, appraising him across the expanse of her curved mahogany desk. "You must be J. Brady Talcott," she observed in her controlled professional voice. "Won't you sit down?"

He didn't move, except for one hand that thoughtfully stroked his chin. For several moments he stared at her, his substantial, impeccably tailored frame filling the doorway of her office. He'd known two lady lawyers in his life. One was a tough feminist with a penchant for man-tailored suits. The other was round and dumpy and wore thick glasses. This woman could have stepped off the cover of a fashion magazine. But it wasn't her clothes that captured his total attention. Her light-colored dress faded into the background. All he saw was the shape of high, full breasts, and the curve of slender hips that would be soft to the touch. The rest of her disappeared below the edge of her desk. He wondered what her legs were like. She was one of those women who made him wonder things like that. Aware that she was waiting for him to say something, he found his voice. "You're Juliet Cavanaugh?"

"Yes," came the crisp reply, "I am Ms Cavanaugh."

"Well, I'll be damned," he muttered under his breath.

Juliet fought a smile. His reaction wasn't unusual, but she particularly liked the fact that it came from him. She was quite aware that she didn't fit the stereotype of a woman lawyer, especially one with her credentials. And that suited her just fine. "Won't you come in?" she asked again, extending her hand toward him.

"I will," Brady agreed, striding across the carpeted expanse to the front of her desk. He still couldn't take his eyes off her. Her face was delicate with high cheekbones and a small, straight nose. She had the clear, almost translucent skin of a redhead framed by a thick auburn mane more brown than red. It wasn't until he got closer that he saw her eyes—really saw them, darker green than emeralds but with the same fire.

He took her hand in a brief, firm handshake. "I must admit," he told her, "you're not what I'd expected."

He wasn't what Juliet had expected either, but she didn't see any reason to tell him so. She had already interviewed a dozen men and screened twice that many more applications. She'd found the normal complement of kooks, a few serious contenders, and no one who even vaguely interested her. But something about J. Brady Talcott set him apart from the others. She found herself standing quietly, letting him study her with deep-set brown eyes, nearly the color of bittersweet chocolate. He made her feel more like a woman than like a lawyer.

From a pocket inside his pin-striped suit he extracted a neatly folded clipping, which he opened, scanned quickly to recheck his facts and then dropped in the center of her desk. "Did you run this ad in the *Bay City Magazine*?"

Juliet caught the frown, no more than an infinitesimal crease in the high, broad forehead, and a cold knot began to form in her stomach. Until that moment her plan for having a baby had seemed so logical. Now she saw herself through his eyes and her confidence wavered. Her cool, professional demeanor threatened to desert her. "Yes, I placed the ad," she replied, keeping her voice calm as she sat down. She gestured for him to take the chair that faced her desk.

"Why?" he demanded. He didn't sit down.

"Why?" she repeated, wondering why she felt so defensive. "I thought the ad was self-explanatory."

"It says paternity."

"Right," she confirmed. She'd been pleased with the ad's wording. It was brief and to the point and quite clear. Or at least *she'd* thought it was.

Brady leaned his hands on the edge of her desk and gave her a probing look. "Do you understand what paternity means?"

Juliet stared back at him for a moment, until the question sank in. "Since I was about twelve years old," she told him, laughing softly. She felt herself regaining control. "If you find it a problem, then what are you doing here?"

Brady was beginning to wonder that himself. When he got no response from her in the week after he'd sent his business card, he'd pretty much dismissed the whole thing. By the time she did contact him, he'd lost his initial ardor and was beginning to have second thoughts. Now that he saw her, the whole thing made no sense at all. He couldn't figure out what she was up to, unless she was working for someone else. Maybe she was nothing more than a go-between, somebody to screen the applicants. That would explain everything.

Casually, Brady sat on the chair across from Juliet and leaned forward. "Let's quit playing games. Who are you working for, Ms Cavanaugh?"

"I don't know what you mean."

"Who is your client—the lady who wants to have the baby?" He watched her carefully, figuring she might try to mislead him, but she probably wouldn't tell an outright lie.

Juliet hesitated, and then decided it was best to be direct. "In this instance, Mr. Talcott," she answered evenly, "I am working for myself."

At first Brady just stared at her. Then he laughed, a deep booming laugh that resounded through her office, echoing off the paneled walls and ricocheting through the silence.

Whatever reaction Juliet had expected, it wasn't laughter. She wasn't sure how she felt about this man. He was making her very uncomfortable. "You find that funny?" she demanded.

"Don't you?" he countered, still chuckling.

"Not at all," she replied coldly.

Brady Talcott shook his head. What was this woman after? If she were dull and plain, which was frankly what he had expected, he could have figured out her reasons for placing the ad. But just about any man would be happy to hop in bed with her, no questions asked. She was either naive as hell or there was some gimmick here he hadn't found yet. He tried again. "You mean to tell me that you want a baby and so you advertised for a father? Haven't you ever heard of adoption?"

"Of course. I've investigated it very thoroughly. The kind of baby I want would require waiting for years and then, as a single mother, I'd be too old to adopt at all," Juliet explained patiently. "Besides," she added, "I want to have the baby myself. Really, Mr. Talcott, I've thought this over quite carefully—"

"Then you must have considered artificial insemination," he interrupted bluntly.

Juliet sensed an uncharacteristic burning in her ears. "I want to know without a shred of doubt who the father is."

"So pick your donor," he told her. "How about that place where they guarantee you the father won a Nobel Prize?"

"You obviously haven't read the stories about the doctor who bragged about fathering hundreds of babies because he routinely replaced the donor sperm with his own," Juliet shot back. "I find the whole idea repulsive."

Brady leaned forward in his chair, his eyes penetrating her. "In that case, Ms Cavanaugh, are you familiar with the emotion called love, followed by the institution of marriage?"

Determinedly, Juliet stared back at him. "As a divorce lawyer, Mr. Talcott, I am intimately familiar with both." She had the distinct impression he was trying to intimidate her, and she wasn't going to let him. A growing irritation swelled inside her. "I am also familiar with the havoc that results when marriages fail, which most of them do," she added stiffly. "I figured out twenty years ago that marriage wasn't what I wanted. And everything I've seen since has proven me right."

Brady listened, his face impassive but his mind moving quickly. He had a lot of groundwork to do before he brought up the trust agreement. Funny, in some ways her situation was actually a lot like his. She wanted something she couldn't have the traditional way, so she'd figured out her own approach. Maybe that was part of what intrigued him about her. Before he mentioned the trust agreement he needed to know a lot more about her hang-up with marriage. After all, a marriage arrangement was a critical part of the deal.

"Have you ever been married, Ms Cavanaugh?" he inquired.

"No, Mr. Talcott, I have not."

"Then what's your problem? I thought every woman wanted to get married—at least once." He knew right away he'd hit a sore spot. Her expression barely changed, but her eyes flashed fire.

"I am not 'every woman,' Mr. Talcott," she retorted. "I'm a divorce lawyer. That gives me a window on a lot of miserable marriages."

He knew that explanation was too simple. There was more to it. "I thought you said you'd made that decision twenty years ago. You certainly weren't a divorce lawyer then."

"That's quite true, Mr. Talcott, but that's not the point." Juliet sat up straighter and folded her hands. "We are here to discuss a business arrangement, not my philosophy of marriage. My requirements are very specific, Mr. Talcott. I want to have a baby when I'm thirty. I want to know its father. And I don't want any long-term entanglements with the man. It's as simple as that."

Good, Brady thought. He didn't want any long-term entanglements either. He drummed his fingers on the desk. "I do believe you're serious," he observed.

"Quite serious, Mr. Talcott." The knot inside Juliet's stomach was tightening. For all the same reasons she instinctively knew this man was the right one, she was also wary of him. It hadn't been like that with any of the other applicants. They'd come before her, some with bravado and some with embarrassment, but all of them applying for the position, waiting for her judgment. She'd been in control. With this man, she wasn't. She waited, unable to predict his response.

"In that case, Ms Cavanaugh," he said finally, "if you really are serious about this plan of yours, do you suppose we might proceed from here on a first-name basis?"

His answer caught her off balance. Then the incongruity of the situation struck her. However brief and businesslike their relationship, producing a child required more intimacy than "Ms" and "Mr." Juliet tossed back her head and laughed; it was a soft, melodious sound that swept away the tension between them.

Their eyes met and held for a long moment. Once again she held out her hand. "I'm Juliet," she said softly.

"That's better." He took her hand and held it firmly in both of his. "Call me Brady."

Juliet looked at him as if she were seeing him for the first time. She found herself studying him, breaking the whole into parts—the full lips drawn into an oddly engaging smile, those eyes deeply set beneath bushy brows, the thick dark hair framing an angular face that was almost, but not quite, classically handsome. Nothing was unusual about him and yet everything was. Something about this man was terribly appealing.

She couldn't decide whether that was good or not. She had purposely sought a stranger to help carry out her plan because she wanted to avoid any involvement later. If she'd chosen someone she knew, perhaps one of the men she'd dated, she would have to see him again. There would be no way to make a clean break. He might even try to make some claim on the child and she'd have a real legal battle on her hands, one she might easily lose the way the courts were moving. She couldn't chance that. This was going to be *her* baby.

Realizing with a start that Brady was still holding her hand, Juliet pulled away. She actually knew very little about him and, in any case, it was important to keep her distance. This arrangement was, she reminded herself again, strictly business, whatever they called each other. She needed to get on with the interview. "Now that you've questioned me about my intentions," she began, "tell me about yours. Just exactly why did you answer my ad?"

Brady hesitated. What would she think, he wondered, if he told her the truth right now? Would she laugh and agree to it? Or would she turn him down cold? It was too soon to tell. He decided to wait, and he gave her his other reason. "Absolutely insatiable curiosity," he replied.

"That's all? Just curiosity?"

"What other reason would anyone have? I assume I'm not the only applicant. What reason did the others give you?"

"Most of them assumed there would be a substantial fee—"

"You mean you're going to pay for this?" he interrupted. "A stud fee?" For some reason, an exchange of money had never occurred to him.

Juliet winced. "That's a crass way to put it. Keep in mind, Mr. Talcott, that this is strictly business." When he didn't answer her, Juliet hurried on, anxious to change the subject.

"Since I don't have your résumé—suppose you tell me abou yourself," she suggested.

Brady shrugged. He couldn't figure this woman out. He wa picking up all sorts of sensual signals, subtle invitations to com closer and get better acquainted. The air hung heavy betwee them. There was no denying the attraction. It had been imme diate, and he knew she felt it, too. But the words coming out her mouth, and even the tone of that carefully modulated voic were calculated to keep him at a distance. Only in those flasl ing green eyes had he caught a glimpse of the woman behind tl facade, and then what he saw was so fleeting that he couldn capture it.

Any fool could figure out that his next move was to leave an put as much distance between himself and this woman as l could. But he knew he wasn't going to, and something told hir it wasn't just because of Talcott Enterprises. He also wasn about to submit to her questioning. If she wanted his life hi tory, she could figure it out for herself.

His mouth formed a half grin. "You have my card, whic lists my name, and address, and telephone number." He looke steadily into her eyes. "That is precisely the same informatic I have about you."

"But Mr. Talcott—"

Straightening his suit coat, he stood up. "Brady," he co rected her. "If you want more facts," he added offhandedl "I'm sure you have the resources to find them."

He covered the distance to the office door in three strid before he stopped and turned to look back at her. Somethir in the way she was watching him suggested a vulnerability l hadn't expected. He sensed her disappointment, but he didn change his mind. If she wasn't interested enough to pursue hir she'd never accept his proposition, anyway. He knew that h plan, in its own way, was as radical as hers.

Juliet stood up, and Brady had a sudden, overwhelming ur to go back to her, to suggest they forget what had passed b tween them and go to dinner like two normal people on a dat But they had already come too far. And they were both carr ing too much emotional baggage for that kind of normal rel tionship to work. He wondered how it would feel to touch tl curves beneath her dress, wondered how long it would take

xpose the softness of the woman that was hidden inside her.
I don't know the Juliet behind those lovely green eyes," he
old her, a huskiness creeping into his voice. "I have no idea
hether I would like her or not."

"Is that important?" Juliet inquired.

"Critical." He started to leave and then turned back again.
When you find out whatever it is you seem to need to know
bout me, and you are ready to have a civilized conversation,
el free to call."

Juliet's voice was icy. "Good day, Mr. Talcott."

"Good day, Ms Cavanaugh," he replied formally, almost
aring himself away from her, not doubting that he would see
er again.

Juliet watched him walk away. Once he had disappeared
om sight, she paced across her office to the window that
verlooked Embarcadero Center and waited until Brady's tall,
nposing form emerged from the revolving doors below. Even
eeing him from high above, she couldn't have mistaken him
r anyone else. There was something about the way his body
oved, the way he walked, that set him apart from the other
ny figures bustling along the street. No matter what the con-
equences, she wanted to know him better.

CHAPTER TWO

THE NEXT STEP in Juliet's plan was to pay a call to Linda Burke. Somebody had to keep the law practice going while she was busy having a baby, and her former roommate was the logical candidate. But the early-morning visit was only partially business. Juliet greeted Linda with a big hug, realizing how glad she was to see her friend.

"You're looking more and more like a successful lawyer, new clothes and all," Linda observed, standing back and admiring Juliet's designer suit. She tugged at the ribbing of her faded Stanford sweatshirt. "I'm jealous," she said, only half joking. "You make me feel like a *hausfrau*."

"Not for long," Juliet answered, "and that's why I'm here." Walking beside her friend through the low, sprawling house where Linda and Steve had lived for the five years they'd been married, Juliet noted the sharp contrast between her own lifestyle and theirs. Linda's existence was comfortable and homey and obviously geared toward children. Juliet picked up a Raggedy Ann doll that had been dropped half under the hall table, wondering if her life would change the same way once she had a baby. "Where are the kids?" she asked, suddenly aware of the silence.

"Jennie's at nursery school—you just missed her," Linda explained, pushing her short, brown hair back from her face. "And the baby's asleep, outside in the buggy. That gives us a few blessed uninterrupted minutes, and we'd better take advantage of it," she said, leading the way toward the kitchen. "Come on. I'll get the tea."

Juliet watched her friend fill the teapot and put it on the tray with the cups. Linda didn't look like someone who'd had two babies. Maybe she was a little thicker around the middle than she'd been before, but she was still petite. And she had the

me sparkle she'd always had. It seemed strange to think of
inda with a family when only a few years ago she'd been as
ee and independent as Juliet; a young struggling lawyer try-
g to build a practice. It was time her friend got back to
ork—they'd both agreed on that. Now, if everything jelled the
ay she'd planned, Juliet thought, it would be perfect for both
f them. Linda could have a part-time practice, and Juliet
ould have someone to shoulder some of the load when she was
regnant and later, when she wanted to spend time with the
aby.

While Linda carried the tray to the large patio looking out
cross the hills toward the city, Juliet tiptoed to the buggy and
eked in. The baby, sleeping soundly beneath lightweight
hite netting, still looked very small and vulnerable to Juliet.

"Sh-h-h, don't wake him," Linda warned. "He'll be up soon
ough. I want to know what's going on with you. You were
ally vague on the phone."

Juliet accepted the cup of tea Linda offered and settled back
the wicker rocker. "I think I may have found the father I'm
oking for," she announced. "He came in yesterday, and I had
is feeling right from the beginning—"

"You're really going through with it?" Linda broke in.

"Of course. I said I would." Juliet was surprised by the
uestion. Linda was the only person she'd told about her plan,
e only one she could count on to listen to her instead of be-
g judgmental.

Linda set her teacup on the table. "So tell me about him,"
e directed, turning her chair toward Juliet. "Everything."

"Well," Juliet hesitated. "Right now there isn't much. His
ame is J. Brady Talcott and he's president of something called
alcott Enterprises."

"And?"

"That's it, so far."

Linda frowned. "I thought you required a résumé and med-
al history and all sorts of stuff from these guys."

"This one only sent a business card. I don't know why I even
ecided to follow up." Juliet took a sip of tea. "But he seems
ke a good choice."

"You can't get involved in a deal like this with someone you
on't know anything about," Linda protested.

"Don't worry," Juliet assured her. "I already called Harry."

Linda nodded approvingly. "Ah, yes, Harry Mechum's one man detective agency. If anyone can tell you everything there is to know about him, it's Harry."

"That's what I figured," Juliet agreed. "Now, how about you? Are you ready to go back to work?"

"Ready? I'm dying to." Linda leaned forward. "I found a agency last week that provides nannies—they sound absolutely wonderful. Except they cost an arm and a leg. Can we make enough money?"

"We should be able to," Juliet answered. "The practice has really taken off in the last couple of years. There's almost enough work for two of us full-time."

Linda's eyes sparkled. "That sounds almost too good to be true." She poured another cup of tea for both of them and slowly her expression changed. "But even with money, it's going to be a juggling act for both of us," she warned, looking directly at Juliet. "Especially for you. A husband can take a lot of the load off sometimes. I know Steve's gone a lot, but when he's home it's really nice to be able to turn it all over to him for a few hours." She shifted in her chair. "You're taking on a lot of responsibility."

Juliet didn't answer right away. Linda wasn't telling her anything she didn't already know. There were going to be a lot of times when single parenthood would be hard. But other people managed. It was the same kind of caution people had given when she got out of law school. "Go into a law firm," they'd advised. "It's too hard to make it on your own." But she had made it, and she'd make it this time, too.

"You know how I feel about marriage," Juliet said slowly. "It's been good for you and Steve—so far at least—but you're the exception." She stood up and walked to the edge of the patio. "I don't see any reason why I should lose the chance to become a mother just because I don't want to get married."

Linda's eyes followed her. "You could adopt a baby, you know. That's an acceptable way to do it."

"But I don't want to adopt." Juliet turned around, her tone unrelenting. "We've been over that, too. I want to have the baby myself."

Linda nodded. "I understand that. Having a baby is probably the most profound thing you'll ever do. I'd be the last person to ever try to talk you out of it. But even if you're determined to have it there are other ways—"

"You're about to tell me there are other ways to accomplish that," Juliet interrupted. "We've been over those, too. But this is the only way I can have the baby and be absolutely certain who the father is."

"In other words, you retain total control."

Startled by the comment, Juliet walked back to the chair. "I suppose so. I haven't thought of it exactly that way."

"You like to be in control, Juliet. You always have, and I'm not knocking that either." Linda shrugged. "I just figured we should run through the options one more time."

"Like always?" Juliet grinned at her friend.

"Like always," Linda agreed. "Which brings up the question of you know, what's-his-name . . . Sam? George?"

"You mean David?"

"Yeah, David. Whatever happened with you and David? You sounded as though you two might actually have been going places. I know it was good . . . that was written all over you . . . I thought maybe he'd be the one. At least you know him," she added, pointedly.

Juliet looked out across the hills. Linda was right. It had been good, at least for a while. But she'd never felt complete—as if there should somehow have been something more. They hadn't quite clicked, not the way they ought to have if they were going to risk anything permanent. The relationship had just gone on and on and grown more predictable until finally, one day, Juliet decided she'd had enough.

She looked at Linda. "I think you put your finger on the problem. How long did I go out with him? Two years, maybe? And you couldn't remember his name."

Linda laughed. "I guess we'd call him eminently forgettable."

"Something like that," Juliet murmured.

They sat quietly for a few moments. It was a comfortable feeling, talking with her friend again, Juliet thought. She would be glad to have Linda come into the practice. She'd had reservations at first, wondering whether she would have a difficult

time sharing something she'd struggled so hard to build her
self. But she and Linda had always been frank and open with
each other, going clear back to those years when they were
roommates at Stanford. That would make everything easier.
And the practice had grown until there was enough work for
both of them.

A litany of baby noises, words that weren't words, poured
into the morning silence. "Quiet time's over," Linda ob
served. "Paul's awake—and damn, there's the phone." She
stood up and started inside. "Pick him up before he cries, will
you?" she called over her shoulder to Juliet.

Juliet folded back the white netting that covered the buggy
and two large blue eyes met hers. The round face broke into a
delighted grin. She leaned closer, slightly in awe of the tiny
creature. "You lost your rattle," she observed gravely, picking
up the small silver rattle she had given the baby when he was
born. She held it against his fist and the tiny fingers closed
tightly around it. He waved both arms and then stared curi
ously at his hand when the rattle made noise.

He'd grown in the weeks since she'd seen him, but he still
looked so little. Juliet wondered if she'd have trouble leaving
her own baby to go back to work when it was still small. But a
good nanny would make all the difference, and at first she
would work only part-time.

Juliet took off her suit jacket and searched for a cloth to put
over her shoulder. She'd learned the hard way that Paul could
be very messy. When she turned away from the baby the happy
sounds changed to cries. By the time she located a towel, the
wailing from the buggy was growing steadily louder. "Come
here, Paul," she said soothingly, slipping her hands under the
baby's back. "I can tell you don't like being ignored."

Paul continued screaming while Juliet sat down in the wicker
rocker and cradled him in her arms. She talked to him softly
while she rocked him and in a few moments he was quiet again,
his blue eyes fixed on her. He was soft and warm against her
body, sweet smelling after his morning bath. Juliet felt a deep
sense of longing as she rocked him, and she found herself
holding him closer and wondering what it would be like if he
were hers.

The baby cooed softly and looked up at Juliet. Yes, she thought, her instincts had been right. She did want a baby, and she wanted one so much that it was worth all she had to go through. She thought about Brady Talcott, framed by the doorway of her office, and hoped Harry Mechum wouldn't find anything damaging about him. The more she thought about Brady, the more "right" he seemed.

Juliet looked up as she heard the patio door slide open. "You two are obviously getting along," Linda observed with a smile. "You'll be a good mother, Juliet. Just make sure you know what you're getting into before you do it."

"I think I do," Juliet answered seriously, "as much as anyone ever does ahead of time."

"By the way," Linda asked, "how are you going to break this to your mother?"

Juliet didn't hesitate. "The same way I'd tell her anything—directly," she answered nonchalantly. "You know how Cass is. She believes in everyone doing her own thing. She won't have any trouble with this. In fact, she'll probably love the idea of being a grandmother."

Linda laughed. "She can't possibly be any happier about her new role than I am about mine. It sounds really good to go into a law practice that's off and running. Mine never quite got to that stage."

"You didn't have time," Juliet replied. Paul wiggled in her arms and she turned him so he was sitting up on her lap.

"Most of the work I had was bar association referrals, and you know how few of those pan out," Linda remembered.

"Bar association referrals," Juliet echoed. She freed her arm from around Paul and checked her watch. "Linda, I'm really glad you said that. I've got a woman coming in this morning—I'd almost forgotten."

"Then you do still take them. If you're already overloaded, why do you?" Linda leaned down to pick up Paul, and the baby reached his arms out toward his mother.

"A couple of reasons, I guess," Juliet said as she stood up and put on her suit jacket. "Sometimes they come to something and . . ." Her voice trailed off. It sounded sort of hokey to say that was the way she paid her debt to society, but in a way it was true. "Sometimes you can help those people without investing a whole lot of time," she continued. "Remember that big Barker case—the one that really got me going?"

Linda nodded. "How could I forget? It was all over the papers for weeks."

"That started out as a bar association referral," Juliet reminded her.

"I guess it did," Linda agreed. "And besides that," she said grinning, "you've got a big heart, even if you won't admit it. But if we're both going to work at this and make any money—especially when you've got a baby to support—we're not going to be able to spend our time on charity cases."

"Don't worry," Juliet assured her. "My heart's not that big."

Still carrying Paul, Linda walked her to the door. "I'm really anxious to get back to work, Juliet. Thanks for giving me the chance."

"You're the one doing me the favor," Juliet replied. "How do you want to start?"

"Maybe I can come in one or two days a week for a while, till I get into the swing of things." Linda suggested. "I'll call the nanny agency this afternoon and see what I can arrange."

"Fantastic," Juliet agreed, giving Paul a parting pat. She left, feeling that the pieces of the puzzle were all falling into place.

As she drove back toward the office, Juliet mentally sorted through the cases she could turn over to Linda. Nothing too complicated at first, she decided, and obviously only ones where the retainer was already in the bank. Linda had made her feelings about money pretty clear. And she was right. But in reality, Juliet thought, she only took one or two cases a year without cash up front, and never anything that would take a lot of time. She also decided to call the building management about expanding her office space. Linda would need her own office right away.

A visual image of Brady kept intruding on her thoughts, and she smiled, catching her bottom lip lightly between her teeth. She really would like to know him better. But she couldn't let personal feelings intrude, she reminded herself, and she needed to wait until she talked to Harry to make any final decision.

This was, after all, a business arrangement, and it was critical that she keep it that way.

When Juliet walked into her office, the reception room was empty except for her secretary, who was bent over a stack of file folders. "I take it my eleven o'clock didn't show," she said, resting her briefcase on the edge of the reception desk.

Alice peered over her glasses. "Oh, no, Ms Cavanaugh. She's been here more than an hour. She seemed real nervous and so I told her she could go sit in your office. I checked first to make sure your desk was locked up and all."

"Did you have her fill out the background forms?" Juliet held out her hand expectantly. "I'd like to take a look at them before I see her."

"She took them with her, but I don't think she filled them out," Alice said. "She wouldn't even tell me her name."

"That's not a very good start," Juliet muttered.

Behind the closed door a woman sat stiffly on the edge of a light blue wing chair. Her fine blond hair fell like a curtain around her face. Her hands were knotted in her lap. She hadn't moved in nearly an hour. Instead, she simply waited, not really knowing how long she'd been there because she wasn't wearing a watch. The time didn't matter much anyway. She would have waited as long as necessary. This meeting was important. She smoothed her camel-colored wool skirt nervously, pressing out the deep wrinkles with her palms. Her clothes had been beautiful once, and she liked wearing pretty things. This outfit was still presentable. She had worked hard to sponge the stain out of the ecru blouse, and now it was barely noticeable.

Hearing muted conversation in the reception room, she glanced over her shoulder. The lawyer must be in. She fumbled with the clasp on her purse and pulled out a gold compact. Her reflection in the small mirror told her that she looked fine. Well put together. She tried out a smile. Almost gracious. She had to be if she was going to accomplish her goal. She dropped the compact back in her purse and fished around until she found a peppermint under some crumpled tissues. Putting the peppermint in her mouth, she closed the purse and took a deep breath. This wasn't going to be easy. She had known that at the onset. But she could do it. She had to.

The door opened and the lawyer entered. Her hair was a deep auburn and she was younger and much more attractive than the woman had expected her to be. The lawyer didn't look very experienced. The woman clutched a wadded twenty-dollar bill tightly in her hand. That was what the man at the bar association had said she had to pay for a half-hour consultation. She hoped he had referred her to a good lawyer.

Juliet assessed the woman quickly, noting how the hands were knotted nervously together, the angle of the head, the tight lines at the corners of the woman's mouth. They were all common signs. When Juliet extended her hand, the woman stood up. "Good morning," Juliet greeted her, looking directly into the pale blue eyes. "Come on over and sit on the sofa. Would you like a cup of coffee?"

The woman shook her head. Wordlessly, she followed Juliet across the room where she sat stiffly on the far end of the sofa. Juliet watched carefully as she set her purse on the coffee table, moved it to the floor, and finally laid it in her lap. This wasn't the time to pick up the yellow pad she always kept handy by the couch, Juliet decided. She'd dispense with taking notes. It was more important to get the woman talking first. "Why don't we begin with your name?" Juliet suggested.

"No," the woman responded quickly. Too quickly. "I don't want to tell you my name until I'm sure."

"Sure of what?" Juliet prompted.

"Sure you can help me."

"All right," Juliet answered. "Let's begin there. Tell me about your problem."

"I want my babies back," the woman blurted out. For the first time since they'd sat down, she looked at Juliet.

"Your babies? How many children do you have?"

"Two." The woman's voice was flat. She looked away.

"Where are they?"

"With my husband." Again, the toneless voice.

"Are you divorced?"

The woman shook her head.

"Has there been any legal action? Has the court awarded your husband custody?"

Again the woman shook her head, a barely perceptible movement. Her knuckles were white from clutching her purse.

Juliet knew they weren't going to get very far unless she could get the woman to open up. The effort was probably going to be fruitless, anyway, but she was so obviously alone and in need of help that Juliet had to try. Juliet asked another question. "How long have you been separated from your husband and children?"

"I'm not separated." She sounded defensive.

At least that was some emotion, Juliet thought. She leaned forward in an attempt to bridge the gulf between them and caught a faint hint of alcohol well-masked with peppermint. "You need to explain more clearly," Juliet told her, beginning to understand at least part of the problem.

For a long moment, the woman searched Juliet's face. "I'm not afraid to tell you, but I want to be sure you can help," she said quietly.

"I can try," Juliet promised, "but I can't do anything unless you tell me what's happened."

The woman took a deep, shuddering breath. "I left last year, one day in the summer. He hadn't been home all week. He never came home anymore."

Now they were getting somewhere. "You haven't been back since?" Juliet questioned.

"I used to go home, but not for a long time now. I miss my children, but when I go back it isn't the same. He won't let me take them anywhere." The woman stared down at her hands. "It's not like really being their mother." When she raised her head, her eyes were filled with tears. "I want to take them home with me. I want them to be mine again."

Juliet pressed her lips together. The puzzle was beginning to take shape and, like so many others, it wasn't very pretty. "Why won't your husband let you take them with you for a few days?"

For a long time the woman didn't answer, and then her voice was barely audible. "He says I can't take care of them."

She was talking now. Before they went further, it was time to lay the cards on the table. "Is it because you drink?"

The woman looked as though Juliet had struck her. Juliet braced herself, not knowing whether to expect anger or denial. She got neither. The woman stared straight ahead.

"I never used to drink. But it got so lonely when he didn't come home. The babies got sick a lot, and I was always so tired, and I never got to go anywhere. I tried to talk to him. But he didn't understand how lonely I was."

The woman's eyes met Juliet's in a plea for understanding. "He sent me to psychiatrists and sometimes they gave me pills, but it didn't help. My husband didn't seem to care about anything but his work. He said I should be grateful because he worked so hard and made so much money. And then he wanted me to have another baby so I would have something to occupy my time. I couldn't stand it anymore." She covered her face with her hands.

"That was why you left?" Juliet probed. "Nothing specific, just because you'd had it?"

"No, not exactly," the woman admitted, placing her hands carefully in her lap, but not looking up. "One day I got really angry at my older boy and I shook him and pushed him against the wall."

"Did you hurt him?" Juliet asked.

"No, but I could have," the woman answered slowly. "The next day, when I thought about it I got really scared." She raised her eyes, her face taut with the pain of the memory. "I was afraid if my husband found out he'd send me away to a hospital. He'd threatened to before. So I just packed and left."

Juliet offered her a tissue from the box on the coffee table, making a mental note to replace the box soon. It was nearly empty again. "Do you want to begin divorce proceedings?" she asked quietly.

A profound sadness settled in the pale blue eyes. "I just want my babies. I want to take them away and start all over again."

"And your husband?"

"I don't know." She blew her nose.

"He hasn't taken any legal action?" Juliet asked.

The woman shook her head. "I don't think so."

"Does your husband send you money?"

"Sometimes," the woman admitted, then added quickly, "but I work as a waitress, too."

Juliet debated briefly about what to do. What this woman needed was some love and understanding from her husband, and if he hadn't cut her off after a year, that was a good sign.

It was obvious that she needed a therapist, not a lawyer, and someone to help her fight the alcohol problem when she was strong enough to do it. Juliet knew she might be able to get a court order allowing the woman partial custody, but in good conscience she couldn't do it. At least not right now.

"My first suggestion," Juliet began, "is that you try to talk to your husband again. If the two of you could work out something together, it would be best for you and the children."

"It has been a long time since I've talked to him," the woman admitted. "I don't think it will do any good."

"You need to try," Juliet urged. She stood up, indicating the meeting was over.

The woman came slowly to her feet. "I brought the money. The man said I had to pay you twenty dollars for a half hour."

Juliet accepted the crumpled twenty-dollar bill the woman offered. "If you need further advice, let me know," she said kindly. "We'll discuss payment then."

"All right," the woman agreed, starting toward the door. Even as her hand touched the doorknob, the woman knew that she probably wouldn't come back again. This lawyer sounded like she understood. She sounded like she wanted to help, but she didn't know what to do. No one did. It was all so complicated. Maybe she would find a quiet place and have an early lunch and a few glasses of wine. Then she could get her head together and decide what to do.

When the office door closed, Juliet took a new box of tissues out of the closet and set it on the coffee table. She hoped that somewhere that woman would find the help she needed. She wasn't going to find it in a lawyer's office.

Every time she talked to a woman like that, Juliet understood a little more clearly why she didn't want any part of marriage. This one was a little different than most. Usually it was the man who walked out, like her own father had. In this case it was the woman. But it was the same pattern. Two people, happy at the beginning, slowly grew apart. When the anger and the disappointment got to a certain level, one of them usually left. Everyone involved got hurt, especially the children. Often they got hurt most of all.

Juliet walked over to her desk. She wasn't going to let that happen. She'd planned her life a different way, and she'd make her plan work. But first she needed to know more about Brady, and that required a visit to Harry Mechum.

CHAPTER THREE

THE STAIRWAY LEADING UP to Harry's office had a smell of its own. It wasn't dirty exactly, but it bordered on that definition. The pungent smell of permanent waving solution from the beautician's shop down the hall mixed with years of stale cigar smoke and the odor of an old mongrel dog that often slept in the corner of the upper landing. It was a dingy old building, in a neighborhood near the Tenderloin district where Juliet never ventured after dark.

She remembered the first time she'd come, the idealistic young lawyer expecting a spit-and-polish private eye of the Paul Drake variety. Then she'd met Harry, with his doleful eyes and ever-present cigar, stationed behind the mound of clutter he called his desk. Mostly he'd grunted, and she'd left disgusted, never expecting to hear from him again. But when he called, it was to tell her that her client's husband was maintaining a double identity with two wives, two comfortable suburban homes, and two sets of children. The story hit front pages across the country, and Juliet's law practice took off. Ever since then, she'd figured she owed Harry. She knocked twice on Harry's office door, carefully, because it made the glass rattle, and then walked in.

"Morning," Harry grunted as usual, barely looking up. He nonchalantly shifted his soggy cigar from one side of his mouth to the other and pulled a sheaf of dog-eared papers out of one of the piles on the back corner of his desk. "Got that info you wanted. The stuff about the Talcott guy," he said, holding the papers out toward Juliet.

"This is *all* about Brady Talcott?" Juliet asked in surprise as she took the papers from the detective and sat down on one of the wooden chairs crowded into the tiny office. She thumbed through the roughly typed papers, turning them occasionally to decipher Harry's scrawled notes in the margins. Harry certainly was thorough. A newspaper photograph caught her attention, and she picked it up.

"Good lookin', ain't he?" Harry commented. "The broad that's divorcing him is gonna lose a lot. Or maybe get a lot with you workin' for her," he winked.

Juliet smiled at the compliment. She studied the photo of Brady in a sleek, smooth-fitting swimsuit. He was poised on the bow of a sailboat grinning at the large trophy he held in his hand. The caption below the picture read, "J. Brady Talcott III wins Bay Regatta."

"He is good-looking," she said as much to herself as to Harry. Well, she thought, that was one of the requirements she had put in the ad. "Obviously Mr. Talcott sails," Juliet mused.

"Among other things." Harry scraped a wooden match across his shoe sole and lighted the remains of his cigar.

"Such as?" Juliet prompted.

"Flying. The guy used to own his own plane. Tried his hand at racing cars a few years back. Apparently gave that up."

"So, he sails, he flies, he used to race cars," Juliet repeated. "What else?"

Harry reached a none-too-clean hand into the pile of papers Juliet was holding and dug out some notes. He rocked his oak swivel chair backward almost to the point of disaster before beginning. "Let's see here," he drawled with maddening slowness. "John Brady Talcott III. Age thirty-four, turns thirty-five March fifth."

Perfect, Juliet silently approved.

"Born in Boston, public schools there, an engineering degree from M.I.T.—that's the Massachusetts Institute of Technology—" Harry explained.

"I know, I know," Juliet said impatiently. "Go on."

"Father died two years ago, John Brady Jr. Mother surviving, name's Amelia. She's sixty-four. One sister, Sheila, lives in Connecticut," Harry droned on. "She's got a husband and a couple of kids."

Juliet's attention wandered. So, she mentally calculated, Brady was born when his mother was thirty. Good age to have a baby, she smiled to herself.

Methodically, Harry continued. "Never been married..." Harry shot Juliet a puzzled look. "Yeah, I remember now, this is the one I wanted to ask you about. If he's not married, how come somebody's divorcing him?"

"Harry," Juliet responded, "the deal is I don't ask how you get the information and you don't ask what I do with it? Okay?"

"Sure," Harry grunted. "Couldn't find much to spice this up. Doesn't seem to play around much. Did go out a lot with one woman a couple of years ago, but she's married to somebody else. Seems to spend most of his time with his business."

"Oh, yes," Juliet interjected. She remembered Brady's business card which she had been carrying in her purse all week. "He's chairman of the board of Talcott Enterprises," she noted. "Just exactly what is Talcott Enterprises."

Harry stopped rocking his chair. He stood up and leaned over his desk toward Juliet, blowing the acrid cigar smoke directly into her face. "Now we come to the interesting part," he chortled.

"I'm waiting, and not very patiently," Juliet muttered. She coughed slightly and turned her head away from the cigar fumes. Harry, as usual, didn't pay any attention.

"This guy," Harry tapped Brady's picture, "is worth a mint. We're not talking a couple of hundred thou. We're talking big bucks here. Millions."

Juliet stared incredulously at the picture and then at Harry. No wonder Brady reacted so differently from the others when she offered him money. She'd figured at the time he must be comfortable financially, but she'd never thought about him being wealthy.

"Are you sure?" she countered.

"Yep." Harry nodded his head.

"Where did Brady, er..." Juliet caught herself, but not before Harry shot her a curious look. "Where did Mr. Talcott get all this money if he's only thirty-four?"

"Got the family business when the old man died. Built it into a million-dollar operation."

"And it's all his?"

"Couldn't quite get a handle on that—something odd about the way it's set up but I couldn't nail it."

"Just exactly what is this family business?" Juliet stood up and paced restlessly back and forth across the carpet. She had fleeting thoughts of a line of cruise ships, diamonds, oil. . . .

"Children's furniture," Harry said matter-of-factly.

Juliet stopped pacing and stared at him. "Children's furniture?" she repeated blankly.

"That's what I said," Harry confirmed. He dropped the sheaf of notes into the rubble on his desk and clamped down hard on his cigar. "He designs lots of it himself. Used to be pretty run-of-the-mill, but in the last year or so he's come out with some ritzy new stuff. You probably heard of it—he's got that TV ad. You know the one, that mechanical toy named Hugo that marches around adding pieces to the furniture to make it bigger." Harry stiffened his arms and began to strut around the office, making electroniclike beeping sounds as he rearranged the chairs.

He looked more like a penguin in a greasy tie than a mechanical toy, Juliet thought, and normally she would have convulsed in giggles at the sight. But not this time. She was searching her memory, trying to put it all together. "Now I remember," she cried out. "Last Christmas. Neiman-Marcus, Bloomingdales, Saks. 'The furniture that grows with your child.' "

"You got it." Harry stopped his penguin imitation and reached in his pocket again. "He's apparently test-marketing some other stuff. Started with a spin-off from his furniture—wooden blocks and then snap-together bubbles. He's added motors and remote control hookups for older kids, and a few months ago he came out with some climbing stuff." Harry consulted his notes. "I don't know where he's headed with that. I got a copy of his balance sheet that shows a profit breakdown—"

"Enough." Juliet held up her hand to stop Harry's dissertation. She already had enough information to know Brady Talcott was way beyond what she'd expected. "Now, how about his medical report?" That was the one critical area Harry hadn't covered.

"Talcott's medical report." Harry scratched his balding head. "Why you wanted a medical report is beyond me." He gave Juliet a penetrating look and waited for a response, but she only smiled. Harry shrugged. "Okay, you're the boss. Whatever you want. Anyway, the guy is in great shape."

"You checked his medical background very carefully?"

"That's what you pay me for." Harry scowled. "He had a complete insurance physical a couple of months ago—X rays, blood tests, the whole works. There's probably not a test around that wasn't done on that guy."

"And there is absolutely nothing irregular?" Juliet questioned.

"No, I already told you that," Harry retorted. "Next you're gonna want an affidavit from his doctor."

Juliet didn't answer. She was focused on Brady. His medical exam sounded even more comprehensive than hers had been. It looked as though he filled all the squares. He was smart, and in the right areas. He had math and science abilities to balance her verbal talents. And he was definitely attractive. She pictured him as she had first seen him, standing in her office doorway—dark hair, deep brown eyes, a powerful build that fit nicely into his custom-tailored suit. He was obviously athletic, which she certainly was not. The two of them as parents could be an absolutely dynamic combination.

"Anything else?" Harry's gravelly voice intruded.

She looked up to find him waiting expectantly. "As usual, you've done a fantastic job," she praised him enthusiastically.

"Thanks," Harry answered with practiced modesty. Juliet stood up and reached for the information folder about Brady. Instead of giving it to her, Harry cleared his throat. "You forgot to pay me," he reminded her.

"I'm sorry," Juliet apologized. She quickly reached into her purse for her tapestry checkbook, wrote a check, and gave it to Harry.

"This is a personal check," he noted. "You always pay me with a business check."

"Right," Juliet agreed.

"It's also a hell of a lot more than you usually pay me," he added.

"Right," Juliet answered again.

Harry gave her an astute look. "I don't ask questions. I just do the job," he muttered, handing her the folder.

"Right again," grinned Juliet. "I'll close the door behind me."

She sailed down the stairs, stopping just long enough to give the old mongrel dog a vigorous pat on the head. Once outdoors, Juliet took a deep breath of air, already heavy with afternoon fog, and considered her next move. She had all the information she needed about J. Brady Talcott. She might as well get on with it. Juliet looked around until she spotted a pay phone and then took Brady's business card from her purse. Her pulse quickened as she dialed the number.

Brady answered his own phone.

"Hello, this is Juliet Cavanaugh," she said breezily. There was a long pause, and Juliet's confidence evaporated. It had been a week since the interview. *My God,* she thought, *he's forgotten me.*

"Well, well," Brady finally replied, the businesslike tone gone. "I thought I'd be hearing from you pretty soon. You must have made up your mind."

It suddenly seemed important to Juliet not to sound too anxious. "On the contrary, Brady," she hedged, "I haven't made up my mind about anything. Just moved a little more in that direction."

"I understand you've done a background check on me that would make the FBI blush." He didn't try to mask the amusement in his voice. "Did you find my house in order?"

Damn Harry, Juliet thought. He could have been more subtle. "Just a few inquiries," she answered, brushing the investigation off as best she could. "I hope you didn't mind."

"As a matter of fact," he answered, "I got calls from people I hadn't heard from in years. My mother said the bank contacted her to find out if I was going to work for the CIA."

Juliet laughed, a soft, throaty sound in the silence. Her own mother would have thought it was funny but, then, Cass wasn't like other mothers. "What did you tell your mother?"

"That someone was doing a credit check—what would you tell her?"

Juliet chose not to answer his question. She was glad she didn't have the problem.

"Well, Brady," she said briskly, "if you're still interested in my offer, I'd like to meet with you in my office as soon as possible to see whether we can agree on a suitable arrangement."

There was another long silence. He must be checking his calendar, she decided. Juliet motioned to a man waiting for the phone, indicating that she wouldn't be much longer. She hoped Brady might be free sometime in the next few days. The contract was ready—all he had to do was sign it, and then ... And then, she thought, after Brady signed the contract ... Juliet shifted her weight uneasily. That part was still hazy in her mind. She realized she hadn't thought much about the period between finding the man and having the baby. But that would come later.

"Are you in your office?" Brady's abruptness startled her.

"Well, no, I had an errand—"

"Fine," he interrupted. "As long as you're out, you might as well come here. I'll be available in about half an hour."

"But I can't," Juliet protested. "I don't have the contract with me. And it doesn't have to be right away," she added quickly. "I was thinking perhaps later in the week." There was another pause. Juliet thought she heard him chuckle, but she couldn't be sure.

"I'm not sure we're quite at the contract stage yet. Do you have my office address with you?"

"Why, yes—"

"Good," he said, cutting her off. "I'll see you in a little while." Then he hung up.

Juliet stared at the silent phone. It would serve him right if she didn't show up. But inside, she knew she would.

THE BEGINNINGS OF afternoon rush hour had already clogged the streets, which made the cab ride to the Jackson Square renovation district take twice as long as it should have. The delay gave Juliet that much longer to question why she was going to Brady's office in the first place. The cab wound along a route lined with sycamore trees and past old, restored buildings that were a pocket of the past in the middle of the city. When the cab pulled up in front of the address she had given the driver, Juliet found herself on a narrow sidewalk in front of a red brick colonial-style building with two shuttered win-

dows. The brass plaque on the front wall said Playspace, by
Talcott Enterprises.

She opened the door and stepped into a quiet showroom
where children's furniture was grouped in several softly lit display areas. The nursery caught her attention immediately. She
stood by a cradle, idly tracing the outline of a bright red teddy
bear on a quilt. She'd need a room like this soon. A sign on a
nearby dresser explained that every piece of furniture could be
disassembled and expanded, to grow with the child. As she
walked past the remaining rooms, she could visualize the
change table becoming part of a toy box and then an easel for
painting and ultimately part of a corner compartment that
housed both a stereo system and a computer center.

The whole concept was ingenious. She wondered whether it
was Brady's design. Juliet approached a receptionist sitting at
a desk on one side of the room. As soon as she gave her name,
the woman directed her to Brady's office, saying he would join
her shortly.

Juliet walked briskly up a flight of stairs and down the hall
to the third door on the right. She turned the knob hesitantly
and found herself frozen in the doorway of the strangest office
she had ever seen. In fact, it didn't look like an office at all. It
looked like a playground. There was color everywhere. A vast
expanse of bright green carpet—grass green, Juliet thought—
blended right into the flower garden stenciled on a wall painted
in the palest of sky blue. A brilliant red dome-shaped climber
dominated one corner of the room. Across from it was a series
of ramps and mazes, which appeared to have been built from
a combination of clear plastic tubing and flat multi-colored
panels. A collection of small airplanes, gliders, and intricate
kites hung from the ceiling. Enchanted, Juliet stepped inside
and put her briefcase down near the door.

For several moments, she didn't move. What kind of man
could call a place like this an office? Despite all the information Harry had given her, there was obviously a lot she still
didn't know about Brady Talcott. At the far end of the room
she spotted a desk and telephones and a small conference area
with chairs and a sofa—definite signs that someone worked
there. But it seemed like a token gesture in the midst of a fantasy.

Slowly, Juliet stepped farther into the room. Walking past an oversized drafting table strewn with drawings and designs, she bumped into a red miniature sports car poking out from behind the table leg. She reached out to touch it and then pulled back, startled when its lights flashed on.

Glancing over her shoulder to make sure no one was watching, she knelt down for a closer look at the car. It reminded her of a toy car she'd seen in a department store window when she was about ten. She'd really wanted that car. But by the time her birthday came, her father was gone and Cass would never have bought her anything like that. She picked up a small remote control that she found leaning against the table leg and curiously pushed a button.

The car doors all opened at once and a horn honked. Delighted, Juliet pushed another button. The car doors closed, the engine revved up, and the car took off, veering to the right and smashing head on into a table leg. "Damn," Juliet murmured. She laid the remote control on the floor and crawled under the table to retrieve the car.

Brady stopped near the doorway, his eyes following her every move. He knew she hadn't heard him come in. There was something very appealing about her in that position, he thought, as he watched her back out from under the table. The way her hips moved, swinging back and forth like that, was definitely sexy. Very sexy. Brady was in no hurry to announce his arrival.

Standing very still, he watched her pick up the remote control and push different buttons, making the car swerve back and forth across the room. There was a spontaneity about her he hadn't seen before. She looked almost fragile to him, not at all like the cool lady lawyer who had interviewed him the week before. His eyes swept across the soft curves beneath her yellow jersey dress and down her legs to her high-heeled pumps. He'd been right. She did have very nice legs. He'd thought she would.

"I see you like the car," he said casually, stepping into the room.

Juliet spun around. "What are you doing here?"

"It's my office," Brady grinned. "I don't usually knock."

"You startled me," Juliet admitted, laying the remote control on the table. "Besides, I don't understand all this. I thought you made children's furniture."

"I do," Brady affirmed. "But after my father died, I expanded the furniture line into a modular system—I assume you saw it on the way in—and now I'm adding toys." He loosened his tie. "Let me show you around."

Juliet shook her head. "Thank you, but I came to discuss business."

"And this is my business," Brady interrupted. He took two steps forward and placed his hands firmly on her shoulders. "Adults are allowed to play, too, you know."

Juliet looked up to find Brady's eyes as warm as his hands. He wasn't laughing at her, she decided, and her body relaxed in the firm pressure of his grip. "This is all foreign to me," she admitted. "I didn't have toys when I was a little girl. My mother doesn't believe in them."

"Doesn't believe in them?" Brady let go of her shoulders. "How can anyone not believe in toys?"

"She doesn't believe in commercial toys," Juliet explained. "Cass thinks children should create their own fun." Juliet could see that he didn't understand at all, but she always had trouble when she tried to explain Cass's theories.

"Cass is your mother?" Brady questioned.

Juliet nodded.

"And you call her by her given name?"

"Well, yes . . ." That obviously seemed odd to him, too, but she had always called her mother Cass.

Brady's rich, mellow laugh reminded Juliet of rare vintage wine. "My mother would faint dead away if I ever called her Amelia." He took Juliet's hand, his touch echoing through her. "Come on," he urged, leading her across the room. "It's time we caught up on your childhood."

"We have to discuss business," she protested, but his hand still covered hers and she walked beside him, realizing that she wanted to accept his invitation.

For the next two hours, Brady introduced Juliet to a world she'd read about and heard about, but never really experienced. They built ramps for the race car, adding bridges and jumps, and Brady produced two more racers along with a tank and a jeep. He found himself as caught up with Juliet as she was with the toys. The tough, self-assured lawyer was suddenly only a cardboard character compared with the intense, vibrant woman underneath. He wanted to know her better.

"Did you really design all of this yourself?" Juliet asked him.

"Just about," Brady answered.

Juliet spread her full skirt around her knees to sit cross-legged on the floor. "You must know little kids pretty well," she told Brady.

"I spent a lot of time with my sister's kids when they were growing up," Brady explained. "I had trouble finding them toys that were fun for more than an afternoon, so I began trying some ideas of my own."

"Do you give them new toys to try out?" Juliet asked him.

"They're too old, now," Brady explained. "But I have a friend living near me with a couple of little boys. They're my official toy testers." Brady watched as Juliet finished building a miniature drawbridge. "You can attach a remote control to that you know." He dropped to his knees beside her, and reached around her to help her secure a connection that would raise the bridge.

With Brady's arms around her, his hands guiding hers, Juliet found it harder and harder to concentrate on what she was doing. He told her step by step how to attach the motor, his warm breath grazing her cheek as he talked. When she finally tried to make the bridge work, it lurched forward, and she convulsed in laughter, leaning back against Brady's chest.

"First drawbridge I ever saw designed to reach out and smack the adversary," he said, laughing with her as his arms tightened around her.

It was a brief embrace and yet it sent Juliet's pulse pounding with the speed of the race cars. She was struck by how easily and naturally she fit into the circle of his arms. He released her, leaving one arm lightly across her shoulders, and moved beside her. She met his eyes, uneasy with what she saw there and even more unsure about her own emotions. But he only smiled and said softly, "You're fun to be with, Juliet." Before she could answer, he squeezed her shoulders lightly and stood up.

Juliet watched his every move. He'd taken off his suit coat and tie and unbuttoned his shirt at the neck. There was something casual and almost familiar about the way he looked, the way he moved. It would be hard not to like him.

"I'll bet you're as hungry as I am," he said, striding across the office and picking up the phone.

"Hungry?" Juliet glanced quickly at her watch. The afternoon was gone. She wasn't quite sure how she'd lost track of time. "I had no idea it was getting so late—" she began, but he motioned for her to be quiet and said a few words into the phone.

Very shortly, Brady was opening the top of a pizza box and Juliet was jabbing straws through the lids of two soft-drink cups. He sat close to her, his knee resting against her thigh. He was pleased when she didn't move away.

"We still have some business to discuss," she reminded him, swallowing a bite of pizza. "Even though I don't have a copy of the contract, I thought we might review the provisions and see whether you have any requirements that aren't included."

He listened, fascinated. She was back to being the consummate lawyer again. He felt her muscles tense as she gathered together her image. Even her speech pattern changed. "You realize this plan of yours doesn't make a whole lot of sense," he said, baiting her.

"It makes perfect sense," she countered. "I thought we straightened that out last week."

He watched her drink her Coke, making hollows in her cheeks as she sucked in through the straw. Her eyelashes were lowered, her thick auburn hair held lightly back from her face with clips. It wasn't just her plan—she didn't make sense, either. "What if a man came along and suggested marriage?" he asked her. "Wouldn't that be a better arrangement?" It was a trial balloon. He waited for her reaction.

"Marriage?" Her eyes, a darker green than before, were hard with determination when she looked up. He could see this wasn't going to be easy.

"I've already told you how I feel about marriage. It tears people apart and makes them hate each other. I see it every day, every time a new client walks through the door."

Maybe he shouldn't mention the marriage arrangement just yet. "You sound pretty set in your opinion," he observed.

Juliet wadded her napkin into a tight ball and dropped it on the empty pizza carton. "When people get married, they make a commitment that's supposed to be for a lifetime and, as often as not, they turn around and walk out on it. I don't want any part of that kind of hypocrisy."

Brady stared at her, thinking about Phil and Eileen and what an apt description that was of their marriage. He wondered how much pain Juliet had seen to make her so bitter—and how much of it had been personal. At the same time, her objections to marriage wouldn't necessarily get in his way. What he wanted was a short-term arrangement. There would be no commitment involved. "You've apparently given this a lot of thought," he said noncommittally.

"I have," she concurred. She didn't like the direction of the discussion. He kept going back to marriage for some reason she couldn't fathom, and that was totally beside the point. Juliet glanced up at the clock over the fireplace. "It's getting late, and I really need to go." She moved forward on the couch. "Why don't I mail you a copy of the contract? That will give you time to go over it, and you can let me know if you have any problems."

"That'll be fine," Brady agreed. Already he was anxious to see her again.

"Do you mind if I use your phone to call a cab?"

"A cab won't be necessary," he told her, pressing one of a series of buttons on a small control board in the center of the table. "I'll send my driver with you. I'd take you myself, except I have to review a project before tomorrow morning."

As Juliet approached the office door, Brady moved in front of her. Swiftly he pulled her toward him and bent his head down to kiss her. When her arms stretched up around his neck, he let his mouth linger until her lips softened and parted. He touched her hair, wishing he could loosen the clips so it would cascade freely down her back. Instead, he pressed her tightly against him, reluctant to let her go.

But at that moment Juliet pulled away. Shaken, she leaned over to pick up her briefcase which sat unopened where she had left it, by the office door.

"Thank you for the afternoon, Juliet," he said hoarsely.

She looked back but didn't meet his eyes. "Good night, Brady," she responded quickly. She didn't know how else to answer him. Nothing that had happened was the way she'd planned. And when he'd kissed her, her whole being had trembled. She'd never dreamed she would respond to him that way. It left her unsettled and very unsure about what lay ahead.

Brady watched her walk through the lit showroom and disappear in the darkness beyond. "Juliet Cavanaugh," he said softly into the silence, "you're quite a woman." With a satisfied smile, he walked slowly toward his desk. He had a feeling this was going to work. In a few more months he would have met the terms of the trust, and Talcott Enterprises would be solely his. But the thrill of impending victory was brief, dimmed by the lingering image of the woman who had just left him.

CHAPTER FOUR

MEETINGS KEPT BRADY in the city all week and it was Saturday before he could get home to his beach house near Half Moon Bay. As he loped along the sand, watching the gulls on his way to see Phil and the boys, he shot a longing glance across the calm ocean. He and Phil had been planning to take Phil's Boston Whaler out to fish for longfins. Even though it was early in the season, the weather had been warm and there were reports of catches close in.

But that was before Timmy came down with the chicken pox. Phil had been at home taking care of him all week. Turning up the sandy slope toward Phil's house, Brady checked his jacket pocket one more time. Inside was the contract Juliet had sent him. That was the real reason he was going to see Phil. He'd been waiting impatiently, knowing he had to put together a proposal of his own before he could see her again. He was counting on Phil taking time to assist him right away.

In the other pocket, he had a new black racing car for Timmy and the motor Michael wanted. He always tried to take the kids something. It had been rough for the boys since their mother had left. Brady slowed to a walk. He still couldn't quite figure out what had happened between Phil and Eileen. They had always seemed like the perfect couple—happy, in love, two great kids. But after Eileen started drinking it was all downhill until she left. He supposed seeing that kind of thing was what had made Juliet so bitter about marriage.

"Brady, Brady," came the yell from above him, and Brady braced himself to catch a bundle of seven-year-old enthusiasm that plunged over the deck rail and into his arms. "Timmy's got the chicken pox and he looks really awful," Michael announced with a big grin as Brady set him on the sand. "Did you bring my motor?"

"Sure did." Brady reached into his pocket. He was glad he hadn't forgotten. "I want you to try this with all the hookups and let me know whether it works better than the old one," he directed solemnly.

"You bet!" He grabbed Brady's hand. "You gotta see Timmy. But Dad says we can't laugh when we look at him," Michael added, looking very important. "It'll be hard because he looks really funny all covered with spots."

They found Phil in the kitchen stirring a pan of beef-a-roni. "Brady—just in time for lunch," he offered, pleased at the promise of adult company. He was beginning to understand some of the complaints he used to get from Eileen.

Michael stuck out his tongue as soon as he smelled the food. "Yuk!" he exclaimed, and went off to try the motor.

"Looks like you've had a long week," Brady sympathized.

"That's an understatement." Phil dished some beef-a-roni into a bowl. "As long as Timmy's got the chicken pox, Mrs. Campanelli won't come near him because she's afraid she'll get shingles." It made him realize how much he depended on the motherly Italian woman who had been his salvation since Eileen had left.

"So that's why you haven't been in the office all week." Brady wondered if Juliet had given any thought to the dependency of single parents on their nannies.

"Did you come to look at me?" inquired a muffled voice. A small figure with a tattered blue blanket wrapped around his head tugged at Brady's sleeve.

Brady knelt down and gently unwrapped the blanket. "No way, Timmy. I just came to say hello."

"Then how come you're looking at me?" Timmy demanded.

Brady stifled a grin and took the racer out of his pocket. "Because I want to see if you like your new car." Michael had been right. His brother did look funny.

Suspiciously, Timmy took the car from Brady's outstretched hand and examined it. "Am I testing it for you?"

"I'd like it if you would," Brady answered.

"All right." Timmy's face was serious. "But it better be stronger than the last one, because that one broke." Hiking up his blanket, Timmy started for the stairs.

"Take your lunch with you," Phil called after him, handing him a bowl. "Can I give you some?" he asked Brady.

"Thanks, but I've already eaten lunch. I've got something I'd like you to take care of for me, unless you've got your hands full here...." He didn't want to push Phil, but he was already impatient. Until he had the contract ready to go, he couldn't very well call Juliet.

"No problem," Phil assured him. "Come on into the study." He was glad Brady had business that needed attention. After a whole week with the kids, it would be a relief to do some legal work. "Really sorry about the fishing," Phil apologized, opening the door to his study. "A fella down the way came in with some nice ones yesterday."

"They'll be around for a while," Brady said conversationally. He stepped carefully around a tipsy block construction Timmy had apparently been working on. He always smiled when he walked into Phil's study. When Eileen had been there, it had been Phil's domain, a haven of books and leather and rich stained wood. But in the year since she'd left, a lot had changed. Now a painted rock held down papers on the old roll-top desk, and the boys' drawings were taped to the glass front of the barrister's cabinet. The floor was littered with toys.

"Sorry about the mess. Timmy's been in here a lot this week," Phil explained.

Not answering, Brady walked over to the antique walnut chest under the window and looked at the grouping of pictures: one each of the children and a picture of Eileen, her blonde hair tousled and her lips pursed in determination as she held out the biggest fish she'd ever caught.

"Have you heard from her lately?" Brady asked, staring at the snapshot.

"Not since I got all those calls a couple of months ago when she was in such bad shape," Phil answered. He didn't add that he'd been trying to find her without any luck. He'd tracked her to a restaurant in the Tenderloin district where she'd worked as a waitress for a while, but they'd told her she left no forwarding address when she quit. It seemed futile after so long. But now that the anger was over with, he couldn't help but think about what might have happened to her.

"Why don't you put the picture away, Phil?" Brady asked "Having it out only makes things harder."

"I suppose I should," Phil agreed. "But the kids would mis it. They keep hoping she'll come back."

"And you?" Brady asked bluntly.

Phil sat heavily in one of the twin leather chairs. "That's tough question," he answered noncommittally. For some rea son he wanted Eileen's picture there on the walnut chest whe it had always been, and he didn't want to have to think abou why.

"I guess when you love somebody, it doesn't go away," Brady mused.

"No," Phil answered sadly, "it doesn't. You can hate wha they've done. Sometimes you even hate them. But then the are other times—" Phil stared thoughtfully at the picture. Thei lives had been such a mess before Eileen left that he didn't se how they could ever work things out. He didn't even know i he wanted her back—certainly not the way she was now. But at the same time, he couldn't quite give her up.

Brady stared out the window at the deserted beach. "Whei you love," he said, half to himself, "you give a part of your self to the person, and you don't get it back." He thought abou the two women he'd loved. Both had faded into bitterswee memories, and yet a part of him belonged to each of them and he supposed, a part of both of them would always stay witl him.

Brady leaned over to gather up a handful of crayons from th chair before he sat down. He could understand why, even afte all this time, it was still hard for Phil to talk about Eileen. Sh was gone, but she was still a part of his life.

Turning away from Eileen's picture, Phil deliberatel changed the subject. "Now," he said, looking at Brady, "wha can I do for you?"

"You can draw me up an agreement," Brady answered, set tling back in the chair.

"More hassle over those patents?" Phil asked.

"Nope," Brady told him. "Remember that ad I showed yo in the *Bay City Magazine*?" He didn't have to say any more Phil snapped to attention.

"You mean the broad who wants the baby?" When he hadn't heard any more about it, he'd thought Brady had lost interest. "Dammit, Brady! You're an ass to get involved in some fool scheme—"

"She may be someone you know," Brady continued, watching Phil carefully. "Her name is Juliet Cavanaugh." The significance of the name registered slowly. Brady listened to the old oak wall clock tick away in the silence.

"Juliet Cavanaugh?" Phil repeated. "The divorce lawyer?"

"You've got it," Brady grinned.

Phil shook his head. "No way. There has to be some mistake." Phil didn't know Juliet very well, but he knew what she looked like, and that was enough. No woman with a body like that had to advertise for a man. "She's probably working for some dame who—"

"Wrong," Brady interrupted. "I asked her about that. She's on the level. She wants a baby, but she doesn't want to get married. She figures this is the way to go."

Phil scratched his head. "Well, I'll be damned." He had to admit that changed the picture, but not much. "She's not going to be a hell of a lot of help to you if she doesn't want to get married," he observed.

"That depends," Brady said, reaching into his pocket, "on how clever you are and how persuasive I am." He handed Juliet's contract to Phil. "She's got all her terms spelled out in there. Take a look."

As Phil flipped through the document, Timmy appeared, still dragging his blanket, and without a word crawled up on his father's lap. Phil instinctively patted him as the little boy wrapped his blanket around his head again and stuck his thumb in his mouth, his eyes drooping. Phil went right on reading the contract, running his finger along the margin as he went. "If I hadn't read it, I wouldn't believe it," he muttered.

"What I want you to do," Brady directed, "is to include all that stuff of hers but add in that we have to be legally married for six months. After that point, either party can terminate the marriage without objections from the other."

Phil leaned back, shaking his head. "And that will get you past your birthday and give you full control of Talcott Enter-

prises." He could see Brady's rationale. He could also see the
pitfalls. "Pretty clever, buddy, except for a couple of loose
ends."

"Like what?" Brady challenged. He'd figured on getting an
argument.

"Like it will never hold up in court."

Brady grinned. That was the least of his worries. "It won't
have to. Juliet won't challenge it—she hates the whole idea of
marriage. It's nothing but a statement of intent."

"Then let's try something a little heavier." Phil tucked the
blanket around the sleeping child on his lap. "How are you
going to just walk away from your baby? Could you go off and
leave Timmy if he were yours?"

"I'll never see the baby," Brady retorted, more sharply than
he'd intended. Phil knew him pretty well, Brady realized. He
looked at Timmy—the dark hair, the round face, the surprisingly square chin—all of it so much like his father. What would
a child of his look like? Brady wondered. Maybe some day he'd
find out. But not this time. This time, he reminded himself, it
would never be real, because he would never see the baby. He'd
have to make damn sure he didn't.

Phil sat silent for a moment, giving his friend time to think.
He knew Brady wasn't as sure of himself as he'd like to appear. He also knew never seeing the baby wasn't the only potential problem. "Now that we know who the woman is," he
added, looking Brady in the eye, "there's another consideration. What if you fall in love with her? She's made it clear she
wants no strings attached."

That had never occurred to Brady. "Falling in love has
nothing to do with this. I'll admit she's damn attractive, but so
are a lot of other women. Hell, if I were in love with another
attractive woman, I'd marry her and I wouldn't have to do
this."

Phil looked skeptical, but he didn't answer.

"Look," Brady said, "she needs me for the baby and I need
to marry her to satisfy the terms of the trust. It's a trade-off.
That's all. Love doesn't come into it."

Standing up along with Brady, Phil shook his head. "For
your sake, buddy, I sure hope you're right. You could pay a hell
of a high price." He wished there were something more he

could say to stop Brady from going ahead with the scheme. Phil watched him leave, knowing that what he needed was a real wife, someone who loved him and wanted to have a family the normal way.

After reading over a few paragraphs in the contract, Phil tossed it onto his desk. Damn! Marriage was hard enough without starting out with a load of bricks tied to your back. Maybe that's what had happened to him and Eileen. The bricks had been too heavy—especially for her. They'd been too young, had kids so soon. He stared at Eileen's picture on the chest. Everybody, even Brady, thought the crazy smile on her face was because she was holding the biggest fish she had ever caught. That wasn't the reason at all. She was lit up with happiness because she was pregnant with Michael. It was their anniversary and she had been saving the news as a present. It was the best present she'd ever given him.

Everything had been so good then, Phil thought bitterly. Why the hell couldn't it be like that anymore? That's all he wanted, just Eileen and the kids. Screw the house, the boat, the club, even the law practice. He'd give it all up for life the way it used to be.

"Mommy?" Timmy's eyes fluttered and his thumb dropped from his mouth.

"Mommy's not here right now," Phil gently reminded him. It hurt him to have to say the words. Timmy had asked for her so many times while he'd been sick.

"Is she coming back pretty soon?" Timmy's voice was sleepy and distant.

"I don't know," Phil answered. He looked at Eileen's picture again. They'd sure as hell messed things up. If Brady thought he could do better with that half-assed plan of his, let him try.

MONDAY MORNING Phil sent a contract by messenger to Brady's office with a note clipped to the top. It read: "You sure are a stubborn bastard. Best of luck, Phil."

Brady laughed out loud and reached for the phone. It was time to get together with Juliet. After several rings, her secretary answered only to inform him that Ms Cavanaugh was in court and wouldn't be back for at least an hour. He questioned the secretary closely and, over her objections, he left a cryptic message for Juliet and hung up.

When Juliet returned from the courthouse, she found Linda sitting at Alice's desk eating a carry-out sandwich from the deli. "Stop," Juliet protested. "This is your first day back to work, and I'm taking you to lunch, remember?"

"Wrong," Linda said, taking a drink of her Coke. "You have other plans."

"What do you mean?" Juliet set down her briefcase and loosened the belt on her raincoat.

"Alice took the call just before she left," Linda explained, handing Juliet the top sheet from a sheaf of phone messages.

Juliet looked down at the yellow memo. "Union Square. Noon. The bench on the north side by the pine tree. Bring your pen. Brady."

It was the message she'd been waiting for. The news brought a heady exhilaration and, right on its heels, a surge of panic. He was going to do it. For some reason Juliet couldn't discern, Brady Talcott had gone beyond curiosity, overcome his reservations, and was about to sign a contract agreeing to father her baby. She was going to be a mother! Juliet was aware she was still staring at the memo, and Linda was grinning at her.

"Got cold feet all of a sudden?" Linda teased.

"Of course not," Juliet responded. "Except I guess I didn't think he'd really do it."

"I've got a funny feeling you kind of like him," Linda probed. "From what you told me, and from the stuff Harry gave you, he sounds like quite a guy. Just one question—why does he want to meet in the park on a day like this?"

Juliet glanced out the window at the murky fog. "I have no idea." She picked up the memo and read it one more time.

"I've also got a feeling you're pretty undone about this," Linda observed. "Your hands are even shaking."

"Yours would, too, if you were about to become a mother," Juliet said defensively.

Linda munched on a potato chip. "Speaking of mothers, what did Cass say when you told her?"

"Cass?" Juliet looked blank.

"Cass—you know, your mother. What did she say about your having a baby?" Linda shook her head. "Boy, are you out of it today."

"I am not. I was just deciding whether to walk or take a cable car," Juliet declared. "Besides, I haven't mentioned it to Cass yet—the opportunity hasn't come up."

"I see," Linda answered. "Maybe you ought to walk to Union Square. The fresh air might bring you back to reality."

"I'm going to ignore that," Juliet retorted. But she slipped out of her brown pumps and shoved her feet into a pair of well-worn running shoes. Pulling her raincoat snugly around her green wool dress, Juliet automatically reached for her briefcase before she realized she wouldn't need it. Brady had the contract, which was all that was necessary. Actually, she thought, there wasn't any reason to take a purse, either.

"Anything I can take care of while you're gone?" Linda offered.

"Nothing on the book till four o'clock," Juliet told her.

Linda finished her Coke and dropped the paper cup into the wastebasket. "Oh, I almost forgot—there was a blond woman here to see you," she told Juliet. "I told her I expected you any minute, but she wouldn't wait. She didn't leave her name."

"About our height, thin, short hair?" Juliet questioned.

Linda nodded.

"She's been here before. Don't worry about it. She'll probably come back." Juliet tightened the belt on her raincoat. "By the way," she added, "you might go through those folders I left on my desk. Another week and the doorway should be finished so you'll have your own office."

"Then maybe I'll really feel like a lawyer again," Linda answered, laughing.

"Sorry about the lunch," Juliet called over her shoulder as she headed for the elevator.

"No problem," Linda answered.

Once out of the building, Juliet walked steadily, and within a few minutes she was glad to be outdoors. The exercise was invigorating and the fresh air felt good. She didn't even mind the heavy fog that clung to her skin. As she approached Union Square Park, the wind picked up from behind her and whipped her hair around her face. With a laugh, she turned and walked backward until the long, auburn locks blew back into place and she could tuck them deep inside her collar for protection. When she turned frontward again, she realized she hadn't done that since she was a little girl.

Her pace picked up as she got closer. Meeting outside on a day like this was objectively a dumb thing to do, but the idea was growing on her. There wasn't any need to be indoors for what they had to do—just a quick signature. Maybe they would talk for a while afterward or go to lunch, sort of get better acquainted before they set up their meetings. But they should take care of the business first, she decided, before they did anything else.

As soon as she rounded the corner, Juliet spotted Brady already sitting on the bench directly in front of a neatly trimmed pine tree, just as he had promised. Her purposeful stride slowed while she watched him feeding popcorn to a flock of noisy pigeons. His tie was loose, his jacket hung open, and his hair fell across his forehead as he leaned over to persuade a plump, gray pigeon to take a popcorn kernel from his fingers. *Business,* she reminded herself. *Stick to business.*

"Hi," he called, breaking into a grin when he saw her. He took her in all at once, the curve of her legs above the running shoes, the hair tucked into the collar of her tan coat, the flush in her cheeks that heightened the delicate cheekbones. Every time he saw her, she was more beautiful. He moved over to make room for her. "Come join me before the pigeons start roosting in your spot on the bench."

Making a conscious effort to control the spring in her step, Juliet approached him slowly. "You really have a following," she teased, shooing the pigeons aside so she could sit down.

"Just my magnetic personality—and my popcorn," he replied. "Have some?" he asked, offering the red-and-white box to Juliet.

"No thanks." Juliet shook her head. Despite her resolve to focus only on the contract, she couldn't help but notice he had a wonderful grin that deepened the cleft in his chin and crinkled the corners around his eyes. Suddenly, she was quaking inside. What was she doing? In a few minutes the contract would be signed and then, well, then what? She hadn't ever really considered the exact logistics before. She had just assumed that somehow everything would happen the way it should and in nine months—give or take a few weeks—she would produce a baby. Just exactly when, or where, or how the encounters would take place... That part was all a little vague. She was going to have to give some thought to the logistics.

Brady leaned over to feed a pigeon and his leg pressed more firmly against hers. Would they go to her apartment or his? she wondered. Would he take her to dinner? That wasn't in the contract, of course. Maybe he would expect her to take him to dinner. The pigeon waddled away and Brady sat back, his shoulder touching hers. She had to get a grip on herself. Everything would work itself out. First the contract.

"Did you bring it?" she asked, trying to sound casual.

"Bring what?" Brady emptied the last of the popcorn directly from the box into his mouth and tossed the empty box toward a trash can, scoring a direct hit.

Juliet took a deep breath. "The contract." Her stomach tightened and she began to feel uneasy. "The agreement for us to...um, ah..." Inexplicably she was at a loss for words.

"Oh, *that* contract." Brady sat up straight and pulled the papers from a pocket inside his jacket.

Relieved, Juliet took the document from him. "I assume you've signed this?"

That was the opening Brady had been waiting for. "Not yet. There's one more thing we have to add first."

Juliet frowned. "I expected you to contact me if you wanted changes. I suppose we can initial them if they aren't major."

"This one may require some discussion," Brady began. "You're entering into this agreement because you want a baby, right?"

Juliet nodded.

"Then it's only reasonable that you should make some concession to get what you want," Brady continued.

"What are you getting at?" Juliet asked skeptically. "If you're asking for more money—"

"We can forget the money entirely," Brady interrupted her. "I don't consider that a concession."

Juliet was growing more and more uneasy. He had lured her to the park with a message saying he was ready to sign the contract, and now he was hedging. She thought back to the exact words her secretary had written down. Actually all she'd said was "bring your pen."

"Exactly what is it you expect me to do?" Juliet demanded.

Brady looked directly into Juliet's eyes. "I want you to marry me."

For a few moments, the word "marry" stunned Juliet into silence. Then she sprang to her feet, positioning herself directly in front of Brady.

"We never discussed marriage as an option, and we're not going to now," she sputtered. "The contract stands as written. I'm hiring you to father my child. Take it or leave it."

Watching her calmly, Brady leaned forward, resting his hands on his knees. "Those are your terms. Now I've added mine," he asserted in a low voice. "If I'm going to father your child, I'm going to marry you first. If you'll sit down and listen for a minute, I'll explain why."

"You can explain anything you want to and it's not going to make a bit of difference." Juliet sat on the bench as far away from Brady as possible.

Brady went right on talking. "When my father died, he left Talcott Enterprises in trust, with me as the beneficiary," he told her. "My father was a real family man, and he wanted me to be the same way. As he got older, he got more and more domineering."

"I don't see what that has to do with this marriage arrangement you've concocted," Juliet declared.

"That's because I haven't told you yet." Brady brushed a stray popcorn kernel off his pants. "When my father wrote the trust agreement he put in a provision requiring that I be married by the age of thirty-five or the company would be sold and the proceeds go to some rather questionable charities."

"But you could fight that—" Juliet interrupted.

"And probably win," Brady added. "But in the meantime I could get tied up in litigation that would drag on for years."

"It's still an insane idea," Juliet argued. "If you think I'm going to marry you just because—"

"Actually, there's another thing to consider," Brady cut in. "Maybe you should think ahead. When the child grows up, wouldn't it be nice to be able to say you were married when he or she was born?" It was part of his preplanned argument, but the words came out with a conviction that surprised him.

Juliet hesitated. She'd never thought of it that way. "Times have changed," she asserted. "Marriage doesn't matter any more." She'd always believed that. She had to believe it. Otherwise, this wouldn't work.

Brady's voice was firm. "I don't care how much the world has changed. It's easier for a child who has a father—a legitimate father."

"And I suppose you would want it to have your name?"

Brady flinched. The idea appealed to him. But if he wasn't going to see the child, that was out of the question. "I don't care what name you give the baby," he answered. He hadn't meant to sound so harsh. He reached into his pocket and took out a neatly folded paper. "I had my lawyer prepare a contract that spells out our revised agreement."

Juliet knotted her fists, her green eyes blazing. "I'm not marrying you or anybody else," she announced evenly. The words barely out of her mouth, she wheeled around and took off down the sidewalk.

"There's a six-month escape clause written into the contract," Brady called after her. Juliet kept on walking, her back stiff and unyielding.

He realized she hadn't heard him. *Now she's mad as hell*, Brady thought. He settled back on the bench and pulled a crossword puzzle out of his coat pocket. Unless he missed his guess, Juliet would be back. But it might take a while.

By the time she turned the corner out of sight of Brady, Juliet was ready to explode. "Damn," she swore aloud. *I should have known he was after something. It was all too easy.* Too angry to even begin to sort the snarl of thoughts, she slowed her footsteps and tried to figure out what she was going to do next.

This is stupid, she lectured herself, realizing she had lost all perspective. What she had to do was take the overall objective, analyze the obstacles, and choose the best option. Same as any other problem. She looked for a place to sit down, but there wasn't a bench in sight. Perching herself on a fire hydrant, which was very uncomfortable, she managed to come up with a pencil stub from her coat pocket and began making notations on the back of an old grocery receipt.

Objective: Have a baby, as quickly and simply as possible.

Problem: Need a father

Solution: Advertise for one

Problem: Nearly 300 replies, ten possibles, but only one really desirable and he demands marriage

Solution:

Juliet scrawled "Damn!" across the sheet. The obvious solution was to accept his terms or find another father. She didn't want to do either one. Juliet shifted her weight, wishing she had found a bench to sit on, and then finally stood up. She wasn't getting anywhere. She began to walk, idly, aimlessly, hands stuffed deep in her coat pockets. It had all seemed so simple until Brady came up with that stupid marriage demand, she thought, kicking at a clump of grass that grew up through a crack in the sidewalk. She scrunched her shoulders and buried her chin in her coat. The air was damp and heavy and the sky leaden, threatening rain.

Juliet shivered. She didn't want to start all over and find another father. Brady was prefect. She thought about him sitting on that bench feeding the pigeons, and about the light in his eyes when he looked up and saw her coming. There was no way she could talk him out of marriage and still get him to cooperate. That was his bottom line, just like having the baby was hers. Well, she thought, if she couldn't refuse his demand, maybe she could modify it. Suddenly Juliet stopped walking and turned on her heel. If she couldn't do this on her terms, she'd do it on his terms—but her way.

In long determined strides, she retraced her steps. Somehow she knew Brady would still be sitting right where she left him. But this time she was going to be in control.

"Hi," she called out to Brady, slowing to a normal pace.

"You're back," he observed, stating the obvious. It hadn't taken her as long as he'd thought it might, and everything about her told him she'd come to some decision.

"That's right," Juliet confirmed. "I'm back." She sat down on the bench next to him, but still as far away as possible.

"Are you ready to read my contract?" Brady asked, putting the crossword puzzle in his pocket and again offering her the papers.

"Not quite," Juliet responded. "I've considered your offer, and I've decided to negotiate."

"It doesn't seem to me there's much to negotiate where marriage is concerned," Brady noted. "You either do or you don't."

"Not quite," she corrected him. "If you expect me to make a concession and agree to marriage, then you can make an equal concession and agree to release me from the marriage at any time."

"Fine," he shrugged.

She stared at him. It was too easy.

"If what you're trying to say is that you want an escape clause, it's already in here," he noted mildly. "It applies equally to both parties."

"Why didn't you tell me all that in the first place?" Juliet demanded.

"I tried to tell you." Brady broke into a grin. "But you stalked off." He laid his contract gently in Juliet's lap. "Maybe you should read this before we discuss it further?"

Juliet slowly picked up the papers and began to read. She wondered if the churning inside her was because he seemed to have the best of her—again. She suspected that wasn't the only reason. If he insisted on marriage, an escape clause was obviously the only sensible approach. But she'd liked it better when it was her idea.

After studying the contract carefully, Juliet had to admit it was simple, to the point and scrupulously fair. It spelled out that after six months either one of them could dissolve the marriage. But the whole thing didn't make sense. She knew she should take a few days to think it over. Instead she turned toward Brady. "Do you have a pen?"

"Sure thing." Quickly he reached in his pocket. He'd won. She was going along with it. He was about to get what he'd gone after, and for an instant he wasn't sure he wanted it. Phil's warning echoed in his ears: *You could pay a hell of a high price.* He handed Juliet the pen.

Within moments the document was signed in duplicate and Juliet was folding one copy to put in her pocket. "Well, that should do it," Juliet said awkwardly. She stood up and extended her hand.

Brady rose quickly to his feet. "Right," he agreed. He shook her hand. What an inane way to seal a marriage proposal, he thought to himself.

"Then I guess that's it." Juliet patted the pocket that held the contract. "I'm tied up in court next week, but my calendar is reasonable after that. Phone me when you've set the wedding date." She started to walk away.

Suddenly he couldn't let her go, not like that. "Juliet!" Brady's hand was on her shoulder, turning her around. "We forgot something else." He gave her no time to think, his lips closing over hers as he pulled her to him. They were alone in the mist, the intimacy of their mouths at odds with the awkwardness of the agreement that separated them. Her lips were incredibly sweet, and Brady sensed the fleeting promise of something that might have been.

He held her very tight before he slowly released her. Juliet didn't want him to let her go. She was frightened by what lay ahead, overwhelmed by the scope of the commitment they'd just made. For those few brief moments they shared the immensity of what they had done, but when she walked away, she'd be on her own.

"I'll phone you, Juliet." She heard the uncertainty in his voice. Then he turned on his heel and disappeared into the mist.

OVER THE NEXT FEW DAYS, Juliet persuaded herself that their compromise was actually quite reasonable. She would have her baby—not exactly the way she'd planned—but the marriage would be only a brief inconvenience. And maybe Brady did have a point about legitimacy. She could decide later how to discuss its father with the child. At least this gave her another option. When Linda called to see how things had gone with Brady, Juliet told her they'd signed the contract, but she didn't mention the marriage provision. She decided she'd explain that part the next time she saw her.

It wasn't until Juliet found herself standing at the door of her mother's art studio in Sausalito that her confidence wavered.

She couldn't quite put her finger on the problem. Cass was a free spirit if there ever was one, accepting of nearly everything. Juliet had intended from the very beginning to discuss the plan for a baby with her, but she kept waiting for the right moment. Now she didn't have any choice. If she was going to be married, her mother had to know. She opened the door slowly, with a gnawing feeling that dealing with Cass on this one was going to be a little tricky.

"Juliet?" Her mother's red head popped up from behind her easel. "Come give me a hug—but don't spill the turpentine. Why didn't you phone and tell me you were coming?"

"So you could stop your work and break out the silver tea service?" Juliet teased. Relishing the familiar smell of paint, she leaned carefully around the easel and gave her mother an affectionate squeeze.

"Silver tea service, my foot," laughed Cass. "I've never owned a silver tea service in my life. Besides, if I don't get these illustrations to the publisher pretty soon, he'll have the sheriff after me." She wiped her brush with a rag and stood it upside down in an old mayonnaise jar. "However," her face lit up, "I do have a brand new juicer. How about some fresh carrot juice?" Without waiting for an answer, Cass breezed into the kitchen, her paint-splotched smock billowing like a parachute around her wiry frame.

Juliet grimaced but followed along behind, ducking low to avoid the bundles of fragrant herbs drying over the kitchen door. Once she got the conversation rolling, she would ease into the subject of the baby and go from there, Juliet decided as she perched on a tall stool next to the butcher-block counter. Her mother would laugh and congratulate her. After all, Cass had been a single parent for most of Juliet's life. And once she got excited about the baby, she'd be able to take the marriage idea in stride. She'd understand why it had been necessary to compromise on the marriage as soon as she found out it was only temporary.

"Why did you drive all the way to Sausalito on a weekday afternoon?" Carrot in hand, Cass gazed intently at her daughter. "It must be bad news," she determined, raising her voice over the hum of the juicer. "My horoscope said this morning that—"

"No, it's not bad news," Juliet interrupted. She took a glass of carrot juice from her mother. As many times as she had rehearsed the speech, she couldn't seem to get into the opening statement.

"What is it then?" Cass prompted impatiently. She took a sip of her juice.

That's my cue, thought Juliet. She took a deep breath. "How would you like to be a grandmother?" she began. She knew immediately it was the wrong approach.

Her mother's eyes flew wide open and her mouth dropped. "My God," she whispered hoarsely. "You're pregnant. I knew it was bad news."

"Oh, no," Juliet reassured her. "No, no, not yet."

Cass heaved a deep sigh of relief.

"But I'm going to be," Juliet forged ahead. "Very soon, I hope."

Cass blinked several times and downed the rest of her carrot juice like it was a well-fortified martini. "Juliet," she said firmly, "you know I pride myself on being liberal—some people might say too liberal—but this tests my limits. Now, you start at the beginning and give me a full and complete explanation. Don't try to spare me. I am in excellent physical condition, and I want all the details."

Juliet felt a smile begin to cross her lips but quickly suppressed it. Maybe a marriage was going to be easier to explain than a baby, after all.

"All right," Juliet agreed. Setting her glass of carrot juice on the butcher block, she looked directly into her mother's worried eyes. "I'm going to get married." She paused to let the concept sink in. After all, she had been proclaiming for most of her life that she would absolutely never get married.

When she saw the slightest hint of a smile on her mother's face, she continued. "And then, I'm going to get pregnant as soon as I possibly can. I got a little ahead of myself with that part," she explained.

Her mother broke into a glowing smile. "Oh, I see," she babbled with great relief. "You're going to get married first and then have a baby. That's perfect. The wedding and then the baby. That's really the best approach." Cass was regaining her usual aplomb. "It's wonderful, Juliet," she exclaimed. "Ablutely wonderful. I can't imagine what was wrong with my oroscope."

Juliet's laugh was hollow, but her mother was too excited to otice. Underneath it all, Cass apparently wasn't the free inker she'd have people believe she was—at least where her wn daughter was concerned. Discussing the agreement she had ith Brady would be a terrible mistake, Juliet realized. In fact, e less said the better. It would be easier to just deal with the ivorce when it happened.

"Aren't you even going to ask me who I'm marrying?" Juet inquired.

"As long as you love him, dear, it doesn't matter," Cass reonded blissfully.

Juliet almost spilled her juice. This wasn't at all the kind of eaction she had expected from Cass. She had no idea what to y next, but Cass didn't seem to expect anything more.

"Now," her mother continued, "we have to make plans. here's a church, a place for the reception, flowers, invitaons, a photographer, and..." She reached out to Juliet and eld her close. "And a wedding gown," she finished in a reamy voice.

Juliet realized she would have to put a halt to that kind of inking immediately. "Cass," she said gently. "I'm not sure ow to break this to you, but I...er, we don't want a big weding. We're both really busy," she hurried on. "We need to eep it simple—there's not enough time for a big wedding."

"Not time for a big wedding? Juliet, you're my only daughr! What do you mean not enough time?"

Juliet had never considered having a problem like this with er mother, and she wasn't prepared. "Brady—that's his ame—Brady and I want to be married as soon as possible. I ave several important cases coming up and he's...well, he's usy, too, and can't take time from work. We thought we'd just ave a small ceremony in front of a judge."

"Juliet!" Her mother looked her square in the eye. "Are you re there isn't something you aren't telling me? This all sounds ther unusual. Very rushed. Are you sure you're not pregant?"

"Of course not, Cass," Juliet answered uncomfortably. he'd always been open with her mother, and she didn't like this

deception. "I just don't want to make a production out of
wedding."

Cass nodded knowingly. "I must remember I'm talking
the woman who vowed she would never get married under a
circumstances."

"That's right," Juliet answered.

"I'm really glad you've changed your mind," Cass sai
softly. "I've always worried that your father walking out an
leaving us had a permanent effect on you. And maybe it did—
maybe it made you wise enough to wait until you were sure."

Juliet swallowed hard. "You're probably right," she ma
aged to agree, momentarily overwhelmed with guilt. Then s
added quickly, "You've been as terrific as any other two pa
ents could have been. I was perfectly happy having a sing
parent."

"Raising a daughter is the most meaningful thing I've do
in my life," Cass told her, and Juliet looked away, seeing t
misting in Cass's eyes.

"Even more than winning the publishers' art award la
year?" Juliet tried to redirect the conversation and escape t
emotion.

But her mother remained serious. "It far surpasses that," s
answered, her voice unsteady. "Bringing a child into the wor
is an enormous responsibility, Juliet. And trying to raise a chi
alone and give it all the guidance and love by yourself..." Cass
voice broke and she hugged Juliet again. "I'm so glad you
have a man to share it with." She was speaking almost in
whisper. "I want so much for you to be happy."

Juliet froze. All these years she'd never known how Cass fe
never imagined that her mother felt doubt or uncertainty. Whe
she'd decided to have a baby, she'd been so sure of her mot
er's support. But Cass would never be able to accept what s
was doing. That didn't matter, she told herself. It was going
work.

"Now young lady..." Cass's tone changed, breaking t
tension between them. "Your nutritional habits will need si
nificant improvement if my grandchild is to arrive in robu
condition." She frowned dramatically and picked up Juliet
untouched glass. "Here," she directed, "drink your carr
juice."

"Mother," Juliet groaned, emptying the glass. She hated carrot juice.

"My name is Cass and has been all my life," her mother reminded her. "Now, let's discuss having this fiancé...Brady, you said his name was? Let's discuss having this Brady to dinner. Is Thursday a good night for both of you, and does he eat sushi?"

Juliet sighed. This was another one of those details she hadn't given much thought to, but she supposed—even if they were going to be married for only a few months—that Brady would have to meet Cass at some point. Thursday dinner was as good a time as any.

CHAPTER FIVE

JULIET WAS SHAKEN when she left her mother's. She thoug
she knew Cass. But it appeared that Cass's libertarian ide
applied to everyone else but her daughter. Regardless, Juli
reassured herself, Cass would be delighted when her gran
child was born. And it was the long term that mattered. T
immediate future wasn't all that important.

Except for one thing. Cass was planning to have them f
dinner Thursday night. That meant she needed to talk to Brad
as soon as possible. She didn't even know whether he'd acce
the invitation. Dinner with in-laws wasn't part of their agre
ment.

She followed the line of traffic around the ramp and nose
her Nissan into the center lane on the Golden Gate Bridge.
Brady hadn't insisted on marriage, none of this would ha
happened. She could have explained him away as an indiscr
tion. As it was, he would simply have to make some sacrifice
too.

Impulsively, she decided to drive by his office on her wa
home and invite him in person. It wasn't really all that muc
out of her way to go to Jackson Square. She changed lan
again, noticing that when she thought about seeing Brady, sh
started to feel a little better.

By the time she got to Talcott Enterprises it was late afte
noon, and Juliet was afraid Brady might already have left f
the day. She was sure of it when she walked in and found t
reception desk empty. Deciding to check Brady's office an
way, she walked hesitantly through the showroom and up t
stairs.

When Brady met her at his office door, looking enormous
happy to see her, a warm glow filled Juliet. She was instant
glad she'd come. He wrapped one arm around her shoulder

:aning down to give her a brief kiss on the lips. "Boy, am I
lad to see you," he told her. "You couldn't have come at a
etter time."

Juliet wanted to believe he'd missed her, and that he simply
ouldn't wait to be with her, but something didn't ring true. She
ooked at him more closely. His shirt sleeves were rolled up, his
e was askew, and he was carrying a bottle of calamine lotion
 his hand.

"I've got a big favor to ask—"

"That's funny," Juliet interrupted. "That was going to be
y opening line."

"I beat you to it." Impatiently, Brady checked his watch.
What do you know about chicken pox?"

Juliet frowned at the bottle of calamine. "A little bit," she
nswered suspiciously.

"Great! Then you can stay with Michael while I catch the last
alf of an important meeting." Brady was already rolling down
is sleeves.

"Wait a minute!" Juliet didn't like the sound of this.
Who's Michael?"

Brady rapidly buttoned his cuffs. "A seven-year-old buddy
f mine who's staying with me because his father's in court to-
ay. Here, hold this." He thrust the calamine into her hand and
traightened his tie. "You'll need it. Michael caught the chicken
ox from his brother. But he's not contagious anymore—he's
ll scabbed over."

"Brady!" Juliet brandished the calamine. "I didn't come to
aby-sit with—"

"Sh-h-h." Brady glanced over his shoulder. "I need you."
Ie was already walking back into the office. "Come meet
im." Reluctantly, Juliet followed Brady. She felt herself be-
ig railroaded.

A loft bed had been attached to standards on the wall near
he dome climber, and as they approached, Juliet saw a small
igure almost lost in a tangle of sheets and blankets.

"Michael, I want you to meet Juliet," Brady said cheer-
ully. "She's going to stay with you while I go to a meeting."

Michael looked at her with obvious hostility. "I don't want
er to stay with me. I want you." He kicked the sheet off en-
irely.

"I won't be long," Brady promised, putting on his suit coa
"And your dad will be here soon." He leaned close to the bo
"Juliet's okay," he confided. "She's my friend."

Michael didn't answer.

"Be back as soon as I can," Brady called over his shoulde
and Michael and Juliet were left alone.

Michael turned toward the wall. Juliet considered telling hi
she wasn't any happier about the situation than he was. N
wonder Brady had been glad to see her. He'd have been glad
see anyone who could take over this job. Michael squirme
uncomfortably. "Have you had the chicken pox long?" sh
asked, for lack of anything else to say.

"Forever," he answered glumly.

"It probably seems that way," Juliet observed. She looke
at the boy more closely. He lay on his back on the bed, starin
at the ceiling, his hands rubbing his pajama shirt rough
against his stomach. His face, his neck, his feet—every e
posed inch of skin was covered with spots. Judging from th
pink streaks of lotion in his short blond hair, he probably ha
scabs on his scalp, too. He was obviously miserable.

Juliet began to feel more sympathetic. "Do you itch a lot?

"Everywhere." For the first time since they'd been alone, h
looked at her, the startling blue eyes still skeptical. "Brady p
calamine on me," he added pointedly.

Juliet hesitated. "Would you like me to do that?" She didn
really want to touch him, but he looked so unhappy she o
fered anyway.

"I suppose," he muttered.

Determined to at least give it a try, Juliet took off her line
suit jacket and rolled up the sleeves of her green silk blous
thinking that she'd have dressed differently if she'd know
about this. She uncapped the bottle. "Where do you want n
to start?"

"My feet. They itch really bad." Juliet dabbed some cal
mine on her finger and began rubbing it gently on the botto
of Michael's left foot, trying not to recoil as her fingers move
across the rough scabs. "Yeah, right there," he encouraged he

She liked making him feel better. "Mr. Talcott said yo
name is Michael. What's your last name?" Juliet dabbed o
more calamine, thinking about Brady. He owed her one f

this. There wouldn't be any way he could turn down dinner with Cass.

"My name is Michael Allen Gentry. And I don't call him Mr. Talcott. I call him Brady. I work for him," the boy added proudly.

Then Juliet remembered. "You must be one of the toy testers Brady told me about."

"Yeah, me and Timmy. He's my brother, but he's too little to be much good. He's the one who gave me the chicken pox." The boy wiggled uncomfortably. "Can't you hurry up? You're still on the same foot."

"This method isn't very efficient," Juliet admitted. At this rate it was going to take her all afternoon to coat his spots. There had to be a better approach. "Maybe if I can find you something to do...." Looking around the office, she saw some brushes and paints in one of Brady's open shelves. "I've got it!" she exclaimed.

"Just hurry up," Michael pleaded.

Juliet dumped the paper clips out of a ceramic box on Brady's desk, wiped it clean with tissue and filled it with calamine lotion. Then she grabbed the biggest paint brush she could find and went to work on Michael's other foot.

"Hey, what are you doing?" he demanded, half sitting up.

"I'm painting you." Juliet ignored the lotion that dribbled on the sheet. "Pull up your pants legs."

Michael appraised her with new admiration. "Even Brady didn't think of that."

Since when was he the ideal? she asked herself. It made Juliet feel good that she was the one who'd come up with a better method. In a funny way, it restored some of the confidence Cass had shaken. She would be able to take care of her own child, just as she was able to take care of Michael. Juliet quickly painted him with calamine, feeling his muscles relax as she worked. He dipped his own fingers in the bowl and rubbed them on his scalp. She finished the job with a flourish of the brush on his chest. "There, does that feel better?"

His eyes were no longer angry. "A whole lot," he said gratefully.

No longer apprehensive about touching him, Juliet patted him on the shoulder. She liked Michael. "Maybe I could read to you," she offered, "if I can find a book."

He watched her search through the shelves. "My mom used to read to me."

"She doesn't anymore?"

"Nope."

Juliet absently continued the conversation. "Why did she stop?"

"She's gone."

No emotion. Just a statement of fact. Juliet began to pay attention. "Is she coming back?"

"Daddy says maybe someday."

Juliet's heart went out to him. She remembered the loneliness after her own father left. It was worst of all when she was sick. "I found a book," she told him, pulling a chair up near the bed. "Has anyone read you *The Lion, the Witch, and the Wardrobe*?"

"Never heard of it. Does it have detectives?"

"No, but it has a witch who turns living creatures into stone. It was written by C. S. Lewis," she added. "He was my favorite author when I was a little girl."

Michael didn't comment, and so Juliet began to read. She had just finished the second chapter when she hard an unfamiliar voice behind her. "Michael?"

"Daddy!" Michael sat up and held out his arms. Stepping around Juliet, the man leaned over to hug his son. She could sense the bond between them. Even as they talked, the boy was still clinging to him. Even if Michael didn't have a mother around, he obviously had one parent who cared.

When the man turned back toward Juliet, their eyes widened in mutual recognition. "Phil Gentry!" she exclaimed in surprise. He had the same brilliant blue eyes as his son.

"Juliet, what are you doing here?"

"She's a friend of Brady's," Michael answered for her. "She painted me all over with calamine lotion and she's reading me a neat book."

"Juliet, I really appreciate this...." He hadn't seen her for months, and than only in passing at the courthouse and at occasional bar meetings. She was more beautiful than he remembered, and he knew by looking at her that his gut reaction had been right. Brady was playing with fire.

"Brady had to go to a meeting, so I stayed with Michael," Juliet explained. "We had a good afternoon," she added, almost surprised to realize that they really had. "I'm sure Brady won't mind if you take the book we were reading—"

"And the paintbrush," Michael interjected.

"And the paintbrush," Phil agreed. "Where'd you learn about that?" he asked Juliet curiously.

She shrugged. "Necessity sparks lots of new approaches."

Right, thought Phil, *and doubly right where you're concerned.*

Once they were gone, Juliet wiped the calamine lotion out of the ceramic dish and replaced the paper clips. She wandered around the office, impatient for Brady to come back. She found herself thinking about Michael and about the kind of man who would offer to keep a sick child in his office all day. She liked the things she was learning about Brady. She was walking over to the bed which was still in a tangle, when she heard his voice.

"Juliet, great, you're still here." Brady burst into the room. "Where's Michael?"

"His father picked him up," she explained, turning toward Brady with a smile.

Brady pulled off his suit coat and tie, watching her straighten the sheets on the bed. "I'll bet Phil looked harried. This is the second time around with the chicken pox." Brady dropped his coat on the chair. "Had you ever met Phil before?"

"Only professionally." Juliet fluffed the pillow and her auburn hair tumbled down around her face. "I understand he's a good lawyer."

"He is," Brady agreed. "And with both kids sick, he's had a hell of a time keeping up. The baby-sitter won't come near them."

"Their mother's not there?" Juliet remembered what Michael had said. She wondered what the real story was.

"Nope." Brady didn't want to elaborate. He couldn't take his eyes off Juliet. When she stood up, her blouse settled over her breasts, outlining them subtly. Brady's mouth was dry. "How did you and Michael do, this afternoon?"

Juliet stretched her leg down from the ladder that leaned against the loft bed. Her calf was slender and shapely, the kind that invited a man to stroke it.

"Just fine. We talked for a while and I read him a book—" She felt Brady behind her, his hands cupping her elbows.

"I really appreciate this, Juliet." He turned her around to face him, his eyes apologetic. "I pushed you into doing it—"

"I'm not angry, if that's what you're thinking," she assured him.

That wasn't what he was thinking at all. He was thinking about her breasts and how they thrust, high and firm. He ran his hands lightly along her upper arms. Her blouse was silky to his touch and her skin warm beneath it. "Well, anyway, thanks for taking care of Michael for me." He was acutely aware of the rising and falling of her breasts when she breathed.

"I didn't mind staying with him, Brady, at least not after I got to know him." His touch warmed her everywhere, a rippling warmth like a slow electric current running through her. His hands tightened on her arms. His eyes were soft as velvet. She opened her lips and found his, cool and sweet, waiting for her. Juliet wanted the moment to last forever, so she could press still closer to him, his arms binding her body against his.

Instead, she opened her eyes slowly and forced herself to come back to the present. This wasn't the answer, not here, not now, not under these circumstances. "What are we doing, Brady?" she whispered, pulling away.

He felt the tightening in his groin and wanted her against him again. He slipped his hand under her hair to find the sensitive skin on the back of her neck. "We're getting to know each other. We're about to get married, remember?"

Juliet's whole body stiffened. "That's turning into a real problem, Brady. It would have been a lot simpler my way."

"Meaning?"

Juliet took a deep breath. "Meaning my mother wants us to come for dinner."

From her reaction, Brady had been expecting a crisis. This hardly qualified. "So why not?" he shrugged. "Can she cook?" He was about to reach for her again when she paced across the office.

"Of course she can cook, but she's a little . . . um . . . original sometimes. She asked if you eat sushi."

"Raw fish?" Brady groaned. "I owe you one for this afternoon, Juliet. I want you to know you're collecting. When do we do this?"

"Thursday night. I can ask her to change the menu."

"No," Brady declined, "let's stick with sushi. At least I know what that is." He made a note on his calendar. "I take it she knows we're getting married?"

Juliet grimaced. "She's very excited . . . full of plans."

Plans. He drew back sharply. "Wait a minute. What kind of plans? You're not going to dress up like a real bride are you?"

The prospect horrified Juliet. "Of course not—why would I do something like that?"

Brady felt better. "I just wanted to be sure," he said. They looked at each other in silence, wondering what they'd gotten themselves into.

CASS CALLED JULIET three times in the next three days about the dinner plans, which was three times more often than she had ever called about any social event. Juliet felt herself getting more and more involved when everything was supposed to be so simple.

She worked late Thursday, and by the time she locked the office door it was already seven o'clock. That was when she was supposed to be downstairs meeting Brady. Juliet had just stepped out of the elevator and was hurrying across the building lobby when she heard someone calling her name. "Wait, please wait, Miss Cavanaugh."

She turned toward the sound of the voice and saw a blond woman hurrying toward her. Juliet recognized her immediately. She was the one who wouldn't give her name, the one with the children. Checking her watch, Juliet decided whatever the woman wanted would have to hold until later. Brady was probably waiting for her, Cass was expecting them, and she was already late.

"I'm sorry," she said as the woman approached. "My office is closed for the day, and I'm late for an appointment."

"But I really have to talk to you," the woman persisted.

For an instant, Juliet wavered. This woman desperately needed help. But there wasn't enough time just now. "If you'll call the office in the morning…" Juliet said, walking faster. She left the woman standing alone in the building lobby, and tried hard to block out the look of disappointment in those pale eyes.

The blond woman watched the lawyer go through the revolving door. The lawyer made her angry. She had said it was all right to come back anytime, but every time she came the lawyer was busy. She probably wouldn't even have time to make a phone call. Just one phone call that could get her babies back.

For a moment the woman considered making the phone call herself. There were pay phones just outside the building. She would just call her husband herself and tell him she wanted the boys. That was what she'd wanted the lawyer to do, because he would listen to a lawyer. But now she'd have to do it herself.

She headed purposefully through the revolving doors and toward the row of phones. When there was no answer at home, she tried his office, but his secretary said he had left for the day. Now she didn't know what to do. It was just like before. He was never there when she needed him. She'd even thought about telling him she might like to come home for a while. But it didn't matter anyway. The last time she told him she might come home he'd wanted to put her in the hospital first. She didn't want that. She just wanted her babies back.

Turning away from the phones, the woman walked briskly, leaving Embarcadero Center behind. She slowed as she passed the liquor store and then picked up her pace again when she turned the corner. That proved she didn't need to be in any hospital. It had been over a week since she'd had a drink, except for a few glasses of wine, and they didn't really count. If she really had a drinking problem she wouldn't be able to stop drinking. She'd be like one of those bums staggering down the street taking swigs from an open bottle. And she wasn't like that at all.

The woman paused for a moment and stared at her reflection in the window of a portrait studio. Automatically she smoothed the fine blond hair back from her face and stood up a little straighter. Inside the studio, propped up on an easel, she could see a picture of two children about the same ages as hers.

Their mother was probably fixing them dinner now. That was how it was supposed to be.

Discouraged, she walked down the street. Her husband was using the children to hurt her, keeping them from her when she had a right to them. She wouldn't let him get away with it. She'd keep calling him and when she got him, she'd make him listen. And, if he still wouldn't, she'd go back to the lawyer and wait no matter how long it took. And, one way or another, she'd get her babies back.

JULIET STOOD ON the corner for several minutes before Brady pulled up. No matter how hard she tried, she couldn't get the woman off her mind.

"You look like you've seen a ghost," Brady told her as she slid into the car.

"No, just a client with some enormous problems," Juliet replied. "She seems so lonely, and so defeated, and there's not much I can do to help her."

Brady found a break in the steady stream of traffic and pulled the car away from the curb. "It must be hard not to get involved in their problems," he said thoughtfully.

"It is sometimes," Juliet agreed. She wanted to tell him more about the woman, because the incident was bothering her. But at the same time, she wanted not to think about it. She turned toward Brady with an apologetic smile. "Enough work for one day," she said. "I'm sorry I'm late."

"It doesn't matter. I got tied up in traffic anyway," Brady answered. "Your mother obviously doesn't commute, or she wouldn't live in Sausalito."

"Cass? Commute?" Juliet laughed, realizing how little Brady knew about her mother. "Of course not. She's an artist."

"What kind of artist?" His BMW purred softly as they took their place in a line of cars stretching back from an interminable stoplight.

"She illustrates children's books."

Brady began to look interested. "And she's good enough to make a living at it?"

The comment struck Juliet as peculiar. She'd always pretty much taken her mother's talents for granted. "Did you ever hear of *The Beetlebob and Ellie*?"

"Sure," Brady revved his engine and made it through the light on yellow. "I read one of those books to Timmy not long ago—he's Michael's four-year-old brother. You mean she illustrates that series?"

"Along with a couple of others." They crested a hill and Juliet looked down to see cars flowing smoothly across the Golden Gate Bridge to about midpoint in the bay where they vanished into nothing as the fog rolled toward the city. Her mother's timing had been perfect. The crunch of traffic was thinning out.

"Has your mother always lived in Sausalito?" The BMW zipped across the bridge and made a turn.

"Since I was little. She has one of those old houses that used to be dirt cheap before all the tourists came. For a while she considered living on a houseboat," Juliet laughed. "She's really kind of... kind of different."

"I knew that when you told me we were having sushi." Following Juliet's directions, Brady turned down Cass's street. "I can promise you that my mother will serve a more traditional meal when you eat at her house."

"Your mother?" Juliet echoed. This was getting more complicated.

"Don't sound so surprised," Brady answered.

"And I suppose she serves roast beef, mashed potatoes, that sort of thing?" Juliet inquired.

"Yeah, Mother's big on roast beef—standing ribs for company," Brady confirmed.

Juliet couldn't remember her mother ever cooking roast beef, and when Cass was in one of her vegetarian phases, she was disdainful of all red meat. Juliet had the distinct feeling Brady wasn't ready for Cass. "Where does your mother live?" she asked.

"Boston," Brady answered. "She went back there to live with her sister after my father died." He slowed the car as they neared their destination. "I'll have to take you there to meet her. She doesn't travel much anymore."

Juliet barely heard him. She was resolving that she would not, under any circumstances, fly to Boston to meet Brady's mother. A paper marriage was one thing. Getting involved with all the relatives was something else. She wished she'd told Cass the truth right from the beginning.

"So this is where your mother lives," Brady observed, turning off the engine. Juliet glanced at Brady, who appeared to be studying the house with great interest. She followed his gaze across the tangle of wildflowers where the front yard should be, and on to the weather-beaten frame structure almost hidden by tall trees.

"Maybe we shouldn't have come, Brady," she said suddenly.

"Why not?" He hesitated, his car door half open.

"Cass isn't at all like the people you're used to."

"I think she'll be fascinating—"

"But Brady, she thinks we're really getting married," Juliet blurted out.

"So that's it." He shut his door and turned toward her, taking her hands in his. "Have you changed your mind?"

"Not about the baby, but all the rest of this—"

"Look, Juliet, it's a lot easier to explain a baby with a marriage than a baby without one. I thought you said your mother was excited."

"She is." Juliet answered glumly.

"Then let her have the fantasy." He held her hands tight. "In the long run it'll be easier for her, too."

Brady wished he felt as confident as he sounded. He squeezed Juliet's hands reassuringly and hurried around to help her out of the car. It was no wonder she was apprehensive. He'd never considered mothers as a part of all this either. Boston was far enough away that they could probably avoid a trip there since they only had a six-month agreement. But Sausalito was just across the bridge.

As they approached the door, which was painted bright turquoise, Brady slipped his arm around Juliet's shoulders. She was tight as a knot. Might as well make the best of it as long as they were there, he decided, reaching for the brass peacock knocker.

"You're here," Cass exclaimed, flinging the door open.

"Cass, this is—"

"I know, I know," her mother interrupted. "This is Brady."
She threw her arms around him and gave him an enormous
hug.

Barely keeping his balance, Brady managed to lean over and
give her a kiss on each cheek. "You're even more delightful
than I'd anticipated," he told her. Juliet had obviously been
trying to prepare him, but he hadn't been ready for a middle-
aged woman dressed in a purple Japanese kimono, especially
one who embraced him like a long-lost love even before they'd
been properly introduced. She was obviously Juliet's mother—
the resemblance was striking—but the similarity stopped there.
"If I were to guess," Brady said with a twinkle in his eye, "I'd
wager that we're having Japanese food for dinner." He wondered if the gardenia tucked into Cass's flaming red hair would
simply continue to wobble precariously or if it ultimately would
drop into the nearby fish tank.

Cass patted his arm. "Indeed we are dining Japanese tonight," she said approvingly, "and I like to create the proper
atmosphere right from the start, so if you two will just leave
your shoes here at the door..."

"Sorry," Juliet whispered to Brady as she bent down to slip
off her black pumps.

"It's okay," he whispered back. "I can tell this evening is
going to fall in the category of 'one of those enriching experiences....'" Brady untied his shoes and set them alongside Juliet's pumps on the terrazzo floor of the foyer.

"Come along now," said Cass, taking Brady's arm and
leading him into the living room.

"Hey, this is great." Brady grinned and dug his toes into the
thick white carpet. She was obviously the eccentric artist, and
he had to admit, despite the effusive welcome, there was
something about Cass he liked.

"I can tell that you and I are going to get along very well,"
Cass told him, "and I am a very good judge of character." She
led the way among piles of bright, multicolored pillows that had
been strewn across the carpet and folded herself into a perfect
lotus position as she sank down on a pink satin cushion. Juliet
and Brady followed her example and settled themselves around
a black lacquer table. Brady choose a green cushion that was
firmer and thicker than the rest.

uliet had long ago accepted the fact that her mother didn't ve chairs in the living room, and had no illusions about Cass anging her style at this late date. She wondered what Brady s thinking and stole a sidelong glance at him. His attention s focused totally on Cass, and he looked as though he was oying himself.

"Now," Cass began, "I want to hear all about these wed-g plans. First of all, when is the big event going to take ce?"

uliet looked at Brady. If he'd set the date yet, he hadn't told about it.

"A week from Saturday," he answered smoothly, as if it had n an accomplished fact for some time.

"A week from Saturday?" Cass repeated. "You mean the urday just after this one?" The gardenia in her hair bobbed gerously.

"I did warn you that we were going to do this soon," Juliet erjected quickly. It obviously wasn't the time to tell her ther that the actual date was news to her, too.

"You did tell me," Cass agreed, "but by 'soon' I didn't re-ce you meant immediately. You were obviously hatching se plans for a while before you got around to telling me." e gave Juliet a pointed look.

"Oh, no... well, yes," Juliet corrected herself. She judi-usly avoided Brady's eyes. "You see, both Brady and I are y busy," she hurried to explain.

"Not too busy for a honeymoon, I hope. You are going to e a honeymoon, aren't you?" Cass demanded.

Honeymoon? The idea had never crossed Juliet's mind. *Honeymoon!* thought Brady. *Damn!* That did follow the dding.

hey opened their mouths simultaneously. "No," answered et. Her higher pitched voice was almost drowned out by dy's deep, resonant "Yes."

"Well, which is it?" Cass looked back and forth from one to other. "No or yes?"

uliet paused, not wanting to get in any deeper than she al-dy was. She could tell her mother was already suspicious of ir relationship.

"It's yes," Brady replied firmly. "We are definitely going
a honeymoon."

"We are?" Juliet looked at him, puzzled.

"It would appear you're not quite of one mind on this," C
noted. Juliet shrugged helplessly, and so Cass focused
Brady. "Where are you going?"

"To Carmel," Brady answered. He hoped the inn ha
room available for the week. "I had been keeping it a bit (
surprise," he added coolly.

"Oh, I hope I didn't spoil anything," Cass exclaimed. "I
to Carmel—" Her deep green eyes, so like her daughte
sparkled with excitement. "How romantic! The ocean,
quaint little shops, the rolling hills...we need to drink a toa:
Quickly she stood up and disappeared into the kitchen.

"Brady," hissed Juliet. "First you didn't tell me when
wedding was, and now you're talking about a honeymoo
never agreed to a honeymoon. There isn't a word about C
mel in our contract."

"Don't blame me," he hissed back. "It was your mothe
idea."

"She's not the one who said we were going to Carmel."
liet's voice began to rise.

"Sh-h-h." Brady warned her. "She is, however, the one v
assumed—and, I might add, correctly so—that there is a r
mal progression from wedding to honeymoon."

"That doesn't mean I've agreed to it," Juliet whispered
fensively.

"Maybe not," Brady grinned at her, "but you're the
who wants the baby. That could be a hell of a good start."

Juliet felt the color rising in her cheeks. Fortunately, C
returned to the living room at just that moment, carrying a
with three porcelain wine cups and a plate of delicate sushi

"Warmed sake," she announced as she handed each on
them a cup. "To a long and joyous future," she toasted h
pily, looking first at Brady and then letting her gaze linger
Juliet. "My goodness, dear," she said after a sip of rice w
"your color is better than I've seen it in ages. Obviously
pending marriage agrees with you."

Juliet thought for a moment she might choke on her dri

"To us," Brady added his own toast, obviously aware of her scomfort and, she realized, no doubt enjoying it. He leaned er and kissed Juliet on the cheek, stirring sensations that ced through her faster than a large gulp of the smooth, warm e wine.

Stop that, Juliet thought. *Stop that instantly.*

"You two are perfect for each other," Cass pronounced. "I n tell just by watching you together. And, in case there is any ubt, I'll do a chart comparison."

"Cass!" Juliet protested. For some reason she didn't want know whether hers and Brady's astrological signs were mpatible. It was all nonsense anyway.

"No kidding." Brady looked up with interest from the sushi had been dipping in soy sauce. "Does that really work? I'm arch fifth—Pisces." He downed the sushi as if he'd been ting it all his life.

"Of course it works," Cass proclaimed, "even for a strong-inded woman like Juliet. But it might take me a few days to ach my astrologer. She isn't always available." Cass stood up acefully. "Now, if you'll excuse me one more time, I'll get the kiyaki."

"Let me help you." Juliet sprang up behind her mother, xious to avoid any more private conversations with Brady.

"I wouldn't think of it—sit down, Juliet," her mother or-red. "You have a fiancé to entertain. I won't be a minute."

Reluctantly, Juliet sank back on her yellow silk cushion, ving Brady a sidelong glance to see how he liked being re-rred to as a fiancé. But his thoughts were elsewhere.

"It's fun to watch you take orders for a change," he com-ented with a wicked grin. "Your mother is fantastic."

"That's not exactly the word I'd choose," Juliet noted dryly.

"Then you underestimate her," Brady asserted. "Just one ing I can't figure out."

"Only one?" Juliet jibed.

"Tell me," Brady continued, "how did an eccentric artist e Cass Cavanaugh end up with a daughter like you?"

Juliet rolled her eyes helplessly. She'd often wondered how e'd ended up with a mother like Cass.

Brady and Cass launched into a lively discussion of children d creativity, while Juliet mostly listened, wishing they didn't

get along quite so well. It was just going to make bookshelve
more difficult when the marriage came to an end. On the wa
home, Brady talked enthusiastically about the illustrations Ca
was doing for her latest book. The doubts that had shadowe
Juliet all evening grew even more disquieting. There would b
no trip to Boston to meet his mother, she resolved again, an
as little contact with Cass as possible until the six months we
over. The marriage was nothing but a formality, and it wou
stay that way.

As they neared her apartment, Brady also lapsed into s
lence. He sensed that the evening had disturbed her, and th
fact that he'd thoroughly enjoyed himself probably didn't hel
He made no move to touch her when they pulled up in front
her apartment building and she quickly got out of the car. He
wait and let her phone him—which, he realized, would have
be soon. Their wedding day was just a little more than a wee
away.

Brady chuckled softly as he drove away. It was going to be
hell of a funny marriage—two people who didn't want to b
married to each other going through the motions. Too bad
a way. He wished he'd met Juliet under different circun
stances. He really did like her. But getting married like th
would no doubt destroy anything that might have develope
between them. Turning the corner, he gunned the engine. Ph
had been right. This whole damned thing wasn't going to be a
that easy.

It wasn't until the next day that Juliet realized she had bee
so preoccupied with Brady meeting Cass that she didn't ha
the basic information she needed to plan her schedule. She ha
spent an entire evening with Brady and they hadn't even talke
about the time of the wedding, or anything about the hone
moon he'd sprung on her.

"Just which details did you want to discuss?" Brady i
quired over the phone.

"Oh," replied Juliet breezily, "a few minor things like t
time and place of the wedding."

"Three-thirty next Saturday afternoon. Judge Baldwi
office on Geary Street," Brady said promptly.

Juliet made a quick note in her appointment book and th
started to laugh.

"What's so funny?" Brady asked.

"Oh, nothing," Juliet said, scanning the page, "except it looks a little odd when you pencil in your wedding the same way you'd write down a trip to the dentist."

"I don't know. You said yourself this was purely a business arrangement," Brady pointed out.

"Yes, I know I did...." Juliet's voice trailed off. Somehow it was different now. "Well, then," she continued briskly, "I also need to know what the honeymoon plans are. I may have to rearrange my schedule."

"Just block out the week following the wedding," Brady directed.

"An entire week?" Juliet gasped, looking at the neat notations sprinkled all across the calendar page. "You've got to be kidding. I've got a load of appointments and two cases I'm getting ready for trial. I can't possibly take a week."

Brady held firm. "A proper honeymoon requires at least a week."

"How about we settle for a long weekend?" Juliet proposed.

"Nope," Brady asserted. "A week at least."

"What will we do all that time?" Juliet regretted the words the instant they were out of her mouth.

There was a long silence on the other end of the phone line. "Apparently we do have some details to discuss." Brady's tone of voice offered no clue as to what he might be thinking. Juliet decided that might be just as well.

"We can talk about it over dinner tomorrow," he suggested. "I'll pick you up at eight."

Juliet frowned. Sitting at her desk, she could maintain a strong bargaining position. But over dinner... "Couldn't we just take care of it now—over the phone?"

"I've got an appointment in exactly...actually I'm late now. See you tomorrow."

Juliet hung up slowly. She'd just have to be firm, she decided. A whole week simply wasn't necessary. She could see if Linda could take over for a few days, but any longer would be asking a lot of her this soon.

Linda should be in by now, Juliet realized. She'd stayed at home for the last week, getting her house in order, as she'd ex-

plained, and waiting for the workmen to finish with her office. Yesterday, movers had delivered knocked-down bookcases, a dozen cartons of books, and a desk, and today Lin
planned to get organized. Although they'd talked on the pho
two or three times, Juliet still hadn't mentioned her upcomi
marriage. It seemed better to discuss it in person.

The door to the new office was open, and Juliet found h
new partner in jeans and a sweatshirt, pounding a recalcitra
bookshelf into position with the heel of her shoe. "Sure gla
saved these bookcases when I closed down my practice," Lin
said, giving the shelf a final smack.

Juliet surveyed a long line of cardboard cartons. "You've g
enough books here to open a law library."

"It just looks like a lot when they're boxed." Linda wip
her hands on the back of her jeans.

"You should be pretty well settled by next week," Juliet o
served. "How's your schedule look for the week after that?

"Free as a bird," Linda answered. "That new nanny is
gem. Jennie loves her and she's wonderful with Paul. Wh
have you got in mind?"

"Well . . ." Juliet hesitated, trying to decide how to lead
gradually. "I told you things went really well when I met wi
Brady—"

"And that's all you said," Linda interrupted. "What's up'

"I'm going to get married a week from Saturday," Jul
announced. There didn't seem to be any way but the direct a
proach.

"Married!" Linda exclaimed. "You hardly know him."

"It's not like it sounds," Juliet added quickly. "His fat
left a trust agreement that says he has to be married by the ti
he's thirty-five. That's the real reason he answered my ad. I
offered to father the baby if I'd marry him for six months."

"You've got to be kidding." Linda stared at her. "I knew
sounded too good to be true."

Juliet paced across the office. "I didn't want any part of
at first," she admitted, "but actually it's not that bad. It's r
really a marriage—it's just an arrangement for six montl
And, as he pointed out, it might be easier this way when
baby grows up."

"I can't believe this is you talking." Linda sank onto the only available chair, which was still covered with brown paper. "Wait a minute—when did you say you're doing this?"

"A week from Saturday," Juliet repeated.

"Oh, Juliet," Linda moaned. "I can't come. That's my Dad's sixty-fifth birthday and my mother is giving him a surprise party. She'll kill me if I don't show up."

"That's okay," Juliet shrugged. "I really didn't expect you to come. This isn't for real. It's just going to be a quick thing in the judge's chambers to make it legal."

"When am I going to meet him?" Linda asked.

"I don't know." Juliet frowned. "It's no big thing, and it's going to be really brief, just till I get pregnant. That's part of the deal. I don't want to get involved."

"It sounds to me like you're already involved, Juliet," Linda observed quietly. "Are you sure you want to do this?"

"Why not?" Juliet questioned, but she didn't feel as casual about it as she was trying to sound.

"I'm not sure why not," Linda answered. "It just seems like you're in pretty deep. How's Cass handling it?"

"She's ecstatic because her only daughter is getting married."

"You didn't tell her the circumstances?"

"No," Juliet said, "and that turned out to be a problem, because she insisted on having Brady to dinner and then asked where we were going on our honeymoon. He said to Carmel, so I guess we are." Juliet sat on the edge of the desk across from Linda. "I thought maybe you could come in for a few days that week...."

"Of course," Linda agreed, "if you'll give me some idea of what's coming up. Stay away as long as you want—if you're going to be married to him, you might as well get to know him."

"A couple of days will do it," Juliet assured her. "I'll put together the background you'll need and we can sit down next week and go over all of it." Juliet started toward the door, and then she paused. "Just one other thing, in case I forget," she said, turning around. "Do you remember that rather subdued blond woman? I think you saw her that first day you came in."

Linda looked thoughtful for a moment, then her face brightened. "Oh, yes—tall, thin . . . could be really pretty?"

"She came back just as I was leaving last night and I didn't have time to talk to her," Juliet said. "There's no file on her because she won't give her name, but in a nutshell, she wants custody of her kids and she's got an alcohol problem. There's something about her, Linda. She's so lonely—"

Linda nodded. "I get the picture. Don't ever let it get around town what a soft heart you have or we'll both starve to death."

Laughing, Juliet went back to her office. It had been time to take in a partner, and Linda had been the perfect choice. She let out a long, satisfied breath. Everything was going pretty much as she'd planned it. Except the wedding, and, in the overall scheme of things, that was only a bump in the road.

CHAPTER SIX

JULIET LET HER BODY slide down the slick porcelain bathtub, wondering how many years it had been since she'd taken a bubble bath. Tonight she was going to dinner with Brady, and next Saturday they were getting married.

Checking her hair, which she had piled high on her head and secured with a ribbon, she sank lower until the water touched her chin and the bubbles tickled her nose. *I'm getting married in a week,* she thought incredulously. Of course the ceremony was just a formality. She blew a long trench in the sea of bubbles. But then ... then they would drive to Carmel and then ...

Despite the steamy water, little chills ran through Juliet. She'd never really thought about getting in bed with the man who was going to father her baby. At least she hadn't thought about it in concrete terms. And it was different now that it was one specific man. *Brady.* She considered what making love with him would be like. She couldn't quite imagine being totally naked with him, but maybe that wouldn't be necessary. She probably wouldn't need to undress. He could slide her nightgown up....

The sound of the doorbell ringing punctured her reverie. She ignored it, wondering what Brady wore to bed. Some men slept in the nude. Sinking just a little deeper in the soft, perfumed bubbles, Juliet thought that over. Under these circumstances, she decided, Brady would probably wear pajamas.

The doorbell rang again, insistently. "Go away," she called out. "Nobody's home."

There was absolutely no one she wanted to see in the middle of her bubble bath. She tried to revive the image of Brady in bed, but whoever was outside her door leaned steadily on the bell. She heard a muffled male voice shouting from outside. Annoyed, Juliet stood up. It was always possible there was a

fire or some kind of emergency. Mounds of bubbles ran down
her slippery skin. "All right, all right, I'm coming," she
shouted, wrapping a huge, thick blue terry towel around her
body.

After making sure the security chain was firmly in place,
Juliet opened the door a crack. "Yes?" she said impatiently,
water dripping around her feet.

"Boy, are you slow," replied Brady's cheerful voice. "How
about letting me in?"

"Brady!" gasped Juliet, pulling the towel tighter. She wondered irrationally if he somehow knew what she'd been thinking. "What are you doing here?" she demanded. "You're not
supposed to come until tonight, and I'm in the bathtub."

"No, you're not," Brady countered. "You are standing at
the front door of your apartment, wearing a towel, probably
freezing, and arguing with me. Open the door."

"Can you wait till I get a robe?"

"Open the door," Brady directed impatiently. "I promise I
won't attack."

"Oh, all right," she agreed. Taking a firm grip on her towel,
Juliet removed the chain, poised for a speedy retreat to the
bathroom.

But after Brady closed the door behind him, he stopped directly in front of her. "You, my dear, are a vision of loveli-
ness," he said admiringly, flicking at the bubbles that still clung
to her shoulder. "I want you to know that it is only because I
am a man of my word—"

"Stop that, Brady Talcott," she demanded. "What are you
doing here anyway? You said you'd pick me up at eight. That's
hours from now."

"I got impatient." His fingers still toyed with her shoulder,
removing the final traces of the bubbles and leaving a tingling
sensation in their place. "Besides, it's a perfect day to fly a kite
and I've got a new one I want to test. Put your clothes on, and
we'll go to the beach. I'll show you my house."

Juliet hesitated. There were probably a thousand reasons why
his suggestion was a bad idea, but she couldn't think of one.
"Make yourself at home," she said with a smile. "I'll go get
dressed."

Brady watched her disappear in the direction of the bathroom, wishing the towel she had clutched around her would flap open a little more when she walked. Then he wandered into the dining room, curious about how Juliet lived. He surveyed the graceful lines of the Queen Anne table and chairs, all in gleaming mahogany. Her taste was impeccable, he decided, but very conservative. The living room was more inviting. He studied the room, a blend of peach and aqua and yellow, coordinated by an expanse of light peach carpeting. They weren't his colors, but he liked the room anyway. It had a friendly feeling about it.

Checking his watch, Brady looked for the kitchen. You got a feeling about people by walking through their houses, he realized. Everybody put things together a little differently. He checked the refrigerator for beer and settled for orange juice. Juliet apparently didn't cook very much, he decided, looking around the immaculate kitchen which was decorated in pale yellow. Maybe because of the subtle striped wallpaper—or maybe it was the shutters—the room didn't look cold. But it didn't look used, either.

Brady wasn't sure what to make of Juliet. She was a series of contradictions. Cold lady lawyer wants a baby, negotiates a contract. But there had been nothing cold about her that day in his office. And she didn't look very formidable in that towel, either. He smiled to himself as he mentally undressed her. Tantalizing was a better word. Yet she didn't seem to be a closet homemaker who had made a nest and wanted a child to complete the fantasy. He was putting the orange juice back in the refrigerator when he heard Juliet's voice.

"If you'd like something to drink, help yourself," she called to him.

Orange juice in hand, he went in search of the sound. He caught her on her way to the bedroom, still in the towel. "You haven't made any progress at all," he complained. "Hurry up."

"I've still got roughly six hours before you're due to pick me up," she retorted, shutting the door behind her. "And I am hurrying," she called out through the closed door.

When she appeared in the living room in a white warm-up suit with a jacket slung over her shoulder, Brady let out a low whistle. Her skin glowed, framed by that thick flowing hair that was pulled loosely back except for a few damp tendrils that had escaped. She smelled fresh and new, like spring flowers. But what drew him most, what always drew him, were those eyes, those magnificent green eyes.

"I take it that whistle is a compliment. Thank you," she told him.

"Well deserved," he murmured, still staring at her. Whatever else Juliet was, she was also beautiful. He was almost sorry he'd decided to take her to the beach. He'd have liked to stay there with her. But he also wanted to fly the kite. "We need to get going," he said, taking her arm.

BRADY WAS RIGHT, Juliet decided, as soon as they stepped out into the sunshine. The day was perfect for flying a kite or for almost anything else, as long as it was outdoors. The blanket of fog that had hung heavily until mid-morning was gone entirely, leaving the city sparkling beneath a brilliant blue sky. With the jutting skyline disappearing behind them, the BMW purred south on Route 1.

The highway rose above the coastline and curled through the hilly farmland emerging atop rocky cliffs where surf crashed below. Brady had left the sun roof open, and Juliet drank in the sea-scented air. "I'm glad we're going to the beach," she said happily. Brady only smiled.

As they approached Half Moon Bay, the cliffs gave way to a gentle slope that overlooked an endless white sand beach. Brady turned the car onto a side road that wound its way through the dunes. Sprawling contemporary homes were scattered along the shoreline high above the water. They pulled alongside a house built of weathered cedar with tall rectangular windows facing the road.

She knew immediately why he liked it, and yet it seemed a strange place for a bachelor furniture maker to live alone. The more she got to know Brady, the more he seemed to be a series of contradictions.

"See, what did I tell you?" Brady demanded as they got out of the car, the wind whipping his hair. "Have you ever seen a better day for kite flying?"

"Never," Juliet agreed. She watched him gather the tightly rolled kite out of the back seat, and followed him down the sandy slope to a flat expanse of beach stretching like a ribbon along the sapphire-blue ocean. She sensed his excitement, and it was contagious. Juliet watched Brady lay the kite train on the sand, three kites in a row—one yellow, one red, and one an electric blue, attached together with an intricate web of kite string.

He was as engrossed in what he was doing as she might have been in preparations for a major trial, checking the wind, adjusting the kite string, freeing the tails. He seemed to do everything with his whole being. A wind gust whipped Juliet's hair, and she shivered, sliding her arms into the jacket she had been carrying over her shoulders.

She steadied the kites for Brady until he tightened the lines, and the kites rose swiftly, their noses pointed into the sun, their tails flowing behind in perfect parallel. They hung dead still overhead, before Brady brought them careening down almost into the sand. At the last moment they swerved sharp right and raced sideways toward the breaker line before climbing again to swirl their tails in graceful loops.

Juliet remembered the last time she'd flown a kite. It had been with her father, one of the last things they'd done together before he left. The kite they'd flown had been a simple diamond; the only challenge had been getting it launched in the first place. From then on it had been at the mercy of the wind. But Juliet could still remember the thrill of watching it fly free, sure that at any moment it might touch the clouds.

As she walked up the beach toward Brady, she never took her eyes off the kites racing in gleaming streaks of color across the sun. They were typical of Brady, in their grace and precision. "They're magnificent," she called out as she approached him. He was clearly proud of them. His cheeks were flushed, his eyes glistening with victory.

"You want to fly them?"

Juliet nodded, reaching for the handles, but then she pulled back. She didn't want to fly a kite. She wanted to keep her memory of the day with her father intact, just as it was. "I'd rather watch you," she told him, her voice subdued.

Brady frowned, sensing the change in her. "What's the matter, Juliet?" Taking a piece of twine from his pocket, he secured the handles to a piece of wood buried deep in the sand, letting the kites soar unattended.

"I just don't feel like flying a kite."

Brady put his hands on her shoulders, his fingers pressing into her fleecy jacket. "You're too serious about life, Juliet. You've never learned to play."

Juliet looked past him, her eyes following the jerky movements of the sanderlings racing away from the leading edge of the surf. The tone of his voice softened the accusation, but the truth of his statement was stinging. "My father used to say things like that," Juliet remembered. "He was an expert at playing."

Brady felt Juliet trembling beneath his hands. "Cass said the other night your father walked out when you were little. Is that why you've never mentioned him?"

"There's not much to say." Juliet shoved her hands into her jacket pockets. She didn't like to talk about her father.

"Is he the real reason you're so opposed to marriage?" Brady asked thoughtfully. "You're afraid the same thing will happen all over again?"

"Don't you dare analyze me," Juliet snapped, pulling away from him. "I'm not afraid. I have my life all planned and I'm not afraid."

Brady reached out and grabbed her arm, drawing her back to him. She braced both hands against his chest but he held on, locking his fingers around her upper arm. "Walk with me for a while," he whispered softly. "The kites will be all right here." She didn't answer, but slowly he felt her resistance lessen. They turned and began to walk together, their footprints stretching far down the deserted beach before either of them said a word.

Gusts whipped the froth from the breakers, spewing a fine spray across the sand. Juliet's mind churned, searching for the reasons behind her sudden burst of anger, trying to understand the memories. "Whatever you're thinking, I don't hate my father," she said finally, raising her voice so the force of the wind wouldn't blow away her words. "I know what the experts say: a daughter abandoned by her father at an early age learns to distrust men. My problem with my father is that he couldn't set priorities. All he wanted to do was play."

"And that's why playing makes you feel guilty?"

"It does not," Juliet retorted. She knew the words were empty, and probably Brady knew it, too. Work had always come easily to her—hard, driving work that had led her to more and more impressive successes. But play seemed so frivolous, so unproductive. There were always so many more important things to do.

Almost as though he'd heard her thoughts, Brady continued, "Playing is how you get in touch with yourself." He reached for Juliet's hand. "I have a hell of a lot of fun with my life. I also work—I work damn hard. But that's not what life is all about."

"Just exactly what is life all about?" Juliet heard herself asking him.

Brady didn't answer right away. It was one of the questions he'd wrestled with since as far back as he could remember. He hadn't come to terms with the meaning of life until after his father died and probably he wouldn't, completely, until the trust agreement was also dead and buried. "Life is about people." His words came slowly. "It's about people and the links that hold them together. It's about families and the kids who grow up to carry it all on."

His answer surprised Juliet. "Then why aren't you married?" she asked bluntly.

Brady didn't hesitate. "The right woman hasn't come along. It's as simple and as complicated as that." Letting go of Juliet's hand, he leaned down to pick up a broken seashell and skip it across the waves. "I want a wife to be the reason for my existence and I want our children to be an outgrowth of our love."

Juliet sifted his words uneasily. In his own way, Brady obviously felt as strongly about marriage as she did. His feelings were a stark contrast to their paper agreement. She walked along beside him, feeling very much alone, watching the breakers froth and curl before they dashed up on the sand. The seagulls screamed into the wind, flying free, diving for their supper and then soaring again to float on the air currents high above the blue-black water. She would be free like the gulls, and she would teach her child to love that freedom. The child. A sense of anticipation stirred inside her. Cass had said raising a child was the most meaningful thing she'd ever done. It would be the same for her. She couldn't get tangled in her feelings about Brady. He was temporary. The child would be forever.

The kites were fluttering in the distance, and Juliet looked ahead to see a tiny figure in a bright red sweatshirt running toward them down the beach.

Brady saw him, too. "Here comes Michael," he said grinning, automatically bracing himself.

Without breaking his stride, the boy leaped into Brady's arms, nearly sending them both tumbling into the sand. Regaining his balance, Brady spun him around twice before setting him down feet first.

"You gain two more pounds, and your human dynamo days are over," Brady warned him sternly. "I can't believe you're only seven years old."

Michael grinned. "I thought you said you were going to take up weight lifting."

Brady groaned. "No amount of weight lifting would prepare me for you, the size you're getting to be." He tousled the boy's sandy hair.

Only then did Michael seem to notice Juliet, who was trying hard not to stare at him. She had forgotten how dreadful children looked on the downhill side of chicken pox when the crusty scabs turned black. But Michael's liquid blue eyes had a sparkle in them now. As awful as he still looked, it was obvious that he felt much better.

"We finished the book," Michael announced, dispensing with any greeting. "Daddy said we could start *Prince Caspian* next week—that's the next one. There's a whole bunch of them."

Juliet smiled. "Did you like the part in the book about Lucy having tea with the faun?"

"Yeah, but I liked the part about Edward running away better," Michael answered. He turned back to Brady. "We came down to the beach right away when we saw your kite. I told them I'd find you, but Timmy thinks you fell in the ocean and got eaten by a shark."

"Then maybe we'd better go straighten him out," Brady suggested.

Michael didn't budge. "Do I get to fly the kite?" he demanded.

Brady smiled. At seven years old, it was obviously necessary to settle the important issues first. "You can fly it as long as you want," he agreed seriously.

"Before Timmy?"

"I suppose," Brady sighed, realizing he'd fallen into a carefully set trap.

"All right!" Michael grabbed both their hands. "Hurry up, will you?" He broke into a half run between them.

With Michael binding them together, Juliet and Brady avoided each other's eyes, staring straight ahead as he pulled them along. Like a flying wedge, the strange triangle moved swiftly down the beach.

Phil saw them coming long before they saw him. *What a perfect family portrait,* he thought, *and how deceiving looks can be.* As he watched them, bittersweet memories flooded back. Eileen's hair was blond, fine and straight like the boy's. And Michael had been smaller then, his short legs pumping furiously. When he couldn't keep up any longer, they each wrapped one arm around him and lifted him up, running in step with the boy between them, laughing together with the wind in their hair. It seemed an eternity ago instead of only a couple of years.

Phil brought his heel down hard on a shell, crushing it into the sand. Those first years after they'd moved to the beach had been so good. Maybe if he hadn't been gone so often, it would have stayed good. He'd warned her that it was going to be a tough commute, and that he wouldn't be home as much. She'd said that would be all right. They'd work it out. But even he hadn't realized how grueling the schedule was going to be and how often he'd end up spending the night in the city.

He'd stayed over more and more often as the distance grew between them, Phil realized. And when he did come home near the end, she was usually asleep, and the empty bottle was in the trash. After a while, he gave up trying to wake her. Maybe he shouldn't have pushed her to have another baby. He'd thought it would help. But it had only made everything worse. The psychiatrists hadn't helped much either. Maybe if he'd encouraged her to go into a rehabilitation program . . .

Hell, none of it mattered anymore, anyway. You played the hand life dealt you. At least he had the boys. He watched

Timmy digging a giant hole near the surf, making his own ocean he called it. God, he loved them. Despite everything else that had gone wrong, his kids made life worthwhile. Even i. they did get the chicken pox, he thought, grinning.

"Daddy!" Michael shouted, dropping both Brady and Ju liet's hands and racing ahead. "I do get to fly the kite. Brady said so."

Phil shook his head as Michael raced for the kite. Brady had been a godsend with the boys. By making them his official toy testers, he'd given them a purpose in life after their mother had first left, something to take their minds off how much they missed her. It had been especially good for Michael. He was older, and he remembered so much more.

As Brady and Juliet came nearer, Phil waved a greeting. They were walking side by side now but a safe distance apart "Brady, Juliet...good to see you again." Phil extended hi hand, and Juliet clasped it briefly. He wondered if she realized he was aware of the arrangement between her and Brady.

"Nice to see you, Phil," Juliet said. "I'm glad Michael feel better."

"Me, too," Phil agreed. "That paintbrush idea of yours wa definitely inspired."

"Paintbrush?" Brady interrupted, looking from one to the other.

"Didn't Juliet tell you?" Phil had figured Juliet probably told Brady all about her time with Michael. Maybe they didn' talk about things like that. He wondered what two people with a relationship like theirs did talk about. "She painted the cal amine lotion on Michael and then gave him the brush to take home," Phil explained. "I could tell right away when he started to get better. He began painting calamine pictures on his stom ach."

They all laughed, but at the same time, Brady found himsel looking at Juliet with surprise. For some reason, that kind o novel approach to a child's illness wasn't something he woul have expected her to think of.

Feeling a pressure on his leg, he looked down to find Timm tugging at his pants. "You look a whole lot better," Brady tol him, "almost as if you didn't have the chicken pox at all."

"I didn't get ugly like Michael," Timmy said proudly. "So I think I should get to fly the kite first—and because I'm only four."

"Not first this time, because I already promised Michael," Brady explained, wishing he'd brought along an extra kite. "You let him do it for a little while and then it will be your turn."

"I'll go tell him that," Timmy announced, racing across the sand toward his brother.

Within moments, he was back. "Michael says I can't fly it till he's through and that will probably be all afternoon," he wailed.

Juliet watched Phil kneel down on the sand and talk to his son quietly. Phil seemed to know exactly the right things to say, because after a while the tears stopped, and Timmy sniffed. Would she know the right answers in situations like this? Juliet wondered.

Phil patted Timmy, not seeming to notice the dirt streaks that appeared when the little boy wiped his face across his sleeve. "We need to go have a talk with Michael," he explained as he stood up. "We'll bring your kite back later, Brady."

"Keep it for a few days," Brady called after them. "Let them give it a good workout."

"Thanks," Phil called over his shoulder.

Juliet smiled as Phil reached down to take Timmy's hand, shortening his stride to walk in step with his son. "He likes being a father," Juliet said softly, "and he's got two really nice little boys."

"It's a lonely road for one person," Brady replied.

"But even alone he's obviously done a good job of it," Juliet pointed out.

Brady tossed a shell at the breakers. There was no arguing that Phil had done well with Michael and Timmy. But no one outside could possibly understand how hard it had been. Brady had caught only glimpses of his friend's agony, a few words over a drink, a look in his eyes when they talked about Eileen, which they rarely did anymore. "He didn't have much choice," Brady said quietly. He took her hand, not wanting to talk about Phil's situation. "It's starting to get cold. Let's head back to the house."

With the setting sun at their backs, they started to climb the slope that led back to the beach house. Without looking up at Brady, Juliet asked cautiously, "Do you think my plan will work?"

"What plan?" he asked.

"My plan for single motherhood."

"If you're asking me if it's all right to back out of this deal, the answer is yes. I won't sue you for breach of contract."

"That isn't what I meant," Juliet answered. Their pace slowed. "I just wondered what you thought about it."

"You're having second thoughts?" he pressed.

"Not exactly." But something was bothering her. "It's just...well, watching Phil with Timmy...I guess it made me think. Babies grow up and, well..." Juliet paused, not sure what she was trying to say and sorry she'd ever begun to explore it. "I guess I was just thinking that another life is a whole lot of responsibility for one person to take on." She reached down to pick up a fragment of shell, polished soft pink in the pounding surf, and rubbed her finger rhythmically across it.

Brady stopped walking and studied Juliet carefully. She looked very vulnerable at that moment, he thought, and very beautiful, with the sun burning red behind her, shimmering off her tousled auburn hair. He resisted the urge to take her in his arms, knowing he needed to answer her.

"Well, Juliet, you are biting off a big chunk," he began. She listened, not moving at all. He understood that it was important to choose his words carefully. "I think a baby is a lot bigger step than most people realize at the beginning," he continued thoughtfully, "although I suppose if anyone can do it well, you can."

Juliet looked relieved. "Thank you," she answered.

He couldn't leave it there. "But it would be easier to do it with two parents."

Juliet turned toward him, her eyes clouded, suspicious. "Are you trying to say something else, Brady—about our arrangement?"

"Not at all," he assured her. "I was simply pointing out that parents normally come in pairs."

Juliet started walking again, bringing her feet down hard on the sand. There it was, the same old argument. The Noah's ark syndrome. The great American dream that wasn't true anymore. "They may start out in pairs—but they don't stay that way." Juliet didn't try to hide the bitterness in her voice. "And you can't tell me that broken homes and broken trust make children better off. They're a whole lot better off with love they can count on—love they can keep."

Brady matched her stride. "Love doesn't come with guarantees, Juliet." He watched her, wondering how many people, if any, had seen the sensitive, frightened woman beneath her polished exterior. She was looking for a way to beat the system, to ultimately make life better for herself and for this baby she wanted so much. If it was a mistake, it was an honest one.

They were still at the edge of the chasm, Brady realized, with nothing tangible between them except a piece of paper that could be torn up. Nothing was irrevocable—yet. They walked faster. The approaching evening had tamed the wind gusts, but brought with it a pervasive chill. "Are you sure you want to go through with this, Juliet?"

Her response was immediate. "Of course I'm sure," she answered with a cool assurance she didn't feel. She sensed his uncertainty. If she wanted out, this was the opportunity. But she'd already made her decision, after months of thinking it through. She wasn't going to change her mind now. "Are you backing out?" she challenged.

Brady hesitated.

"Well?" Juliet prompted. She turned toward him, her eyes flashing.

"No," he said finally. "I'm not backing out. The contract stands."

"Good," she answered smoothly.

He took her extended hand but held it instead of completing the handshake. "We'll take it one day at a time," he said evenly. "First we'll be married. Then you'll probably get pregnant—"

"No probably about it. Definitely," Juliet interrupted. "I've got it all figured out, the timing and everything. There's no reason why it shouldn't work."

Brady couldn't suppress a laugh. "Sometimes the best plans in the world have to be a little flexible—"

"I know that, but—"

"But you figure if you've got it all mapped out ahead of time, you've got a better chance," Brady chuckled.

His response didn't faze her. The wall of doubt between them was thinning, for some reason Juliet couldn't quite put her finger on. Nothing had changed. But she saw an acceptance in his eyes that hadn't been there before. "You're getting to know me," Juliet smiled back. "Maybe you'll pick up some of my good habits."

"Don't count on it," Brady answered softly. He let go of her hand and wrapped his arms around her. All afternoon he'd wanted to do that.

Juliet buried her face in his chest, giving in to the unexpected pleasure of feeling sheltered and protected. A steady wind off the ocean swirled around them, but in the circle of Brady's arms, Juliet was secure.

The embrace tightened, and she knew he was going to kiss her. Brady barely touched her at first, holding back until she moved her head toward him. Then his mouth pressed down hard on hers.

At first she savored his salty taste and then she felt the warmth all through her. It might have been heat from the late-afternoon sun burning into her back, except it moved when his hands moved, stroking her rhythmically. Gently, his tongue parted her lips and traced a tantalizing path across them. She opened her lips wider, letting him explore the softness within.

When she felt Brady's hand against the curve of her breast, inside her jacket against the soft, fleecy fabric of the warm-up suit, it seemed right and natural. But then he moved away. She wondered how much he could read in her face.

"The air is getting colder, Juliet," he said.

"I guess I hadn't noticed." She lowered her eyes.

"There's a fireplace in the house. We can warm up there and have something to eat."

"I'd like that," Juliet agreed. She wanted to be with him for a little while longer. Turning toward the sprawling beach house, its weatherbeaten siding blending in among the sandy hills dotted with mossy ice plant, they walked silently, hand in hand in the deepening twilight.

Juliet followed Brady into a large room that stretched all across the back of the house. The sun, sinking toward the horizon, poured through a wall of glass. Brilliant streaks of red shimmered off the crashing surf that pounded the beach below. Juliet caught her breath.

"Like it here?" Brady asked, and Juliet was aware of him standing beside a white fireplace that seemed to recede into the stark wall behind it.

"How could anyone be less than enchanted?" Her eyes followed the sun rays across the room, watching them dance in splendor on a myriad of tiny silver seagulls suspended from the ceiling. "If I had a place like this, I don't know whether I'd ever go anywhere else."

"I guess that's the real reason I moved out here," Brady admitted, as he stacked wood in the fireplace. "It's damn inconvenient, but it's worth the drive." He dusted his hands together before wiping them on his jeans. "Maybe we should come here instead of going to Carmel for our honeymoon," he mused.

His suggestion brought Juliet back, away from the hypnotic surf, to the memory of why she was with him. They were supposed to be talking about going to Carmel. Maybe it would be better to honeymoon at his house, instead.

She looked at the room itself more carefully. It was simply decorated but all the more striking because of it. The only chairs, if you could call them chairs, were huge blue beanbags. Several small glass tables with driftwood bases were placed among them on the natural-fiber area rug. Brady's house was casual. And close. And not as much like a honeymoon as a trip to Carmel. "This would be a nice place to spend a couple of days," Juliet agreed.

"A week," Brady corrected, striking a match to the paper strips he had stuffed under the logs.

Juliet winced. She wasn't ready for a week. Actually, she wasn't ready for a honeymoon at all. What she'd expected was a paternity agreement and then a few arranged meetings, carefully timed. "We obviously have some things that need discussing," Juliet observed.

Brady put up the firescreen. "First, we eat," he determined. "That'll give the fire time to get going."

Juliet couldn't argue. She'd been hungry for an hour. Brady's kitchen turned out to be well stocked—actually better than hers. They took thick, meaty lentil soup from the freezer, then prepared a large salad and hot buttered bread. They both ate hungrily after the day outdoors, not slowing down till the end of the meal when they wiped out their soup bowls with the last pieces of bread.

Brady took a swallow of coffee, studying Juliet over the rim of his mug. He still couldn't figure her out. She seemed so damned together most of the time, as though she didn't need anyone or anything. But out on the beach, when he'd touched her, she'd wanted more. He'd seen it in her eyes, and he never misread that in a woman. He'd wanted her this afternoon, when she'd greeted him in that towel. Brady set down his coffee cup. "I like you in blue," he told her.

"But, Brady—" Juliet's eyes dropped to the warm-up suit. "I'm wearing white."

"You weren't this afternoon."

At first Juliet was confused. Then she felt the heat in her cheeks. She'd known he was studying her. Now she knew what he'd been thinking. It didn't make her angry—that would have been easier to deal with than the unmistakable sensation stirring deep inside her. "I guess I *was* wearing blue," she acknowledged.

Anxious to change the subject, Juliet stood up abruptly and took her dishes to the sink. "I feel much better after eating," she told him as she rinsed off her plate. "But we still haven't settled anything about next week—"

"Then come sit down and we'll discuss it," Brady invited as he pulled a dark blue beanbag chair in front of the blazing fire.

Juliet stopped at the edge of the room. "This doesn't seem like a very businesslike atmosphere."

"Honeymoon discussions are rarely businesslike," Brady said laughing. "They go more like this." He crossed the room in a few strides and scooped Juliet up in his arms.

"Put me down," she protested, kicking the air.

"In just a moment," he promised. But as he leaned over to drop her in the beanbag chair, she grabbed him tightly around the neck and they tumbled down together in a laughing, tangled heap. "That was supposed to be a classy maneuver," he noted.

Juliet tried to shift her weight off him, but he pulled her back. "You're not heavy," he told her. "Unless you don't like it here—"

"Well . . ." She lowered her thick lashes till they brushed her cheek. "It is warm," she murmured.

Brady stroked her hair, smoothing it into place. He liked her this way, so open and free. He trailed his fingers along the side of Juliet's face, and then, with one finger, lifted her chin and leaned down to cover her lips with his. Her mouth was soft and yielding. "You seem happy, Juliet," he whispered, sliding his arm under her and cradling her head against his shoulder.

"I am happy," she confirmed, smiling up at him. He was leaning over her, the deep red of the sunset bathing his face, softening his rugged jawline and illuminating the darkness of his eyes. She felt very close to him. "The last thing in the whole world I'd have done on my own today was to come to the beach," she admitted. "But I liked it. I liked the kite, and I liked the way the wind felt in my hair, and I like . . . I like being here with you."

Juliet stopped talking because she didn't know what else to say. She didn't understand her own happiness and she didn't want to analyze it. She didn't want to lose it. Not forever, but just for the moment, she wanted to be here, with him, just the way she was.

For a long time they lay together, quiet and content, watching the darkness gather and the orange and yellow flames dance in the fireplace. After a while, Brady began to stroke the smooth, fair skin of Juliet's cheek, slowly and gently with the back of his hand. Juliet turned slightly in his arms and snuggled closer to him. She ran the tips of her fingers up and down the length of his arm, enjoying the feel of his coarse, springy hair.

His body felt so different from hers, so firm and hard. His scent was as masculine as he was, a musky smell Juliet realized she had come to associate with Brady. His breath was warm, barely grazing her ear. Juliet closed her eyes. She could hear the ocean waves rolling up on the beach and then sliding back to the water's edge. Up and back, up and back. Over and over in a rhythm as old as time itself. Juliet felt her body begin to undulate in rhythm with the waves. She reached around Brady and pressed close to him, tilting her head up, waiting, knowing how delicious his lips would taste.

"My God, you're lovely, Juliet," he whispered into her ear.

Juliet floated in his arms, trailing kisses down the side of his neck. He tasted salty from the sea breeze and the afternoon by the ocean, a delicious taste. She twined her fingers in his hair and pulled him down, until his mouth covered the hollow in her throat. Still the ocean waves rolled up and back on the shore and Juliet continued to match their rhythm.

Brady buried his face in her breasts for only an instant. Then he raised up to look at her, a debate raging inside him. He had to decide quickly or there would be no decision. His body was straining, ready. He thought he might explode when she rocked against him.

But when he reached down to touch her, she changed, her muscles drawing taut, the gentle rocking gone. *Oh, God,* he thought, *not now.* She didn't push him away, or offer any real resistance, but he knew. She might have let him take her. Under other circumstances, he'd have tried. But she wasn't ready, and he knew it. She might not even realize it herself, but she would afterward, and they had too far to go together. For one more moment he pressed hard against her, his body screaming for relief.

When he drew back, Juliet caught her lower lip between her teeth, biting down, waiting. The passion that had engulfed her, almost strangling her, had ebbed. She was disappointed but not surprised. It was what usually happened.

But he didn't move back against her. "No," she found herself protesting. "Don't stop." In a strange sort of way she still wanted him. She opened her eyes wide and saw Brady above her, silhouetted in the firelight, looking down at her.

"The rest will have to wait until the honeymoon," he said softly.

What had happened? No man stopped at that point. "Why?" she asked, her voice barely audible.

"Because it isn't time now." He kissed her lightly on the lips. "I want it to be good for both of us."

Again Juliet heard the breakers crashing against the sand and the low whistle of the rising wind outside. She reached up to touch Brady's cheek, and felt the tension in the hard set of his jaw. When he turned his head slightly, she saw the fire in the dark brown of his eyes.

"About the honeymoon, Brady," she began slowly.

"Yes?" His voice was choked.

"I think I can clear my calendar for a week." Right then, she wasn't sure a week would be long enough.

CHAPTER SEVEN

STILL IN HER SLIP, Juliet tucked a sweater in the corner of the suitcase that lay open on her bed. Shoes, lingerie, robe, slippers—slippers! She couldn't go on a honeymoon without slippers. Juliet hurried to the closet. Maybe it would have been better not to have left the packing until the last minute, she thought, feeling almost panicky. She always packed at the last minute but for some reason, this time, she couldn't seem to get it all together. And she couldn't be late for her own wedding.

The sharp jangle of the phone startled her so much that she dropped one of the wedge-heeled satin slippers on the floor.

"Yes, Mother, I'm ready...no, I haven't left yet...well, yes, I'm almost packed . . . no, I'm not quite dressed . . . yes, I know you're already there." Balancing the phone on her shoulder, Juliet started pulling clips out of her hair. "Look, if I don't get off the phone I'll never be ready." She stretched the phone cord to its very limits and grabbed her brush off the dresser. "No, of course I'm not nervous," she added defensively, hearing the laughter on the other end of the line.

Tossing the slippers toward the already bulging suitcase, Juliet dashed back to the closet. Still struggling with the buttons and loops on her organza blouse, she stepped quickly into her suede pumps and then took them off again to pull on her white wool skirt. The zipper stuck and she tugged at it, already on the way back to her dresser to get her pearls. Catching sight of herself in the dresser mirror, she stopped and slowly counted to ten.

"Get hold of yourself," she commanded aloud. This wasn't really her wedding day, she reminded herself for the tenth time, only a brief arrangement, a necessary formality.

The doorbell rang, and Juliet raced to answer it, glancing nervously at her watch.

"Delivery for you," said the uniformed messenger, handing Juliet a shamrock plant wrapped in floral paper. As she closed the door, Juliet fumbled with the card, wondering who had sent it. She knew the moment she saw the handwriting.

"For luck," Linda had written. "Relax and enjoy. I'm thinking about you." Juliet smiled, wondering if Linda could have guessed she'd be coming apart. *She's right,* Juliet decided, touching a tiny white flower. *If I could just relax—pantyhose!* she thought suddenly, when the hem of her skirt brushed her bare leg. She hurried back to the bedroom and kicked off her shoes one more time. At this rate, she thought ruefully, Brady will end up marrying my mother because she's the only one there.

ON HANDS AND KNEES, Brady shoved his hand as far as it would reach under his dresser and patted the thick gray carpet. It had to be in there somewhere—a cuff link didn't just disappear. "Damn," he sputtered, crawling to the other end of the dresser to try again. The doorbell rang, and he ignored it. He could almost feel the fuzz from the carpet coating his charcoal-gray suit pants. The bell rang again, steadily, until Brady finally withdrew from under the dresser and shouted angrily, "Can it, will you? I'm coming."

"Say, buddy," Phil noted calmly when Brady's unfastened French cuff flapped in his face at the front door, "you seem to have forgotten something."

"Stupid cuff link dropped in the carpet," Brady muttered. "Look for it, will you, while I close the suitcase?"

Phil folded his arms across his chest and grinned. "I'm your lawyer, remember, not your valet."

"Well, today you're my best man," Brady corrected him, leading the way to the bedroom. "It's somewhere over there by the dresser—start digging."

Phil couldn't remember ever seeing Brady this way. "You sound almost like a real groom." He crouched down and studied the carpet. "I thought this wedding ceremony was just filling a square in your father's trust agreement."

"That's exactly what it is," Brady said explosively. He brushed vigorously at the carpet fuzz on his pants.

THE ARRANGEMENT

"Then why are you so nervous?" Phil casually picked up the lost cuff link from behind the leg of the dresser. He reached for Brady's shirt cuff. "You haven't answered my question," he persisted.

Brady wished Phil would leave him alone. He couldn't answer. He had no idea why he felt the way he did. He'd been like that since he got out of bed. "Anyone would be nervous if he had to rely on you for help," Brady muttered. He shoved his arms into his suit coat, which Phil held for him.

"Now, do you have everything?" Phil asked, more and more amused. He remembered the day of his own wedding when the situation had been reversed. Except his marriage had been for real. He dismissed the memories and grabbed the suitcase off the bed.

Brady dug in his pockets, still muttering to himself. "Let's see...got the license in here, the hotel reservations here, the ring in this pocket—"

"Ring?" Phil interrupted. "You got her a ring?"

"It's a wedding, isn't it?" Brady retorted.

Phil frowned. "It's supposed to be a business arrangement. You didn't have to get her a ring."

"Well, I did." He hoped it wasn't a mistake. It had seemed the right thing to do when he bought it yesterday.

"I suppose you got her a bouquet, too?" Phil's voice was heavy with sarcasm, but Brady didn't notice.

"A bouquet? Damn! Never occurred to me." Brady grabbed Phil by the arm. "Come on, we've got to hurry."

"What's the rush?" Phil inquired mildly, nearly running to keep up with Brady. "We don't have to be in Judge Baldwin's chambers for more than an hour."

"Yeah," said Brady, "but first we've got to find a florist willing to put together a wedding bouquet on short notice."

ALL THE WAY up Geary Street Juliet mentally reviewed the contents of her suitcase, absolutely certain something vital was missing. Money! She'd meant to stop at the bank and pick up some traveler's cheques. They hadn't discussed how they were going to pay for this honeymoon, but she assumed since it was Brady's idea he'd pick up his half. Too late now—at least she had her credit card.

After she paid the cab driver, Juliet stood for a moment at the curb, her crimson leather suitcase in one hand, her makeup case in the other, and her purse tucked tightly under her arm. The street was nearly deserted. She didn't know what she'd expected, but it seemed that maybe Brady—or somebody—might be around.

When she walked into the reception room outside the judge's chambers and found Cass waiting for her, Juliet felt an enormous surge of relief.

"You are absolutely lovely, dear," Cass bubbled. "I'm so glad you wore that white suit. Here, put down your things and smile while I take your picture."

Feeling like a little girl on display at her birthday party, Juliet obediently gave the camera a radiant smile.

"No, no," Cass told her, shaking her head. "You aren't buttoned." Juliet looked down to find the entire center section of the organza blouse gaping open. "You obviously need a mother's touch," Cass clucked, quickly going to work on the buttons. "I had no idea you'd be so nervous, but I should have expected it. It isn't every day a girl gets married."

No, thought Juliet, *and it isn't happening today, either, not really happening.* The whole thing was absolutely ridiculous. She hadn't had this many butterflies the day she took the bar exam.

After giving her daughter a final once-over, Cass resumed the picture-taking session and Juliet posed patiently. "Good," Cass beamed. "Now turn your head to the right just a tad."

Juliet followed Cass's instructions and, in doing so, caught a glimpse of a clock on the wall of the reception room. Brady was ten minutes late. What if he didn't come? In some ways, it might be better if he didn't.

"That should do it," Cass declared, setting the camera on a nearby table. "Now, one more thing." She produced a flat white box which she handed to Juliet.

Both surprised and deeply touched, Juliet untied the ribbon. She hadn't thought about presents because this wasn't a real wedding. But Cass didn't know that. Cass was giving away her only daughter with the same hope and joy and tugs at the heartstrings that any mother would feel. Juliet lifted the lid and slowly unfolded the tissue paper inside.

"Oh, Cass," she gasped. "Grandmother's mantilla." She blinked back tears. How could she wear the exquisite lace veil, with all the meaning it held, to her wedding which wasn't really her wedding at all?

"I knew you'd be pleased," her mother said, glowing. "Hurry and put it on so I can take some more pictures. Brady will be here any minute."

"Oh, Cass," Juliet began, "I can't—"

"Nonsense," Cass dismissed her protest. "Just because this isn't a church wedding doesn't make it any less real." She took the delicate mantilla from its bed of tissue and draped it gracefully over Juliet's silky auburn hair. "Perfect," she declared, picking up the camera. "Now, smile."

Juliet produced a wavery smile, but inside she was quaking. She'd never bargained for all this.

"Once more—lift your chin a little," Cass directed.

Juliet sighed. Whatever she should have done, it appeared she was going to have to deal with what she had done. Like it or not, she was going to look like a bride—veil and all.

As the camera flashed again, Judge Baldwin appeared from his chambers. "I see the blushing bride has arrived," he commented jovially, still fastening the front of his voluminous black robes. "How about the groom?"

Right on cue, Brady strolled through the reception room door looking for all the world as though he got married every day. But when he caught sight of Juliet, he stopped, his lips parted, and he didn't say a word. What was she doing? She'd promised she wouldn't dress up like a bride. But, God, she looked beautiful. He stood transfixed, unaware of the others gathered silently around them.

"Hello, Brady," Juliet said softly. "I'm glad you're here...I was beginning to worry about you."

"I...I'm sorry I'm late," he stammered. "I...Juliet you're beautiful."

"Thank you," she answered.

"I have something I wanted to give you....." Brady looked helplessly at Phil, who produced a nosegay of pastel flowers edged in lace, with white satin streamers flowing almost to the floor. "Here," Brady said, holding the flowers toward Juliet.

Juliet stared at the bouquet. "Brady, you didn't have to... I mean... Oh, Brady, I love them." Suddenly, everyone in the room was talking at once. When the chatter settled, they all had been introduced to each other and Brady was standing beside Juliet, his arm tightly around her waist.

"Now," began Judge Baldwin, with an expression that said he clearly enjoyed weddings, "let's get down to business. We'll complete the preliminaries first. Choosing to be married in a civil ceremony does not diminish the sanctity of the institution of marriage," he added sternly.

Juliet avoided looking at Brady, and she sensed that he wasn't looking at her, either. Her hand was shaking as she signed her name and then handed the pen to Brady whose usual ruddy complexion was several shades of gray. *He looks like he's as scared as I am*, she thought, waiting silently while Phil and Cass signed as witnesses. Why are we doing this? Juliet asked herself, and at that moment she almost backed out. Then she looked at the flowers clutched in her hand and lightly, almost reverently, touched the lace mantilla that flowed gracefully to her shoulders. She'd come too far. She wouldn't change her mind now.

Judge Baldwin talked for several minutes about the commitment of marriage and the responsibility a husband and wife have to one another. Juliet clutched her bouquet tighter and tighter, trying to shut out his words, wanting to scream for him to get on with it. Everything was so real. She had thought when the papers were signed, it would be over. But this—this was like really getting married.

Juliet heard herself almost inaudibly repeating the vows the judge recited, and she heard Brady's voice break when he said the same words. But when Brady took her left hand to slip a gold band on her finger, her response was loud and clear. "Brady! You never said anything about a ring." She pulled her hand back. A ring was so... so tangible.

"I suppose if you don't want one—" Brady answered.

Juliet realized everyone was staring at her. "It's not that," she added quickly. "It's just, well, I guess I was surprised." Feeling very foolish, she extended her hand and Brady slid the ring on her finger.

She was still staring at the shining gold band when she heard Judge Baldwin say, "Now, Brady, you may kiss the bride."

For the first time since the ceremony began, their eyes met and held. Brady lowered his mouth to hers.

THEY WERE in the car on their way down the coast before Juliet stopped shaking. She glanced sideways at the man next to her. The radio was set to a pop rock station, and he was tapping his fingers on the steering wheel in time to the music. His eyes were fixed on the road, a curving, twisting highway that hugged the coast. He had been quiet for a long time, but then so had she. It didn't make any difference that they'd gone through the ceremony. You couldn't be married to someone by just signing some papers and repeating empty words. Not really married. Still, she'd done the thing she'd sworn she'd never do, with a man she'd known only a few weeks. Even if it wasn't a real marriage, it was a sobering experience. The sun glinted off the gold band on her finger.

Brady saw her staring at it. She looked frightened and unhappy. Buying the ring had apparently been a mistake, probably one of many. "I'm sorry about the ring, Juliet," he apologized. "I walked by a jewelry store yesterday and saw it in the window. I bought it on a whim. You don't have to wear it."

Juliet didn't answer right away. In fact, she didn't want it. But she didn't want to take it off, either. "I guess maybe I'll wear it for a while, while we're in Carmel, anyway. It'll remind us we're on a honeymoon." Juliet winced. She hated that word.

Brady tuned the radio to a classical station. "Do you think we'll need reminding?"

"Well, we barely know each other and here we are—"

"You're sorry, aren't you, Juliet?"

She looked out the window at the rocky cliffs rising from the ocean far below. "I don't know." She twisted the ring on her finger. "I didn't expect so much...so much wedding. I thought we were just going to sign some papers and that would be it."

"So did I."

"You mean you didn't arrange all that?"

"Hell, no." Brady slapped his hand down on the steering wheel for emphasis. "All I did was phone the judge and set up the time. Phil told me he liked to do weddings."

"Obviously." Juliet frowned. "But, Brady, what about the flowers . . . ?"

Brady squirmed uncomfortably. "I got them on the way. Phil brought the idea up, and I thought maybe it was something I should do. And then when I got there and saw you—" His face softened as he remembered. "You were beautiful. But you told me you weren't going to dress up like a bride."

"I didn't!" Juliet exclaimed, suddenly defensive. "At least I didn't mean to. My mother brought Grandmother's mantilla and there wasn't anything I could do."

"I didn't mind, you understand," Brady added. "You looked—" He stopped. How could he tell her that when he walked in and saw her, she was like a fantasy, like a beautiful dream? "You looked nice," he finished lamely.

"Thank you," Juliet murmured. The wedding had apparently had an impact on him, too. "Were you nervous?"

"Nervous?" He remembered the missing cuff link and how irritated he'd been with Phil. "No, not really. How about you?"

Juliet thought about the haphazard packing job, the pantyhose she'd forgotten. "Well . . . having my mother there was sort of unsettling."

"At least it's over," Brady sighed. He didn't add that the good part was still ahead of them. Ever since the night at the beach, he'd wanted her. She'd crept into his fantasies, soft and sensuous, her body moving rhythmically against his, an invitation to soothe the raging heat that drove him. Whenever he thought about Juliet, he felt the familiar aching in his groin.

They lapsed into silence again. Juliet stared out the window at the ocean whipping by. It wasn't over. Getting married was a carefully programmed activity, with a very specific set of built-in expectations. The next one down the line was the wedding night. They were speeding toward it, drawing closer with every passing mile. She couldn't back out now. That was the whole reason she was doing this. The faster she could get pregnant, the faster all this would be over, and the sooner she could quit pretending, she reasoned. But logic didn't help at all. Her stomach tightened and she felt almost as though she might be sick. "How much further?" she asked. The voice didn't sound like hers at all.

Brady glanced at her. She was huddled as close to the door as her seat belt would allow. "We're just coming in to Monterey," he answered. "Is something wrong, Juliet?"

She swallowed, her throat dry. "No, nothing's wrong. I just wondered." But he hadn't quite answered her question. "Is the place we're staying at far from here?"

"The inn? Maybe twenty minutes." He looked at her again. "Are you sure you're all right, Juliet?"

"My stomach feels sort of odd," she admitted.

So that was it. "Nerves and a long car ride," he diagnosed. "I was going to suggest dinner, but maybe you'd like to stop and get some fresh air. We can walk down on the wharf."

Juliet gave him a grateful smile. "I'd like that, Brady." She relaxed slightly. A walk would give her a little more time.

The sky was cloudless blue when they stepped out of the car. Juliet tilted her head upward, drinking in the fresh salt air. The wind off Monterey Bay whipped around her legs and tossed her hair playfully across her shoulders. "Maybe we can eat some squid while we're here," she suggested.

"That's the fastest transformation I've ever seen." Brady brushed a long auburn strand of hair from her face, noticing how Juliet's emerald eyes sparkled in the sunlight. "You sure your stomach's all right?"

"Fine," she assured him. "Except I'm hungry."

"That's easy to fix if you can handle dinner out of a cardboard box on your wedding day." He laughed easily. "Of course I don't see any reason we can't make our own rules. We have up to now."

Juliet wasn't sure why, but she suddenly felt better than she had all day. They ate fried squid and drank coffee from Styrofoam cups balanced between them on a wooden bench. Juliet could hear the seals barking and the haunting sound of the fog horn that signaled the coming of evening and, with it, the approaching fog. When the last bite of squid was gone, Brady chucked the box in a trash can and took her hand.

"Are you ready?" he asked.

"Oh, no." The answer had been too quick. "What I mean is, I'd like to go out on the pier and look at the seals."

"You couldn't possibly have a case of bride's jitters, could you?" Brady asked.

She saw the amusement in his eyes. "Of course not," she snapped. "I'm not even sure what you mean."

"Good." He put his arm around her waist, slipping his hand under her suit jacket to brush her breast suggestively. "Because anticipation's half the fun."

Juliet's cheeks flamed and she didn't answer him.

His arm still around her, they walked out on the wharf, moving slowly so that Juliet's heels didn't catch between the rough hewn boards. A mixture of smells, laced with caramel corn and frying fish assailed them. As they drew near the end of the wharf, Juliet wrinkled her nose. "Ah, fresh ocean air."

"That smell, my dear, is coming from those very picturesque seals off to your right," Brady informed her.

She leaned her elbows on the railing and scanned the horizon. In the distance she could barely make out a group of seals on a pile of dark rocks. She supposed if their barking carried that far, their smell could, too. Her eyes drifted upward to follow a seagull, and then she felt Brady behind her, his body pressing against hers. She tensed, her thoughts moving ahead. The anticipation, he'd said. She shivered.

Seeing something floating in the water, Juliet leaned over the rail for a better look, relieved when the movement separated her from Brady. "I think it's a sea otter," she said.

Brady bent over the rail beside her. "Sure enough, and she's got a baby."

Juliet stared at the brown furry creature bobbing on its back. It was a mother cradling a tiny baby with black beady eyes that stared fearlessly at them. She felt Brady's arm around her as he leaned close to watch. He didn't seem so threatening now, sharing the same fascination she felt.

"She seems totally contented, doesn't she?" Juliet observed. "Like she had nothing better to do than just lie there and let the waves rock them."

"Maybe she doesn't." Brady held Juliet tighter. "She's got a full belly, and probably a place to go for the night. What more could she want?"

Juliet nodded silently. It all seemed so simple.

Brady straightened, putting his hands on her shoulders. "We've got a place to go for the night, too. Are you ready?"

Juliet turned toward him, and his eyes, dark as midnight, locked with hers. His meaning was clear. Silently, Juliet looked away, staring out at the rolling ocean. The sun was setting, a glowing red ball fading beyond the horizon, and the sky had turned to a smoky-purple dusk. He was waiting for an answer, and there was only one she could give him. "Yes, Brady," she said softly. "I guess it's time to go."

THE ROOM WAS DECORATED in a modified country theme, a delicate balance of casual and elegant. Juliet didn't notice. Her eyes were riveted on the bed. A huge bed with ornate posts rising at its corners to support an arched lace canopy. The bed dwarfed everything else in the room, and the longer Juliet stared at it, the bigger it got.

"I hope everything is all right," the bellboy said politely. His job finished, he stood near Brady, waiting.

"Just fine," Brady assured him, reaching for his wallet.

Juliet didn't say anything at all. She glanced around the room, but found her attention drawn almost immediately back to the bed.

"Well, here we are," Brady said conversationally after he handed the bellboy a tip and the young man left.

"Yes, here we are." *And what in God's name are we doing here?* she thought.

Brady laid the room key the bellboy had given him on a small table near the door. He looked around. The room was everything the desk clerk had promised on the phone. "Do you like it?" he asked Juliet.

"Like it?" She hadn't moved. "It's really big."

"Big?" Brady looked at her curiously. That was an odd comment for someone as cosmopolitan as she appeared to be. "Well," he said skeptically, "I suppose as hotel rooms go..."

"Oh! You mean the room." She hadn't been paying attention. Looking around carefully for the first time, she managed a weak smile. "It's a lovely room," she answered sincerely.

Brady walked toward her, still puzzled by her response. "What did you think I meant?"

"Well, I don't know...." Juliet searched for a graceful way out. "This is a really nice inn. Have you been here before?"

Maybe her thoughts had been elsewhere, Brady decided. "I took a trip down here when I first came to San Francisco," he replied, "and I made up my mind right then if I ever went on a honeymoon, this was the place."

"I see," Juliet murmured. This was an insipid conversation. Why was she so flustered? Obviously, it had something to do with going to bed with Brady. But why? She was no prude. That night in the beach house she'd wanted him, really wanted him. She thought back, trying to recapture those feelings. It didn't work.

Brady put one hand on her shoulder and then lightly stroked her arm. She could feel his eyes on her, but she didn't look up. Maybe if she had just a little more time.... Her eyes darted around the room, she searched for something, anything, to divert him.

"Oh, Brady!" she exclaimed enthusiastically. "This room has a fireplace."

Brady frowned, moving his hand away from her arm. "Of course it has a fireplace. Did you just notice it?"

Juliet approached the corner fireplace, a prominent feature in the room with its raised hearth and rough-hewn mantel. Developing a sudden interest in the decor, she touched the patterned blue-and-white tiles that bordered the sides of the hearth. "How pretty," she said. "Maybe we can have a fire."

"A fire?" Brady gave the wood box a cursory glance. "I guess it *is* a working fireplace," he conceded, "but why don't we wait till tomorrow to build a fire?" Raising his arms over his head, he stretched expansively. "It's getting late, and it's been a long day." He approached Juliet again, standing behind her, his hands on her upper arms. "You must be tired, too."

"Oh, no," Juliet answered quickly, turning to face him. "I'm not tired at all." She noticed a bouquet of mixed flowers in the center of a table between two large, blue chairs. "I like the flowers," she commented to fill in the silence. "Did you order them specially?"

Brady turned to see what she was talking about. "No, they must come with the honeymoon suite."

"Honeymoon suite?" she repeated. "We're in the honeymoon suite?"

"It seemed appropriate," Brady remarked. "After all, we are on our honeymoon." He scrutinized her carefully. This had gone far enough. "Juliet . . ." he began, his fingers tightening on her arm. He waited till she looked up at him. "Juliet, are you . . ." he began again. Something stopped him, as though he sensed she was begging him not to push her and not to ask the intimate questions that were on his mind. "Juliet," he asked gently, "would you like a glass of champagne?"

"Yes." Her eyes were grateful. "I'd like that very much."

While Brady picked up the bottle of champagne that had been chilling in an ice bucket near the fireplace, Juliet sat down in one of the blue chairs, slipping out of her shoes and tucking her feet underneath her so she occupied the whole chair seat. She was going to have to come to terms with her problem, whatever it was—and quickly. Maybe it was getting married, she speculated, but quickly realized that while the ceremony had been profoundly disturbing, it was over and she didn't feel any more married than she had before.

Here at the inn, with the day behind her, she should be breathing a huge sigh of relief. Instead her hands were icy cold and her stomach was in a knot again. Juliet watched Brady unwrap the foil from the top of the champagne bottle. Again, she thought about that night in his beach house, that night when she had felt so very differently.

Brady popped the cork and it shot to the ceiling, bouncing off a beam and landing across the room. "To us," he said, handing her a glass of the bubbling champagne and taking a sip of his own.

Juliet took a large gulp. "Brady," she asked suddenly, "which side of the bed do you sleep on?"

"Well—" he grinned, sitting on the edge of the other blue chair and leaning toward her "—it just depends. Most nights, I sleep right in the middle."

"Oh." Juliet replied in a small voice.

Brady worked hard to control a smile. "Do you have a favorite side?"

"I always sleep on the right side," she proclaimed. "But maybe that's just because my night stand is on that side, and I like to be near the phone...." Her voice trailed off.

"That's all right," he assured her. "You can have the right side. It shouldn't be much of an issue after a night or two anyway."

Juliet shifted in her chair and took another large drink of champagne.

Brady drained his glass and set it on the table with a deliberate clank. "Juliet, we've had a full day. It's time we got ready for bed."

Juliet's eyes widened. In one quick motion, she emptied her glass. "Do you think I could have some more champagne?" She held the glass out to Brady who promptly refilled it. He did not, she noticed, pour any more for himself.

"Would you like to go into the bathroom first or shall I?" he inquired.

"Well, if you're really tired—"

A fleeting frown shadowed Brady's eyes and he looked hard at Juliet. "I'm not 'really tired,' and neither are you," he asserted flatly. "That has nothing to do with it. Now, would you like the bathroom first?"

"No, no," Juliet demurred. "You go ahead. I'm still finishing my champagne."

"I didn't know you liked champagne so much," Brady remarked as he opened his suitcase.

"Oh, yes." She took another sip, drawing it straight down so it didn't touch the sides of her tongue. "It's so bubbly," she added. She watched Brady loosen the straps that held his clothes in neatly folded stacks. He removed a robe and a shaving kit, then walked back across the room and set them on a table beside her. She didn't see any pajamas. Maybe he did sleep in the nude, after all.

Brady began casually unbuttoning his shirt. "Today has been a lot to handle, Juliet—more than either one of us expected." She watched his fingers move with agility as he progressed to the next shirt button. It was hard to remember the day. She had a flash of her loneliness when she'd stepped out of the cab onto that deserted street; of that look in Brady's eyes when he first saw her just before the wedding; of Cass near tears when she lovingly arranged the mantilla.

The last button unfastened, Brady pulled out his shirttail. "We haven't had very long to get to know each other, Juliet."

She watched him pull his arms out of the shirtsleeves and wad the shirt into a ball.

"Even if this is only a short-term arrangement, I guess it's natural we might have some qualms about it," he continued, pulling his V-neck T-shirt off over his head.

His chest was broad, Juliet noted, and covered with thick, tightly curled hair. She'd never seen him without his shirt before. She watched in fascination as he slipped the undershirt inside the wadded shirt and tossed both in the direction of his suitcase. He leaned over her, naked to the waist, not touching her. Juliet lowered her eyes, waiting. He lightly brushed her hair with his fingertips and asked softly, "Juliet, would you like some more champagne before I go into the bathroom?"

Juliet look at the half-empty glass on the table and then up at Brady. "No, thank you, I don't want any more." Whatever her problem, more champagne wouldn't solve it.

He picked up his robe and shaving kit and kissed her lightly on the cheek. "I won't be long," he called back to her before he closed the bathroom door.

Juliet sat perfectly still, watching the bubbles rise and burst in her champagne glass. The night in the beach house, Brady had stopped. He had sensed the change in her. No other man had ever done that. Most men were satisfied with a willing participant. Brady obviously wanted more. Again her eyes were drawn to the bed, its French-blue coverlet trimmed in lace that matched the edging on the dust ruffle. Deep inside, Juliet knew what Brady wanted. It was a part of her she had never been able to give any man. The problem was, Brady knew the difference. That made the wedding night like a command performance, one Juliet knew already she could never complete.

She stood up, stretching her stiff, tight muscles. She could hear water running in the bathroom. Slowly, she began to pace diagonally across the room and then back again. Her legs were shaking. Passing the bed, she stopped and pushed on the mattress with her hand. When it didn't give under the pressure, she

entatively sat down on the edge and bounced up and down a
ew times. Then she poked at the pillow.

Juliet swallowed hard, trying to contain the turmoil inside.
Maybe she should have talked to Brady, told him ... told him
what? That she liked sex even though she couldn't let herself go
completely? That he shouldn't expect so much of her?

She picked up the edge of the coverlet, tracing the patterns
n the lace with the tip of her fingers. Her attitude shouldn't
make any difference anyway, she told herself. She could still get
pregnant, and that was the point of all this. Or was it?
Abruptly, Juliet stood up and walked across the room to open
er suitcase. That was the heart of the problem, she realized
uddenly. However all this had started out, it wasn't strictly
ousiness anymore. Brady had made his way into her life and her
houghts. Even after everything she had said about no entan-
lements ...

Juliet rummaged in the suitcase until she located her white
vatiste nightgown at the very bottom and pulled it out with a
wift tug. Frowning, she held it up in front of her. It was per-
ectly plain except for a sprinkling of tiny yellow flowers at the
eck and eyelet lace at the armholes. Hardly the right thing for
. wedding night. Juliet wished she'd planned ahead.

She was still holding the nightgown when the bathroom door
pened and Brady emerged wearing a deep blue velour robe.
His hair, damp from the shower, was curly. He smelled of soap
nd shaving lotion and yet, as he came closer, Juliet realized
hat he still smelled like Brady.

"Sorry to take so long," he apologized, "but that shower felt
ood."

"I ... I didn't mind," Juliet answered quickly, bending over
he suitcase in search of her other slipper.

Brady laid his trousers across his open suitcase and put his
hoes on the floor under the ledge before he turned toward Juet. "Your turn," he prompted.

"You mean in the bathroom?" Juliet asked. She stood in
ront of him, her nightgown over her arm, her slippers hugged
gainst her body, and her small case filled with toiletries
lutched firmly in her free hand.

Brady tried to control his impatience. "From the looks of things, that would appear to be where you're headed," he noted wryly. "I'll be waiting."

"Right," said Juliet. She hurried toward the bathroom.

For several moments after she disappeared, Brady stared at the locked bathroom door, shaking his head. "I'll be damned," he muttered to himself. The signs were unmistakable. For some reason that was beyond him, Juliet Cavanaugh was scared to death. Only she wasn't Juliet Cavanaugh any more, he reminded himself. She was Juliet Talcott. "Damn!" he swore out loud. What the hell had he done?

Stuffing his hands in the pockets of his robe, Brady paced back and forth in short, quick steps. Except she wasn't Juliet Talcott either. That was only on paper. No wonder she was confused. He went to the side of the bed and turned back the coverlet, leaning across to smooth the other side. Her side. She said she always slept on the right.

He began pacing again. He should have taken her that night at the beach house. Then making love now wouldn't be such an issue. He thought about her body, soft and beautiful in the firelight, and the texture of her skin, like spun silk, and her hair that glistened in the red of the sunset. His body stirred, and he pulled the belt on his robe tighter. Methodically, he turned off all the lights in the room except for a small hurricane lamp by the bed, and then he sat down by the fireplace to wait. Damn, she was slow.

CHAPTER EIGHT

THE BATHROOM DOOR opened, pouring light into the darkened room. Brady sat forward expectantly. Juliet was a study in hesitation, emerging barefoot, her auburn hair flowing to her shoulders, the nightgown dropping in soft folds to the floor. She stopped when she saw Brady and reached back to turn off the bathroom light.

Instantly Brady was on his feet, moving toward her. She watched his approach as if in a dream. "You're beautiful, Juliet." His voice caressed her. Still studying her face, he slipped a hand under her gleaming hair.

Feeling very shy, Juliet avoided his eyes. "I'm sorry I didn't get an appropriate nightgown," she told him. "I guess I didn't think about . . ."

Brady held her at arm's length, a puzzled expression on his face. "What could possibly be more appropriate?" he asked her. When she didn't answer, Brady continued, "But if you don't like it, we'll take care of that right now." In one swift motion, he caught the hem of her gown in both hands and pulled it off, dropping it on the floor beside her.

"Brady!" she gasped.

He never took his eyes from hers. "You are now more lovely than you could possibly be in any nightgown ever created," he assured her. His hand brushed her cheek. "If they were giving awards for wedding night attire, you'd be the unanimous choice for best dressed."

Juliet's mouth quivered, but she forced a smile. "I do feel very naked."

"You didn't turn and run."

Her smile widened, slowly becoming genuine. "I never even thought about it," she admitted.

Brady's eyes crinkled at the corners. "That means we'
halfway there." He scooped her up in his arms and carried h
across the room.

"That's twice, Brady," she warned mischievously. "I'm g
ing to begin to expect this kind of service."

"Your turn next time," he promised glibly. "Equality, y
know." He put her down gently on the crisp white sheet ar
stood above her. "I know, wrong side," he muttered pla
fully. "You always sleep on the right. But I'll share just th
once."

He untied the belt and let his robe fall backward off h
shoulders. Juliet caught her bottom lip between her teet
watching his every move. His body was trim and strong in t
soft lamplight. Dark hair curled in a soft, springy mat on h
chest, thinning toward the flat muscles of his abdomen. Sl
could see those muscles, flexed and taut, drawing in at h
waist.

Juliet averted her eyes. "Do you think we could turn out t
light?" she asked in a small voice. Except for the flush high c
her cheekbones, her skin was almost as white as the sheet.

Sitting beside her on the bed, Brady frowned. The moon ha
set early, and without the dim lamp they would be in tot
darkness. Brady wanted to taste and touch Juliet, but he want
more than that. He wanted to relish her with all his senses. H
wanted to watch her face, as he had in the firelight, when b
touch and his kisses consumed her. "Why do you want the lig'
off?" he asked her.

"Well, I just thought it might be more . . . more . . ."

"It would make you more comfortable?"

"Maybe . . . well, yes . . . no . . ."

Brady moved closer to her, his lean hip pressing against b
gentle curves. "I don't want the light off, Juliet." He strok
her cheek with two fingers, which felt cool against her burni
skin. "I want to see your face. I want to savor all of you." H
lowered his mouth to hers and flicked his tongue across her lip
softening and moistening them until they melted into his.

He touched her, gently at first, his hands moving and e
ploring. As fire rose rapidly within him, he grew insistent an
then demanding. He could feel her breath coming in litt

asps, and he stretched out his body until he was lying against
er.

Something wasn't right. Brady opened his eyes and looked
t Juliet. Her eyelids were squeezed shut, and her hands were
lenched into tight fists at either side of her head. He sensed she
vas literally holding her breath, waiting.

"Juliet," he said hoarsely. "What's wrong?"

Slowly she opened her eyes and in the jade-green depths he
aw that he'd been right. Her little gasps had not been breaths
f passion. She was scared.

"Talk to me, Juliet," he demanded, forcibly restraining his
esire.

She turned her face away. "I don't know what to say, Brady.
'ou expect so much of me and I—I don't think I can do it."

"Look at me, Juliet," he demanded. Slowly she turned her
ead. She looked so fragile, so vulnerable, her green eyes huge
a that fair, fine-boned face. "Juliet," he asked gently, "are
ou a virgin?"

"No," she said in a barely audible voice.

His forehead wrinkled. He tried to sort it out. "Then what
s it? What is it you think I expect of you?"

Juliet wanted to crawl away and hide. She had to try to tell
im, but she didn't know how. These were intimate, hidden
celings she had never verbalized. "It's just that when
ou...we...get to a certain point, I don't...I don't feel the
ame anymore. It isn't that I don't like it...I just don't feel quite
s...quite the same." It was so hard to talk about. His eyes were
ark as midnight, inscrutable. She had no idea whether he
ould even begin to understand, but she couldn't seem to go on.

Brady sat silently for a moment, thinking over what she had
aid. "What you're telling me is that you have a shut-off but-
on, and when I hit it, it's over for you."

Relief washed through Juliet. In an odd way, he did under-
tand. "But I want you to go ahead," she added quickly. "I
ust—it doesn't work to wait for me."

"But you weren't going to say anything about this, were
ou?" he demanded accusingly. "You were just going to let me
o ahead—"

"That's what I want you to do," she interrupted. Maybe he
idn't understand after all.

Tenderly he stroked her hair back from her face. "Oh Ju
liet, Juliet," he murmured softly. "You're so damn dete
mined to be superwoman and handle everything on your ow
that you have no idea what it can be for two people t
gether...." His voice trailed off. "Trust me, Juliet," he d
rected. "For this one time, this one night, let yourself tru
somebody else."

Juliet wasn't sure what he meant. "I'll try, Brady," s
agreed tentatively. "I'm not doing this very well."

"Dammit, Juliet! We're not having a contest," he e
ploded, raising his body almost to a sitting position. "This
one area where your standard measures of accomplishme
don't apply. There's no right or wrong. Think you can hand
that for a little while?"

He was so intense he frightened her. "Are you angr
Brady?" She almost wished he wouldn't answer.

"No, not angry." He shook his head. "Just trying to figu
out how to get to you. My grandfather had this saying. He sa
there weren't any cold women—just bad lovers. You need
start by believing that. Grandfather was a very wise man."

"I...I'm not cold, Brady," she answered defensively.

"No, Juliet, you're not cold. But I don't think you have a
idea how really passionate you are. I think it's time you fou
out."

"I guess I can try," she agreed again, this time reaching h
arms around his neck to pull him back to her. But he didn
move. "Not that way, Juliet. This way." He took her han
patiently unclenching her fist, and very gently stroked h
palm.

She wasn't sure what he was doing, but he kept on un
slowly her hand began to relax and Juliet found her entire b
ing focused on the sensation. "M-m-m... That feels goo
Brady." She didn't try to hide the surprise in her voice. The
wasn't much point in trying to hide anything from him now.

"All right," he told her. "It's your turn. I want you to strol
my hand just the same way."

His suggestion seemed easy enough. Juliet cradled his han
against her stomach and gently touched him. After a while, sl
was amazed to feel a stirring deep inside her. She was almo

disappointed when he took his hand away and touched the inside of her arm.

He moved his hands with deliberate slowness, until the shell of fear melted away and he found the softness of the woman waiting for him. She was sensual and lovely, and it took all his determination to harness the passion building in him. He could have touched her, but to share, she had to also give to him. He took a deep breath, anticipating the delicious agony.

Juliet was beginning to drift into a pleasant oblivion when Brady stopped and lay back on his side, waiting. She raised up one elbow, her fingers outlining the roughness of his jaw and then moving quickly to explore the thick hair on his chest. Brady seemed willing to let her go on touching him, but she was growing more and more restless. She moved her hand downward, to the taut skin at his waist, and felt him draw a sharp breath. His response was like a lightening bolt that shot through her in an incredible burst of heat.

"Touch me, too, Brady," she urged him. She pulled his hand down to her breast. "Oh . . . oh, Brady, that makes me feel like—"

"Like more and more," he breathed.

"Oh, yes."

"Not quite yet," he whispered, feathering kisses downward until Juliet gasped with pleasure.

He wrapped one leg around her, and she lay back on the pillow, moving against him. Her hands began to explore Brady hungrily, twining in the tightly curled hair on his chest and then running downward along his firm, taut hips. Juliet's entire body seemed to be on fire. The more she touched him, her hands, her mouth, her tongue flicking across his skin, the more the driving, burning sensations welled up in her.

"Don't you feel it?" she whispered in desperation. "Don't you know what's happening inside me?"

"Tell me," he commanded in a hoarse whisper. "Tell me how you feel."

At first she didn't answer, unable to focus on anything except his hand on her waist.

"Talk to me, Juliet," he demanded. "Tell me what you're thinking."

"I'm not thinking." She fought to form the words, reaching downward, touching him as he was now touching her. He moaned softly.

"Oh, Brady, more . . . I . . ." His fingers were moving rhythmically upward along her thigh. Juliet arched her back, her body writhing against his.

"Brady," she cried out. She felt it happening, her response unbearable, consuming. Driven by a passion that exceeded all her fantasies, she dug her fingernails into his shoulders. "Don't stop, please don't stop," she pleaded.

"God, no, Juliet," he rasped. "I want you." His mouth found hers, open and ready, as she clutched him, grasping his hips to pull him down. He plunged deep inside her, and she cried out again, a piercing cry amidst the shuddering gasps pulsing through her.

Finally, her body trembling, she dropped back against the pillow, overwhelmed by him and by herself. She felt his hand gently enclosing her breast. His breathing slowed until it was deep and steady, and when she opened her eyes, he was watching her, his face peaceful, his eyelids heavy.

"It was good," Brady said.

"Very good," she murmured, her voice dazed and soft.

He studied her, sharing the peace that had settled around them. "You trusted me, Juliet. You let yourself be you, instead of fighting."

"But I didn't make it happen, Brady. When I touched you, I had these feelings—"

He smiled, knowing she couldn't describe her feelings because there were no words. He also knew that what they'd done had forged a bond between them that was irreversible. A man and a woman couldn't share together what they had shared and come out of it unchanged. However much they might someday want to, they could never go back. He stroked the damp tendrils of hair away from her face. She smelled of musky springtime, a delicious smell that tempted his senses. He leaned over to kiss her breast, moving with the heaviness of approaching sleep.

"Can I stay nestled here against you Brady?" she asked him, knowing it would produce a grin.

He nuzzled her lazily. "You mean on the wrong side of the bed?" He liked the sound of her melodic laughter.

"I guess I hadn't noticed." She snuggled closer to him, her eyelids fluttering and falling closed. "I think I'd like to sleep right here tonight."

BRADY AWOKE WITH Juliet in his arms. He felt his body stirring even before he opened his eyes. Her breathing was light and regular. He knew she was still asleep, although the sun already streamed through the windows. He shifted slightly against her soft, warm flesh. Her hair was draped across his arm, glistening in the early light, framing a face innocent in sleep. She'd bared her soul to him. He'd asked for trust, and she'd given it all. The heat was building in him. He kissed her lightly, knowing it would awaken her.

When Juliet felt his lips brush her mouth she sighed softly, opening to him, inviting him. She never was sure when she crossed the threshold of consciousness, or whether she ever did. Afterward, when she lay against him, she could only remember the passion that had consumed her and the fulfillment that followed. It took great effort to finally open her eyes.

Brady lay beside her, looking as languid as she felt. "Good morning," he greeted her. "Almost good afternoon."

"Is it that late?" She was surprised, but not the least bit concerned.

"Do you suppose we should get up?" he asked, propping his head on his elbow so that he could see her face.

Juliet didn't feel very ambitious. "Why should we get up? Is there somewhere we have to go?"

Brady laughed softly. "That's right. You were the one who was worried about what we were going to do for a whole week."

Juliet lowered her eyelids seductively. "I guess I wasn't fully aware of all the available activities."

"There are others," Brady suggested. "But I can't promise any of them will be quite as much fun." He ran his fingers slowly through her hair. "For example, we could get up and go eat. Or even take a walk."

Juliet gave him a look of wide-eyed innocence. "You mean before we go back to bed?"

Brady chuckled, and gave her a hard whack on the back-side. "You don't do anything halfway, do you Juliet?"

"Ouch!" she yelped, grabbing for him as he sprang out of bed.

It was early afternoon by the time they both dressed. Brady ordered sandwiches and soft drinks from room service while Juliet took a shower. She ate with him, wrapped in a large terry towel. "I'm beginning to think that's one of your regular out-fits," he teased her, eyeing the beige towel. "But I think I pre-fer you in blue."

After they'd dressed and left the room, they wandered aim-lessly around Carmel, poking through the shops, exploring the tiny art galleries that dotted the narrow, sloping streets. They lingered in a toy shop, rearranging an entire display of wooden soldiers much to the amusement of the owner, who had been having a very slow day. By sundown they were both incredibly hungry. Juliet was ready to stop for a sandwich, but Brady in-tervened.

"We ate out of cardboard boxes for our wedding dinner and off a tray for lunch. Tonight," he announced, "we will dine."

After a glass of wine and some cheese and crackers from room service to stave off their hunger, they showered and dressed. When Juliet emerged from the bathroom with its combined dressing room, Brady let out a low whistle. He started at her feet, letting his eyes move from her high-heeled sandals up the shapely curve of her legs. He lingered on the midnight-blue dress that draped her hips and torso above the soft folds of the skirt. Finally, he let his eyes rise to her face—fair skin framed by thick, flowing auburn hair and those eyes—those magnificent green eyes.

"You are absolutely smashing, my dear." He kept his tone light and playful.

She gave a low curtsy. "Thank you, kind sir."

"Shall we go?" he asked, offering his arm, knowing that if they lingered, they wouldn't go at all.

The evening air was sweet with the smell of flowers that lined the long stairway up to the restaurant. Inside, candlelight flickered across the faces of the diners in the softly lit room, and the subdued conversation faded into the sound of the grand piano, which filled an entire corner of the intimate restaurant.

The maître d' seated them at a table near an expanse of windows where they could see the moon rising across the bay.

From the wine, through perfect Beef Wellington, to fresh fruit, the moon turned from soft yellow to silver, its reflection shimmering on the foaming surf. The moonbeams turned the sun-cured grasses white beneath the rugged silhouette of a single Monterey Pine. Juliet stared at the stark outline, letting it form shapes and patterns in her imagination. The man at the piano played a familiar love song that touched a chord deep within her. She felt Brady's fingers curl protectively around hers as he asked her to dance.

Juliet stood up slowly, his hand warm and sensual on her back. Once on the dance floor, Juliet moved in his rhythm, letting him lead her with his eyes and his body until nothing else mattered but the music, and the night, and the two of them. Her fluid movements matched his as he whirled her, light as a feather, in perfect time to the music. The piano player chose a slow love song, and their tempo kept pace with his. Brady silently pressed his cheek against her hair, and Juliet closed her eyes, drifting with him on a cloud of music. In those moments, untouched by the world outside, her life was perfect.

She became aware slowly that the music had stopped, but Brady was still holding her. For a long moment, neither of them moved. In the soft amber glow of the lights above the dance floor, Juliet caught a glimpse of her own feelings reflected in Brady's dark eyes. She sensed that something had changed between them. But she refused to think beyond that.

She felt Brady's hands on her shoulders, guiding her toward their table. Quickly Brady paid the check, and they hurried back to the inn.

It was past noon nearly every day when they emerged from their room. One morning they did wake up with the dawn, and by ten o'clock that same day they were on their way south, driving down toward the Big Sur to look for migrating whales. They both knew it was too early in the season, but they went anyway.

Once the soupy fog that shrouded early fall mornings finally burned through, Juliet felt like they were emerging from a damp cavern into the splendor of the open air. Brady pulled off the road along a deserted stretch of coastline, and they climbed a grassy knoll that rose above the surf where they could look out across the water. High above the desolate beauty of the land, the cries of the birds mixed with the whisper of the wind, nature's symphony underscored always by the dull roar of the ocean. How far away they seemed from San Francisco, Juliet thought, and how much farther still from the rest of her life.

Brady shaded his eyes and searched the vibrant blue expanse of water beyond the breaker line. "Too bad it's not a couple of months from now. We might really see some whales." He turned toward her. "Have you ever watched them?"

"When I was a little girl," Juliet answered. "I used to spend hours along the water when they were migrating."

Taking her hand, Brady led her to a large flat rock, warmed by the sun, and watched with amusement as she unzipped her jacket and lay down flat on her stomach to soak up the heat. Slipping his hand beneath her loose jacket, he rubbed his palm lazily across her back. "Juliet," he said thoughtfully, "when you first came up with that hare-brained scheme to have a baby, did it ever occur to you that you might have—" he searched for the right words "—some problems?"

"What do you mean, 'problems'?" Juliet responded sleepily.

"You know damn well what I mean." She didn't answer. He tried another approach. "Did you ever consider the process of getting pregnant?"

Juliet opened her eyes, propped herself on one elbow, and looked at him. "Well, sort of. I guess I didn't worry too much about the specifics." She shaded her eyes against the sunlight "What I wanted ... what I *want* is to have a baby. I kind of thought we'd have some meetings, very carefully timed, of course, and then, well ... I'd be pregnant."

Brady frowned. "That wouldn't have been much fun."

Juliet eyed him curiously. "It wasn't supposed to be fun. It was supposed to be productive."

"Damn." Brady swore softly. "Is that what you think about sex, Juliet?"

"Well..." Her eyes twinkled mischievously. "Maybe *though* is a better word than think." Playfully, she pulled his head down and found his mouth. She teased his lips with the tip of her tongue until he kissed her back. He shifted his weight so that he was lying next to her and let his fingers trace the curves underneath her yellow knit shirt.

"Oh!" Juliet gasped in surprise. Those now familiar sensations, never far from the surface when she was with Brady, sprang to life again. "Let's go back to the inn," Juliet whispered. Her thighs were pressed against his hip.

"Why?" Brady asked, burying her answer beneath his lips.

Juliet pressed tighter against him. "Because what we're doing makes me want—" She gasped as his tongue blazed a trail down the side of her cheek and his breath, hot and moist, grazed her ear.

"And then again," Brady murmured, "we could stay right here." He slipped his hand under her shirt.

"Right here?" What he was suggesting suddenly sank in. Her whole body quivered. "Brady, stop," she pleaded. "We can't. What if someone—"

"No one will. It's just us and the seagulls," he assured her, his voice almost lost in the lone piercing cry of a bird.

"But, Brady..." Juliet struggled one last time, and then his fingers were stirring a throbbing, pulsing passion that blotted out her reservations. She heard the barking of the sea lions above the roaring surf and felt the wind brush across her bare skin. The sun's warmth became an intense heat all around her, and then, it seemed to be coming from inside her.

Afterward, she stayed a part of him, their bodies joined together even as they lay still. A long time later, Juliet felt the wind ruffle her hair and she shivered with cold as Brady moved away from her. "The sun's gone behind a cloud," he told her, rearranging her shirt and jeans.

She sat up. "Is that why it feels colder?"

"Not entirely." His lips brushed her cheek. "We were generating a lot of heat on our own." He took her hand and helped her to her feet, again wrapping his arms around her and holding her close. Then, hand in hand, they walked slowly down the steep slope, the whales forgotten, as they got in the car to head back toward Carmel.

On their last day they went back to bed after breakfast. It wasn't until noon, when Brady was drying Juliet's back after a long, luxurious shower, that he decided it was time for them to plan what came next. "I've been thinking...." He paused to kiss the back of her neck. "I'm not sure where the best place is for us to live." He soaked up the droplets of water clinging to her shoulder blades and then rubbed the towel across her hips. "My apartment in the city is a small studio—I only keep it for nights I can't get out to the beach. The house there is perfect, except for the commute. I don't know if you're going to want to drive that far. I suppose we could try your apartment—"

Juliet tensed, resisting the urge to clasp both hands over her ears to shut out his words. "Wait a minute," she said quietly. Then she took a towel and wrapped it firmly around her body. "What do you mean *we?*"

He drew back, frowning at her. "Just what I said. We. We—that's you and I—we have to figure out where we're going to live when we get back to the city."

With her back toward him, Juliet slipped quickly into her robe. "I presume," she said without looking at him, "that 'we' will live where we've always lived—you in your house or apartment, or whatever you have, and me in my apartment."

The change in Juliet registered instantly with Brady as he followed her out of the bathroom. This was the lawyer talking. Not cold, exactly, but distant. Determined. Not at all like the woman who had spent the last week with him. "That's a rather unusual arrangement for two people who are married," he noted dryly.

"But we're not married," she countered, concentrating on the slacks and heavy cotton sweater she was removing from her suitcase. "We have an arrangement."

Brady paced across the room, walking past the unmade bed to sit in one of the wing chairs near the fireplace. "Ah, yes. An arrangement." He crossed his legs and sat back. "And if I recall correctly, your purpose in the whole affair is to get pregnant. That requires some contact."

His voice was controlled, but not sarcastic. Juliet wasn't quite sure what to do. It had never occurred to her that he would expect to live with her. That was carrying things too far. She had her own apartment, her own routine, her own way of doing things. Besides, her apartment wasn't big enough for two people. But that wasn't the only thing bothering her, and she knew it. Ever since they'd started getting ready to go home, Juliet had begun to feel differently. For the first time in a week she'd thought about the office, the work that was waiting for her, the life she'd left behind. She turned toward him, her clothes over her arm, her robe clutched tightly around her. "We can't live together, Brady. Neither apartment is big enough and the beach is too far."

"Then what's the alternative?" Brady kept all emotion out of his voice. She was obviously trying to be reasonable.

"We can see each other. Maybe spend the night together sometimes. I already know when I'm most likely to get pregnant." She reached down in the corner of her suitcase and produced a pink engagement calendar. "I've got it all charted in here."

Brady just stared at her.

"Is something wrong?" she asked.

"No, Juliet, I guess not. We just have two different pictures of the way we were going to proceed." He stood up slowly and walked toward the door, making no move toward her. "Why don't you get dressed while I go down to the office and settle with the inn?" he suggested.

"Wait, Brady," she stopped him. "Shouldn't we split the bill?" She hadn't really thought about the expenses all week when he automatically picked up the tabs. Suddenly she felt she needed to ask.

For a long moment Brady looked at her, silently. He couldn't figure out the unfamiliar and unpleasant tension between them. "No, Juliet, we don't need to split it. This one's on me." He closed the door firmly, leaving Juliet feeling very much alone. She walked into the bathroom, locking the door behind her.

They said very little during the drive home. Brady put a cassette of classical music on the tape deck, mostly to fill the silence. When they arrived at Juliet's apartment, he offered to carry her suitcases up for her. He wasn't surprised when she thanked him but refused. Before she got out of the car, she slipped the wedding ring off her finger and wordlessly handed it back to Brady. He took it without comment and put it into his jacket pocket. He didn't want it back, but there wasn't much point in making an issue of it.

Brady waited, the car still running, until her apartment light switched on, glowing along with hundreds of others in the early-evening darkness. He sat quietly for a long time, staring at that light, watching for shadows of movement. His fingers idly traced the gold band in his pocket. Finally he gunned the accelerator and headed for his apartment. He didn't have it in him to drive all the way to the beach.

CHAPTER NINE

BRADY TOOK ANOTHER sip of coffee. He was damn sick of seeing Juliet by appointment only. It had been like that for weeks, ever since they got back from Carmel. If she wasn't busy, he was. She claimed she wasn't avoiding him. In fact she'd accused him of avoiding her.

He ran his finger down the listings in the real estate section of the morning paper. "Two bedroom, beautiful view.... Sublet, available immediately.... Dream pad near Golden Gate Park...." Occasionally he picked up the pencil that kept getting lost in the newspaper spread all across his kitchen table, and marked a likely-looking apartment. If he could find a couple of good ones, maybe he could persuade Juliet to go look at them. He checked his watch. He was picking her up at one. He would call ahead and arrange to see the few that looked like the best prospects, and if she refused to go look at them—well, then she refused.

But they were going to have to figure out something. She'd informed him that according to her pink book they'd totally missed out on prime time last month. He wasn't wasting any sympathy over that one. He didn't like scheduling his sex life by some woman's little pink book.

Disgusted, he went back to the listings, copying phone numbers and addresses on a separate sheet of paper. He barely looked up when the back door banged.

"You considering going into real estate?" Phil looked over Brady's shoulder at the real estate section.

"Hell, no," Brady growled. He kept writing. "Get yourself some coffee and have a seat."

Phil tossed his jacket on a chair and opened the cupboard to find a cup. Brady was in a lousy mood. Marriage obviously wasn't agreeing with him, although it wasn't much of a mar-

riage with him out here and her in the city. Of course, Phil re
minded himself as he poured the coffee, their union was only
paper agreement. From what he'd seen of Juliet Cavanaugh,
relationship with her would be damn hard to keep on paper.

"So what are you up to?" Phil prodded. He pushed the fron
section of the newspaper aside and sat down across from Brady
"Is the lease up on your apartment?"

Brady scowled. "No. I'm going to try to convince Juliet tha
we should rent an apartment together. I saw more of her be
fore we got married."

"It would put you in a better position legally if you were liv
ing together," Phil observed. "This looks suspicious. But
thought you told me she refused to live with you."

"She did." Brady slammed down his pencil. "And she'
never going to get pregnant this way."

Phil eyed Brady skeptically. He had the distinct impressio
that getting Juliet pregnant had very little to do with the rea
problem, at least from Brady's perspective. "I take it that's th
excuse you plan to use," he needled his friend.

"Got any better suggestions?"

Phil started to give him a flip answer, and then he stopped
"Yes," he answered, "maybe I do."

Brady looked at him with renewed interest.

"Why don't you buy a house?"

"Don't be funny," Brady snapped. Sometimes Phil irr
tated him.

"No, wait a minute, I'm serious." Phil shifted in his chai
"I have a client who's got to unload one of those old Victor
ans up in Pacific Heights in a hurry. He bought the thing fo
investment, was planning to renovate it. Then the IRS caugh
up with him. If he doesn't get hold of some cash in a hurry, it'
all over."

"Probably a good deal," Brady muttered. "But it doesn'
solve my problems."

"Your brain's in neutral," Phil complained. "We're talkin
about an investment—you know, money to make money?" Fo
someone with as much imagination as Brady, he sure wasn'
picking up on this one.

"Huh?" Brady stared at him.

"If Juliet won't live with you, maybe she'll invest with you. If you'd live in the thing for a few months and get it decorated and furnished, you could sell it for a tidy profit. You could put your earnings in trust for the baby—that should appeal to her."

Brady wadded up the piece of paper he'd been writing on and pitched it at the wastebasket. "By God, she might go for it. Then can we move in?"

"As soon as you can come up with the earnest money," Phil told him. "My client's about to list it with a realtor, but I've got the keys now if you want to go take a look at it."

"You're on!" Brady grinned. "I'm picking up Juliet at one. Say, how about coming with us? I could use an advocate. If you tell her what a good deal it is, maybe she'll bite."

"Sorry, Brady, I can't make it. Eileen's coming by to see the kids." Phil took a drink of coffee. The compassion in Brady's eyes was too close to pity. He didn't want it.

Brady sensed Phil's discomfort. He wished again he hadn't said some of the things he had after Eileen left. "Is she any better?" he asked cautiously. He knew how hard it was for Phil to talk about his wife.

"She seems to be." Phil's tone was noncommittal. "She claims she hasn't had a drink for a couple of weeks and she's got a new job."

"Still as a waitress?"

"This one's in a bar and grill—lousy neighborhood."

Brady winced. Eileen working in a bar sounded like a bad idea to him.

Phil finished his coffee and carried the cup to the sink, preoccupied. "She said there was something she wanted to talk to me about," he continued, putting on his jacket.

"Any clues as to what?" Brady asked.

"Not really. The build-up sounded like she wants the boys."

Brady shoved his chair back and stood up. Phil lived in constant fear that Eileen would take him to court and try to get at least partial custody. It would be wrong, all wrong. When she was drunk, there was no telling what might happen to Michael and Timmy. "You think she's considering legal action?" Brady asked.

Phil zipped his jacket, making a harsh, grating sound. "I don't know."

"Hell, Phil, even if she did, no court would—"

Phil cut him off, his eyes hard. "When you're dealing with a mother and children, you can't even start to predict what court might do."

Brady backed off. He was right, and they both knew it. They could only hope Eileen had enough sense to let well enough alone. Brady wasn't betting on it. Any mother who would walk out on her children would do practically anything.

"Stop by on your way into the city and I'll give you those keys," Phil called over his shoulder. He vaulted lightly over the deck rail and took off at a dead run down the beach.

"Damn!" Brady muttered, slamming the back door.

BRADY PICKED JULIET UP at one on the dot, surprised that she was ready. "The last time I showed up here at this hour on a Saturday afternoon you were dressed in bubbles," he teased her, brushing his hand across her hair. Whenever he saw her he wanted to touch her. Even hearing her voice on the phone unsettled him.

"The last time you came at one, you weren't due until eight," Juliet retorted, "and I practically set a speed record getting ready." The words weren't what she wanted to say to him. What she'd wanted to say was that she'd missed him terribly, and she'd been ready for an hour, and she'd hoped he'd be early.

Linda had been expecting her at the office to go over a new case, but as soon as Brady called, Juliet had postponed the meeting with Linda. They could do that anytime. What she really wanted was to see Brady. Ever since they got back from the honeymoon, they'd had one problem after another getting together.

"I've got something I want you to look at," Brady said casually. He'd slipped his arms around her and was looking down into her eyes. Her invitation was blatant. She'd been waiting just like he had. Maybe just for a little while... God, he wanted her. He knew it was crazy. There wasn't going to be any little while. "We need to see it now, in the daylight," he told her.

"Need to see what?" Juliet asked. She ran her fingers along the line of his jaw, slowly, suggestively.

"I want us to go see . . ." He paused. He had to do this just right and it was so damn hard to concentrate with her so close to him. "I want us to look at an investment," he said finally.

Juliet took her hand away. "An investment?" The only investment she was interested in was right here.

"Yes," he continued speaking quickly. "Phil told me this morning about a great opportunity, and I thought you might be interested, too."

Juliet stepped back, feeling disappointed. "Exactly what kind of investment did you have in mind?"

Brady sucked in his breath. He hadn't meant to approach the subject like this. He'd wanted to ease her into it. But now he was going to have to level with her. "One of those old Victorian houses in Pacific Heights." He quickly added, "Phil says it'll go cheap."

"You're suggesting we buy an old Victorian house?"

"Right," Brady affirmed. "As an investment. We can fix it up, sell it in a few months, and make a good profit." Before Juliet could protest, Brady took her hand and started for the door. "We can at least look at it. Come on—we'll talk while we drive."

Juliet was irritated all the way to the car. Ever since she woke up, she'd been fantasizing about the afternoon with Brady. None of those fantasies included going to look at an old house. Her frustration mounting, she tried to discourage him. "Brady, this is an exercise in futility. In the first place, where are we... or at least, where am I going to get the money to buy a house? Up there, cheap costs a fortune. And besides that, we're so busy we can't even find time to get together. And you want to renovate a house in the spare time we don't have?"

Brady kept his eyes on the road. It was a little easier to think now, with her belted on her side of the car and him on his. So, she was concerned about the cost of the house. He could give her the money, but she'd never go for that. Then he remembered. "At the beginning you talked to me about a..." Damn! She'd said it was crass to call it a stud fee, but what else could you call it? "You talked about paying $25,000 to the baby's father." That sounded better. He glanced sideways at Juliet. She appeared to be listening attentively. "I told you I didn't want to be paid—and it's not in the contract—so maybe you could use that money as part of the purchase price of the house."

Juliet was floored. When she thought about it, she realized he was right. They'd signed his contract, not hers, and the fee wasn't mentioned. How had she overlooked that? She'd never intended to drop it. "I fully expect to pay you Brady," she insisted. "That's the only way to carry out this arrangement on a business basis—"

She really is stubborn, Brady thought. But he was on the right track presenting this as a business investment. Pulling up at a red light, he reached over and took her hand. "Tell you what," he proposed. "If this house looks good, you put the $25,000 into it, and I'll come up with the rest of the purchase price. When we sell it, we'll each take back our investment, and the profit can go into a trust fund for the baby."

The light changed, the car behind them honked, and Brady turned back to his driving, guiding the car carefully up the steep hills along narrow, winding streets. Juliet sat frozen, her mind racing. This was one more involvement with him. She could see herself getting in deeper and deeper. And yet it was such a reasonable offer. Not just reasonable but generous. She stole a sideways glance at Brady. Maybe he felt some obligation to the baby even though he would never see it. He was that kind of person. This might help him meet that obligation and make things easier later.

Brady drummed his fingers on the steering wheel. The silence meant she was at least thinking about it. "So, how does that sound?" he inquired.

"It's very unexpected." She hesitated. "But if you want to do it—"

"I do," he cut in quickly, then he pulled the scrap of paper with the address on it from his jacket pocket. "Should be just another block or so...." Brady hit the brakes and swerved forward into a large parking place. "There it is," he announced, checking the address once more.

Juliet stared out the window at a slate-gray house, its columned front porch outlined in wooden filigree. A witches' turret rose high on one side with a curved window outlined in white. The place looked like an expanded version of the gingerbread house in *Hansel and Gretel*, except for the candy. In its day it had no doubt been lovely, and beneath the peeling paint she could still see possibilities—and a lot of work.

"Not bad," Brady commented. He hoped the contractor who had checked out the house had been reliable, because from the outside the place looked like it had problems. Phil had shown him the estimates and there hadn't been anything major. If it weren't for the circumstances, he'd think long and hard about buying this one. He opened his car door. "Let's go in and take a look."

"Inside?" Juliet questioned. "I thought we were just driving by."

"I got the keys from Phil this morning," Brady explained. "It looks as though it could use a little paint," he observed as they climbed the steps to the front porch. One corner of the porch was sagging, he noted silently.

"Brady, renovating this house would be a major project," Juliet said dubiously.

Brady was concentrating on the lock, finally getting it to work after several attempts. "We can't tell for sure until we've looked inside." He quickly opened the door, not ready to discuss the details quite yet.

Juliet was pleasantly surprised when she walked in. The sun streamed through a fan window above the doorway, making a rainbow of color on the wooden floor of the foyer. The drab walls and dirty wallpaper couldn't hide the beauty of the dark-stained wood and the graceful arches that invited them from one room to the next. The kitchen was spacious, with natural wood cabinets and up-to-date appliances, and the bathrooms were in reasonable condition. They even had claw-footed bathtubs. Obviously, someone had begun work on the house, probably over a period of several years, and then been interrupted before the job could be finished.

Brady found himself looking more carefully at Juliet than at the house, which appeared to be in line with the contractor's estimates. But that wasn't important right now. What did matter was Juliet's opinion. As they climbed the stairs, their footsteps echoing through the empty rooms, Brady could feel her excitement. He said nothing until they climbed the final staircase to the rounded turret which looked out across the rising hills of San Francisco. Standing behind her, one arm around her waist, he asked casually, "Well, what do you think?"

When she looked up at him, her eyes were sparkling. "I really like it, Brady," she said softly. "I know that's no reason to go into an investment, but...but maybe if I like it, someone else will." She hesitated. "What do you think?"

He looked down at her, studying her eyes and the shape of her face in the late afternoon sunlight that filtered through the window. His hands ringed her waist and then slid down over her hips. "If you like it, I think it's perfect," he agreed.

"But, Brady, how will we ever have time to oversee all the work that has to be done?" She felt his hands moving back and forth, and her response, immediate now whenever he touched her.

"There's more to do than I'd expected." His voice was deliberately casual. "Probably the best approach would be for us to live here."

Juliet stiffened, but Brady didn't move his hands away. "You mean together?" she asked him.

"I mean together." He pressed her closer to him, his hands wandering up her back.

"Wait a minute!" She put her hands on her hips and pulled away. "Was that what you had in mind all along?"

A slow smile settled across his face. "It had occurred to me," he admitted. "Will you think it over?" He pulled her to him again, and she didn't resist. Privately, she knew she wasn't going to resist the house, either. It would be far better than the uncertainty about when they might see each other. She pressed her hips against him and felt his rising passion.

Brady tried to gather his thoughts. He knew there were other keys out for the house. When he'd picked up this set, Phil had said something about a realtor looking at the place today. But he didn't care. Right now they were alone. Then she tipped her head back and he saw her eyes. He didn't want to wait till they got back to her apartment to make love. He pushed up her sweater and kissed her.

Juliet felt like a volcano about to erupt. Her breath coming in short gasps, she opened her eyes. It was at that moment she saw the man in a business suit walking briskly up the front sidewalk.

"Brady," she cried, grabbing his shoulders. "Brady, someone's here to see the house."

"Oh, God," he groaned, his arms tightening around her. He mentally calculated how long it would take for someone to get in the house and find them up on the third floor. He felt her tremble. "We've got time, Juliet." His voice was tight, raspy.

"Brady, no..." she cried out. "I can't..." Then she felt her legs shake uncontrollably, and she sank slowly down to the bare wooden floor, aware of Brady's arms around her, breaking her fall.

Far below them a key rattled in the front door lock. "Brady, do you hear that?" she whispered. It rattled again.

"Ignore it," he whispered. He knew this was a damn fool chance he was taking, but he couldn't stop himself. He wanted her beyond all reason.

Trying to shut out the sounds, Brady pulled her to him. He heard the key again, and then nothing else. He was driven by a compelling need, desire pushing him beyond the razor's edge of reason.

Juliet gripped him tightly, listening, too. A sound, the click of the latch, broke the silence. She dug her fingernails into Brady's shoulders, struggling for control, but she was already too much a part of him. She began to soar outside herself and nothing else mattered anymore.

Almost as quickly as it had begun, it was over, and yet Juliet felt complete. Brady collapsed on top of her, his breathing deep and ragged and she lay beneath him, holding him in her arms. Once again she heard the sound of footsteps echoing through the house.

Jarred back to reality, Juliet opened her eyes. "Brady!" she whispered.

"It's okay," he reassured her. "He's just starting up to the second floor."

Brady got up quickly and Juliet scrambled to her feet. With trembling hands she adjusted her sweater and straightened her skirt while Brady stuffed his shirttail inside the waistband of his pants. They heard heavy footsteps on the stairs.

"We're about to have company." Brady grinned and put his arm around Juliet, drawing her closer.

"Are you ready?"

Juliet looked up at him, nodding. Now that she and Brady were safe, she could almost, but not quite, return his smile.

They were standing calmly by the stair rail when the man started up the last flight. "Who are you?" Brady demanded.

The man jumped, obviously startled. "I . . . I'm a realtor, preparing a listing on the house. I didn't realize anyone was here," he added apologetically.

Juliet suppressed a grin. Brady had him on the defensive. A few minutes sooner, and the situation would have been very different.

"That's quite all right," Brady told the man, at the same time making a mental note to call Phil right away with their decision before a realtor got in on the act. "We were just leaving," Brady added, taking Juliet's hand.

As they started down the stairs, Juliet saw the lace edge of her underpants peeking out of Brady's pocket. She started to reach for them, and then thought the better of it. She'd just hope they didn't fall out and land right in front of the realtor.

Once in the car, both Brady and Juliet burst out laughing. "That was really dumb," she told him. "I can't imagine what ever made you—"

"Made me?" he asked. His eyes crinkled, and his mouth formed a broad, mischievous grin. "Just exactly who was it who didn't want to go home first?"

Juliet's cheeks flamed. "Oh," she said softly, and contritely folded her hands in her lap. Before Brady, she could never have done anything like that. But now . . . now a lot of things were different.

Brady made a quick call from Juliet's apartment to tell Phil they wanted the house, and then he and Juliet spent the next several hours planning. They decided not to sublet their apartments, because their time in the house wouldn't be long enough to really make it worthwhile. Brady suggested Juliet try to find someone to house sit, as though she were going on a long vacation. She smiled, quietly, and snuggled into his shoulder. That, she decided, was an extraordinarily good description of what was about to occur.

By the time Brady returned the keys to Phil on Sunday night, he and Juliet had decided to move in the following weekend if the arrangements could be made. The bell was still chiming when Phil opened the door. "Come in," he urged, "and tell me about the house."

"I owe you one for this," Brady said, dropping the keys on the table.

Phil took a closer look at him. "You look a hell of a lot more relaxed then you did yesterday morning," he observed pointedly.

"Weekends can do that for you," Brady answered with a smug expression on his face as he thought back over the last two days with Juliet. Before Phil could follow it up, he added, "Did you get any word on exactly when we can move into the house?"

Phil got the message. Apparently their sex life was good, and Brady didn't want to discuss it. "You should be able to move within a week," Phil answered. "We'll work out a temporary rental agreement until you close. All you need is some up-front money."

"No problem," Brady assured him. He turned to leave.

"I'll keep an eye on things out here while you're gone," Phil offered.

There was a crash as Timmy appeared in the doorway and an armload of cars clattered to the floor. "Where's Brady going?" he demanded. "He's got to fix my racer." He held up the black car, which was minus one headlight and three of its four wheels.

Brady took the car and gave Timmy a rough pat on the head. "If I can make one that survives you, we can advertise it as indestructible."

Timmy picked up the rest of his cars. "My mommy was here yesterday," he told Brady. "She said we should tell you hello." Cars in hand, he disappeared up the stairs.

Brady had been so caught up with Juliet and the house that he'd forgotten about Eileen coming. "How'd she look?" he asked Phil.

"If you mean had she been drinking, the answer's no." Phil shoved his hands in his pockets. He'd only seen Eileen a few times since she left and it got harder every time. The woman she was now didn't match his memories of his wife.

Brady proceeded cautiously. "Did it go all right?"

"A little strained." Phil paced slowly across the hallway as he talked. "The kids aren't sure how to react to her anymore and she doesn't quite know what to do either. I talked to her alone before she left. She wants the kids, Brady. A weekend for starters, and then . . ."

"What did you tell her?" Brady prodded.

Phil paced faster. "I told her no. What the hell was I supposed to say? I'm not going to give them up, Brady. She can come here and see them and if she stays on the wagon, maybe after a while she can take them for a day." Anger glinted in his eyes. "But, dammit, she's the one who walked out."

"Yeah, I know," Brady muttered. "Do you think she'll do anything?"

Phil stopped pacing and leaned against the staircase. "I don't know. She was pretty angry when she left."

Brady knew that meant the answer was probably yes. "Do you think you ought to see a lawyer, Phil?" It wasn't the first time he'd made the suggestion, but this time he went farther. "Maybe you could talk to Juliet."

For a long moment, Phil didn't answer. He wondered if Brady thought he had his head in the sand. The fact was, he didn't want to talk to a divorce lawyer, because he didn't want a divorce. He didn't want to get the courts involved at all. And he kept hoping against hope that Eileen wouldn't either. Maybe eventually, one way or another they could work out something themselves. Maybe she'd finally agree to get help. "Thanks, Brady," he answered. "I think I'm going to let it ride a little longer."

The response didn't surprise Brady. He only hoped Phil wouldn't wait too long. "Let me know if there's anything we can do," he offered, reaching for the door. "I'll come by your office and sign the papers on the house whenever they're ready."

"If this is going to be joint ownership, you'll have to bring Juliet," Phil reminded him.

Brady grinned sheepishly. "Yeah. I completely forgot."

ONCE THE PAPERS had been signed the next week, Juliet spent most of her free time getting her apartment in shape to leave it. Linda offered to come over and help her, but she declined. She had already decided not to take much with her, other than her clothes. She and Brady would be basically camping out while they got the house fixed up.

Until she'd realized that fact, Juliet had had serious second thoughts about buying the place with Brady. The possible ramifications of what she was doing hit her hard one afternoon after she'd had three appointments in a row with new clients who broke down and cried when they talked about starting out full of dreams, only to have their lives crash down around them when the marriages soured. Two of them had lived with their husbands before marriage. They said they'd been so sure of their long-term commitments and they simply couldn't understand what had happened.

When the last client left, Juliet stood up and paced over to the window to stare out at the gray rainy day. She knew that her relationship with Brady had advanced well beyond the "purely business" arrangement she had once envisioned. And there was nothing wrong with that, she supposed. It was probably better that the baby's father be someone she liked because, after all, he was going to pass his genes on to the baby. She even wondered sometimes what it would be like to be really married to him, not just on paper but really married. What would it be like to plan a future with someone, to watch a child grow together, to furnish a house and plant a garden, and grow old together?

A knock on the door interrupted her thoughts, and Linda walked in, pulling on her coat. "Think I'll call it a day," she told Juliet. "I seem to be spending more time here than I do at home."

"I've about had it, too," Juliet agreed. "Hold on a minute and I'll go downstairs with you."

Linda looked surprised. "You have another client waiting. Didn't you know?"

"I thought Mrs. McDowell was the last one." Juliet quickly checked her calendar. "Who's here now?"

"That blond woman, you know the one who always refuses to give her name," Linda said. "I forgot to tell you—she came in again while you were in Carmel. She refused to talk to me—said you knew all about her problem and she'd wait till you got back."

Juliet shook her head. "Alice says she's been back a couple of other times, too. Apparently she sat here most of Monday morning while I was in court. Alice offered to make an appointment for her, but she said no."

"She obviously needs help... I see what you mean," Linda said. "What are you going to do about her?"

"Talk to her, I suppose." Juliet sighed. She was tired. It already had been a very long week. And it was unlikely she could do much for this woman, anyway.

Linda smiled sympathetically. "Don't stay too late," she said, partially closing the door behind her.

THE WOMAN HELD herself perfectly straight as she walked into the lawyer's office. She wasn't drinking much at all now, and she was tired of her husband always using that as an excuse. And she had followed the lawyer's advice. She had tried to talk to her husband, but he had shut her out. Again. Even when she told him she wasn't drinking, he kept talking about her going away to a hospital for some sort of rehabilitation program. That wasn't what she needed. What she needed was her babies, and it was the lawyer's job to figure out how to get them for her.

"Won't you sit down?" Juliet motioned to a chair near the desk. The woman looked better than when she'd been there before. She was wearing a soft peach-colored dress, and Juliet saw a spark of life in the pale blue eyes. "What can I do for you?" Juliet asked.

The woman sat on the very edge of the chair. "I followed your advice." Her eyes were almost accusing. "It didn't work."

"I don't understand." Juliet tried to remember what advice she had given the woman. She had no notes to jog her memory.

"I went to see my husband and talked to him about taking the babies, just for a weekend at first. He said no." The woman fidgeted as she talked, twisting and untwisting a handkerchief around her fingers. It wasn't as hard as it had been the first time, but she wanted to make sure the lawyer understood she'd done everything she was supposed to.

"Did he give you a reason?" Juliet inquired.

"He said it was because I drink. I told him it wasn't a problem, but he still said I need to get help. He always uses that as an excuse . . . like a drink now and then was going to make me an unfit mother."

Something about the way she said the words put Juliet on guard. If the woman had a serious drinking problem, she probably did need help to stop completely. But at least she was trying. "You say you have two babies?" Juliet began.

The woman nodded.

Juliet picked up her pencil and began to write. It was almost time to get the woman's name, but she'd let her talk a little more about the children first. "How old are they?"

"Four and seven." The woman brightened. "They gave me pictures when I was there. Would you like to see them?"

"Of course," Juliet answered politely.

The woman already was digging in her purse. She produced two slightly bent pictures.

Juliet stared at the images on the film, a towhead with a huge grin on his face, and his little brother with dark hair, clutching a tattered blanket. "My God!" Juliet blurted out. "You're Eileen Gentry!" She was immediately sorry. It was the most unprofessional thing she could ever remember doing.

The woman drew back, a hostile uncertainty in her eyes. "How do you know that?"

Juliet tried to placate her. "I know your sons. They're very nice boys."

The woman was still suspicious. "How do you know them?"

Juliet hesitated, searching for the best explanation that still was true. "I know them through Brady Talcott."

"Then you know their father."

Juliet could see the anger building. "Well, yes, but only professionally . . . and as a friend of Brady's."

Enraged, the woman stood up. "You lied to me," she accused Juliet. "You're on his side too."

"That's not true, Mrs. Gentry," Juliet protested. "I didn't even know who you were until right now."

Her words made no impression on the woman, who was shouting now. "You're just like all the rest of them. You want to keep my babies from me." She snatched the pictures off Juliet's desk and clutched them in her hand. "I thought you might understand because you're a woman, but you don't either.'' She glowered at Juliet with a frightening intensity. "I just want you to know I'm going to have my babies—and there is nothing you can do to stop me."

Eileen ran out of the office, slamming the door behind her. She was down the hall and into the elevator before she stopped to think. She shouldn't have gotten so angry. The lawyer was probably telling the truth when she said she didn't know her. But it wasn't fair that everywhere she turned, everyone was against her.

She looked down at the pictures she still held in her hand. She felt so awkward with Michael and Timmy now. Timmy had given her a big hug before she left, but Michael ... He seemed so grown-up now, and so shy with her. She didn't know what he liked to do or even what to talk to him about. She watched the lighted numbers on the elevator panel descend toward one. Obviously this lawyer wasn't going to be any help, and she wasn't sure any of the others would be any better. They probably all knew Phil.

The doors opened, and she walked past a faceless crowd waiting to enter the elevator, and on through the lobby to the street. It was still drizzling. She pulled up the collar of her raincoat. She didn't have any umbrella. For several blocks, she walked aimlessly, obsessed with the idea of having the children with her but without any notion of how to accomplish it. She slowed as she passed a bar where she used to go after work. She knew the bartender and all the regulars. Now that she didn't go in anymore, she missed the company. It looked warm in there, and dry. On impulse, she turned and walked inside.

For the next several days, Eileen's agonized face haunted Juliet. It had never occurred to her that the woman was Phil Gentry's wife—until she saw the boys' pictures. And then she had handled the situation badly. Eileen was obviously trying very hard to fight the drinking and the loneliness. She needed help, and frightening her off had probably only made things worse. Eileen was desperate. Juliet wished she knew enough about her to be able to guess what she might do next. She considered talking to Brady about it, or even to Phil, but immediately rejected the idea.

Juliet found herself thinking about Eileen and Phil as she sorted through her closet to choose the clothes she would take to the new house. People made such a mess of their lives. She hoped she wasn't making a mistake by living with Brady. But the more she thought about it, the more it was something she wanted to do.

Moving into the house turned out to require no more than one carload and a few trips in and out. Juliet and Brady had agreed they wouldn't need furniture, except for a kitchen table and chairs and a bed which Brady had promised to take care of. When the bed arrived, it turned out to be a massive four-poster from an antique store. As they watched the workmen assemble it, Juliet felt Brady's hand wander across her back until his fingers slipped ever so slightly under her sweater and settled just inside the waistband of her jeans. She knew that as soon as the workmen left they were going to try it out. The longer she stood next to Brady, the better an idea that seemed.

Once they were settled, the weeks slipped by quickly. Juliet liked sharing the house with Brady, and overall, things were going very well except for one problem. She still wasn't pregnant. Juliet was temporarily hopeful, and she even bought a home pregnancy test. But her optimism turned out to be premature. She got more and more impatient. One night while Brady sat tinkering with a toy bulldozer, Juliet flipped through her pink datebook, studying the careful markings she had made. She looked up to find him watching her.

"Is something the matter, Juliet?" he asked.

"Sort of." She marked her place on the page with her finger. "Brady, I really ought to be pregnant by now." She'd talked to Cass about it, and her mother had told her to be patient. But she had been patient. By now her approach should have worked.

Brady grinned. "Is that all? Sometimes getting pregnant takes time."

"But after that first month, we've been right on schedule—"

Brady jumped to his feet. "Wait a minute! You mean to tell me you've kept track of every time..." His voice rose as he snatched the book from her.

"But how else are we going to know—"

"Damn!" Brady exclaimed, scowling at Juliet's neat entries. He stalked over to the fireplace and pitched the book into the flames.

"Brady! Stop! You can't do that." Juliet reached him just as the paper caught fire.

Brady's jaw was set. "The hell I can't." He turned to Juliet, his eyes blazing. "There are some things you don't do on schedule, and this is one of them." He took her roughly in his arms, and kissed her hard. Meshed with hers, his lips softened, and his irritation melted into desire.

Juliet never mentioned the book again. Secretly she knew that what Brady had said, and what her mother had told her, was true. There were some things that shouldn't be scheduled, and now that she and Brady were living together, scheduling had actually turned out to be totally unnecessary. Spontaneity covered all the bases.

She found that both of them were beginning to spend more time at home. It was something that had happened gradually, but it had happened. There seemed to be fewer night meetings and less work that was important enough to keep either of them late at the office. Juliet liked the evenings in front of the fire, curled up in the beanbag chairs Brady had brought from his beach house when he got tired of sitting on the floor. Despite its lack of other furnishings, the living room felt like someone lived there. But the rest of the house was still drab and shabby, which had started to bother Juliet.

"You know, we're not moving along very fast with this house," Juliet observed one night, as she eyed the cracked plaster on the living room ceiling.

Brady closed the wallpaper book he had been studying. "You're right and I haven't told you the latest. That guy Simmons who was supposed to show up next week? He fell off a ladder yesterday and broke his leg."

"Fantastic," Juliet muttered. "Of course the people I lined up didn't work out any better. You know," she mused, "I've been thinking about it. Maybe we ought to do some of it ourselves."

Brady shot her a skeptical look. "You mean decorate the house? Have you ever painted?" He surveyed the ten-foot walls.

"Well, no," Juliet admitted. "Except I did help Cass with a bathroom once." She sat down and picked up a strip of paint samples. "How about you?"

"Not for a long time. I worked for a painter one summer when I was in high school." Brady sat down cross-legged on the floor facing her. "But that doesn't make sense, Juliet. Any work we have done by professionals will be a tax write-off when we sell the place."

"We can't write it off if we can't get anyone to do it," she noted pragmatically. "Besides, it might be kind of fun."

Brady had never thought of painting walls as much fun, but it might be with Juliet. "Maybe you're right," he agreed. "We can at least give it a try."

Juliet's eyes sparkled with anticipation. She'd always thought it would be fun to fix up an old house, or any house. "Who do you suppose we might get to help us?" she asked.

"Any number of people," Brady answered. "Steve and Linda, Cass, Phil . . ."

"Cass would be super at selecting the paint colors, but I think Steve and Linda are out. Their enthusiasm for decorating is definitely lacking since they remodeled their kitchen last summer. They were knee-deep in plaster dust for weeks." Juliet laughed at the memory.

"Phil's probably the answer then, at least for the big jobs like wallpapering." Brady shoved the book of wallpaper samples over toward Juliet. "What do you think about these stripes for the hallway?"

Juliet barely glanced at them. "Phil does know that our marriage and living together in this house is nothing more than an arrangement, doesn't he?"

"Of course. He drew up the contract. Does that bother you?"

"No," Juliet answered slowly.

"What's the problem then?"

Juliet hesitated. She wanted to tell Brady that ever since she'd discovered it was Eileen Gentry who had come to her office seeking help she had been uncomfortable around Phil and the boys. But she couldn't talk about it without breaking a client's confidence. And she never did that. "There's no problem," she answered.

Brady looked at her carefully. There was something Julie wasn't telling him. "Are you sure?" he asked.

"Absolutely positive," she replied. She slid the heavy wall paper book between them. "Now, show me again which stripe you want to put in the hall."

CHAPTER TEN

PHIL HAD BEEN genuinely glad to help Brad and Juliet with the house. He had missed the casual camaraderie of such projects. Since Eileen had left, he hadn't done much of that sort of thing at home, because working alone was sheer drudgery.

But as he hung up the phone, he wished he weren't going. Eileen's anger echoed in the silence. "They're my babies, too, and I have a right to be with them," she'd shouted. "You're just using them to get back at me."

It was the third call he'd had from her in a week, all of them emotional confrontations. He'd told her he wasn't going to be home today, that he'd be glad to have her come tomorrow. But that wasn't good enough. She didn't want to wait. She wanted the children while he was gone. No, he'd said, that wouldn't work out. The hell of it was that would have been a better plan all the way around. He'd be able to do a lot more at Brady's if the kids weren't along.

He'd been tempted, but only briefly. Eileen's voice hadn't sounded right. Maybe it was his imagination. Or maybe he did want to hurt her because she'd made such a mess of all their lives. But if she drank, and something were to happen to the boys...

"Daddy, I'm hungry," a small voice whined. Timmy was standing in the middle of the kitchen floor in his pajama bottoms and bare feet.

Simultaneously Phil smelled the oatmeal, and it was too late. He snatched the burned pan from the stove. "Timmy!" he roared. "I told you to get dressed."

Frightened by the unexpected anger, Timmy dropped his glass of grape juice, splattering the floor with purple. He ran out of the room sobbing.

Phil leaned back against the stove and covered his face with his hands. He didn't know how much longer he could go on, how much longer he could do it all alone. He was juggling the boys and his law practice, and now, with Eileen calling all the time, it was too much. Slowly he took the roll of paper towels out of the holder and began to soak up the purple puddles and gather up the shards of glass. The mess looked endless, just like the rest of his life.

By the time he rang the doorbell at the old Victorian, Phil felt slightly better. It was a cloudless blue December day, and the boys were excited about visiting Brady. Michael had brought his newest C. S. Lewis book along, in hopes that Juliet might read some of it to him. Whatever she'd done that day in Brady's office when Michael had had the chicken pox, she'd won him over. He was always trying to think of some reason to see her.

Juliet answered the door, dressed in paint-spattered jeans and one of Brady's old shirts. She looked radiant, Phil thought. There wasn't a hint of that cool lady lawyer he sometimes saw striding down the corridors at the courthouse.

"You're just in time," she told them. "I'm painting trim, and Brady is trying to build a scaffolding. From the sound of it, he could use some help."

"I'm ready," announced Timmy, holding up a hammer half as big as he was.

"You're too little to do anything," Michael scoffed. "You'd get the nails all mixed up in your dumb blanket."

"Michael!" Phil took the boy firmly by the shoulder.

Juliet tried not to smile. "Why don't you go on in, Phil, and let me show the boys what Brady brought home from the office last night." She knew the surprise was going to solve a lot of the problem. She and Brady had hauled in half a dozen cartons and set them in one of the empty bedrooms, purposely leaving them packed so the boys could have the fun of discovering what was inside. Except for one. Brady had shown her a new building system he was working on with large-size nuts and bolts and color-coded wrenches, and she had pulled the whole thing out and spent more than an hour building a fort.

As she had expected, the boys were equally fascinated. "I'm still going to help you paint," Michael promised, "but maybe I'll play here for a while first."

Juliet laughed and gave his shoulder a squeeze. "Stay as long as you want," she told him. "We'll be painting all day."

The scaffolding went together quickly under Phil's direction, and with the men wielding paint rollers and Juliet using a brush on the trim, the dining room was quickly being transformed. Juliet's choice of a light-colored paint with just a hint of peach turned out to be perfect. Even Brady gave his approval. "This color was grotesque in the can but it isn't too bad on the walls."

"Told you so," Juliet answered smugly.

"Women must all be alike," Phil sighed. "That's what Eileen said when we had a big fight over painting the bathroom pink, and it didn't look half bad."

Brady watched Phil soak his roller and swipe it across the wall. Something had been bothering his friend all day, and it was a good bet that Eileen was behind it. Maybe if he could get Phil talking about it, Phil would ultimately ask Juliet for legal help. That wasn't going to solve the problem, but at least it would give him some protection if Eileen went to court. "Did Eileen call again?" Brady asked innocently.

"This morning." Phil's words were clipped. "She wanted to see the boys today."

Juliet flinched, painting furiously. She didn't want to hear about it. She wanted to keep as much distance between herself and the Gentrys' problems as possible.

"What did you tell her?" Brady prodded.

"That we couldn't do it today. I told her tomorrow, any time, but she wasn't interested. She got mad and hung up on me again."

Juliet could almost see Eileen's face, and pale blue eyes so full of pain, boiling over with frustration and loneliness. Phil laid down his paint roller and continued almost as though he had forgotten she were there. "Dammit, Brady, I was tempted to just tell her to take them for the day. But they're still little kids. If she's drinking, anything could happen to them."

Brady continued to paint, slowly, methodically. This was the time to bring in Juliet. "You know, Phil, we've hashed this over a hundred times and we never get anywhere. Maybe we need another opinion." Phil didn't answer. Brady knew he was treading on dangerous territory. "Maybe Juliet can come up with an approach—she's a woman." He purposely didn't point out that she could also provide specialized legal advice. One step at a time.

Juliet kept painting. The less she said, the better. "I don't know that being a woman gives me any special insight," she commented.

Brady frowned. He had expected her to cooperate. "Well, give us an opinion anyway. What do you do with a wife who walks out, has a drinking problem and wants to see the kids?"

There it was, in a few short phrases, the anatomy of one more marriage that had fallen apart. Tucking a stray lock of hair under her bandana, Juliet searched for an appropriate nonresponse. She knew what Eileen Gentry wanted, and she knew what Phil wanted. She didn't know what was right. "It sounds to me like Eileen needs help," she suggested cautiously.

Phil turned toward Juliet, his interest piqued. She'd gone right to the guts of the problem. Maybe it was worth talking to her. "But how do you persuade somebody to find help when she won't listen, when all she can say is you don't understand? She says I'm using the children to hurt her."

Juliet couldn't find any way at all to change the subject. "Has she tried Alcoholics Anonymous?"

"I don't think so. I've brought it up, but she says she isn't like those people."

For the first time, Juliet noticed the deep lines etched on Phil's face. They formed a pattern of disillusionment that made him look far older than his years. It was such a stupid waste. He'd done a fantastic job with the boys. He should be pleased with his life, but instead he was bitter and discouraged. On the other side of the fence stood Eileen, lonely, afraid, seeking comfort from a bottle. In the middle were the boys, the innocent victims, who could ultimately bear the brunt of it all.

Phil wiped his sleeve across his forehead, streaking the paint that had splattered. "I've tried so damn hard to figure this thing out. She claims she has a right to the boys, and I suppose in a way she does. She is their mother. But what if she gets drunk? She's already totaled one car and now she's got her license back and she's driving again. I'm afraid to let them go with her."

Brady broke the ensuing silence. "I don't know much about the legalities of this, but it looks to me like Phil needs a lawyer who specializes in family law. Do you suppose you could help him out, Juliet?"

Juliet froze, her paintbrush dripping on the drop cloth under the window. Brady was right, of course. Phil probably was going to need a lawyer, eventually if not right now. And she wasn't a candidate. Even though she wasn't representing Eileen, she was far too emotionally involved.

"I don't think so," she mumbled. "I always try to keep business and friendship separate." It was a lame excuse, but the only one she could think of. She scraped the paint off her brush on the side of the paint can and covered the bristles with plastic wrap to keep them from drying out. "I think maybe I'll go check on Michael and Timmy. They're probably getting hungry, and I bought some peanut butter yesterday."

Juliet spent the rest of the afternoon with the boys, avoiding Phil and Brady, who had moved the painting operation to the living room. It wasn't until after Phil left that she saw the anger glinting in Brady's eyes.

"What the hell was your problem this afternoon?" he confronted her.

"My problem?" Juliet hedged. She took the remains of their Chinese carry-out dinner out of the living room and dumped them in the kitchen wastebasket. She knew exactly what he meant.

"I've tried for months to get Phil to go to a lawyer. I finally got him talking...he was receptive to you. You could have helped him and you refused. Why, Juliet?" he demanded.

"I told you. I keep business and friendship separate." Juliet busied herself putting away the peanut butter and jelly she'd left on the kitchen counter.

Brady scowled, towering in the doorway. "That's a bunch of bull and you know it. Phil's been my lawyer ever since I needed one and he's also my best friend. Lawyers always represent their friends."

Not saying anything, Juliet closed the refrigerator.

"Answer me, Juliet!" Brady demanded. "What's the problem? Is it because he's a man and in your book the man's always wrong?"

Juliet spun around. "That's not true and you know it," she snapped.

His voice rose. "Then what is it, Juliet?"

She took a deep breath. "I can't represent Phil Gentry. I've already been contacted by his wife."

The heavy silence between them had a texture of its own. Brady stared at her, unmoving. Slowly, she crossed the kitchen and sat down at the table. She hadn't wanted to tell him, but there wasn't any choice.

Brady sat down across from her, his face grim. "Then you're representing Eileen?"

Juliet shook her head. "No, I'm not representing anyone. She's so frightened and upset that she refused to tell me her name. When she showed me pictures of the boys, and she found out I knew them, she walked out." Juliet stared out the window at the city lights far below. "Brady, there's no way I can represent Phil after his wife talked to me. And in good conscience I can't tell him why."

Brady picked up a napkin and methodically folded it into triangles. This meant Eileen had sought legal advice. He'd been right. Phil did need a lawyer. "Is she going to do something immediately?" he asked Juliet.

"I don't know what she's going to do." Juliet found herself relieved to finally be able to talk about it. "She really needs help. She thinks that the whole world is against her, conspiring to keep her from having her children."

"But she's drinking..." Brady interjected.

"Probably," Juliet agreed. "I don't know the answer. I'm not sure there is one." She looked up at him and found him no longer angry with her. "She's desperate, Brady," Juliet added. "I don't have a good feeling about her."

Brady thought about the boys and about the agony Phil had already endured. "I don't have a good feeling about the whole damn thing." He stood up abruptly and walked out of the kitchen.

JULIET AND BRADY didn't discuss Eileen and Phil again. One drizzly Sunday afternoon, nestled in a beanbag chair in front of the fire, Juliet considered asking Brady if Eileen had called Phil or tried to see the boys. But she didn't ask. It would have created discord, and they didn't need that. They were simply too happy just the way they were.

They were not, she noted, making love at the moment. Nor had they been all afternoon. When they first moved into the house, they'd wound up in bed at every available opportunity. But sometimes now, just being close was enough. Juliet had never been able to share her innermost thoughts with anyone, but with Brady, it was easy. She watched the orange flames dance in the fireplace, wondering if Brady ever imagined pictures in the fire the way she did. She thought about asking him, but he was engrossed in a book. Instead, she laid her head on his chest, rubbing her cheek against the scratchy wool of his shirt. She was very content.

Lazily, Brady reached around Juliet and stroked her hair. He liked the quiet times with her. Usually they didn't do much of anything. Sometimes, like now, they didn't even talk. But the silence was comfortable. He supposed that was an outgrowth of living together. A man and woman were bound to grow close when they spent a lot of time under the same roof. Brady laid his book down on the floor beside him.

"Juliet," he whispered. Her eyes were closed, and he didn't want to wake her if she was asleep.

"Mmm." Her head stirred on his chest, and her eyes fluttered open. In the glow from the fire, their brilliant emerald color softened to a subtle jade.

"I've been thinking about Christmas," Brady began. Actually, the subject had been bothering him for several days and he knew he had to deal with it soon. His mother was expecting him in Boston for the holidays.

"Christmas?" Juliet asked in a sleepy voice. "That's a long time away."

"Less than two weeks," Brady pointed out. "How do you celebrate Christmas?"

Juliet yawned. "No particular way. Last year I went to the ballet and saw The Nutcracker Suite. Sometimes I go to Linda's, except this year she and Steve and the kids are going to her parents' Christmas day."

Looking at her curiously, Brady asked, "What about your family? And the presents and the tree and all that?"

Juliet sat up and laughed. "Cass is my only family, and she's gone to Yosemite skiing the last few years. When I was little we had a special dinner and a few presents—but a Christmas tree?" Juliet shook her head. "That was out of the question."

"You've never had a Christmas tree?" Brady hadn't known anyone who celebrated Christmas without a tree.

Juliet wrapped her arms around her knees and looked up at him with a serious expression. "I know this is going to sound strange, but Cass thinks that killing trees to celebrate the season of eternal life is insane. She won't have a Christmas tree in the house."

"Didn't you miss it?"

Juliet shrugged. "How can you miss what you've never had?" Then she grinned at Brady. "But I don't even have to ask you. I'll bet your mother always has an enormous tree and piles of presents and a traditional family dinner with enough food for an army."

"You've got it," Brady answered. "And don't forget my sister, her husband and kids, my Aunt Elinor, her yapping schnauzer, and usually a stray cousin or two."

Juliet's eyes sparkled. "You make it sound like a lot of fun." She paused, and Brady realized he'd just made a major mistake. She was waiting to be invited, but there was no way he could possibly take her to Boston. His family didn't even know they were married. He'd always figured there wasn't any point in bringing it up since the marriage was going to be so brief. But it was awkward not having explained all that to Juliet. "I don't think I'll go to Boston this year, though," he said nonchalantly.

Juliet frowned. That didn't sound quite right. "I thought you always went."

"I do," he admitted. "It might be fun to do something different for a change."

Juliet had talked to enough people about family Christmases to know that tradition ran strong. Brady didn't seem to have any reason at all for not going home. Unless . . . "Brady, if you're not going to Boston because you don't think I'd want to—"

"Oh, no, nothing like that," he cut her off. "There's a lot of noise and confusion. . . ." That didn't sound very convincing, he realized. He held his breath, hoping Juliet would make an alternative suggestion which meant she'd accepted his explanation. But she didn't say anything. The silence deepened. He shot a sidelong glance at her, and saw she was staring into the fire. He had the distinct impression she didn't believe him, and if she'd say so, he could at least defend himself. Brady picked up his book, but he couldn't focus on the page. He felt rotten. He was lying to Juliet and it hurt her.

"This is no good, Juliet," he muttered. "It's time I told you the truth."

Apprehensive, Juliet watched him. But she didn't say anything.

"We can't go to Boston for Christmas because my family doesn't know we're married," he announced flatly.

Juliet dropped her eyes. After thinking about his flimsy excuses, she'd suspected as much. "I see," she responded quietly.

Brady stood up and shoved his hands into his pockets. "It seemed easier not to tell them under the circumstances," he continued. "Except now...now I wish I had." He knelt down beside Juliet, taking both her hands in his. "Things have changed between us, Juliet. It's not like it was at the beginning."

Juliet met his eyes, not needing any more explanation. She'd felt them growing closer, just as he had. Sometimes, when she woke up early and lay beside him, she wondered what it would be like if they were really married, whether anything would change.

"Do you ever think about the future?" Brady asked her.

"Not very often anymore," Juliet answered truthfully. The future used to be almost all she thought about—the time after she got pregnant and then had the baby. But that had changed, too. "I guess I've been too caught up in the present," she continued slowly. "I don't think I'm ready to look ahead right now."

Gently, Brady touched her cheek. He understood, and he was willing to wait.

"If you want to go to Boston for Christmas—" Juliet started to suggest.

"We can both go to Boston," Brady interrupted, "but it may be awkward. Instead let's stay here together, and we'll create our own traditions."

"I'd like that, Brady," Juliet answered softly. "I'd like that very much." Lying back on the beanbag chair, Juliet reached for him. She sensed a bonding between them that had grown out of the words that were spoken and those that weren't.

Something very special had happened between them that December afternoon, but Juliet mused about it only briefly before Brady's mouth was on hers. She might have suggested they go upstairs, but she didn't. The late afternoon darkness was gathering rapidly, and the only light in the living room came from the glowing embers of the fire. She knew he wanted her, and her whole being was alive with desire for him. They came together quickly and in the fading light their passion burned with a brilliance that left an indelible imprint on them both. They stayed there together long after the fire burned away and the last of the daylight was gone.

FOR THE FIRST TIME since she could remember, Juliet was counting the days until Christmas. Ever since they had decided to stay home together for the holiday, she'd been excited. She'd made a wreath for the front door and had spent an entire Saturday baking cookies. She had to admit you couldn't tell the angels from the stars, but Brady assured her they tasted wonderful and the shape didn't matter.

"Maybe we can give Phil some cookies to take home to Timmy and Michael when he comes tonight for eggnog," Juliet suggested.

"Terrible idea," Brady answered immediately.

Juliet put both hands on her hips. "Now wait just a minute. I thought you liked my cookies."

"That's the problem," Brady admitted, still crunching. "I just ate the last one."

"The last one?" Juliet was outraged. "I baked six dozen only a few days ago. Now what are we going to give Phil with his eggnog?"

Brady kissed her lightly on the tip of her nose. "Slice up some of that vile fruitcake your secretary gave you. Phil says anything is better than his own cooking. Let's call his bluff."

"We can't do that!" Juliet argued. "Maybe I'll bake one of those loaves of cinnamon bread we bought."

"Suit yourself." Brady pulled on his jacket.

"Where are you going?" Juliet asked.

"Out to run a couple of errands," he answered nonchalantly.

"Good." Juliet started for the closet. "I'll come with you instead of baking cinnamon bread. I need some sage for tomorrow anyway."

Gently, but firmly, Brady took hold of Juliet's shoulders and stopped her. "I'll get the sage for you. Why don't you stay here and bake?"

"Wait a minute!" Juliet called as he hurried out the kitchen door. "That's not fair." Brady obviously had plans that didn't include her. That was odd, because they'd agreed not to give each other presents, so he couldn't be doing last-minute shopping. She hoped he was going to stick to his word, because she had.

She took a cookbook out of the kitchen drawer and turned to the section on poultry. It was funny—they'd also decided to keep the entire holiday season spontaneous and just do whatever they felt like doing at the moment. But they seemed to be doing most of the same things everyone else did, including cooking a turkey, which was ridiculous, considering it was for two people. They'd be eating leftovers for a month.

Juliet flipped the pages in the cookbook to the section entitled "Creative Uses of Turkey." Running her finger down the recipes gave her a pretty good idea why Cass didn't ever cook turkeys. She wondered if Eileen was going to fix dinner for Phil and the boys—he'd said she was going to come for Christmas. Phil would probably take care of it himself, Juliet decided. He was actually a pretty good cook.

Her eyes wandered to the refrigerator door which was almost entirely covered with the painting Michael had done of himself for Juliet. His hair was bright yellow and standing straight up on the top of his very round head. He had a big red grin on his face, probably because he was happy about the kite he was flying. In fact, Michael generally seemed like a pretty happy little kid. So did Timmy. Juliet wondered how it would affect them if their mother ever moved back into the house.

A heavy pounding on the front door interrupted her thoughts. "Hey, Juliet," Brady shouted. "Come open the door for me."

Juliet didn't rush. "What happened to your key?" she asked as she pulled open the heavy oak door.

Brady's face was red, and beads of perspiration stood out on his forehead. "Couldn't get to it." He gasped for breath between the words.

"Are you all right?" Juliet stepped out on the porch.

"Don't come out here," Brady warned sharply, and Juliet immediately retreated. "I'm fine. Just prop the door open, and go wait in the living room."

"Are you sure?" Juliet questioned. He didn't look fine, leaning against the door frame in a definitely unnatural position. But he didn't look sick, either.

"I'm positive," Brady panted. "And close your eyes when you get there."

Aha, thought Juliet, *he's playing a game.* She had no idea what it was, but she was willing to go along. Walking to the exact center of the living room, she closed her eyes and listened carefully. Whatever he was doing, he was making a lot of noise, thumping and bumping and dragging something in the hallway. "Brady," she called out, "be careful of the new wallpaper." There was no answer, only more bumping. As the sound came closer, a pungent fragrance filled the room. It was very familiar, something like—no, exactly like pine.

Cautiously, Juliet opened her eyes. There, in front of the bay window stood the most beautiful evergreen tree she'd ever seen. "A Christmas tree," she breathed. "You got me a Christmas tree!" She stood absolutely motionless in front of the tree, just staring at it.

"Yep," Brady said proudly. "That's exactly what I did, and it's not dead, either." He patted the burlap-covered dirt ball around the roots of the tree and grinned. "I remembered what you said about Cass not wanting to kill a tree to celebrate the season of life. She may be a little eccentric, but some of her ideas aren't all that bad."

He looked expectantly at Juliet. She hadn't said a word, and she still hadn't moved, except to cover her mouth with her hands. That wasn't exactly the reaction he'd expected from her.

Maybe she really didn't like Christmas trees. "Juliet?" he said apprehensively. "It's all right to have a tree, isn't it? It's alive, and we can plant it in the backyard after Christmas."

Juliet never took her eyes off the tree. She couldn't believe Brady had thought of getting her a live Christmas tree. All at once she threw her arms around him. "It's perfect," she whispered, burying her face in his neck, "absolutely perfect. I've never had such a wonderful present."

"You're sure?"

She hugged him tightly. "Oh, yes, Brady, thank you."

Brady heaved a great sigh of relief. She liked it. That was all he cared about. He wanted to get her something special for a present, something she would never dream of getting, and he'd done it. He kissed her tousled hair and held her close. "Next comes my favorite part," he told her. "We get to decorate it."

Juliet looked up at him in amazement. "Did you buy ornaments, too?"

Brady let go of her and went out into the hall. He returned carrying three large boxes. "I only have lights," he answered. "We'll have to use our imagination for the ornaments." He opened the first box and, while Juliet watched, he clipped dozens of tiny white electric candles to the branches. "They are imported from Germany," he explained. "I thought you should have very special lights for your first Christmas tree."

"Then you've been planning this!" Juliet exclaimed.

"I guess you could say that," Brady admitted. He finished clipping on the last string of lights and plugged them in, bathing the whole room in a mellow glow.

Juliet was enchanted. "It's lovely, Brady," she told him. Her eyes swept up the perfect symmetry of the tree. Now all it needed was ornaments. "I know!" Her voice was full of excitement. "We can put a star on top and some little red birds nesting in the branches." She disappeared into the hall closet and returned dragging a carton of art supplies Cass had given her to keep Michael and Timmy busy when they came to visit.

"I'm sure there's some silver paper in here somewhere," she muttered to herself as she dug around in the box. "Here it is," she called out triumphantly. Within moments she had cut and folded a multi-pointed star which Brady attached to the very top of the tree.

Next, she found some origami paper and spent a considerable amount of time trying to teach Brady to fold the delicate Japanese animals. "That's not bad," she said when he pulled his bird's tail to make the wings flap. She finished her pink turtle, strung some translucent fishing line through it, and hung it on the tree.

"These origami animals are for graduate students in fine arts," Brady grumbled good-naturedly. "I'm going back to the kindergarten level where it's easy." Before long, he had constructed a chain of thin strips of gold paper and looped it around the tree. "Not bad, at all," he remarked, as much to himself as to Juliet. "But next year we're going to—"

Brady stopped in mid-sentence. There might not be a next year for them. He kept forgetting that. The only thing that was certain was now, this moment.

A heavy silence settled in the room. Juliet had heard Brady and noticed the meaningful pause, but it was easier to pretend she hadn't. She picked up the last scraps of paper from the floor and dropped the scissors into the carton. She didn't want to think about next year. She stood up, her eyes resting on the shimmering Christmas tree. She'd wanted a baby by next Christmas, but now... She wasn't sure anymore that a baby would make her life complete.

"Why don't you build a fire before Phil comes, and I'll go put some cinnamon bread in the oven," she said to Brady. It was as good an excuse as any to escape the thoughts of the future. All she wanted was to go ahead with this Christmas, right now, just the way it was.

CHAPTER ELEVEN

EILEEN GENTRY HAD been driving aimlessly for hours, thinking about why she was alone on Christmas Eve. The car was dark and quiet. There was nothing on the radio but Christmas carols. She'd turned it off right in the middle of Perry Como singing "I'll Be Home for Christmas." She used to love that song. This year it was depressing.

Home. That's where she should be. At home with Phil and the boys helping them hang the stockings and fix a plate of cookies for Santa Claus. But she wasn't. She was all alone, driving around in her car. And it was rotten.

She drove past a bar, watching its pink neon light flash on and off, and thought about stopping for a drink. A bar was always a good place to find someone to talk to, especially tonight. There would probably be a spillover from office parties, people who wanted to do a little more celebrating. She glanced at the bottle of wine in the brown paper bag next to her on the seat and decided not to bother. Instead, she turned her car south and headed down the coast.

When Eileen swung onto the beach road, she wasn't sure what her intentions were. All the homes along the road glowed with the warmth of Christmas. Tree lights sparkled in every window, and she could see people inside, some still decorating their trees. In almost every home there were children.

Eileen stopped the car alongside the curb down the street from her house. Like the others, it had a sparkling Christmas tree in the window. She could see Michael inside, already in his pajamas, sitting next to Phil on the couch. She watched as Timmy appeared, dragging his blanket, and climbed up on Phil's lap. An ample woman was hovering in the background, probably Mrs. Campanelli from down the street. Eileen wondered if she'd come in just to be with the boys on Christmas Eve or if Phil was planning to go out somewhere.

Eileen reached for the bottle of wine and unscrewed the plastic top. One thing about cheap wine. It was easy to open. She should be in the living room with the boys. They were hers and another woman was taking care of them. She took several swallows of wine, savoring the warm, almost burning sensation in her throat, and continued watching the scene before her.

Phil was reading to the boys now from a big, flat book. There was a catch in Eileen's throat and she drank some wine to get rid of it. She knew what Phil was reading. It was "The Night before Christmas." He read it every year, even the first year they were married, before there were any babies. It was a custom in his family. She could imagine his deep, resonant voice but she ached to really hear it.

The wine was nearly gone. Phil had finished the story and Eileen watched him kiss her babies good night and send them off with Mrs. Campanelli. Eileen felt the first flickers of anger. She wanted to be the one to hold them close and kiss them good night. They were hers. That was her right.

She finished the last drops of wine. Phil had his coat on now and was checking for his keys, the way he always did before he went out. She watched him hurry down the stairs and drive away in his car. Eileen clutched the steering wheel until the taillights of Phil's car disappeared around the curve at the end of the street. The anger inside her grew. He had no right to keep her away from her babies. It was her house, too. She fumbled in her purse for the key to the back door, the one nobody knew she had.

Unsteadily she approached the house and walked to the back. She'd thank Mrs. Campanelli and send her on her way. Then there would be no one to keep her from her babies. Popping a mint in her mouth, Eileen turned her key in the lock and the door opened easily. Silently she slipped inside.

PHIL PARKED HIS CAR and climbed the steps to the porch of Brady and Juliet's house. Even as his hand reached for the doorbell, he had reservations about being there at all. It was a long-standing tradition, having eggnog together on Christmas Eve. But it had always been Brady who came to his house bringing the toys he'd kept for Phil from the time Michael got old enough to dig through the closets. This year Brady had been adamant about his coming to see their tree, wanting him to share Christmas Eve with them.

Phil hadn't minded, except he wished Mrs. Campanelli had told him earlier that she was going to midnight mass. He checked his watch. He couldn't stay very long. He'd promised her he'd be back home by ten-thirty.

"Merry Christmas," Brady greeted him, opening the door. A wide arc of light beckoned Phil inside. Christmas music played softly in the background and the smell of something baking wafted out of the kitchen.

Juliet gave him an exuberant hug. "Come in and see our tree," she urged, leading the way into the living room. "We just finished decorating it."

An aching loneliness swept through Phil when he looked at the tree sitting proudly in the front bay window, its limbs cradling homemade ornaments and twinkling with tiny lights. Phil knew it wasn't only the tree itself that made him feel wistful, but also the love and sharing that had created it. Objectively it wasn't nearly so impressive as his huge tree with its ten-year accumulation of ornaments, but there was a different feeling about this one. "You did this?" he asked.

"Yep." Phil could hear the pride in Brady's voice. "All tonight."

"It's really beautiful." Phil coughed to get rid of the catch in his voice. "I'd say you two make a pretty good team."

Smiling, Brady handed him a glass of eggnog with a touch of rum, and gestured toward the beanbag chair next to a small table where Juliet had placed a plate of hot cinnamon bread. He wanted to tell Phil what was happening, how he felt about Juliet now. But he hadn't even really told her, and he wasn't sure it was quite time. Instead he asked, "Are the boys asleep?"

"Probably, by now. Mrs. Campanelli is very firm," Phil replied, sitting down. "We read 'The Night before Christmas' three times, and I issued the warning about Santa stopping only at houses with sleeping children." He sipped his eggnog and took a piece of bread. "I can't stay long," he added. "Mrs. Campanelli wants to leave at ten-thirty for mass."

Juliet listened with an odd sense of longing. Cass had already explained to her about Santa Claus when she was Timmy's age. "I'll bet they're really excited—we've got the toys all ready and Brady added a few more."

"All of which Juliet wrapped," Brady added, squeezing her hand.

"Thanks...to both of you," Phil told them gratefully. He took another drink of eggnog. It made no sense, but he felt uncomfortable, as though he shouldn't be there. Maybe it was because he knew too much about Brady and Juliet. He could see what was happening. Without expecting to, without wanting to, they were creating a marriage. A real marriage.

Brady turned over the cassette tape in the portable tape deck and Bing Crosby's voice, smooth as honey, crooned "White Christmas." "Is Eileen still coming tomorrow?" he inquired.

Phil shifted in his chair. "As far as I know. She told me on the phone that she had presents for the boys. Timmy is really happy about it. Michael isn't so sure." He hesitated, wanting to stop and yet needing to talk about it. "Michael says he wants her to come back when she isn't going to leave again."

"That's a tough one," Brady sympathized. "There's not much you can say to him. He's too young to understand."

It wasn't just Michael who didn't understand, Phil thought, staring into the fire. "I've been thinking about it a lot lately," he told Brady. "For a while I thought I wanted to talk to her, maybe try it again, but I can't handle the drinking anymore. It's too hard on the kids, on all of us."

They lapsed into silence, with only the crackling of the flames punctuating the soft Christmas music from the tape deck. Juliet wished she knew some way to help ease Phil's pain. At least he recognized the folly of starting over again. The sooner he and Eileen could make a clean break, the better off they'd all be.

"How about some more eggnog?" Brady offered, picking up the pitcher.

Phil stood up. "No thanks," he declined. "I have the feeling I need to go home."

Brady and Juliet helped him carry sacks of brightly wrapped packages until the trunk and the back seat of the car were verflowing. Phil said goodbye quickly. He was in a hurry to ᴇ home.

When he arrived there, the outside lights were blazing but the ᴏnt window was dark. He wondered why Mrs. Campanelli ᴀd turned off the tree. He grabbed one sack of presents and ᴏund his house key to unlock the front door. Dropping the ᴀck on the hall bench, he called to Mrs. Campanelli.

There was no answer. He checked his watch. Ten thirty-eight. ᴇe was late, but not that late. Irritated, he called her name ɢain. He knew she was anxious to get to mass before the ᴜurch got crowded, but to leave the boys alone . . .

He tiptoed noiselessly up the carpeted stairs. Everything was ᴜiet, and their bedrooms were dark. He peeked inside cauᴏusly, smiling when he saw the familiar lumps under the ᴅlankets. They slept in some of the strangest positions. He ᴀnted to go in and kiss them good night, but children slept so ᴦhtly on Christmas Eve. He was afraid he would wake them, ᴀd then it might be an hour or more before it would be safe to ᴜt the presents under the tree.

He hesitated a moment more and then tiptoed back downᴀirs. Things seemed to be all right, but he still couldn't unᴇrstand Mrs. Campanelli leaving Michael and Timmy alone. ᴀipping on the Christmas tree lights as he passed through the ᴠing room, Phil walked to the car to get the rest of the presᴇts. They were all wrapped but Timmy's rocking horse and the ᴦt bike for Michael. He arranged the presents carefully ᴦound the tree, and then stood back to admire his work. His ᴠes traveled upward to the star that glowed softly at the top of ᴇe tree. He and Eileen had bought that star the first year they ᴇre married. It had been outlandishly expensive, but she had ᴀllen in love with it. They would keep it forever, she'd said, ᴀd a hundred Christmases down the road it would still be ᴀining for their children's children.

Phil felt sudden rage. He wanted to tear down that star and ᴀash it in a million pieces, the same way she had smashed his ᴦe. He stood perfectly still, his jaw clenched, his hands in tight ᴀsts. The fury passed, and he turned off the lights. It was a long ᴛe before he slept that night. He tossed restlessly, kicking off ᴇe blanket and then pulling it back again, slipping in and out of an uneasy sleep. Christmas was a hell of a time to have to celebrate by yourself, he thought bitterly.

Sunlight was streaming in the bedroom window when Phil awoke. He lay quiet, listening. An eerie silence filled the house. He checked the clock on his nightstand. Nine o'clock. Michael was always up at dawn on Christmas. The routine was the same every year. He'd peek downstairs and then come racing in and bounce on the end of the bed, yelling that Santa had really come. Phil shoved his feet into his slippers with an odd sense of urgency. Halfway down the stairs he leaned over the railing. The presents hadn't been touched.

He opened the door to Michael's bedroom and saw the lump still under the covers, but in the bright morning light the bed didn't look right. Fear gripped him, and he crossed the room in two strides and tore back the blankets. Except for wadded up pillows, the bed was empty. Phil froze, his palms clammy, his breath coming in short, hard spurts. "Michael," he shouted. "Michael where are you?"

With a sick feeling in his stomach, he raced into Timmy's room. Before he even touched the bed covers, he knew. He sank to his knees beside the bed, his face in his hands, dry sobs wracking his body. "My God," he whispered into the silence. "They're gone."

He had to think. He had to do something immediately. He dropped his face into the crook of his arm and lay against the bed, paralyzed with fear. They'd been gone for hours. But where? And why? He lifted his head and something cold and hard raked against his cheek. He tried to pick it up but it was hooked under the blanket. Frowning, he looked at it more carefully. It was the bracelet, the gold bracelet he'd given Eileen when Timmy was born. Then he knew. The fear mixed with a helpless rage. Eileen had taken the boys.

Phil raced downstairs and snatched the telephone receiver, hurriedly running his finger down the list of numbers by the kitchen phone until he found Mrs. Campanelli's name. The phone rang three times and then four. "Answer it, dammit," he muttered. When she came on the line, he could barely hear her over the excited shouts of children in the background. "It's Phil Gentry," he said, trying to fight the note of panic in his voice.

"Merry Christmas! And to the boys, too," she exclaimed joyfully.

"Mrs. Campanelli." Phil's voice was grim. "Were Timmy and Michael all right when you left?"

There was a pause and more shouting in the background, and then Mrs. Campanelli's voice yelling for everyone to be quiet. "They were sound asleep," Mrs. Campanelli told him. "Mrs. Gentry came in just before I left and said she was going to be with you for Christmas. Mr. Gentry, is something wrong?"

He wanted to shout at her. How could she have been such a fool? But he realized it wasn't her fault. She couldn't possibly have known. "I'm sure everything is all right." Phil forced himself to be calm. "Mrs. Gentry has apparently taken the boys out for a little while."

"Oh, Mr. Gentry—"

The noise level in the background was building again, but he could hear the concern in her voice. He didn't need her showing up with half a dozen relatives and lots of advice. "You go back to your Christmas, Mrs. Campanelli." He tried to sound cheerful. "I'm sure everything will be just fine."

Phil hung up the phone, trying to decide what to do next. At least he knew where Michael and Timmy were. Actually, he didn't know at all. He knew who they were with, but Eileen had refused to tell him where she lived and she didn't have a telephone.

He started to dial the police emergency number and then put down the phone. That wasn't going to work. Eileen was their mother. And even if he could persuade some sympathetic cop that the children might be in danger, it still probably wasn't the answer. At least not yet.

He stared through the archway at the Christmas tree, still surrounded by mounds of presents. The bicycle, all glistening chrome and knobby tires, stood to one side, blatantly alone and unused. Michael had wanted it more than anything. He had talked about that particular bike for weeks, persuading Phil to detour past the sports store every time they were in the neighborhood so he could look at it again. What had Eileen told Michael when he woke up this morning? That Santa Claus had forgotten?

Phil felt sick to his stomach. In desperation, he dialed Brady's number. His friend's sleepy voice answered.

"Brady, wake up!" Phil commanded. "She took them. Eileen took the boys."

Brady sat bolt upright in bed, jarring Juliet out of a sound sleep. "When?"

"Last night, after Mrs. Campanelli left. I didn't know they were gone till this morning."

Brady let out a long, slow breath. "Jesus Christ," he muttered. "We'll be right there."

Juliet grabbed his arm. "What's happened, Brady?" When he told her, she closed her eyes, bombarded by images of Michael and Timmy, their faces open and innocent, of Eileen driven by loneliness and frustration, and of Phil who must be frantic with worry and guilt. "Has he called the police?" she asked Brady, who was already pulling on his jeans.

"I don't know. I just told him we'd come."

Juliet dressed quickly and then fumbled through her purse, which was hanging on the doorknob. "The police won't help anyway," she muttered. She found Linda Burke's unlisted number and picked up the phone. "The police would tell Phil to sit tight and see what happens. After all, Eileen's their mother and there's been no court action."

"What are you doing?" Brady asked as she dialed the number.

"Calling Linda Burke. Eileen talked to her once. I doubt that she knows anything, but just in case . . ."

When Linda answered with a cheery "Merry Christmas," Juliet told her briefly what had happened. The only thing Linda could remember was Eileen saying she wanted her boys more than anything in the world and she'd do anything to have them. At the time Linda had assumed she was referring to her efforts to quit drinking. Later she'd wondered briefly if the woman had meant something else, and then she had forgotten all about it.

Juliet thanked her and wished her a Merry Christmas. She hung up the phone slowly. Eileen had made virtually the same threat to her. She wished all of them had paid more attention to the warning signs.

"Linda doesn't have any information that will help," Juliet told Brady. "I knew Eileen was desperate," she added, "but I never expected anything like this."

"Nobody did." Brady tied his shoes, his mouth set in a firm, straight line.

Juliet grabbed her coat and followed him down the stairs. The only thing left to do was go to Phil and wait with him. On Christmas Day, there weren't any other options.

CHAPTER TWELVE

MICHAEL WASN'T SURE where he was at first. He stared at th patterns in the cracked plaster ceiling. Without moving h head, he could tell that Timmy was beside him, wadded up i a ball around his blanket. There didn't seem to be anyone els around. Tentatively, he raised up slightly, his hands clutchin a rough green blanket against his chin. The room was old an kind of dirty. It had a window, but there was nothing except brick wall on the other side. He was sure he'd never been ther before.

Timmy stirred beside him. "Did Santa Claus come?" H rubbed his eyes sleepily.

"I don't know," Michael answered, his voice barely mor than a whisper.

"Isn't it Christmas?" Timmy looked around. His eyes wid ened and he clutched his blanket. "Where are we?"

"I think we're at Mommy's," Michael answered. Feelin braver, he sat up all the way. "She came last night, remem ber?"

"No she didn't," Timmy asserted. "She's coming today Santa Claus was supposed to come last night."

"No, stupid. You were asleep, and she was carrying you. don't think Santa Claus came, because there wasn't anythin under the tree. You probably don't remember."

Timmy put his thumb in his mouth. "I don't like this place, he announced.

Neither did Michael, and he was the oldest so it was up t him to figure out what to do about it. "Come on," he sai "We're going to phone Daddy." He grabbed Timmy's fre hand and led him down a short, dark hallway into a tin kitchen barely big enough for the two of them to stand be tween the sink and the refrigerator. He didn't see a phon nywhere, but there was a door at the end of the kitchen. Still arefoot, they tiptoed out onto a wooden porch with stairs ading up to the floors above them and down to the alley be-ow.

"I don't think there's a phone out here," Timmy said, shiv-ring in the cold air.

"No, I guess not," Michael agreed, peering through the roken slats of the railing. The porch smelled bad from all the arbage spilling out of the old, rusty can. He chipped at the eeling paint with his thumbnail. "Let's go back inside, immy. We really need to call Daddy."

Michael led his brother back through the kitchen and past the edroom where they'd slept. Moving cautiously, they ap-roached an open doorway a few steps farther on. "There's Mommy," Timmy announced, pointing to the woman lying on lumpy flowered couch. "She's still sleeping."

"Sh-h-h." Michael put his hand over his brother's mouth. heir mother didn't move. He stared at the empty bottle on the able beside her. He could remember her at night sometimes vhen she used to be at home, sleeping so he couldn't wake her p. His father had told him once it was because she drank too nuch.

"Santa Claus didn't come here," Timmy whispered. "I want o go home."

Michael looked around for a telephone, but there wasn't one. le turned toward his brother. "Why don't you see if you can vake up Mom?" he suggested.

Timmy looked terrified. "What if she gets mad?"

That was the same thing that had been worrying Michael. "She won't get mad if you wake her," he assured Timmy. "I'll ive you a jawbreaker when we get home if you do it."

"Give me two," Timmy negotiated.

"Okay, two," Michael agreed grudgingly.

Timmy tiptoed hesitantly toward the sleeping form. "Mommy," he whispered. "Mommy." He put his hand on her houlder and shook gently. She groaned and he jumped back.

"Three jawbreakers," Michael promised.

Timmy tried again. This time his mother opened her eyes and tared at him with a dazed expression. "Timmy! What are you loing here?"

Confused, Timmy blurted out, "But Michael said you brought us here."

Eileen rubbed the palms of her hands hard against her temples to dull the throbbing. "That's right, I did bring you home with me." It was Christmas and her babies were going to spend Christmas with her.

She looked at them standing there, shivering in their thin pajamas. They looked alone and frightened, like she was, and they didn't look much like babies any more. "We can spend Christmas together." She tried to sound reassuring, but her head was pounding and nothing was very clear.

Michael studied his mother carefully. She was still wearing her clothes, the same ones she'd had on the night before when she came to their house. She had black smudges under her eyes. Michael wasn't sure what to say to her, so he didn't say anything. His mother sat up and smiled, but it was a funny, crooked smile.

"Did you guys just wake up?"

Timmy looked helplessly at his brother.

"Yes," Michael said firmly.

"Then, if you'll wait just a minute . . ." Eileen stood up unsteadily and walked to the bathroom, closing the door behind her.

Timmy looked at Michael, his eyes wide with fright. "She's not going to take us home. She said we have to stay here and spend Christmas. I want to go home."

"Daddy will know what to do," Michael said, still looking around for a phone. "Maybe there's a telephone outside." he crossed the room to the front door and turned the knob as quietly as he could.

Timmy scurried up behind him. "I'm coming, too." They leaned out the open doorway, and saw a long, dark hallway dotted with doors. Timmy jerked back. "But I'm not going out there." He grabbed the bottom of Michael's pajama shirt and pulled his brother back inside. Michael quickly closed and latched the door.

"Then we're going to have to figure something else out," Michael told him, "because we can't stay here. You tell her we want to go home and I'll give you the whole bag of jawbreakers. Deal?"

Before Timmy could answer, the bathroom door opened, startling them both. "You must be hungry," Eileen said, feeling more in control of herself. "I think I have some orange juice." She led the way to the kitchen and both boys reluctantly followed, watching as she took a pitcher of orange juice from the nearly empty refrigerator. She poured three glasses and handed one to each boy before she opened the cabinet and reached for the bottle of vodka.

Her hand gripping the neck of the bottle, she stopped and looked at the boys. They were holding their glasses, watching her. Methodically, she unscrewed the cap from the bottle. Then she looked at the boys again. A drink would make her feel so much better. Turning away from them, Eileen wrapped her fingers around the edge of the kitchen counter and closed her eyes. She'd promised to stop drinking a hundred times, but this was different. This time it wasn't for her. It was for them, because she loved them—and because she didn't want to lose them.

With a shaking hand, Eileen poured the liquor down the sink, holding the bottle upside down until the last drops were gone. Then she threw the empty bottle into the trash. It was one of the hardest things she'd ever done. Both boys' eyes were wide, but for a long minute neither of them said a word.

Hesitantly, Timmy broke the silence. "Mommy?"

Eileen turned around.

"We want to go home." Timmy wasn't looking at her. "Michael said he'd give me a whole bag of jawbreakers if I told you."

"I did not," Michael protested.

"Yes, you did. You said—"

"Is it true that you want to go home, too, Michael?" Eileen questioned.

Michael stared at his feet.

"I want to," Timmy piped up, "because Santa Claus didn't come here."

"No," Eileen admitted, "but I have presents for you—"

"You're not Santa Claus," Timmy interrupted.

"But I'm your mother," Eileen said gently, "and I love you very much, and I'd like to spend Christmas with you just like we used to."

Michael looked up, his eyes full of hostility. "If you want to be with us so much then why don't you come home and live there like you used to?"

Eileen could feel the anger pouring out from deep inside him. "I . . . I can't right now, Michael—"

"Then it's not fair to take us away and make us come here. You don't love us, or you wouldn't do that." Michael turned his back to her and stood perfectly straight, staring at the wall.

She looked down at Timmy. "Please take us back to Daddy," he whimpered, large tears rolling down his cheeks.

"But I'd hoped . . ." she began to explain, and then she stopped because she could see it was another dream gone wrong. They weren't babies any more. She couldn't just take them and have them like she did when they were little. She looked back at Timmy's tear-streaked face. He was standing there crying for his daddy and there was nothing she could say. And Michael. She walked over to him and put her hand on his shoulder but he jerked out of her grasp. She wanted to tell him not to hate her, that she couldn't help what had happened. But there was no way to make him understand.

"I guess," she said slowly, "if you both want to go home, that's what we need to do. We can see if Santa Claus came."

Timmy brightened substantially, but Michael didn't turn around. "Does that make you happy, Michael?" Eileen asked him. She thought about the vodka. She was glad she had poured it out.

"I guess," Michael answered grudgingly. "Are you going to stay?"

Eileen hadn't thought about that. She had been supposed to spend Christmas with them. "Do you want me to?" she asked Michael.

Slowly, he turned around. "I guess," he said.

Eileen looked down at her wrinkled skirt and the blouse she'd worn for two days. She couldn't go looking so disheveled. She wanted to look nice, nice like she used to look when she had a whole closet full of clothes and could shop at any store. There was one dress, the green one, that she'd kept hidden away. It would be all right. She didn't have the necklace that went with it anymore. She'd sold that. But she did have the pair of plain gold earrings and the bracelet—she looked down at her wrist.

She always wore the bracelet, but it was gone, too. So much was gone.

Eileen opened a door to one of the lower cabinets which was empty except for two brightly wrapped packages. "You can open your presents now, and then I'll go get ready." She handed one package to each boy.

Timmy's face broke into a wide grin. Michael remained more skeptical. She watched them untie the ribbons with a queasy feeling in her stomach. She had bought the presents at the dime store a week ago, one night when she was working and got a lot of tips. She'd been really excited at the time and had come home the same night and carefully wrapped each box. But now she wasn't even sure the boys would like the things she'd bought them. She barely knew them anymore.

Timmy ripped into the paper with a vengeance, and his present was open in seconds. He took out the brightly painted metal box inside and looked at it curiously. Finding the small handle on the side, he turned it, and the box played "London Bridge Is Falling Down." The faster he turned, the faster the music played. All of a sudden the top popped open and a grinning clown head popped out with a bang. "Yikes!" yelled Timmy, jumping backward. Even Michael laughed.

"Let me try," Michael demanded, reaching for the jack-in-the-box.

"Open your own," Timmy retorted, hugging the present to him.

Michael jerked at the ribbon he had been meticulously untying and opened the box. Inside was a miniature fort and a bag filled with tiny plastic figures of soldiers, Indians, and horses. "Wow!" he exclaimed, and for the first time since Eileen could remember, she saw the light in his eyes that had once brought her such joy. He ripped open the bag and dumped the figures in a heap in front of him. "This is neat. I never saw one of these."

Timmy stopped cranking. "Lemme see." He leaned over Michael.

"Go play with you own toy." Michael covered the figures protectively with his hands. "This is mine. Mommy gave it to me."

With tears in her eyes, Eileen knelt down behind the boys, putting one arm around each of them. "Merry Christmas," she whispered.

Both boys looked up at her, and for just a moment Timmy rested his head against her shoulder.

"Merry Christmas, Mommy," Michael said quietly. He didn't pull away.

Joy flooded Eileen, sweeping through her to fill the emptiness. How long she'd waited for this moment. Her babies, her boys, were with her, and a halo of happiness surrounded them all. She'd missed them so desperately, and she wanted to be with them so much. "Do you two think you could share your toys for just a few minutes while I change my clothes?" she asked as she stood up.

The brothers glared at each other. "I guess," Michael said.

Eileen took a quick shower, humming all the while. She wished she had dusting powder or perfume, but there wasn't any. She rubbed the bathroom mirror with her towel to wipe away the steam and then brushed her hair hard until it seemed to take on a new luster. She wanted to look her very best today. The green dress was loose when she zipped it, and she pulled the belt a notch tighter than usual to gather it in at her waist. She was relieved to find the dress was long enough to cover the run in her only pair of pantyhose. Wishing she had a full-length mirror, she studied her image again in the small mirror in the bathroom. She didn't look perfect, Eileen decided, brushing her hair one more time, but it was the best she could do.

"Mommy you look different," Michael observed, when she reappeared in the kitchen where the boys were apparently waging war with Michael's new fort.

"Yeah, you look pretty," Timmy seconded.

It wasn't just their words, but the way they looked at her that filled Eileen with a new kind of courage. She'd lost so much, but maybe all of it wasn't gone forever. "How about calling a temporary truce and putting all your men into the fort?" she suggested. "We're going to..." She paused, and then she said simply, "We're going home."

The boys followed her down to the car, each with a blanket wrapped around his shoulders and his present clutched in his and. Eileen shook her head. It had been stupid to bring them without clothes or even shoes. She hadn't been thinking. For a long time she hadn't been thinking. It was time she started.

She buckled Timmy firmly in the front seat beside her, and let Michael get in the back where he promptly began to set up his fort. The street was empty. Everyone was inside, celebrating Christmas. She considered calling Phil to let him know they were coming. He was probably worried. But the phone she usually used was in the bar down the street, and she didn't want to go in there this morning.

"Do you think Santa Claus has really come to our house?" Timmy asked as they started out.

"It won't be long till we find out," Eileen promised, knowing that he had indeed come. Phil would have seen to that, just like he'd always taken care of everything. Maybe that was part of the problem, she realized suddenly. She'd always seemed so unnecessary. Nothing she did was ever very important.

"I hope he brings me a whole lot of neat stuff." Timmy began cranking out "London Bridge."

"What do you want most?" Eileen asked.

"I know what I want," Michael interrupted. "I want this really neat dirt bike. It's silver and blue and it's really fast."

"You don't know it's fast. You just think so," Timmy countered smugly.

"Mommy! My soldier got lost down in the seat!" Michael exclaimed.

Eileen took a quick look over her shoulder. "I'll help you get him as soon as we stop—"

"Mommy!" Timmy shrieked.

Eileen turned her attention back to the road quickly and for an instant she froze in fear. An enormous truck was hurtling backward down the hill ahead. They were directly in its path.

"Stop!" Timmy shrieked again.

Eileen slammed on the brakes and spun the steering wheel. The car lurched to the left. Everything moved in slow motion, the truck bearing down on them, getting bigger and bigger until there was nothing else. Then came the sickening crash. Eileen felt the car begin to spin and from somewhere behind her she heard a long, piercing scream.

THERE WERE QUIET sounds, voices talking, dishes clattering in the distance. And an odd smell, like the school room after the janitor leaves with his bucket and mop. Her head was pounding, an incessant throbbing pain. The voices got louder. She opened her eyes, just a flicker, to find a bright light glaring down at her. Then she heard his voice.

"Eileen? Eileen, can you hear me?"

It was too much effort to answer. She wanted to go away again to somewhere that her head wouldn't hurt so much.

"Eileen? Please answer me, Eileen," the voice repeated.

He was calling to her. He wanted her. She had to answer. Using all her energy, she forced her eyes open, squinting against the brilliant light overhead. "Yes?" she said, her voice barely audible.

The pounding inside her head increased when she turned slightly. A hazy image of Phil's face bending over her came into focus.

"Eileen, are you all right?"

She knew he must be talking because his lips were moving, but his voice sounded hollow and far away. She thought about his question. Why was he asking her that? "I don't know," she murmured.

"Do you remember what happened?" he questioned. "You were in an accident, Eileen, in the car. You and the boys."

It began to come back. They'd been riding in the car, going somewhere, and then— She closed her eyes again, trying to shut out the image of the truck. It kept coming and coming at them and then the noise— Letting out a low moan, she clamped her hands over her ears.

She felt Phil touch her arm and slowly she opened her eyes and moved her hands back down to her sides. She was awake now, and she felt like she might throw up. Suddenly she grabbed Phil's hand and clutched it hard. "The boys," she whispered. "Are the boys all right?"

Phil nodded, squeezing her hand. "Yes," he nodded. "The doctor is checking Michael now, but he seems fine. Timmy has a broken arm and a nasty cut across his forehead. They want to keep him for a few days to make sure it doesn't get infected, but it's not too serious."

"Thank God," she breathed. She looked up at Phil, tears welling up in her eyes. "I didn't mean for it to happen. I didn't mean to hurt them." She could hear him telling her not to take the boys in the car. He'd told her when she was drinking it was so dangerous. Suddenly she had to make him understand. "I didn't have anything to drink, Phil. I didn't—"

He stroked her hand. "It wasn't your fault, Eileen. It was that damn truck. Some idiot didn't set the brakes. You did everything you could. The ambulance driver told me about the tire tracks. He said they were almost at a right angle." His voice broke, but he went on, having difficulty with the words. "When you swerved like that, it saved your lives."

Eileen remembered looking back at Michael and then Timmy's scream and the truck— She shut her eyes. "Oh, Phil, I've made such a mess of everything. All I wanted was for them to be happy," she sobbed softly. "All I wanted—"

"Sh-h-h," he whispered. "I know."

"No," she protested, her voice stronger, "you don't know. You don't know how close I came to taking a drink. I could have killed Timmy and Michael." The tears rolled freely down her cheeks and she didn't try to stop them. Her words came pouring out. "I shouldn't have taken them. I know I shouldn't. I hadn't had anything to drink for so long and then when it was almost Christmas I felt so bad. I saw you leave the house and I wanted my babies more than anything in the world. But then, this morning, I realized they weren't babies any more. They've grown up and I haven't been a part of it."

"Eileen," Phil interrupted her. "Don't do this to yourself. We'll have time to talk when you feel better."

She tried to sit up, but the pain in her head was too intense. "I don't want to wait, Phil. I've already waited too long." Her voice was choked with sobs. "I've lost everything that really mattered. I left because I was so lonely. You were never home anymore, and you didn't care. Nothing I did was right, and then you wanted another baby and I just couldn't do it anymore.... I thought if I went away you'd realize how much you needed me." She closed her eyes against the pain. "Except it didn't work that way."

Phil stared at her, stunned by the barrage of emotion. "I did need you, Eileen," he answered softly. "We all did. We thought you didn't want us anymore."

Her body was still, the crying over. "I guess I didn't, at least not like that. And now you don't want me."

Phil didn't know how to answer her. He remembered the months before she left, the hostility and the screaming rages. They couldn't go through that again. And yet the boys needed a mother. And he needed a wife. There had been too many lonely times. But he wanted the woman he'd married, not the stranger she'd become.

When he didn't answer, Eileen went on, speaking slowly and painfully. "I thought I had the drinking licked. I'd done really well until the last few days. I need help."

Those were the words Phil had hoped to hear for so long, but he wondered now whether it was too late. He reached out and gently took her hand again. "I don't know whether we could make it work again, Eileen." He paused, thoughtful, tracing the pattern on the back of her hand as he'd done so many times before. "I don't know if there's anything left for us."

She looked up at him and met his eyes, searching with an understanding beyond words. "I don't know either, Phil," she answered.

"Maybe we could try," Phil said softly. He looked toward the window where the sun was slowly sinking toward the horizon, signaling the end to a long mid-winter afternoon. "And maybe, when you're better, you could come home to recuperate for a while." He stopped, knowing what he was saying, not knowing if it was right or wrong. "After that, I don't know. We'll just have to take it a little at a time."

Eileen closed her eyes, trying to shut out the intense throbbing in her head. "Let me think about it, Phil."

He took her hand once more and held it gently, but her eyes were still closed and her breathing was slow and regular. He turned and walked quietly out of the room.

Juliet stood up when she saw him approach. "Phil, is she all right?"

"I think so." He sank heavily on a bench, and she sat next to him. It seemed to Juliet as though she'd been waiting to hear about Eileen forever. "She's kind of groggy from the blow on

e head, but she seems all right," Phil said. " She's sleeping
w."

"At least none of them is badly hurt. From what the police
id—" Juliet knew it was better not to go on. The policeman
e'd talked to while she was waiting for Phil had bluntly told
r it was a miracle they all weren't killed. If the truck had hit
e passenger door instead of the rear fender, the car would
ve been crushed and no one could have survived. "Will she
hospitalized for long?" Juliet asked.

"Probably not." Phil hesitated. "I think she may come home
r a while when she's released."

Juliet frowned. "Are you sure that's wise?" She was imme-
ately sorry she'd asked. It was absolutely none of her busi-
ss and an area she'd been determined to stay out of.

"I don't know whether it's wise or not," Phil answered.
The whole damn thing's tough either way."

And tougher this way, Juliet thought. It was a no-win situ-
ion. She wished she could believe it would work out for them.
it it was more likely that everyone would get hurt again. She'd
en the pattern in families too many times.

"Juliet, look, they gave me a Santa Claus pen!" Michael
me bounding from around the corner with Brady close bend.

"I like it . . . does it write?" she asked, as he thrust it at her.

"Two colors at the same time," he answered proudly. He
rned toward his father. "Can we go home now?"

Phil patted Michael's shoulder. "In just a few minutes. First,
ady's going to come with me while I take care of some busi-
ss. Why don't you wait here with Juliet?"

Michael sat down on the bench by Juliet, who produced a
emo pad from her purse. "You want to draw with your new
n?" she asked him.

"Yeah, I guess so."

She watched him fashion the shape of a car and then a big
uck on top of it. "Is that how you remember the accident?"
e asked him.

Michael started to push his hair out of his face and then
imaced with pain when he touched the big purple lump on his
rehead. "Sort of." She could still see the fear in his eyes.
This big truck came barreling down the hill and Mom didn't

see it at first and then I got down on the floor in the back s[e]
and there was this awful screeching and then a big crash a[nd]
then we were spinning and spinning." He buried his head in [her]
lap, his whole body trembling.

Juliet's heart went out to him. It had been so awful for hi[m.]
First his mother took him and then the accident and now t[he]
hospital. "At least everybody is all right and you're goi[ng]
home," she soothed him, gently rubbing his back as he [leaned]
against her.

"Me and Dad are going home," he corrected her.

"But Timmy will be all right in a few days," she told hi[m.]
"And then you'll all be together."

There was a long silence. Juliet felt Michael's musc[les]
tighten. "We won't all be together. Not anymore."

"You mean because of your mother?" Juliet asked. "Wh[at]
if she came home, too?"

Michael kept his face buried. "She won't come," he said [in]
a muffled voice. "And even if she did, it wouldn't matter, [be-]
cause she'd just go away again," he added bitterly. "It wou[ld]
be better if she would just leave us alone." His whole bo[dy]
shook. Juliet could tell he was crying.

She held him for a long time, hurting for him, hating wh[at]
was happening to him. She would never let this happen to [a]
child of hers, she vowed silently. This was the fallout from [ru-]
ined marriages. People weren't satisfied with destroying ea[ch]
other. They had to take the children along, too. Michael w[as]
right. Better one parent you could count on than two to te[ar]
you apart.

When Phil and Brady appeared, Michael sat up quickly a[nd]
rubbed his face on his sleeve. "You ready?" Phil asked hi[m,]
offering his hand. Wordlessly, Michael took it and followed [his]
father.

"Thanks to both of you—for everything," Phil called [to]
Brady and Juliet as they walked away.

Brady slipped his arm around Juliet's waist. "It's been a lo[ng]
day," he said, pulling her close to him. "Let's go home."

Juliet tensed. She was going to have to talk to him. No[w.]
She'd let herself just go along with him, relaxed her guard, [let]
the walls come down. She'd even pretended sometimes that th[ings]
might be different, and lately she'd been thinking about wh[at]

t might be like if they were really married. She kept getting in deeper and deeper with Brady, slowly, one day at a time. And he had to stop it.

All the way home, Juliet stared out the window at the ribbons of house lights running up and down the hills. So many people chasing rainbows with lead weights at the end. The pot of gold was only a fantasy. Brady glanced sideways at her several times but didn't try to get her to talk. She was upset about the accident and maybe she needed some time alone with her thoughts. When they got home, he'd take her to bed, and afterward they'd both feel better. They always did.

CHAPTER THIRTEEN

BRADY TURNED ON the tree lights as soon as they walked into the house, and the living room took on the soft, warm glow of Christmas. Juliet watched uncomfortably as he tossed his jacket on one of the beanbag chairs and opened the fire screen. She was tired, and she longed to curl up with him in front of the fire. But she couldn't forget Michael's face, the bump on his head, his cheeks streaked from crying, his eyes old beyond his years from carrying the weight of his parents' ruined marriage.

She watched Brady methodically stack the wood, two logs across, three on top, tinder underneath. People didn't start out to hurt their children or each other. Juliet knew that. They started out the way she and Brady were starting out, happy and full of dreams. She should never have let their relationship come this far. And waiting would only make things worse.

The match flared. Brady touched it to the wood curls he'd shaved, and the flames crept steadily along the logs. He watched until the fire built in intensity, and then closed the screen and stood up. It was a small fire, but he didn't expect to stay downstairs very long.

Without a word, he turned to Juliet and took her in his arms, leaning down to nuzzle beneath the auburn hair and kiss the sensitive spot along the side of her neck. She smelled good. It was a natural fragrance that reminded him of spring mornings. He raised his lips to playfully kiss her earlobe.

"Brady..." The first stirrings of desire already rippled through Juliet, and she realized again how much a part of him she'd become. It required a conscious effort to hold her body away from his. "Brady, I need to talk to you."

He kissed her behind the ear, smoothing back the flowing ~~h~~air. "Fine," he murmured. "Come sit by the fire." His arm ~~ti~~ghtened around her, guiding her toward the beanbag chairs.

Juliet stiffened and pulled back. "No, Brady, not here. Let's ~~g~~o into the kitchen."

"Why the kitchen?" He took a good look at her. He'd never ~~se~~en her eyes like that, as dark as tree moss and full of appre-~~te~~nsion. *It must be the accident,* he decided. It had shaken him, ~~to~~o. "We can talk here." He sat down in the beanbag chair and ~~he~~ld his arms out to her. "The fire's warm and we can look at ~~th~~e tree. After all, Juliet, whatever else has happened, this is ~~st~~ill Christmas."

Juliet wavered. It was so hard to say no. He'd become a res-~~er~~voir of strength for her. But that had to change, too. "I'd like ~~to~~ go into the kitchen, Brady," she said again, without expla-~~n~~ation.

Puzzled, he followed her.

She sat down at the table, poised on the edge of the chair. ~~B~~rady didn't join her. He walked to the refrigerator and found ~~a~~ carton of eggnog. Then he took two glasses from the cabinet ~~an~~d poured a drink for each of them.

Juliet took a deep breath. The sooner she got this confron-~~ta~~tion over with, the better. There wasn't any gentle approach, ~~at~~ least none she could think of. She might as well be direct. ~~"~~Brady, this isn't going to work," she said simply.

He put the eggnog carton back in the refrigerator. "What ~~is~~n't going to work?" He placed a glass in front of each of them ~~an~~d sat across the table from her. She was beautiful sitting there ~~w~~ith her hair loose, still dressed in the bright green sweatshirt ~~an~~d jeans she'd pulled on in such a hurry this morning. He ~~p~~icked up his glass and then paused, holding it toward her. ~~"~~Before you tell me, let's drink a toast to us—and to better ~~w~~ays to spend Christmas," he added, smiling at her.

Her response was an uncomfortable silence. Juliet's face re-~~m~~ained impassive and her eggnog sat untouched on the table. ~~B~~rady put down his glass. "What's going on, Juliet?"

She lowered her eyes. Now was the time to lay it out, clearly ~~an~~d simply. A clean break was the only answer. "Brady, what's ~~h~~appened between us isn't what I'd expected. I never antici-~~p~~ated getting so involved." She hesitated, waiting for him to

affirm what she'd said, or perhaps to discuss how he felt abou
her. He'd never really told her that, not in so many words. B
Brady didn't say anything. She could feel him watching her, an
she kept her eyes riveted on the table.

"When we signed the contract," she continued slowly, "
was with the understanding that the marriage was an arrang
ment for the convenience of the baby." Juliet took a dee
breath and lifted her eyes to meet his. "What I'm trying to sa
Brady, is that I can't live with you anymore, and it's time w
move on with the divorce."

Brady stared at her, trying to figure out what could hav
caused such a radical change in this woman virtually ove
night. Yesterday everything had been fine. Before the accide
suddenly complicated everything, he'd planned to talk to h
about extending their living arrangement indefinitely. He'
figured that would be easier for her to accept than dealing wit
the future of the marriage which, of course, would also hav
been extended indefinitely. Now, suddenly, she was talkin
about ending it all. His stomach lurched.

"Aren't you going to say anything?" she demanded. She'
expected him to at least answer her.

Brady chose his words carefully. "I don't know what to sa
A lot has happened between us, Juliet, or at least I thought
had. It may not be the way we'd planned things, but it's the wa
they are."

His words hurt her still more, and she didn't know wh
"That's my whole point, Brady. This isn't right."

"Why the hell isn't it right?" he demanded. "Aren't yo
happy?"

Juliet stared at her glass, turning it around and around wit
her fingertips. "It isn't a question of happy or unhappy. It's
question of the future and what we want." She spoke delibe
ately. "I told you the first time I met you that I didn't want
get married. I agreed to it—" She stopped. Right now it was
puzzle to her why she'd ever gone along with it. She'd sense
even then that it was a mistake, but somehow she'd manage
to persuade herself that it was an innocuous one. "I agreed
it because it wasn't a real marriage. We put in the escap
clause—"

"That probably wouldn't hold up in court, you know," rady interjected.

Juliet managed a wry smile. "I know that. I wasn't sure you d." She looked up at him again, a profound sadness in her es. "But does it matter? Would you fight it if I wanted out?"

Then it was Brady who looked away. "Of course not, Ju-t. Marriages aren't made in the courts. They're made in ople's hearts." He tapped his fingers against the table. The hole damn thing made no sense. "But why, Juliet?" he de-anded. "Why?"

Juliet shook her head. His was the hardest question of all. I've already told you why. You know how I feel about mar-age." Her eyes pleaded for understanding. "I'd like to think e're different, but that's what everybody wants to think. I'm re Phil and Eileen thought they were different. You told me urself what an ideal couple they seemed to be at first—"

"Juliet!" Brady interrupted. "We're not Eileen and Phil. ou're trying to tell me because they have problems, we will, o?"

"It's so many people, Brady, and you're never sure till it ppens."

Brady ignored her answer. "Besides," he added, "Phil told e Eileen is going to come home for a while until she's feeling tter and they're going to see how it works."

Juliet sighed. "I already know that. But they've got the same oblems they always had. And look what they're doing to the ys." Her voice took on a hard edge. "Michael has it all apped out. He said he didn't care if she came home because e'd just leave again." She paused, remembering how Mi-ael's body trembled as he lay against her. "And then he cried, rady. He hid his head in my lap and he cried. How many ghts do you suppose he's fallen asleep crying like that?"

For several moments, Brady didn't answer. "It has been hard the boys," he admitted finally, "especially on Michael." He as beginning to understand what had happened, and he felt en more powerless than before. What Juliet was telling him d nothing to do with how she felt about him. She must care, she wouldn't even have tried to explain.

"Can't you see, Brady?" Juliet appealed to him. "This is all rong for us."

Brady reached across the table and took her hand. "We g married for some pretty flimsy reasons, Juliet. Sometim things seem a lot different when you look back at them." F took a deep breath. "But what about us, Juliet? Aren't we reason to be married?"

"I...I'm sorry, Brady." It was harder to say what she need to with him holding her hand.

The silence gathered around them, a heavy, uneasy silenc "I can't believe you're ready to throw it all away, Juliet. Wh you're telling me doesn't make any sense at all."

"I'm sorry." Her voice was almost a whisper. She was afra to try to say anything more.

Brady watched her. There had to be some way he could rea her. "Will you do one thing for me, Juliet?" he asked. "W you give it a little time and think about it? You're reacting what happened today—"

Juliet gave her head a vigorous shake. This was one of th things she had determined at the outset she wouldn't do. It h to be a clean break. "I can't stay here with you any longe Brady. I don't know what we're going to do about the hous We can try to sell it like this. At least we shouldn't lose a money."

He lifted her hand and cradled it in both of his. "I don't gi a damn about the house. And I'm not even asking you to st: here with me. Go to the beach house, if you like. All I want y to do is give it a little time."

"Brady," she argued stubbornly, "I'm not going to chan my mind."

"No, you're probably not, certainly not if you go back your apartment and back to your law practice and shut yo eyes to everything else." His voice was firm and steady. "That not fair, Juliet. It's not fair to you or me. You may not li what's happened between us, but not liking it doesn't make simply vanish. Whoosh!" His hand streaked through the air

"I know it doesn't, but—"

"Go to the house at the beach, Juliet. Spend some time alo and think about it."

Juliet couldn't quite decide whether his request was reaso able or simply a ploy that she would regret later. He'd ma aged to persuade her to do some very uncharacteristic thin;

ver the past few months. "I don't know, Brady," she hesitated.

"I promise not to disturb you while you're there, if that's what's bothering you, Juliet. You can stay as long as you like."

It was a tempting offer. Juliet knew realistically that making he break with Brady was going to take a lot of rethinking. This meant there would be no baby, at least in the near future. And ll those hazy dreams, that had somehow included Brady, were o more. "I suppose it wouldn't hurt to spend a few days at the each," Juliet relented.

"Thanks Juliet," he responded softly. A shadow of a smile ouched his lips.

"Wait a minute," she stopped him. "All I said was I'd go to he beach house."

"And that's all I asked."

"It's a transition, Brady," she warned. "I'm not going to hange my mind."

Brady knew the odds of Juliet reconsidering her decision ere no better than fifty-fifty, if that. But any odds were betr than none right now. He might as well lay it all on the line. his could be the last chance. "There's something I need to tell ou, Juliet, something I've never said, but I guess I thought you new." He took her hand again and looked directly into her yes.

She watched apprehensively, afraid of what was coming.

His voice was soft when he spoke. "I love you, Juliet, more han I knew it was possible to love a woman. I told you once vhy I hadn't married—that the woman had to be my reason for eing, my family would be my life."

"Please stop," she cried out. "You're only making this arder."

"No," he replied, his gaze never wavering. "I won't stop, ecause I want you to hear this. You have to do what you feel a your heart is right, Juliet. But I'm not going to let you deny he truth."

"I'm not denying anything." Her voice rose. "I just don't ant to hear it."

"Of course you don't. You are ready to destroy something eautiful because you don't have a crystal ball. There aren't any crystal balls, Juliet. We can't live in the future and we can't live in the past. We have to live right now. That's all there is.''

Juliet buried her face in her hands. ''Don't do this to me, Brady,'' she pleaded. ''Please don't. Please just let me alone.''

He stared at her, wanting to take her in his arms but afraid to touch her. There was nothing he could do now. It was up to her to drive out whatever demons haunted her. Nobody could do it for her, least of all him. If he lost her . . . he couldn't even bear to think about it. The only thing he could do was wait.

''I'll leave you alone, Juliet,'' he told her quietly. ''I already promised I would.''

She heard his chair scrape against the bare floor, then the clank of the fireplace doors shutting and the click as he turned off the switch on the Christmas tree lights. The front door opened and closed softly. The deadbolt snapped across and a pervasive silence filled the house. Juliet knew without looking that she was alone, very much alone.

THE WEEK AFTER Christmas was sun-dappled and warm, a perfect week to spend at the beach. Juliet hated it. She'd already made her decision. She wasn't sure why she was there.

For the first two days she got up early, took long walks, ate regular meals, and whiled away the long evenings watching old movies on television. She did very little thinking about anything other than having her apartment redecorated and taking a late spring vacation in the mountains to look at the wild flowers.

There wasn't any hurry about anything, really. She didn't particularly want to be at the beach, but she didn't want to go back to her apartment, either. When she'd called Linda to say she wouldn't be in the office for a few days, her friend had urged her to take as much time as she needed. Knowing how much in favor of marriage Linda was, Juliet had expected a lecture, or at least an opinion. But she didn't get either. ''I can't give you any advice on this one,'' Linda had told her. ''I'll listen if you need to talk, but you're the only one who has the answers. Just keep thinking till you figure it out.'' But Juliet couldn't even decide what she was supposed to think about, and after two days she was as confused as when she'd first arrived.

When her alarm went off on the third day, Juliet rolled over and went back to sleep. She awoke with the sun high in the sky and sleepily reached for Brady. He wasn't there. Suddenly she was wide awake and everything came into sharp focus. He wouldn't be there, not ever again. And God! How she missed him!

Pulling on her jeans and an old sweatshirt, she went into the kitchen to make a pot of coffee. Everything reminded her of Brady. His old running shoes, riddled with holes, were sitting by the back door. Two jackets and an old fishing hat had been slung over the wooden rack on the wall. A pottery mug with a picture of two ducks flying sat near the coffee pot. It was Brady's favorite.

She wandered into the living room with her coffee and sat cross-legged on the floor in front of the window wall to watch the surf. She missed the beanbag chairs, but they were back in the house in San Francisco. She remembered the first time she'd seen them, that night Brady had brought her to the house before they got married. Beanbag chairs had struck her as an odd choice, even for a beach house, when she'd looked at them then. That seemed such a long time ago.

That night had been the first time Brady had made love to her. Except he didn't. He'd wanted her to be ready, too, and so he'd waited, and then he'd shown her things about her body she might never have known. Restless, Juliet stood up and walked back to the kitchen. He'd asked her to think about it, but what was there to think about? You either wanted to be married or you didn't. It was easy to delude yourself and pretend that the path would be smooth and you'd walk off into the sunset together holding hands. With Brady that would be so easy. But she'd seen marriages fail so many times.

Grabbing her jacket, Juliet went outdoors, kicking at the sand as she headed down toward the water. The sanderlings were skipping across the beach in tiny steps, a little society all their own that looked suspiciously like a microcosm of San Francisco pedestrians in rush hour. She watched a gull swoop and dive, then she carefully scanned the horizon. She knew there had been whale sightings along the coast. Of course, it was logical that there would have been. It was the time for them, unlike the day she and Brady had gone looking for whales. But that had been as good an excuse as any to go off together. She thought about that sun-warmed rock high on the grassy knoll, and Brady's hands on her back and then all over her body. Picking up a seashell from the beach, Juliet hurled it with all her strength into the waves and then took off running along the water's edge.

She ran past people walking in the sunshine and skirted around children with buckets and shovels digging deep holes in the sand. Farther along she passed a small shark that had washed up, its carcass picked almost clean by the gulls. She studied it all with extraordinary interest, filling up her mind with sights and sounds and smells of the beach so there was no room for anything else.

Her eyes traveled up to the beach houses nestled into hills covered with ice plant. Phil's house was up there. She wondered if Eileen had gone there after being discharged. She looked upward, and on Phil's deck saw two small figures, men probably, by the way they were standing, leaning over the rail. She stopped to study them more closely, and then the one on the left moved. She knew immediately it was Brady. The slope of the shoulders, the way he turned his head, those common, familiar movements she knew so well. It couldn't be anyone else.

She wanted to wave to him and start running up the hill. And then he would come home with her and they'd fix dinner together. Maybe he'd grill steaks and she'd make a salad like they did sometimes. And then they'd spend the evening reading or taking a walk or maybe he'd show her a toy he was working on. Sometimes she gave him pretty good advice. Juliet turned around and began walking back down the beach past the dead shark and the children with their buckets and shovels. The piercing cry of a gull echoed close behind her, but she didn't turn around.

Through the binoculars, Brady could follow Juliet's every move. He'd seen her hesitate. She'd probably recognized him. Even without the binoculars, he'd have known her. But she hadn't come toward him and he supposed he didn't expect her to. He watched her turn back, making her way slowly along the water's edge. She was lithe and graceful, but there was no spring in her step. She walked heavily, like someone carrying a great burden. Brady kept the glasses trained on her back until she was little more than a wisp of color in the distance.

"Any whales out there?" Phil inquired.

Brady grunted, still studying Juliet.

Phil looked at him curiously. "Hey, there aren't any whales that direction. You pick up a good-looking broad or something?"

"Something like that," Brady muttered, lowering the glasses and handing them to Phil. The days had stretched endlessly since Juliet had left. He'd spent Christmas night in a hotel, sleeping very little, mostly pacing the floor and thinking. When he went back home the next morning, he was still clinging to a shred of hope that she might have changed her mind. But he found the house empty. Most of her things were still there, except her toothbrush was missing from her cup in the bathroom and her pale pink robe was no longer hanging in the closet. He'd assumed she must have taken a few clothes and gone to the beach house, but it made him feel better to actually see her and know for sure she was all right.

"Doesn't seem to be much out there," Phil observed, running the binoculars slowly along the horizon and then moving in to scan the beach. "Looks like Eileen and the boys down that way." He studied them for quite a while. "The kids seem to be building one of their sand forts for her." He lowered the binoculars. "She used to love to build with them."

"Isn't she supposed to stay in bed?" Brady inquired.

"That's what the doctor said, but she seems to feel better. I suppose sitting on the beach won't hurt her."

"Is she drinking?" Brady asked.

Phil shook his head. "Not so far. I dumped all the liquor I had in the house, and she hasn't been able to go out." He laid the binoculars on the table. She talked to somebody from Alcoholics Anonymous yesterday. They said they'd help her, but it's going to be a tough battle."

"Yes, but it's a beginning," Brady said. He leaned on the rail, looking out at the pounding surf. He remembered Juliet's conviction that things would never work out for Phil and Eileen and he hoped she was wrong.

"Have you heard from Juliet?" Phil asked him.

Brady hesitated. It was hard for him to talk about their separation. "I didn't really expect to," he answered. "She needs some time."

"And she's at the beach house? Why don't you walk down and see her?"

Brady shook his head. "I promised not to."

"And it's tough as hell, right?"

"Yeah." Brady left the rail and paced across the deck, drinking in the salty wind that gusted off the ocean. "I may have lost it all, Phil. Juliet, the company, everything." He paced back again, his hands stuffed in his pockets. It was hard to admit that it was all gone, everything he cared about. But too much time had passed now and Juliet hadn't called or come home. He'd figured if she was going to change her mind, she'd do it in the first twenty-four hours. After that, the chances were pretty slim.

"I did have one thought," Phil ventured, "not about Juliet but about the company."

Brady paced back across the deck. He didn't want to talk about the company. Right now he didn't give a damn about it.

But Phil persisted. "Don't you personally hold all those patents for the toys and the new furniture line?"

"I guess so," Brady answered absently. "I've been going to transfer them, but—"

"Think about it, Brady," Phil insisted. "If you hold the patents, then what is Talcott Enterprises really?" When Brady didn't respond, he answered his own question. "It's nothing but a shell. As long as you hold the patents, you call the shots, Brady, and there's not a hell of a lot anybody can do about it."

"I guess you're right," Brady answered slowly. "I'd never really thought about it."

Phil was disappointed. He'd solved a major problem and he'd expected at least a thank you. "You don't sound very enthusiastic," he observed.

"I'm sorry, Phil." Brady turned toward him. "I really do appreciate you working it out. It's just...I guess my mind is on other things."

Phil shook his head. "I guess it is. Six months ago you'd have given anything for that kind of a handle on Talcott Enterprises. Now you're telling me, 'Gee, that's nice.' What the hell are you doing, Brady?''

Brady leaned against the rail again, idly watching the birds march across the sand. "I don't know." He ran his fingers through his hair, trying to find an answer. "Everything's changed. Nothing much seems to matter any more. Nothing except..." He stopped, knowing he might as well lay it on the line. "You warned me, clear back there at the beginning, and I laughed at you. So I guess it's your turn to say, 'I told you so.'"

Phil put his hand on Brady's shoulder. "What are you talking about?"

"I'm in love with her, Phil. Really in love with her. I don't give a damn about anything else. All I want is to have Juliet back."

Almost sharing Brady's pain, Phil closed his eyes. He remembered those feelings all too well, the agony of losing the woman you loved, the sense of powerlessness because there was nothing you could do to get her back. And yet you hoped that somehow, someday... If she'd died, at least it was over. If you'd walked out, you still had some options. But when she was the one who ended it, there was nothing left. "Have you told her how you feel?" Phil asked gently.

"I told her. Not soon enough, but I did tell her."

"And?"

"And she said she didn't want to be married." Brady picked up the binoculars and scanned the beach, looking for any patch of bright green that might be the sweatshirt Juliet was wearing.

"Did she give you any particular reason?" Not wanting to be married didn't seem to Phil much of a reason for getting a divorce. There had to be more to it than that. He couldn't believe she didn't care about Brady. He'd seen them together too many times. You could tell about a man and a woman, just by the way they were when they were together. And with Brady and Juliet, it was written all over them.

"She's got a lot of reasons." Brady was still studying the beach. "Or at least she thinks she does. She's a divorce lawyer, remember. Most marriages don't look very pretty once they get to her." Brady paused, thinking about some of the other things Juliet had said. "I'm not sure that's all of it. Her father walked out when she was ten. She jokes sometimes about how a psychologist would tell her she hates men.''

''Does she?''

''Hell no,'' Brady retorted, ''or at least you couldn't prove it by me.''

Phil smiled. ''That's what I figured.''

''What she wants is some guarantee that this will last forever, and there aren't any guarantees.''

''No.'' Phil's jaw tightened. ''There aren't any guarantees.''

They watched Eileen and the boys walking slowly up the hill toward the house. One boy was on either side of his mother, each holding one of her hands. All of them, Eileen included, were streaked with sand, and they were all smiling. They waved when they saw Phil and Brady, but neither of the boys broke away to run ahead.

''It's nice to see you, Brady,'' Eileen called out as they approached. ''I'm really out of breath,'' she admitted, sitting down for a moment on the stairs before she climbed up. ''Maybe the doctor had a point about a few days in bed.''

''Why don't you go take a nap?'' Phil suggested. ''You've got time before dinner.''

''I think maybe I will,'' she agreed, holding on to the rail to pull herself up.

''I'll help you,'' Michael offered, taking her hand.

''Me, too,'' seconded Timmy. Both boys walked with her into the house.

Brady's eyes followed them. ''The boys obviously like having her back.''

''But they're still afraid she'll leave again,'' Phil answered.

Brady looked directly at his friend. ''Do you want her to stay?''

Phil hesitated. ''I'm not sure. We've spent a lot of time talking, more than we have in years. Every so often I catch a glimpse of her the way she was when I first met her... when I fell in love with her.''

''That should be good,'' Brady observed.

Phil stared off into space. ''I don't know, Brady. I have a feeling we need to go at this pretty carefully. She's still sleeping in the guest room....'' Phil's voice trailed off. ''It's almost

starting over again," he said finally. "Even if she does stop
king, we've got a long way to go."

aybe Juliet was right, Brady thought bitterly. Maybe mar-
e was a bad bargain all the way around. But, if that was
, why was he so miserable? There had to be a way to make
ork, if two people only loved each other—and trusted each
r enough.

NEXT DAY Brady stayed home from work. He told himself
gs were slow during the holidays and there wasn't much
on he really needed to be at the office. But he knew that
t he told himself had nothing to do with it. He simply didn't
t to go anywhere.

e puttered around the house, mentally cataloguing the work
left to be done. In the small room off the master bed-
n, which they had immediately designated the nursery, he
across a box of pink-and-blue wallpaper rolls waiting to be
g. It had been a ridiculous choice for a house they were
ut to sell. For a couple with older children, or no children
l, that room would have been a dressing room or a study or
be a sewing room. He knew that and he'd assumed Juliet
too. He'd taken the choice of wallpaper as an unspoken
ement that maybe... Maybe what? If he'd said something
, instead of making assumptions, things might have been
erent.

rady walked through the other bedrooms and downstairs to
main floor. They'd made a surprising amount of progress
e time they'd had, maybe because they'd enjoyed working
ther. It had been fun to paint with Juliet. He'd figured that
right away. But the thought of doing it alone was dismal.
ectively he hated painting. He wandered into the kitchen
rummaged through a drawer until he found a list of con-
tors. As he ran his finger down the names, the phone rang.
rady stared at it. It could be Juliet. She was the only one his
etary might have told where he was. He picked up the re-
er on the second ring.

Brady, what are you doing at home?" Cass's cheery voice
ired. "You aren't sick, I hope."

No, nothing like that," he assured her.

"I'm certainly glad to hear that. I assume Juliet must there, too, since she isn't in her office. Just wanted to let know we all got back from Yosemite—wonderful skiing year, and only one broken leg. Fortunately, not mine.''

"Actually, Cass, she's not here,'' Brady told her. "She's the beach house.'' The silence was so long that he wasn't s Cass had heard him.

"What's she doing there?'' Cass asked suspiciously.

"She . . . ah, well . . .'' Cass was so damn blunt it was har soft-peddle anything with her. "The weather was nice she—''

"How long has she been there?'' Cass interrupted.

"Oh, a few days,'' Brady answered vaguely.

"Now, Brady!''

Brady winced. Only rarely had he heard Cass use that t of voice.

"You can't tell me Juliet's at the beach and you're in the c staying home from work, and everything is normal. Wh happened? Did you have an argument?''

"Well, no,'' Brady replied. Actually, they hadn't argued. wished it were that simple.

"Well,'' Cass continued, "you two haven't been marr long enough to have any serious problems. Give Juliet a days, and she'll probably cool off.''

"Yeah, I suppose so,'' Brady said, deliberately keeping reply casual. He said goodbye and hung up the phone, turn again to the list of contractors. Cass was smart. He proba hadn't fooled her a bit.

CHAPTER FOURTEEN

RLY THE FOLLOWING morning, Juliet sat at the kitchen ta-
in the beach house staring into her cup of coffee. She had
akened before dawn and couldn't go back to sleep. It seemed
tter to get up and get busy than to toss and turn. But busy
ing what? She had no idea. There wasn't anything to do, or
en anything she wanted to do. And so she sat at the table
nking coffee and listening to the raucous gulls quarreling
er their morning catch.

A sound, different from the other beach sounds, intruded on
liet's solitude. She listened carefully. It was a car, driving
wly down the beach road. There were never any cars out
re this early. Maybe it was Brady. For one long second Ju-
t's heart stopped. He had promised he would leave her alone,
d she was sure he would keep that promise.

She listened again. The car was pulling into the driveway
ongside the house. It had to be Brady. There was no one else
o would come, especially so early. Juliet stood up and went
the door, waiting for the familiar sound of his footsteps on
e deck stairs.

The coffee mug shook in her hand and she set it on the
unter. That's when she realized there were no footsteps on the
irs. If it was Brady, he apparently wasn't coming into the
use. She hurried into the living room, carefully positioning
rself off to one side of the glass wall. No one could see her
t she had a clear view of the beach. After several moments
she could see were the birds, and the white-capped surf, and
e lone jogger far down the shore.

She was just beginning to feel uneasy, knowing the car was
ll there alongside the house, when a slim energetic figure ap-
ared in her field of vision. She saw the flaming hair, the bil-
wing gauze blouse. *Who else but Cass?* Juliet watched her

mother settle in a secluded spot in front of a sand dune and ta
a large drawing tablet out of her Kenya bag. Obviously she w
preparing to sketch. But Cass wouldn't have driven down t
coast before dawn unless she had a very specific purpose
mind. And it was unlikely that purpose was sketching.

Her hands on her hips, Juliet turned away from the w
dow. The only way her mother could know she was here wa:
Brady had told her. She hoped that was all he'd told her. C:
had zeroed in on the fact there was a problem, or she would
have come. That meant she might have put pressure on Brad
Cass was good at getting information out of people.

Irritated, Juliet pulled on her jacket and headed toward t
back door. She wasn't ready to talk to Cass. She already f
dishonest because she'd misrepresented Brady, the marria
everything. It would make telling Cass about the divorce th
much harder. But the sooner she got it over with, the bett
Juliet decided, quietly closing the door behind her. She'd si
ply explain that things weren't working out with Brady a
they'd decided...no, she'd decided...it had been decided th
getting a divorce now was better than dragging things out.

Juliet saw her mother look up and wave her hand in gre
ing. With a lightness she didn't feel, Juliet waved back.

"I didn't expect you to be awake this early," Cass called c
as Juliet approached. "I thought I'd take advantage of t
morning sunlight and work for a while."

Juliet stuffed her hands in her pockets. So, Cass was goi
to take the casual approach. But she wasn't in the mood t
playing games. "You didn't drive all the way down the coast
sketch in the morning sunlight," Juliet said, challenging he

Cass set her tablet and charcoal beside her on the sand. "
course not," she answered quietly. "Why don't you sit do
and join me?"

Juliet didn't want to sit down. She wanted her mother to
home and leave her alone until she got herself together. E
Cass wasn't offering that option, and Juliet couldn't very w
just stand there. Slowly she lowered herself to the sand a
wrapped her arms around her bent knees. She stared straig
ahead, not saying anything, waiting for Cass to give her t
opening she needed.

"All you need to do is stick your lip out and you'll look as [sul]len as you did when you were six years old," Cass laughed [sof]tly.

Juliet didn't answer. She didn't like it when her mother saw [thr]ough her. Besides, she was cold and wrapping herself up was [a g]ood way to keep warm. She watched the ocean, studying [eac]h wave as it crested to a foamy white peak before it broke [and] rolled up on the smooth, wet sand.

[I]t was Cass who finally broke the silence. "Would you like [to] talk?"

Juliet shrugged, still studying the ocean. "Not really. There [isn]'t much to talk about."

"I see," Cass replied. "Well, maybe I will sketch for a little [wh]ile, then."

Cass picked up her tablet, and Juliet heard the rasping of a [ch]arcoal stick as it moved across the lightly grained paper. The [sou]nd evoked sharp memories of her childhood, the hours [she]'d spent in the studio when Cass worked. She could close her [eye]s and smell the pungent turpentine. She could see the myr-[iad] of paint tubes on the table next to the easel, and she could [he]ar the soft classical music in the background blending into [the] rhythm of the rolling surf. "Whatever happened to that [lum]py old chair in the corner of your studio—the one I used to [cur]l up and read in?"

Cass stopped drawing. "I gave it to the Salvation Army right [aft]er you passed the bar exam."

"Oh," Juliet answered. It had been years since she'd thought [ab]out that chair. She didn't even know she liked it.

"Juliet?" Cass touched her lightly on the back. "I want you [to] look at my sketch."

Curiously, Juliet took the sketch pad from Cass. Her mother [rar]ely showed her unfinished work. "You sketched me!" she [ex]claimed.

"That's right."

Juliet studied the stark, hunched figure on the paper, the [hol]low eyes staring out toward the ocean. "I don't like it." She [ha]nded the tablet back to Cass.

"I didn't expect you to," her mother replied. "Art isn't al-[wa]ys beautiful, and neither is life."

Juliet hurled a broken shell across the sand toward an a
proaching wave. "You don't need to lecture me about t
seamy side of life. I see it all the time in the office, remen
ber?"

"Maybe too much, Juliet," her mother observed.

"And you're telling me I've set myself up to fail?" Julie
face was grim. "Look, Cass, if you'd talked to all the peopl
have who started out full of hope—"

"Just like you," Cass interjected.

"No." Juliet traced a pattern in the sand with her forefi
ger. "Not just like me. I'm smarter than that. I went into ma
riage with my eyes wide open. I knew what I wanted and we
for it."

"Exactly what was that?" Cass inquired.

"A baby. I wanted to have a baby."

Cass raised her eyebrows. "I didn't think marriage was
prerequisite for having babies nowadays."

Juliet turned and looked sharply at her mother. "How mu
has Brady told you?"

"Only that you came to the beach house to be alone a
think for a few days."

Juliet remained skeptical. "That's all?"

"Yes, Juliet, that's all," Cass answered. "I gather then
more to tell."

Juliet turned away from her mother's penetrating eye
looking down at the swirled patterns in the sand. "I've rea
made a mess," she said in a small voice.

Cass reached out and took Juliet's hand. "You aren't alo
dear. We all do it—some of us on a larger scale than others.

"I thought I had it all planned. If only Brady hadn't
sisted on marriage...."

"Maybe you should begin at the beginning, Juliet. Ther
obviously a lot I don't know."

In a slow, toneless voice, Juliet related what had happene
She was barely through the part about advertising for a fath
for her baby when Cass picked up her tablet and began
sketch again. Juliet knew it was her mother's way of cha
neling the shock, anger, disappointment—whatever emotio
were stirring—while her face remained impassive. The m

liet talked, the faster the charcoal moved across the paper in
oad, bold strokes.

"And so it didn't work out for either one of us," Juliet fi-
lly summed up.

For several minutes, Cass continued to sketch without com-
nt. "I'm not sure you've quite come to terms with the prob-
1," she said mildly, laying the charcoal on the sand and
rning toward Juliet. "Are you unhappy because you're not
egnant?"

"No," Juliet answered quickly. "I was for a while. But now
n not even sure anymore that I want to have a baby. I don't
m to be sure about much of anything."

Cass smiled. "You're more sure than you realize, Juliet. You
st aren't being honest with yourself."

"I don't know what you mean," Juliet retorted. She wasn't
any mood to have Cass analyze her.

Ignoring Juliet's obvious irritation, Cass asked, "How did
ady feel about you leaving?"

Juliet hesitated. She'd gone this far; she might as well tell
erything. "He didn't want me to go. He persuaded me to
me to the beach for a while, supposedly to think it all over. I
d him I wasn't going to change my mind."

"Exactly what is it you want, Juliet?" Cass asked her.

Juliet's eyes flashed deep green in the morning sunlight. "I
1 tell you what I don't want," she proclaimed. "I don't want
be married. Getting married means getting hurt. I've seen it
er and over again."

Cass studied her thoughtfully. "And so you figured if get-
g married means getting hurt, conversely not being married
ans you won't be hurt, right?"

"Right," Juliet agreed, surprised at how quickly her mother
emed to understand.

"Juliet, did you ever study logic?"

Juliet eyed Cass suspiciously. "Of course."

"Well, you should have studied harder. You're asking your-
f the wrong questions, Juliet. That's why you're getting the
ong answers."

"I am not," Juliet snapped back.

THE ARRANGEMENT

Cass took Juliet's hand again, and Juliet struggled again the urge to pull it away. "Does Brady love you?" her moth asked.

The question was like a weight bearing down on Juliet. She felt so guilty when he'd told her he loved her, guilty and ang because it all seemed so unfair.

"Well, does he?" Cass prodded.

"Yes." Juliet braced herself for the next question.

"And do you love him?"

She wanted to deny it. That would solve everything. It al would be a lie. "Yes, I love him," she admitted slowly. "Bu lot of people love each other when they start out, and th doesn't keep them from destroying their marriages and th children and each other before they're through. How can I sure we'd be any different?"

"You can't ever be sure," Cass replied quietly. "But that is the problem, Juliet. What you don't understand is that it's n the marriage that hurts. It's the love, the profound emotio commitment to each other." Cass's face clouded. "That's wl tears people apart. You can choose to live with Brady or n You can choose to divorce him or not. But if you really lc him, you're going to hurt sometimes no matter what you dc

Juliet stared at the surf, her head pounding like the brea ers. "I've thought about it until I can't think anymore, Cass still don't know what to do."

Cass patted her on the shoulder. "You're looking for swers in the wrong place. This isn't the kind of decision y make with your head. You can't make a list of pros and cc the way you do when you're preparing a case."

Juliet frowned. "So what's the alternative?"

"On this one," Cass told her, "you have to follow yc heart. It's the only way you'll come up with any real answer

"But that's not how I make decisions," Juliet protested.

Cass smiled. "Maybe you've never faced a decision li this." She picked up her sketch pad and stood up. "Come and walk me to the car."

"You're leaving?" Juliet rose slowly to her feet. "Would you like to come in and have some tea? Or I could fix breakfast?" As unhappy as she'd been to see Cass arrive, n she didn't want her to leave.

"Not this time." Cass gave her daughter a hug. "Brady was right. You do need some time alone. He knows you well."

Juliet walked with Cass up the dune and around the beach house to the car. She watched Cass's car until it became a tiny red dot in the distance, and then she turned back to the house feeling very abandoned. She wandered around the kitchen for a while and then walked into the living room and sat cross-legged, staring out at the pounding surf. She tried to think, tried to make some sense of everything that had happened, but she couldn't. She only knew that she hurt deep inside, and that as the days passed, the hurt didn't go away.

MICHAEL WAS BORED. He lay on his back on the family room couch and kicked his feet in the air. He'd ridden his new dirt bike all morning, and he was tired of it. There was nobody to play with. Even dumb old Timmy was taking a nap with Mom. His dad had been shut up in the study all afternoon. There was nothing to do.

His eyes wandered to the window. The sun was shining on the beach. Maybe he could go outside and skip stones. But that wasn't much fun alone. He stared at a thin crack in the ceiling. He really wanted to do something neat with someone who was fun. Brady was fun, but he wasn't at the beach house. It seemed like he was never there anymore.

But Juliet was there. He'd seen her walking on the beach. Michael sat up. That was the first good idea he'd come up with. He'd go see if Juliet wanted to do something. She was a whole lot of fun. Pulling on his windbreaker, Michael slipped out the back door and ran down the beach.

As soon as Juliet heard the sound of feet pounding up the stairs, she knew it was Michael. He was the only person who hit those stairs like the lead runner in a marathon. She smiled as she hurried to answer his impatient knocking on the door.

"Hi, Juliet." He was gasping for breath. "I knew you were here."

"Come on in," she invited. His arrival was the brightest thing that had happened to her in days.

Michael shook his head vehemently. "I don't want to come in. I want you to come out."

"All right," Juliet laughed. She pulled on her old green sweatshirt and followed him down the stairs to the beach.

"Do you want to skip stones?" he asked eagerly. "The water is pretty calm today." He began to scuff the sand with the toe of his sneaker, searching out the smooth, flat stones that were best for skipping. "Here's a good one," he announced, handing Juliet a pale pink stone.

Juliet watched him, amazed. Michael looked as though he'd never had a problem in his life. It was hard to believe that this was the same child who had been in a recent automobile accident, the same one who had dissolved in tears because his mother had rejected him. How could he bounce back so fast?

"Watch this!" Michael yelled. He drew back his arm and pitched a stone across the sapphire ocean, laughing aloud when it skipped in three perfect arcs over the top of the waves. "Wasn't that great?"

Juliet knew he wasn't asking; he was stating a fact. Michael was brimming over with confidence today. "My turn now," she announced. She drew back her arm in what she hoped was an imitation of Michael and threw her stone. Instead of skipping, it plopped on top of a kelp bed and sank out of sight. "Not my best skill," she laughed.

Michael skipped another stone across the water. "You should get Brady to teach you. He's really good at this kind of stuff. He taught me."

Brady. Juliet hadn't thought about him the whole time she'd been with Michael. That was some sort of a record.

"How come Brady didn't come to the beach with you?" Michael asked.

"He had to work," Juliet explained casually.

"It doesn't seem right, you staying here all this time without Brady," Michael observed.

Juliet didn't answer. She felt the same way, and she still didn't know what to do about it. Absently, she tossed another stone toward the ocean.

"That was a little better," Michael said, praising her. "It must be harder for girls to skip stones. My mom isn't very good at it either."

"How is your mom feeling?" Juliet asked, relieved to change the subject.

Michael's face lit up. "Okay, I guess. She still gets tired a lot." He picked up a shell and examined it before tossing it away. "She made waffles for breakfast this morning," he volunteered. "Real waffles in that waffle-cooking thing. My dad always gets the frozen kind you put in the toaster." Poking at the sand, Michael added, "I hope she'll make real waffles for us all the time now—like she used to."

Juliet looked at Michael sadly. How easily children were taken in, she thought. How quickly they believed. In Eileen's condition, anything might happen. And here was Michael, letting himself hope that because things had been better for a little while, they would always be. "You really like having your mom home, don't you?" she asked.

"Yep." Michael crouched down in the sand, digging for more stones. "I think she's gonna stay this time, too."

Juliet wanted to protect him. He was opening himself to so much hurt. "How can you be so sure she'll stay?" Juliet asked gently.

Michael stopped digging and looked up. "I'm not," he answered quietly. "I just hope."

"And if it doesn't work out, then what?" Juliet prodded.

Michael shrugged. "Then at least we had today."

At least we had today. At least we had today. At least we had today. The words pounded in Juliet's head like the breakers pounded the sand. It sounded so simple. But, then, Michael was only a child. He didn't have the perspective to look ahead, the maturity to be concerned about his future. He couldn't possibly understand the risk he was taking by loving someone who might leave him.

A stiff breeze blew up from the ocean, and gulls started to squawk. Michael had stopped skipping stones and stood contentedly next to Juliet looking out toward the horizon. "I think I need to go home," he announced. "It's getting late, and my mom might be worried about me."

"Good idea," Juliet agreed.

Michael took off at a dead run along the water's edge. "See you around," he yelled back over his shoulder.

"See you around," Juliet whispered to herself. Maybe it was time for her to go home, too.

Juliet walked slowly up to the beach house. She kept thinking about what Michael had said: "At least we had today."

It was a simplistic approach, a child's way of dealing with uncertainty. But maybe it was more than that. She'd spent all her life planning tomorrows—growing up, working toward law school, preparing for the bar exams, building her law practice so it would be more and more successful. All tomorrows. Even her marriage had been for tomorrow, a way to make a baby who would grow up and have its own tomorrows.

Today, the right now of things, always got shoved aside. All she'd ever done for the moment was make love to Brady. It was the only time in her life when the future hadn't existed for her. She hadn't thought once about whether they would ever make love again or whether it would be better or different. What was, was. It was complete and total and all-consuming.

Juliet went into the house, closing the door behind her. She'd always been so sure of what she wanted—and so determined to have it at any price. But that was before. She sank down on the kitchen chair, her head in her hands. That was before she fell in love with Brady.

Now her whole world had changed. Her life was empty without him. She'd tried to deny it, but it wasn't any good. She didn't want to go back to her apartment. She didn't want to go to work. The only thing she'd been able to muster any enthusiasm for in a week was walking on the beach, and that was because when she got close to Phil's house she always hoped she might see Brady.

Standing up abruptly, Juliet hurried into the bedroom and stuffed the few clothes she'd brought into her canvas bag. She wasn't sure what she was going to do when she got there, but she knew she was going home.

JULIET'S PALMS WERE DAMP against the steering wheel as she turned up the steep street toward the house. When she got closer she looked for Brady's car, but she didn't see it. It was early. He might not even be home. It bothered her that he hadn't called or made any attempt to contact her since she'd left. He'd promised not to disturb her, but she'd thought he might at least check to see how she was getting along. Maybe he'd done some thinking, too. She felt the cold knot in her stomach. It hadn't been there in a long time.

She found a parking spot and started up the front walk. With its new lighter gray paint, and gleaming white trim, the house looked very different from when they had bought it. Having the footing replaced under the corner of the front porch had helped, too. Now everything seemed solid and square as if the place was ready for another hundred years.

As she approached the front steps, Juliet caught sight of something alongside the porch and went to investigate. In the fading light she couldn't see it very well, but she was sure it hadn't been there when she left. When she rounded the corner of the porch, she knew immediately what it was and she cried out.

Their Christmas tree, stripped of its lights and its ornaments, was on its side, discarded and forlorn. From the way it was lying there with the burlap hanging off the root ball, it was apparent that Brady had dragged it that far and left it to die. An overwhelming sadness surged through her. The tree was alive. Brady had proudly told her that when he gave it to her. She'd thought they were going to plant it in the yard where it could grow.

She stood staring at the tree for a long time before she understood. No wonder he'd left it there. This was their tree, the symbol of their first Christmas together, and now Brady didn't want to plant it. She couldn't really blame him. Christmas was over, and maybe everything else, too. With brimming eyes, she reached inside the branches and took out a paper bird Brady had missed. Carefully she straightened out one of the crumpled wings.

Slipping the bird in her purse, Juliet inspected the tree. She didn't want it to die. Until right then, she hadn't known how much it mattered. She walked all the way around it. The ball of dirt was dry and crumbling, but except for a few brown needles, the tree itself still looked healthy. Maybe she wasn't too late.

She found a discarded paint can near the back door and filled it with water. It took a dozen trips before she was satisfied that the roots were thoroughly soaked. She tried to prop the tree upright so its branches wouldn't get bent or broken, but it was too heavy for her. It would take Brady, or better yet both of them, to maneuver it. Dusting the dirt off her hands, she walked back around the house. At least their tree would live for a little while longer.

When she walked into the house, she felt its emptiness. "Brady?" she called out from the foyer. Her voice echoed through the rooms. She knew without asking that Brady wasn't home.

With the silence clinging to her, Juliet went up to the bedroom and dropped her canvas bag on the unmade bed. When she hung her robe back on its hook in the closet, her eyes were drawn down to the jumble of shoes on the floor. His shoes had started out on the left and hers on the right, but somewhere along the line they'd gotten all tangled up together. She and Brady had talked about building a rack to keep them separated, but they hadn't done it. It hadn't seemed too important.

Juliet wandered into the adjacent room they'd decided should be the nursery. She knelt down beside the roll of wallpaper laid out on the floor and traced the pink and blue design. They'd laughed when they'd chosen it. You needed both colors, Brady had said, because you never knew whether it would be a boy or a girl. She'd thought at the time maybe one or the other might already be growing inside of her. But that had been another dream. Maybe they weren't intended to have children. There was no way of knowing. As Juliet walked out of the nursery, it occurred to her that the room would make a wonderful study for someone without babies. They'd made a really dumb choice of wallpaper if they were going to sell the house.

She went down to the kitchen and considered fixing dinner, but she didn't know whether Brady even came home for dinner now. At loose ends, she made herself a peanut butter sandwich and since there wasn't any milk, she drank a Coke. She wished Brady would arrive, and at the same time she was almost afraid to see him. She didn't know why.

The kitchen was almost finished, she noted with satisfaction, except for painting a couple of door frames and the chair rail. Then all it would need was curtains and maybe some hanging copper pans. Juliet stopped herself. This wasn't the time to be planning homey touches for the kitchen. She was facing other decisions first. But at least she could paint the chair rail.

She opened the paint can and stirred it patiently, until the swirls of blue blended into one solid color. She could understand why Cass took such pleasure in painting. Of course, Cass created pictures. Juliet just liked the feel of the brush in her hand and the way the paint flowed onto the wood. She had finished the wooden strip of chair rail along one wall and was starting on the next when she heard Brady's key in the lock. She kept on painting, a chill spreading inside her. She didn't know what to say to him. She didn't know what to say to herself.

Brady's heart was pounding as he fumbled with the deadbolt. The lights were on inside. That meant Juliet had come home. Maybe it was only to pack, to leave for good. But she was there. He jiggled the key impatiently. It was the first time for months he'd had trouble with the lock.

When he finally got it open, Brady literally ran inside. "Juliet!" he shouted. "Where are you?"

"In the kitchen," she answered. Her fingers were trembling and the paint oozed over the edges of the wood onto the wall. She put down the brush and dabbed at the splotches with a damp rag.

When he reached the kitchen door, Brady stopped dead still. "You're painting!" he exclaimed.

She didn't know how to answer. Obviously she was painting, and she was doing it because she wanted to. Still on her knees in front of the chair rail, she wiped a blue streak off the wall and picked up the brush again. "I thought we needed to get it done. And I guess I like to paint." It was an easy thing to say while she forcibly calmed her trembling body. She focused totally on her brush strokes, never looking up, never meeting his eyes.

Brady wasn't quite sure what was going on. Whatever he'd expected to find when he walked in, it wasn't this. He'd thought she might be packing. Or maybe she'd be at the table waiting for him. Or she might be pacing the floor agitated and upset. But from the way she was acting, she might never have left. On the other hand, she might have come back only to work—to hold up her end of the bargain. That would be like Juliet. Either way, she didn't seem in any hurry to talk about it. "When did you get back?" he asked her.

"This afternoon. I was going to fix dinner," she explained, "but I didn't know whether you would come home." Home. As her lips formed the word, it echoed in her mind. This really was home. They'd made this house a home, by sharing it and working on it and caring about it. But home implied so much, such an enormous commitment.

"I always come home," he said softly. "I always hope maybe I'll find you here." Unwilling to wait any longer, Brady crossed the kitchen in three long strides and gripped Juliet's shoulders. "Juliet, talk to me," he commanded. "What's going on? Why did you come back?"

Her paintbrush zig-zagged across the wood in a wavy line before Juliet pulled it away and set it down on top of the paint can. "I thought about it for a long time, Brady." Her voice was barely louder than a whisper. "I wanted to come home."

He dropped on his knees beside her and took her in his arms. He hadn't lost her. All those nights he'd waited, so sure that she wasn't coming back, were over now. "I've missed you, Juliet," he whispered. "Oh God, how I've missed you!"

She rested her head against him, feeling full and complete for the first time since she'd left. If only life could be this simple, if she could just live one day at a time. "I'm all snarled up, Brady." Her voice dropped lower until it was barely audible. "And I think I'm afraid."

He stroked her hair, cradling her against him. "Afraid of what, Juliet? Not afraid of me?"

"I think I'm mostly afraid of me." She leaned hard against his shoulder. "I'm changing, Brady. What I always wanted, or at least thought I wanted, isn't the same anymore."

His arms still around her, Brady leaned back against the wall and looked at her. She'd obviously struggled over the last few days. At least she'd faced her fears. That was the first step. He stroked her hair. "But what are you afraid of, Juliet?"

"I'm afraid of marriage." She hesitated. "And I'm afraid because of how I feel about you. I'm afraid because I love you." She'd never admitted all that before, and it was very hard to talk about now. "I've always made my own decisions, set my own goals. I go after what I want. But this is different, Brady."

e met his eyes. "I didn't decide I wanted you. It just hap-
ned. And now I don't know what to do about it. I don't
ow for sure we can make it work."

His arm tightened around her. "But if we don't try, we'll
ver know. We'll never know anything beyond what we have
w unless we try." He paused, wanting her too much to make
omises to her that he couldn't keep. "There aren't any guar-
tees, Juliet. We have to trust each other."

She moved away from him slightly, wrapping her arms
ound her knees and hugging them tightly to her. Brady let her
, sensing that he'd touched a raw nerve in her. "I don't know
I've ever completely trusted anybody, Brady," she said
oughtfully, "except maybe myself." She buried her face in
r hands. "Oh, Brady, why does it have to be so compli-
ted? Why can't I just get married and have babies and take
chances like everybody else?"

"Because you're not like everybody else." He gently took her
nd. "And, you know Juliet, maybe it isn't marriage that's the
oblem. Maybe you're not ready to have a baby."

Startled, Juliet sat up straight. "But having a baby was the
ole reason for getting married in the first place," she pro-
ted.

"I know," Brady agreed, "and not a very good reason."

"But I've always wanted to have a baby by the time I was
rty—"

"And if you don't, then what?"

Juliet thought that over. Having a child had been one of her
als, like making the dean's list and passing the bar exam. A
w smile lighted her eyes. "I guess, if I didn't, maybe I could
ve a baby when I was thirty-five."

"Right." He laughed and gave her a hug. "We aren't in any
rry, Juliet. We've got years and years to have babies if that's
at we want to do."

Juliet hesitated. "I don't know, Brady. That's how I'd
anned it for so long—"

He shrugged. "Plans change." He looked at her for a long
e. "Do you love me, Juliet?" he asked her. He had to hear
r say it again.

"Of course I do, Brady," she answered quickly. "I already
d you. That's partly why I'm afraid."

He put his hand under her chin and turned her head gent‑ toward him until their eyes met. "No, Juliet, I mean really lo‑ me, the kind of love that lasts forever."

Juliet hesitated. She knew what he meant. He was asking f‑ the kind of commitment she'd been afraid to make all her lif‑ It was the question she'd wrestled with all those lonely days‑ the beach. But it wasn't until she looked into his eyes that s‑ found the answer. "Yes, Brady," she finally told him. "I ‑ love you. That's why I had to come home."

He pulled her close to him, and held her, rocking her gent‑ back and forth. It was what he'd wanted to hear. "Then we‑ make it work, Juliet." His eyes were dark with emotion. "B‑ it will take both of us." Brady gently touched her cheek. "‑ haven't had much time together, Juliet. Most people start o‑ going to dinner and taking walks in the park. They do it f‑ months, or even years. We started out by getting married."

Juliet laughed, seeing the irony. "I'm glad I didn't get pre‑ nant, Brady. That would have been all wrong."

"It needs to be just the two of us for a while," he agree‑ "and then maybe we'll know each other well enough by t‑ time the baby comes along—"

"That we could be three without losing each other?" Juli‑ finished for him. She felt like a weight had been lifted off he‑ "But we can keep the wallpaper for the nursery just in case‑ she added happily.

Brady laughed. "In the meantime, we'll buy some boo‑ cases, and I'll use the room as my study," he announced.

"Wait a minute!" Juliet's eyes flashed and she sat u‑ "Whose study?"

Brady's eyes were still twinkling. "We'll argue that o‑ later," he said taking her in his arms again. "And if that's t‑ biggest problem we're facing, you can be damn sure we'll ma‑ it."

Juliet snuggled against him, letting his lips feather tiny kiss‑ down the side of her face. "Brady," she said tentativel‑ "There's one more thing."

"What's that?"

"Our Christmas tree. I don't want it to die."

Brady stood up, pulling Juliet up with him. "Then I su‑ pose we should go out and give the root ball a good soaking

Juliet smiled. "I already took care of that."

"You watered the tree?"

"I did, and now I want to go plant it in the backyard.

Brady looked out the kitchen window. "It's starting to get dark. Couldn't we wait until tomorrow?"

"No, I want to do it right now. I want to plant it, and water t, and feed it—"

"And watch it grow over the years?" finished Brady.

"Yes, that's exactly right. I knew you'd understand."

"Of course I do." Brady pulled on his jacket. As he reached n his pocket for the key to the garden shed he felt something lse. "Hey, look what I found." He grinned as he took out Juliet's gold wedding band. "This doesn't belong in my pocket."

"No, it doesn't," she whispered.

Brady took her hand in his and slipped the wedding band on er finger. "That's more like it," he said, kissing her gently.

Juliet held him tightly. "I'm glad you kept it, Brady," she nurmured. "I didn't feel right wearing it before, but now it eems to belong there."

"It does belong there, Juliet." His voice was husky. "It belongs there, just like we belong together."

Juliet smiled up at him. "I love you, Brady."

He stood quietly studying her for a moment. "The last time gave you that ring, we had a ceremony, and went on a honeymoon . . . do you want to do those things again, Juliet?"

"Once in a lifetime is enough," Juliet answered emphatically.

"Good," Brady agreed. "Then this time we'll do it our own way."

"Our own way?" She wasn't sure what he meant.

With a broad grin, he pulled her toward the door. "What's e most romantic way you can think of to celebrate a marage?"

Suddenly understanding, Juliet leaned up to kiss him, and er laughter blended with his. "Get the shovel, Brady. Let's go lant a tree."